THE BATTLEFIELDS OF
PAX AMERICANA

THE BATTLEFIELDS OF PAX AMERICANA

A novel set in the troubling times of the new millennium.

GEORGE H. STOLLWERCK

Copyright © 2004 by George H. Stollwerck.
First American Edition.

Library of Congress Number:		2004093099
ISBN:	Hardcover	1-4134-5618-9
	Softcover	1-4134-5617-0

All rights reserved. No part of this publication may be reproduced, stored in a retrieval system, or transmitted, in any form or by any means, electronic, mechanical, photocopying, recording, or otherwise, without the written prior permission of the author.

This is a work of fiction. While it is history-based and contains references to historical events, personages, organizations and locales, those have been included solely to lend the fiction a historical context.

Events, conversations, media product and sequence may have been created and/or modified to make the narrative flow more interesting to the reader.

Characters in this book have no existence outside the imagination of the author, and have no relationship whatsoever to anyone bearing the same name or names. Those characterizations were not inspired by any individual known to or by the author.

Names, characters and incidents, as well as dialogue and the storyline, are wholly products of the author's imagination, research, training, and experience. The overall scenario has been interwoven with the documented history of the United States of America.

Any resemblance to actual persons, either living or deceased, is entirely coincidental.

This book was printed in the United States of America.

To order additional copies of this book, contact:
Xlibris Corporation
1-888-795-4274
www.Xlibris.com
Orders@Xlibris.com
24919

Contents

THE BATTLEFIELDS OF PAX AMERICANA 11
ACKNOWLEDGEMENTS 17
CAST OF CHARACTERS 19
PROLOG : DAY 001 25

CHAPTER ONE 43
    THE AMERICAN NAVAL BASE—CAMP DELTA
    GUANTÁNAMO BAY, CUBA

CHAPTER TWO 55
    THE AMERICAN NAVAL STATION—CAMP AMERICA
    GUANTÁNAMO BAY, CUBA

CHAPTER THREE 59
    THE AMERICAN NAVAL BASE—THE WAR ON TERROR
    GUANTÁNAMO BAY, CUBA

CHAPTER FOUR 66
    THE AMERICAN NAVAL BASE—GITMO VULNERABILITY
    GUANTÁNAMO BAY, CUBA

CHAPTER FIVE 72
    HOOVER DAM—THE INTELLIGENCE ASSESSMENT
    NEAR BOULDER CITY, NEVADA

CHAPTER SIX 81
    HOOVER DAM—MICAP MEETING ON THE THREAT
    NEAR BOULDER CITY, NEVADA

CHAPTER SEVEN 99
    HOOVER DAM—HOMELAND SECURITY'S THREAT APPRAISAL
    NEAR BOULDER CITY, NEVADA

CHAPTER EIGHT 124
    HOOVER DAM—THE MYSTERIOUS INTRUDER
    NEAR BOULDER CITY, NEVADA

CHAPTER NINE 144
    HOOVER DAM—LAKE MEAD RESERVOIR
    LAKE MEAD, NEVADA
CHAPTER TEN 169
    ON A NEVADA STATE HIGHWAY
    APPROACHING CLARK COUNTY
    THE MIDDLE OF NOWHERE
CHAPTER ELEVEN 195
    SOMEWHERE IN THE DESERT
    MOHAVE COUNTY, ARIZONA
CHAPTER TWELVE 211
    FBI HEADQUARTERS—THE DIRECTOR'S WRATH
    935 PENNSYLVANIA AVENUE, N.W.
    WASHINGTON, D.C. 20535
CHAPTER THIRTEEN 223
    ABOARD A SAM FOX FLIGHT—DESTINATION CUBA
    DEPARTING ANDREWS AIR FORCE BASE
    CAMP SPRINGS, MARYLAND
CHAPTER FOURTEEN 247
    JOINT TASK FORCE 160 HEADQUARTERS
    GUANTÁNAMO BAY, CUBA
CHAPTER FIFTEEN 268
    ABOARD A U.S. NAVAL WARSHIP
    SOMEWHERE IN THE CARIBBEAN SEA
    NORTHWEST OF HAITI
CHAPTER SIXTEEN 290
    ABOARD A STOLEN RUSSIAN SUBMARINE
    SOMEWHERE IN THE CARIBBEAN SEA
    NORTHEAST OF JAMAICA
CHAPTER SEVENTEEN 299
    JOINT TASK FORCE 160 HQ—THE INFILTRATION DISCOVERY
    GUANTÁNAMO BAY, CUBA
CHAPTER EIGHTEEN 335
    MOHAVE COUNTY—0900 HOURS—THE SABOTEURS
    LAKE HAVASU CITY, ARIZONA

CHAPTER NINETEEN 356
    MOHAVE COUNTY—1100 HOURS—DAY OF ATONEMENT
    LAKE HAVASU CITY, ARIZONA
CHAPTER TWENTY 383
    MOHAVE COUNTY—1200 HOURS—THREAT ERADICATION
    LAKE HAVASU CITY, ARIZONA
CHAPTER TWENTY-ONE 408
    THE AMERICAN NAVAL BASE—THE INFILTRATION
    GUANTÁNAMO BAY, CUBA
CHAPTER TWENTY-TWO 428
    THE AMERICAN NAVAL BASE—SABOTEURS PLANT SEMTEX
    GUANTÁNAMO BAY, CUBA
CHAPTER TWENTY-THREE 440
    THE AMERICAN NAVAL BASE—ASSAULT ON CAMP DELTA
    GUANTÁNAMO BAY, CUBA
CHAPTER TWENTY-FOUR 465
    THE AMERICAN NAVAL BASE—DAMAGE CONTROL
    GUANTÁNAMO BAY, CUBA
CHAPTER TWENTY-FIVE 479
    THE AMERICAN NAVAL BASE—PURSUIT OF
    THE SCORPION OFF THE BAHAMAS
    THE SOUTHERN ATLANTIC OCEAN
CHAPTER TWENTY-SIX 500
    HOOVER DAM—HIDDEN IN PLAIN SIGHT
    NEAR BOUNDER CITY, NEVADA

EPILOGUE 525
GLOSSARY 533
REFERENCE MATERIALS 543
ABOUT THE AUTHOR 545

[1. Al-Qaeda hierarchy—Fiction. 2. Federal Bureau Of Investigation—Case management procedures—Fiction. 3. Government investigators—Fiction. 4. Fugitives from Justice—Fiction. 5. Guantánamo Bay—Fiction. 6. Hoover Dam—Fiction. 7. Lake Havasu City—Fiction. 8. Female Investigators—Fiction. 9. Soviet (Russian) submarines—Fiction. 10. U.S. Navy warships—Fiction. 11. Mystery and detective stories—Fiction. 12. U.S. military aircraft—Fiction. 13. Military weaponry—Fiction.] I. Title.

THE BATTLEFIELDS OF PAX AMERICANA

The United States has been the world's only superpower since the fall of the Berlin Wall, perhaps longer. International political strategists refer to the current condition as 'Pax Americana.'

Pax Americana is summed-up in a thirty-one-page document of political philosophy that some of our leaders have been touting since it was reported in the September 23, 2002 edition of the *Christian Science Monitor*. It asserts American dominance, as the lone superpower—a status no rival power, if one existed, would be allowed to challenge. Namely that only America has the means, motivation, and political will to stamp out terrorism.

American leaders promoting this U.S. strategic doctrine, point out that the "dangers in the post-9/11 world come not from the strong states, but the weak ones that nurture terrorists with the capacity to create great chaos "for less than it costs to purchase a single tank."

Bin Laden, and one of his older sons, Saad, who has recently taken a more active part in the command structure of al-Qaeda, and always have been more in tune to what is going on in America than our average citizen, realizes the threat this philosophy represents. After all, the bin-Laden's muse, what if the American President was able to act against terrorist organizations unilaterally, without the necessity of having to first form coalitions of countries, who with exception of Britain, offer limited military credentials, and rainy day commitments.

The al-Qaeda leader and his son, and their allies in Hamas, Hezbollah, and Jemaah Islamiyah, recognize that unless they can immediately bring massive disruption, confusion, and suffering to America, to convince her people to rise up and confront their national leader who is up for reelection in November 2004, extremist terrorism in the world may be defeated without achieving the victory they all seek so feverently, the destruction of the Great Satan.

Beginning in the early morning hours of 2003, al-Qaeda undertakes actions that will bring disruption and confusion to America—to our nation's power-grid infrastructure; against one of America's most-critical military bases existing outside CONUS; and unbelievably, and brings havoc on a small resort community in the American Southwest.

A NOVEL BY:
George H. Stollwerck

PUBLISHED:
Summer of 2004

OTHER BOOKS BY THE AUTHOR

Terrorism: America's Incurable Disease!
2002

The Vanishing Hero!
2001

Nine Lives Minus One!
2000

ACCLAIM FOR THE AUTHOR'S PREVIOUS NOVELS

Pre-Publication:

"... the author's professional and psychology application to *TERRORISM: America's Incurable Disease!* is gripping and logical! I look forward to (novel) number four!"

Edward R. Wolfe
Lt. Colonel—USAF
Fighter Pilot—Retired.

"... it has been indeed a pleasure to read *TERRORISM: America's Incurable Disease!* It truly fits the present world scene. The characters and the role they portray are realistic and exciting. They also show the (commitment) of the Government personnel that are dedicated to conquer(ing) the ever present threats we face. This is a must read for all those who wish to promote security in our country."

Marvin J. Lokkesmoe, Chief

USS West Virginia
Pearl Harbor Survivor
U.S. Navy—Retired.

One of several examples of Post-Publication—Media:

"Those who enjoy high technology suspense novels (*TERRORISM: America's Incurable Disease!*) will find the book absorbing and revel in its wealth of detail."

TODAY'S News-Herald
Lake Havasu City, Arizona
21 February 2003

ACKNOWLEDGEMENTS

In writing a technical thriller where every sentence must seem to have just leaped from next week's morning newspaper, an author only has his/her own experiences, education, training, the historical past, vivid imagination, and thousands of hours of detailed research, as a foundation on which to bring life to a host of believable scenarios.

Sometimes, as in the case of this and my other books, the presented situations and facts are so firmly based on historical fact, achievable situations, available methods/tools/tactics/tactics, and state-of-the-art technology, that just reading the book seems to bring each frightening scenario into our lives.

However, in my case, that still leaves amazing gaps of knowledge in the area of customary publishing practices, and the never-ending battle to stay ahead of the word processing function. Pitifully I must admit to be a neophyte in the former, and on-life-support on the latter.

Therefore, I would be remiss if I didn't acknowledge the occasional advice I have been fortunate to receive from Michael A. Hawley, the respected author of the police thrillers *Silent Proof*, and *Double Bluff*.

I also owe a word of thanks to Sharon Poppen, author of the

excellent novel *After the War, Before the Peace*, who has provided valuable advice to me in publishing matters which is just one of her many areas of expertise.

Another expression of appreciation goes to Heather McCormick and Jeff McCormick—no, it isn't just coincidence that they have the same last name. Heather, despite recently graduating law school, keeping up with their son Sam, and managing to find time for her husband, Jeff, still has managed to provide invaluable advice to me in computer crises when I thought all was lost—really, really lost!

I thank you all for being so considerate to provide your valuable advice. This book, nor any of its siblings, would exist today without the above-and-beyond-the-call-of-duty-friendships of knowledgeable persons such as these.

Last but not least, I must again thank Eleanor Poppe for always brightening what might otherwise be a bleak day. And for her willingness and skill in researching the wide breadth of the Internet to obtain access to otherwise unavailable information. That is when she can be located at home in between her numerous golfing forays. Thank you, Ellie.

This novel includes an alphabetical Glossary of terms and acronyms at the rear of the book. Enjoy the Read!

CAST OF CHARACTERS

U.S. Senior Command:
Bush, George W: 43rd President of the United States.
Eisenhower, Dwight D: 34th President of the United States.
Johnson, Lyndon Baines: 36th President of the United States.

The U.S. Cabinet:
Key, John W. (III): Commissioner of the Department of the Interior.
Norton, Gale: Secretary of the Department of the Interior.
Page, Calvin: Secretary of the Department of State.
Rice, Condelezza: National Security Advisor.
Staples, Ted: Secretary of the Department of Homeland Security.

The U.S. Congress:
Calvert, Kenneth: Chairman, House of Representatives—Resources, Water and Power Committee.

U.S. Bureau of Reclamation:
Casterbottom, John: Western States Regional Manager.

U.S. Federal Bureau of Investigation:
Mueller, Robert: Director.

Savage, William "Bill": (ADC) Assistant Director In-Charge/Counterterrorism.
Davis, Diane A.: Supervising Special Agent. Acting Head of TTIC—U.S. Terrorism Threat Integration Center. Appointed to serve at the pleasure of the President in 2002. Dotted line reporting relationship to President's NSA. Solid line reporting relationship to ADIC/Counterterrorism Savage.
Gordon, Carlene: A PhD in charge of the Bureau's Profiling and Behavioral Assessment (PBAU) Unit.
Douglas, John: Retired Supervising Special Agent, Profiling Consultant and Author.

U.S. Central Intelligence Agency:
George Tenant, Director.
Kennedy, Jim: Deputy Director/Plans.

U.S. On-Shore Military Counterterrorism Task Force:
Stalwart, Jennifer: Commander, US Coast Guard Counterterrorism Taskforce.

U.S. Ship-Based Military Command—USS *OSCAR AUSTIN*—DDG 79
Smith, Jethro: Commander—US Navy. Captain of the AEGIS Guided Missile Destroyer.
Daliinez, Jose: Lt. Commander—US Navy, Executive Officer (XO) of DDG 079.
Lockwood, "Crissy" Christine: Lt.—Weapons Systems Officer (WSO) DDG 079.
Stevens, Anton: Lieutenant—Command Plot Division—DDG 079.

Cuban Principals:
Ruz, Fidel Alejandro Castro: President for life of the Nation-State Cuba.
Ruz, Raúl Castro: Vice President of the Nation-State Cuba.
Bello, Manuel Lopez: Managing Director—Jose Marti Airport—Havana.

Chaviano, Lazaro: Jose Marti Airport Cargo Manager.
Rivero, Robert: Jose Marti Operations Director.

Cuban Commando Force:
Barbosa, Luis Hernando: Lieutenant—C.O., Cuban Navy UDT Commando Team.
Garcia, Manuel: Master Chief—Cuban Navy UDT Commando Team.
Gonzales, Julio: Master Sergeant—Cuban All-service Commando Team.
Hernandez, 'Perky': Underwater Specialist—Cuban All-service Commando Team.
Jaminez, Jorge: Master Chief—Cuban Navy UDT Commando Team.
Lopez, Hector: Underwater Specialist—Cuban All-service Commando Team.

Hoover Dam, U.S. Bureau of Reclamation:
Hammer, Edith: Dam's Resident Manager.
Beebout, Paul: Human Relations Manager.
Benson, Abigail: Operating Log Yeoman.
Conduit, Jefferson: Public Relations Manager.
Castro, David: Hydraulic engineer and self-appointed employee spokesperson.
Davis, Billy Joe: Power Plant Post-Design Manager.
Donoho, Peter: Administrative Oversight Manager.
Fox, Jesus: Quality Control—Leadman.
Frisbee, Marvin: Preventive Maintenance Manager.
Harkat, Mohammed: Physical Inspection Manager (Acting).
Ness, David: Assistant Hoover Dam Chief of Police.
Robinson, Joseph: Exterior Power Cabling Unit—Leadman.
Zubaida, Elizabeth: Public Relations Office Secretary (Acting).

Al-Qaeda Kilo-class SSK submarine—*The Scorpion*:
Moqod, Majed: Operational and Political Captain of the vessel.
Al-Adil, Saif: Weapons Systems Officer (WSO).

Al-Motasseded, Farouk: Vessel's Executive Officer—2IC.
Al-Shihhi, Marwan: Al-Qaeda Special Operations (SOF) Team # 2 leader.
Hof, Abu: Engineering Officer.
Jarrah, Zaid Samir: Al-Qaeda Special Operations (SOF) Team #1 leader.

Lake Havasu City/Mohave County—Arizona—Civilian Command Structure:
Hazard, Chief: Fire Department Chief, Lake Havasu City.
Lion, Chief: Police Department Chief, Lake Havasu City.
Sheahan, Tom: Sheriff—Mohave County.
Whelan, Bob: Mayor, Lake Havasu City.

Al-Qaeda terrorist cell in Lake Havasu City:
Mohammed, Mohammed: Team Leader.

Camp Delta **Detainees:**
The Skagit Eight:
    Alghamdin, Hamza (Saudi)
    Alghmdi, Saled (Saudi)
    Al-Haznawi, Ahmed (Saudi)
    Alomari, Abdulaziz (Saudi)
    Al-Sugami, Satan (Saudi)
    Barghouti, Marwan (Palestinian)
    Qayoon, Abdul (Saudi)
    Oms, Mohammed (Palestinian)

Al-Qaeda High Command:
Bin-Laden, Osama: Age 47, Commander, Visionary, and Leader of Al-Qaeda (Saudi).
Bin-Laden, Saad: Age 23, Elder Son of Osama (Saudi).
Al-Zawahiri, Ayman: Age 52, Chief al-Qaeda planner and bin-Laden's chief deputy.
Al-Sha'ir, Abu Hazim: Lieutenant over Persian Gulf Operations (Yemeni).

US Joint Taskforce 160—US Naval Station—Guantánamo, Cuba:
Al-Halabi, Ahmed I.: USAF Airman, a translator assigned to JTF at Gitmo.
Battle, John: US Army Master Sergeant in JTF 160 at Gitmo.
Hehalba, Ahmed Fathy: Civilian contract linguist assigned to JTF at Gitmo.
Johnson, Jason: US Army 1st Lieutenant. Aide to General Montrose—JTF at Gitmo.
Lewis, Jeffrey NMI: US Army 1st Lieutenant. Aide to General Montrose—JTF at Gitmo.
Lokkesmoe, Marvin: USMC Colonel—NCIS/JAG Taskforce into al-Qaeda spies.
Montrose, Geoffrey: Major-General USA, JTF Commander.
Stark, David: Brigadier General, USA, JTF Executive Officer (XO).
Yee, Yousef: US Army Captain. Muslim Chaplin assigned to JTF at Gitmo.

PROLOG

DAY 001

United States Central Intelligence Agency: *Factbook—Cuba.* (excerpts from)

(In general, information available as of 01 January 2003. Selected pages were updated by the Agency on 18 December 2003.)
CUBA: "Fidel CASTRO led a rebel army to victory in 1959, his iron rule has held the country together since then. Cuba's Communist revolution, with Soviet support was exported throughout Latin American and Africa during the 1960s, 1970s, and 1980s. The country is now slowly recovering from a severe economic recession in 1990, following the withdrawal of former Soviet subsidies, worth $4 billion to $6 billion annually. Cuba portrays its difficulties as the result of the US embargo in place since 1961. Illicit migration to the US—using homemade rafts, alien smugglers, or falsified visas—is a continuing problem. Some 2,500 Cubans attempted the crossing of the Straits of Florida in 2002; the US Coast Guard apprehended about 60% of the individuals."

Land mass: 110,860 Sq. km.
Area comparative: Slightly Smaller than Pennsylvania.
Coastline: 3,735 km.
Maritime claims: Exclusive economic zone: 200 NM.
Territorial sea: 12 NM.
Land boundaries: Total 29 km.
Border countries: **US Naval Base at Guantánamo Bay, 29 km—Contested.**
Terrain: Mostly flat to rolling plains, with rugged hills and mountains in the SE.
Climate: Tropical; moderated by trade winds; dry season (November to April).
Natural resources: Cobalt, nickel, iron ore, manganese, salt, timber, silica, petroleum.
Irrigated land: 870 km (CIA's 1998 est).
Natural hazards: The east coast is subject to hurricanes from August to October.
Geography note: Cuba is the largest country in Caribbean and westernmost island of the Greater Antilles.
Population: 11,263,429 (CIA's July 2003 est.)
Median age: 34.5 total.
Life expectancy at birth: 76.8 years total.
People livings with Aids: 3,200 total.
HIV/AIDS deaths: 120 (CIA's 2001 est.)
Government—Country name: Republic of Cuba.
Government type: Communist state.
Administrative divisions: Fourteen provinces.
Legal system: Based on Spanish and American law, with large elements of communist legal theory.
Suffrage: Sixteen years of age, universal.
Executive branch: President of the Councils of State and Ministers; Fidel CASTRO Ruz. First Vice President of Councils of State and Ministers; Gen. Raul CASTRO Ruz.
Economy overview: The government continues to balance the need for economic loosening against the desire for firm political control. It has undertaken limited

reforms in recent years to increase enterprise efficiency and alleviate serious shortages of food, consumer goods, and services but is unlikely to implement extensive changes. Major feature of the economy is the dichotomy between relatively efficient exports enclaves and inefficient domestic sectors. The average Cuban's standard of living remains at a lower level than before the severe economic depression in the early 1990s, which was caused by the loss of Soviet aid and domestic inefficiencies. High oil import prices, recessions in key export markets, damage from Hurricanes Isidore and Lili, and the tourist slump after 11 September 2001 hampered growth in 2002.

Radio stations: AM 169, FM 55, shortwave 1 (CIA's 1998 est.)

Telephones—main lines: 473,031 (CIA's 2001 est.)

Television stations: 58 (CIA's 1997 est.)

Paved airports: 70.

Military branches: seven.

Military manpower availability: 3,120,702. (25% of population including women.)

Transnational Issues: **(Disputes) US Naval Bases at Guantánamo Bay is leased to the US and only mutual agreement or US abandonment *(emphasis added)* of the area can terminate the lease.**

Prepared and maintained by the US Central Intelligence Agency
Last updated 18 December 2003.

Author attests the above document to be an exact copy of selected excerpts contained in the US Central Intelligence Agency's *World Factbook—Cuba*.

HOTEL PRESIDENTE LA HABANA
PENTHOUSE 2-A
Thursday—02 January 2003
GMT—5

The shrill sound of dueling alarm clocks roused Manuel Lopez Bello from a deep, alcohol-induced sleep. Cursing, he crawled first to one side of the king-sized bed, then, after having to first shove last night's conquest onto the floor, to the other. As he shut off both clamoring alarms, Manuel noted unsurprisingly that both proclaimed it to be 5 a.m.

The penthouse was large, 12 meters by 12 meters, or 144 square meters. The carpets were rich looking, royal blue, with a 30.5 centimeters wide, gold-colored emphasis strip around the floor-covering's perimeter. The bedding, drapes, and other fabrics were a pastel yellow, edged with gold trim. In the large bath, all the fixtures were of plated gold, and the over-sized towels, yellow to match the room decor. Futuristic yellow-colored telephone instruments were located on the tables on both sides of the large bed, and another wall-hung between the commode and bidet in the bath. A HP top-of-the-line commercial-grade laptop, a Sony fax machine, a sixty-inch Samsung big-screen TV, a theater-quality sound system, a tan-leather vibrating recliner, and two matching leather armchairs completed the room furnishings.

Dear Mother of God, he thought, *how much rum did I have to drink last night?* After a moment of contemplation, he remembered where he was—The Hotel Presidente La Habana. Located at Calzada 110 Esq Avda de Los Presidentes, the Hotel Presidente was one of the top three-star hotels within reasonable driving distance of Jose Marti Airport, where he worked. Only a three-star, because the American's continued to punish his country, with their groundless embargo which kept the tourists away. No tourists, no four-or-five star ratings for La Havana hotels.

Jose Marti International, Cuba's flagship airport, was located on the Rancho Boyeros, eighteen km from Midtown Havana.

Bello, forty-five years of age, five foot five and weighing a trim

150 pounds, often was mistaken for a movie star in the clubs of Havana. His dark good looks, flashing white teeth, and workout-hewn physique, seemed to attract young, beautiful women like moths to a flame. While not wealthy, he managed to maintain his lifestyle through countless small schemes and sizable bribes throughout the year. Last night's bounty, a young, aspiring but no-talent blond-haired nightclub entertainer, had bought his empty promises—hook, line and sinker. Her promise to satisfy his every desire, had earned her a place on that night's A-list for the evening bedding. And, as an important man who could grant many favors, the hotel has been more than willing to comp the penthouse for his personal use.

Normally, Lopez Bello didn't attempt to reach his desk at the airport until a more reasonable hour. However, Presidente Fidel Alejandro Castro Ruz was adamant that the top officials in the government be productive and accountable. As Managing Director of Cuba's largest civilian airport, Bello was by default included in that select group.

Today would be especial. That much had been graphically made clear to Bello by the mid-day visitor to his office on New Year's day. Raúl Castro Ruz, Fidel's brother, was someone prudent people never antagonized, never offended, and never disobeyed.

The fifth of seven children of Angel Castro y Argiz and Line Ruz Gonsález, Raúl was the son of a landowner. He, like his older brother of five years, Fidel, had married well, Fidel into one of Cuba's wealthiest families, and both could have assimilated themselves into the island's oligarchy.

Yet today, Raúl was one of Cuba's most feared officials. Both men had collided with fate following an attack on the Mancada Barracks in Santiago de Cuba. The attack was an attempt to overthrow an "oppressive government." But it had been a dismal failure. Raúl and Fidel were captured. Many of their 160 followers were executed. Both brothers were imprisoned and Raúl given a

13-year sentence. Both were released in a general amnesty in May of 1955. The Mancada raid gave birth to Fidel's '26th of July' movement.

Over the years, both brothers had attained new heights of brutality. Perhaps because Fidel was an attorney by education, the younger brother harvested a far worse reputation for brutality, sadism, and cruelty. Of course, he was essentially doing his brother's bidding. But on numerous occasions since 1955 Raúl had ignored Fidel's orders. One example was in the summer of 1958, when Raúl kidnapped forty-seven Americans and two Canadians. The kidnapped had been stationed at the Guantánamo Base. Fidel, disagreeing with the justification Raúl gave him, ordered that they be immediately released. Raúl did not comply until months later.

Today, in 2003, Raúl was the commander of Cuba's two military intelligence organizations. He literally made people disappear. Especially those he categorized as being counter-revolutionary. Which in the new millennium included almost anyone Raúl became annoyed with.

Was the General Manager of Jose Marti Airport intimidated— you bet! That was the reason he had set *two* alarm clocks to insure he was at his desk by seven am. He personally was responsible for making sure every order Raúl had given him, was carried out in the extremis. The alternative—no doubt, would be a very unpleasant death if historical rumor was to be believed.

After Bello had received his marching orders from Raúl yesterday, the feared despot and his entourage had departed, leaving the General Manager shivering in fear. The fact that Manuel could just pickup the phone, and call Fidel, did nothing to mitigate the fear. Raúl did what he wanted anyway, and Fidel apparently supported him, blood being thicker than water. And no doubt, an order of this magnitude had come directly from Presidente Fidel Castro Ruz, himself.

Manual Lopez Bello had quickly summoned his staff by punching the speed dial buttons, first for extension # 666151, and then # 454576. Bello admitted, but only to himself, that the only reason the Cuban international airport operated so seamlessly, was solely due to the tireless efforts of his two subordinates, Robert Rivero and Lazaro Chaviano.

Robert Rivero was the airport's Operations Director. His actions insured that the passenger-related activities in the three terminals functioned without complaint. Although only slightly over five foot tall in height, and constantly fighting a battle with an imaginary fifteen pounds of weight, Robert modeling himself on his mentor. This extended to the careful study of his boss's mannerisms, dress, and personal methods of conduct. Unusual for a Cuban, the thirty-year-old Rivero was blonde-haired and blue-eyed. He was married. He and his wife had nine children, somewhat explained by the fact that triplets ran in his wife's gene pool. Robert was a graduate of one of Havana's Universities, with an advanced degree in International Marketing.

Lazaro Chaviano, the airport Cargo Manager, on the other hand, seemed an odd addition to Bello's team. He was nearly six-foot, six-inches tall, and weighed in at more than two hundred ninety pounds. He had been an excellent and talented baseball player in his youth. However Chaviano's shot at the big time had come to a crashing halt. While serving his obligatory stint of compulsorily military service as a revolutionary Army conscript, drill instructors jealous of his potential had staged a late-night-hours 'blanket party' in the recruit barracks. With a heavy olive green wool blanket being held over his head, and his massive arms restrained by ropes, his fellow recruits, anxious to curry their drill instructor's favor, had proceed to break every bone in those powerful hands. A Cuban Special Forces Captain, who was familiar with the stories of Chaviano's talent, had stumbled upon the beating, Once he ascertained what was going on, he had drawn his pistol, and killed five of the young athlete's attackers. Then he had personally driven the young man off the training base, and to the home of a nationally acclaimed orthopedic surgeon he knew was a baseball enthusiast.

Unfortunately the beating had been too severe. Those wonderfully talented hands would thereafter be relegated to more menial tasks. The captain returned to the base, woke up the drill instructor one of the pleading recruits had fingered, and saw that he was placed in a dungeon without trial.

The Army Captain asked his father, who had been with Fidel in the Mancada Barracks attack, to seek out appropriate compensatory action from El Presidente. Once Fidel heard about the incident, he sent his even-then feared brother to investigate the circumstances behind the attack. Raúl had ordered the jailed drill instructor, and the other recruits that were known to have participated, taken out to a nearby crocodile farm, and fed piece by piece to the hungry twenty-foot long animals, beginning with their still-attached testicles.

Fidel made further arrangements. Lazaro Chaviano was discharged, and sent on an all-expenses paid scholarship to one of Cuba's premier technical schools. Upon graduation, Lazaro was sent to Bello. The Managing Director had been ordered by Fidel to employ him as the airport's Cargo Manager. The young man had by that time set aside his personal tragedy. Managing Director Bello had to admit Chavaino did an excellent job in coordinating the dozens of daily air freighter flights into and out of Jose Marti. Their importance was paramount. Cargo flights were the lifeblood of a poor communist island-nation.

Manuel Bello admitted to himself that he was paranoid. In a communist state such as Cuba, that preoccupation was the only thing that insured his longevity in the position. He used the airport's significant operating funds to pay for a rotating squad of plainclothes detectives to tail both Rivero and Chaviano, during their off-hours. The surveillance team, were former Cuban interrogators that he had recruited from the Cuba's Revolutionary Armed forces, fired for brutality. The on-going surveillance of his subordinates had thus far reveled no tendencies towards corruption or disloyalty towards himself.

Yesterday, by the time Rivero and Chaviano had appeared in his spacious office located immediately below the air-traffic-control-complex, Bello had swallowed several large mouthfuls of rum, popped a breath mint into his mouth, and managed to bring his visible emotions back under control.

The office of La Havana—Jose Marti Airport's (world airport designator HAV/MUHA) General Manager, had been furnished by Bello over the ten years he had occupied it. The large rooms had hardwood flooring, with Persian carpets separating the desk from two conversation areas, including an eight-foot-long cherry conference table. All the armchairs were dark-green leather, as were the intricate inlaid surfaces of the conversation pit and conference tables.

Over the years, Bello had managed to upgrade the room by 'diverting' a few pieces of high-end furniture here and there from airfreight shipments destined for foreigners here in Havava. His paid strong-arm team, if pressed, quickly settled the occasional complaints of missing cargo. And likely as not, the end result was completely to the dissatisfaction of the complainers.

When his Operations and Cargo managers entered the room, he gestured to the conference table for them to sit, and took a seat himself in a armchair having a taller back. Briefly he explained to them what Raúl Castro Ruz had ordered of him.

"At exactly 8 am tomorrow, Thursday, 02 January 2003, a civilian jet with the tail number of N901FJ will have priority clearance to land on all-weather runway 06/24." The airport's main runway was full IFR-certified and equipped, 4,000 km long and certified for all aircraft types. Bello continued, "The airport will be closed for fifteen-minutes before the landing, and for fifteen-minutes immediately following the jet's subsequent departure."

"Other passenger and cargo flights are not to be pre-warned of the closing. If still on the ground, ground control will direct them to hold at their gates. If aloft, departure control will order them to hold in the traffic pattern, until the airport again reopens permitting them to land. I have been assured the delay will not be so lengthily as to impact the commercial passenger flight FAA-mandated fuel minimums."

Bello continued, "Thirty-minutes prior to the VIP landing at 0730 hours, an armored convoy from the Cuban Revolutionary Army will arrive at the airport. They will take up prearranged positions around a then-unoccupied 'large aircraft' maintenance hanger. From that point, until the time the VIP aircraft again departs the airport, no one except that aircraft and a vehicle convoy from the Palacio de Las Revolutiones, will be permitted entry. No passage will be permitted within ninety-one meters of the secured hanger, no exceptions. I have been warned that any violators will be shot," Bello warned his men.

"The VIP jet will not be taxing to one of the three airport terminals. Instead, it will be led by a FOLLOW-ME jeep, driven by you, Lazaro, to a designated maintenance hanger here on-airport, on which the rolling doors will have been left open. The pilots of the executive jet will 'power it' into the hanger, pivot the aircraft on its main gear, and come to a stop with its nose facing the now-rapidly closing rolling doors."

Bello, consulting his hastily scribbled notes, continued, "In order to not restrict airborne commerce, the airport will be reopened at that point. However, the Army's protective screen of guards will remain around the hanger, until the VIP's aircraft and the Presidente's convoy, depart."

Checking his notes to make sure he had forgotten nothing, the Airport's Managing Director concluded, but only after asking if the men had any questions. Bello then answered some routine questions as to the permissibility of unscheduled on-airport movements such as fire trucks, field security, postal trucks, and emergency maintenance vehicles.

Then Bello, in a rare moment of openness, shared with his staff that "General Raúl Castro Ruz has given me no more information about the VIP visit," but reminded them of Raúl's reputation for being the most hot-headed, impetuous, and violent member of Fidel Castro's government.

Shrugging his shoulders in a involuntary display of the stress he was under, Bello said, "Everything will go smoothly if we do exactly as we have been told—but I must advise you, as I am being held accountable, I will hold each of you accountable—collectively and individually responsible—for any failures to adhere completely to the orders of Presidente Fidel Castro Ruz, and General Raúl Castro Ruz. Now get back to work—and make sure that tomorrow goes off without a hitch. If absolutely necessary, you may call me on my cell phone for any reason, as long as it is connected with this VIP matter. I have plans for dinner tonight at the Hotel Presidente la Habana, as my wife is out of town for a few days visiting relatives in Cientuegos."

After an afternoon of repeatedly checking and double checking the notes that had come from his noon meeting with General Raúl Castro Ruz, Manuel Lopez Bello looked at his gold Rolex Presidential, and found it to be already 4 pm.

Long before Raúl's visit, he had made plans to take advantage of his wife's infrequent visits to her family down country in Cientuegos. A young sultry performer he had caught the show of several times in the past month, was performing in the cocktail lounge at the hotel Presidente that evening.

Twice, following her shows at several of Havana's few remaining nightclubs, he had sent his flowers with a note offering to 'help her career' if she was interested. The girl claimed to be twenty-one in her publicity posters. Through his connections with the tourist police, Manual had learned that she yet had to turn fifteen, which excited him greatly.

Learning that the Presidente Hotel had booked the teenager for a singing gig on a slack night at their ailing tourist bar, Manual had leaped into the breech. He had a trusted secretary send the girl flowers, with a note saying, that he "just happened to plan to be in the neighborhood of the Presidente hotel. And that he would be willing to consider interviewing her that evening, to determine if she met the rigid standards he maintained, for the introduction of fledgling entertainers to his important recording company contacts."

Within five minutes of the girl's receipt of the flowers, she had called on his private telephone line, assuring him that she "would be honored to interview with you, Señor Bello, this evening."

With that heady anticipation in mind, Manual changed his suit in his office dressing room, grabbed a small pre-packed overnight bag, and had one of his security men drive him over to the elegant hotel, for what he anticipated was going to be a primo night of sex and debauchery. Before getting out of the ten-year-old black, Soviet-era ZIL limousine at the Presidente Hotel, he reminded his security guard to pick him up no later than 6:30 am the following morning at the valet parking curb out front. While he felt that his two trusted subordinates could handle the VIP assignment the next morning without any problems, he nevertheless reminded himself that *he* was the one Raúl would hold responsible for any foul-ups. He intended to be in his office when the executive VIP jet landed to insure nothing untoward happened. Raúl's reputation gave ample warning that any deviation from his brother's carefully conceived plan would have life-threatening consequences for him, even if the failure had been beyond his control.

The following day, following his rather jarring wakeup call from the two alarm clocks he had prudently set the night before, Bello hurried dressed, electing to forego a shower. Before leaving the room, he tossed the girl one hundred convertible Cuban pesos, the equivalent of the $3.70 US dollars. This, she obviously considered an insult of the highest degree. She vaulted out of the huge bed and to her feet, still naked at the proverbial jaybird, and began to scream at him, and assault him with her hands and feet. Bello tried to push the strong girl aside with one hand, as he attempted to finish putting on his expensive alligator leather shoes, with the other.

He had almost reached the door, when she landed like a tiger on his back. She was scratching, spitting on him, and screaming at the top of her lungs about his offer of help with her career he had promised her the night to attain her performance of a specified act of oral sex. As he had never intended to make good on his part of the bargain, Bello shrugging her off his shoulders and fled the room running down to the hall elevator.

There with the girl's screaming threats echoing in the hallway behind him, now being enhanced by the inclusion of the words *pig* and *rapist*, he darted in front of an astounded elderly couple who had just been stepping into the elevator, and began to frantically punch the 'lobby floor' button, forcing the couple to retreat and wait for the next car.

Bello forced himself to walk with his customary strut across the large lobby of the opulent hotel, and out though the shiny brass doors where his security officer awaited him, holding the rear door open to the highly polished, near-antique, Soviet limousine. As soon Bello had dived into the car, all the while imagining the girl suddenly materializing at the rear window screaming insults regarding his manhood, the security man slammed the rear door, and jumped into the front seat.

The car today was being driven by a duty security officer who 'had seen that, done that' many times since Bello began to taking the indiscriminate 'popping' of Viagra, chased by up to a bottle of potent Cuban rum, several months ago. Lately, the officer had taken to wondering if Bello would suddenly die of a massive heart attack. Or whether some well-deserving but angry father would manage to castrate Bello with a machete. In any case, the officer tromped on the accelerator and sped off for the 18 km trip, taking the sidewalks when required to get through Central Havana's morning gridlock traffic and out to Jose Marti International Airport.

Less than thirty minutes later, the heavy ZIL limo ran the open gate at the Airport's employee entrance. That action avoided a blast from one of the guard's AK47s, only because the car was a one-of-a-kind, and thus was easily recognizable as belonging to the Airport's Managing Director. The security officer drove, as the now-terrified Bello, fast approaching being late for the VIP landing, screamed in his ear to "Hurry! Hurry! Hurry!"

The now-equally frantic limo driver cut across parking lots, dodging parked vehicles. The ZIL swerved at 100 km/hour dangerously along the narrow, weaving airport's surface roads where the posted speed limit was 40 km/hour. By this time, all four of the heavy vehicle's hubcaps had popped off in collisions with traffic islands and road curbs.

As the car raced along the perimeter road, it caught the attention of the just—arrived Army armored convey. The Army was already in-place surrounding the maintenance hanger, that stood empty, with the huge rolling hanger doors gapping open, waiting for the VIP aircraft. As the Russian ZIL continued past the hanger, the Army elected to let it go and remain in-place as ordered. The Army convoy detachment's commander reasoned that it wasn't his responsibility to play traffic cop. And if it was, he was too smart to make any effort that could result in his having to apprehend, which he incorrectly assumed, was one of the few remaining Russians officers yet to flee Cuba.

At exactly 7:48 am, the now smoking and sputtering ZIL, screeched up to the main administration building at Jose Marti International Airport. Bello, livid, jumped out and barged past the two-armed guards holding the entrance doors open for him. Reasoning the elevator would be too slow he darted up the stairs two-at-a-time, until he reached the back door to his private office. Fumbling with the key, he wrenched the door open, and ran to the floor-to-ceiling windows. Shielding his eyes from the glare of the morning sun, which was raising in the east, he noted that the large flashing light atop the control tower was indicating that Jose Marti Airport was closed to all air traffic, a fact the in-bound VIP aircraft would of course ignore.

Bello decided that he did not have the time to contact his subordinates by phone. He would just have to assume they had done their jobs, and everything was in-place to receive the VIP aircraft and the Presidential convoy from Castro Palace.

Approaching from over the Straits of Florida for a landing at Jose Marti was a white Dassault Falcon 900 manufactured by the Country of France. The aircraft's tail number, clear and readable in the rising morning sun—N901FJ. The Falcon 900 was in a carefully controlled descent from 10,000 feet, and still more than 100 miles southeast for a straight-in landing to runway 24.

The Falcon 900 was one of the more expensive executive transports jet at $27.9 million each. The Falcon 900 was also one of the fastest. The payload capacity was a maximum of nineteen passengers. And she can carry over 3,000 pounds in cargo, without cutting down on her 3,900 mile range. Today, this Falcon 900, leased to a Muslim charity in Afghanistan, had taken off from a country sympathetic to the Muslim cause, less than 2,000 statute miles distant. The 900 had a low/swept wing; three tail turbofans; and a mid-mounted tailplane. The upper fuselage hull was painted white, the lower gray, with a blue train line separating the two colors.

There were only four passengers besides the two pilots onboard. One of them was a young man, 24-years in age, who wore an Iranian-style turban, flat black in color. The word 'turban' is thought to have come from the Persian word *dutBand*. His name was Saad bin-Laden, an elder son of Osama bin-Laden. He had emerged in recent months as part of the upper echelon of the al-Qaeda network. Western intelligence has identified them as a small group of leaders that is managing the terrorism organization from Iran, according to U.S., European, and Arab officials.

Although Saad bin-Laden was not the top leader of the terrorist group, his decision-making presence on today's mission, acting as a representative of al-Qaeda, demonstrated his father's trust in him and an apparent desire to pass on the mantle of leadership to a family member.

The other three passengers were heavily-armed bodyguards. They were part of an elite, radical Iranian security force loyal to the nation's clerics and beyond the control of the central Iranian government. The group was known in U.S. and European intelligence circles as the 'Jerusalem Force.' Each had pledged their lives to protecting Osama bin-Laden's son, Saad. That was the reason each of them was present on today's flight.

They wore threadbare black suits, over-starched white long-sleeve shirts, and well-worn black silk ties. Each, surprising, carried a 9 mm Uzi machinegun, a cheap weapon built in quantity by the Israelis. They also each carried a lightweight, hard-hitting Glock .45 caliber automatic handgun. Each of the three bodyguards was electronically wired up in a manner similar to American secret-service agents. The exception being that none of the American's ever carried a ten-pound block of Semtex formed to be a part of a deadly waist belt. The detonator for the explosives was located directly over the hearts of the each of the three men. In that location, studies had shown that even a dying man would be able to strike his chest with enough strength to detonate the charge. Al-Qaeda had designed the explosive charge to bin-Laden's specification that it be capable of destroying anything within 91 meters. In Bin-Laden's obsessed mind, this could be the greatest gift he could give to his son, should the group be captured. Extremist terrorist zealots are skilled practitioners in the methods of human torture. Knowing the beast well, bin-Laden owed it to his son and family to prevent Saad from having to experience it, first hand.

The fast jet continued its descent into a smooth landing on the 4,000m runway at Cuban's Jose Marti Airport. As it touched down and began its roll out, the pilot could have easily braked the jet, and taken the first turnoff. The Falcon 900 required less than one-half the Cuban runway's available length. However, per plan it continued to high-speed taxi to the far end of the long runway. There the Falcon 900 was met by a FOLLOW-ME Jeep, and escorted to the open doorway of an empty commercial aircraft hanger.

The French jet slowly powered itself into the hanger, and locked its portside wheel brakes. This permitted the aircraft to pivot until it was facing the way it had entered. Almost instantly (one had to assumed that the entrance had been choreographed for diplomatic reasons) a convoy consisting of three, shiny, black French-made Citroen sedans, pulled in alongside the parked aircraft.

The occupants of the sedans waited for the jet's three turbofans to spool down. Then the portable airstairs module folded out of the starboard side of the aircraft, and snapped into place. The final view to be had, as the large rolling hanger doors closed, was Fidel

Alejandro Castro Ruz, and his brother, Raúl Castor Ruz, exiting the middle sedan. Once the heavy rolling doors had clanged shut, Fidel and Raúl, holding on to the handrails, pulled themselves up the steep airstairs. Presidente Fidel's progress up the Falcon's self-contained air stairs into the aircraft's spacious cabin, was slow and with the difficulty brought on by advancing age. Raúl, five years younger, did little better.

It would be months before the ramifications from the January 2nd, 2003 meeting came to light. It had been a meeting between representatives of two of America's fiercest enemies. The meeting between the Castro brothers and the son of Osama bin-Laden would serve to fan the flames of revolutionary extremism. And was destined to elevate world terrorism to an entirely new level. A new level far beyond even the highest level of the American's color-coded terrorist-threat assessment system. Far above the 'Imminent threat level.'

CHAPTER ONE
THE AMERICAN NAVAL BASE
CAMP DELTA
GUANTÁNAMO BAY
CUBA

"*Humane but not comfortable*"
          Commander—US Joint Taskforce (JTF) 160;
          Guantánamo Bay, Cuba.

NEWS BULLETIN (Excerpts from)
Associated Press
09 April 2002
(Accompanying photo-redacted by Website owner)
CAMP DELTA
By Beth A. Keiser/AP
CAMP DELTA: Construction workers build a security fence around the new, permanent detention facility for Taliban and al-Qaeda prisoners at Guantánamo. The structure is

capable of housing up to 2,000 men in individual cells—potentially for the rest of their lives.

30—END OF BULLETIN

NEWS BULLETIN (Excerpts from)
The Chris Science Monitor
30 April 2003
By Warren Richey / Staff Writer
HOW LONG CAN GUANTÁNAMO PRISONERS BE HELD?
The building of a permanent detention facility highlights an emerging US tactic: Long-term holding of captives.
WASHINGTON: Within the next two weeks, all . . . suspected terrorists in US custody at Guantánamo Bay, Cuba, are set to leave their makeshift cells at *Camp X-Ray* and move to a new detention facility on a rocky bluff overlooking the Caribbean Sea.

The view is spectacular. The ocean breeze is balmy. But that is where any similarity to a seaside vacation will end for al-Qaeda and Taliban fighters who find themselves behind bars at . . . *Camp Delta*.

The new terrorist detention facility is being built as permanent structures, capable of housing up to 2,000 men in individual cells—potentially for the rest of their lives.

Construction of the new camp highlights an emerging tactic in the Bush team's war on terrorism; the open-ended detention of large numbers of terror suspects. While the prospect of military tribunals has sparked extensive debate, this move toward indefinite detention has drawn relatively little attention . . .

30—END OF BULLETIN

GUANTÁNAMO BAY—US NAVAL STATION, CUBA.

The duty station was known in the U.S. military by its

website name *"The Least Worst Place in the world."* If you feel that term doesn't adequately cover it, feel free to visit Guantánamo Bay Naval Base in Cuba. You can tell them I sent you. See if you can find one *good thing* to say about it.

It is a very disagreeable spot located on northern shoreline of the Caribbean Sea. Typically just the place in the past, that the Pentagon 'star-fighters' felt would be a "ideal location" for a U.S. military base. Well, I guess it is better than Adak Naval Air Station in Alaska, but it would be a tough call either way.

Guantánamo Bay, Cuba. Actually, the U.S. Naval Base in Cuba really isn't located anyway near the City of Guantánamo. Guantánamo City is more than eight miles north of the U.S. Naval station. Who knows what the current population of Guantanamo City is? Fidel Castro Ruz hadn't permitted anyone to do a census count since 1994. At that time the city boasted a population of 200,000 souls. The infrastructure growth of Cuban cities is tied to politics and Presidente Castro. Not to the needs of the local economy. So the real time population figure now could be higher, or lower.

If you are one of those technical device geeks, the global satellite position (GPS) of Guantánamo City is 20°10'N, 75°13' W. The longitudinal location is represented by the east-west coordinate, and latitude by north-south coordinate. Both coordinates are measured with respect to the Prime Meridian at some place known as Greenwich, England or the equator, in the case of latitude. Look at one of those neat glass world globes they had in every geography classroom when you were in high school. Longitude is the scribed lines that run left and right, with latitude being the lines running up and down. OK, you didn't purchase this novel to get a navigation lesson—I'll move on.

That's almost enough about Guantánamo City. The city is a processing center for the sugar and coffee agribusinesses. However, it also has furniture factories and publishing houses. Guantánamo City has railroad connections to the larger hub city of Santiago de Cuba. But let's get back to the U.S. Naval Air Station where this tale begins anyway.

Guantánamo Bay (or 'Gitmo' as the U.S. Navy and/or master techno-thriller writers Tom Clancy, and USAF Captain Dale Brown,

Retired, refer to it) is a U.S. Naval base. It is located on a sheltered Caribbean Sea inlet, which also serves the Cuban ports of Caimanera to the west, and Boqueron to the east.

For you linguistics experts (or not) the base's formal name is pronounced (gwahn-TAHN-ah-mo). The U.S. Government leases it from the Cubans for about $4,500 USD/year, and has since 1903. The lease was renewed in 1934. Fidel Castro would love to see the Americans "go missing" from there. He has in fact refused to accept the nominal annual rent payment since 1960. That happened to be the year the U.S. cut off relations with Cuba. Sounds like a marriage made in Heaven, right?

The base is a forty-five-square mile parcel of treaty-leased land. The exterior perimeter security fence is seventeen miles in length, or about twenty-six kilometers (km). The perimeter has interesting specifications, including two parallel security fences separated by a no-man's land, liberally planted with Cuban land mines. A small army of highly trained guard dogs accompanied by human handlers, patrol the perimeter fence. There is only one formal passage gate in the security fenceline separating the base from the communist country of Cuba. It is located in the north perimeter fence line. The gate is well patrolled by heavily armed U.S. Marines and aggressive guard dogs, as are most areas on the base.

The U.S./Cuban relationship concerning Gitmo is a bit strained. In recent years, the trained security dogs have effectively— even literally—eliminated any incidents of on-base trespassers. The great majority of Cuban males do not like dogs, let alone growling ones. Most Cubans aren't surprised that their people attempt this very dangerous breaching of American defenses. The near hopeless attempts are easily understood when you realize that a high percentage of Cubans in Castro's revolutionary utopia are starving to death.

Presidente Castro Ruz insures that the Americans at Gitmo remain under the close scrutiny of his Eastern Army. It is headquartered at the Cuban Camagüey Army Base. U.S. Intelligence experts maintain that the few remaining Russians in Cuba are based at their own intelligence base at Lourdes, outside Havana. The

Russians also have established human intelligence (HUMINT) networks which spy on Guantánamo Bay U.S. Naval Station.

The Cuban Army is broken up into three distinct and separate military units, and further broken down into seven sub-groups. This was done to prevent coup attempts against the Castro Regime. The mission of the Eastern Army quite simply is to surround our naval base at Guantánamo Bay. Its Cuban counterparts are known as the Western Army. It protects the capital city of Havana. The Cuban Western Army also has orders from El Presidente to keep a jaundice eye on the remaining Russians at Lourdes, and San Antonio de Los Banos bases. The Cuban Middle Army's mission is responsibility for routine military functions associated with Cuba's national security.

Why doesn't Fidel Castro Ruz evict us from Gitmo? After all, Cuba has a population of 11,178,000 persons, 96 percent of them literate, and its landmass includes more than 3,700 islands. The United States remains a tenant at the Guantánamo Bay Naval Station, solely because in 1934 some pencil pusher in the State Department modified the lease language. With his devious pen, he inked in the proviso that "the consent of both parties is required to revoke the agreement."

The U.S. Navy has been there for seventy-five years, intends to be there another seventy-five hundred years, or until the proverbial cows come home. How will this tenant/landlord relationship be impacted when Castro's dies, should the replacement regime turn out to be staunchly democratic? That's above my paygrade—I can truthfully say, I don't know.

Guantánamo Bay Naval Station is located on the southeastern tip of Cuba. That's approximately 500 statute miles southeast of Miami. You remember Miami—the city that Dade County Sheriff's department; the TV reality show COPS; and the actor Don Johnson made into a household word. Gitmo can be approached via the Windward Passage from the north, or the Caribbean Sea from the south. It is the largest bay on the far southeast coast of Cuba, and has admittedly fantastic 'blue water' ship anchorage capability.

The bay itself is potato-shaped, and measures twelve miles

long in a northeast-southwest direction. The bay is about 2.5 miles across its girth. Contour elevation-wise, Guantánamo Valley is a unremarkable area with relatively junior-league hills running north by northeast along the Sierra Maestra. The water outside the bay proper is very deep. It descends to a depth of 200 meters, once traffic passes Windward Point, headed south out into the Caribbean Sea. Sharks come in all sizes and are plentiful. The deep bay is protected by the Cuzco Hills, which reaches an elevation of nearly 500 feet Mean Sea level (MSL) to the south and east, and by the mountains to the north.

The entrance into Guantánamo Bay is located between the landmarks designated Leeward Point and Windward Point. It is accessible through a navigational channel less than a mile wide. That entrance is restricted controlling the passage of any vessel for security considerations. The United States' restriction of the area is based on lessons hard learned at the U.S. Naval Base at Pearl Harbor on December 7th, 1941.

The bay entrance has been dredged and is maintained at a depth of forty-two-feet, from the entrance north to Fisherman's Point. From that landmark, the passageway continues north to Caravel Point. The designated navigational channel is maintained at only slightly more than thirty feet in depth.

The Guantánamo Bay complex is actually two logistical harbors—an Inner and Outer Harbor. The Outer Harbor, which is the northeastward limit of the U.S. Base's leasehold, extends only to Palma Point, the entrance into the Inner Harbor. At Palma Point, the harbor narrows until it is 750 feet wide. As the harbor waterway continues north, it deepens, and then widens into two separate bays totaling five miles in width. The inner section, called *Ensenada de Joa*, forms the Upper Harbor. There, two Cuban commercial ports are located on opposite sides of the Inner Harbor.

U.S. Guantánamo Bay Naval Station is located completely within the Outer Harbor, and includes seven designated anchorages. The U.S. Naval Base is sited on the east shore of the harbor, about 1.75 miles north of Windward and Granadillo Points, which is located slightly more than 2.5 miles to the northeast.

There are many peninsulas, a number of coves, and a small number of islands in that section of the harbor. Much of the land on the east shoreline of the harbor rises rapidly above sea level.

This, as opposed to the west side of Guantánamo Bay, which is very close to sea level. The east shore consists mostly of mudflats and mangrove trees adding to U.S. Base's already considerable security challenges.

Fortunately, the coves between Corinaso and Deer Points were ideally suited for the construction of waterside port facilities of the Guantánamo Naval Station. As one proceeds inland, the land remains fairly flat for about 700 feet. This made it an acceptable site for the construction of the two airfields that originally served the U.S. naval complex.

Leeward Point field is the superior airfield, and is currently the base's only active flight facility. The military jetport is ringed with many valuable support facilities, and is heavily guarded at all times.

McCalla Airfield on the other side of the harbor entrance has been inactive for years, due primarily to the logistical limitations of the field, that would be necessary to support the extension of its runways to provide for use by heavy military jet aircraft.

To insure the Guantánamo Bay's continued ability to support the berthing of capital U.S. warships, the main entrance is maintained by the U.S. Navy to about sixty feet until you enter the forty-two-foot depth of the Outer Harbor. As ships do proceed northeast up the bay, contract dredgers maintain the depth to about thirty feet, as you enter Eagle Channel in Granadillo Bay's east navigation lanes. The tidal range between Mean and Low tidal flows, does not routinely exceed more than one foot. However, variations of up to four-five feet have been recorded during tropical storm conditions.

The tidal current in the bay has been measured to be from less than a quarter knot on the flood stage, to a little more than a half knot on the ebb. At the Guantánamo River entrance more robust currents are recorded. Three-to-five-foot swells in the afternoon and evening hours are typical at the river mouth, from the Outer

Harbor entrance to a coordinate off Fisherman's Point. When waves in the Outer Harbor reach six feet in height, the Navy's ferry service between the Leeward and Windward sides of the base is forced to temporarily discontinue service. Waves well over that height have been experienced during occasional tropical storms. And of course, such is the case frequently during the hurricane season.

The Outer Bay at Gitmo is essentially U.S. Navy leasehold territory while the Inner Harbor is a Cuban commercial port complex. The Outer Harbor extends from Palma Point (entrance to the Inner Harbor) south to the Guantánamo Bay entrance off Windward Point. The Outer Harbor includes the U.S. Naval docking facilities located at Corinaso Cove, between Radio Point and Corinaso Point.

Currently there are five active piers, running between 180 feet to 900 feet in length, which offer moorage limited by a dredged depth of only twenty to thirty-five feet. Only three wharves, the largest slightly more than one thousand feet in length, offers dredged depths of thirty-eight-feet, and those docks when designed, were constructed six-to-ten feet above Mean Sea Level. In any case, vessel maneuvering is considered difficult, as some of the actual depths are inconsistent with the published bottom clearance information. Ship pilots find that the actual dredged channel width is limited.

The U.S. Navy Port Service Officer at Gitmo assigns wharf space. Seven deep-water authorized anchorages are available in the Outer Harbor. Use of a harbor pilot is mandated for all commercial shipping vessels, but is an option for U.S. Navy ships. Limited tug service is available through Port Control 2400/7 upon telephonic or radio request.

Cuba, an island of 42,804 square miles, was discovered by Christopher Columbus over five hundred years ago, and was once if not currently considered by the Russians to be the "finest aircraft carrier in the Atlantic." You don't have to be a U.S. naval academy graduate to understand the implications of that observation.

The U.S., under the multi-service umbrella of Guantánamo Joint Task Force 160, has constructed modern prison facilities at

Gitmo, which eventually could accommodate up to two thousand detainees. A number of temporary camps were used initially for detaining al-Qaeda prisoners, such as the relic Camp X-Ray. Those outdated camps have since been replaced by new construction— Camp Delta. This is a maximum-security, modern (expandable) confinement facility. It is designed to house the detainees for as long as the rest of their natural lives.

The U.S. Naval Base is divided into two separate functional areas by Guantánamo Bay. There is a much-improved airfield on the Leeward side (west) and the main base on the Windward side (east). The U.S. Navy maintains ferry service across the bay. Its mission is to provide for movement of personnel, supplies, and equipment. The Guantánamo Base's primary naval mission is to serve as a functional logistics base for the U.S. Navy's Atlantic fleet. Its secondary mission is to support counter-drug operations in the Caribbean Sea. Its new tertiary mission is the War on Terrorism.

The U.S. Coast Guard, specifically Port Security Unit (PSU) 307 at the time of this novel's editing, provides the 'on-water' security inside the Outer Harbor for the base. The PSU is equipped with a total of six, twenty-five-foot radar-equipped Boston Whalers. Each boat has M-60 machine guns mounted on each wing, and a .50 caliber heavy machine gun on the bow. The PSU element also provides surveillance and interdiction capabilities on the water.

International and Cuban commercial ship traffic utilize Outer Bay for access to the Cuban ports up in the Inner Bay to the north. All commercial vessels including sport fishers and Cuban fishing boats, are shadowed during their transit through the U.S. Base's leasehold waters by no less than two heavily-armed PSU 307 patrol boats.

When off-duty, the 307th sailors have access to diving, sailing, hiking, mountain biking, cookouts and outdoor movies activities for relaxation. A grand duty station it isn't—but it is critically necessary to America's War on Terrorism.

Naval Reserve Mobile Inshore Undersea Warfare Unit (NRMIUWU) 106 is headquartered out of Miami. (You've got to *love* the Navy's acronyms.) It is their mission to guard the waters around outside Guantánamo Bay proper, to prevent non-authorized activities by terrorists and Cuban nationals, alike.

Over the years, Gitmo has served as an unscheduled temporary stop for Haitian refugees. The U.S. Base has also supported two contingency operations involving Chinese immigrants—namely Operation Marathon in 1996 and Operation Present Haven in February 1997. These 'no notice—no lead time' operations both involved the illegal smuggling of the Chinese immigrants into the United States.

In 1994, temporary rudimentary camps for this influx of migrant civilians were set-up at 'Radio Range.' The area got its name because it is also the site of the base's 'antenna farm' (radio antennas) on the south side of the facility. However, massive numbers of unplanned, and unforeseen illegal immigrants forced the United States to set-up additional camps on the north side of the base. The only remaining camp in the base's northern area in 2001, even minimally able to meet the requirement for housing al-Qaeda prisoners, was Camp X-Ray. And that location, to speak frankly, was realistically assessed by a former JTF Commander as a 'grim, nasty place'.

Another former Base Commander, Brigadier General Lehnert, certified the somewhat renovated Camp X-Ray as failing even the "humane, (but) not comfortable" test. The existing prison facility didn't have running water in the cells. The detainees had to use a 'slop bucket' for bathroom functions.

Another limiting factor at Camp X-Ray was that it only had housing capacity for 320 detainees, far smaller in size than the eventual anticipated population. Preparatory to the in-coming requirement for up to 2,000 detainees, a new more humane facility was designed and built by military contractors, Navy SeaBees, and U.S. Marine engineers. Camp X-Ray was deactivated when a state-of-the-art confinement facility came on-line in April 2002. It is located about five miles south of X-Ray at a new facility named Camp Delta.

Compared to X-Ray and all previous facilities designed and constructed at Guantánamo for the housing of detainees, Camp Delta is a modern facility. Even the ICRC (International Committee of the Red Cross) agrees the accommodations there are much nicer than any of the detainees were accustomed to at home. Camp Delta was built at the south end of Radio Range, on the crest of the highest real estate on the Gitmo base. The ICRC has free and unannounced access to monitor camp conditions, subject to security restrictions for their own safety. All of the detainees are capable of extreme violence. Something the ICRC staffers sometimes forget or ignore.

At nearly five hundred foot elevation, the weather at Camp Delta is generally mild. The camp is blessed with balmy ocean breezes. The view is stupendous as Delta is perched on a rocky bluff overlooking the Caribbean Sea.

Each individual detainee's elevated eight foot by six-foot-eight-inch expanded metal housing unit at Camp Delta has a flush toilet, a sink with running water, and a roof. A welded steel bunk was built into the design for each unit. Each detainee is provided with a typical military mattress, blue-colored blanket, sheet, towels, washcloth, sandals, and a set of orange coveralls, which can be exchanged weekly for a clean set. Detainees are permitted two hot showers weekly.

There are also two fenced recreation/exercise yards available per detention block. Each block has a fully equipped First Aid Station. Access to a fully staffed, on-base hospital for the seriously ill is available. A communal 48-man covered unit is provided where the detainees may visit, eat, and pray together.

Of course the fact that readers must keep in mind, is that pleasant or not, Camp Delta is a prison. Each one of the detainees earned their incarceration at Gitmo for being caught bearing arms against the United States, and/or the Coalition. The detainees must behave and cooperate with the two-hour interrogations, to be afforded the communal privileges. The entire detainee population (nearly seven hundred detainees currently, from forty-two countries, as of this editing) is generally between the ages of twenty-one and thirty-five.

Previously there were even a half dozen teenagers between the ages of thirteen and fifteen who were captured in combat—carrying and/or using loaded weapons, killing American or Coalition troops. However, American compassion served. These teens were kept separate from the camp's general population. Guards monitored them hourly to insure their individual safety and welfare. Depending on their conduct, they were permitted additional privileges such as educational classes, counseling, and afternoon opportunities to view ancient 'Gilligans Island' videos.

In the later part of 2003, all six of these teenagers were repatriated to the lands of their birth. There they continue to be detained. Assumedly they will be held until some appropriate action can be taken to insure they will not return as enemy combatants in the War on Terrorism.

Detainees at Camp Delta are offered three meals daily, at least one of which consists of a U.S. military meals-ready-to-eat (MRE). The same ration American troops eat in the field. Breakfast for the detainees at Camp Delta consists of bagels and crème cheese, the preferred fare for most of the detainees when they were at home.

Camp Delta as a detention facility replaced Camp X-Ray and also a portion of Camp Bulkeley. Both the old camps were being used initially for temporary incarceration facilities to house al-Qaeda and Taliban detainees. The new camp was built on the cinder block foundations of a previous 'temporary' camp, which shortened the construction schedule to some degree. Although not perfect, and certainly in no way comfortable, the facility goes a long way to showing the world America's compassion, even for those who are its self-avowed enemies.

CHAPTER TWO
THE AMERICAN NAVAL STATION
CAMP AMERICA
GUANTÁNAMO BAY
CUBA

The U.S. completed construction of "humane, but not comfortable" facilities for the detainees at Camp Delta. Now it was time to turn to the construction of adequate housing for the U.S. military element required to administer and operate the detainee facility. Some U.S. Marines and related personnel, were still having to use a rundown housing section of the Camp Bulkeley facility. However, more permanent living quarters were required for the personnel who physically operate, administer, and see to the health and welfare of the detainees in the new camp.

The minimum overall staffing levels for operation of an U.S. overseas military detention facility depends on many factors. In this case, the number of troops is significant, as all detainees are first and foremost considered 'combatants.'

The exact number of U.S. contract-civilian and military support personnel stationed at Guantánamo Naval Station, is then and now considered a matter of national security. Thus, those figures are not available to the media. But it is likely the number is significantly in excess of fifteen hundred trained and fully equipped combat-ready troops.

Camp America was designed and constructed at Guantánamo Bay, strictly to address this need. It is modern although utilitarian in design. Still, normally no one could be offered enough money to volunteer for Gitmo as a duty station. The end result is that the U.S. military troops assigned there have been well provided for.

Camp America opened for the housing of U.S. multi-service support personnel in April 2002. Unlike Freedom Heights (temporary quarters for U.S. support personnel adjacent to the temporary detainee Camp X-Ray) and the section of Camp Bulkeley being then used by other U.S. camp support personnel, Camp America is a full-service housing facility.

The new housing has hot showers, laundry rooms, workout/ recreation areas, medical stations, air conditioning, big screen TV, computers, phones, and ultra-fast Internet connections. Everything the modern U.S. military specifies for its permanent housing facilities.

Camp America is located between Kittery and Windmill beaches, on the south side of Guantánamo Naval base. The new housing consists of fifty-five foot by thirty-two foot plywood, air-conditioned and insulated structures, called 'SeaHuts.' The former housing structures the JTF troops had been living in at Freedom Heights were called GP-Ms, or General Purpose—Medium tents. A total of one-hundred-five SeaHuts were constructed in ninety-days by the 'SeaBees.' The SeaBees are the highly skilled engineering and construction branch of the U.S. Navy. Each of the SeaHuts is designed to house up to ten people, and each is built to military standards (MilSpecs.)

The new SeaHuts are weather-resistant and equipped with dual access/egress doors at either end of the structure. The DoDs (U.S. Department of Defense) design for Camp America permitted amenities not found at Freedom Heights. Modern features like a Local Area Network (LAN) SeaHut with phones, and fast access to the Internet.

Camp America also has basketball courts, a library, a first-aid Station, secure phones and special Internet computers that interface directly with the Guantánamo Naval Hospital facilities, which are located over on Hospital Cay. Another SeaHut serves as a mini-theatre for a top-of-the-line big-screen TV, showing of first-run movies, and seating for up to twenty persons. The Navy calls these structures Morale, Welfare and Recreation huts (or MWRs.) Generally each MWR is located adjacent to two other MWR SeaHuts and are linked by a common porch. Other MWRs provide Chaplin's areas and medical stations to treat the troops domiciled there.

Additional facilities deemed necessary by the Army to adequately support the troops at Guantánamo, include three tension frame systems (TFSs) at Camp America. The first includes a free-weights gym, with Nautilus-type exercise machines and rubber mats on the floors for sports such as Judo.

The second TFS contains a mess hall, grandly named *The Seaside Galley*, which is air-conditioned. This galley is mission-capable of feeding a battalion-sized element. In other words it is ready to generate up to 4,000 hot, nourishing meals daily.

The third and last TFS is a freestanding hall for training, meetings, and OJT (on-the-job training) educational activities.

The design of Camp America is unique in the fact that it centralized Command Services, by placing the Platoon Headquarters facilities among the troop's living quarters. This was similar to the Freedom Heights headquarters facilities layout. The Freedom Heights facility had been the first JTF troop housing constructed when the detainees began to arrive. Due to time constraints and having no other options, it had been constructed immediately adjacent the site of the Camp X-Ray detention center. The Command complex served to provide U.S. JTF troops with additional MWRs. These units provided the troops with even more call-home phones, and computer access to the Internet.

Future planned construction (phase two) at Camp America involves extending the facilities another quarter mile down the beach. However, at the present time, additional troop housing is not currently required. Thus, phase two will be delayed until all 'future' detainee-housing needs are fully met.

On 24 June 2002, a full-service JTF First-Aid facility became operational at Camp America. This facility also has direct phones lines and Internet access to and from the base's hospital complex.

Facilities at Tierra Cay, formerly used for family housing, have also been renovated permitting a limited number of troops to move in there. This action served to relieve the non-housing building needs at Camps America and Bulkeley. The renovated housing at Tierra Cay is generating building vacancies elsewhere on the base. As SeaHuts are vacated, and become available, they will be used for storage and office space, both of which are currently in short supply at Camp America.

Kellogg, Brown and Root Services (a division of Halliburton Company which acts as the government's general contractor at Guantánamo) construction jaggernaught continues. November 2002 brought additional hard-roofed quarters with indoor latrines on-line for the use of the JTF staff at Guantánamo. The new facility will be called Camp America—North.

CHAPTER THREE
THE AMERICAN NAVAL BASE
THE WAR ON TERROR
GUANTÁNAMO BAY
CUBA

It was slightly before dawn and a beautiful chilly morning at Camp Delta. The camp is located on a bluff at the 495-feet elevation. It looks out on the Windward Passage from its vantage point on the Cuzco Hills. If it weren't for the circumstances, perhaps the detainees would have found the view from the tall bluff stupendous. By midday the sun would warm the balmy breezes blowing in from the Caribbean Sea. At exactly 0530 that morning the U.S. Joint Taskforce guards began morning reveille. They came around, banging their nightsticks against the individual detention units, to wake any of the detainees who might still be sleeping.

The brisk morning air was fresh and filled with the fragrance of salt. The sun had started to raise its blindingly bright orb over the eastern horizon. Signaling the beginning of a new day.

As the sun came up, the prisoners easily determined which

direction they would knell for Islamic prayers. Commercial hotels throughout the world generally indicated the direction of Mecca for Islamic prayers by clearly marking it on the walls. That was for the convenience of their Muslim guests. No such amenity had been provided here at Camp Delta. The International firm of Kellogg, Brown and Root Services had designed and constructed the new U.S. detainee facility. The firm's designers had explained that their omission was intentional. The justification—the designers felt that there was a possibility that some persons detained there might not be of the Muslim faith. The Department of Defense's design specifications were clear in any situation where that could be the case. The designers were to take steps to avoid culturally offending the devotees incarcerated there, wherever possible.

The U.S. Joint Task Force troops administering, operating and guarding the new detainee facility would have been surprised to learn that less that six of the Taliban and Al-Qaeda detainees there were of the Christian faith. And that a like number were agnostic.

Those few detainees that didn't completely spurn the idea of God's existence nevertheless felt more comfortable believing in the 'Sheik' than any other deity. That was the form of address Osama bin-Laden preferred.

The topography of Camp Delta was one of gentling rolling hills. The finished elevation for the camp included some mounds of earth that had not be excavated during construction. It was a well thought out design. Delta currently held nearly seven hundred detainees from forty-two countries. The always-active al-Qaeda prison 'grapevine' was saying additional terrorist combatants were on the way to join the camp.

The now awake detainees finished their morning ablutions. The JTF guards handed out the morning meal, fresh bagels and cream cheese.

In a short time, the list of those to be interrogated this morning would be read aloud over the camp's P.A. system by an Arabic-speaking JTF guard. In order of scheduled appearance on the today's interrogation list, each detainee would be shackled. This was accomplished without any of the detainees having to leave, or have a guard enter their individual confinement units. Each detainee, on command, would lean back against the inside of the steel access gate, and extend his hands backward through a pre-engineered rectangle metal opening in the gate. The guards would snap-on the military handcuffs. The prisoner's feet were shacked in a similar manner.

The terrorist detainees were then permitted to sit on their welded steel mattress racks. As their names came up on today's interrogation schedule, which was randomly rotated daily, the guards came to individually escort them blindfolded to their daily interrogation sessions elsewhere in the Delta Two and Delta Three maximum-security areas of the camp.

Depending on the amount and quality of the interrogation product each detainee provided and/or divulged that day, a red or green check was placed alongside their name on the list. Those with green checks, absent any other demerits, would be escorted back to their individual confinement unit, where their blindfolds and shackles were removed. Then, those deemed 'cooperative' were escorted to join their comrades. After morning meal and interrogation sessions, one of the communal forty-eight-man day rooms was opened for the detainees use. Activities that typically took place in the day rooms were religious prayers, afternoon and evening meals, conversation or limited exercise. Each day's 'special privileges' pass had to be re-earned each day.

Those detainees unluckily enough to be considered uncooperative (U.S. intelligence interrogators have bad days also, you know) would be escorted—blindfolded, back to their individual confinement units. Their blindfolds and shackles would be removed and they would spend their day in isolation. Without any human contact except for the JTF guard that brought them their meals.

No detainee was ever permitted access to a television, radio, newspaper, uncensored mail, e-mail, writing supplies, tape recorders—nothing. If the detainee wanted sign up to see a Red Cross inspector to complain, his name was added on the bottom of the 'whiners list' for the week.

The al-Qaeda and Taliban detainees at first had been assigned to various temporary holding facilities throughout the forty-five-square-mile Guantánamo Base. Later they all had been centralized at the new Camp Delta facility. All the captured terrorist combatants (which had resulted in them occupying the facilities at Gitmo in the first place) were under the age of forty.

There originally had been an handful of teenage terrorists detained at the U.S. Naval Base. Those detainees were guarded by a special detachment of Arabic-speaking guards. These U.S. troops had demonstrated the people skills necessary for counseling, coordinating sports activities, and settling petty arguments.

The specially qualified JTF guards would run a VCR and show approved videotapes in the afternoon for the boys. Assuming their morning interrogation sessions had been productive and the kids cooperative. If so, they were permitted to watch old *Gilligans Island* reruns.

The teenagers, most who had first killed their first American or coalition member before age ten, seemed amused and joked among themselves about the similarity of the show's purported locale (an island), and their own situation here at Guantánamo.

The head U.S. JTF guard carefully observed the kids. He or she made note of when the kids were getting bored, between the education classes offered them, and their own interactions. A couple of the younger guards, after removing and locking up their security hardware, might challenge the young killers to an impromptu volley ball game. The playing court was inside the secure compound. And the game was always under the watchful eyes of the other guards who were still armed with Tasers and nightsticks.

As usual the kids usually waxed the guards, resulting in laughter and rude gestures being exchanged by both sides.

There were eight detainees at Camp Delta who were watched more closely than the other prisoners. These men, by plan, had been sprinkled among the general population throughout the camp. None of them was ever permitted to get close enough to another of the 'eight,' to communicate.

The U.S. Joint Task Force guard personnel didn't really know if these specific eight prisoners were any more dangerous than their other colleagues at the camp. What they did know, however, was that these each of these 'special' detainees came with a intelligence file nearly three inches thick. It was filled with photocopied reports on their terrorist activities before they came to become the guests of the United States at Camp Delta.

Each of the 'high-security risk-classified' detainees had been captured during an attack on the United States' homeland, specifically the Pacific Northwest. Their attacks came down in the county of Skagit, in the state of Washington.

On 28 October 2002, these eight detainees had been a small part of a larger al-Qaeda attack force that sought to demolish the levies along the Skagit River in Washington State. If they had been successful, it could have resulted in the deaths of hundreds of local county residents. The terrorist plan had been to eradicate the road base, on which Interstate highway, which passed through the county, had been constructed. The blowing of the swollen river levies would cause massive uncontrollable flooding. The flooding would in turn wash out the Interstate highway's compacted roadbed.

However, the terrorist's attack scenario had been war-gamed by Washington State law enforcement years previously. It was no secret that the only way the Canadian fast-response REACT teams, and the Washington National Guard's own heavy-wheeled Bradley fighting vehicles and Abrams tracked vehicles, could provide support to the population and infrastructure of the Greater Seattle area, was over the north-south running I-5 highway system.

Many uncontrollable floods over the years in Skagit Valley had shown engineers that once the levies gave way (or in this case, were blown up) the released water could quickly undermine the I-5 freeway. And that Interstate was the only road through the Skagit Valley, built strong enough to support the massive weight of military's heavy-wheeled and tracked equipment.

The San Juan Islands, Boeing Field in Everett, Deception Pass Bridge, access routes out of the Navy's Whidbey NAS, and the Space Needle at the Seattle Center had already come under terrorist attack that year. Without the Canadian REACT teams, and the

Washington National Guard troops and firepower, Seattle and King County would be helpless to adequately protect its many at-risk venues, infrastructure, and landmarks. Continuing al-Qaeda attacks the summer of 2002 even targeted the historical landmarks in the Pacific Northwest. The Space Needle had been demolished into a pile of steel and concrete rubble. An al-Qaeda suicide crew had turned a stolen Boeing 747-400 into a weapon on 31 July 2002, bringing the structure down.

Fortunately, for the protection of the critical river levies, the Skagit County Sheriff backed up by the FBI's best, the Washington State Patrol, and municipal police departments operating under 'mutual aid' had stopped the terrorists cold. The law enforcement strike force had counter-assaulted the terrorist teams. This action prevented all but one of the crude but highly explosive ammonia nitrate fuel oil (ANFO) bombs, placed by al-Qaeda, from detonating.

The eight 'special watch' prisoners currently being detained at Camp Delta were all of the surviving terrorists that had been taken alive following that failed attack.

Abdul Qayoon and Abdulaziz Alomari, both Saudi al-Qaeda team leaders, had headed up two of the terrorists explosives teams involved in the explosives attack in Skagit County. Their captured al-Qaeda subordinates, also explosives experts, included Mohammed Oms (Palestinian), Marwan Barghouti (Palestinian), and Ahmed al-Haznawi, Satan al-Sugami, Hamza Alghamdin, and Saled Alghmdi, all Saudi citizens.

The eight terrorists had proven to be uncooperative since their arrival at Camp Delta. One of them had even bit a JTF guard in the throat nearly severing his jugular vein when the guard had allowed his attention to wander. There were no punishment facilities here at Camp Delta by intent and design. So all the JTF could do was restrict those eight terrorists to their individual housing units, as they would any uncooperative and combative detainee. One of the JTF camp psychiatrists ventured an opinion. He said, perhaps the 'Skagit-Eight,' as the detainees had come to be called, harbored embarrassment from failing in their assigned mission. They feared the consequences should they ever be repatriated, and sent home where they again would be subject to Bin-Laden's harsh discipline.

The guards assigned the Skagit-Eight accepted that opinion as being as good as any other. But deep in the logic centers of their minds, the seasoned guards still worried. The Skagit-Eight had developed an aura of arrogance about them. A perceived feeling that seemed to shout that he "Don't expect us to be at Camp Delta very long, you pitifully stupid Americans."

Each of the eight forced themselves to eat every morsel of food they were given. No matter how disagreeable it may have been to their fundamentalist Muslim palates. Almost as if they were maintaining their physical well being for a strenuous task whose demands lurked just around the corner.

Ever since the eight detainees had been incarcerated at Gitmo, they had allowed themselves to be lead around by the arm like blind men. Which of course they were as no detainee moved outside the center of the camp without a blindfold. The Skagit Eight appeared to be conserving their strength. Due to their complete refusal to cooperate with the interrogation specialists, they had not been permitted access to the exercise yard.

However the JTF guards frequently noticed them doing pushups or isometric exercises in their containment units. All the U.S. guards could do was observe, report what they saw up the ladder, and worry some more.

While depression, and even attempts at suicide were not new at Camp Delta—nearly two dozen detainees had tried it, a few of them twice, unsuccessfully—the Skagit Eight seemed immune to the pressures of the camp. They seemed to revel in its orderly procedures, and 'zero surprises' atmosphere. That these were very dangerous men was never disputed. But how they planned to escape from this escape-proof prison camp was yet unknown. Making the group the subject of many speculative 'what if' discussions that occurred daily within the U.S. JTF guard directorate.

CHAPTER FOUR
THE AMERICAN NAVAL BASE
GITMO VULNERABILITY
GUANTÁNAMO BAY
CUBA

During the massive influx of terrorist detainees, construction of new holding facilities resulted in steam roller-driven construction. The needs for providing for ever-increasing numbers of both prisoners and JTF support staff drove life at the U.S. Naval station.

The remote U.S. Naval Base had been through 'no-notice' detainment programs like this before. First came the Cuban fence-climbers. The Haitians closely followed them. The Chinese followed both groups. The rush-rush-rush environment the around-the-clock construction created high levels of stress for the Base's 'regular party.' Regular party consists of officers and enlisted involved in the physical operation of the base, excluding the detainment operations.

The natural fear was that Cuba or some other nation-state would learn the true staffing levels of Gitmo. And an enemy would take the opportunity to attack, kill or capture the remote, underprotected naval base's operators. Few of the permanent party listened to the rumors that America had no nation-state allies willing to come to their assistance in the event of such an attack.

But the concern caused some of the base personnel, those not directly involved in that terrorist detainee activity, to purposely attempt to isolate themselves from it. A supposedly informed 'rumor mill' occupies every military base in the world. More times than not, the information generated by such a 'mill' is unsubstantiated bull crap. Those that accepted the validity of the negative information they heard around the their barracks, and the enlisted men's club from the rumor mill at Gitmo, were seriously infected with a terminal case of negative thinking. Of course the 'mill' existed. But the rumor that 'no one stateside cared the Gitmo was at-risk' was totally untrue.

The Gitmo base permanent party had experienced the disruption before, and surely would again, after this latest crisis was over and when the next assignment steamed their direction from over the horizon.

Guantánamo is the oldest U.S. base overseas. And the only permanent one, to date, located in a communist country. The base is located in Cuba's Guantánamo Province. The bases' terrain and climate made it a haven for iguanas and banana rats.

President Dwight Eisenhower severed relations with Cuba in 1961. Many Cuban trespassers in those days sought refuge by climbing over the U.S. Base's perimeter fencing. Some were successful, despite the barbed and concertina-wrapped U.S. perimeter fence lines and Castro's minefields. The seventeen-mile perimeter fence line is guarded today 2400/7 by the U.S. Marines on the U.S. side, and the Cuba's elite 'Frontiers Brigade' on the other.

Guantánamo Bay provides access to the Upper Harbor for Cuban commercial vessels. Cuban commercial fishermen must use the Outer Bay for access to Windward Passage. It is not physically possible by treaty or otherwise to barricade access-by-water through the U.S. base.

U.S. Guard patrol boats protect the waters surrounding the

U.S. base at Guantánamo, and the waterways adjacent. These twin-engine, twenty-five foot Boston whaler-type patrol boats, are nimble, quick, and outfitted with both sonar and Doppler radar.

On the base proper, trained sentry dogs have eliminated the threat of Cuban trespassers. For whatever reasons, the Cubans have a healthy fear of those animals.

Guantánamo Naval Station—the aviators call it the Naval *Air* Station—was formerly a 'dependants permitted' service billet. However in 1962 during the Cuban Missile crisis, when the Cuban's permitted the Soviet's to install ballistic missiles on the island, the bases' dependants were evacuated to the U.S. mainland. The U.S. mounted a naval quarantine of Cuba until the Russians removed the ballistic missiles.

By Christmas of 1962, the U.S. dependant families were permitted to return. Then fourteen months later, before many of the families had fully settled back into their day-to-day lives, Castro struck again. This time the Cubans cut off all potable water and electrical power supplies to the base. Castro claimed the interruption was justified because U.S. authorities had issued citations and fined Cuban fishermen for fishing in water that belonged to the U.S., under the terms of the base's leasehold agreement.

The U.S. authorities by then had decided that any dependence at all on Cuban officials was too much dependence. A huge desalination plant was constructed on the Guantánamo Bay naval base. Today, that plant produces 3.4 million gallons of drinking water and more than 800,000-kilowatt hours of electricity, daily.

In 1991, the Haitian refugee crisis reared its ugly head, again disrupting the base. In 1994, Operation Sea Signal was implemented to deal with the incursion. The U.S. Naval Base at Gitmo was tasked with providing humanitarian aid and housing to the fleeing refugees from Haiti. Temporary housing facilities were constructed on 'Radio Range' to accommodate the refugees. That site would later serve as the location for the permanent Camp Delta.

By September 1994, the Haitian migrant population housed at Gitmo had increased to 45,000. This caused the Navy to again return the base's military dependents to safe haven on the U.S. mainland. By the end of January 1996, the military had managed to facilitate the relocation of all the Haitian and Cuban refugees to safe havens, elsewhere.

U.S. military dependants again returned to Guantánamo Bay in October 1995. Military service-family facilities, which had been rundown by the interloping refugees, were either renovated, or new construction replaced them. Support facilities, such as a child development center, a youth center, two schools, and a Sunday school to American standards, were renovated. When completed, they were made available for use of the dependant families. The on-base revitalization of both genders' Scouts programs, along with an enhanced Guantánamo Bay Youth organization, was provided by the U.S. Department of Defense (the DoD).

After the refugee expulsion, Operation Sea Signal at Guantánamo became fairly quiet with never more than about forty refugees on base at any particular time. That all changed in 1996. Two separate operations (Marathon and Present Haven) began. Both of which dealt with an influx of Chinese refugees, intercepted while being smuggled into the United States.

In 1995, Guantánamo Bay Naval station began to lose some long-time U.S. tenants. Ending a tenancy of fifty-two-years, The Atlantic Fleet Training Command moved to Mayport, FL in July 1995. Another major tenant, Shore Immediate Maintenance Activity, was disestablished in 1995 after ninety-two-years of service.

As of the date this novel was edited, the Guantánamo Naval Base still includes the separate Commands of a Naval Hospital and a branch Dental Clinic. There exist detachments of the Personnel Support Activity, the Naval Atlantic Meteorologic and Oceanic Command, and the Naval Media Center. A few smaller tenants remain including the Naval Communications Station, Department of Defense Dependent Schools, and a Navy Brig.

In direct support of the NAS as individual departments, are the U.S. Naval Criminal Investigative Service (the NCIS), and the Resident Officer in Charge of Construction. The Human Resources Office, Family Support and Service Center, and the International

Committee Red Cross, Gitmo Base Security, and the Naval Exchange/Commissary also remain.

In 2001, JTF/GTMO (Joint Task Force—Guantánamo) was tasked with providing services and shelter to house incoming Taliban and al-Qaeda detainees. That requirement has been escalating weekly, ever since. The detainees are transported to, and occasionally out of, out of Guantánamo on C-17 (Boeing Globemaster II) USAF cargo planes, accompanied by (Lockheed Martin Fighting Falcon) F-16 fighter support.

The free world has entered into a new era. A single terrorist wielding a small nuclear weapon such as a 'suitcase' bomb can threaten an entire city. That makes the continued operation of the active U.S. Naval installation at Guantánamo Bay, along with its controversial detainment camps, absolutely critical to America's national security. This despite the fact, that the isolated U.S. base has lost nearly fifty-percent of its major tenants in the recent years.

Guantánamo Naval Station is currently considered self-reliant. This is based on the criteria of having the in-house capability for the production of potable water, and the generation of electricity. Foodstuffs, and nearly all other supplies have to be flown or shipped in by aircraft, freighter or barge. This makes the U.S. base potentially vulnerable to a naval blockade. However, that scenario would require the involvement of a major unfriendly world power. Currently, nations that meet that definition do not exist. Or if so, they are not considered viable 'players' by America's intelligence community at this time.

The question remains whether a surprise enemy invasion of Gitmo in an attempt to rescue the detainees is potentially possible. The U.S. Naval Base's anti-siege defenses would make an invasion by water very costly to the belligerent. Such an attempted invasion would likely not succeed. Or at least would not, if the enemy's intent were to maintain a presence long enough, to remove *all* the Taliban and al-Qaeda detainees, and make good an escape by air or sea.

The wild card in the deck would be whether Presidente Fidel Castro Ruz would get Cuba actively involved in the rescue assault.

Or would he simply be satisfied to be a passive participant, by his willingness to grant the escapees 'political asylum.' This assumes the enemy assault team is at least momentarily successful, permitted them to breech the Naval Station's perimeter fencing, for egress.

American airborne combat response from the U.S. mainland is less than two hours away. Any enemy invasion with the grandiose goal of rescuing and spiriting away *all* the terrorist prisoners detainees off the island would be futile. This is not to say, the Pentagon admits, that such an escape mission might not have limited temporary success, if the enemy's mission goal were significantly reduced in-scope.

CHAPTER FIVE

DAY 121—01 MAY

HOOVER DAM

THE INTELLIGENCE ASSESSMENT

NEAR BOULDER CITY

NEVADA

SECRET
NO FORN
Intelligence Assessment Report
Homeland Security Department
Washington D.C.
01 May 2003

FROM: Secretary, U.S. Homeland Security Agency
DATE: (Redacted, as authorized under U. S. Patriot Act—2003.)
SUBJECT: Hoover Dam, Strategic Analysis and History
TO: George W. Bush
      President of the United States
      The White House
      George W. Bush Washington, D.C.

In compliance to the Presidential memorandum to the Secretary, Homeland Security Agency, dated 30 May 2003, the following information is furnished:

Strategic Analysis and History—Hoover Dam

Since the early 1900's, businesses such as lumber mills have employed thousands of American workers in their manufacturing operations in Arizona, Nevada, and California. Those were the bygone days when forests in the western U.S. were still abundant, filled with huge girth trees, just begging to be cut down and turned into lumber to feed America's insatiable growth.

While raw wood product was widely available in those days, sources from which to obtain cost effective power to run those operation's large equipment, were not. Lacking other options, the mills routed the 'off-fall' waste from the lumber and plywood-making operations, back into the process. Every bit of sawdust and waste wood from the mill operations was 'blown' by mill pneumatic systems to an enclosed storage facility, called a fuel bin, which was as large as a tennis court.

Necessary to protect the power generating fuel operation from any accidental mechanical spark, the concern for the high-combustibility of the material was paramount. Little external source ventilation was provided, and workers wore dust masks to protect their lungs. Inside the large cave-like rooms, combustion-engine crawler tractors fitted with spark arrestors collected the volatile wood waste from where the large mill blowers had dumped it onto the fuel storage room floor. The 'pusher' and 'front bucket' tractors accumulated the off-fall waste into piles, which were then loaded onto large belt conveyors. The conveyors, in turn, fed the waste fuel into massive furnaces. There the fuel was burned, turned into energy in the form of 'steam,' and steam was used to generate electricity. This electricity was utilized to run the sawmill operation. In some of the larger well-planned facilities, there was even a surplus of power, and electricity would be distributed to the entire company-owned town.

American lumber companies, at the time, viewed this process as a dangerous but necessary evil. In the workplace, company safety officers preached ad infinitum to the sawmill workers, warning them that an accidental spark could ignite the airborne sawdust, which would cause at least *two* consecutive explosions.

Large Red Emergency 'Call-for-Help' mushroom buttons were located abundantly throughout the storage bin. However, in the real world, it is always too late to react once the 'balloon has gone up.' The primary explosion was the result of the initial ignition of the uncontained dust on the floor. The second explosion was directly attributable to the sawdust that had been collecting in the roof support structure overhead, for decades. That dislodged sawdust was thrown into the air by the force wave of the primary explosion, where it readily mixed with oxygen and ignited, thereby producing a much greater and far more damaging fuel-air secondary detonation.

The sawmills, plywood 'planer' operations, and the 'door and box shook' factories were diligent and worked hard to prevent these catastrophes. However, every couple of years that unique set of environmental conditions seemed to again materialize, and another powerhouse fuel bin blew up. Often the explosions blew off the building's roof, and the now-unsupported walls fell in, killing or severely injuring the employees whose bad luck it was to be assigned to the fuel storage processing operation that day. A good number of the casualties were workers who were hideously burned by the explosions.

At the beginning of the 20th century, large amounts of non-allocated electricity were not available for purchase in the Western United States. Those lumber mills that could generate their own electricity, did, and possibly would have continued to produce their own nearly cost-free power, if stringent Occupational Safety and Health (OSHA) legislation had not been enacted by Congress.

Until the mid-to-latter part of the century, sawmill operations as a whole remained very inefficient. Perhaps American lumber operations were not anymore inefficient than those in any other manufacturing industry, but the equipment was nowhere near state-of-the-art. Raw wood product was certainly more available in those days, as hundreds of thousands of acres of American forests had yet to be harvested. Admittedly, it is the nature of American industrialists to defer the spending of large capital sums of money required to 'update' something, until one absolutely must. An applicable adage (if it ain't broke, why fix it?) was often repeated in 'Obsolete Equipment Replacement' request meetings, in boardrooms throughout America.

As America moved into the mid 1970's very few capital dollars were being approved by CEOs for the replacement of antiquated sawmill equipment. This is not to say that there were not plenty of young, dedicated, safety-and profit-oriented MBA's available to the wood products industry, conducting feasibility studies, and preparing replacement equipment requests for capital funding.

Modernization came first in the Southern and Eastern United States, where the large-girth raw wood product had already been logged off, leaving only smaller diameter trees, and those in far lesser number. In the Southern United States in particular, a lot of smart guys in wood products corporations started to introduce automated equipment that could produce the desired end product cost-effectively, while consuming considerably less raw material, and managing to do so with fewer workers. The new methodology was far more worker-safe and used available raw product in a far more environmentally friendly manner.

This was especially true in America's paper products industry. Large corporations such as International Paper Company (IPCO) one day found their mills running out of available or acceptable raw product. And when raw product was available, mill operations were killing their company's profitability. This was due to having to rely on old, inefficient manufacturing equipment, growing environmental concerns, and the staggering costs required to comply with The Occupational Safety and Health Act (OSHA).

One of the first inefficiencies targeted by big lumber was their on-site electricity generating operations. Scrap wood product 'off-fall' was still being used in an attempt to make the mills self-sufficient. It was nearly economic suicide when companies were forced to purchase prohibitively expensive electrical power off the 'energy spot market.' Safety, profit considerations, and the impact of regulatory legislation, demanded that the wood products industry immediately find another safer, less polluting source of electrical power to run their saw and paper mills. By then, most CEOs had reluctantly come to accept that their companies either spent the money now to modernize, or as hundreds of other sawmills would in that era, simply go out of business. This would have caused massive unemployment across America. And that situation was something the U.S. Government had to avoid at all costs.

Although introduced to deal primarily with providing irrigation to arid and semi-arid regions in the seventeen western states, relief was on the way, beginning first in the very early 1900's. The U.S. Bureau of Reclamation had been tasked with providing affordable electricity collateral to the design and construction of flood/irrigation control projects in the Western United States.

A handful of like projects were to be undertaken to prevent flooding, and as a much valued side product, provide the vital electricity needed to support the U.S.'s fast-growing industries, and ballooning population growth.

The Bureau of Reclamation is part of the U.S. Department of the Interior, and as such is one of the primary construction agencies of the Federal Government. Its record of accomplishment is outstanding, and it has produced quality projects, despite government's inherent bureaucracy.

The Bureau of Reclamation designed and built what, at the time, were the world's five largest concrete dams. Of those five, they first completed four in the Western United States. They were the Shoshone Dam (328') in 1910 on the Shoshone River in Wyoming; the ArrowRock Dam in 1915 (349') on the Boise River in Idaho; the Owyhee Dam (417') on the Owyhee River in Oregon in 1932; and in 1935, the Boulder Dam (726') on the Colorado River in Arizona and Nevada. Boulder Dam, after a name change in 1947 by Congress, would come to be known as the *Hoover Dam*.

The largest at the time, *Hoover Dam*, is perched on Black Canyon where the Colorado River forms between Arizona and Nevada. The dam contains between 3.25 and 4.4 million cubic yards of concrete, depending on which U.S. government agency's calculator you chose to accept. Despite the questions that surfaced after-the-fact over its alleged over-design, *Hoover Dam* was critically important in permitting Americans to farm and raise food in the Western United States. Dedicated by law to irrigation and related flood control projects, it and its sister dams brought water to literally millions of acres of otherwise arid land, permitting the building of hundreds of thousands of homes.

As a collateral result of ingenious systems design, the dams also provided the electricity required to give birth to dozens of new American communities, and provide power to support the resident's livelihoods. Without *Hoover Dam*, a comparatively less productive society would exist today in Southern California, Western Arizona, Southern Nevada, and even portions of old Mexico.

The daunting physical hazards that hindered *Hoover Dam's* construction decades ago still are evident today. Located in the center of a southwestern desert, the nearest towns of any size to the fledgling dam were Boulder City in its infancy, eight miles west; and Las Vegas, Nevada thirty miles to the northwest. The construction of *Hoover Dam* proved to be an almost unbelievable engineering accomplishment. Construction crews had to overcome killer temperatures from the desert's summer sun bouncing off the inner walls of Black Canyon. The unpredictability and ever-changing quirks of one of the world's largest rivers initially taunted the designers. The extraordinary hazards, while attempting to perform dangerous construction tasks on the high sheer walls of the canyon, threatened to fill the cemetery in greatly expanded Boulder City, to capacity. Despite these many barriers, *Hoover Dam* (then called Boulder Dam) was completed in 1935.

The reservoir created behind *Hoover Dam* is Lake Mead. The lake is 500 feet deep and 110 miles long. Actually the deepest depth behind the dam is 589 feet—that bottom eighty-nine-feet was and is a planned de-silting area. Lake Mead contains enough water to cover the State of Connecticut ten feet deep or supply 5,000 gallons of water to every person on the planet. The total powerhouse generating capacity is 1,344,800 kilowatts.

The powerhouse complex at *Hoover* is equipped with seventeen large generators, of which one is rated at 95,000 kilowatts; fourteen at 82,500 kilowatts each; one at 50,000 kilowatts; and the remaining unit at a mere 40,000 kilowatts. The Powerhouse's seventeen large turbines represent 1,850,000 horsepower, excluding two very old small station service turbines rated at between 3,500-4,000 horsepower each. N-2 was machine designation for the first 95,000-kilowatt generator that went on-line at *Hoover Dam* in 1935.

Water for the production of the electrical energy, supplying the downstream anti-flood system requirements and normal regulation of the reservoir, flows through four intake towers into penstock headers. The massive flows are then routed through outlet headers and outlet conduits to permit the flow to the reach the needle valves in the dam's outlet 'works.'

The four intake towers, in themselves engineering masterpieces, resemble huge fluted columns. According to the U.S. Bureau of Reclamation's published specifications, "each tower is a hollow cylinder of 29 feet 8 inches, internal diameter, and 75 feet average outside diameter, from which twelve 'fins' project." Those fins prevent debris from entering the complex's power generation process. Two of the intake towers are on each side of the canyon, "one set 135 feet from the dam face, and the second set 185 feet further upstream. All are equal in height to a 34-story building." The power generation facility (the Powerhouse) is the heart of *Hoover Dam*, and perhaps even the life-giving organ responsible for the welfare of the seventeen Western United States.

Without *Hoover Dam*, the communities downstream would lack flood control, locally grown food, power for industrial and residential use, and a endless list of other must-haves. If it remains unfettered, the operation of *Hoover Dam's* Powerhouse is capable of generating millions of watts of power for transmittal to Southern California, Western Arizona, and Southern Nevada.

The distribution of the power generated at *Hoover Dam* is defined by contractual agreement. The user recipients of this largeness (for a contractual fee) by percentile are the State of

Arizona—17.6259 %; The State of Nevada—17.6259 %; Southern California Edison—7.9316 %; Metropolitan Water of Southern California—35.2517 %; City of Burbank—0.5773 %; City of Pasadena—1.5847: and the City of Los Angeles—17.5554 %.

If the 1,400-mile length of the Colorado River were shutdown for an extended period for any reason, the following losses would result, according to the projections of the U.S. Bureau of Reclamation, Department of the Interior:

- There would be no electricity for lighting in Las Vegas.
- Southern California's agriculturally rich Imperial Valley would dry up.
- All major cities in Arizona, and San Diego and Los Angeles would be devastated.
- Colorado's front-range cities would die.
- Electrical power to twenty-five million people would be seriously curtailed.
- The action would result in $2 billion dollars of economic loss in Arizona, California, Colorado, Utah, Nevada, Wyoming, New Mexico, and the country of Mexico, annually.
- The CAP (Central Arizona Project) canal would run dry, and the concrete riverbed would soon crack, break apart, and erode.

The lack of dead-necessary electricity in the short haul, would mean terrible food shortages, breakdown of law and order, the loss of millions of jobs, a tremendous loss of this lives of those citizens whose health requires constant or periodic mechanical medical intervention, and eventually the likely exodus of a majority of the population to elsewhere in the United States. The then-homeless population would only have the Eastern U.S. into which to migrate. Most homeless could die before reaching any type of safe haven. The *Hoover Dam* is that important!

In the long-term, if the loss of the generated power from Hoover Dam was permanent, or even denied the user population for more than a ninety-day period, the beginning of the abandonment of the residential communities and the debilitation of the level of civilization currently enjoyed in those areas, may be irreversible. While it is possible that flood control systems could be marginally maintained below Parker Dam, the loss of electricity could eventually cause those portions of the United States to revert to conditions last experienced over one hundred years ago.

Glen Canyon Dam would be significantly unable, due to the routing and flow characteristics of the source rivers, to come to Southern Nevada and Western Arizona's aid. Possibly Parker Dam could continue to pump water over the mountains, via the 336-mile California Aqueduct Project to Southern California, and perhaps transmit curtailed amounts of electricity to Los Angeles. Five pumping station lift water from the Colorado River Dam system over mountainous barriers, totaling 1,617 feet in height, between Colorado and the California's coastal plains.

In a pro-active, anti-terrorism move, the U. S. Government in 2003 began construction on 3.5 miles of four-lane highway, including a 2,000-foot long bridge, approximately 1,700 feet downstream from Hoover Dam. The *Hoover Dam* bypass is scheduled for completion in 2007. It will accommodate any traffic that officials feel needs diverted off vulnerable *Hoover Dam* crest roadway.

Signed: *Ted Staples*
Cabinet Secretary,
U.S. Department of Homeland Security

(End of Document)

NO FORN
INTELLIGENCE ASSESSMENT REPORT
SECRET

CHAPTER SIX

DAY 135—15 MAY

HOOVER DAM

MICAP MEETING ON THE THREAT

NEAR BOULDER CITY

NEVADA

The location of the weekly Mission-Capability (MiCap) was, as usual, at the dam's Operating Complex, Central Power Generation (CPG) department conference room. Included, were self-invited guests from the U.S. Justice Department.

It wasn't yet 8:50 A.M. in the CPG department's conference room, and already the facility's air conditioning had cooled the room down to a point where, arguably, most thought it could be alternately used for chilling 'hanging beef.' The casually dressed professionals around the table, excepting of course the dark suit-wearing Federal agents who were still fuming about having been instructed to lock their handguns in their cars "if they wanted to attend this meeting," all wished they had brought a sweater or jacket. Here, buried deep in the bowels of Hoover Dam in a windowless tomb theoretically safe from any nuclear attack, the dam's regular staff members could only fantasize that the facility would have included *one lousy working thermostat.*

As the meeting room filled, both the attendees who had been invited and the interlopers who had not, helped themselves to the 200 calorie, glazed donuts provided by the federal agents from Washington D.C. Krispy Krème pastries were becoming a frequently offered bribe by certain federal agencies, to insure a neutral acceptance of their presence at meetings to which they typically invited themselves, with very little prior notice or approval from the host organization. Even though they'd never admit it, the Feds ran into the 'gun' issue at almost every U.S. facility, and always tried to bluff their way past security, sometimes unsuccessfully.

The uninvited federal agents scrambled to help themselves to the fast-disappearing, calorie-laden donuts, and belatedly took the remaining open seats. The Department of Reclamation's Regional Director, 'Big John' Casterbottom, called the MiCAP meeting to order. Standing 6'10 inches tall, and weighing in at over 275 pounds, very few people made fun of Big John's nickname, at least to his face. A Navaho Indian by birth, not surprisingly John seemed to always manage to obtain willful cooperation, even from the most self-important bureaucrats. Awarded the Congressional Medal of Honor by LBJ for single-handedly rushing a Viet Cong position during the Vietnam conflict to rescue six kidnapped American Army nurses, John tended to be pragmatic in his approach to his job, which was to oversee the safety and welfare of the U.S. dams in the Western United States.

Stubborn he was, but generally fair, assuming everything went his way. His subordinates occasionally referred to him as "My way or the Highway," most assuredly behind his back. John was a rough-dressed man, especially when he left his office in Denver to come out into the field. His usual public demeanor concealed most evidence of the doctorate he had received from the Harvard School of Business, and four years of intensive exposure to the CIA Operations Directorate, when he had been recruited by that agency as soon he stepped off the 'freedom bird' coming back from Vietnam, in 1975. A rumor persisted that his hobby was growing championship rose bushes, but most pooh-poohed that, as being just too impossible considering whom they were talking about.

Regional Director Casterbottom, was a hands-on manager, as the resident management heads of the dams located in the Western United States soon found out, some while they were in-place in their job assignments, others as they were leaving the job at the mandatory exit interview with 'Big John.'

Among the invited guests in the conference room for today's regular MiCAP meeting, were Hoover Dam's resident manager Edith Hammer, and the heads of her management team representing Power Plant Post-Design, Maintenance Engineering, Preventive Maintenance, Quality Control, Powerhouse Operations, Physical Inspection Services, Security, Safety, Procurement, and Human Relations. The only department head missing from today's meeting was Jefferson Conduit, the 5'2" well-dressed Press Officer (often described by the media as the Bureau of Reclamation's on-site mouthpiece) who claimed to have a non-deferrable dental appointment in Las Vegas that morning.

Conduit had asked his new secretary, Elizabeth Zubaida, to attend and take notes for the department. She was a Saudi, graduated at the top of her class, and claimed a Water Dynamics advanced engineering degree awarded her by Saudi Arabia's prestigious School of Hydraulics, located in the capital city of Riyadh. Having a degreed registered engineer on his personal staff, greatly pleased Conduit, even if she had been an unbudgeted 'walk-in' hire. Primarily because Press Officer Conduit didn't consider himself to be technically proficient in the slightest, despite what his resume said. So Ms. Zubaida took advantage of the situation, while at the same time dodging calls from U.S. Department of Reclamation's Human Relations department. Seems they were still having difficulty obtaining transcripts from her graduate school.

Edith Hammer had been with the Bureau of Reclamation for twenty years, and previously had run smaller dams for the Bureau throughout the United States. She was in her fifties, in excellent shape, about 5'2" inches tall, and athletic to the consternation of the dam's other softball team players. Edith's credentials were impeccable as were her past performance evaluations from the Bureau's upper management. Her current assignment at Hoover Dam had not been of her own choosing—she had been perfectly happy with less stressful duty assignments, being the matriarch of a large immediate family that worshipped their Mom and wife. However, in the last management change here at the one of the world's most significant dams, a handful of influential in-house job applicants, who had inflated opinions of their importance, turned contentious when negotiating with the Bureau's Human Relations Manager. In response, the Bureau had brought in Edith Hammer, reassigned the warring male applicants, which shocked the shorts off both them and the rest of the U.S. Bureau of Reclamation. Ms. Hammer was extremely well educated, with a handful of professional engineering degrees, and almost over night had been accepted by the rest of the Dam's management team. They who frankly had been tired of all the infighting and uncertainty brought on by the now-past application process.

The Power Plant Post-Design Manager, Billy Joe Davis, was currently filling in for the open positions for Managers of Maintenance, Preventive Maintenance, and the Quality Control Departments, vacated when the previous occupants had been summarily reassigned to remote Bureau of Reclamation duty stations throughout the United States. Billy Joe was the most experienced in-house Bureau of Reclamation professional at the dam, and that fact alone made Edith Hammer silently breathe a sigh of relief.

The punitive reassignments also generated management openings in the Power Plant Operations billet, and the all-important management position over the Physical Inspection Service unit, whose sole task was detecting and exposing any potential structural problems in the dam, well before they occurred. The Denver Bureau office had fortunately (although they were keeping mum as to the 'how') brought in an outside consultant from Bechtel, the firm that was part of Consortium that constructed the dam. The out-source consultant would temporarily cover the critical Physical Inspection management slot, while Edith Hammer did her best to keep Hoover Dam's Power Plant Operations department on-line, on-schedule, and within budget.

The consultant, Mohammed Harkat, was previously unknown to anyone in the Bureau of Reclamation, and had never previously interfaced directly with anyone on the Hoover Dam management team until his arrival a month ago. But he had a handful of glowing reference letters, adequate copies of well-worn college transcripts, and seemed knowledgeable. He had endeavored to make himself instantly welcome by offering to provide a often non-requested but much appreciated helping hand to the other over-worked department heads. Casterbottom had been frankly surprised to find the Denver office had made such an apparently excellent selection, as he himself had never heard of Mohammed Harkat, even in the notoriously small field of collateral power generation. From the way the rest of Hoover Dam's management team was now singing the consultant's accolades, Big John was beginning to feel moderately at ease having a new previously unknown professional occupy the critical position, even if it was only temporary until a permanent department head could be hired and brought on-board.

The Safety, Security, and Procurement management slots were deemed less technical, and had temporarily also been out-sourced. Those temporary consultant contracts were figuratively being overseen by Jefferson Conduit, the currently absent Press Officer. Edith Hammer figured that what the flashy Press Officer didn't know, his secretary, Elizabeth Zubaida, who apparently was a trained Hydraulics Engineer, did.

Casterbottom in his usual curt manner called the MiCAP meeting to order. He introduced the Hoover Dam staff setting around the large rectangle-shaped conference table and then asked Ms. Hammer "What is the status on the replacement service station generator?" Hammer stood up and gave Casterbottom what was obviously a longer explanation than he had desired, before getting around to directly answering his question.

"About six months ago" she began "one of the two small 3,500 horsepower service station generators self-destructed for unknown reasons. The dam's contractor finally was able extract the decades-old unit out of the Powerhouse, and onto a heavy-duty transporter, for the short trip through the dam's internal maintenance tunnel to Boulder City. When the faulty generator arrived in Boulder City, contractual inspection personnel noted that the casing of the huge generator was permanently cracked, and excessive corroded, ending all hopes of rebuilding the unit."

Hammer continued "Fortunately, a procurement manager at the Bureau of Reclamation's Washington headquarters managed to find a new replacement unit that was just being assembled in Guanajuato, Mexico, when economic conditions had forced the previous customer to file for bankruptcy. The Hoover Dam Preventive Maintenance department has managed to get by for nearly five months, deferring one critical project after another, until the new generator is available for installation."

"At that time, the machinery vendor and the Bureau's HQ Maintenance Director decided to have the generator moved by rail from Central Mexico, to the harbor at Long Beach, CA. There the 200,000-pound unit was trans-loaded onto a specially designed fifty-wheel carryall, and trucked to Boulder City. The $1,000,000 piece of critical electrical equipment is currently very slowly en-route Boulder City. As with every shipment of national security-sensitive machinery in these days of terrorism, a heavily-armed security crew is both following and leading the gigantic hauler across California."

"The truck, upon arrival at Boulder City, will be signed for a member of my management team, permitting the guards to return to Long Beach. The fifty-wheel transportation rig will be held over and used by the Bureau of Reclamation's installation contractor to move the heavy generator from Boulder City to the dam's Powerhouse. The contractor will utilize the dam's internal access road, specifically designed and constructed for that purpose back in the early-1930's. The dam's maintenance department will then go on 24/7 duty until all the deferred preventive maintenance projects have been satisfactorily completed."

Edith Hammer completed her verbal report to Regional Director Casterbottom, and the group. She asked the group if there were "any questions?" Receiving no requests (service station equipment 'change-out' was considered routine maintenance, due to the advanced age of all Hoover Dam's generators) she again took her seat.

Then Casterbottom also abruptly sat down, making it clear that he expected the interlopers to introduce themselves. After a ripple of chuckles from staff quietly bubbled from around the table, the spokesperson for the Federales stood up, shot a glare at Casterbottom, smiled at Edith and wiped a host of donut crumbs off his suit coat. William 'Bill' Savage was a large, well-dressed man, and a highly educated one. It was well known that he personally booked no B.S. and expected his staff to conduct themselves likewise. Savage's particular job, similar to the job slot the dapper Secretary Ted Staples occupied over at Homeland Security, was a thankless one—after all, we all learned in school that it is impossible to refute 'a negative'. Attempting to deal logically with that fell into the job descriptions of both of the Savage and Staples. Savage opened his presentation.

"Ladies and Gentlemen, I am FBI Assistant Director/Terrorism, William 'Bill' Savage, and I'm here to help you." His use of the antique government joke generated few laughs. Not nearly the number it had when the CIA's Assistant Director/Plans Jim Kennedy had used it break the ice, and kick off the CIA's portion of the Pacific Northwest Terrorism taskforce meeting in Seattle on July 11, 2002. *Well, my wife has told me I wasn't stand-up comic material, more than once,* Savage thought.

Before Savage started to introduce his people, he asked a short question of Casterbottom. "So Ms. Hammer is saying the generator change out is a routine maintenance item, and doesn't require post-inspection by the Bureau's Internal Security Unit?" he asked.

One of the dam's engineers jumped up uninvited, and explained to Savage that "The generator is a sealed turnkey purchase and to open it in any manner will void the warranty." Savage thought about that answer, then he thanked the engineer, who by then had retaken his seat.

Bill Savage continued, "The federal agents you are about to meet today, including myself, are here on the express orders of the president of the United States, George W. Bush. I apologize to Regional Director Casterbottom from the Denver office of the Bureau of Reclamation, and Hoover Dam's on-site manager, Ms. Edith Hammer, for the lack of adequate notice of our no-notice attendance at today's MiCAP meeting, and other niceties."

"Although my opening remark to you was an old government joke to be sure, it is nevertheless our intention today to help you, and all the people of the United States, specifically those in the Western United States. First, it will be better if I introduce my team today, since you all will be spending a lot of time with them in the coming days," he concluded. (Mock groans from the audience.)

Savage slightly shook his head in simulated disbelief, and said, "Despite the FBI's occasional disagreements with the Central Intelligence Agency (laughter) we all are very fortunate to have with us CIA Assistant Director/Plans Jim Kennedy from Langley." Kennedy briefly stood up, then sat down and continued to sip his coffee. Kennedy was a tall, lanky Washingtonian in his early 50's who usually wore glasses that tended to make him look professor-like. The general state of Kennedy's clothing at any time could be classified as 'casual/rumpled.' Kennedy was a former professor at prestigious MIT and allegedly had one of the highest IQs of anyone currently working at the 'spook house.'

"The second person I want to introduce to this group is FBI Inspector Diane Davis, out of the HQ of the President's new Terrorism Threat Integration Center (TTIC), located in Washington D.C. Inspector Davis is here today to acquaint us with the latest terrorist intelligence that has only this week has became available to TTIC, Homeland Security, and the Administration. This information has been culled from HUMINT sources, the NSA phone intercepts, and interrogation product from JTF-GTMO (Joint Task Force—Guantánamo) straight from Camp Delta. We'll get to Inspector Davis in a minute," Savage continued.

Inspector Davis smiled, instead of standing to be recognized. She was a medium-height, attractive, African-American woman, reportedly a 'fast mover' in the FBI due to her stellar performance in 2002, facilitating the Seattle Anti-Terrorism taskforce. Davis had been assigned to head up that taskforce, some alleged, because President Bush had the foresight to anticipate the difficulties anyone might have directing a bunch of contentious multi-service experts. He had decided to put someone in there who had demonstrated she could deal with the hassle, especially when quietly backed by the president's unspoken but well-apparent authority, to make personnel changes as she saw fit. Few persons knew that Davis was a full-fledged, paid-up member of the FBI's vaulted Hostage Rescue Team, operating out of the Quantico Marine Corps Station, and that made her a very dangerous young woman.

Savage introduced last but not least "U.S.C.G. Commander Jennifer Stalwart." Instantly all the male attendee's attention was drawn to the only uniformed officer in the room. The Commander was a 6'1" tall, weight proportionate to height, attractive dark-haired woman. She appeared to be in her mid-twenties, but most felt that impossible, due to her elevated rank. She was a college-educated flight officer, certified to fly any fixed-wing aircraft the U.S.C.G. and U.S. Navy had to offer, and was command-qualified. She also was qualified in a long list of jet-turbine rotorcraft—helicopters. Reportedly, Commander Stalwart was also being considered for astronaut training by NASA.

To say Commander Stalwart was just on a fast-tracked, military career, was to badly underestimate the extent of her accomplishments and the respect she enjoyed from military commands up to and including the Joint Chiefs of Staff (JCS). Stalwart briefly stood, waved her hand, and re-took her chair.

After the introductions, Savage began to address the reason behind he and his counterterrorism specialists attending Hoover Dam's MiCAP meeting. "Two days ago, at the request of the president, and on the recommendation of Secretary Staples of the Homeland Security Agency, the four of us here today before you, were called to the White House at 2215 hours, or 10:15 P.M. for you civilians. This was to attend an emergency meeting with President Bush and Cabinet Secretary Staples."

"CIA Assistant Director/Plans Jim Kennedy, FBI Supervising Special Agent Davis, and Commander Jennifer Stalwart—were on the Pacific Northwest Federal Taskforce last year. That federal taskforce, which was established by President Bush, directed the United States' response to a dozen or more bloody terrorist attacks perpetuated by al-Qaeda in the Pacific Northwest. Inspector Davis was involved, close and personal, in one of the counter attacks by the FBI's Hostage Rescue Team. In that incident, HRT prevented a 747-400 passenger jet from being hijacked from Paine Field in Washington State, after the terrorists had already commandeered it, killing the Boeing cockpit crew."

"We are here today to consult with you, the dam's professional staff. The subject of today's discussions is a persistent rumor that continues to circulate throughout the world's terrorist communities. This threat allegedly targets Hoover Dam in some manner. Few details concerning the specifics of this alleged attack have been harvested to-date, using traditional U.S. Intelligence sources. We don't know if the threat is upstream, downstream, or at the dam proper. Edith Hammer has told us that anything other than light trucks and cars have been prohibited since 9/11 from using the roadway over the dam's crest. Trucks, buses, trailers, campers, and mobile homes—except those approved loads coming *directly* to the dam on Department of Reclamation business—get detoured from Las Vegas onto Highway 95. Then southbound to Interstate 40 where they can head north and southbound," said the CIA's Kennedy.

"The Hoover Dam highway bypass won't be completed until late 2007. So there you have it—an ambiguous threat, agreed. But one the Homeland Security Department, the president, and some ranking members in Congress think is real enough. One that begs an immediate exploratory investigation, working had-in-hand with you, the professional experts." Savage paused, before continuing.

"At this time, I'm going to turn this meeting over to CIA's Assistant Director/Plans Jim Kennedy. He can give us a briefing on the various directions from which such an attack could be expected to come," concluded AD Savage. With that, Savage turned to the CIA's Jim Kennedy, gestured 'come up' and returned to his chair.

Kennedy stood, and approached the podium. Initially he had been exercising a great deal of manual dexterity to keep the ten-inch thick stack of paper he carried in his long arms, in order. Finally with a deep sigh, he gave up the futile effort. He dumped the entire stack onto the conference table. Some of it continued its slide off the highly polished oak table, and onto the carpeted floor of the conference room. He threw up his hands, and made a gesture that could only mean he was abandoning his carefully prepared speech, in favor of speaking off the cuff.

Kennedy began to speak, "I had planned to come before you folks today, and attempt to present some orderly textbook scenarios for the threatened attack. But that dog won't hunt! In one way, any threat against the overall dam operation on this portion of the Colorado River is fairly well limited by geographic factors. It has to be attacked upstream of the dam, which certainly makes sense. Or at the dam proper, which make less sense due to a number of hard facts. Or downstream from the dam, which makes even *less* sense. However, this is the subject matter on which your valued input is being urgently solicited." Kennedy walked over to the coffee urn, refilled his Styrofoam cup, and return to the table.

"To properly evaluate the risk here, we must establish some parameters. After all, the length of the Colorado River is about 1,400 miles from the Colorado Rocky Mountains to the Gulf of California."

"There is no way this group can put their hands around that," Kennedy said shaking his head. "So the 'finding' that President Bush signed this week, assigns everyone in this room the responsibility to address only those potential terrorist threats with a parameter from one-mile upstream of the dam, the dam proper, and one-mile downstream of the dam crest. Still no small task, I'm sure you'll agree."

"Lets theoretically eliminate some of the possibilities. If any of you think we are missing something, for Heaven's Sake, lets get it out on the table now," Kennedy went on. "Discussing the downstream threat probably is as good place to start as any. Any terrorist threat more than one mile of the dam downstream likely won't impact Hoover Dam directly. Not one iota. Certainly it could impact the hydraulics of water distribution and hydroelectric concerns for the hundred or so miles south of the dam, but not Hoover Dam proper. Are we all in agreement with that?" Jim Kennedy asked. After five-minutes of intense discussion centering around the staff's self-elected spokesperson, David Castro (the same hydro-engineer who had spoken up to FBI Assistant Director/Terrorism Bill Savage earlier), the dam's management team and technical team group, reluctantly agreed.

But only after Castro qualified his statement by saying "We are considering the powerhouse to be part of the dam proper. The only functions downstream within the mile limit are the penstocks, the canyon outlet works, both 'Stoney' gates, and the spillway exits. All of those are buried deep inside Black Canyon's granite walls."

Kennedy moved the discussion along, once again, "Okay, now let us address the upstream side of the dam. What threat exists there? What presents a possibility for attack at one of the at-risk points in the upstream threat window?"

The noisy technical conversations among the group again started, this time running on for nearly ten minutes. Jim Kennedy patiently stood and waited.

Again, David Castro spoke for the group. "Actually on further discussion, we now don't exactly know why we said that the percentage of risk 'upstream' was any greater than the minimal risk downstream. But to answer your question, what we have upstream of the dam face, within the parameters that have been established for this discussion, are two of the Arizona and Nevada fifty-foot diversion tunnels and spillways. They are sealed with concrete tunnel plugs. But I guess those could still be removed using some very high-explosive charges, but highly unlikely."

Castro continued, "Both entrances to the Arizona and Nevada canyon banks, include a 'trash rack.' The fifty-foot-wide diversion tunnels (two on the Arizona and two on the Nevada sides) are firmly anchored in place with steel bulkheads, set in granite. Below that point, downstream of the reservoir intake, but upstream of the dam face, is the cofferdam, which certainly could not be at-risk. And the four intake towers, again upstream of the dam face, connect with those diversion tunnels on either side of the canyon."

David Castro stopped talking, only long enough to take a big gulp of water from one of the stainless-steel bottles sitting on the conference table. Then he continued, "Now, water is drawn into each of the four intake towers. Then it travels underground, alongside the foundation of the dam proper, and 'downstream' as discussed previously. The only parts of the system at—risk, are the fifty-foot diversion intakes. Other exposed piping, past the reservoir-side cofferdam, but above the dam face, below the upper cofferdam, are the four intake towers. Even though two of the four diversion tunnels are currently plugged, water still can enter through the intake towers to the penstocks, and into the powerhouse. It will be discharged through the canyon wall works, Stoney Gate, and the tunnel portals."

"Oh," remembered Castro, "remember there is also a cofferdam on the downstream side of the dam."

David Castro took another large gulp of water. "The use of the lower portal road is strictly regulated, and can be accessed only from the Boulder highway. It has direct access to the powerhouse for maintenance purposes."

"Highway 93 forms the upper access road, over and past, the dam crest. As you know, Highway 93 continues south from the dam, to Kingman, Arizona. But that route has zero vehicle access to the dam's inner structure."

Castro self-importantly stretched, and went on, "There are, of course, several elevators from the crest level, down into the dam's lower operating spaces. Those were originally used both for visitor tours, and our own operating staff's access and egress. Following 9/11, all visitor access to those particular elevators has been prohibited."

With a tremendous sigh of importance, typical of someone who likes to hear himself talk, Castro shrugged. His non-verbal body language conveyed the message that his impromptu presentation was something that *even a dunce at the CIA* should be able to understand. Enjoying the limelight, he briefly remained standing, then retook his seat.

Kennedy stood staring at David Castro for almost a minute before again taking control over the meeting. "Thank you again, Mr. Castro. That was very informative of you. I know myself, and my colleagues from the Federal Bureau Of Investigation, appreciate your expertise."

Turning to the group, Kennedy addressed them. "Basically what I heard Mr. Castro saying, and please speak up if he wasn't talking for all of you (first came a groan from the group, then good-hearted laughter) was that there is no threat either upstream or downstream of the dam within our parameters—is that correct?"

When Castro failed to pop up and answer promptly, Kennedy again asked the question, this time directly to Castro, whose face by this time was flushed red. He was hanging his head hoping Kennedy would give him a break. But now he had been asked a direct question. Castro, embarrassed, having no other choice, slithered up out of his chair like the snake he was, and mumbled the seemingly unrelated response, "I guess so—Parker Dam is 155 miles south of here," and quickly again took his seat.

Jim Kennedy stretched and continued, "Lets assume for a minute that all the facts presented by Mr. Castro are factual and pertinent. (More laughter) And that we are figuratively safe, from attacks both upstream and downstream, of Hoover Dam."

"Please permit me to briefly digress here," Kennedy requested. "I'm sure you all know what alarmists are saying. The media is calling it the 'what happens if terrorists take Hoover Dam down' scenario. Basically, they are manipulating facts, and coming up with WAGS, wild-ass-guesses. The facts have long been published by the Bureau of Reclamation in Washington D.C., but lets review them briefly anyway."

"If Hoover Dam loses its ability to generate electricity, there will be no lights in Las Vegas. The all-important, food-growing Imperial Valley region in California will dry up and blow away. All the major cities in the state of Arizona, plus San Diego and Los

Angeles are forfeit—gone, good-bye, 'its been good to know ya.' All the State of Colorado's front-range cities will die—dead, gone," Kennedy read, shaking his head.

"There will be little or no power available for up to twenty-five million people who live in the Western United States, presumably including some of your mothers, fathers, brothers, or sisters. It is entirely possible that the California and Arizona Aqueduct Projects will simply dry up, and end up looking like a vacated stretch of abandoned, under-maintained drainage ditch. The states of Arizona, California, Colorado, Nevada, Wyoming New Mexico, even parts of Old Mexico will suffer tens of billions of dollars in annual economic losses."

The CIA Assistant Director/Plans first looked pointedly at David Castro, and then each person seated in the room. He cocked his head sideways with look of simulated disgust. "Now," Kennedy said, "Do you understand the magnitude of the threat here? The reason you all have been included in this meeting? And exactly how important each of your frank and freely voiced opinions are to the survival of the Western United States? If there is still some confusion as to the mission of this group, please stand up and bring it up now, Ladies and Gentlemen."

After standing with his hands on his hips, looking individually at each member in the assembled group, Kennedy turned to Regional Director Casterbottom of the Department of Reclamation, and asked him the same question. Casterbottom briefly remained seating, then surged to his feet like Polaris rocket, and begin to speak in the 'no bullshit' tone of voice he was well known for.

"Jim, it isn't as though we don't understand the gravity of the matter. I guess we bureaucrats do get a little complacent at times. But lets get back to discussing the problem, Okay? All you are doing is pissing people off here with your bullshit."

Kennedy smiled at Casterbottom; as if that was exactly the answer he had been looking for, and with a courtly gesture, motioned for the large man to take over the meeting. Then the CIA man took a seat and attempted to drink some coffee, which by now was cold and bitter.

Casterbottom begin to speak in a low resonant voice. "Okay, tempers are understandably short—after all, this is America we are talking about here. Well, we have pretty much moved from upstream, to downstream, and into the highly improbable category. What about the risk to the dam proper?"

Casterbottom turned to Agent Davis, who coolly watched him as she sipped from a cup of the dam's awful coffee. "Diane," he asked, "Bill Savage tells me that you have a photographic memory. How about turning it on? Refresh our minds as to the dam's overall specifications. Would you mind? I know the dam's operating personnel can do this in their sleep, but lets see if we get a new perspective by having an outsider do it." With that comment, Big John sat down and Davis, after first setting her cup down, stood up. She was heard to mutter something less than inspirational about a 'dog-and-pony show.'

Agent Davis began with the basics. "Hoover Dam is 726 feet tall; and the crest is 1,244 feet long. The top of the crest is forty-five feet thick—the bottom is 660 feet thick. Parts of the dam, for whatever reason at the time, was over-designed by up to fifty percent. While the structure was not a monolithic pour, it does contain between 3.25 to 4.25 million cubic yards of concrete. Nothing short of a massive nuclear bomb would take out this dam. Even taking out a single diversion tunnel would take over a 1,000 pounds of deep-drilled Plutonium explosive, I am told. The dam system has redundant fail-safe provisions."

"Water can be directly bypassed through the intakes towers, and out the discharge piping. Every drop of the river's water taken in through the intake towers can be bypassed on a continual basis, assuming the entire hydroelectric function was disabled. And frankly, I can't see terrorists even being interested in taking the entire dam out permanently. Okay, perhaps temporarily disrupting its flood control, irrigation, or generating capacity, but why go scorched earth?" Davis smiled, and continued, "Osama is thinking big, and who says that despite his intelligence, he is planning on someday moving into to our neighborhood. Al-Qaeda keeps on saying that they will someday occupy our lands. If so, wouldn't the dam's capacity be something you'd want to use for your own people?" With that surprising remark, Special Agent Davis again took her seat.

Casterbottom scratched his head, rotated away cramps in his shoulders, and continued. "This is what we are going to do people—this afternoon, I want you to go back to your offices and complete everything in your in-boxes that you can. Put the rest of the non-critical work on-hold, for at least the next four days. Then, at 9 A.M. tomorrow morning, we'll all meet here, again no excused absences, and form into study groups. We'll cover every single terrorist possibility inside the parameters we been given, logical or not. The day after, you'll each be here with your study groups, at 9 A.M. sharp. Be prepared to give a formal presentation to the group, outlining your group's findings and proposed solutions."

Then, Casterbottom pausing for effect, proceeded, "The following day, we are going to sit here and fine tune our findings, recommendations, and a prepare a final list of exactly how we can defend against these hypothetical attacks. We'll roll it all up into a comprehensive plan, for the president of the United States, and Secretary of Homeland Security, Ted Staples. Attendance on all days, each day, everyday will be mandatory."

"Forget about bringing your lunch. My Denver office will make arrangements for the week to be catered, so no one has any excuse to be absent, including the missing Press Officer who had such a important dental appointment this morning—Agent Davis, get with the Press Officer's staff and make sure he is both told and understands everything I have said here."

With a covert wink at Kennedy, Casterbottom released everybody to go back to either offices or homes to prepare for the next four days. He told them to "Tell your family you will be at an emergency management retreat here at the Dam for the following four days, and not to attempt to call except in the case of an absolute life-threatening emergency."

Casterbottom gave an infrequent smile, and said, "Do not discuss the terrorist threats we discussed today with anyone not in this room. Now get out of here, and I'll see you all tomorrow.

Please apologize to your families for me, in advance. As if they will let me off the hook that easily. Come dressed casually the rest of the week, as we may need to crawl around the facility to make some inspections. And Edith, get that damn service generator installed as soon as it arrives on site—I'll approve any necessary overtime. Okay? You never know when you might need it to back up the Arizona powerhouse, if everything goes to hell in the proverbial hand basket."

With that, everyone in the room hurried out, and the Federal law enforcement officers all headed to Boulder City to secure hotel rooms and call home.

CHAPTER SEVEN

DAY 136—16 MAY

HOOVER DAM

HOMELAND SECURITY'S THREAT APPRAISAL

NEAR BOULDER CITY

NEVADA

The second day of Hoover Dam's Study Group meetings, called to evaluate terrorism target possibilities, had begun. The digital read-out on the clock on the conference room wall indicated it was 9:00 A.M.

Regional Director John Casterbottom was already at the podium, anxious to get this morning's MiCap/Counterterrorism meeting started. There was a busy agenda for this week's meeting. A magnitude of needs had to be addressed. That was the only way to make sure they accomplished the overall goal. They would attack the problem head on, something Casterbottom was well known for.

"Ok, people," He began, "I see you all have brought your departmental experts with you today. Great! You know what today's agenda is. But for Mr. Conduits benefit, having missed the beginning of yesterday's *mandatory* meeting, here it is again."

"There is a reported imminent terrorist threat against some facility on the 1,400 mile length of the Colorado River system. Hoover Dam is just one of the more likely possibilities. This group will gather information concerning, and form action and contingency plans for, any potential of attack that terrorists might be planning for Hoover Dam."

Casterbottom continued, "Today is day two of this exercise. We are going to look at upstream threats as well as downstream threats. The threat footprint will consist of a logistical parameter of one mile above and below the dam proper. We will also be assessing any perceived terrorist threats at Hoover Dam proper. Even though the technical experts here claim the dam to be terrorist-proof. That frankly is the dumbest statement I have ever heard. At least ever since my previous personal favorite best, when the Dixie Chicks opened their collective mouths to demean the President of the United States."

Opening his briefing manual, he went on, "Now, I said this all this yesterday. But I'll review it once again now for Mr. Conduit's benefit. We have broken the problem up into three study groups—upstream, downstream, and the dam proper. Each study group will have a facilitator. Facilitating these groups will be Commander Jennifer Stalwart for 'upstream threats.' FBI Agent Diane Davis will handle 'downstream threats.' Deputy Director Kennedy will work with the 'dam proper' team. I will be circulating between the groups as a technical source. I will deal with any disagreements or unnecessary home-turf-protecting that detracts from our mission here today. Are there any questions about any of this?" Casterbottom asked, looking intently at the group.

"On the morning of day three, each study group will prepare a presentation addressing the potential weaknesses they perceive to exist. Those will be restricted to the area of their assigned group's responsibility."

"On the morning of day four, the once-again combined group will hear each group's presentation. After which each group's presentation will be discussed and fine-tuned."

The Regional Director proceeded, "The afternoon of day four, we will all participate in condensing everything into a comprehensive contingency plan. It will include all the possibilities you've come up with. Next week, FBI Director Mueller will present our finished report to President Bush and Secretary Ted Staples. Are there any questions? Okay, breakup into your groups. Each group has been assigned one of the small conference rooms in this wing. Ms. Hammer has made arrangements for three members of the administrative secretarial pool to be available. They will be assigned one per study group. Thank you for that, Edith—it slipped my mind completely. The lunch and supper meals will be catered. Ok, lets roll!"

THE 'UPSTREAM THREAT' STUDY GROUP; ROOM 3-A; COMMANDER STALWART FACILITATING:

The half-dozen people filled into the small conference room. Hot coffee and donuts appeared as if by the young officer's command. Actually the largeness was the bequest of Regional Director Casterbottom. He knew what it took to get people loosened up and talking.

Commander Stalwart sat down, grabbed a Krispy Krèam donut, and to no one in particular, said, "These are low fat, right?" She had previous tossed her briefcase into a nearby empty chair. She reached over and opened it, removing a bound legal-sized white pad. Displaying one of her obviously well-practiced winning smiles, the commander spoke. "First things first. Let's introduce ourselves. Not because *you* don't know the names, but because *I* don't."

The self-introductions went around the small oak table. Jefferson Conduit, Press Officer; Elizabeth Zubaida—Acting Press Secretary; Jesse Keith—Power Plant Safety Officer (Lead); Alan Johnson-Security Security Officer (Lead); David Bitterstone-Maintenance Engineering (Lead); and Alan Kidd—Procurement (Lead). All stood up and introduced themselves and their department's responsibility.

Stalwart began the discussion by saying," We discovered something important during the Seattle Counterterrorism taskforce last year. That being that no one spoke his/her mind when their boss was sitting in the same room. So today, everyone in this room is current promoted or demoted. To whatever position makes everyone here a peer, position-wise. No bosses, or non-bosses. Just us 'folks'. Got it?"

After a brief muttering, mostly by the 'former bosses' Jennifer noted, everyone agreed. Each of today's facilitators had been delegated authority to run each of the study groups as they saw fit. This included the authority to evict anyone they felt was not adding anything to the group, either in substance or spirit.

After the pause, Coast Guard Commander Stalwart revealed some new intelligence, yet unknown to the rest of the group. "TTIC (the Terrorism Threat Integration Center that President George W. Bush ordered into existence in early 2003) has 'ears' all over the Middle East. One of those 'ears'—fortunately one that was literate—passed along the following article earlier this year. Everyone on this taskforce needs to be aware of the contents."

As the commander handed out a sealed document clearly stamped SENSITIVE INFORMATION, she said, "This is what it says. Go ahead, open and read it. Commit it to memory. Then I'll pick up the copies in put them in my personal burn bag." The article read:

> CAIRO, Egypt (AP)—An Arabic-language magazine quotes a senor member of Al-Qaida (the Associated Press's preferred spelling for al-Qaeda) as raising the possibility that the group might poison U.S. water supplies.
>
> The Saudi-owned, al-Majalla weekly also reports in its latest edition that al-Qaida militants are in the ranks of Saddam Hussein loyalists who are attacking U.S.-led forces in Iraq.
>
> The reports are based on e-mail correspondence that al-Majalla exchanged with Abu Mohammed al-Ablaj, whom the magazine identified as a senior member of al-Qaida.

"It is something that would have to be viewed seriously," said a U.S. counter-terrorism official in Washington (D.C.), speaking on the condition of anonymity.

The London-based Al-Majalla began receiving al-Ablaj's e-mails earlier this (last) month, and a U.S. counter-terrorism official said previously that al-Ablaj was believed to be an al-Qaida operative.

In an earlier email exchange with the magazine, al-Ablaj said that al-Qaida was going to carry out major attacks in Saudi Arabia. Al-Majalla published the warning on May 11th—a day before suicide bombers detonated explosives at three housing complex occupied by westerners . . . 30

"What are your thoughts relatively to the potential likelihood of that threat?" Stalwart asked with obvious interest. "Take a few minutes to ponder it. Grab another cup of coffee. Then please share with the rest of us, your first impressions regarding what you have just read." The commander rose, and led the group to the large stainless steel urn in the corner. There she refilled her borrowed 'Hoover Dam Rules!' ceramic visitors cup.

When the seven returned to their places at the oak table, Jesse Keith, the dam's Safety Lead spoke up. "Commander, this is an area I feel qualified to speak to. Most of you don't know it, but I completed pharmacy school a couple of years ago. Can't remember now why I decided not to take the test for certification, but I didn't. But please permit me to briefly speak to this aspect of the threat."

"First," Keith continued, "Lets look at the wide-range of possibilities concerning contaminates that conceivably could be introduced into Lake Mead upstream. I think we can eliminate 'Sarin' right off. It is far too dangerous to manufacture. And in the quantity that would be needed to be even marginally effective. Frankly even the Russians and the United States combined couldn't produce that much product, especially covertly."

Keith continued, "That leaves a virtual laundry list of legal chemicals that are more or less available on the commercial market.

They include Antivan, which is a paralytic substance. And Xactil, which is a non-voluntary muscle relaxant. Then there is what is referred to as the date-rape drugs (assuming anyone had the contacts to obtain huge quantities of chemical compounds that would be required) such as Versed, GHB, Ketamine, Burundang, or Rohypol. That was the bad news. Here is the good news."

Keith continued, "Last night I worked up some calculations. I wanted to determine exactly what quantities would be required for any of these chemicals to effectively poison the water in Lake Mead."

"First, here is a quick and dirty explanation of why this contamination really can't be considered a doable threat. Lake Mead, or rather Lake Mead National Recreation Area, is a very damn large body of water. From the Town of Logandale, down to the face of the backwater crest, the lake contains thirty million acre-feet of water. That is nearly twice the annual flow of the Colorado River. Taking the minimum toxic dilution rates, or parts per million (PPM), to the best of my admittedly dated knowledge, that scenario simply wouldn't be possible."

"Secondly, and to my thinking, just as important," said the trained chemist. "Why would terrorists, of any ilk, want to employ this, a scorched earth action? At a minimum, it would directly and collaterally affect over twenty-five million people. Lets say, conservatively, that ten percent are of the Muslim faith. In round numbers, that means they would be killing or seriously incapacitating over 2.5 million persons of their own religion!"

Keith, continued, "Thirdly, the chemical itself, say it was used in the quantities necessary to contaminate the water, has a short lifespan. It is easily diluted and readily breaks down when exposed to oxygen. So you have one or more highly dangerous chemicals, difficult to manufacture under the best of Level Four Bio-Lab conditions. Any of which likely won't last six hours, once dispersed. Sorry, even in a worst case scenario, I can't buy that." Keith thanked the group for listening to his ideas, and sat down.

Commander Stalwart, without rising from the chair she had taken when Keith began to speak, asked "Any other opinions on the chemical contamination possibility?" No one apparently disagreed with Mr. Keith's assessment of the possible threat.

Elizabeth Zubaida, the dam's Acting Press Secretary (cum hydro-engineer) spoke up, "I think the most at-risk part of the overall facility within the one mile parameter, would likely be the four upstream intake towers."

Her boss, who just had been advised he wasn't a boss for the purposes of this meeting, Jefferson Conduit, snapped his head around to look at Ms. Zubaida. Since she came to work here in his department, Elizabeth had always been extremely reserved. She was soft spoken and never volunteered anything. Zubaida especially refrained from voicing technical opinions she felt her boss was uneasy with. Zubaida held an advanced hydro-engineering degree. Conduit did not. But just now, the woman had jumped into the technical discussion with both feet, which both surprised and shocked him.

Feeling an opportunity to shine (something Jefferson Conduit always endeavored to embrace) was slipping away because of someone he considered a mere secretary, he hastily spoke up. "Oh, come on Elizabeth, this is the Hoover Dam we are talking about here, for Christ Sake."

Zubaida, insulted at Conduit's demeaning tone of voice, and the negative comment Conduit had less-than-flatteringly espoused, turned to her boss. She looked him in the eye, saying, "Mr. Conduit, I tell you now, and a dozen other times previously, you are not to talk to me in that manner. Do you feel superior because I am a Saudi, a woman, or both? That sexist, demeaning language is discriminatory. It is not permitted in the American business place. I am surprised you do not know this."

Commander Stalwart quickly came to the woman's defense. "Mr. Conduit, I must agree totally with Ms. Zubaida's description of your manner of speaking. If you had directed the comment to me, I would also have taken it to be sexist and demeaning. After all, I understand that Ms. Zubaida is a degreed hydro-engineer who graduated at the top of her class. So why do you object to her expressing her opinion?"

"Yeah," Alan Johnson, acting Lead in the dam's security department, said. "I also would like to hear her thoughts, Jefferson—do you mind?"

Then consecutively, the other department 'leads,' Jesse Keith and Alan Kidd, added their support to Johnson and Stalwart's comments.

"Okay," shrugged Conduit, "I apologize Elizabeth, will you accept that? I spoke hastily without thinking."

"Mr. Conduit," the Assistant Press Officer said, "I will accept your apology but I wish you would not use my given name in addressing me. In my country we find that extremely rude in conversations between professionals—do you understand?"

"Okay, okay, Ms. Zubaida, I understand." replied the frustrated Mr. Conduit. "Now can we continue this god damn dog-and-pony? Especially since it obviously is so important that Casterbottom felt it necessary to embarrass me in front of my peers. And for a minor thing, like having to go to a routine dental appointment. Christ almighty! Opps, sorry again, I apologize, Ms. Zubaida. You people are acting like I committed high treason."

After allowing a minute for tempers to cool down, Commander Stalwart asked Ms. Zubaida to repeat what she had said just a few minutes earlier.

"Okay, Commander Stalwart, and you men. I have been thinking of the information we received in yesterday's meeting from the CIA and Mr. Savage. I went over to Engineering and reviewed both the architectural and mechanical plumbing drawings. You know, to make sure that the idea I express today is not faulty."

"Now, I will explain how the intake towers work on the upstream side. Sorry if I bore you, Mr. Conduit," she said giving her boss a parting shot. "There are two diversion tunnels on each side of the canyon. Below that is a small cofferdam. It was used during construction to isolate the construction site from the upstream water flow. Below that are four intake towers. There are two each on the Nevada and Arizona sides of Black Canyon."

Pausing to refer to her mental notes, Ms. Zubaida continued, "From an engineering standpoint, I do not see how anyone can harm the diversion tunnels. They were all drilled through the granite rock of the canyon walls. Also, the cofferdam is small. Not nearly high enough to hold back the five-hundred-or-so-foot-tall wall of water flowing out of Lake Mead to the upstream face of Hoover Dam. So I am thinking, that only leaves the four intake towers. They are not accessible from the walls of Black canyon. In theory, they do not have any access from Lake Mead proper. Nothing guards the portion of them that is below the normal water level of Lake Mead. So you see what I am thinking now? Any terrorists would have to use a boat to get to the tops of the intake towers to attack those intakes. I think that means the dam is okay, right?"

"Ms. Zubaida, I am the first to admit that most of what you are discussing here is 'French' to me," Commander Stalwart declared. "But Mr. Johnson, Mr. Kidd, and Mr. Keith, you men are dam experts. How would you evaluate Ms. Zubaida's theory?"

"Commander," Alan Johnson spoke up, "almost everyone on the dam's engineering team got together last night after work. We had a beer or two. Now I know we weren't supposed to discuss this but we were at one of the men's houses. So there weren't any unauthorized people there. Our wives routinely use our meetings as an opportunity to drive into Las Vegas to see a show, so we are clear there."

Johnson continued, "Most of us here on the Hoover management team are pretty experienced and long-in-the-tooth. After all, the U.S. Department of Reclamation isn't known for having a lot of opportunity for advancement. What I am trying to say is most of us have been in our jobs for decades, some longer. That also means that some of us even have accumulated a copy or two of the actual construction plans at home—you know, for emergency maintenance callouts and alike. We'd appreciate it if you did not mention that to Mr. Casterbottom, or any members of the big brass."

After Stalwart placed her finger over her lips indicting their secret was safe with her, Johnson continued. "We looked at the upstream side of the dam, from stem to stern. Realistically there isn't any reasonable way to damage the dam from the upstream side. Excepting a nuclear bomb. And even then, we would have to assess every remote possibility, on a case-by-case basis."

"But to cut to the chase, the unlikelihood of risk that Ms. Zubaida discussed is the same conclusion we reached. The upstream steel cable security nets keep all boats from approaching the dam's upstream face. The steel nets also protect the four intake towers, and to a lesser degree, the old cofferdam. Without access from the water to the dam face or those towers, there is no significant threat on the upside of the dam. Do you guys agree?" he asked, retaking his seat. Everyone indicated they did, by nodding their heads up-and-down.

After which, the group spent another couple of hours listing all the pro and con factors of their finding. Then the catered lunch arrived.

During and after lunch, they brainstormed the threat once more. And once again came to the same conclusion. There was only a single caveat or qualification to that conclusion. That was unless fictional terrorists found an alternate method of getting to the base of the towers on the upstream side of dam. Should that happen, then all bets were off.

Commander Stalwart, and the other six 'upstream threat' team members continued throwing around alternative ideas for the next several hours. Until even those got so absurd no one wanted to further prolong the brain storming exercise. With Jesse Keith at the flip chart, the team then began to summarize their thinking into a comprehensive presentation. The arguments, for and against the probability of such a threat, were summarized in a PowerPoint format, aided by the group's temporary secretary.

THE 'DOWNSTREAM THREAT' STUDY GROUP; ROOM 3-B; FBI AGENT DAVIS FACILITATING:

The six-person study group charged with identifying the downstream counterterrorism needs of Hoover Dam quieted down, and gave their full attention to the group leader. Agent Diane

Davis, this group's facilitator, had extensive experience in getting the maximum productivity out of this time-proven FBI threat-definition method. She had headed up the Seattle counterterrorism taskforce during the Pacific Northwest's multiple-threat terrorists attacks in 2002.

Nearly a thousand Pacific Northwest residents had been either killed directly, or collaterally, in those attacks. The Pacific Northwest suffered loses in the tens of billions of dollars in infrastructure damage, and loss of economic viability. However, the president believed the hastily formed governmental taskforce under Davis's facilitation, had been fortunate to fight to what most considered a draw. Against the fanatic, well-planned and amply funded al-Qaeda.

Davis, a young light-skinned African American woman, felt she knew what was required to get this study group moving. Her personal commitment was to do whatever was necessary to ensure the taskforce members would be productive in the limited time available. Priding herself on being always gracious, Davis invited everyone to help themselves to the fresh coffee, cold soft drinks, and tasty pastries the caterer had just placed on the oak meeting table. Then she walked around the room, smiling, and introducing herself to each of the study group members.

This study group consisted of Mohammed Harkat, the consultant that was representing the dam's Physical Inspection team. Jesus Fox, the dam's Quality Control Lead, was in attendance. Also taking their places, were Paul Bebout, head of the dam's Human Relations department; Joseph Robinson, Leadman from the dam's Maintenance Engineering group; and Marvin Frisbee, the Leadman in-charge of Preventative Maintenance at Hoover Dam.

Agent Davis thought to herself that "*this study group won't require my standard 'everyone is the same level—there are no bosses in this room' orientation speech. They are all from peer departments in the dam's operating stru*cture.

Davis began, "Anyone want to start by giving us an overview of potential threats to the physical support structure, downstream from the dam? But within the one-mile limiting parameter Mr. Casterbottom and Deputy Director Savage established yesterday?"

When no one else jumped up to assume the task, Marvin Frisbee, the Leadman from the Preventive Maintenance department at the dam, stood. He said, 'Yeah, I'll take a shot at that, agent." Davis smiled at Frisbee. Then took her seat, turning over temporary control of the meeting to the man.

Frisbee, a long-time employee of the Bureau of Reclamation, had been up and down the command structure at several U.S. dams. He was a highly knowledgeable engineer, about 5'8" tall. He was considered to be prone to needlessly worrying about the politics involved in the day-to-day operation of the dam. He smoked too much and thus was not in the best of respiratory health. However, he was considered a mild-mannered, hard-working family man from Tennessee, and respected by his bosses.

Frisbee began, "Actually, in my opinion, the downstream side of Hoover Dam is the most interesting. And it no doubt is the more totally concealed side to the operation. On both sides of Black Canyon, most if not all of the vital plumbing has been tunneled through the granite of the canyon walls. In each canyon wall, there are two, fifty-foot wide, rock-encased, concrete-lined spillway tunnels that were used during construction. One of the two on both sides, have concrete plugs in-place. The spillways themselves are guarded by massive one-hundred-foot by six-foot drum gates."

Frisbee, now in his element, continued, "Then there are the 395 foot-tall intake towers, two per canyon wall. Those are located on the upstream side of the dam face. These feed two, thirty-foot diameter steel penstocks that were tunneled through each side of canyon wall, on the downstream discharge side of the dam. Their individual length, from drum gate to discharge, is twenty-two-hundred-feet."

"The thirty-foot penstocks connect with thirteen-foot penstocks, four of which feed each powerhouse. The powerhouses are connected by a center structure, and overall are shaped like a huge U-bolt. The foundations for the powerhouses had to be blasted into the rock face of the canyon walls."

The man continued, not bothering to refer to his notes, "The remainder of the water flows from the intake penstocks. That which cannot be accommodated by the smaller power plant penstocks, continues downstream. There, the powerhouse plumbing branches into five, nine-foot diameter steel outlet pipes, which feed the canyon wall outlet works."

"There the outlet works, potentially processes a water flow large enough to fill a two hundred-nine-foot by forty-one-foot, by sixty-nine-foot room, through six, eighty-four-needle valves. And then again through six, seventy-two inch needle valves. All before being discharged downstream through what is called a 'Stoney' gate."

Frisbee continued, "Now bear in mind, everything I just described to you except the Stoney gate, the canyon wall outlet works, and a powerhouse on each side of the canyon wall, has been tunneled though solid granite rock. And that plumbing system is duplicated on both sides of the canyon wall," Frisbee concluded.

"Er," he spoke up briefly again, "The only other structural detail on the downstream side of the dam is an small cofferdam. That hasn't been utilized since the dam's completion in 1935. Any questions? If not, thanks for your time," as he retook his chair, and attempted to take a swallow of the now cold coffee in his cup.

Special Agent Davis stood up, and said "Thanks, Marvin, I had no idea that we were talking about such a complex system here. And here I still am trying to figure out how to add water to my bucar's radiator," she said, shaking her head. Frisbee just sat there and grinned.

Davis stood inviting the group to help themselves to the fresh coffee the caterers had delivered during the dam's Preventative Maintenance lead's presentation.

Once seated back at the table, rest room breaks and snack breaks completed, Davis began once more. "I just have a few questions, Marvin, if you will—please excuse my ignorance. You say there are those fifty-foot spillway tunnels on each state's side of Black Canyon. But how do we know the concrete plugs are still there? Didn't you say that they haven't been used since the dam opened? Wasn't that nearly sixty-five years ago? Please help me here, guys—Jesus, Paul, David, Joseph, or Mr. Harkat?"

Mr. Harkat spoke up first, saying "First, you can call me Mohammad—using my last name isn't necessary. I'm not easily offended, you see. My inspection crew occasionally, as often as possible considering our small crew, 'virtually inspects' all the penstocks, with our electronic equipment. Do we ever physically enter the downstream ends of the spillways, and go into them for a physical inspection? Not since I came aboard, and according to the inspection records, never previously."

"However, as Marvin said, those spillways were plugged nearly seventy years ago. The plugs are made of concrete and are huge, and they were 'press fits.' The spillways theoretically are abandoned—what would we gain by entering those spillways from both ends, and x-ray them up to the concrete plugs? It would be costly, time-consuming, incredibly dangerous, and a waste of time."

Harkat continued, "Think where you are. This is the desert. It is only common sense to expect those long-abandoned pipes to contain carnivorous coyotes, poisonous Mohave snakes, Diamondback rattlers, brown bats, scorpions, desert tarantulas, tarantula hawks, chuckwalla lizards, if not bigger predators in that twenty-two-hundred-feet of tunnel. And remember they are duplicated on both sides of the canyon wall. I wouldn't ask my men to go into there. We'd have to out-source it. That would take ninety-days alone, just to advertise for bids."

Now, his comments rapidly escalating in pitch to a near-rant, he went on, "Think of the possibility of accidents, or fatalities. Consider the remote chance the contractor disturbed or dislodged anything we are not aware of that may be in there. We must avoid any action that could conceivably cause the concrete plug to slip or disintegrate. It would be catastrophic. Please, Lady, do not suggest that," Mohammed Harkat concluded shaking his head helplessly, then loudly plopping down in his chair.

Jesus from QC; Paul from Human Relations; Robinson from Exterior Cabling; and Frisbee from Preventative Maintenance, each seconded Mohammed's dire warning. Jesus, ever the 'ladies man,' even grinned at Davis, saying, "What you want to do that for Lady? It is just like crawling into the center of the Earth—no good, I say, no good. Very few mens were killed building this dam. And you would risk a unnecessary adventure such as that—you are perhaps Jules Verne?" Jesus shook his head, and slumped down in to his chair. With an expression on his brown face, suggesting that he personally had been ordered to head-up the supposed dangerous, reconnaissance mission.

THE 'DAM PROPER—THREAT' STUDY GROUP; ROOM #3-C, CIA'S JIM KENNEDY FACILITATING:

Kennedy invited his study group's five members to help themselves to the hot coffee, pastries, and chilled soft drinks. This conference room was also being kept well supplied by Casterbottom's caterers.

Everyone helped themselves and grabbed a chair around the standard-issue oak conference table. Due the six HP PC's cluttering the top of the table, this room appeared to be smaller than the other meeting rooms in the Powerhouse's administrative complex. But it was not.

Kennedy went around the table introducing each member. The attendees included FBI ADC/Counterterrorism, Bill Savage; Ms. Edith Hammer, Hoover Dam's Resident Manager; Billy Joe Davis, head of dam's Post-Design Unit; Mr. Marvin Larson, Manager of Powerhouse Engineering; and Peter Donoho, the Dam's Administrative Manager. Only Donohue was outfitted in his usual working attire, a expensive dark business suit. The remainder of the group had gone to great pains to dress casual—jeans, golf shirts, usually a belt with a cowboy buckle, and low-cut steel-shank safety shoes. In most cases, this had required a quick trip to the sportswear section of the just-opened Wal-Mart store in Boulder City.

Kennedy began, "You know our assignment. And you may have noticed, our group is weighted pretty heavily with technical expertise and management types. Personally, at the risk of being called a 'brown-noser,' I have to admit that I consider the dam proper to be the most likely target of any terrorist attack. So does the president. By front ending loading the expertise into this study team, we hope to maximize our group's performance. Our goal is to address President Bush and Secretary Staples' top-priority concerns. The protection of the dam proper, in this case, and the powerhouse apparatus itself."

He continued, "I can see the logic in addressing the problem in this manner. Hoover Dam is huge, and is almost bulletproof. But don't quote me on that. We, as the superior technical and administrative study group on this taskforce, were given the most difficult assignment. That being the protection of the physical dam's structure, and its infrastructure—the critical operating systems contained within it. Any questions?"

The other five-team members had not failed to take notice of the qualifications of the personnel delegated to each of the three study groups. They had already begun to suspect what Kennedy had just confirmed.

The CIA DD/Planning said, "Okay, lets break this into two parts; the 'dam structure', and 'other'. We'll address the dam structure first, as it appears the most numerically logical, as to risk and effect. Anyone want to jump in at this point to get the balling rolling?"

"Yes, I'll address the dam's structure," replied Peter Donoho, of Administrative Management. He and his department served as the Bureau Of Reclamation's oversight function here at Hoover Dam. Based on Donoho's advanced engineering degree from MIT, there was little doubt he was the man most qualified for the job.

Donoho hauled his 6'6", 245-pound frame erect. He was a large person. In his early college days, he had played football for the likes of 'Bear' Bryant at Alabama. He still retained his love for sports. Although these days he preferred to watch them the games on his home entertainment center.

Peter began, "Let's see if I have been listening all those years. For some reason, unknown today, somewhere during the design phase in 1928-1930 this dam ended up being fifty-percent over-designed as to structural needs. I have no inclination nearly seventy years after-the-fact, to awake that sleeping dog. Anyone here, disagree?"

After waiting a moments for any response, Donoho continued, "What we have today is a well-maintained, seventy-year-old structure. Hoover appears to have no major structural flaws, according to the experts. This doesn't mean the dam structure is perfect. In fact, the general public isn't even aware that this huge concrete dam was not the product of a monolithic pour, as thought. The excessive temperatures, generated by 'curing cement,' being but one of the many reasons for that."

"The dam was constructed in what today would be called 'pouring modules,' each about fifty feet square and about five feet high," said Donoho. His presentation manner was much like a computer tutorial, as he downloaded the facts from the appropriate storage bank of his cranial memory. "Each module had to cure out, before another was poured on top of the previous 'lift.' In order to wick-off the heat from the curing cement, crews installed nearly six-hundred-miles of steel piping in the structure. Ice water, or alcohol, was circulated through the piping. This served to draw off the contaminant (heat). The concrete-pouring process ran around the clock for two years."

He proceeded, "During the dam's construction, the river was diverted around the worksite by the drilling of four, fifty-foot diameter tunnels, two on each side of the river. After construction, two of the tunnels were converted to spillways, one inside each canyon wall. The remaining two outboard diversion tunnels, one per canyon side, were sealed off with a 'press-fit' concrete plug. They remain in-place today."

Without once referring to a written note, Donoho proceeded. "The physical dam structure is six-hundred-sixty-feet wide at the riverbed. It tapers outward as it rises towards the dam crest. There it is over twelve-hundred-feet across, and nearly seven-hundred-thirty-feet tall. The powerhouse, although appearing from the dam's crest to be a single structure, is actually a three-section building shaped like a horseshoe. There are individual powerhouses on each side of the river, which are connected at their upper ends by a two hundred, forty-five-foot-tall mating structure. The center section conforms in shape to the downstream face of the dam. Any questions?" Donohue asked, as he looked around the table before retaking his seat.

The single comment quietly came from Edith Hammer, the dam's Resident Manager. It was directed to no one in particular. "And to think, in the past, I've actually have accused Peter of *sleeping* through MiCap meetings!" Donoho took his seat, turning a triumphant grin in Hammer's general direction.

Kennedy, in his always-amicable manner, stood saying "Okay, anyone who doesn't agree with the assertion that there are no credible threats to the dam's concrete structure?"

One by one, the other members of the study group agreed. But they all expressed the proviso that their agreement excluded the possibility of a nuclear explosion. Since 9/11, Homeland Security had out-sourced a series of tests using some barely flyable 'hanger queens' that had been parked in the desert at China Lake. No one was saying into what test structure the remote-controlled airliners had been smashed. But the findings from those tests had been touted as proof of the dam's lack of vulnerability, should an airliner crash into the crest, or either face, of Hoover Dam. Reputedly, the qualification had since been enhanced. Now the results included the stipulation that the subject airliner was carrying the virtual equivalent of a twenty-kiloton nuclear bomb, and it still would have not caused any major structural damage to the dam's structure.

Kennedy, checking off another one of the boxes on the to-do-list he carried everywhere with him, spoke, "If all of you are satisfied we can put that concern to bed, lets move forward to the dam's operating concerns. Who wants to address that?"

Marvin Larson, a well-worn, highly experienced Master Engineer with a wealth of experience covering all the various disciplines, stood up. He said, "I'll take a shot at that. Okay, beside the structures we either have heard about today, or know about from personal experience, education, or training, the main mission of this dam is two-fold. It provides irrigation water and the generation of power. Lets take on the most important first, as we always get thirsty long before we worry about the lights going on the fritz."

Larson continued, "As Pete told us, Hoover Dam was constructed using diversionary tunnels, bored deep in the granite walls of Black

Canyon. After the dam's construction, the outboard two tunnels were closed off using huge concrete plugs. This left the inboard diversion tunnels, which were turned into spillways. One on each of the Arizona and Nevada sides, of the Colorado River.

"However, water to drive the turbines for the generation of power is handled by a separate system. It consists of four intake towers on the upstream side of the dam, which feed the power-generation process. These turbine/generators don't require all the water the intake towers bring in."

"The excess is discharged from the thirty-foot penstocks that run under the powerhouse. The water that is used in the generation process is taken to the generators through progressively smaller diameter penstock, before reaching the generators."

Larson stood a little straighter now, indicating by his body language that he was getting to the interesting part of his presentation. "Now, a generator is one of man's most unique tools. It takes water, and converts that water into electricity, then discharges that water downstream without damaging it—cool, huh? For you non-wrench heads, here is how it works. Water enters the four intake towers, and flows through the penstocks to the powerhouse."

The engineer had by now warmed to his speech, which was the reason everyone always found his verbal dissertations interesting. He went, "The powerhouse, or plural powerhouses for you purists, can be considered the first step of the process. These are seventeen turbine/generators of various sizes here at Hoover Dam. We have nine generators in the Arizona powerhouse, and eight on the Nevada size. For various reasons, a majority of these machines have a varying capacity for output."

"Okay, now to the second step of the process. The force of incoming water rotates the turbines, which turns the connecting shafts and magnetic coils inside the turbine/generators, which creates electricity. The incoming water enters into the process laterally from under the turbine/generators, and returns to the river vertically. The electric current they produce is 'stepped up' using a transformer to 230,000 volts for distribution through the Western Electric grid. And there you have it—a simple process, one using extremely technical complex mechanical and electrical mechanisms, to serve mankind."

As he started to sit down, he stood again said "Oh, one more thing—for routine maintenance and related functions in the power house, we utilize a couple small 3,500 horsepower turbine/generators. These things are old—old—old. In fact, because one of these recently if unexplainably self-destructed, the dam is currently deferring non-essential maintenance. And will continue to do so until a replacement is installed. Once the replacement is on-line, we'll being working 24/7 to catch up with the lengthy maintenance backlog. It takes quite a bit of effort to remove and replace a seventy-year-old piece of equipment, I can tell you. They don't build them like that anymore, my wife Barbara tells me." With that aside, Larson concluded his briefing, and sat down.

Kennedy then stood to reassume facilitation of the study group, saying "So it appears the abundance of brainpower lavished on the 'dam proper' facets of this study project has solved all Uncle Sugar's problems, huh?" he queried? "Okay, then lets summarize it, and get it on paper."

Kennedy began to tick each item off his fingers, "First, the original design specifications for the structure of the dam itself, protects it from anything less than a airborne-delivered nuclear warhead of at least twenty-megatons. Agreed?" The five-team member nodded affirmatively. "Secondly," he continued, "common sense holds that a 'scorched earth' action like that wouldn't be in the best long-term interests of the terrorists—after all, they want the riches of America, not just our corpses. Agreed?" Again, there were five positive responses from the team members.

The CIA's Deputy Director Kennedy again began "There are redundant systems for handling the discharge of river water, both from the intake tower system upstream, or the overflow though the 'outlet works' downstream. So, to paraphrase, since the penstocks are tunneled into granite, those systems are not at-risk. Even if we had to temporarily shutdown the powerhouse, all the in-coming process water could be bypassed. Is that correct?" Again, agreement from all present.

"On this power plant concern, we have seventeen generators in a protected environment. The powerhouse is nearly six-hundred-feet below the crest of the dam. The powerhouse is not accessible from that point, by anyone who is not a dam employee. Is that correct? So, if no unauthorized person can access the facility, we can consider that area to be secure, is that correct?" Again, everyone agreed, except Bill Savage who nodded his head affirmatively, but said "With the proviso that the bad guy isn't one of the powerhouse employees carrying very large lunch pail."

Edith Hammer glared over at ADC Savage with a 'if looks could kill' glance. She said, "Yes, Bill, if and when the balloon goes up, and the threat it isn't already in the powerhouse. I might add, that is a complete impossibility. Any device of unknown type or origin can't be brought into the powerhouse. We have exhaustive procedural safeguards to insure that. Now stop verbally trashing my employees, will you?"

Savage look back at Edith, nodded his head to signify that he understood her exasperation. Then began dumping his reference materials back into his briefcase, which had been sitting on the table.

The following day, promptly at 9 A.M., all parties again convened in the main powerhouse conference room. Their mission for today was to review the findings of the individual study groups. Then they would be condensing them into a single report for Homeland Security and the Bush administration. The summarization had been requested by the FBI's Bill Savage, and seconded by the Bureau of Reclamation's John Casterbottom.

After catered coffee, donuts, and soft drinks had been once-again been made available, everyone took their seats, and Casterbottom brought the MiCap/counterterrorism study group to order.

"People," began Casterbottom in his normally gruff manner, "I understand that yesterday's meetings went well, and that the dam appears to be in better shape, counterterrorism-wise, than the naysayers in Congress had feared?"

The Regional Director hesitated briefly for a moment, as if trying to remember some obscure point. He then continued, "Okay, folks, I want each of the facilitators from each of the three study groups to give a fifteen-minute summary of your group's findings."

Casterbottom went on, "Then we'll discuss each of the group's findings. I expect each of you to be looking for unexplained discrepancies between yours and the other group's findings. If that proves unnecessary, we'll then attempt to consolidate them. The final report, annotated by the typed notes you already have made in your group yesterday, will be drawn from that. Edith has promised to make available whatever secretarial support is required. Lets start off with Commander Stalwart, from the 'upstream threat' study group. Commander . . ."

The tall, attractive, intelligent 'fast tracker' stood, and began. "Briefly, we considered the contamination of the reservoir, though the hypothetical interjection of bio-chemicals, or any proscribed controlled chemical substances. But based on known chemical dispersion rates, that proved not to be a viable threat. We came to this conclusion, primarily due of the shear immensity of the volume of water in the equation, reportedly some thirty million-acre feet. The physical volume of Lake Mead is huge."

"Then," the U.S.C.G. Commander continued, "we also considered any potentially at-risk facilities within one mile on the upstream side of the dam. We could only come up with the four intake towers. Our position on those is that as long as terrorists are prevented from reaching those, neither the towers, nor anything else upstream of Hoover Dam, can be considered to be at-risk."

Stalwart continued, "The plumbing, or whatever you call the water delivery penstocks and bypass systems, were tunneled out of granite rock. It isn't accessible, and therefore isn't a risk as long as all accessibility is denied. Any questions?" When no one stood to address any comments to the 'upstream' study group's presentation, Commander Stalwart retook her seat.

Director Casterbottom, seeming surprised at the brevity of the presentation, thanked the Coast Guard officer. He then invited the 'downstream' threat study group's facilitator, FBI Agent Diane Davis, to discuss her group's findings.

Davis began, "The 'downstream' threat environment has been limited to one mile by someone above my paygrade. Therefore, our finding is virtually the same as the one voiced for 'upstream.' In fact, even smaller if any potentiality exists at all. Every bit of essential plumbing, anything conceivably of interest to terrorists, is deeply embedded in faultless granite tunnels. Therefore, we can't identify nor define any risk factors."

She continued, "The one thing that some in the group felt potentially at-risk, primarily because there is nothing on-file supporting the existence of an inspection in the past decade, are the reportedly plugged diversion or spillway tunnels."

Davis briefly consulted her notes, before continuing, "Now, we acknowledge that it may be dangerous to go into these old tunnels to inspect them further. At least dangerous for the inspectors, who would have to go into those long-ago abandoned tunnels. We therefore don't recommend using the dam's maintenance or physical inspection experts. But we felt it was worth a look, especially as it seems no one has been in there for decades, so we put it down."

She quipped, "Heaven knows—perhaps they'll find the lost gold treasure of the Sierra Madre." After receiving no questions, other than the snickers at her joke, she retook his seat. Again, Director Casterbottom, who had been lead to believe that serious threats from terrorism existed at the dam, was again surprised by the report's brevity.

Next Casterbottom called up the CIA Deputy Director/Plans, Jim Kennedy. "Well," Kennedy began, "you probably aren't going to like this either, John. But our group also, upon reviewing all the facts, felt our assigned area of study wasn't at-risk from a non-nuclear attack. For the following reasons: First, Homeland Security simulated crash tests following 9/11 indicated nothing less than an airliner carrying a twenty-megaton nuclear warhead could do anything but scratch the paint on the 'dam proper.' And the dam crest forms a semi-protective umbrella for the powerhouse."

"Secondly, the dam's powerhouse experts have assured us that there is nothing in the powerhouse that in-itself could cause catastrophic damage to the degree they'd lose more that a portion of their power generation ability. And further that no unauthorized personnel, materials or device could gain access due to strict management controls put in-place since 9/11. Questions?" Receiving none, Kennedy sat down.

John Casterbottom stood, stretched his large frame, and shook his head, and said, "You mean Hoover Dam isn't the 'terrorist playground' a couple of U.S. Senators have been claiming?" He asked.

Edith Hammer, the resident manager of the dam, stood and fielded that one. "No Sir. The dam's security controls take everything we've discussed into consideration. It addresses each potential threat."

"We damn sure aren't planning on letting anyone violate the security barriers on the upstream size of the dam. Therefore the intake towers aren't at-risk. We watch them with close circuit T.V., and patrolling armed guards, 24/7, using night optics after dark."

Hammer continued, "The powerhouse is the most heavily-guarded facility in the complex. Nothing is getting in there. You can tell the president for me that he can bet his last dollar on that. The only significant access into the powerhouse is from the lower access road. Since 9/11, the lower access road has been barricaded. The heavy steel barricade must be movable, for passage of maintenance vehicles. But it is monitored 24/7 by armed guards and closed circuit TV. Persons using the upper access road across the dam's crest can't get access down the six-hundred-feet to the powerhouse facility."

Hammer, taking a defiant posture, asserted, "We run a tight ship here, Director Casterbottom. Now, after reflection, that idea of going into the plugged diversion tunnels, although risky, isn't bad idea. But I don't want to have to use my highly skilled engineers for that relatively lo-tech job. They could be bitten by something, or otherwise injured. But if you'll get me a handful of Marines out here, I'll ask my crew for a volunteer to lead the troops into tunnels. If there are no volunteers, I'll go myself. Is that satisfactory, Sir?" Ms. Hammer starred at Casterbottom, as if in defiance, and then retook her seat.

Casterbottom, for once, was shocked into silence. He thought some more, and then asked Hammer if he could now borrow the promised secretarial staff to complete the Presidential report. She indicted with her body English, 'Be my guest,' and the two women, and one male secretary walked up to where he was standing at the podium.

Before speaking with the clerical pool, Casterbottom thanked Edith and the assembled staff that had participated in the terrorism exercise that week. He then asked the three facilitators from the study groups, which were staying in the same hotel as he, over in Boulder City, to remain behind and assist in the completion of the report.

CHAPTER EIGHT

DAY 152—01 JUNE

HOOVER DAM

THE MYSTERIOUS INTRUDER

NEAR BOULDER CITY

NEVADA

It was a pleasantly warm afternoon on the massive 28,537,000 acre-foot Colorado River reservoir that formed Lake Mead. Lake Mead, largely located in Nevada, was upstream of the famous Hoover Dam. At the time the dam was constructed, between 1930-1935, Hoover was the largest concrete dam in the world.

Lake Mead exceeded most of the common measurements of largeness. All which explained why both the dam and Lake Mead were considered critical to the national security of the United States.

A fisherman would tell you that the area's greatness was all due to the outstanding fishing. There were miles and miles of coves and inlets where one could drop a line at his/her leisure. At least seven types of fish populated Lake Mead. They consisted of striped bass, the bluegill, rainbow trout, largemouth bass, channel catfish, the threadfin shad, and the sunfish.

Boaters on the other hand might swear it was the indescribable beauty of the pristine blue water. One could water ski to his or hers heart's content. Or morph yourself into a rude, disaster-magnet with a noisy, over-powered personal watercraft.

For the more traditional recreator, it might just be the absolute magnificence of the massive dam itself.

The more practical citizen might wax endlessly on how regionally important the great dam was. A dam that essentially supported the hope, aspirations, and the lifestyles of the nearly twenty-five million persons who choose to live in the desert Southwest, Southern California, Arizona and Old Mexico.

The dam, seemly magically, provided irrigation water for the growing of food. Its secondary priority was the generation of electricity. Its construction had imposed flooding control measures that all but ended a long history of seasonal flooding in the region it served. And of course, all these advantages had encouraged employment. And that had brought posterity throughout the region beginning back in 1935.

The upstream view of Lake Mead, from the 726-foot crest of Hoover Dam, especially though the powerful U.S. Navy ship binoculars she had talked a junior-grade admiral out of years ago, was damn exhilarating. Edith Hammer, for the past six months, had been filling in as Hoover Dam's Resident Manager. She had initially been promised that the no-notice assignment was a 'temporary, emergency' posting.

Hammer thought she would never tire of this magnificent bird's eye view from the dam crest. However, throughout most of the year, fierce summer temperatures held sway here in Black Canyon. The dam was located in the southwestern United States. Temperatures of 120 degrees and up were not uncommon. Therefore the view she saw today was mainly only enjoyed during the cooler months of the calendar year.

As was typical in earlier-constructed concrete hydroelectric dams in the United States at the time, most of the physical operating and administrative spaces had been incorporated into the dam proper. Thus working offices there had no windows.

Oh, there were exceptions such as the former visitor's center, now being used as an administrative annex, located adjacent to the dam proper. But due to her task-filled work schedule, she and most of her co-workers rarely took the opportunity to stop and enjoy the view from the dam's crest.

She, herself, stayed off the crest top of the dam, or at least as much as her duties permitted her to, during those furnace-like summer months.

As she enjoyed the view of Lake Mead, Edith was always amazed at the unusually low incidence of fatalities among the construction workers on the project, that took five years it took to plan and build. Hoover was acknowledged at the time as the 7th *greatest engineering feat in the world*. Certainly, as with projects of far less magnitude than this particular gravity-arch dam, there had been unavoidable worker deaths. The dam had suffered a small, but still regrettable number of construction deaths, nevertheless.

Some of the deaths had been due to the hostile construction environment. Others due to the inherent hazards involved in building this marvel. On a massive, and dangerous project like this, the only applicants normally were men who possessed the rough, tough egos and strengths a dam-building job required.

As far has Hammer knew, none of the relatively-small number of deaths that had occurred 1930-1935 had been attributed to the consumption of alcohol. Little of any liquor had been permitted in the Boulder City, Nevada, at the time. That was the 'company town' the dam's contractor, Six-Companies Consortium, had enlarged mainly to provide a base for the workers on the dam project.

The actual dam site was located deep in Black canyon. It was remote from any other reasonably priced housing accommodations. All of the construction workers, most of whom worked 12/7, really had no other option other than to relocate to Boulder City for the duration of the project.

The rules in Boulder City were unforgiving, and strictly enforced by the Six Companies' security force. If you lost your job at the dam site, you were gone from Boulder City within twenty-four hours, or rumor has it, suffer the consequences.

Actually, the awkward method the workers were forced to employ to get the concrete down the seven hundred feet to the initial site-of-the-pour can be given some credit for the low death rate. An excessive amount of time was required to complete just a single pour cycle.

The difficulty was getting the concrete-filled buckets from the huge batch plants located high atop Black Canyon's cliffs, lowered the hundreds of feet down to the pour location just above the newly-dry river bed bottom, by hydraulic-controlled cranes. There the buckets were empted into the wooden forms. Then the empty buckets were pulled back up to the batch plants on the cliffs. Even when using multiple batch plants sources to support the sequencing of the pour, each round trip element still took, on an average, at least five minutes time.

That five-minute window had proved a blessing, despite the implied inefficiency. That window permitted co-workers time to jump in and rescue any worker who had lost his footing and slipped into the freshly poured concrete inside the form.

Ms. Hammer had worked at Hoover ever since an unplanned personnel problem had reared its ugly head. It had occurred when there had been unexpected change in management at the facility.

The young, ambitious 'Turks' on the dam staff at the time of the sudden vacancy, had permitted their aspirations and lack of common sense to get out of hand. They had gotten self-centered and infected with tunnel vision. Each intractably was adamant that only he or she 'had the right' to be selected for the temporarily vacant resident manager's billet.

Each of the young applicants had permitted themselves to become dangerously distracted. Their routine responsibilities at the dam began to suffer. Instead of working their respective job-responsibilities, many, typical of human nature, tended to spend a lot of time in backstabbing their fellow applicants for the job.

Finally, it had been brought come to the U.S. Interior Department's attention. The whistle blowers had been a small but talented group of technical engineers. Those individuals expressed their opinions that they couldn't adequately perform their responsibilities unless the political in-fighting was terminated immediately.

The Department of the Interior is, in-effect, the folder holder of the Bureau of Reclamation. Therefore it was only hours before the whistle blowers silent employee rebellion came to the attention the president's cabinet in Washington D.C.

The group that had given the 'heads-up' to the Interior department consisted of the mid-level staff at Hoover Dam. These normally low-profile professionals were responsible for the successful, cost-effective, and safe day-to-day operation of the dam.

When pressed, the engineers had told the cabinet-level administration aides frankly, that the unworkable management situation at Hoover Dam was a disaster looking for a place to happen. That would be a crisis of apoplectic proportions, considering that Hoover was the United States' largest concrete dam. And therefore was vital to the country's national security.

By then, the U.S. Bureau of Reclamation had gotten wake-up calls from their big boss over at the Department of the Interior, as well as from the president's chief-of-staff. The bureau's boss, a long-time political insider, had been made aware in the strongest language, that there was serious trouble on the horizon over at Hoover.

Or would be unless *he* immediately brought in a 'trouble-shooter' to head up the dam, who could hit the ground running. The replacement would have to be authorized to bring a broom, and permitted to clean house wherever necessary. The person that was brought in to resolve the crisis, would have to be authorized-in-advance to make whatever changes were deemed necessary.

The U. S. Department of the Interior's head had been informed by the presidential aides in no uncertain terms, that *he* was expected to have the day-to-day operations of the critical facility back on track quickly. Existing staff was making sure that the routine day-to-day maintenance of the dam was being accomplished. The 'existing staff' being those that had chosen to not get involved in the race-for-the-gold.

But the important functions relative to planning the long-rang goals necessary in the areas of preventative maintenance, capital equipment replacement, and technology upgrades, were being ignored, and had all but fallen by the wayside.

As things tend to run downhill, the actions that followed all happened in a matter of hours. The Interior Department's chairman had informed the Bureau of Reclamation's regional operations director, located in the Denver office, that *he* "damn well better identify an experienced and proven management person by 'yesterday.' That 'someone' would have to be capable of getting the operation back on its feet. Plus having the talent for hitting the ground running. Or that the Bureau of Reclamation would *also* have a vacancy." The Interior Department Chairman hadn't needed to elaborate further on whose position that opening would involve.

The necessary management shakeup at Hoover Dam was the Reclamation Bureau's baby. There was no doubt that they would be the designated scapegoat unless the Nevada/Arizona facility was promptly brought back on-track. The Bureau's head was personally was expected to fix it. If he couldn't, his boss at Interior assured him that "he would have someone deposited on Hoover Dam's crest road by government helicopter within twenty-four hours, that could!"

Another bureaucrat, this one in Reclamation Bureau's Human Relations Department, Betty Jo Hunter, then had the bad luck to receive a tense phone call from her 'higher command.' Hunter's boss, a man who never would be accused of being a 'people-person', informed Betty of the near-crisis situation over at Hoover. He waxed endlessly about the potential for disaster if "you don't do your job, Betty!"

Duly advised of the crisis, Hunter was rudely informed that she was to immediate drop everything she was currently doing. She was being reassigned. It was now *her* job responsibility to resolve the management problem at Hoover Dam, like *yesterday!*

First, she conferred with her equally shocked staff. Then, Betty Jo Hunter, the hapless Human Resources manager, acknowledged that her status in the hierarchy had suddenly deteriorated to that of someone sentenced to the proverbial barrel.

Hunter researched both her files and excellent memory numerable times. Finally, she realized that the individual they needed was Edith Hammer. Hammer was currently in facility-level management at Reclamation. And she had a past track record of getting the job done. In the past, Hammer had demonstrated she was someone capable of jumping in and taking the wayward bull by the horns at Hoover.

However, the individual that Hunter and her staff had unanimously agreed was the only person they felt could do the damage control job, wasn't available. Betty nervously called her direct superior to inform him of fact.

Hunter ran over the background facts with the supervisor. Edith Hammer, a well-experienced, well-respected long-time engineer in the Bureau of Reclamation, had earned the reputation of being a proven 'go to' employee in times of many crises in the past. Hammer was well known throughout the Bureau, as having excellent trouble-shooting skills that had permitted her in the past to be plunked down in a dogfight of egocentric professionals of differing opinions and goals.

Hammer had the people skills to resolve major differences in management style. She had never, in the past twenty-years of her impressive tenure with Reclamation, ever failed to return operational harmony to the desired norm in contentious situations such as that current being experienced at Hoover Dam.

The only problem, as her Betty's staff had reminded her, was that Hammer—a couple of years ago—had been assigned to a smaller dam in a staff position far below her experience level, at her personal request. It was the Reclamation Bureau's collective opinion that Hammer had taken a significant pay cut, and far lesser responsibility, to prepare her family for her impending retirement to the 2,000-acre family ranch in Colorado.

Betty, considering the zero options her boss had give her earlier, decided her own future was at-risk if she failed to perform as demanded. Hunter couldn't permit Hammer's personal plans to stand in the way of the Bureau's ability to obtain the timely resolution of the Hoover problem.

Uncomfortably, guiltily, but firmly, Betty Hunter had informed her staff that their careers were likewise at-risk. That was unless they could convince the renowned trouble-shooter to accept the new assignment, at least on a temporary basis. Hunter initiated one of the very rare known instances of an Emergency Budget Variance Request. She knew the chain-of-command above her would sign off on the pay scale deviation without question, having already heard the flack from the 'mother ship' over at Interior.

The authorization was required to give management and Betty some wiggle-room to do whatever was necessary to entice Hammer away from her current job assignment. The task would be difficult. All the Human Relations staff remembered that Hammer did not suffer surprise well. She would quickly realize the Bureau was figuratively forcing her to vacate the position she currently occupied, to assume responsibility for resolving the Hoover problem.

After much haggling, Hammer's acceptance of the reassignment to Hoover had been obtained. Bureau management had thrown large bundles of salary and cash bonuses in her direction, and dared her not to catch them. Whatever Hammer asked for, no matter the absurdity, she was given without question. If she wanted it, it was hers. But as with everything, there was a price.

The bosses at Reclamation had initially promised her that the assignment to remedy the disruptive atmosphere at Hoover Dam would only be "temporary." But less than two months later, that all changed. Surprisingly to herself, she soon discovered that she had unconsciously permitted her outstanding reputation, people skills, bottom-line performance, and negotiating talents to be prostituted to make her 'irreplaceable' at Hoover.

Months following the emergency appointment, Hammer had been summoned to the Denver office. Transportation both ways out of McCarran Field in Las Vegas was provided via a fancy leased jet. That should have been her first clue. In the office, Hammer was informed that her accomplishments had improved the Hoover facility to such exceptional levels of operating efficiency that the Reclamation Bureau would have to rescind her position's 'temporary' classification.

She was told that Hoover Dam was so important to the united States, indeed the country's national security, that higher ups in the administration had decided that she could not be permitted her to resign from her new 'temporary' position. At least until the Bureau had found an acceptable replacement. Even then, Hammer would be expected to spend the necessary time to bring the chosen applicant up to speed. Thus with abject apologies from her bosses, Hammer's 'temporary' job at Hoover had been converted to a permanent posting, essentially without anyone asking for her concurrence.

Edith Hammer mentally reviewed the efficiency and dispatch of some six-months ago by which she had been politely yanked out of her old job on two-hours notice. She was told to pack and kiss her family goodbye, telling them she would be on a thirty-day 'temporary' assignment at Hoover Dam. Typically a tool of panic-stricken bureaucracies world wide, she had been told "further details of your temporary assignment are being assembled in a package for your subsequent review. We'll get that out to you as soon as you get settled in at Hoover Dam."

It had been hard for her not to be impressed with the Bureau's speed and efficiency. She and her hastily packed luggage had been picked up by one of the U.S. Government's most expensive helicopters, and ferried to the nearest airport with a jet-capable runway. There, one of the Air Force's executive high-speed jets, normally only available to White House staff, waited impatiently for her arrival.

Her luggage has been hastily loaded on-board the white Gulfstream, empty except for her, her luggage, and the flight crew who all looked jaunting, wearing dark blue Air Force flight suits. She had been boarded and seat-belted into a plush reclining passenger seat, as if she was a hick-from-the-sticks, and never had flown before.

With engines screaming, the expensive jet pivoted on its nose wheel assembly, and began a normally forbidden high-speed taxi to the airport's sole 3,000-foot runway. Shortly before the executive jet turned onto the designated departure runway, she heard the flight crew belatedly clearing the aircraft's priority departure with the control tower.

The Gulfstream V accelerated as if shot out of a cannon. It literally screamed down the minimal-length runway. As the plane raced down the runway, its speed was ever increasing as the aircraft pasted the decision points of V-1, and V-2. Then the cabin floor abruptly rotated, and she seemed to leap off the runway into the astute blue sky. Edith watched from one of the six small port windows on her seat's side of the craft, as the runway dropped further and further away.

The Gulfstream's flight crew then made some minor adjustments in trim, which reduced the aircraft's unusually high-angle of attack for the climb to cruising altitude, en-route Las Vegas's McCarran field.

Shortly following takeoff, the co-pilot, a Lt. Colonel, whom Edith had secretly thought looked scrumptious, brought her a pre-packed VIP lunch in a white Styrofoam box. She thanked him and asked about their arrival time in Las Vegas. He hesitated in thought for a brief moment, then telling her the Gulfsteam's anticipated time of arrival time at the airport's general aviation terminal.

Smiling, he told her to push the buzzer located in the seat arm if she needed anything. Then, abruptly, as military officers are wont to do, he turned on his heel and walked back up to the flight deck. He removed his cap, stepped over the center instrument console, and retook his seat on the starboard side of the aircraft. He deftly bucked himself into his seat, and reached back with his left arm, and pulled the reinforced cockpit door closed, effectively separately her from the cockpit.

Those initially twenty-four hours in her new assignment had been exciting despite the mess she had found waiting for her at Hoover Dam.

Returning her thoughts to the present, Hammer crossed the two-lane crest road carefully, avoiding the ever-present motoring tourist, gawking instead of watching his or her driving. She successful managed the crossing of crest's concrete forty-foot wide road without incident, and stepped up on the six-foot wide sidewalk.

Taking a deep breath, she cautiously walked over to the immaculate brushed aluminum railing, revealing a childhood fear of heights she thought she had conquered years ago. She realized she was blushing slightly, but reasoned that no one she knew had watched her trek to the chilling proximity of the dam railing.

Shrugging her shoulders, Hammer attempted to release the tension she knew was carried in them. She looked a hundred feet upstream, past the four intake towers everyone found so beautiful. Then she expanded her gaze past the upstream security barrier located nearly 1,500-feet upstream of the dam's face.

The net barrier was constructed of strong wire cable, strung between the two shorelines, adorned by the equally spaced, orange-colored flotation buoys. The security cable was intended to keep boats and floating debris away from the upstream face of the huge dam.

By forcing her excellent vision to focus even further beyond the cable, she could see almost a mile north from the dam face. There in Lake Mead, apparently at anchor, she glimpsed a large barge. On its large deck rested two gray-colored Tuff-Sheds, of the type she had in her backyard at home.

Around the sheds were stacks of equipment and supplies. For the distance of a mile, her eyes had little difficulty identifying the piles of carefully positioned equipment, compressors, dead-leg hoists, and stacks of aluminum-colored 72-cc diving air cylinders.

Bolted alongside one of the sheds, was a first-aid module which included an expensive gray-colored chamber. Hammer assumed it was there to save the lives of divers who push the envelope a little too much, relative to excessive bottom-loitering time. From her experience as a scuba diver in her earlier years, she knew that overstaying your dive time on the bottom was a sure way to get a fearfully painful case of the bends. The situation caused bubbles of nitrogen to become trapped in the diver's joints.

When Hammer reported aboard, she had taken the time required to read each page of the dam's master operating log. It also included all entries on the 'snivel list'—a list of needed repairs that could place any dam's efficient operation at risk. Every commercial power-generating dam in the world religiously kept and maintained both logs.

Financially, the key to success for any Resident Manager was to keep a proper balance between the categorized needs, and abilities of the contract maintenance department, and its schedule. Any failure to maintain that delicate balance could result in an operational shutdown—the surest way to lose your job in the high-stress environment of hydroelectric generation. And earn an industry-wide blackball while you were at it.

Hammer reviewed the master log weekly to keep herself up-to-date on the dam's long-term needs. Also entered into the log, were reports of what were referred to as 'the unusuals.' Any non-normal situation or occurrence fell under this category. Sure enough, Hammer located an entry made several weeks earlier, over an unreadable signature. The written explanation in the log was nearly nonexistent. It was a single sentence stating that a "Silt survey barge was setting up shop above the dam's upstream face." Other than that, the scribbled entry was completely without further detail, a violation of the spirit, if not the letter, of U.S. Bureau of Reclamation policy and procedure.

When she had spotted the large barge anchored upstream of the dam face, she had been prompted to check the log for a so-noted 'unusual.' Procedure required the presence of the barge to be listed, along with an explanation for its presence.

It was a fact of life in the hydroelectric business, that silt accumulation upstream of all dam intakes, was a frequently audited concern. Nearly one hundred feet of 'accumulation provision' space had been factored into the initial 1930 engineering calculations for silt build-up in the Lake Mead reservoir. And more importantly, silt accumulations levels at the underwater intake towers of the dams, which were periodically monitored.

The Colorado River's 1,400 miles of muddy, red headwaters were ever changing. Silt buildup could greatly reduce the efficienty of a hydroelectric dam. And in extreme cases, shut the dam down completely, as it was in danger of doing at several smaller dams throughout the United States. Excessive silt buildup, exceeding the dam's engineering allowances for same, was deemed an immediate critical situation which characteristically hoisted red flags, rang bells, sounded sirens, and blew whistles.

So reading that another crisis-inspired survey was underway into the silt levels of Lake Mead hadn't greatly surprised Edith Hammer. In fact, she admitted that she would love to switch jobs for a month or so with those lucky souls who dove the waters of Lake Mead to measure silting levels. Instead of being stuck behind the dam's operation desk, fielding the never-ending problems involved in operating a seven-decade old, aging hydro-generating facility, such as Hoover Dam.

Having already exceeded the longest 'work break' she thought a manager ought to be allowed, Hammer turned, walked back across the crest road. She hurried along the downstream sidewalk to the pair of highly polished, decorative brass doors that concealed the elevator car entrance.

The massive elevator, one of two, previously had been utilized to take tour visitors down into the dam's complex innards, before 9/11. However, Bureau of Reclamation staffers such as she and her staff were its primary passengers these days. She often felt like an ant, occupying the huge car, as it transported her down to the dam's operation offices.

While the dam's administration office where she also had an office, was located just off the crest on the Nevada side, all the working operational offices were deep in the bowels of the massive concrete and steel structure.

Edith Hammer, as a certified Bureau of Reclamation dam operator, was well familiar with everything relating to the performance of hydroelectric dams. That fact alone, possibly agitated her logic process, and caused her to wonder about some of the equipment she had seen on-board the silt-level survey vessel.

Frankly, although acknowledging new survey methods are always evolving in the industry, some of the top-of-the-line equipment she'd seen only partially covered by tarpaulins on the deck of the vessel had surprised her. One such observation was that even though rarely are such vessels set up for a 24/7 sampling schedule, this one apparently was. Or so the evidence she had observed of the apparent provisions for on-board sleeping accommodations.

Early in her chosen career, she had taken the time to become a certified scuba diver herself. So, remembering her diving days, she had been surprised when she observed that the survey divers seemed to be using the heavy triple-tank, 72-cubic inch air tanks. This alone was unusual in an activity where stringently monitored and enforced Federal OSHA safety procedures, limited the survey's contract fresh-water divers, to a maximum dive duration of an forty-five minutes, or less.

She had glimpsed a couple of 'parked' underwater diver propulsion vehicles, partially submerged, bobbing alongside the dive platform to which they had been secured. Apparently this survey had been tasked with some special application study assignments. Even though she had observed the barge at some distance, her interest in diving allowed her to recognize the underwater transporters. They appeared to be of the same general size and type she knew the U.S. Navy Seals employed on their covert enemy harbor-reconnoitering missions.

Why expensive underwater devices like those were required for a simple silt survey was beyond her understanding. And also none of her business, she reminded herself. However, being a conservative person through family influence, she hated it when a government contractor screwed the taxpayers. There was probably a very good reason for the extra expense required for the acquisition of the expensive sleds.

But, even with her extensive experience, she couldn't fathom why. Perhaps it would turn out to be yet another example similar to the Air Force $300 toilet seats—another example of what NBC calls the Fleecing of America.

Leaving the cavern-like elevator car when it finally reached the bottom of the shaft, Hammer walked down the short hallway leading to the operations command post. She entered her spacious but windowless subterranean office, which was located mid-point in the various levels that make up the forty-story-tall-gravity-arch structure. She glared at the office's large oak desk, floor and cabinets.

They all were still covered with stacks of paperwork left behind by the dam's previous resident manager. Edith pulled on a light wool sweater she always wore at her desk, necessary due to the administrative areas' overzealous air conditioning. She flipped on her computer, after peeking into her wallet to retrieve her new password.

Then the woman began attacking the piles of over-due reports, requests, and status reports. Before turning her attention totally to the current paperwork task at hand, she made a mental note to call someone over at the Denver regional office of the Bureau of Reclamation, and ask about the need for the unusual costly equipment she had observed on the silt survey barge that was parked in her front yard, on Lake Mead.

It was early evening the following day, when Hoover Dam's Resident manager finally found a few minutes to call over to the 24/7 Regional B of R office in Denver. She felt driven to satisfy her inherent curiosity as to the necessity for the unusual equipment she had observed yesterday on the anchored survey barge.

Hammer was confident she had not been mistaken in the identification of what she had observed. She had been using a pair of powerful Navy binoculars. The same type that the Navy used on the bridge of its warships, designed to ascertain distant details and ship class identification on vessels sometimes twenty miles away. The survey vessel, on the other hand, had been serenely floating less than two miles way from her 726-foot elevated observation point, on the sidewalk just off the two-lane crest road which spanned Hoover Dam.

Unsurprising to a person of Hammer's long tenure in the government bureaucracy, she wasn't concerned when her direct supervisor at the B of R regional office in Denver said she had no idea what survey contract Hammer was referring to.

After all, hydroelectric dam silt survey contracts around the United States were pretty much contracted out on a turnkey basis. And only to firms which had a long and satisfactory history of impeccable performance with either the Bureau of Reclamation, or in some instances, with the Department of the Interior.

Like the major construction contracts let for the building of the Federal Interstate highway system, only proven contractors were solicited for bids. And the contracts were only awarded to those the government knew could, and would, do the job exactly to the contract's written statement of work.

Such contracts awards permitted the vendor firm to accomplish the work on their own schedule, as long as it wasn't deferred. And as long as the company assumed 100% turnkey responsibility for the notification of all impacted parties. The successful contractor also was responsible for supplying whatever level of project security, the U. S. General Accounting Office (the GAO) had established for all U.S. Government-issued construction projects following 9/11/01.

Hammer hung up the phone, and turned on her PalmPilot, which contained the many megabytes of information, she had accrued over her twenty-plus years in management at the B of R. She quickly found the GAO's unlisted procurement information line number, and dialed it. The number was just one of the many 'discrete' telephone numbers, which the B of R procedure manual stated were "never to be given out to civilians," (read, non-management government employees).

The unlisted phone number was answered on the first ring, naturally by a computer, which then gave Hammer a full litany of choices. After punching selection after selection, she finally was connected to a real person.

Before Edith could ask for any information, she had first to provide the 'human' with full verbal details as to her identity, federal position code number, agency affiliation, and why she was calling. Managing to work her way through that maze without losing her cool, Edith asked the person on the opposite end of the line, if she would please pull up all open contracts for Hoover Dam that exceeded $100,000 in gross valuation. Then she requested the GAO do a sub-search of the federal database using the keywords 'Survey/Silt.'

This information would provide Hammer with the details of who the contract had been awarded to, with the accompanying contract numerical designator. That specific information would then give Hammer enough data to permit her to research the survey contract's statement-of-work-scope via her own authorized access to the federal GAO database.

However, as Hammer continued to hang on the line, no matter how many times the 'human' said she ran the data through the GAO's master database, Hammer was told that there was no such open contract. Now irritated in the extreme, Hammer, biting her tongue, politely asked to speak to the woman's supervisor.

Seemingly a half-hour, but more than likely less than five-minutes later, a horse-voiced man came on the line, and asked Hammer again to identify herself. Then Hammer had to repeat answers to all of the questions she had previously given to the first person answering the phone.

And again, after a seemingly thorough search through the data base, she as told "Sorry, dear—there is no open survey/silt contract pending for Hoover Dam—are you sure of your information?" Now, unhappy with the non-politically correct verbal gender-oriented slight, Hammer slammed down the receiver on her phone, hoping to break the bureaucratic bastard's eardrum.

After the steam quit pouring from her ears, Hammer, giving the matter some additional thought, decided to try plan "B". She picked up the phone again, and called the dam's duty yeoman, Abigail Benson, who per Bureau procedure, was charged with maintaining physical custodianship of the dam's operating logs.

Edith asked Benson to please look up the 'Unusual' that had been entered into the log. The same one Edith herself had noted during her earlier inspection of the dam's operating logs.

A member of Hoover Dam operating and/or technical administration was required, by policy, to verify the credentials, authorization, and contract number of any contractor requesting access to the hydroelectric facility. This included all waters adjacent, which certainly encompassed the whole of Lake Mead. The approval would identify which member of the Hoover Dam administration, by affixation of his/her signature of approval, had been responsible for doing the required background check with the B of R's Regional office in Denver. That step would have had to be satisfactorily executed before any dam employee would permit any contractor to go to work in an unsecured area that had been designated as an area at-risk, ever since the disaster on 9/11/01.

After a just a few minutes, the duty yeoman Benson came back on the line. She began to apologize profusely, but admitted she couldn't determine the identity of the signature. The team member's signature, whom had accepted responsibility for double-checking the contractor's authorization before permitting the work to begin. Apropos of nothing, the woman volunteered to Hammer that the handwriting on that particular entry in the dam's operating log, was worse than that belonging to her gynecologist.

Now thoroughly agitated, but still not over concerned, she dialed the extension for the Hoover Dam police chief. The security dispatcher answered the phone, and informed her that the Chief was back in Washington D.C. at a mandatory Homeland Security meeting. A fact Hammer now remembered from her weekly operational briefing, now that she thought about it.

The dispatcher, instead, connected her to the Dam's Acting Police Chief, David Ness. He had walked into the security control center, when the dispatcher had been on the phone with Hammer. The Assistant Chief had just returned from one of the constant management-by-walking-around inspections, that all mid-level B of R managers were expected to religiously perform daily.

When Ness came on the line, they spent the obligatory three minutes inquiring as to the wellness of each other family—a 'team building' communications tool introduced by management consultants from Japan, that the Bureau had contracted with for 'productivity improvement' seminars five-months earlier. At the time, the bosses had been attempting to defuse the personnel crisis that then existed in the Hoover head-shed. Once completing that activity, the two employees would get down to business.

Those preliminaries out of the way, Hammer began to review the concerns that had been building in her head, since her observation of the alleged Survey/Silt vessel yesterday. Today, before she began to make her inquires Hammer had noted the vessel remained under dual-anchor about a mile above the Dam's do-not-enter security zone, upstream of the dam face.

Edith methodically went over with Ness exactly what she had observed the previous day. She took the time to painstakingly explain why her experience lead her to believe the equipping of the vessel was excessive, considering the contractor's scope of work.

Hammer felt comfortable discussing her thoughts with in detail with Chief Ness. However, they both agreed that Hammer could be mistaken. And her suspicions could be unfounded. Perhaps the barge belonged to someone who had contracted with the Bureau of Reclamation, for some unusual work she was unaware of. If that was the case, she told Ness, she damn well wanted to be included in the information loop, before the fact.

Feeling she owed Ness an explanation for the unusual call, she explained that initially the query had just been curiosity on her part. But that feeling evolved, as she kept on running into stonewalls, every time she attempted to verify the contract.

Hammer explained to Ness that the GAO tracking system showed no record of the scope of work being authorized, or contract being issued. Also, she told him about double-checking with the custodian of the dam's operating log to determine who on her staff had authorized the work to proceed.

Only to be told the authorizing signature was unreadable. Chief Ness replied that his department, noting the approval written in the Operating log, which was discussed in every weekly dam management meeting, had not bothered to contact the vendor's vessel or crew directly. Ness, sighing, said honestly that he "now could only hope that his department had not been derelict in the performance of their assigned duties by not doing so." With which Hammer silently concurred.

Both Hammer and Ness knew that only an authorized member of the Hoover Dam's direct administration could gain access to the logs. Therefore, if the work had been permitted to proceed without the procedural verification being executed, then it would be obvious that someone on Hammer's staff was responsible. That individual would be guilty at the least of making a falsified entry.

In that case, the possibility followed that the 'doer' may have even attempted to disguise his or her identity, through the hastily scribbled, unreadable signature Hammer had found in the log.

Edith reached over to yank her copy of the Bureau of Reclamation's crisis contingency 'book' out of her briefcase. Over her career, she had learned to never permit the expensive Halliburton aluminum case to be more than fifty feet from her, whether she was on and off-duty. Crisis situations at hydroelectric dams can get serious, rapidly. Sometimes having contingency plans at your fingertips is the difference between a calamity that disrupts the lives of millions of people, and being able to calmly return home at the end of your regular shift.

Thumbing to the applicable section, she quickly, as Ness was doing, sped-read the narrative. Both of them knew they had to move fast. The barge, in control of some unknown party or group, was currently out in Lake Mead, less than two miles away from the dam's face. Ness asked her if she wanted him to call the Homeland Security 'Go Center' to alert them, or would she?

Hammer responded by telling him to get his team deployed along the dam's 1,244-foot crest. He was to go ahead and activate the emergency floodlights on both sides of the dam face once dusk fell, and barricade the crest roadway. She would alert the two State Police check points that had been established since 9/11. The checkpoints were located a mile in either side of the dam crest, on Highway 93.

Hammer instructed Ness to meet her in her topside office in the administration wing on the Nevada side, post haste. Then she plumped back down into her chair indelicately, which caused her to fart and utter a suspicious sounding gasp. Embarrassed at the involuntary outburst, she quickly severed the telephone connection with Chief Ness without explanation.

CHAPTER NINE

DAY 153—02 JUNE

HOOVER DAM

LAKE MEAD RESERVOIR

LAKE MEAD

NEVADA

Edith Hammer had just finished the procedural call that activated Homeland Security's crisis notification tree. Following 9/11, the cumbersome list, as far as the Resident Manager of Hoover Dam was concerned, had been reduced to a single telephone call. But before placing that call, she had alerted the Bureau of Reclamation's Regional office in Denver, and her immediate supervisor directly, to inform them of the potential crisis.

She had just hung up the phone, when a six-foot, six-inch tall black man in combat fatigues burst into her office, holding a M-16A1 assault rifle threateningly at port arms. Her first reaction was to scream in uncontrollable fear. Then she forced herself to take a second look at the gunman. This time she thankfully identified the man as Lt. Colonel David Ness, the dam's assistant Chief of police. The 'Super Chief', as his men like to call him, was in Washington D.C. attending another one of the endless security conferences.

"Shit, David," Hammer shouted, "you Goddamn near gave me a heart attack. Have you ever heard of knocking before you barge into a lady's office?"

"Yeah," Ness replied, "I guess I was a little over enthusiastic. However, but you did tell me to get my ass up here 'yesterday' didn't you? Just before you gasped and our phone connection went dead. Christ, I thought someone was attacking you. I'm sorry. It won't happen again, Ms. Hammer."

"No, no, please David," Hammer began, "I'm the one who should be sorry for what I said. If you ever think someone is attacking me, you have my complete permission to run through walls, doors, jump off tall buildings in a single bound, or whatever. Anything you have to do in order to perform a heroic rescue to save me. Please accept my apology, OK," Edith asked? Allowing a very slight grin to shine through onto her flushed face.

Colonel Ness acknowledged her apology, and then came rigidly to attention in front of her desk. Hammer, told him to "Sit down, David—you look foolish—standing like that in front of a woman who is only five-foot tall, on a good day."

As soon as Ness had done so, Hammer began. "I just finished talking with Homeland Security, or rather their command post. This is what Brigadier General Edgar Davenport—Homeland Security's Crisis Center duty officer—told me was going to happen right now. Their plan is more or less, chapter and verse, as it appears in the B of R's contingency manual. With a few play pretties thrown in because the possible enemy vessel is currently only a mile or so physically removed from the dam, perhaps ready to jump down our throats."

"Homeland Security," Edith continued, "has learned that the large barge we see out in front of our dam was rented for a two-week period. From up at that touristy Callville Bay Marina, on Lake Mead's north shore, just off Highway 167. According to the manager, read *harbormaste*r, whom the Center rousted out of a local bar, a small group of tanned, athletic-appearing young men, rented the barge about three days ago."

"The men claimed they would be using it as a platform for a diving job. According to the men, the diving job was being funded by a grant from the U.S. Government. The divers said they had been hired to perform some underwater measurement functions, somewhere north of the face of Hoover Dam."

Referring to her scribbled notes, the Resident Manager went on, "The old guy that Homeland Security talked to, said the guys that had rented the barge said something about performing silt level analysis."

"Now hear this, David," Hammer continued. "The rental was paid for in cash. The harbormaster, seeing that it was Homeland Security that was talking with him, appears to have found religion. He claims to be very eager to help. He now admits that he charged the men an outrageous rental fee. And demanded a $18,000 cash deposit, to boot."

"The old salt said he was surprised the group would pay such an exorbitant deposit for an old barge, long beyond its prime. He claims he later felt remorse, for about a nanosecond. And when the men asked, he had given them permission to temporarily mount a couple of those 'Tuff Shed' storage structures you see advertised on TV, on the open deck of the old barge."

"The group told the old guy they had already paid cash for the sheds," Edith Hammer said. "They had arranged for them to be trucked in from Las Vegas, in hopes they would be permitted to use them on the barge to protect what they claimed was their expensive equipment. The now-reformed harbormaster told Homeland Security that *what* really swung the deal, was that the new sheds were his to keep when the rental was over."

"General Davenport said the old man told him that the barge was a very old, but still plenty seaworthy. Back in its heyday, it had been constructed out of rough-hewn timbers. The harbormaster thought the barge had originally been built to transport mine ore to market, back around 1915."

"The group also had a new commercial-sized air compressor, a decompression chamber, a lot of fancy scuba diving equipment, and some very large wooden crates." Hammer read from her notes. "The old duffer said the crates must have contained valuable and sensitive equipment, as the divers insisted on handling themselves. Even though he offered to load them aboard using the marina's forklift."

"The apparent leader of the group, a dark skinned, tall, humorless type of guy, told him that the Tuff Sheds were insurance against any rain that might fall while they were on their ten-day diving expedition."

"The 'rain' comment, especially this time of year, and the fact that in the harbormaster's extensive experience, their willingness to pay for the rental in cash was unusual, normally would have raised all kinds of red flags. However, the old guy said his only thought was, and I quote, *Hell—they are just rich college kids—it ain't none of my worry how they spend their money.*"

"Oh," Hammer remembered, "the old guy said they also asked his permission to over-spray the entire above-water surface of the old barge with some surplus navy-gray paint. That also seemed odd to the harbormaster, but the men offered to pay additional for the painting, and he figured what the hell—the barge needs painting anyway, what could it hurt?"

After taking a deep breath, Hammer told Lt. Colonel Ness that one of the CIA's KH-11 'Keyhole' electro-optical imaging, intelligence surveillance satellites, had been maneuvered on-station into a geosynchronous orbit periodically passing over the dam. Soon it would be beaming real time imagery to the Homeland Security Crisis Center, using equipment from the National Security Agency.

She said, "I imagine that about now, the NSA analysts are seeing down-linked real-time images of whatever is going on, on and around the barge. Feedback we've received from their Crisis Center so far, says that despite the hour, a handful of scuba divers are currently in the water around the barge. The imaging reveals that the rest of the suspects are unpacking material from those mysterious large wooden crates they loaded on-board when they rented the barge."

"The satellite's infrared lasers are bouncing beams off some of the brick-sized, wrapped objects they are unloading from those crates. The NSA Image Assessment Team feels the packages might have been recently waterproofed. As quickly as the packages are removed from the crates, the suspects are carefully handing them over the side to the divers already in the water. The diver's underwater transport sleds appear to be stacked with these packages. The weight of the packages have caused the sleds to sit slightly lower in the water, but they remain moored to the barge."

The dam's resident manager continued, "The Homeland Security Crisis Center, exercising the presidential authority granted them for use in expediting their response in these matters such as this, have ordered the respective Nevada and Arizona sheriffs to immediately roll units to our general location. Fortunately, it appears that both of those two counties regularly patrol Lake Mead enforcing safe boating laws, and their equipment includes several fast patrol boats."

"Upon reaching a point within five hundred yards of the barge, the county cops' boats will stop to coordinate with one another, via radio. Homeland Security has strongly suggested the two county's 'first responders' utilize a combined approach, which will permit both departments to board concurrently, for purposes of backup."

Lt. Colonel David Ness raised his hand, causing Hammer to pause. He said, "I assume that the Powers-That-Be are hoping the interdiction confrontation will turn out to be a cake walk. The deputies will board, inspect the barge, and check their identification and paperwork. Then they'll get on the horn to Homeland Security and advise them what the hell is going on out there, if anything. I am assuming the deputies have orders to detain the occupants, until it is determined whether there is probable cause justifying further action. Then the Homeland Security head shed will give you a call on your-encrypted cell, with the word."

Resident Dam Manager Hammer nodded, sifted through her hand-written notes once again, and continued, "Both county sheriffs have committed to immediately dispatching a second team, consisting of a four-deputy, two-cruiser contingent, armed with

Colt AR-15 semi-automatic assault rifles, just in case. Actually, it would be my guess that the deputies that the sheriffs are dispatching, were off-duty."

"So, I assume that means that the units will be 10-8 as soon as he can contact them, and get them on the road. General Davenport advises he is routing those deputies directly here to the Nevada-side visitor's center. The fact that the deputies have probably only just been recalled to duty, means you may have to have someone else temporarily cover their assignments. I mean the ones you had plan to assign the deputies when they arrive on-scene."

Lt. Colonel Ness again broke interjected himself into Hammer's briefing and said, "Edith, I'm concerned that even with the AR-15s, or M-16s, these guys are likely inadequately trained to deal with this. I mean if everything goes to hell in a handbag, and the balloon goes up. I damn straight don't want any blue-on-blue incidents if this situation goes 'critical.' That being said, I'll just have to keep that in-mind when making their assignments. Perhaps my prayers will be answered, and there is a combat veteran or two among them."

Hammer continued her briefing, flipping over the scribbled-filled pages of her notebook. "The Clark County Sheriff from Nevada apparently has made good use of all that tax money from gaming receipts the State collects from the casinos. His department has a Bell, model 206-4, LongRanger, jet-turbine helicopter at his beck and call, 24/7. That model carries two-pilots, and is rated with full-fuel for the transport of up to five passengers. In about thirty minutes, you can plan on it being aloft, and en-route our location with a fully-equipped SWAT team. I've advised Homeland Security that the team is to report directly to you, and operate under your orders."

"The pilots have orders to land on dam's visitor's center parking garage, ETA one hour. Since that version of the Bell LongRanger is a civilian model, the ship won't be armed. However, the sheriff has assured Homeland Security that the SWAT team she'll be transporting definitely is. As soon as the 206-4 lands here, Colonel, I'd suggest you pull the sheriff's SWAT team off her, and have the pilots lift back off and reposition the bird up on the lake, over the suspect's barge."

Hammer said, "As you no doubt are aware, the Bell LongRanger is thin-skinned so I'd suggest keeping her high enough that she doesn't present an attractive target for small-arms fire from the barge. Until the military gunships arrive, the 206-4 will be our only means of maintaining an airborne observation post. Any questions?"

"No, Ms. Hammer. I understand what you want and understand your plan. What we've just covered is nearly chapter-and-verse with the manual's contingency planning for confronting and repelling a potential threat like this one. So no surprises. I assume the FBI will also be rolling on this, Boss?" Ness asked.

"Yes," Hammer continued, "Homeland Security Crisis Center's notification tree has notified the FBI. And their response is underway. Unfortunately for our present situation, the closest FBI SWAT team is headquartered out of the Las Vegas field office. That makes the team and their equipment about thirty-five-miles from Hoover Dam. Don't expect them to be here anytime in the next hour, to an hour and a half."

"The notification tree also alerted two U.S. Navy Seal teams from the Marine Air Station at Miramar, who had just completed their bi-annual Basic Underwater Demolition/SEAL School (BUD/S) refresher course. Their training facility is located on Coronado Island. Down on what San Diego residents refer to as the Silver Strand. The Homeland Security Crisis Center has dispatched two U.S. Army Boeing MH-47E Chinook helicopters to Miramar. They were already in the general area of operations (AO), having just dropped off some big-shot Marine general and his staff at a meeting over at Camp Pendleton," Hammer said.

"As soon as they are refueled, those two Army birds are under revised orders to get the fifty air miles down to Miramar, flying at full military power. There they will top off their tanks again, upload the Seals and their equipment, and get them here to Hoover, most 'ricky tick.' In addition to terrain-following radar (TFR), the—47E has mid-air refueling capability, if push comes to shove."

Hammer reached over to the pick up a chrome-plated insulated bottle of ice water sitting on the edge of her desk, and poured herself a drink. She didn't bother to offer Ness any. Not because she was rude, but rather because she believed a former Army Special Forces Green Beret, with a Silver Star and two Bronze Stars along with numerous other decorations, was capable of filling his own glass, thank you. After taking a deep drink from her glass, Hammer resumed her spiel.

"Homeland Security appears to have planned for every contingency. That includes deploying a KC-135 fully fueled Stratotanker in the next thirty-minutes out of Edwards Air Force Base, which is northwest of Los Angeles. That Stratotanker will serve as the 'Texaco' station to provide mid-air refueling, if necessary, for the two *dash* 47E choppers, who have the job of airlifting the Seals and their equipment here to Hoover."

Hammer continued, "Having the KC-135 'Texaco' as a back up, the—47s will be able to proceed here at their top military speed of 196 mph. That will get them on-scene as fast as possible, even if they have to drag that fuel tanker with them, their fuel probes still locked into the tanker's receptacle baskets."

Lt. Colonel Ness broke into her briefing once again. He said, "Ms. Hammer, may I suggest that the Chinooks drop everything off on the Arizona side of the dam crest. That'll give us some flexibility over here on the Nevada side, which will be getting very crowded about then. The—47s are 'space-takers' and we can't get them both in on that side. The outside dimensions of their rotors, fore and aft, are one-hundred feet by sixty foot respectively." The dam's resident manager nodded, approving the plan change, and made another scribble on her notepad.

"And for situational awareness, Colonel, Homeland Security indicted that those two MH-47E's have been already morphed with the standard Chinook ALQ-156 ground-to-air missile defensive system. In case some gomer launches on them, while they are making what undoubtedly will be a very hairy approach into that small crest pad, on the dam's Arizona-side."

"Ok, Colonel, lets roll. Oh, I almost forgot to mention the one additional arrow in our quiver. The 'big sticks,'" Hammer said, "will be two AH-64 Apache helicopter gunship 'flights.' Each flight will consist of two birds. The Apaches are armed with TOW and Hellfire missiles, heat-seeking Stingers, StarStreak, and AIM-9 Sidewinder air-to-air rockets."

"The four Apaches are being deployed from the closest military base, that being Nellis AFB outside Vegas, home of the fabled Area 51, even as we speak. One of these flights, once on-scene, will be deployed to establish an overhead recon pattern on the suspect's anchored research vessel, until we find out what in the blue Jesus is going on out there."

"The Apache pilots are aware that the bad guys, in the worst scenario, might have heat-seeking SA-7 or Stinger missiles, so you can bet they'll be 'jinky and loose,' and will keep their distance. The second AH-64 flight will set down wherever they can find some room on the Nevada side of the crest. That flight of Apaches will serve as a backup, on-demand. They also will replace the first AH-64 two-bird flight, when their fuel reaches the 'bingo' fuel state."

Hammer continued, "Due to the Apache's lousy fuel consumption rate, Home Security has ordered a aviation-gas tanker truck from McCarran International. It will be one of the few they own capable of operating at highway speeds."

Thinking out loud, Hammer stopped to jot a note down on her pad reminding her to verify the critical fuel tankers deployment with McCarran, before she resumed speaking, "Oh, and I'll have to get someone over to Boulder City to grab a couple of those fancy orange, portable Ingersoll-Rand, diver-air certified, air compressors out of that rental yard on Main Street, to make sure the Seals don't lack for breathable air refills for their bottles if they have to go in the water to search for explosives."

"Following behind the first responders, will be a radioactivity detection team, from the U.S. Department of Energy, and various other technical types to take apart that vessel if anything threatening is found aboard her. Do you have any questions, Colonel?"

"No, Ms. Hammer," Ness replied. "That pretty much follows the contingency manual, which thanks to your insistence, each one of us can recite in our sleep. What specific assignments do you have for me, and our security team? By coincidence, due to this being a scheduled in-service training night, we have twenty of our people on-site, now armed, locked and loaded, and ready to rumble."

"Your assignment, and hear me clearly on this Colonel, is to do exactly what the Emergency Contingency Manual says, relative to our reaction and response to a threat of this type. No more, no less. I've informed the Homeland Security duty officer that you are to have 100% control here, as delegated under my authority. And that your primary priority is to do whatever is necessary to insure this dam is totally protected at all times. Don't worry about what is going on upstream at those dams, or what is going on, down towards Parker Dam. That isn't your responsibility. I'll back you in whatever decisions are necessary."

"And, Colonel, I expect you anticipate some minor difficulty keeping the more aggressive FBI SWAT teams members in-line. But you are a former Green Beret, if my recollection serves me, correct?" Ness stopped making notes long enough, to nod in the affirmative to at her. "So, I'm going to assume you can handle that potential problem." she said.

Hammer continued, "As soon as the Seal Teams arrive, I want them in the water. Have them inspect everything from the dam's upstream face, and then as far down as they can inspect on the four intake towers. Completing that, and failing to come across anything that can go boom, have them pull a grid search out to the dam's upstream Do-Not-Enter security barrier."

"The Seal team leaders have been advised that their teams are subject to your authority. They are to follow it without deviation. I don't think you'll have much problem with the Seals. They are professionals, only want to get the job done safety, and go home."

"Now hit the streets, Colonel, and please be careful out there. I don't want my potentially heroic rescuer injured in anyway," she smiled, as Ness barged out the door of her office nearly as fast as he had barged in, a few minutes ago. Watching the officer hurry off, Hammer could only think *I'll have to get that door replaced for sure after this is over.*

Then she picked up her phone to tell the dam maintenance supervisor to dispatch two of his people with pickup trucks set up for towing a trailer, immediately the seven-miles down into Boulder City, to 'borrow' critically-needed, diver-air-quality-certified, air compressors from that town's only rental equipment yard.

As the flurry of action, driven by Homeland Security's mission moved ahead rapidly, the suppositions upon which the mission had been war-gamed and pre-planned, began to come apart like a flimsy soiled piece of cheap government single-ply toilet paper, dropped into a flushing toilet bowl.

First, the darkest of nights seemed to have come to Lake Mead on that date, or at least that is how it seemed to the first responder teams. Perhaps the stress of the moment, as they attempted to identify, verify, and successfully interdict an attack on the country's most valuable hydroelectric facility, caused their normally fine-tuned perceptions to be tested. In actuality, dusk probably came no sooner or later than was common this time of year, here in the Black Canyon.

Even before the county sheriffs reached the Lake Mead shoreline to launch the patrol boats, the sudden brilliance of the dam's emergency flood lighting was activated by the dam's security contingent, bathing both sides of the 1,244-foot wide, 726-foot tall, road crest, not unlike that of a mid-summer's noonday sun. Anyone not prepared for the sudden unscheduled light, was temporarily blinded, at the very least momentarily losing his or her night vision.

If that action wasn't a bad enough omen, the State Patrol officers from the security check points, that had been set-up a mile either side of the dam since 9/11/01, were rapidly approaching the dam crest with their patrol vehicles' sirens screaming, their headlights on-bright, naturally still wearing the obligatory dark highway patrolman-style sun glasses, and running at high speed.

The officers had been recalled by the dam's security team, and ordered to block off both ends of the 1,244-foot wide dam crest. Someone had neglected to factor into the orders that civilian and commercial traffic over the dam's crest, even in the early evening, continued to be was brisk.

Several wailing State and Highway Patrol cruisers, on both ends of the road crest, arrived simultaneously, without any advance warning, and followed what they assumed were their emergency orders. At an imaginary point, three hundred-feet before reaching beginning of the crest, the responding patrolmen on both sides of the dam's span, intent on 'looking smart,' suddenly applied their vehicle's brakes. This caused all the four cruisers to lock up their wheels, slide sideways, and come to shock-absorber-bouncing stop. The resulting roadblock maneuver was one they all had learned at basic cop school. Back when they had been fledging police cadets. And one they, of course, had never been able to practice and gain proficiency with, since.

This well-intentioned if ill-timed maneuver had the collateral effect of instantly and without any warning, stopping all vehicular traffic in both directions over Highway 93, the crest road crossing Hoover dam. After a few minutes, the motorists managed to recover from the unpleasant shock. The more agile-minded among them, sometimes aided by the efforts of an equally surprised State Highway patrolman, attempted to turn their vehicles around, and retrace the route they had just come.

The cruisers themselves were now entangled in the gridlock. They also could not move an inch. Blocked in by the very traffic that had rolled up behind their cars, following the establishment of the roadblock. The backup behind the now grid locked patrol cars, was estimated to be fast approaching a mile, from both end of the centerspan.

The Hoover Dam vehicle bypass highway, planned after 9/11/01, but limited in funding to the extent where only a single-shift of construction could be funded daily, was not scheduled for completion for another two years. So the bypass highway was not operational. If it had been operational at the time of this current tangle, the police knew that it may have taken a half-dozen hours, but the gridlock could have been overcome with diligent work in marshaling the vehicles, to and fro, until they were turned around, and free to take the alternate route around Hoover dam. That was Congress' original intent for the bypass project in the first place.

Highway patrolman from both states quickly found out any attempt, by anything other than a motorcycle, to a reposition itself, turn it around and re-route it back the way it had come, was utterly hopeless. It became obvious that the maneuvering room required to turn any vehicle around, from cars to single-axle delivery vans, in order to accomplish an escape from the gridlock, was just not going to work. It was also obvious, this time to cops and motorists alike, that the traffic-stopping maneuver that had just placed them in an untenable position, one that had never been anticipated by Hoover Dam's planners some seventy four-years previously.

The blockading of Highway 93, at both ends of the 1,244-foot span of Hoover Dam's crest road, had been intended to make sure no explosive device(s) managed to get out onto the crest span of the gravity-arched dam, once the dam had been placed on red-alert.

But the just-executed maneuver, by two vehicles each from the two State and Highway Patrol departments, now inadvertently served to make significant portions of Homeland Security's interdiction plan, worthless.

Additionally, the four county patrol cars, responding on the orders of their respective sheriffs, were also now blocked by gridlock. Thus they were unable to reach their assigned destination to protect the vulnerable dam crest. The country teams had elected to use 'slick-back' unmarked cruisers, with the reasoning that they would draw less attention and cause less disruption, than using marked patrol units. Unfortunately, the reality of all this was that it only served to make the grid-locked motorists, already fuming as their progress in getting home for dinner was halted, totally pissed.

This hatched a citizen's show of rebellion to authority, as the civilian motorists made it impossible for the unmarked sheriff's cars to force their way through the grid-locked traffic to provide backup and prevent the crisis that could be rapidly unfolding.

If that wasn't enough, the gridlock also meant that the critical aviation fuel tanker, long-before dispatched from McCarran International Airport in Las Vegas, was also stuck in traffic, nearly five miles west of Hoover dam. That meant the protective Apache gun ships, their fuel capacity already heavily limited due to the weight of their armament and unexpended ordnance, were not going to be able to orbit the suspicious survey barge. Once their initial load of fuel that had brought them here from Nellis AFB reached 'bingo,' the aircraft would instantly be transformed into some of the heaviest paper weights in the world, unable to respond to their nation's needs in time of dire crisis.

The County Sheriff's patrol boats, and a cabin cruiser commandeered by the FBI, launched from the closest marina to Las Vegas, would arrive very shortly to confront the suspicious group of unidentified divers aboard the barge. But once the Apache's reached a 'bingo' fuel state, the law enforcement officers would be left to defend for themselves. The deputy's personal weaponry consisted of semi-automatic 9 mm handguns, a few M-16As or AR-15s. This was augmented by the inclusion of their department's standard-issue Winchester 12-gauge riot guns, with 18.5 inch shortened barrels. The shotgun's shell-quantity restriction magazine plugs had been 'removed, and mislaid,' perhaps just minutes after their departments had issued the shoulder weapons to their officers. Thus their shotguns carried five rounds in lieu of the civilian, three.

Not a smidge of daylight remained when the 'first-responder' gunships aircraft arrived on-scene. Due to the dam's illumination, the pilots elected to go to night vision goggles (NVG) before first performing the mandatory procedural flyby over the dam crest. And once again before the fast birds rolled into a 180-degree bank to return on a reciprocal heading for their landing approach to the visitor's center parking garage roof.

The use of the NVG, and the stress any approach into an unfamiliar landing zone (LZ) posed, prevented the pilots from visually identifying much of the dam's detail. In the best of situations, the most that would register on their detail-oriented brains, was what appeared simply to be a colossal-sized chuck of concrete plugged into, what at that altitude/speed/and ambient lighting levels, to be nothing but a convenient slot between Black Canyon's steep granite walls.

The pilots likely wouldn't even have the time to contemplate that the 'convenient slot' they were observing, had over millions of years ago been gouged out of the nearly impregnable granite rock by the Colorado River. Or that the slot was a result of the river's 1,400-mile headlong run down from the Colorado Rocky Mountains, en-route the Gulf of California. Or that the seeming small, when viewed from altitude, concrete dam, constructed some seventy-four years previously, caused the thirty million acre-foot lake Mead reservoir to extend 110-miles back toward the Grand Canyon. Or that Lake Mead had the static capacity to hold two year's worth of the Colorado River's flow. But all in all, the view was still impressive.

Preoccupied with their approach procedures, the pilots, both not even appearing to be old enough to buy beer without being regularly carded, would not register on their high-intellect brains, through the armored cockpit windscreen, the dam's four 395-foot 'deep' water intake towers, which were located a hundred yards downstream from the canyon wall 'spillways' and upstream from the upstream dam face.

And that those four buttons-sized structures, each seemingly jutting from a nearby canyon wall—appeared to be only connected by a tenuous piece of thread, which in actuality were walkways to the dam's forty-two foot wide, 1,244-foot long crest road. Surely the pilots wouldn't notice that the crest structure of the dam, being represented in their minds as a simple piece of thread, bowed backwards in a reverse arch.

And the left side of their brains would fail to interpret and identify the fact that the arch served to interrupt the flow of the river and restrict it, until again bidden, redirecting it back into the thirty million acre-foot Lake Mead, where it would wash up lazily along the reservoir's 550-mile long shoreline.

Nor that on the downstream side of the dam crest, was a stomach-grabbing 726-foot drop, ending in a horseshoe-shaped structure that represented the dam's combined 2,080-megawatt powerhouse. And finally, past that, the trailrace, which was the point where the water that had just been utilized to generate enough electricity to support the lifestyles of twenty-five million people, joined with the excess unneeded water that flowed through the dam's multiple, fifty-foot-wide penstocks, and was reintroduced into the downstream river bed, to be recycled until it evaporated or was otherwise consumed.

The US Army MH-47E Chinooks arrived nearly fully fueled, thanks to their in-flight refueling probes, and the KC-135 Stratotanker Homeland Security had caused to be dispatched. The sophisticated *dash* 47E Chinook troop transport helicopters had very 'long legs,' a virtual necessity that permitted them to excel in the accomplishment of the mission for which they had been designed.

The dam's contingency plan, as modified by Ms. Hammer and Assistant Chief of Police David Ness of the federal facility's Security Force, was that the Chinooks would disembark the Navy Seals and their gear on the Arizona side of the dam's crest road. Despite their exotic war-fighter enhancement features such as the terrain-following radar (TFR); forward-looking infrared imaging (FLIR); and electronic countermeasures (ECM), the—47Es weren't intended to be an infantry ground-support platform.

The large, twin-rotor craft was capable of transporting fifty-five troops, but only fielded a pair of M-60 door guns with which she could provide covering fire for the two county sheriff's REACT units in the patrol boats, and the FBI SWAT team, aboard the commandeered cabin cruiser.

A short time after the dam's turn-night-into-day emergency floodlights were activated, the security personnel on the dam's crest observed that the law enforcement boats were now approaching the site of the anchored barge. They also noted, due to the not-inconsiderable illumination coming from the barge's own floodlights, that the persons on the suspect craft were now running around on it, throwing off everything that was not bolted down overboard into the deep waters, where the heavier items no doubt promptly sunk to the bottom.

Four of the suspects on-board the suspicious vessel, were currently attempting to sever the greasy three-inch thick rope anchor hawsers, which had been secured tied to barge's capstans. They were using a couple of small hatchets only intended for chopping wood. Those massive lines, secured on-board the barge, ran over the sides and down to the industrial-size anchors, which had been deployed by the crew days earlier, far below on the reservoir bottom.

Suddenly, all the activity frantically going on the barge's deck seemingly vanished into the darkness, as all the barge's lights were suddenly extinguished. Only the reflection from the dam's floodlights, reflecting off the waters of the deep reservoir, still hinted at the fact that the boat's occupants had become even more frantic in their furtive off-loading activities. This despite the fact that the sudden darkness must have made the barge deck seem invisible, in the period required for their eyes reacquire their night-vision.

By that time, the four, AH-64 heavily-armed Apache helicopter gunships from Nellis AFB arrived over dam crest, heralded by the characteristic *pop-pop-pop-pop-pop* sound of their powerful four-bladed rotors spanking the night air.

Since the gunships liftoff from Nellis AFB outside Vegas, Homeland Security's defense plan had been revised, due to the delay in the arrival of the Av-gas fuel truck, which was still stuck in gridlock traffic five-miles west of the dam on Highway 93. A single Apache gunship now took up station, hovering in the near-dark sky over the suspect's barge, while the remaining three birds were directed to shoehorn their ships in to land on the dam's visitor's center parking garage roof.

The helicopter commander was advised via encrypted radio, that the tanker from McCarran carrying their go-juice hadn't yet arrived. That being the case, the mission commander had no option other than to break up the two flights into individual ships, hoping to extend the duration of their on-board fuel loads as long as possible.

And according to Acting Police Chief Lt. Colonel Ness's encrypted cell-phone communication with the tanker's driver thirty minutes earlier, currently there was no expected time of arrival (ETA) for the critical aviation fuel. The tanker had already been slowed by the post-rush hour traffic snarl, when the both the Nevada and Arizona State Police units, acting under Homeland Security's orders, had blocked the Highway 83 dam crest in both directions, stopping all traffic which effectively stopped any further movement of the heavy fuel truck.

As soon as the Apache gunship which had drawn the first watch and was now orbiting over the survey vessel's location, approached the 'bingo' fuel state, she would be relieved by one of her sister ships. As the on-station bird's fuel was consumed, each of the remaining helicopters would rotate individually and separately into the holding pattern over the barge, while the chopper being relieved would come off station, and land on the parking structure roof, to await the planned arrival of the aviation fuel from McCarran International.

In that situation, the US Army mission commander calculated that the four Apache gunships maximum possible time-on-target (TOT) would be a little less than three hours. These figures reflected gas-gulping high rate of fuel consumption the high-technology birds had expended, flying out from Nellis AFB at full military power as ordered by the Nellis' duty officer.

The lone Apache gunship left to orbit over the suspects barge was armed to the teeth. Over the pilot's mission radio net with the other Apaches, he heard someone pass on the word that the suspects had been observed continuing their attempts to sever their vessel's anchor lines. Once the anchor lines were severed, if the suspects on the barge didn't immediately start their engines to permit the barge to maneuver under its own power, it would drift downstream. And carried by the Colorado River's substantial current, it would either become entangled in the dam's floating security barrier, or breach it. Those two frank possibilities only brought more doom and gloom to an already threatening situation for the dam's defenders.

Due to that unthinkable possibility that the heavy barge would breach the floating security barrier, the last protection between it and the dam's upstream face, the three law enforcement agencies charged with making sure the dam was not threatened in any manner, were ordered by higher command to reposition their boats between the dam and the barge. The separation distance between themselves and the barge was not to exceed 300-yards. Even though three football-field-lengths might seem to be an adequate standoff position for the police, it was still well in range of anything the bad guys wanted to throw at them, with the possible exception of hand-thrown grenades. And all acknowledged that a M79 grenade launcher or 'blooper,' if the barge had one, would certainly eliminate that qualification.

Even if the people on the barge were only in possession of handguns, they could be used with reasonable accuracy at the separation distance that 'higher' command had specified, depending on the skill of the marksman. It would be noted after-the-fact, that even that distance of separation only served to save a lives of two of the twenty-two law enforcement officer's lives aboard the 'first responder' boats that night.

Eight minutes after the suspects had extinguished all lighting aboard the barge, its anchor lines were finally severed. And the large flat-bottomed vessel began to drift downstream toward the dam's vulnerable security barrier. The only reason the factual history of what happened next, exists at all, is due to the dedicated efforts of one of the dam's civilian clerks who had remained atop the dam crest, sacrificing his own safety.

The man was sixty-year-old retired member of the U.S. military, whose meager army pension forced him to seek alternative employment following his retirement. This is the man who provided the 'facts behind the story,' as Paul Harvey used to say. Those facts would turn out to be invaluable when the after-action Federal Incident Investigation Board was convened.

Based on his years of extensive military experience, the clerk couldn't imagine any instance in which an incident such as the current one, wouldn't result in 'the *mother* of all Incident Investigations.' So the brave clerk, heedless of the risk of danger, had remained at his duty station documenting the conflict. The latter would turn out to be the nexus of the government investigation that was to follow.

As the two Country Sheriff patrol boats, and the large cabin cruiser commandeered on an hour ago by the FBI regional SWAT team, maneuvered in a coordinated effort to block the now-drifting barge, a series of horrendous explosions shattered the calm of the otherwise peaceful evening! Instantly, the structures that had been added to the survey barge's deck were blown hundreds feet up into the air. A secondary larger explosion seemed to vaporize the barge completely. The mushroom-shaped fireball cloud the explosions generated, rose into the heavens, turning night into day, as the shrill screams of unfortunate men and women pieced the dark night air.

The eyes of those nearby who had been looking in that direction had their retinas seared. The eardrums of anyone within a one-mile radius, not wearing ear protection, were ruptured.

The pressure-wave from the detonation of the two explosions was so horrific, that even the eardrums of the security force posted over one mile away on the dam's crest, received lesser, but no less painful, injuries. The first explosion blew out and shattered every piece of glass on the three police boats. A second later, an even greater explosion closely following the first, arrived to capsize the police craft.

In a nanosecond, the ambient air was filled with flying shards of shattered glass and metal debris, horizontally at speeds nearing that of sound. The brain-rattling sound generated by the explosion was not unlike deafening claps of thunder, as it bounced off the adjacent granite-hard walls of Black Canyon. The officers who had been catapulted off the boats, most burdened down with the weight of night vision goggles, weapons, ammunition, flash-bang grenades, first-aid kits, and their bulky SWAT helmets—already dead after the concussion had ruptured every vital organ inside their bodies—quickly sank to the silt-covered bottom of the deep reservoir.

Ammunition and grenades, mostly from the overturned law enforcement vessels, was now adrift on top of the flotsam floating on the waters. There, it selectively seemed to ignite from the white-hot 2,000-degree heat generated by the violent explosions. A few seconds later, a thermal pulse swept the lake's surface, igniting any floating fuel that had been leaked from the capsized boat's engines and fuel tanks. The few officers, attempting to cling to what was left of their overturned boats in the 54° degree water, had the flesh stripped off their hands, arms, and faces.

A second nanosecond later, a debris hurricane consisting of flying glass, melted plastic fragments, burning marine fuel, pieces of equipment, twisted weapons, and body parts, suddenly seemed to change direction. It now rushed back towards the explosion's vortex, completely shredding, abrading, and roasting any human flesh that had been left behind on the victim's bones, in the earlier inhuman assaults, as the violence trumpeted its full fury.

A small number of the recently-arrived US Seal teams, those which could be spared from their primary duty of inspecting the facilities upstream of the dam's face, having brought their Vietnam-era, fiberglass-hulled Seal Tactical Assault Boats (STABS) with them on the—47E troop transports, finally reached the site of the fiery explosions. Out of the twenty-two-law enforcement officers that had been aboard the three boats, only two men were found to have survived the explosion. Both were barely conscious, badly burned, in-shock, half-drowned, and nearly catatonic. Other than the two men the Seals 'rescued'—although due to their highly-critical medical condition, one wonders if the correct term might be 'recovered'—no other bodes were found floating in the area.

However, dozens of small clumps of boiled flesh bobbed in the debris fields from the fragmented boats, causing the Seal veterans to say a brief prayer of thanks that Lake Mead did not also have sharks, among the many bountiful fish species hopeful fishermen sought there daily.

Two LifeLine helicopters, based at hospitals thirty miles northwest in Las Vegas, arrived over the scene of the explosion less than forty-five minutes later. They winched the two critically injured officers off the decks of the Seal's STAB craft, up into their cargo bays, for the brief flight to the hospital ER in Vegas for a continuation of the emergency medical care already under way.

Paramedics from nearby fire departments from the Nevada towns of Laughlin and Boulder, operating under the provision government entities call 'mutual assistance,' arrived in boat-towing-trucks at a nearby marina, upstream of Hoover Dam. They completed the orderly launching of their boats, and reported to the scene of the explosion within ninety minutes of being called-out.

Additional law enforcement support boats from local communities, including the fabled Las Vegas Nevada Crime Scene team, who was the focus of a new CBS TV crime drama show, also provided evidence technicians. Body parts were recovered, tagged, bagged, and laid out on a medium-sized, wooden barge, for cataloging.

The barge had formerly used by the dam's maintenance crew to inspect the upstream dam face, and above-water surfaces of the four intake towers. It had been tied up at the small dock the dam maintained on the Nevada side, inside the upstream security barrier containment zone. To remain out of the ever-moving crime scene, the small dam barge had been passed around the barrier, and anchored 200-yards upstream of Ground Zero.

Lake Mead, at the location where the vaporized barge had been anchored, was 589-feet in depth, the deepest point in the entire reservoir. There would be no attempted recovery of bodies and anything else that sunk into those waters under later that day. Special hard-hat diving equipment would have to be airlifted in and put to use by the law enforcement and U.S. Navy Seal divers.

In the meantime, a hastily procured, small-mesh nylon net of the largest overall dimensions available locally, weighed down with lead weights, was stung across the floating security barrier. It was an attempt, perhaps futile in nature, to keep the body parts, remaining corpses that might surface, and any surviving debris that could be used as evidence, from drifting towards the dam face. Where the offal would be sucked into the water intake towers, and flow though the dam, either via the powerhouse, or through the penstocks, which are used for the bypass flow of the Colorado River.

While all this was going on, the remainder of the Navy Seals that had been flown in, were totally immersed in the most dangerous work imaginable. There, working hand-in-hand with certified bomb-squad divers from the Las Vegas Police Department, Clark County Sheriff's Office, the Nevada State Police, and the FBI's now on-scene dive-qualified crime scene bomb assessment team, they sought to determine whether the upstream dam face, the four intake towers, the spillways located on either side of the canyon, or the area between the dam face to the floating orange security barrier, had been mined.

It was extremely dangerous job, even for these tried and tested professionals. The dive team from the U.S. Bureau of Reclamation had been notified, and would be flying in from Washington via a charter transport aircraft, landing at Las Vegas' McCarran Field later that day. Due to the gravity of the threat, no one suggested the law enforcement and Seal divers should hold off until Reclamation's divers arrived from Washington, D.C., six-eight hours hence.

A master, grid search plan had been promptly developed by the Navy Seals. They, without dispute, were the most experienced of the divers present that night, early morning. Each of the civilian divers, after presenting their credentials proving they were bomb-squad-certified, was assigned a specified grid to search. A total of six of the more experienced divers were designated as Safety Officers, and would circulate among the divers working their respective underwater searches areas, to insure no one's enthusiasm got themselves or their fellow divers, injured or killed.

The crews inspecting the underwater surface of the dam face, found nothing but the routine organic plant growth attached, and made a almost-believable effort to look very disappointed at coming up empty.

The four, three-man crew of divers, all decorated U.S. Navy Seals, had been assigned to the four, 395-foot tall intake towers.

The bases of the four water intake towers were anchored into the bedrock of Black Canyon. Naturally the inherent restriction of their scuba equipment would preclude the divers from performing inspections down to that level. On the other hand, any bad guys couldn't have gone that deep without specialized equipment, none of which had been observed on the suspect's moored barge.

The Seals by nature are very competitive, and had begun their search with vigor. Bound and determined to show up their fellow divers who had been assigned the dam's face. Each of the three-man teams had only been just begun their detailed inspections, when one of the designated safety officers noticed a unnatural-appearing bulge, seemingly attached about fifty feet down the side of one of the elaborate-crafted intake towers.

Her reaction, as she had been trained, was to activate a water-piercing electronic silent vibrating alarm. All Seals now carried the newly introduced $2,300 communications device as part of their diving gear load-out. That alarm, as was intended, ordered all the Seals to immediately back off away from whatever they had been doing, and return to the surface.

The U.S. Navy Diving Safety Officer, who had activated it, saved the lives of every diver in the water within two hundred feet of the dam face and intake towers that morning. She also prevented prevent literally billions of dollars in collateral damage to the Southwestern United States that would have resulted, had the 'budge' she noticed detonated, as the terrorist diver who had affixed the limpet mines to the intake towers had intended.

In the ensuing visual inspections, the Seals found all four of the intake towers had been mined. Surprisingly, there was no evidence that there had been any attempt to conceal the powerful explosive devices where they had been fastened to the tower's cylindrical surface. All however, had been equipped with a depth-sensitive booby trap that would have caused the device to explode, had a inexperienced driver just cut its tether and taken it to the surface for inspection.

Seals, and the law enforcement divers, had seen a lot of bombs in their careers. But rarely did they come across an effective, sophisticated bomb, designed by mid-eastern terrorist organizations such as Al-Qaeda, designed exclusively for underwater use.

A great amount of Arabia is a desert. The simple logistics that would be required for them to design, trouble-shoot, test, retest, and market such a unique device would have been costly. Al-Qaeda, if nothing else, was very frugal in how they spent their limited funds.

As soon as the master divers and bomb deactivation experts on the scene at Hoover had deactivated the pressure-sensors, all the limpet mines were removed, transported carefully to the surface, and placed on the wooden barge for further disassembling and study.

A day's more of diver's time turned up no additional explosives anywhere in the areas designated for inspection. It was assumed that one or more of the now-departed terrorists had, either purposely or because of their inherent poor underwater explosives training, managed to set off the two explosions that destroyed their barge, and themselves.

The collateral loss of the twenty dead law enforcement officers and FBI agents, all due to the self-inflicted explosions by the terrorist themselves, was devastating, as was the ruined lives of the two officers who had thus far survived the ordeal.

But for Homeland Security Secretary, Ted Staples, and few other more deeply thinking of the 'first responders', was the sobering fact that no timing device had been found when the four tons of limpet mines had been fully disassembled, and studied. In short, absent the pressure-sensing booby traps, there had been no provision designed into the powerful explosive devices for the detonation of the underwater bombs in any other manner.

This could only mean that al-Qaeda had always intended that mines be discovered. Further proving that in this instance, their real goal had been kill all the 'first responders', and that any collateral damage to the dam's intake towers would be considered a bonus.

If the brave 'first responders' in America, be they military, policemen, firemen, medical staff, or a dozen other job descriptions of those who were responsible for being first on the scene of disasters, could be psychologically brain-washed into shirking their critical responsibility to respond on-demand, then the America's critical first line of defense could be eliminated.

CHAPTER TEN

DAY 233—20 AUGUST

ON A NEVADA STATE HIGHWAY

APPROACHING CLARK COUNTY

THE MIDDLE OF NOWHERE

The weather was terrible, screeching, hailing, lightning, thunder claps and blinding horizontal rain. KERBAM! KERBAM! KERBAM!

The lightening strikes out of the dark heavens into the empty desert surrounding the road to Boulder City came fast and furious. One after another, seemingly without end.

Like a gigantic worm, the Caterpillar-yellow, fifty-wheeled heavy hauler inched its way slowly towards its destination.

Its load required use of the entire width of the two-lane divided highway road surface. Flanking and leading the lethargic monster slithering through the sheets of horizontal rain, were fourteen U.S. Army military police, state police, and private contractor vehicles. Their emergency red and blue light bars lit up the road like an out-of-control *wildfire*.

Most of the vehicles were Nevada and Arizona State police sedans, each crammed with officers wearing light body armor. Also in the gaggle of rolling stock were several olive-drab Special Operations Force (SOF) vans festooned with antennas. Each Humvee was filled with heavily-armed and fully body-armored, California National Guard troops. Not so unusual in today's terrorist environment, some of the soldiers were combat-tested, only recently having returned from the bloody battlefields around Iraq's capital city of Baghdad.

Since 'post attack' 9/11, all high-value U.S. Government over-the-road shipments were moving with armed escorts. As were some being transported via private carrier, consisting of loads judged vital to the national security of the country.

Hoover Dam's unexpected equipment failure, and its potential risk of disrupting nearly twenty-five million residents in the southwestern United States, had been reported directly to the attention of U.S. Interior Secretary Gale Norton, the 'folder holder' of U.S. Bureau of Reclamation. Commissioner John W. Keys III, his theoretical subordinate, had immediately issued orders to all government purchasing departments. All over the U.S., procurement officers and their staffs scrambled to find a replacement for the one-of-a-kind 3,500-H.P., model-specific 'service station' turbine/generator set. It was nearly a month before a replacement unit was located.

That the new generator was available at all on such short notice was completely by happenstance. A new unit to those specifications had been nearing completion in Guanajuato, Mexico. The manufacturer had just been notified by its customer—the Mexican government—that the order was cancelled. The government, due to unforeseen financial difficulties brought on by the recession in North America, had no choice other than put stop-losses on its accounts payable obligations.

The small company that had all but completed manufacturing the unit would be forced into bankruptcy. Rather than wait years for the matter to be adjudicated in the Mexican Court system, the fabricating company elected to sacrifice it for immediate sale to the Americans for one million U.S. dollars, f.o.b. its Central Mexico factory.

Aware of the reality of the hatchet figuratively hanging of the heads of both the U.S. Department of the Interior, and the Bureau of Reclamation due to the political implications, Secretary Gale Norton immediately ordered his office to set-up an emergency conference call to address the matter.

Present on the call was himself, Commissioner Keys, the Governors of Nevada, Arizona, and California, and U.S. Representative Ken Calvert, (R-Calif.), Chairman of the house Resources—Water and Power—subcommittee.

Secretary Norton took the lead on the call, calling everyone's attention to the specter of imminent interruption to the lifestyles of upward of a twenty-five million residents, should the mechanical unit not be immediately replaced. The other decision-makers present on the call quickly realized Norton's call was in reality a telephonic 'Come-To-Jesus' meeting. They all agreed with the Secretary that it had become an instant matter of U.S. national security. And that the unit's acquisition, transportation, and security should be given the highest priority.

Thus down the chain of command, came the support order for the transportation and security during cartage, of the replacement generator for Hoover Dam. Norton's ties to the White house gave the matter one of the highest priorities in the land.

The 'Powers-That-Be' instantly translated that directive, upon receipt. Their interpretation convinced them that the directive meant a full security and cartage contingent would be required. Immediately, open-ended funding was authorized for an emergency cost-plus 10% contract, skirting the Government Accounting Office's requirements for competitive bidding.

In this case, the escort would consist of heavily-armed security personnel provided by the ANG, and Federal and State agencies. The physical job of cartage was under the responsibility of a private cartage firm, well known to the Department of Energy (DoE). The well-proven firm that had been selected routinely transported shipments of nuclear-materials on our country's highways without incident since the 1990s.

In fact, the sizing of such security contingents was becoming an art into itself, as the intended goal of the extra security was *prevention*, not *provocation*. Imagine if you will, the instance when the U.S. Government, after evaluation of all the risk factors, decides to detail an entire Army or Marine company to safeguard the security of a particular shipment.

How inviting or enticing that could be to one or more of the major paramilitary extremist groups in the United States that wanted the show its muscle and capabilities. Even if this 'showing of the flag' by the rebel organization, was at the expense of the lives of a hundred or more of U.S. servicemen. Men and women who just had been following orders and doing their duty.

A armed A-64 Apache gunship CAP unit (combat air protection) had been promised the convoy, along the entire length of the mission route. The equipment movement would begin in Long Beach Harbor, continuing on for five days until it reached Boulder City, Nevada. The shipment would then resume, with the final destination being the Hoover Dam powerhouse, located on the Colorado River.

The only air cover exception would be over heavily populated areas. The Apache's machine guns and Hellfire missiles couldn't be safely employed there. The potential for collateral damage would be unacceptable.

The high-priority convoy only had been scheduled to move during daylight hours—that was up until that evening. Apparently, law enforcement and ANG National Guard officials felt that haulage of the shipment through California and Nevada would be too risky after dark. The Apache gunship pilots, whose SOF's (Special Operation Force) motto in Vietnam had been *"We Own the Night!"* apparently weren't consulted in the government's decision-making process.

Under brilliant sunshine, the special convoy had pulled, albeit very slowly, out of the Port of Long Beach onto fabled Long Beach Harbor Freeway, days earlier. Its route had been planned to follow that section of freeway, then US 91 east to San Bernardino. At that point the convoy would transfer to I-15, and head eastbound to Barstow, California, before continuing on to the intersection of I-15 with SR 93, at Las Vegas.

The unwieldy procession would continue on SR 93 east to Boulder City, Nevada. Then the final portion, under the supervision of the U.S. Bureau of Reclamation, required reversing the direction of the shipment's travel, back up Boulder City Highway a short distance. There, the BCH intersects with Hoover Dam's mile and one-half long lower portal road. That over-width road connects with a deep-rock tunnel, leading to the south end of the Nevada section of the Hoover Dam powerhouse.

At the end of each day of the schedule convoy, the federal and state Gold (day) crew security contingent and civilian truck operators were relieved by the Blue (night) crew. 'Blue' were combat troops of the U.S. Marines bought in by large green H-60 Blackhawk helicopters at-dusk, to the convoy's designated night bivouac location.

The just-relieved Gold crew would enjoy their dinner of U.S. Army MRE's (meals-ready-to-eat). Then they would attempt to get as much rest as much possible in the troop transports. The transports, usually referred to a 'cattle trucks,' had been pre-staged at the night laager position earlier that afternoon. They had been reasonably out-fitted as night accommodations, for field use in emergency situations.

The troop transport trucks headed off each morning, once the Gold crew had relieved the Blue crew. The Blue contingent was retrieved by the H-60 Blackhawks, who ferried them to the nearest permanent military installation to bunk out for the day.

The now vacated 'cattle trucks' would speed off to the next planned nighttime bivouac laager. Sometimes the new laager was less than a hundred miles further east. This was due to the maximum, but no less maddeningly, slow creeping speed the heavy hauler convoy hauling the two hundred-thousand pound load was able to maintain.

It had been early that morning when a change in orders had come down. U.S. Government weather forecasters, tasked with monitoring the convoy's progress relative to any inclement weather, learned that one of the year's worst summer storms was en-route their remain-overnight (RON) location. The storm was forecasted to bring up to twelve inches of rain with it, targeting the location the convoy had previously planned to stop for the night.

The convoy's wide-load effectively tied up whatever Interstate highway over which she happened to be rolling. None of the off-ramps on that particular stretch of highway, weight capacity-wise or width-wise, could handle the load of the heavily burdened hauler.

After taking the reported summer storm into consideration, the 'Powers-That-Be' in the Pentagon cancelled the helicopter gunship CAP. The convey commander was ordered to make a run for shelter. The convoy was expected to utilize their own resources to successfully protect their critical load during the expected vicious storm. In other words, in civilian-speak, the convoy was on its own.

It never had been the government's plan to work the security or convey transportation crew for twenty-four hours straight. However, the weather would also ground the H-60 garrison relief helicopters scheduled to ferry in the relieving Blue, or nighttime, crew.

So the 'run for the sun' as the more jaded convoy drivers were referring to it, would require that the 'cattle truck' drivers and their security crews break the rules, and leap frog further up the planned route, acting as a point element for the convoy.

After months of Hoover Dam's maintenance department being unable to accomplish a full one-half of the critical 'do-not-defer' programmed preventive maintenance jobs, the need for the replacement unit had gone 'critical.' The risk that a potential powerhouse failure would take 'down' the entire western power grid, not just in the Southwest, had grown exponentially. The replacement shipment was needed desperately at Hoover Dam, and it was needed *now!*

The U. S. Government's Bureau of Reclamation managed Hoover Dam. The Bureau was solely responsible for maintaining the facilities' uninterrupted level of power generation. The day-to-day lives of twenty-five million residents depended on that.

So, in the eyes of the government mavens, there were no rules that couldn't be bent. And only a few that could not be broken outright. Especially if the breech in regulations would ensure that the mission of delivering the replacement equipment to the dam was accomplished in a timely manner, without damage to the heavy hauler's load.

As the heavy hauler and its accompanying security contingent, continued to pick its way through the pitch-black night, they activated their emergency lights and sirens to scream warnings to the uninformed freeway traveler, unaware that the jaggernaught was either close behind or dead ahead. Then the huge summer storm hit in earnest.

The slashing winds and rain even further taxed the already sleep-deprived hauler crew. The storm affected the troops assigned to the 'point' and 'flank' patrolling segments of the convoy's security forces, even more. The four-wheel drive Humvee flanker patrols were attempting to maintain their patrol position, to either side of the highway procession. Having to maintain their position in the jet-black storm conditions meant that in some cases, they were unable to avoid crushing a road culvert or ripping out farm fencing, as they slowly crept forward.

The first casualty occurred to the occupants of an armored army Humvee. It had been assigned to run 'point' on the two-lane highway about a mile ahead of the convoy. Out of the blackish heavens the 'mother of all lightning bolts' had struck the olive drab vehicle, instantly turning it into flaming scrap metal, and its four occupants into carbon.

Due to the mission's priority, one of the army trucks merely pushed the flaming wreckage aside, and a backup vehicle took over the point position, all in a matter of less than three minutes. There was nothing anyone in the convoy could do for the troops. Their time to die had just rotated to the top of the firing chamber. Their death had been preordained by career choice, years previously.

The next casualty was another one of the Humvees. This time a light command/ scout vehicle carrying the convoy's ranking military commander, a paygrade O-6 Colonel. The Humvee also contained his pregnant Executive Officer (XO), a Major, and their Samoan driver. The unarmored command-model of the Humvee had been picked up by a particularly strong gust born out of the fierce horizontal rain deluge. It had then been tossed over the edge of the highway overpass they had been crossing at the time. That bridge had been the only means of crossing the two hundred foot deep ravine, which ran under it.

Several of the military MP vehicles screamed up onto the slick bridge deck to provide emergency assistance to the command car occupants, but it was all for naught. Several blindingly bright, and ear-splitting explosions from fuel detonation were observed, as the jeep-like vehicle impacted upside down on the boulders at the bottom of the deep ravine.

Per establish army procedure, the next-senior officer in the convoy automatically assumed command, and the procession of vehicles continued crawling into the darkness, wetness, flashes, and deafening thunderclaps, of the killer summer storm.

Despite the horrific events, at no time did the driver of the heavy hauler downshift and slow down. It would have taken too long and too much distance to re-achieve the maximum eight-to-ten mph speed the rig was capable of. And nothing could be done now for the soldiers who had so abruptly lost their lives.

The first civilian injured was a Nevada State Police sergeant. He was the father of five young children, and the spouse of a severely disabled wife. He was being driven by a young police officer, just three-weeks out of the Police Academy. She had been battling a urinary tract infection for nearly a month now. It had become so uncomfortable, she had seriously considered calling in sick for the current deployment. As it was, she was forced to wear the heaviest DEPENDS absorption pad available.

But her failing to call in sick was too late now. A gust of wind, even greater than the level-four category winds that the convoy up to this point had been dealing with, bodily picked up their shining new white Ford Victoria patrol unit. The wind twirled it around several times before slamming it into the heavy-hauler's unprotected cab, killing the truck's civilian driver and his helper, and injuring the two police officers.

That forced the unscheduled stop of the convoy. Two of the convoy mechanics broke out the *Jaws of Life* and an acetylene torch, to cut away the tractor's damaged sheet metal. Then they extracted the hauler crew's bodies. Urgent medical attention was given to the two state highway patrolmen, who remarkably were found to be alive in the wreckage of their demolished patrol car.

Once the heavy hauler had been opened up like a sardine can, sheets of thin malleable steel, carried on the hauler's trailer bed for just such an eventuality, were screwed and tack-welded into place. The sheet metal work would make the hauler's tractor cab as weatherproof as possible. The heavy-hauler had been designed for extremely rough-use. The designers wisely envisioned this to include the possibility of unanticipated damage to its operating equipment beyond the control of its operators. Due to this foresight, the hauler's relatively simple mechanical, electrical and hydraulic systems still functioned. In fact, the one-piece shatterproof, well-pillared front cab window had escaped damage.

In forty-three minutes, the convoy was back on the road. But the deadly storm had worsened. Now, none of the civilian or military 'communicators' they carried could get through the storm to access anyone. The convoy's radio personnel continued to make contact attempts every five minutes, per procedure. Not even the Satellite-Communicator (SAT-COM) telephone the convoy commander by-default, had brought with her, a model routinely used by U.S. Special Operation Forces in Somalia, Iraq, the Falklands, and other foreign war zones, would utter a proverbial peep.

With this news, the flinty-eyed, hard-ass convoy crew and its combat-hardened armed protectors finally admitted they had graduated to being 'extremely worried.' The convoy had relied on their electronic capability to communicate freely with the troop transports and other civilian police units along the designated route. The convoy urgently needed that communications-ability to keep them advised on what bridges, viaducts, and other structures might have already suffered disabling damage.

Any significant damage to those structures could make them impassible. For the load of over one hundred-tons of replacement generator, not to mention the seventy five-tons of heavy hauler on which the load was chained.

An attractively tall, dark African American female Captain,

now the senior surviving convoy officer by-default, despite her 'alpha hotel' heterosexual-husband recently 'outing her' to her co-workers, yelled to her now communications-deaf troops. She urged them to "keep the convoy moving" as the partially-repaired heavy hauler began its laborious thirty minute-long crawl back up to its best 'top speed' of ten mph.

By now, sleep-deprivation was taking its toll on every member of the convoy. When they had woke up that morning at 0600 hours for reveille, no one had anticipated still being on-duty nearly sixteen long hours later. They also had missed two of their scheduled meals of MREs.

That the crew had anything to eat at all was largely due to the sharp-eyes of an old sergeant. He happened to notice that a double box of king-size Snickers and Milky Way candy bars was being hoarded by one of the convoy's civilian mechanics. Upon discovering the missing sweets, the obese, wet and hungry mechanic had been pissed off to find his stash had been seized. The MPs were supposed to enforce the law, not break it. He made a silent vow to turn in the old sergeant at the first opportunity. When they got back to the California base, and he could do so without the fear of getting his butt kicked by the rest of the convoy crew.

To combat the sleep-deprivation, the convoy's civilian supervisors started 'hot-seating' their drivers, every thirty minutes. A dangerous practice at best, it required the 'relieving' driver to hastily switch places with the co-worker being relieved—all without stopping. Both the relieving driver and the driver being relieved, had to exercise extreme caution when mounting and dismounting. No one could risk breaking an ankle, jumping on or off the hauler.

Should that misfortune happen, the severe weather conditions might obscure a inadvertent stumble. It was dark, very dark. And very, very windy. He or she could be inadvertently left behind alongside the highway, and forced to fend for themselves. Or perhaps even run over by the next truck in the convoy, being operated by another tired and inattentive driver. In any case, the net result would be leaving the abandoned individual without provisions or medical care to survive the tumultuously stormy night.

On the other hand, most of the military drivers, long accustomed to twelve-to—eighteen-hour shifts while on convoy duty, just drank more coffee. The coffee that was hot enough to give the recent Golden Arches' personal injury lawsuit, a run for its money. They simply strived to cope as they had been trained.

After about an hour, the rain and wind although still very vigorous, seem to lighten to some degree. One of the army's encrypted GPS receivers began to chirp with in-coming data. After redundant encoding checks, the satellite-driven device indicted that were less than forty statute miles from Boulder City, Nevada. That was the point where the U.S. Department of Reclamation would accept responsibly for their load.

In Boulder City, the convoy's civilian crew, less the heavy hauler crew, would be released to grab a hot meal. Perhaps a few forbidden brews, before finding a warm bed in which to crash. When they woke to a hot breakfast later in the morning, they'd all head back for their barracks outside Long Beach. Using the vehicles that had managed to survive the in-bound convoy leg, this time driving at a more normal pace. They could be back at their California barracks by 'happy hour' if some officious if well intentioned supervisor didn't change their orders in the meantime.

About twenty minutes later, the convoy turned east on a windy, rain-inundated section of Highway 93 that bypassed the Las Vegas strip. As they headed southeast for the Boulder City turnoff, the expensive Motorola walkie-talkies and COM-SAT phones came back on-line.

The U.S. Bureau of Reclamation personnel waiting at Boulder City, Nevada were relieved to learn the beleaguered convoy would arrive there in several hours time. No one on the receiving end in Boulder City even inquired as to whether the convoy had suffered any casualties or fatalities due to the freak summer storm.

This omission actually didn't surprise the battle-hardened troops and hard-core truckers very much. You accepted your dollar, and took your chances. Sometime the bear gets eaten, and sometime the bear ate you.

It was the law of all special-elite units, of which both groups considered themselves a part. Unforeseen shocking misfortunes on heavy-hauler assignments on-road can always happen. But they are always impossible to either predict or prevent.

The more senior members of the road crew deferred any expressions of celebration. Further messages from Boulder City told them to remain on alert. The weather was expected to briefly worsen, as the heavy hauler got closer to its next waypoint.

Specifically contained in the alert notice, were multiple reports of now-almost continuous lightning strikes. The crew knew the lightning would be attracted by the metal they were driving, riding in, or hauling. A number of local Boulder City residents reportedly had already been electrocuted. Including the local Sheriff who had been assisting a stranded young female motorist at the time. The fact that the female had chosen to drive into flood waters on the road too deep for her vehicle to forge, despite adequate signage telling her and other drivers to *Keep Out,* didn't make the news anymore palatable.

The convoy struggled on in a southeasterly direction on Highway 93, towards the safe haven of Boulder City. Now, they simply now halted the procession and waited when the electrical storm activity increased. After nearly twenty-hours on the road, those that weren't scared, on-break, or driving, had drifted off into a much-needed twilight-zone nap. Their respective subconscious jolting them awake every time the thunder signaling a particularly close lightning bolt strike, rattled the shatter-proof windshields of their vehicles.

Probably the only thing preventing further crew casualties due to excessive fatigue was the fact that the thunder, lightening, and sheeting horizontal rain, combined to keep the most fearful of the crew, trembling in their boots. It is well known that the most fearful always seem to be the more inexperienced junior crew and younger troops. In this case, fear seemed to work well as a motivator keeping everyone alert.

At exactly midnight, Nevada time, the convoy and its surviving eleven vehicles pulled into a large unpaved Boulder City parking lot, which had earlier been cleared for their use. Only then did the utterly exhausted convoy crewmembers permit themselves a sigh of relief. What remained of this portion of the commercial firm's cartage assignment, now depended solely on the U. S. Bureau of Reclamation's inspectors. They were scheduled to do a cursory inspection of Hoover Dam's new 3,500-H.P. 'service station generator' to insure its factory-affixed 'no tamper' seals were undisturbed and remained in-place. The Bureau of Reclamation's security team would then accept possession and responsibility for the package.

Immediately upon the inspection and turn-over being completed, the surviving convoy personnel, except for a small contingent consisting of the replacement heavy-hauler driver, two master mechanics, and one of the relief drivers who were all being held over to deliver the mechanical unit the remainder of the way up to the Dam's powerhouse later in the day, would go to a pre-arranged hotel in Boulder City. There, a conference room had been previously reserved by the transportation contractor's Long Beach office.

The crew would find it well stocked with cold beer, snacks, sandwiches, and key to a single-occupancy room for each of them. The driver, mechanics, and relief driver who had been ordered to 'stay-over' were invited also to the conference room, but with the proviso that they not partake of any liquor. At least during the remaining early morning hours, until after the convoy's last movement of the shipment to the powerhouse of the world's second largest concrete dam had been successfully completed.

The 'stay-overs' sleeping accommodations were likewise waiting for them. Unofficially, their lodging included two ice-cold beers one of the managers from the cartage company, thoughtfully had a bellhop smuggle into each room. A large steak sandwich with 'freedom fries' had also been freshly prepared, and sat warming under a commercial 'hot-cover' in each of the stay-over's rooms.

Every off-duty cartage company employee, hopefully reminldful of their co-workers who hadn't survived the trip, was to receive first class treatment compliments of their grateful employer. The crew, after eating and sleeping, would return to their home office in Long Beach. The crew's civilians would return to Long Beach in the surviving trucks, leaving the heavy hauler behind temporarily for the dam maintenance crews to use. The convoy's military contingent was scheduled to catch a chartered flight out of Las Vegas' McCarran Airport later that day.

By a somewhat different procurement method, 'higher command' of the military contingent had also made arrangements for their people to be treated in a similar manner. But in a different hotel, far across town from the lodging of their civilian brethren.

After first writing out the obligatory military 'after-action' report, those who chose were also provided access to cold beer or non-alcoholic beverages, supplemented with heaping plates of barbequed ribs and fried chicken, which spilled over the platter's edges onto the table.

But this was a military mission, and as such, still demanded discipline. So higher command had arranged for a U.S. Army top sergeant to be flown in the day before by army helicopter from a Las Vegas military facility. The 'top kick' stood around the conferencing room joking, drinking coffee, and dispensing advice. The sergeant also was there to ensure that everything went exactly as the Army intended.

Surprisingly, the top sergeant thought, *none of the troops brought up the names of those who had lost their lives on the recent mission. He thought that it seemed to be a group-wide unofficial agreement, not influenced by command presence or authority.*

The convoy had turned out to be a damn long mission for everyone. Soon the men and women soldiers drifted off to their individual rooms after consuming their fill of food, and sampling a few beers. All the lodging, food and drink expenses were paid for by the top sergeant. Rest assured, the invoice would eventually find its way across some army procurement officer's desk, albeit with a modified explanation, for authorization and payment.

About mid-morning, the Top Kick from the early morning security watch at the conference room, contacted each member of the 'stay over' contingent. He told them to grab a shower and some breakfast, and report back to the parking lot within ninety minutes where the 'package' had spent the night parked under the protection of Bureau of Reclamation's contract rent-a-cops.

When the crew returned to the parking lot, they were amazed to find a dozen or so energetic men and women crawling all over the heavily tarped turbine/generator set. They were removing only those hold-downs had been added solely to meet California or Nevada State Highway requirements. The actual 'hold-downs' deemed necessary to properly secure the load were checked for wear, and left alone unless they needed repair or reinforcing.

The game plan was to get the heavy hauler turned around, without incident. And then get it headed back up Boulder City Highway to its intersection with Hoover Dam's lower portal road. The dam's 'lower portal road' led to the Nevada powerhouse. Inconsequentially, at least to the accomplishment of the current assignment, the lower portal road also provided access to the Nevada side's bypass 'Stoney' discharge gate.

Hoover Dam's lower portal road included the hard-rock tunnel, which provided the only road access and egress to the massive horseshoe-shaped powerhouse. Personnel access to the powerhouse was via one of two forty-story tall elevators, which could only be entered from the middle abutments high on the dam's crest. Back in the early 1930's the elevators had been designed and ornamented for the vertical transportation of visitors and staff personnel. Therefore, it was impractical to move anything but the very lightest of supplies via anything other than the dam's lower portal road/tunnel. Since 9/11/01, no one but authorized employees of the dam were permitted access to the crest elevators, without exception.

The Bureau of Reclamation's planners and designers selected the town of Boulder Dam, Nevada in 1929 as the project's focal point. That meant many infrastructure improvements had to be designed, established, expanded, extended, and financed to make the then-Boulder Dam Project a reality.

When dam construction began in 1930, the Bureau of Reclamation's planners and schedulers had laid out a seven-year schedule. Initially, the contractor was known as 'The Six Companies' which was just that.

At the time, the Department of the Interior, the Bureau of Reclamation's folder-holder, felt no single company claiming an interest in bidding had the resources to adequately handle 'turnkey' responsibility for the project. However, as the project progressed, several of the individual contractors would earn excellent performance reputations and assume a greater share of the responsibility. This consolidation of responsibility, more than other factors, would end up bringing the highly technical, complex project in two years ahead of schedule in 1935.

Boulder City, Nevada was chosen as the project hub for logistical reasons. First, the city was only seven miles from the dam site chosen. Secondly, it was over 2,000 feet higher in elevation than the sweltering dam site in Black canyon. Hence, the town experienced ambient temperatures nearly ten degrees cooler than the construction location.

To fully understand the importance of that fact, it is important to be aware that while the climatic conditions at the Black Canyon site are considered excellent for eight months out of the year, the remaining four months (most easily described as *hell on earth*) May 15th to September 15th, could result in the project being placed 'on-hold' annually, until the torrid environmental conditions improved. Shade temperatures in Back Canyon historically rose as high as 128° F, as the reddish Black Canyon walls reflect furnace-like waves of heat.

The dam has been described by pixel pundits as "being the center of a inhospitable desert of mammoth dimension; complexity of design; intricateness of construction; a victory of man over the desert's summer sun; built despite the vagaries of the United State's most treacherous river; and the extreme hazards of great heights on the Back Canyon's sheer walls."

The dam's name was later changed from Boulder to Hoover Dam by an act of the United States Congress in 1947.

To support the dam workers residing in Boulder City, over 1,000 individual homes were built and at peak construction, a dozen dormitories also housed nearly 5,000 dam and support workers who had come to live and work in a single-status. Four churches, a grade school, shops, stores, garages, a 700-seat theater, tourist camps, recreation halls, and later a beautiful hotel, would be built to compliment the construction of other trade facilities.

But in the beginning, the Bureau of Reclamation project team was dealing with management, engineers, estimators, planners, and schedulers from all six private entities. The main task, before anything else could move ahead, was redeveloping Boulder City to the point where it would serve to support the project. Originally, the project schedule ran from its beginning in 1930 until the then-anticipated completion date of 1937.

As Boulder City became the project's primary support and operations base, the small Nevada town seemed to blossom. In a seemingly shotgun manner in the eyes of the uninitiated, but actually one of superb coordination, foresight, and scheduling, the following years saw a figurative explosion of activity in Boulder City. Facilities to house up to 6,000 dam-builders and support personnel were constructed.

A seven-mile long road from Boulder was constructed to what would be the 1,244-foot wide upper crest of the 'arch gravity' dam. To give you some degree of relative magnitude, the dam had to be constructed out of concrete and reinforcing steel to a height of 726-feet. It would extend from the bedrock of the Colorado River bed to the roadway on its crest.

While this was being accomplished, other crews were building thirty-two miles of standard-gauge railroad track from the main line in Las Vegas, to the dam site and Boulder City.

Another crew undertook the task of building 222-miles of 88,000 volt power transmission lines from San Bernardino, California to the dam site and City of Boulder, to provide power for the required construction.

The first major 'benchmark' project undertaken, outside the town, was the construction of what was envisioned by the designers as the nexus—the connection or link. That was the dam's lower portal road. The road included the 1,900-foot hard-rock access tunnel.

There was no other practical way for the contractors to reach the riverbed. Reaching that riverbed was necessary to permit construction of the all-important upstream cofferdam, four massive fifty-six-foot tunnels necessary to fabricate the fifty-foot spillways, and the thirty-foot penstocks. It was also necessary to permit men and equipment to clean the riverbed down to base rock. Only then could the structural forms be built, and millions of yards of concrete, poured.

Additionally, the road provided access for thousands of shift workers; nine hundred pieces of heavy construction equipment; one dozen, 3.5 cubic yard power shovels; and one hundred ten-ton dump trucks. All the rolling stock was necessary to evacuate the canyon stone, after it was laboriously removed with drills, shovels, and high explosives from the gorge's sides and riverbed.

Every inch of the mile and one half-long 'lower portal road' from the Boulder City highway, including the hard rock access tunnel, has at one time or another, been described by dam workers as "primitive, hot, crawling with poisonous snakes."

The day the yellow heavy hauler bearing the 3,500 horsepower replacement unit, was to be trucked through the tunnel, a security crew with shotguns loaded with buckshot had walked along the road, and through the claustrophobic tunnel earlier that morning, to insure those legends hadn't been understated.

Potentially dangerous creatures inhabiting the tunnel, and found along the lower portal road included coyotes, brown bats, scorpions, desert tarantulas, both Mohave and Diamondback rattlesnakes, and the eighteen-inch-long Chuckwalla lizard.

The Nevada-side generation wing had been readied for the delivery earlier that morning. The automated, anti-terrorism security detectors and shields set-up at the road's intersection with the Boulder City highway, had been temporarily disabled. This was necessary to permit the installation crew and their equipment access to the power plant. As soon as the heavy hauler had delivered the load to its final destination, it would be off-loaded, lifted by bridge cranes, which would transport it to the installation site, to be bolted into its foundation, and wired up. The operations crew was ready to test, and activate the critically needed unit.

The now-faltering Arizona powerhouse service station turbine/generator was well beyond any reasonable expectation of continuing to carry the 24/7 maintenance loads much longer. The dam's electricians and maintenance teams had their fingers and toes crossed for luck.

The physical clearance for the Caterpillar-yellow heavy hauler, especially in the 1,900-foot tunnel, although adequate, would be tight—more for length rather than width. No one wanted to rush the equipment movement and risk damaging the replacement unit. Not after literally millions of dollars, and thousands of hours at the Teamster Union's overtime rate, had already been invested in its acquisition and transport.

One or two of the dam's oldest 'old timers' claimed to remember the dam's original west wing 'service station' turbine/generator set that this new unit was replacing. The original set had been installed in the middle 1930's. However, as far as research personnel at the Dam, and Bureau of Reclamation knew, none of the original 'installers' were still alive to provide their sage advice on handling the replacement unit today.

Hoover Dam, up until July 14, 2003, held the bragging rights as the world's largest dam. Until that day when most sections of the Three Gorges Dam, on the Yangtze River near Yichang in Central China's Hubei province, came on-line. Among other bragging rights the Chinese dam automatically assumed, was the world's widest turbines for the generation of electricity; the world's longest ship lock—a five-stage ship lock to be specific; and the world's highest ship lift.

In 1935, and continuing until today, Hoover Dam has never needed the ship lock and ship lift features of the Chinese dam. The dam for this Colorado River water project was unique. Only a single powerhouse access and egress truck route had been constructed to permit the building of the all-important powerhouse. It also provided for the installation of equipment necessary to facilitate the dam's multi-functions of irrigation, power generation, site stabilization and recreation.

The Hoover Dam powerhouse is a massive horseshoe-shaped building, with ten-acres of paved concrete floors under roof, having a central section, and two long wings. The entire powerhouse serves as a monolithic operating system, even though the wings—one on the Nevada and the other on the Arizona riverbank—are capable of operating individually, but in a coordinated environment.

The curved center section of the dam's powerhouse immediately abuts the dam's lower concave face. The entire powerhouse roof is heavily reinforced to protect against possible damage from rocks falling off the canyon walls. It was at an elevation of two hundred, forty-five feet above the downstream level of the Colorado River. The center section of the powerhouse is approximately six hundred feet in length, and roughly seventy feet in depth. The dam's center section and the two powerhouse wings are each equipped with independent acting, three hundred-ton bridge cranes. Each of the two wings of the powerhouse, referred to as the Nevada and the Arizona powerhouses, are over six hundred-feet in length, and vary in width/depth from sixty-seven to seventy-three feet.

Since September 11, 2001, visitors to the dam have generally been led to believe by tour guides that the 'only' way down to the ten acres of powerhouse floors, besides the non-public-access 'lower portal road' that connects to the south end of the Nevada powerhouse out of Boulder City, is via two forty-story tall, large elevators entered only from the dam's two middle towers located on its 1,244-foot crest. These both were secured from public access following 9/11.

Each of these load-certified lifts, descend five hundred, twenty-six feet to a beautiful-tiled gallery constructed deep inside the massive dam. Before 9/11, visitors could walk downgrade for a block and a half, which would lead them to the central section of the huge horseshoe shaped powerhouse.

Given no overt publicity since September 11, 2001, more from casual omission rather than a premeditated intent to deceive, is the fact that Hoover Dam has nearly two miles of paved shafts and galleries. Those seemingly subterranean routes were included in the original engineering design to provide access for accomplishing grouting repairs, drainage, and for inspection purposes. The passageways pierce the multi-million cubic yard structure at various levels, in circumferential and radial lines.

For instance, one of these access shafts begins near the west-most middle abutment on the dam's crest, and continues very, very far down to within five to thirty feet of the Colorado river's millennium-old bedrock. There, it laterally crosses the six hundred foot lower dam, and begins a very long, arduous climb back to the dam crest entrance, located near the second middle abutment, just east of the first entrance.

Returning to the powerhouse proper, the three heavy-duty bridge crane systems combine, to functionally link all of the three sub-structures together. The lower portal road/tunnel enters the south end of the Nevada powerhouse wing. Any equipment or machinery, off-loaded there, can be picked up and placed anywhere in the horseshoe-shaped facility, including at the far southern end of the Arizona powerhouse wing.

The design specifications on the powerhouse structure alone have been alternatively called gratuitous and mind-boggling. Acknowledging there may have been debatable elements of over-sizing during the dam's project-design stage, it is noted that there are a total of seventeen turbine/generator sets installed in the two powerhouse wings, plus two smaller 3,500-H.P. turbine/generator sets, which are allocated strictly for maintenance, and preventive maintenance of the powerhouse critical complex.

For the detail-minded, it is briefly noted that each of the turbines have a forty-foot 'spiral scroll' case on the lower turbine floor, which is driven by the hydro-power of 28,537,000 acre-feet of water which has accrued in Lake Mead reservoir since 1935.

The seventeen sets of turbines are coupled to their respective generators via an ascending shaft. The shaft is located between the seventeen turbines and their generator sets, in the space between the turbine and generator floors of the powerhouse.

The overall dam contains millions of cubic yards of concrete, twenty-two million pounds of reinforcing steel, and eleven-miles of pipe and conduit. Then there are the seventeen, fourteen-foot butterfly valves. The dam includes over ten acres of Italian-tiled floors.

The combined Nevada and Arizona powerhouses have the ability to raise the voltage from the 16,500-volts generated to a transmission voltage of 287,500-volts. The powerhouse production capacity is 1,344,800 kilowatts daily, or an annual supply of four billion kilowatt-hours.

The equipment being delivered, off-loaded, and installed on this date was a replacement for one of the 3,500 horsepower 'service station' turbine/generator sets. The original-equipment units had been installed in 1935. In the subsequent years since 1935, those units as had all the dam's original equipment, were rigorously subjected to a very expensive, all encompassing preventive maintenance program, as recommended by the manufacturer.

Thus, it had been an unpleasant surprise to both the Bureau of Reclamation, and the unit's manufacturer, when the one of the two original service station generators had unexpectedly 'failed' a number of months previously. The dam's maintenance engineers removed the failed unit.

Both the Bureau of Reclamation engineers and the experts from the turbine/generator set manufacturer, then rigorously had inspected the unit. Following the inspection, they were uniformly shocked to find that the well-maintained unit had unexplainably self-destructed.

As the unit was obviously beyond repair, a replacement unit had been needed quickly, regardless of the expense. Critical preventive maintenance, designed to rely on the inoperative 'western' wing service station generator, would have to be deferred, until the replacement set's arrival and installation. As one of the manufacturer's more sarcastic engineers had declared, "That broken puppy needs replacement, Praise the Lord."

The broken 3,500-H.P. 'service station' unit might become instrumental in the disruption of the lives of nearly twenty-five million residents in the American Southwest and Southern California, unless it was replaced promptly. As it was, the experts from both the Bureau of Reclamation and the units manufacturer, had put their respective heads together, and came up with a temporary plan—one that worked solely on absolute priorities, and historical breakdown performance.

The decision-making engineers, months before, had felt that regardless of what 'work around' plan they came up, it could only guarantee that the Hoover Dam power-generation capacity would hold together, short term, or less than thirty days. Today, those same engineers in retrospect found it remarkable that the work-around plan had kept the dam limping along, generating its full committed load, for a little over four month's time.

The process by which hydroelectric power is generated, will soon reach its 100th birthday. The scientific theory is simple, but complicated and costly to implement. A quantity of water from a reservoir propels fluid under pressure into spiral turbine 'scrolls,' where it passes between the inner rims, striking the horizontally rotating turbine runner, which turns the turbines. The turbines, on the turbine floor, are attached by ascending shafts to the generating units above on the generation floor. This occurs, while the now-once-utilized water from the hydroelectric process, is discharged back to the downstream source river via various penstocks and gates.

Electricity is generated by rotation of the rotor field in the stator windings in the seventeen generators. The newly generated electricity exits the generator, and goes directly to a power distribution panel. There the 16,500-volt power is stepped up to the 230,000 volts required for long-distance transmission to the desert southwest and Southern California.

Now that the replacement unit had arrived on-site, the Bureau of Reclamation maintenance crews would install it immediately, without regard for the dam's already abused overtime labor budget. The long haul along the lower portal road had progressed slowly, but thus far without incident.

It was when the heavy hauler began to inch its ways into the beginning of 1,900-foot deep-rock tunnel that things could get dicey. No significant piece of 'in-coming' heavy equipment had been moved through the lower portal tunnel, since the final turbine, number N-8 was installed on December 1st, 1961.

Except for the occasional maintenance rig, little in-coming equipment had traversed the tunnel northbound in the past forty-three years. The hard-rock tunnel as designed, was very primitive and contained deadly venomous snakes of several types, not to mention abundant populations of scorpions, and tarantulas. The 'spotters' or 'marshals' on-foot, assigned to guide the hundred-foot long, wide-load trailer, had a job none of them had volunteered for.

Now that the rain and wind had finally stopped, the deadly summer storm had moved on and the southwest desert was back to its over-bearing 120° F temperatures. Those temperatures produced heat waves, which were further heated by the black asphalt of the road, which made the access-road surface appear to ripple. Its undulating movement was hypnotic, causing the convoy walkers as well as the seated operator's minds, to drift dangerously.

The entire trip by heavy hauler only took two hours from Boulder City to the 'lower portal road' intersection. Another hour was expended just getting the mile and one half to the entrance of the 1,900-foot tunnel. There, the hauler procession slowed to a pace that occasionally resulted in the walking marshals in front unknowingly walked away from the rest of the convoy, so intent was their concentration on exactly where they were placing each individual step.

After an additional forty-eight minutes, the procession finally reached the south entrance to the Nevada powerhouse. Then, another hour was expended attempting to maneuver the long hauler in the very limited space available. Once that had been accomplished, the heavy-hauler was backed deep into the south portal of the Nevada powerhouse. The stale air of the powerhouse was blue with profanities. The entire maintenance crew generously directed well-meaning, if unnecessary, advice to the hauler driver.

Finally, the seemingly madcap activity came to an abrupt halt. The pre-positioned Nevada three-hundred-ton overhead bridge crane was securely coupled to the 200,000-pound, rust-preventative coated mechanical load.

The operation was now solely in the dam's 'lifting crews' domain. They routinely moved huge machinery, using the three bridge cranes in unison, throughout the large horseshoe-shaped powerhouse. To date, the powerhouse crew had never dropped anything, from the time the first huge N-2 turbine/generator had been off-loaded and installed back in 1935.

The new hole-pattern required for the replacement units forty gigantic foundation bolts had been previously determined. The mating plates had already been drilled accordingly. The heavy load was lifted off the heavy hauler with a screech. It began its swaying and creeping 'float' far over the installer's heads. Well over the rest of the existing behemoth generating equipment, to its final resting place on the generator floor at the north end of the Nevada powerhouse. Everything had gone exactly as planned, to everyone's relief. The replacement 'set' was gently positioned in its designated location in the Nevada Powerhouse, next to one of the older 82,500-kilowatt, turbine-generators. All involved then uttered a long-overdue sigh of relief.

The cartage contractor's heavy hauler driver and crew had left their now-outward-pointed rig. They watched the transition of their load from being just a piece of innate equipment, to a working element of the power generation system of the U.S.'s largest concrete hydroelectric dam. It seemed to be almost anti-climatic.

Over a dozen stalwart, wrench-toting men immediately jumped on the flanges of the service station turbine-generator to bolt the unit firmly in place. The electricians concurrently began to wire-up the various critical high-voltage connections, so that pre-operational testing could immediately begin.

Some twelve hours later, everyone on the installation crew had all signed off on the inspection and installation. Then Edith Hammer, the dam's resident manager, gave the order that would introduce Lake Mead water to the turbine.

And without a sound other than that of well-meshed innards, the new unit began to earn its keep. The fresh Preventative Maintenance hotshot crews, out of the regional Bureau of Reclamation office, began to attack the work order backlog with ferocity.

In the Arizona powerhouse some six hundred feet away, the duty maintenance crew, that had been sleeping fitfully every hour of every day with the antique Arizona service station 'twin,' would soon be relieved. They could finally call it a 'long couple of months.'

The men would be released to head home to their families for a hot meal, a warm bed, and perhaps a cold beer. All of the mechanics, from the git-go, had agreed to abstain from alcohol for as long as it took to obtain and install a replacement unit. They knew their skill and expertise had been the only thing preventing total disruption of the power supplying the southwestern United States, and Southern California.

The crew being relieved was so tired that none of them gave a passing thought to the greatly increased size of their family's savings accounts. The significant sums of money came from overtime wages, while manning the 24/7 emergency shifts in the Arizona wing of the Hoover Dam powerhouse.

So tired, for that matter, that they had no thoughts of the handful of men and women on the convoy, who had ended up giving their lives to insure the replacement unit reached the dam. But the convoy had gotten through. Despite the fact that they had to forge through the worst summer storm to hit the California-Nevada-Arizona borders in years.

For several weeks, the Bureau of Reclamation hot-shot maintenance teams would stand-in in for Hoover Dam's regular maintenance crew, who had spent most of the recent months on-duty.

The dam's Manager, Edith Hammer, yearned for the time when day-to-day operations at the facility could return to normal, and she could return to a ordinary existence with the family she loved so much.

Despite today's victory with the replacement's units activation, Hoover Dam's Police Chief, Rich Melin, a very conservative and respected professional, continued to subject the various terrorist threats discussed by the FBI under heightened evaluation. Once the risk factors were determined, and hopefully eliminated, his security team could get back to their day-to-day routines. Unless further unscheduled 'panic attacks' kept their lives from returning to normal.

CHAPTER ELEVEN

DAY 298—25 OCTOBER

SOMEWHERE IN THE DESERT

MOHAVE COUNTY

ARIZONA

Highway 95, running more or less north/south through the states of Nevada and Arizona, is mostly a two-lane road. When constructed many years ago, it appeared to have been slapped onto the existing topography, much like a raw beef patty slathered in a hot skillet of grease. Or a dollop of fresh pancake mix plunked down onto the hot surface of an old range stove. Then trimmed as to width.

The narrow road wove its way through the desert areas like a meandering Mohave rattlesnake. The snake ever mindful of its ultimate destination, only deviating to avoid one of nature's many obstacles, in life.

In a noble if misplaced struggle to keep road construction costs down, very few dollars had been spent to maintain any approximation of a level roadbed. Bulldozers had simply cut the tops off of the highest crowns of the rolling terrain. Dump trucks filled in old 'washes' that were only wet for an hour or two annually, for the past hundreds of years. The resulting road surface undulated gently across the sandy, arid soil which only had value to the occasional human desert rat, venomous snakes, scorpions, and tarantula spiders, to name but a few of the desert's full-time occupants.

However, the bleakness and frying-pan-heat along Highway 95, like its more infamous sister road—Route 66—of days gone past, seem to draw scurrying motorists. Each intent on getting from point A to point B in the fewest strokes of the atomic clock of time. This seemingly self-destructive urge driving those that surfed the narrow pavement of Highway 95, often lead to very serious, avoidable auto accidents. The crashes were significant occurrences where one or more of the parties often expired due to their acute injuries. Compounded by the lack of reasonably available emergency medical care.

All along Highway 95, grows a forest of little white crosses, hung with either fake flowers, or long-since dried out garnishments. Loved ones have planted them. Loved ones who are attempting to symbolize the foolishness resulting from the premature earthly departure of the now-decreased family members. The heavy-footed drivers who "just had to get to Las Vegas, Kingman, Phoenix (fill in any of a hundred other destinations) with utmost dispatch."

To achieve their goal, the deceased had made one dangerous vehicle pass after another, knowing deep in their brains that there was not room to safely get back in line. But hope sprung eternal that the oncoming driver was not in as large a hurry as they were. And as such, would back down in the age-old game of 'chicken,' gambling the speeding driver could avoid a head-on collision.

The one fact those motorists refused to factor into their calculations was that the other guy in the on-coming car was in as big a hurry as they were! The other driver was also thinking that they'd "God Damn had it up to here, with these God Damn trailer-pulling, motor-home-driving seniors, and the other obviously mentally deficient drivers who thought they owned the God Damn road."

The numbers of little white crosses continued to increase along both roadsides, the entire length of Highway 95. As if to provide an endless winner's circle for the survivors of the massive vehicular jousts. The collisions went on endlessly over and over again. Not unlike an old 78-RPM record of Elvis that has been played for decades until its every groove has been turned into a virtual vinyl wasteland.

The on-going vehicular carnage continued weekly, monthly, annually, through one decade and into the next. The loss of life on Highway 95 was unusually high, as it is on all other rural highways crossing the superheated desert. Motorists whispered and *pooh-poohed* about the tragedies, but continued to drive like a bat out of hell.

Government officials, when they could tear their attention away from continually campaigning for reelection, refused to work with one another for the common good. Politicians across the nation's western and southwestern states, when in public, lamented the on-going loss of life of the motorist, which also constituted members of the voting public.

But this was modern America. The motoring appetite of the population was just too large to be satisfied. There was never enough money to fund all the various special interest and social projects. Hell, who could justify putting State Police into assignments where they, hour-after-hour, day-after-day, patrolled the same wasteland of boring two-lane highway. The cops countered by responding that their goal was the education of drivers to good driving practices, and the avoidance of poor habits.

Law enforcement sought to break the motorist's current mindset of disregard for the traffic laws of the land, the practice of ignoring general road safety, and tendency to defend their birth-given privileges to speed recklessly all the way to their graves.

There just wasn't enough tax money for everything—such as protecting motorists from other motorists. Why didn't the public see and appreciate that?

So, after a gnashing of teeth in the State and Federal legislatures, more and more funding began to find its way past the dams of fiscal constraint, ear marked for the improvement of the national infrastructure, which including our highway and byways. If we couldn't retrain the motorist, perhaps we could make improvements to the highway configuration that would protect the motorists from their own worst enemies, themselves.

Thus highway improvement programs such as the State Route 95 project, having a price tag of a mere $19 million dollars, began in 2003. The project ran from I-40 to the north, and extended south through the city limits of Lake Havasu City, Arizona. In 'funding-speak' the scope of the yearlong project was identified as "SR 95 from McCulloch Boulevard South (mp 176.76) to London Bridge Road (mp 190.40)."

The scope of work, scheduled to begin 07 April 2003, called for "the widening of the existing two-lane paved roadbed to five-lanes; to mill and pave existing five-lane roadway; and construct a new parallel southbound roadway resulting in a four-lane divided highway."

The work would have to be accomplished at night. It was important to the local economy to avoid any road restrictions that would otherwise hamper tourism and hinder commercial vehicle movement. Thus the resulting extra efforts on the part of the contractor, greatly increased the project's cost, and meant the project would take twelve months to complete.

The Arizona Department of Transportation's (ADOT) overall goal for the project was making at least that stretch of Highway 95 safer. That, in spite of the self-centered, self-absorbed motorists that continued to bust the double-nickel the length of its byways. The work was going to take a lot of construction equipment, and more importantly, manpower.

The latter requirement would permit the infiltration into Mohave County of terrorists of the worst ilk. They managed to blend in with the influx of incoming construction workers seeking jobs. Highway construction projects in the desert, even the low desert, often went wanting for skilled workers required to facilitate construction of the roadwork project. Often, those doing the hiring occasionally were less than exacting in completing the required background investigations that have been required by Homeland Security since 9/11.

An even dozen of these dedicated and trained Muslim extremists had arrived in Lake Havasu City. There they would straggle into the project's construction hiring office in small groups of two to three persons. All spoke perfect English, more importantly, American English. Indeed, half of them had even attended various California community colleges. But all had given their souls to Allah, bin-Laden, and al-Qaeda.

Demographically, the group was made up of young, physically fit men and women, mostly of Saudi Arabian linage. None of the males fit the traditional Arabic stereotype by wearing any type of thin, narrow beard around the chin bone, or a mustache. All falsely claimed a birthplace within the contiguous United States, which was supported by forged birth certificates, social security cards, driver's licenses, and other 'pocket litter.'

By intent, team selection had included a small number of blue-eyed, blond—haired individuals. In hot, humid, stinking desert training camps, each of the potential 'construction workers' had been well taught. Then repeatedly tested by unforgiving al-Qaeda instructors in American culture, trivia, dialects, wear, hairstyles, and customs, including the non-Islamic practice of partaking of alcoholic beverages.

The women, those not already having facial makeup skills being typical Muslim women, actually had a weeklong seminar in the camp taught by a ex-film makeup expert from Paris. They had been instructed in application, in what quantity, and more importantly, why the application was necessary, even for construction jobs out in the elements. They were amazed when told that American workingwomen always wore lipstick, and perhaps a little eyeliner, even on construction-related jobs.

All the al-Qaeda men and women had been thoroughly 'Americanized' during their desert camp training. Not even an experienced CIA expert, a student of author Kanade's *Comprehensive Database of Facial Expression Analysis*, would have questioned the identity of the few individuals that did have more Arabic features.

The team had been carefully instructed that the entire group was to never be seen together, as it could foster facial comparison.

During the application process, most of the women produced forged construction safety training certificates, and were prompt hired by the contractor as 'flag persons' at scale. The men found employment as heavy equipment operators, as they had been trained back in the Saudi desert camps, or as common construction day laborers.

As is the custom in the American construction industry, the 'new hires' invariably were paired with a more experience worker, and dispatched to differing work locations along the fifteen-mile work site. The new hires were to communicate with their American counterparts, as was necessary. But the al-Qaeda team's mission commander forbade all but unavoidable conversation between the individuals of the undercover group.

The mission commander's job was to lead these warriors into battle against the Great Satan. Each member of the action team would act independently on a rigid pre-established timetable. Up to the moment when they re-grouped to achieve their tactical and strategic objectives and goals. They all prayed to Allah that their actions would cause the Americans to shudder and soil their undergarments as had been the case back on 9/11/01.

Their al-Qaeda leaders had beat into their heads that infidel Americans "were to be considered targets and objectives, not people. Everyone of the Americans, from the oldest elder to the youngest infant was Allah's enemy—there are no innocent civilians or noncombatants in a Jihad."

As the construction project began, the new employees blended into a homogenous crew with the older, more experienced tradesmen and supervisors. After a week on the job, the company's Human Resources Supervisor had performed a preliminary personnel evaluation of all employees. She subsequently reported back to the company's head office that "all new hires were bright, intuitive, self starters, were performing well, and appeared to get getting along with, and had been accepted by, the more seasoned workers."

The masquerading 'new hires' had been trained well by al-Qaeda in the camps. Conversation, interaction and contact, other than that mandated by their construction assignments, was discouraged. They showed up for work, were polite, instantly followed orders, performed well, and went home promptly at quitting time, like the rest of construction crew.

The project workweek was six-days long unless an unforeseen construction emergency came up. The construction crew worked mostly nightshift, due to traffic concerns and worker safety considerations.

Like the rest of the crew, the 'new hires' had found room accommodations at the four inexpensive motels that accepted weekly guests in the Lake Havasu Area. Two members of the group, always of like gender, shared each of the sleeping rooms suites around the city.

One member from each team would purchase the necessary food, everything that typically was required to prepare American dishes. The selected team members would shop locally in Lake Havasu City at Safeway, Bashas, Smith, Food City, or Albertson's grocery stores.

The undercover al-Qaeda operatives had been forbidden to congregate with one another outside their hotel rooms. Even though drinking is contrary to Islam, not to drink in small qualities could appear suspicious to their American co-workers. The team members as individuals attended local movies. In small groupings of two, they frequented local bars consuming small quantities of beer—solely to fit in with the public's expectations of a construction crew.

They visited the public library being careful to read only non-Arabic newspapers and publications. Having no library cards, an intended precaution, not an oversight—they never checked out a book.

When not working or at a movie, they sat around their rooms smoking Marlboro cigarettes (the only thing the operatives enjoyed that was American), and practiced isometric exercises. The latter to ensure they stayed in good physical and mental shape.

As they had been ordered back in the desert camps, they suspend their Islamic prayers to Mecca, to avoid being overheard. The rooms they could afford to rent were not well constructed, let alone soundproof.

All the explosives the teams would need had been covertly brought into the area previously. It had been couriered into the Lake Havasu area by parties unknown to the teams.

The al-Qaeda courier agents had no problem renting an older wooden 34-foot Chris Craft day cruiser for a week. The boat had four bunks and the obligatory chemical head, or restroom.

The boat dealer renting them the boat had been pleasantly surprised to receive their payment cash-in-full upfront. Their offer to pay in advance was an unusual one. The boat dealer's regular rental customers—mostly rich, spoiled, and binge-drinking college kids from the California—always tried to run out on the rental bill. To maintain the deception, the four-man al-Qaeda courier cell proceeded to outfit the rental cruiser with enough food and beverages to last a week, and motored out of the marina as night fell on Lake Havasu.

Approximately an hour later, the al-Qaeda operatives landed at a then-deserted beach in a small natural cove not visible from SR 95. The inlet was a short distance north of Parker Dam. They sat around waiting for nightfall.

Then, they carefully but swiftly unloaded the hermetically sealed equipment and supplies from the back of a beat-up dark van, which had been parked in an adjacent parking area. The van had only that afternoon been left at the small beach. Someone had placed a hastily written, undated message board on the locked van's dashboard, declaring that the occupants had "Gone Fishing." For security reasons, the driver leaving the van had taken the time to prepare an elaborate booby trap in the vehicle, before removing its battery (which was tossed into the water) and locking the van's doors

The explosives were already securely packed in waterproof containers. The four men on the wooden boat concealed the transloaded equipment and explosives below decks, until it could be taken to the underwater cave. When the night was the blackest, they would secret them under water at the site of an old mine. The mine entrance was located a short distance away from Lake Havasu unique island's area, Site Six.

When the boat arrived at the site where cave existed nearly forty feet below, the men were already in their scuba gear. The explosives had been carefully off-loaded, taken below, and concealed deep at the rear of a natural cave, now underwater since formation of Lake Havasu by the construction of Parker Dam.

The day before the team's day-of-execution, the same scuba divers would return to the submerged cave and reverse the process. In the meantime, all they could do is wait for the 'go' order from al-Qaeda.

It was nearly a week later that the al-Qaeda team commander Mohammed felt it safe to get the covert team together. The team needed a final briefing to insure everyone was fully prepared to act on a moment's notice. Since the only day of the week the construction crew had off was Sundays, plans were made to meet on that day, somewhere out in the desert. Not somewhere so remote as to draw suspicion from occasional off-roaders. But far enough off the beaten path to guarantee the group remained anonymous until the target day. The al-Qaeda teams were utilizing an age-old technique—that of hiding in plain sight.

It was like a ghost town that had fallen out of a malfunctioning time machine and landed in the middle of nowhere. Assuming that 'nowhere' was found in a very remote part of desert at the base of the Buckskin Mountains below Lake Havasu City. It was five miles north of the town of Parker, AZ.

The Nellie E. Saloon, or the Desert Bar, as it had come to be increasingly called in the recent decade, was primarily known only to desert rats, four-wheelers, bikers, wannabe criminals and the risk-taking locals. They had learned about the place through word-of-mouth.

Only the very hardy attempted to visit the Nellie E. The only highway access was east of SR 95, off the Cienega springs Road exit. It was a place where you could arrive and leave by four-wheeler, dirt bike, dune buggy, horseback, and horseless carriage. But only if you knew the way to the old camp, using the narrow, rough, pothole filled, unmarked cross-desert rock trails.

No one ventured out to the old camp without heeding to the desert's caution—always, always, and then always again, take lots and lots of water. Those greenhorns that chose to venture out into the northern Arizona dessert without taking that advice, generally never had a second chance to reconsider their foolishness. At all times except during the dead of winter, the Nellie E. was hot as hell. And it was located at least five long miles away from even a semblance of civilization.

The place had been built over the years on land that had once been a prosperous mining camp. The mining camp was deserted and had all but vanished, when the current owner in 1975, had decided to take a chance. He bought the rights to the land, and had set up shop. Then, as now, the area could only be described as rough and tumble, primitive, hot, dirty, and full of venomous Mohave snakes, tarantula spiders, and scorpion critters you certainly hoped you'd never meet. And then there were the always-hungry coyotes. Who prayed to their God for a helpless victim, four or two-legged, made them no matter mind. Their prayer for a human feast was usually answered several times each year.

Over the years the rugged place had been fitted with a solar-powered well pump. The owner had drilled to a depth of nearly 400 feet before striking water. The outpost was a couple of buildings seemingly slapped together in the middle of nowhere, not serviced by electrical, sewer, streets, and plumbing utilities. Whatever the place required to survive either had to be purchased, or manufactured on-site.

Solar power was used for the essential electrical needs. After being collected, it was stored in batteries and run through inverters. Except for the owner's cellular phone, there was no telephone service.

The unique air conditioning, what little there was of it, was by way of an evaporative (swamp) cooler, modified to operate without fan. When the pads on the top of a tall tower were wet with cold well water pumped up to them, the cool air fell. The end result is a nice cool airflow. And in desert temperatures that exceed 120 degrees Fahrenheit, any cooling breeze however unsophisticated, is appreciated.

Closed, except during the day from Labor Day to Memorial Day, the saloon as a collateral benefit of the cooling tower, could be reasonably habitable. Everything in the old saloon building was made from scraps, left over and dug up from the old mining camp. The windows are old glass refrigerator doors. The ratty old bar stools are made of metal tailings, and swayed from side to side. The top of the bar was brass. The ceiling made from stamped tin, which originally came from a factory in the sovereign State of Missouri.

Construction on an ersatz non-denominational church was begun in 1993, and completed in 1996. The structure was nothing but cast-off pieces of steel with the walls and ceiling made from the same stamped tin as that used in the saloon's ceiling. The open-air church was located to the left, once you enter the Nellie E's dirt parking lot. Access from the parking lot, across a ravine to the saloon, is via a narrow desert bridge, which was completed in 1991.

A very limited selection of cold and hot sandwiches (the stove is propane—powered) and cold drinks are available for purchase. The cost isn't too unreasonable considering the cost and difficulty getting it to the Nellie E. saloon in the first place.

Outside the saloon in the arid heat, you'll find a dance floor and a musician's stage partially covered by a rickety overhang. The outside bar is located beneath the unique cooling tower. And its coolness makes it a convenient place to purchase a tasty hot dog, hamburger, and alike. But be advised that none of the sandwiches and finger food on the menu will be found in any Weight-Watchers cookbook. Instead, it is a Adkins-Diet kind of establishment—lots and lots of red meat.

Set off to one side of the outside bar is a horseshoe pit, which is largely unprotected from the sun's blistering rays. As such it is rarely frequented by mere mortals unless those individuals seek absolute isolation, and privacy.

Such was the case with the masquerading al-Qaeda terrorist team. They showed up at the Nellie E. on that bitterly hot Sunday afternoon. They arrived in pre-arranged pairs at ten-minute increments using differing modes of transportation. Two teams riding four-wheelers, suddenly appeared out of the desert. Two more arrived on dirt bikes after riding overland from the direction of the nearby town of Parker. The remainder arrived in a clunky old jeep one of the team had purchased from a drunken miner for eleven dollars. The team had heard about the miner, who continued to eek out a living from one of the few remaining working mines, from one of their American co-workers on the job.

In the group were four women in their mid-twenties. Their already coarse completions had suffered from performing their flag duties, buffeted by the desert's hot winds. The eight men all employed as journeymen equipment operators and an occasional powder monkey, seemed to thrive performing their jobs in the Arizona desert environment.

All were casually dressed in American jeans and t-shirts, appropriate to Nellie E's environment. The team commander needed to ensure that no civilian customer or saloon employee would attempt to approach the group. So he sent two of the men up to the saloon first thing, and purchased a six-pack each of cold Budweiser beer longneckers, and Coke Colas. (Arabs do not drink Pepsi, which they consider to be a Jewish product)

As the men were paying for the drinks, they explained to the bartender that they were celebrating a few birthdays. Further, that the group would appreciate being left alone. The young egregious bartender had to laugh silently. He certainly never intended to walk down to the horseshoe pit in the breath-robbing heat anyway. So he smiled, graciously agreed, and accepted the five-dollar gratuity the men left behind on the bar as they left the saloon.

The two men returned to the horseshoe pit. After opening a few of the cold drinks, they initially sat around trying to remember how to play the American game they had read up on, only last week. Not one of them had ever seen much less played 'horseshoes' back in the Middle East. Not even when they had attended college in California.

Every one of the dozen Arabs crowded under the overhang seeking protection from the hot sun, although the heat didn't bother them. Anyone who had not yet partaken of the cold drinks opened either the soft drinks or beer and took a thirst-quenching swallow.

The team leader, referred to as the commander, confident that no one could overhear them, began to review the plan's execution scheduled for the following Sunday. He would permit today's meeting to only continue for an hour, now 57 minutes. Then they would all casually depart in the manner they arrived. After pouring out any unused drinks in the gravel. And bundling up all the cans and anything else they had touched in a plastic bag. That would go with the jeep driver who would drop it down one of many deep mine shafts as they four-wheeled out of the area.

The team was prepared if an off-duty cop or customer up in the outside bar or saloon observed something suspicious about them. And escalated that suspicion into a hurried call to local authorities on a cell phone.

Fortunately for the al-Qaeda team, Northern Arizona's budget constraints prohibited their use of quick-response police helicopters. This insured the assembled team could make good on any necessary escape. They'd be long gone before any cops could get to the saloon from the town of Parker or Lake Havasu City.

But just in case, a staged eighteen-wheeler, tractor-trailer/motorcycle accident was on stand-by, which would cause a road closure southbound on SR-95 below Lake Havasu City. The potential, on-demand accident had been set-up by an al-Qaeda sympathizer operating separately of the action team. Her job was to make sure that any potential police response wouldn't arrive in time to catch the terrorists. After all, the responders would have to carefully negotiate the narrow, rough desert roads leading the five miles from SR 95 to Nellie E, once they left the highway.

The team was advised that the explosives and other devices were already in safe storage. All they had to do was recover and place the deadly ordnance. The pre-prepared explosives packages would be recovered by the same methods that they had been hidden. Several scuba-trained members of the action team would rent a small power boat to retrieve the waterproof packages from the underwater mine shaft off Site Six.

American law required that prosecutors must prove that all components of a bomb were present at a common location, in order to secure an Intent-To-Bomb conviction. Therefore al-Qaeda had arranged to store the detonators at another location.

The second site was concealed just inside an underwater abandoned copper mineshaft in less than twenty-five feet of murky lake water on the California side.

Both sets of packages would be retrieved from the well-concealed caches after dark, twenty-four hours before the scheduled attacks. Once all the California and Arizona State boating patrols had gone off-duty. And the recreational boaters had secured from their historically nefarious nocturnal activities.

Absolute airtight operational security was vital to the success of the planned surprise attacks on the Great Satan. In this regard, al-Qaeda planners at home had insured that the four-man courier cell, nor the twelve members of the action cell, would ever meet.

The overall team al-Qaeda field commander was only known by the name of Mohammed, as was the majority of the world's Muslim male population. He casually sat with the team at the Nellie E. that afternoon, quietly discussing each of the simultaneous targets with the group. Team responsibility and assignments were verified, and questions answered.

Established al-Qaeda procedures required that the planners in any proposed strike action first prepare a detailed, written plan. This operations plan had already been approved by al-Qaeda leadership. The planners were in Osama bin-Laden's headquarters, currently in a well-hidden cave in the rugged mountains of northern Afghanistan.

A copy of the written plan was always given to the mission's team commander. This was not done because the leadership was worried that one of the action team leaders would forget something.

But rather as a formal indictment under which the entire team would be disciplined in the event of failure.

Muslim fanatics and extremists don't fear death, only failure. After the team commander insured each one of the individual members understood each of the required interactions, the list would be burned and the ashes disposed of appropriately.

The overall mission goal was to confuse, disrupt, and cause disorganizing chaos and unrest in the region. Each of the specified targets was to be attacked simultaneously at dusk on Sunday.

Destruction of the fabled London Bridge was assigned to three of the explosives experts on the team of operatives. That act would be an attempt to isolate the island from any rapid response from Lake Havasu City authorities, in addition to causing serious damage to one of the most important infidel tourist attractions in the region.

The specified task of sinking the *Dreamcatcher* water shuttle was strictly preventative in nature. The act was intended to both confuse, and hinder any cross-lake rapid response from the Tribal police at Havasu Landing on the California side.

Disruption of the weekly Sunday flea marketplace was planned mainly for chaos-creating purposes, with a few randomly placed, timer-controlled smoke bombs in various sales displays. One team member was assigned this task, and when completed, he or she would join up with the London Bridge team.

A major target had been assigned as the secondary assignment for two explosive experts on the al-Qaeda action team. They had orders to bring down one of the cell towers in the vicinity on Sunday. But only after they had placed C-4 explosives with the terrorist's trademark cheap Casio watch timers, on the entrance and egress cables which provide major electrical service, Isleside. Thus the residents and tourists on the island would be isolated. As usual, the terrorist's best friend, chaos, was the operational objective.

Five timer-controlled explosive devices were to be placed on randomly chosen private aircraft (especially any helicopters) at the municipal airport. If the regional air carrier had an unoccupied aircraft on RON (remain overnight) status, and only if it was found to be unguarded. Then the explosive's experts were to place explosives aboard that aircraft, after setting charges to take out the airport's emergency generators.

The combined attacks were strictly a diversion exercise to cause total disruption in the adjacent 'four-corners' area of northern Arizona. The diversion would serve to tie-up the Infidel's response to a larger al-Qaeda target attack. For security reasons, due to the elevated likelihood of apprehension and capture, this mega-target was unknown to the members of the action team in Havasu, as ordered by al-Qaeda's mission planner, Ayman al-Zawahiri.

Male and female devotees of al-Qaeda literally hate America. The FBI had been cautioning the world about that since 9/11. Now many al-Qaeda males were choosing martyrdom to Allah in Paradise. Many had already given their lives. The availability of fanatic Muslim males was not infinite.

Soon, it was necessary for bin-Laden to begin using young educated devote women, who were no less fanatic. They and their Muslim families had also watched American bombs falling on the Middle East destroying their country's infrastructure and killing thousands of men, women, and children.

That the Muslim leaders of their own countries had brought this hell down on their civilian population was either unimportant or unknown to them. The American and their hated Coalition had inflicted on-going grievous destruction and death throughout the Muslim world. Not to mention the Great Satan's support of the Israeli terrorists who continued to attack the Palestinian believers of Allah, even after they agreed to honor a 'Cease Fire' called to give the Infidel's President's *Roadmap to Peace* Plan time to work.

A Jihad was a no-holds-barred religious war. One that must now be modified to include female believers as the attrition among the young males continued. Even those women who were already mothers and wives would be called on to do their duty.

CHAPTER TWELVE

DAY 299—26 OCTOBER

FBI HEADQUARTERS
THE DIRECTOR'S WRATH
935 PENNSYLVANIA AVENUE, N.W.
WASHINGTON, D.C. 20535

In late 2003, reports summarizing detainee behavior coming out of Gitmo's Camp Delta begin change in tone and content. The CIA raises a Red Flag for the presidential administration in Washington D.C. President Bush wants to know 'why' the detainees, and their guards appear to be displaying marked changes in behavior.

The FBI's Assistant Director In-Charge/Counterterrorism, William "Bill" Savage, is ordered by FBI Director Mueller to find the answer to the president's question. Once Savage and his staff have responded, the FBI Director will report his findings to POTUS, and the president's National Security Advisor, Condolezza Rice.

Unknown at that point to the Director Mueller, is that ADC Savage, all along has had access via a back channel, to the DBR reports coming out of Guantánamo. And the ADC has begun to sense a gradual change in the verbiage, narrative, and tone used by those who prepare the periodic Camp Delta DBR reports.

Savage's heightened concern caused him to request further interpretation of the reports from one the of bureau's specialist assessment divisions. He has quietly enlisted the aid of the head of the FBI's Profiling and Behavioral Assessment Unit (PBAU), Dr. Charlene Gordon.

Gordon, a PhD in criminal psychology, is having her people go back through the Detainee Behavior Reports (DBRs) that have already been evaluated by the Central Intelligence Agency. Savage hopes that the FBI's psychologists will come up with a theory for the perceived deviation.

An experienced JTF detachment supervisor at Guantánamo prepared each of the DBRs under review. Those are the knowledgeable personnel that prepare the camp's raw data intelligence dispatches. Then those reports are disseminated back up the Military Intelligence chain-of-command.

NEWS BULLETIN
AL-QAIDA'S FINANCES ARE STILL HEALTHY, PROBERS SAY
By Douglas Farah
Washington Post
14 December 2003

WASHINGTON—Governments around the world aren't enforcing global sanctions designed to stem the flow of money to al-Qaida and impede the business activity of the organization's financiers, allowing the terrorist network to retain formidable financial resources, according to U.S., European and U.N. investigators.

Several businessmen designated by the United Nations as terrorist financiers, whose assets were supposed to be frozen more than two years ago, continue to run vast business empires and travel freely because most nations are unaware of the sanctions, and others don't enforce them, the investigators said. Several charities based in Saudi Arabia and Pakistan that were reportedly shut down by the governments there because of the groups' alleged financial ties to Osama bin-Laden also continue to operate freely, they said.

As a result, al-Qaida continues to receive ample funding not only to carry out its own plots but also to finance affiliated terrorists groups and to seek new weapons, the investigators and terrorism experts said.

30 END OF BULLETIN

The telephone call came to the FBI's Counterterrorism Assistant Director Bill Savage, in the early morning hours of a normally quiet Sunday. He was at his home in the Virginia countryside. Savage and his wife were startled by the not uncommon, but still damn irritating, phone call. It had come in the early morning hours. And on what to that point had been an otherwise perfect weekend.

A past directive from the U. S. Attorney General's office increased communications security for mid-to-upper FBI management. The list of agents the new ruling impacted, was nearly a thousand in number in the FBI alone. Included were Special Agents In-Charge (SAC) and above. Also some Special Agents assigned to handle matters of national security. And matters of extreme sensitivity, such as background checks on presidential Cabinet or Judicial nominees.

The ultra-secure, joint-NSA/AT&T designed, STU-III communication device was installed in each their respective primary residences, in addition to the one in their bureau offices.

Once the classified equipment had been installed, the Department of Justice (DoJ) procedure had been revised. Official calls were only to take place over the new, allegedly untappable, phone-like device. Even then, most of the FBI's top brass assumed that the STU-III would soon be replaced with the next-generation secure video-audio telephone.

After the device's unique third piercing ring, Savage threw aside his covers, and got out of bed. Groggy with sleep, he stumbled into the bathroom closing the door, again pissing off his wife, Delia, of 25 years. It was her combative nature to get demonstrative whenever she felt excluded from anything. Especially, as she put it, by "the God Dam FBI!"

It was her mistaken perception that the bosses her husband worked for at the Bureau apparently didn't consider her a very good security risk. The truth of the matter was that every spouse, or significant other, of every member of the Federal Bureau of Investigation was equally subjected to the same security procedures. But in Delia's mind, that didn't mitigate the insult she imagined in any manner.

After twenty-five stressful, but wonderful years, Savage was accustomed to his wife's tantrums. Especially whenever the STU phone rang at night. Sighing, Savage sat down on the throne. The device had been installed at his request, on the wall of the master bedroom's toilet. Which pissed off Mrs. Savage even more. Savage inserted the requisite key that now always hung on a chain around his neck night and day. Then he picked up the secure device's handset.

The usual 'pain-in-the-buttocks' code words were exchanged. Then it was time for the Bureau's remote voiceprint identification computer located in the J. Edgar Hoover building in Midtown Washington D.C. Its job was to verify that it was indeed ADC Savage of the FBI to whom the caller would be speaking. Then and only then, did Savage hear the alert but tired-sounding voice of the FBI Director Mueller over the handset.

"Bill," the conversation began. The Director considered himself a people-person. As such, he addressed everyone by his or her given name, at least initially during each contact. Never was it 'Assistant Director Savage' or some other formal form of address—always just 'Bill.'

The Director began, "I know it is early, Bill. Please apologize to Delia once again for awaking you both at this ungodly hour. But as they say in the movies, we've got a situation here."

"I've just been directed by the White house to bring in a couple of John Douglas' pshrinks on a consultancy, to monitor everything that comes out of Camp Delta down at Gitmo. POTUS again reminded me of a fact I've heard only about a dozen times since he appointed me to this job. That Douglas himself trained all the profilers in his firm. Since the president feels that retired-FBI agent Douglas is the crème de la crème, relative to past and present FBI profilers, his consulting firm got the nod."

Mueller hesitated briefly, before continuing, "Douglas' current contract with the FBI is to monitor and evaluate everything related to Camp Delta. And by related extension, the al-Qaeda/Taliban detainees."

"That is the interpretation of the President's National Security Advisor, and has been agreed to by Douglas. It will cover several areas of concern. The assessment will include the evaluation of everything from the Camp Delta commander's status reports to the 'puzzle palace' (Pentagon), to the twice-weekly interrogation product summaries of the small number of cooperating detainees."

With a note of exasperation in his voice, the Director added, "For good measure, the president also tossed in copies of the intelligence reports generated by those CIA pukes that the 'Company' managed to slip into the JTF guard force. Back when there was the mad rush to staff up security at Camp Delta for detainee management."

Savage had been privy to the existence of that tour de force. The CIA had never informed the Guantánamo Joint Task Force commander of the controversial action.

Because the CIA would then have to acknowledge that the U.S. Government thought it necessary to covertly monitor the conversations and actions of Camp Delta's highly qualified Joint Task Force Guard personnel. That certainly wouldn't have indicated the proper degree of trust in what was proving to be a very difficult assignment.

The JTF's mission was 'protective-custodial-duty.' The general public had been made aware of that. But less well known was how frequently other preventative and corrective actions were necessary. Over two-dozen detainees had attempted suicide over the past eighteen months. Each attempt had been fortunately interdicted. But nevertheless, the attempts had still resulted in serious injuries to the detainees. There had even been related injuries to the U. S. Security personnel charged with the detainee's security and well-being.

"Boss, how can I be of help in this?" asked Bill Savage. "You know all that intelligence data and product flows directly to CIA Director Tenant's office out at Langley. Then, after his analysts have reviewed it, select portions of their pshrink's evaluations are passed on to the president in his daily morning intelligence briefings, the DPBs."

Savage pushed on, "We, the FBI, are never supposed to see that stuff. That is unless some mucky-mucky over at Langley feels the Bureau can add something to the analysis. The quantity of such data-sharing exceptions, to date, number exactly *zero*."

"And then, only after the product has been evaluated by the CIA, summarized to the president, and he personally has directed further specialized review. By us, the NSA, DIA, or one of the other alphabet soap agencies."

Savage worked to calm himself down before continuing. He prided himself on being a professional that never let his personal opinions taint the way he did his job. So at this time, he just paused to await his boss's reply.

"Well, Bill," began Director Mueller, "apparently the president has decided that a second evaluation of the intelligence product the CIA is presenting to him each morning, would be of value, even if it is after-the-fact."

"The president was very favorably impressed by the successes our counterterrorism task force in Seattle achieved last year. The taskforce defending against a well-prepared, well-planned, and well-funded enemy. Despite all the damage al-Qaeda managed to inflict on the west coast before they pulled up their tent stakes, hopped on their camels, and fled Washington State to parts unknown. Your people managed to get in a few good licks."

Mueller continued, "The Washington State's Governor joined the president in expressing admiration for your team's accomplishments. And the president appreciates the FBI minimizing America's human and infrastructure losses during the al-Qaeda terrorist attacks of 2002."

"The president called me an hour ago to request I immediately implement a parallel and concurrent evaluation of the raw Gitmo intelligent product. And now I'm calling you!" He sounded peeved that he had felt obligated to go into such detail with a subordinate. Director Mueller then quietly asked, "Do you have any problem with that, Bill?"

"No, no, Mr. Director, I don't," replied Savage. "In fact, I was wondering how long it would take the CIA 'experts' to came to the same conclusion that our own PBAU folks have, Sir. We've been looking at a back-channel copy of all of the Gitmo intelligence product the CIA is receiving and . . ."

"Just a God Damned minute, Bill," interrupted Mueller. "Did you just say your people have had access to the same intelligence product out of Camp Delta, as the CIA? That same stuff the president apparently feels I, as the FBI Director, do not need access to, because it allegedly is beyond my *need-to-know*?"

Savage, invisibly to the Mueller, cringed, thinking *here is where my career implodes* as he responded to the Director. "Yes, Sir, I guess I am saying that."

"My counterterrorism division works with all the agencies involved in the suppression of terrorism. That ranges from Homeland Security to the bosses of the beat cops on the street. With all this interaction, sometimes our agents establish unofficial back-channel relationships with their peer co-workers. Even when those co-workers report to different intelligence or law enforcement agencies."

Savage took a deep breath, before rushing ahead, "Mr. Director, you no doubt remember Special Agent Diane Davis. And that she was instrumental in getting the job done when she led the 2002 taskforce in Seattle? She managed to get the job done without disrupting the chain-of-command. She never once exercised the 'dismissal of a incompatible party(s)' powers that came with the assignment. As you are aware, that unusual authority had been given her with the formation of the Seattle Regional Counterterrorism Taskforce, by the president."

"Once the Seattle 'furball' had wound down enough, to shift from the 'rescue' to the 'recovery' phase, Davis was up for reassignment. Due to her success in coordinating the taskforce, the president 'suggested' that she be assigned the task of developing the new U.S. Terrorism Threat Integration Center (TTIC) he envisioned. The new agency that today is headquartered out of leased offices on the beltway here in D.C."

The director fairly sputtered his next words. "Savage, are you telling me that you and your people has been covertly reading the CIA's intelligence product without anyone's knowledge, approval, or authority?"

"Well, Yes sir, I guess I am," Savage managed to say. "That is exactly what Agent Davis has been providing the PBAU boss, Dr. Charlene Gordon, with. You might say the FBI is kind of running a proactive concurrent parallel evaluation, off the books. You know, to make sure nothing slips by us this time. We all know how much finger pointing there was after 9/11. And how much of that was pointed at the FBI. I know it is illegal, and I know my ass could be grass for authorizing Davis to do that. I'm willing to accept whatever discipline you determine is appropriate, Sir."

There was a long moment of silence on the FBI Director's end of the secure line, a pregnant pause magnified by the STU-III device's circuitry, which didn't tend to accept lapses in conversation well.

Finally, the Director again spoke. "Bill, I assume Dr. Gordon's Behavioral Science pshrinks also voiced some pointed concern which supports the CIA's assessment? They also feel that the overall mood, morale and confidence level of the Camp Delta guard detachment, seems to unexplainably be slowly deteriorating?"

Savage replied, "Yes, Sir, for the past week it has been raising red flags in the Behavioral Science's head doctors evaluations. But no one has been able to specifically pin down the why, where or whatever. It is obvious that something unexpected is going on down there. But not something so flagrantly noticeable that the JTF guard personnel is consciously beginning to sit up and take notice. Since they don't notice it, couldn't quantify it if they did, they aren't going to mention in their reports."

"Whatever it is, it seems to be non-quantitative currently. It hasn't become so persuasive or obvious that the JTF command staff would begin to mention it in their reports. But the pshrinks say that 'something' could get serious quickly. And it has the capability of rearing up and biting us on the ass in the very near future. Problem is, as of yet no one has been able to isolate what that 'thing' is, Sir."

"Savage," the Director said softly, "Just when you were planning on bringing this highly significant fact to my attention? You, I assume, understand that the God Damn FBI director has a responsibility of keeping the White House advised at all times!"

Realizing his otherwise exemplary career might be on the line now, Savage worked to control his response. So it was with a calm voice that he replied to the Director. "Sir, if you'd consult your appointments calendar, you'll see that Agent Davis, Dr. Gordon and myself have an appointment with you here at Headquarters at 1300 hours this afternoon. We'd planned on bringing you up-to-date at that time, Sir. The early afternoon timing of the meeting was intentional to provide you the opportunity, if you so wished, to get back to the president before end-of-business today. The agenda includes our preliminary opinions as to what this all may mean, Sir."

There was another thirty-second pause, during which the STU's circuitry again tried repeatedly to reacquire the digitally encrypted conversation. Finally, the FBI director, speaking in an rough, cold-sounding voice, said "I'll see you all at 1 p.m. today in my conference room. None of you is discuss this matter with anyone else until that time. You have that, Bill? And I'd recommend that none of you, including Dr. Gordon, should make any future career plans before then either. I'm sure you understand, Assistant Director

Savage," Mueller shouted over the delicate secure transmission unit before hanging up the headset with a bang. The absolute silence over the line that followed, told Savage that he would have to remember to make arrangements with Director Mueller's wife to gain access to his home. A new STU would have to installed at the FBI Director's home, after he left for the office later that morning.

FBI conferences rooms designated for upper-management-use-only are located on the sixth floor of the J. Edgar Hoover building. The FBI headquarters is located Midtown on Washington D.C.'s busy Pennsylvania Avenue, as are some of the other more security-minded facilities in the Nation's capitol. However, admittedly, the Hoover building's sixth floor conference rooms are not as secure as the White house situation room.

But neither are they buried one hundred feet under the Rose Garden of the most well-protected building in the free world. The president's situation room under the White House is literally a room suspended within a room. Where copper wall cladding, white noise generators, and the full gamut of the finest anti-eavesdropping devices ever designed by man are constantly at-work.

The decision FBI Director Mueller has just made, electing to remain on the sixth floor—that housed his own private office—and use his own conference room, might seem to be petty and self serving to those who where not insiders in the Washington D.C. intelligence community.

But the top-secret Bureau counterterrorism team's presentation that day could well be incrementally expanded to include members from America's other six enforcement agencies. And although remote in the extreme, that could include POTUS, the president of the United States. The bottom line was that like all good administrators, Director Mueller valued being on his own turf in such times of potential crisis.

What was to be discussed this afternoon was a matter that was so sensitive it would be classified NOFORN (no foreign dissemination allowed). It could potentially represent an al-Qaeda decision to deal America yet another devastating blow. One that would be at least equal to, if not greater than, that which had nearly driven the Pacific Northwest into near financial bankruptcy in 2002. Or the attack that had taken 3,000 American lives on September 11, 2001.

Some of the finest brains in the FBI and CIA had detected an anomaly in the status reports coming out of the most hi-security facility of its kind in the world today, Gitmo's Camp Delta. That was the facility in the Caribbean where almost seven-hundred al-Qaeda and Taliban terrorist combatants were currently being detained for further investigation, interrogation, and debriefing. The facility was located on the grounds of Naval Station—Guantánamo Bay, or Gitmo, as it was referred to in the world media.

Joint Task Force 160, which reported to the U.S. Southern Command, headquartered out of Miami, administered the day-to-day custodial requirements at Camp Delta. Delta was a new detainment center, which had been hastily constructed on a 485-foot high bluff, looking seaward from the western shoreline perimeter of the Guantánamo Naval base.

Guantánamo Naval Base had been either vacated, and or their presence downsized, by a number of other U.S. commands over the past twenty years. Budgets had gotten tight, and continuing to use Gitmo was growing increasingly inefficient for some of the base's long-term Navy tenants.

As a military base's support structure is based on a formula of its utilization, several critical Gitmo service organizations had gone wanting. Included in that classification, among others, was Base Maintenance, and Base Security. This left the base understaffed and unprepared to handle much more than the routine operational duties of a U.S. military bastion. Especially one situated deep in enemy territory on Fortress Castro—on the island of Cuba.

The Chief of Naval Operations, a military academy graduate, or anyone else with a rudimentary grasp of strategy, tactics, and logistics couldn't ignore the losses to Gitmo's infrastructure over the past two decades. No one knowledgeable would go on-the-record to claim that today's base could be successfully defended against all comers. Let alone remain impregnable, should a dedicated, sizable, well-equipped enemy assault it.

Even a dedicated holding action, which admittedly would costly in terms of United States' lives, would be ineffective after a couple of hours of determined enemy assault.

Of course, Pentagon strategist's had ago long told the pixel pundits (newscasters in the media) that "on-call armed air support from the U.S. mainland could arrive over the battlefield within the first hour of such an assault, which would tilt the engagement back into America's favor." As with so much in the downsized military, that largely was just so much optimistic bullshit.

Attending the Come-to-Jesus meeting in the FBI Director's secure conference room that day, was FBI Supervising Agent Diane A. Davis, currently on-loan to the president's newly established U.S. Terrorism Threat Integration Center headquartered on the beltway in Washington, D.C.

Also attending was Dr. Charlene Gorton, the PhD heading up the FBI's profiling assessment department. Arriving last was FBI ADC/Counterterrorism, William Savage. All had arrived for the 1:00 pm meeting with FBI Director Mueller, twenty-five minutes early, in order to set up their PowerPoint presentation.

The Federal Bureau of Investigation, indeed the entire US Justice Department, was on the leading edge of utilizing proven management tools to increase the efficiency of their diverse operations. PowerPoint was just a single example of the tools, which have been enthusiastically embraced by the world's leading law enforcement organization. Another modern tool, more investigative in nature, is Rapid Start, a case management tool.

All the FBI agents worked on the presentation until it was complete. Then they grabbed a cup of Mueller's special blend Columbian coffee, took their seats, and settled in for the brief wait for the Boss to arrive.

CHAPTER THIRTEEN
DAY 300—27 OCTOBER
ABOARD A SAM FOX FLIGHT
DESTINATION CUBA
DEPARTING ANDREWS AIR FORCE BASE
CAMP SPRINGS, MARYLAND

NEWS BULLETIN

GUANTÁNAMO
TRANSLATOR FACES
SPYING CHARGES
By Staff Writer
New York Times
17 November 2003

WASHINGTON—A former civilian translator at the Guantánamo Bay naval base was indicted by a federal grand jury Wednesday on charges of improperly gathering military information and lying to the FBI.

The case against the Arabic-language translator Ahmed F. Mehalba has attracted wide attention since his arrest at Logan Airport in Boston on September 29 because he was the third person linked to security breaches at Guantánamo prison.

(Next two paragraphs—Redacted)
Officials said a CD with 368 documents marked 'secret' was found in Mehalba's bags.

In the other two episodes at Guantánamo, military officials have charged Ahmad Al Halabi, an Air Force translator at the base, and Captain James Yee, a Muslim chaplain at the prison, with mishandling classified information.

30—END OF BULLETIN

It was eighteen hours later when the big Gulfstream V (U.S. Armed Services model designation, C-20H) 'SAM FOX' long-range executive jet rotated the weight off her nose gear. This action served to hydraulically 'unload' the two oleo strut extensions on the front gear assembly with an audible *thump* as the nose wheel began to retract into the craft's forward wheel well. Once completed, the hydraulically operated, aerodynamic carbon-fiber wheel doors would begin to close. The sleek aircraft picked up her fiberglass nose. Then lifted gracefully off from the restricted 9,751-foot-long runway 19L at Andrews Air Force base outside Washington D.C.

The specially configured, dual turbofan Rolls Royce engine-powered jet swiftly climbed to its initial assignment of 37,500-foot cruising altitude.

The $40-million-dollar, ninety-six foot, five-inch long speedster then banked on its ninety-three-foot, six-inch low-swept wingspan to come to south-southwest heading for the flight out of the Washington air traffic control (ATC) area.

Guantánamo Bay is located on the southeastern tip of the island-nation of Cuba. With an advertised flight duration range of some 6,500 nautical miles, the trip was well within the C-20's capability, especially since she carried a limited passenger load. Even with baggage and personal equipment, she was carrying far less that the aircraft's advertised 6,500 pound of cargo-lifting capability.

Yesterday's Gitmo-concerns meeting now seemed to have occurred weeks ago at FBI Headquarters. It had taken place with the FBI Director Mueller on one side of the large oak conference table, and FBI Assistant Director In-Charge (ADC) Savage, and Supervising Agents Gordon and Davis, on the other. The meeting, after the obligatory 'Come to Jesus' speech by the Director, had been very productive. Davis, who was rumored to be on the fast-track at the FBI, noted that the director's enthusiastic ass-chewing of the group for failing to keep him in the information loop, lasted a mere twenty-three minutes.

Robert Mueller was a respected FBI Director in times when they seem to come and go, at the whim of their benefactor. He was prone to wearing well-starched button-down blindingly white dress shirts, and single-hand knotted contrasting color ties. Director Mueller preferred to be photographed in his shirtsleeves and often appeared with his starched cuffs buttoned, exposing only the leather watchband for the non-designer-name timepiece he wore inverted, as do a number of men his age. He was clean-shaven and had a longish sensitive-looking face, which tended to support his believability. He had a full head of mostly dark hair, parted on the extreme left, and combed over and back to the right, with medium bushy eyebrows. He tended to gesture only using his left hand, although there was no evidence that this was anything other than habit and not the result of any medical problem.

There was no explanation necessary for the emergency meeting. No excuses from his subordinates were offered or expected. Each of the three FBI agents felt fortunate to have at least temporarily escaped the Director's legendary fury with just a medium-sized ass chewing.

As planned, ADC Savage began the Camp Delta presentation to the Director. Special agents Davis and Gordon followed his introduction. Gordon was the director of the FBI's Profiling and

Behavioral Assessment Unit (PBAU) division. The presentation team expressed the fact that the intelligence reports coming out of Camp Delta, while certainly factual, in all cases seemed to have an added indescribable something—an unpleasant odor—something that wasn't being voiced by the JTF report's authors. A nebulous something that the Joint Task Force's soldiers and interrogators hadn't yet been able to put their respective fingers on.

Camp Delta was Operation Enduring Freedom's austere newly constructed, state-of-the art, high-security prison on the US Guantánamo Bay naval base, located on the southeastern tip of the island of Cuba. Thinking persons considered it a potential powder keg. The Republican administration, the U.S. military, and the U.S. Congress were sometimes included in that category.

The 'Coalition' (read, the Americans) was currently detaining nearly 700 foreign national, enemy-combatant, al-Qaeda/Taliban prisoners at Guantánamo. Although the detaining facility was located on a U.S. Naval Base, the fact remained it was outside the confines of the continental United States. The detainees were being held there without due process of law.

Yesterday's hastily scheduled meeting had been held in conference room C603 at FBI headquarters in Washington D.C. The subject matter was seen by all as possibly being the harbinger of a long-anticipated, blood-red flag-raising, bell-ringing, siren-wailing alert that neither they, nor FBI's respected Director, could either ignore or minimize.

Supervising Agent Diane Davies at age thirty-two was fast becoming a minor legend in the FBI. Only a few years previously she had been assigned as a rookie Supervising Special Agent to Seattle's regional FBI field office. She had recently returned from receiving extensive training in evaluating and addressing counterterrorism incidents. Where she had completed a yearlong syllabus in counterterrorism training, while being temporarily assigned to FBI headquarters in Washington D.C.

Her direct superior was an ADC whose office was located at the Bureau's Peninsula Avenue headquarters in Washington. Upon her graduation for the extensive training, and only after he had conferred with the Seattle Field Office SAC, FBI Assistant Director/ Counterterrorism William Savage had reassigned Special Agent Davis.

Davis' new job held first-line supervisory responsibility for anticipating, evaluating, reporting and interdicting any terrorism actions in the FBI's expended Pacific Northwest region. As it turned out, Davis didn't have long to wait to be rigorously tested in her new assignment.

As the Seattle Field Office is itself an FBI division, located in a larger region, Davis' responsibility covered a lot of territory. Her responsibility ran from the Canadian border on the north, and south to the California border. It included the states of Oregon and Idaho, and of course, Washington State. It was admittedly a lot of responsibility for the young FBI Special Agent. She was only five-years post graduation from the FBI Academy in Quantico. However, Savage noted that Davis had been at the head of her normally male-dominated class.

Davis was a Governmental Affairs Masters graduate, as a number of successful FBI agents were, of the renowned Brigham Young University in Utah. As might be expected, she also happened to be a practicing Mormon. She continued to tithe ten percent of her FBI salary to the Latter Day Saints church, which was no less or no more than the LDS church's expectations.

When Davis found herself excelling at the FBI male-oriented academy, she had set a number of career goals for herself. First, she wanted to be the first African-American woman assigned as Special Agent in-Charge (SAC) of a major West Coast FBI Field Office (FO). Davis figured if she achieved that, then her second goal was to be appointed Director of the FBI by age fifty-five.

Among the extensive training she had received for her new assignment, was the tough physical and mental, if elective, road to certification as a member of the FBI's elite Hostage Rescue Team (HRT) that also trained at Quantico. Her completion of the course to the amazement of her male peers had been something that at that time had been an unknown accomplishment for a female agent. Not even the high-profile agent, Candice Delong, a former FBI agent and profiler, had chosen to take on the men in that particular deadly specialty.

Davis, upon graduation from the toughest the FBI could throw at her, returned to the Seattle Field Office. Being single, she bought a small condo in the somewhat esoteric University District, north of the city.

She was considered by the majority of her co-workers to be extremely hardworking, and freely admitted her weaknesses. The greatest that at five-foot, six-inches tall, she felt short. And there was her tendency to arrive late at office meetings, which were no street agent's favorite activity. Her inborn tendency to be late meant that she had a rather impressively thick file in the Seattle City clerk's office. The file was filled with copies of parking tickets, all stamped PAID, which her latent tardiness had earned.

Diane was attractive and single. Earlier in her career at the Seattle field office, she occasionally dated a Special Agent on the office's regional SWAT/REACT team. Since she had been back in D.C. for training, he had retired and reportedly was happy running a hunting guide business in Eastern Washington. Theirs had always been a relationship that ran both hot and cold.

Davis' career had taken a major leap in mid-2002. The president of the United States had received credible intelligence from the CIA of another threatened al-Qaeda attack. The report came almost a year to the day, following 11 September 2001.

The president, POTUS—his official designation, BUCKSKIN—his Secret Service handle, 'suggested' to FBI Director Mueller, that he assign Agent Davis as head of the Pacific Northwest Counterterrorism taskforce. The taskforce was being hastily formed at that time, based on the new intelligence the CIA had carried to the president.

The president reasoned with Director Mueller that the proposed assignment "was definitely inside the limits of Davis' new job description. Director Mueller, privately felt that the important appointment of an African-American female could bring him the president political benefit in the upcoming 2004 national elections.

During the year following, Davis' leadership in the Seattle

counterterrorism taskforce, which operated out of the Seattle Field Office, was exemplary. She had personally headed up a bloody but successful FBI-HRT counter-strike action. Her team's actions had prevented the hijacking of a $200M dollar 747-400 out of Paine Field in Everett, Washington. Al-Qaeda terrorists planned target for the hijacked Boeing widebody, had been the destruction of America's newest and most-expensive capital warship, the *USS Ronald Reagan*. The brand new next generation nuclear-power aircraft carrier at the time, been tied up in the Bremerton Naval Shipyards for post-maiden voyage adjustments and repairs.

Agent Davis' leadership skills and direct involvement had also saved the valuable Skagit Valley farming community in Washington State from certain flooding and economic ruin.

Her careful assessment of even unlikely threats had also prevented a US Army aircraft filled with two Green Beret A-teams from being blown up during their planned landing on what turned out to be a heavily-mined runway. The A-Teams had been responding to terrorist attacks on two critical mountain passes between Eastern and Western Washington.

Davis had gone on to operationally participate in one of the two terrorist mountain pass infrastructure attacks. In this latter case, her bosses—known to be politically gender-insensitive—made sure her bravery and efforts had not been without some criticism from FBI headquarters in Washington D.C. The Bureau was changing, but it still was a male-dominated organization that cringed whenever a woman won recognition.

Of course, the taskforce's counteractions had certainly not been a clean sweep by the forces of good. Hundreds of al-Qaeda dormant agents, living under deep cover in the Pacific Northwest, had still managed to bring down the landmark Seattle Space Needle with another hijacked aircraft. They had managed to disable the vital I-90 and I-520 bridges over Lake Washington for nearly six-months.

Submarine-transported al-Qaeda Special Operation Forces (SOF) staged a mildly successful attack on the Everett Naval Station, in Washington State. And had been successful using a number of explosive devices to bring brought down the Deception

Pass Bridge. The bridge had been the only land route onto Whidbey Island, home of Whidbey Island Naval Air Station. All of which had thrown the Pacific Northwest into a severe economic and military crisis.

Opposing what the FBI HQ's sixth-floor naysayers were saying, the president credited Davis' aggressiveness with providing the necessary wiggle-room the PNW needed. The region would have to strive to work itself out from under the current financial cloud brought on by the terrorist attacks.

The president continued her defense saying that without Davis' leadership, and the accomplishments of the multi-agency taskforce in Seattle, things could have gotten far worse, perhaps beyond recovery. The attacks in the PNW had killed nearly one thousand victims. In the president's opinion, Davis and her action teams were responsible for avoiding thousands of additional American deaths.

Dr. Charlene Gordon PhD was the forty-five-year old head of the FBI's Profiling and Behavioral Evaluation Unit. Along with Crime Scene Investigation, PBAU was another field of law enforcement currently popular with American television viewers and crime buffs. Gordon was a skilled professional with a combined medical degree and criminal psychiatry doctorate from the impressive Harvard School of Medicine. At six-foot tall, the fragile-appearing, northern European pale-skinned Scandinavian blond was an impressive woman, rumored to possess a phenomenal photographic memory, as coincidently, did Agent Davis.

The FBI PBAU units highly educated staff served as a invaluable support organization in preparing suspect profiles for the nation's law enforcement agencies. Often the PBAU profiles aided under-funded police departments in the apprehension of America's most brutal and dangerous criminals, those involved in violent crimes, including the forcible abductions of children, serial rapists, and serial murderers.

Charlene Gorton's department and the FBI were widely praised for their work. PBAU's profiles, prepared using the division's years of experience in developing leads, determining strategies, and taking each piece of evidence down to its lowest common denominator, had saved victim's lives. And by doing so, had indirectly supported the capture of America's most violent criminals.

ADC Savage had gone to Dr. Gordon for help. The PhD was a fifteen-year veteran of the FBI. Therefore she was no stranger to the often bitter, inter-agency conflicts than the CIA and FBI seemed to endlessly perpetuate. Gordon, having seemingly a endless-fountain of on-going curiosity, had said she'd be more than happy to review whatever raw intelligence ADC Bill Savage had. And she'd at least temporarily overlook the questionable methods by which Savage's subordinates had gained access to the product.

ADC/Counterterrorism, William "Bill" Savage, a newly appointed but well-experienced former HRT Team leader, now reported directly to FBI Director Mueller in his new job. A big man, six-foot, four-inches tall, still bearing the physique of the former college star linebacker he had once been, Savage having only recently begun to become acclimated to the FBI's corporate-like headquarters power structure. He was considered by his subordinates to be an agent's agent, a FBI poster-boy. Since he had 'been there—done that', he tended to not be as autocratic and cover-your-ass-oriented as were his peer ADCs on the sixth floor of Washington D.C.'s FBI headquarters.

Savage had graduated magna cum laude from the famed Harvard School of Law. He later would also earn a Doctorate in Business Law from that revered institution. It was generally assumed within the tight-knit world of the Intelligence Community, that one day he would add the position of 'Director of the Federal Bureau of Investigation' to his already impressive resume if he kept his nose clean. Savage was aware that his subordinate, Agent Diane Davis, had similar career aspirations. ADC Savage was said to speak seventeen languages, and was fluent and able to write in fifteen of them.

In the crisis meeting on the sixth floor of the John Edgar Hoover building headquarters held eighteen-hours previously. Mueller had patiently listened to the three agents as they presented, reviewed and summed up their reports. Then the director had asked each to respond to some very pointed questions.

Their respective answers would be invaluable in preparing a briefing document he would take to POTUS later that afternoon. Director Mueller huddled with his staff to come up with a suggested action plan for the president.

Basically the Director, the ADC, and the two federal agents agreed that the FBI had to make an immediate on-site evaluation of Camp Delta. Politically, The JTF's commander would have to be informed of the discrete investigation.

The FBI is not considered to be an expert in federal penal facility security. Thus the FBI team being sent to Guantánamo would restrict itself to investigating pending accusations of espionage.

That task would involve the careful review of the past work habits at Gitmo of three specific individuals. Each at the time was being detained stateside. All three either had been or still were, employed as either Arabic translators or U. S. military Muslim Chaplains at Camp Delta. All of the suspects were male and had been apprehended by the U.S. Transportation Security Agency (TSA) during routine security inspections at U.S. commercial airports. Two of the suspects been stateside at the time, on scheduled vacations. The exact status of the third individual was unknown to the FBI at the current time.

The two FBI Special Agents dispatched on today's SAM FOX flight, were tasked with determining exactly what each of those three individuals had been up to at Camp Delta. And whatever it turned out to be, was it significant enough to generate collateral damage that would hinder the United States' war on Terrorism? The two women had prepared a preliminary list of possible lines of the inquiry. The executive jet aircraft out of Andrews had departed for Guantánamo eighteen hours after the trip request had been faxed over to the Pentagon. The request had to be approved by the Air Force's Chief of Staff.

Davis had hacked a typewritten draft copy of the meeting out on her laptop. It had been electronically sent to a remote laser printer at a clerical station on the floor, adjacent to the conference room they were using.

As soon as the sheets of still-warm paper fell into the laser printer's out-tray, one of the Director's security-cleared administrative assistants promptly hand-carried it back into the meeting. The assistant then waited for Davis to proofread and initial it, then turned and left quietly the room, closing the solid oak door.

As soon as Director Mueller had signed off on the travel request, and initialed the agent's preliminary plan, copies were distributed to the ADC and the two FBI Agents. Director Mueller excused himself, left the room, collected his always-present security contingent and walked rapidly to his office. There Director Mueller inserted his key, and grabbed the handset off his STU-III. And initiated a priority call to the president's Chief of Staff, telling him he needed to talk with the President *now!*

Twenty-five minutes later, Director Mueller returned to the conference room. He informed the agents that the president, without consulting anyone else on his Cabinet, or the CIA Director, had made the decision to approve the deployment of FBI Supervising Agents Davis and Gordon (Dr.) ASAP to Guantánamo Bay NAS.

POTUS had concurred with Director Mueller's recommendation that one of the Air Force's fast executive jets be utilized to get the two women to Guantánamo. It was critically urgent that the agents investigate the three subject's past work habits. And to attempt to ascertain if the suspects had any help in obtaining the supposedly secret information that had been found on their persons. The White House travel office, once nearly eliminated by Hillary Clinton, changed some existing senatorial 'junket' plans, to insure an Air Force C-20 would be available within eighteen hours. It would depart from Andrews Air Force base in Camp Springs, Maryland.

A more detailed review of Camp Delta's security procedures would have to be developed by a far larger joint JAG/NCIS (Judge Advocate General/Naval Criminal Investigation Service) taskforce. The joint taskforce was currently being formed under the orders of the U.S. Southern Command in Miami, Gitmo's folder holder. But its commander, USMC Colonel Marvin Lokkesmoe, would report directly to the Pentagon.

The joint JAG/NCIS taskforce was hurriedly getting all their ducks in a row. A US Air Force C-17 was scheduled to fly the combined team, their equipment, and necessary rolling stock into Guantánamo Naval Station less than twelve hours after the FBI agents first touched the ground. Once the two agents had arranged for an initial 'meeting of explanation' with the Joint Task Force's commander, Major General Montrose.

Space capacity aboard the C-17 aircraft would not be a problem for the combined JAG/NCIS task force. The huge Air Force Boeing Globemaster II cargo plane had a payload of 170,400 pounds, and could carry 154 troops, or a M1 Abrams Main Battle tank, or three AH-64 Apache helicopters.

ADC Savage was concerned by the Director's decision to send the two FBI agents to go to Gitmo without backup. It was a dangerous assignment, and he said so to Director Mueller. The Director again contacted the president, and they tossed 'what if' scenarios around briefly.

Then POTUS called the Pentagon. They were to order the U.S. Southern Command in Miami, to instruct General Montrose of the their 'expectations' concerning the following: The General was to be given the factual explanation as to why the two FBI agents were there. However, he was ordered to tell his subordinates or anyone else who might inquire, that the two agents were members of the International Red Cross (the IRC—the International Committee of the Red Cross.). The mission of the IRC inspectors was a Pentagon-approved, no-notice surprise inspection of conditions at Camp Delta.

The two agents were also to make sure that the JTF commander, General Montrose, received a 'headsup' about the incoming JAG/NCIS joint taskforce. It was preferred that it came from his folder holder, or from two-star General Montrose's Command in Miami, but if that had not occurred, then it would be passed on diplomatically by two FBI agents.

The JTF commander was to be advised, if he had not already been, that two dozen JAG/NCIS investigators, operating on the express orders of his bosses in the U.S. Southern Command, but reporting directly to the Pentagon, would be 'wheels dry' at Guantánamo within the next twelve hours. The president explained to Director Mueller that he was hopeful that revealing this fact to the General, would buy at least grudging cooperation from him for the FBI team. Without qualification or reservation, General Montrose was to make whatever arrangements the FBI team requested, and provide for their security 2400/7.

The Joint Chiefs of Staff (JCS) Chairman was to make sure the U.S. Southern Command contacted the JTF's commander after his meeting with the 'International Red Cross inspectors,' to insure the General understood the Pentagon's and hence the president's expectations.

The Southern Command C.O. would brief the JTF commander on what the JAG/NCIS investigators were going to be doing. Also the level of support he was expected to provide without reservation to accommodate the large en-route multi-specialty investigative team. Montrose's boss, the Southern Command C.O., would also attempt to answer any questions the general had. And attempt to make the General understand that there was no suspicion directed at him personally in this highly unusual surprise inspection.

The FBI Director himself was to immediately contact George Tenant, the CIA Director, in person. He would discuss the president's orders with him. He was to inform Tenant of the FBI's highly unorthodox actions in obtaining documents for which the Bureau had no specified mandated need-to-know.

A inter-agency confrontation was sure to follow over the intervention by the FBI in a CIA-directed mission. But it would have to wait until the damage assessment report was couriered back to Washington by the investigating FBI agents now en-route to Camp Delta.

The U. S. Air Force's SAM FOX C-20H aircraft had departed from Andrews AFB at 06:54:00 Local time. As soon as it arrived at the cruising altitude called out in the flight plan the pilot had filed with the Federal Aviation Administration (FAA), the seat beat light was extinguished.

A 'Chuck Yeager-drawling' Air Force pilot's voice soon was heard over the cabin speakers, correcting one of their misassumptions. The PIC (pilot-in-command) advised them their trip to Guantanamo would be extended to 1,300 nautical miles. The additional distance was due to the necessity of first making a brief touchdown at the Miami International's Dade County Airport to pick up some anti-toxin medicine. Apparently, six JTF guards were ill at their eventual destination. The guards were reportedly suffering from severe food poisoning, of an unknown nature and source. The men were fighting for their lives in Guantánamo's hospital dispensary on Hospital Cay.

Secondly, the fast C-20H leaving CONUS (the Continental United States) for Guantanamo, would be forced to take a roundabout flight path to their intended destination, to insure they avoided Cuban air space.

Lastly, in the current day, there was the not unexpected threat of Cubans outside the U.S. compound attempting to 'down' U.S.A.F. aircraft. Several times in the past month, unidentified persons had fired one or more surface-to-air missiles at incoming aircraft landing at Gitmo.

The particular aircraft they were currently riding in had not yet been 'scheduled down' for the maintenance period, required to permit the installation of the Air Force's tried-and-proven, heat-seeking missile diversion package. The package was relatively lo-tech, and consisted of the co-pilot's manual ejection of multiple aerial flares that burned hotter than the sun's surface. To disrupt radar if the missile so equipped, tin-foil-like reflective chaff could be command-ejected by the flight crew from specialized dispensers mounted under the jet's belly.

The pilot drawled on, informing the three passengers and his fellow crewmembers that when they initiated their approach into

Gitmo's military airfield, the aircraft would be at its most vulnerable from the enemy missiles. Therefore, the passengers should expect that the pilots would bring the sleek aircraft down in a steep, accelerated descent onto the runway at Guantanamo's Leeward Field. As was mandated by the U.S. Air Force regulations in any high-risk environment.

Even with the stop in Miami, the overall flight took less than four hours. Then after a heart-stopping, stomach-dropping high-speed descent onto the main Gitmo runway at Leeward Field, the forty million dollar jet kissed the runway smoothly. Albeit a bit faster than the Air Force's operating manual specified.

The bird had just began its rollout down the long runway, when the pilots braked hard. Abruptly, they steered the aircraft off the runway onto a high-speed taxiway. From there, the aircraft rolled at an unusually high rate of speed directly in the open portal of a immense, otherwise empty, high-bay aircraft hanger. They had arrived at the heavily fortified Leeward Field, at Guantánamo Naval Station.

Once the screaming twin turbofan, tail-mounted engines had been shutdown, the exit doorway on the port side of the aircraft opened. Only then were the two civilian-clothed agents, accompanied by the class-A uniformed Naval MSC (Medical Services Corps) officer carrying the refrigerated vaccine in an aluminum Halliburton-type briefcase, permitted to disembark.

They were met by an armed U.S. Navy five-man Base Security contingent. All of who were wearing body armor. The agents both noted that the body armor worn by the guards included the optional substantial ceramic insets that slid into front and rear pockets in the black vest. That served to answer everyone's unasked question as to the magnitude of the perceived risk that currently existed here at Gitmo.

The armed security detail, dressed in dusty fatigues caked in dried sweat, was equipped with locked-and-loaded M249 light machine guns. The MGs weighed in at close to fifteen pounds without the ammunition. Apparently the risk factor had caused the Navy to replace the customary and lighter M-16s the guards normally carried. It was obvious that the chain-of-command was expecting trouble here at Guantánamo.

There was little doubt in the two FBI agent's minds. The guards had not been provided for their personal safety. But rather to insure that both FBI agents promptly and with all due dispatch immediately reported to the JTF protocol office, across the bay, on the windward side of the base.

The two women agents and the male naval officer barely had time to grab their luggage, before the three were hustled into a pair of idling Humvees. The uncomfortable ride down the southeast side of the Leeward Air Field took but a few minutes. During which time, their welcoming party totally ignored them.

It was hot, humid, sticky, and the ride bumpy. None of the models of the U.S. military Humvee were known for their air conditioning excellence. Or, for that matter, having a reasonably comfortable chassis suspension.

The base security patrol, again totally without comment, stopped only to drop the passengers and their luggage off in front of a shack. Apparently, they were now under the command and control of a rugged, armed U.S.N. Master Chief. When the Humvee had driven up, he had been leaning against a guard shack that had obviously seen better days. The guard post was the restricted entrance to Gitmo's Leeward side ferryboat dock.

The U.S. Naval officer was courteously asked to show his military I.D., and traveling orders. Both agents were totally ignored, as if they didn't exist. Surprised, they returned their apparently 'invisible' fake IRC credentials to their pockets, wondering what the hell was going on. A uniformed naval officer gets asked for I.D., but two women in mufti who were both carrying concealed service .40 caliber semi-automatics, are waved through as if their presence was of no consequence.

Gitmo Naval Station was unevenly bisected by Guantánamo Bay. Thus, a handful of old dilapidated vehicle-capable ferryboats were the only method of surface transportation across the harbor. Each was powered by an old single-cylinder Atlas engine, which was noisy, but dependable.

The old, 'single-lung' boats plied the bay on a more-or-less regular schedule. Their ponderous routes took them across the water, which extended between the airfield field on the Leeward side, and the equally well-guarded Windward side. The bulk of the base infrastructure was located on the Windward side. The base's combined size totaled forty-five square miles.

In the situations where fast response by Base Security, the commander, or other transportation needs were deemed to be urgent by the Powers-That-Be, there were armed military helicopters of several types. The most ominous airships currently visible were a pair of heavily-armed and rocket-hung AH-64 Apache gunships. They appeared to hover over and follow the ferry's route of travel. Other military helicopter types, all armed the two agents noted, seemed to flit to and fro in the air above the base. Guantánamo was deemed, by treaty, to be American territory.

The navy ferry had room for a couple large vehicles, such as six-by trucks, or a single Bradley fighting vehicle. Then the remainder of the main deck space dedicated to dozens of grimy, uncomfortable, canvas benches, some exposed to the weather.

In relative short order, the ferry arrived and docked at the busy, if rundown waterside terminal, on the Windward side of Guantánamo Bay. The terminal was located due east of the Gitmo's other airfield. That airfield, McCalla, was now largely abandoned due to its runway length limitations. The short runway was unsuitable for modern, shit-hot, military jet aircraft. As a general but not always hard and fast rule, military aircraft, unlike their civilian brethren, were not equipped with thrust-reversing clamshells on their powerful turbine engines.

At Windward, the ferry was met by another enlisted contingent of armed U.S. Marine guard escorts. The MSC officer was meet by an old 1959 Cadillac ambulance, painted navy gray. It had large red crosses adorning all four sides and the roof. The military messenger was borne away with dispatch, presumably en-route the base's hospital with his life-saving vaccine.

The transportation provided for the two tired FBI agents consisted of two more shop-worn Humvees, driven by armed marines. Agents Davis and Gordon apparently were expected to carry their own luggage. Even though under U.S. military protocol, each agent carried the assimilated rank of Colonel. The camouflaged Humvees swallowed their luggage, as the two women sank into the rear well-worn, dusty canvas bucket seats in the lead vehicle. Surprising, as the vehicle departed the Windward wharf, they picked up an escorted of armed U.S. Army outriders on ancient-looking, but obviously well-maintained, 500-cc British Norton motorcycles.

In less than fifteen minutes, the tight convey of vehicles pulled up in front of the JTF Commander's headquarters. The naval buildings the two women had the limited opportunity to observe thus far, although heavily defended, looked shabby. Realistically this reflected the climate. It was nearly impossible to adequately maintain such facilities in a tropical humid climate.

The structure's poor condition probably more importantly, indicated the U.S. Government's unwillingness to throw good maintenance dollars after bad. After all, the US Navy was attempting to maintain a base that Cuba's President-For-Life Fidel Castro and his demonic brother Raul, probably could wrestle away from the American defenders in less than twenty-four hours, albeit with a significant loss of soldier's lives on both sides.

Davis and Gordon entered the once-majestic building, again lugging their gear. There they decided to ignore the brusque orders of their armed escorts. The guards apparently been told that the two 'IRC' women were to be taken directly to the General's office to check-in.

But, in defiance, Davis and Gordon had stopped, stared the troops down, walked to a nearby rest room door, and had entered, slamming the door for emphasis, and locking it behind them.

After about twenty-minutes of doing whatever female law enforcement agents do in women's rest rooms, they exited smiling. They permitted the now frustrated guards to escort them the remainder of the way to meet Gitmo's JTF commander, Major General Montrose.

In the general's reception area, they checked-in with the aide-de-camp, easily recognizable by the MOS device he wore on his uniform shoulder. Then, they stacked their luggage in a convenient corner, and asked when they might see the General.

The aide had already been briefed to expect the 'inspectors' visit. As ordered, he forced himself to forego the normally-obligatory check of their credentials. He picked up one of his several multi-line desk telephones, and briefly spoke into the mouthpiece.

When the aide softly returned the headset into the phone's cradle, he politely informed the women that Major General Montrose would see them immediately. He rose from his cluttered desk, and walked to an adjacent connecting door. He knocked, waited for the reply, then opened it, and stepped in.

Backing to one side of the doorway, the aide proceeded to announce the two women as apparently nameless "Inspectors with the International Red Cross."

The women walked into the room, and directly up to the desk behind which sat an impressive officer, and took up a 'hard brace.' The General seemed amused, and gestured to a couple of cracked and patched vinyl military-vintage side chairs. The agents ignored the gesture, and remained standing at attention.

The aide, after receiving a nod from the General, hurriedly left the spacious if plain office, closing the door firmly behind him.

Both agents, having been taught military protocol as part of their training, remained standing. General Montrose rose, and invited both of them to be seated, before again taking his chair behind the massive old wooden desk. That piece of furniture would have looked more appropriate at the head office of the Chase Manhattan Bank in New York City. Both agents removed their FBI credentials from their jacket's inner left chest pockets, and handed them to the General Montrose.

After he had studied both of the oversize, small gold badge-inset black leather cases for a moment, he shook his head. He tossed the 'box tops' back across the desk to the agents, who returned them to their pockets.

The general turned and looked out the rear window of his office. His bullet-proof view included several well-manicured softball fields, which extended in a westerly direction. In the general direction of the newly constructed state-of-the-art Camp Delta.

The camp housed nearly 700 al-Qaeda and Taliban detainees. They all had been captured in combat, during the War on Terrorism. The prisoners were all considered violent, and were being detained under rigorous guard. The camp was under the direct control of the Coalition's Guantánamo JTF, Joint Task Force 160.

There were some short weather-cracks in the thick but aging bullet-proofing material used in the general's rear office windows. Both of the agents in their earlier assignments for the FBI had noted that this was typical of America's military buildings. Which often had been thrown up overnight in tropical climates such as Cuba.

General Montrose was a trim, efficient-looking Army officer, six feet or so in height, whom Director Mueller had told them was well-respected by both the military at-large, and the president. Despite his close-cropped military haircut, tending toward the color of gray, he looked quite at home, looking slightly like Douglas McArthur, sitting behind a desk in his freshly pressed Class A uniform, however he was not toying with a unlit corncob pipe.

Reportedly, it had been this outstanding, can-do reputation of the General's that had prompted the president to volunteer him for this thankless assignment, hundreds of miles away from his home in Florida. The hastily constructed Camp Delta detainment facility at Guantanamo was a critical part of the president's War on Terrorism. As such, its command mantle must be borne only by proven, the best, and most loyal officers in U.S. military service.

In General Montrose's wife's mind, it was more a case of 'no good deed goes unpunished.' Currently, all Gitmo billets were sans dependents. Mrs. Montrose had been forced to remain behind at their Miami home. Like any other good military wife, she attempted to not trumpet her frustration with their current assignment.

However, being only human, She fumed daily. She knew that if this god-forsaken assignment hadn't untimely interrupted her husband's career, she would have taken her place in Washington D.C.'s social circles.

The rumored 'word' at the Pentagon was that her husband would soon be appointed to the Joint Chiefs of Staff. But both the general and Mrs. Montrose had been in the army a long time. They knew better than to complain about the current assignment. No one in history has ever gotten away with telling a president of the United States 'no', and gone on to bigger and better things. Five-star Army General Georgie Patton to name but a single example out of many.

When General Montrose did turn back and speak to the FBI Agents, they could tell he was past the point of being just tired. His command staff's 'pointy end' was being blunted. It had been the leading edge of the America's War on Terrorism for several years now.

Last night, long after the general had returned to at his well-guarded residence on the Guantánamo Base, he had received an unexpected call from the President's National Security Advisor, Dr. Condelezza Rice. The call had gone to his headquarters, as the bases' telecommunications people had not yet been able to debug a problem with the STU-III at his residence.

To receive that secure telephone communication, he'd have to redress. The general, by that time comfortably in-bed because he hated to watch the bases' cable television unless there was a sportscast scheduled, complied without comment. That required that he roust his security detail from their office behind his residence. Four heavily armed troops were required to accompany him by procedure, anytime he traveled anywhere on the forty-five square-mile base.

There really hadn't been any other option. The Pentagon demanded that all official conversations must be conducted over the STU-III secure phone. That device was to be used exclusively for all security matters.

As it was after midnight, he had already given his personal aide and driver the rest of the night off. Which Montrose knew meant they were probably perching on a ratty bar stool down at the Senior Enlisted Men's club, kicking back a few 3.2 brews, before the start of another hot, humid day on Cuba's southeast coastline.

So Montrose had hurriedly redressed in a pair of old black shorts, ratty tennis shoes, and a spiffy new gray t-shirt. It had logo lettering 'Commander Navy Region SE' lettering over the left breast pocket, and CNRSE's Motto 'Enabling Warfighter Readiness' on the back. The general purposely left the t-shirt untucked, to cover of the butt of his service-issue 9 mm Beretta. His handgun was stuffed into a ballistic nylon clam holster, hung on the reinforced elastic band of the athletic boxer shorts in the small of his back.

Picking up his direct telephone line to Base Security, he asked that the duty officer roll out his security detail. The men would pile into several of the armored Humvees parked behind the residence. Then they would transport him to his office for the stateside call.

By procedure, the transportation detail would remain on standby at the near-vacant HQ, awaiting his for further orders.

When the call finally came through on the STU-III, the message turned out to be from the president. It served to fully awaken him, despite the hour. The president had told him that normally reliable sources had put the administration on heightened alert.

Reportedly, there was a possibility (as one of the White House's more aged housekeepers used to say) that something "wasn't kosher" down at Camp Delta.

Further, that the source of the information behind the alert was so sensitive that the president hesitated to even discuss it over the secure STU-III device. POTUS apologized to General Montrose for being so cloak-and-dagger. But told him that he was sending to a couple of ranking FBI agents down to see him early the next day. To brief the general on the president's concern.

The president gave the commander an unofficial headsup that he could expect the agents, who would be wearing civilian clothing, to do some snooping around, of course with the general's concurrence.

Montrose readily agreed—things in his estimation had been

far too quiet at Gitmo—for far too long. The general and his bosses at U.S. Southern Command in Miami were well aware that if Castro wanted their butt, it was figuratively his for the taking.

Castro was well aware that any assault on the Guantánamo Naval Base, which included Camp Delta, could only be accomplished at a great cost of manpower on both sides.

Everybody in the U.S. Southern Command knew that such a opportunistic raid by Fidel Castro would result in the complete eruption of the region's relative stability. This referred to the tense cease-fire-like atmosphere that both sides had been forced to live under, on and off for decades.

Specifically, Gitmo's western perimeter, at the base the bluff on which Camp Delta perched, would be a bitch to defend. To one degree or another, the detainee camp was always at-risk. But it would require a substantial enemy assault launched from the base's southern shoreline perimeter to breech Camp Delta's fenceline and bunker system.

Precautions had already been taken. The new JTF-guard force compound, Camp America, had been specifically sited and constructed to place a major obstacle to any such assault. 'America' was located less than two hundred yards east of Camp Delta, on the base's vulnerable southern shoreline.

Camp Delta sat on the bluffs, which oversaw the beach. Realistically, there was little question that eventually, a well-equipped, well-supported enemy assault force would eventually prevail. The general had no doubt that directly or in-directly, that is where the enemy assault could be expected. But as of yet, the president had not indicated that any attack was imminent. Montrose calmed himself, and vowed to take things as they came.

General Montrose had respectfully asked for further details. But the president, just as respectfully, asked him to wait until the FBI team arrived at Guantánamo Naval Station the following day.

Then, the president had told him, "If then if you have any concerns you feel may being overlooked after talking with the FBI, I want you to feel free to place a personal call to me here at the

White House. I'll have the Chief-of-Staff instruct the White house switchboard to find me, anytime, at anyplace, to take your priority call." Montrose thought that sounded fair enough, so he thanked the president for the 'headsup' call.

The general, once it became obvious that the president had terminated the call, carefully replaced his headset back on the cradle, and locked the STU phone with the key that was constantly on his person. Then he sighed and called the base dispatcher to make sure his security team was standing by, as he had ordered.

He locked up his office, said goodnight to the detail of sentries, which roved the interior and exterior of the building 2400/7. Montrose walked out and got in the idling olive drab armored Humvee, behind which were clustered the vehicles of his security detail.

He asked the enlisted driver to drop him again at his residence. On the brief ride back to his quarters, and his previously warm if lonely bed, he thought it probably would be for what promised to be a very short remaining night of troubled sleep.

CHAPTER FOURTEEN

DAY 301—28 OCTOBER

JOINT TASK FORCE 160 HEADQUARTERS

GUANTÁNAMO BAY

CUBA

F BI agents Davis and Gordon had taken seats across the large oak desk from Major General Montrose. The women identified themselves to him, and waited to begin their briefing. The general was again reminded why no military officer ever welcomes surprises.

The two federal agents waited respectfully for the General to open the conversation. He used the brief moment of silence to review the facts to-date, as was his habit. *Christ all mighty,* he thought, *how has this slip by my interrogation and detainment experts at the camp?*

Is my U.S. Joint Task Force embedded with foreign spies and provocateurs, and if so, how badly? How many al-Qaeda enemy agents or sympathizers are involved? How deep are they submerged in JTF 160's operations here at Gitmo? How long have they lain dormant? Who are they, and how big of pile of feces has our complacency permitted the JTF to step into here?

Shaking his head in disbelief at his unanswered thoughts, he leaned forward in his chair and welcomed the two agents to Guantánamo. He asked if either of them would "like a cup of Guantánamo coffee, prior to proceeding." Both women answered "no," but were quick to thank him for the offer of hospitality anyway.

There was no debate about who had seniority on the FBI side of the desk. However, Gordon had decided to permit Davis to take the lead with General Montrose. After all, the intelligence reports had been obtained through Davis' excellent back-channel contacts in the first place.

Dr. Gordon planned to just to sit back and listen to Agent Davis brief the general. She'd only jump in if she thought that providing additional background detail was necessary. Or if her input was requested by either.

After Diane finished, the PhD would explain PBAU's assessment of the intelligence product. And her group's best guess as to cause and effect. Gordon saw her role as a mentor to Davis. As such, she'd do her best to assist Special Agent Davis in answering the JTF Commander's questions.

General Montrose, having deciding the FBI agents could wait a little longer to begin their presentation, reviewed some of the thoughts he had earlier that morning.

He thought, *I understand the logic behind the president's concern that something is amiss, security-wise, here at Gitmo.*

In fact earlier this morning, after talking with the president, I put out some subtle feelers on my own to some of my old military friends. I was pleasantly surprised to receive a number of prompt responses.

Back channel scuttlebutt had been passed on to him from his former WestPoint classmates. Some were now assigned to the U.S. Southern Command. They had informed him that both the CIA and FBI had uncovered what they classified as "serious security breeches" at Gitmo. He carefully thought through what his old classmates had told him.

Those agencies had apparently performed independent reviews of Gitmo's intelligence reports, under presidential directive. The intelligence summaries had been prepared from the interrogation product collected from the detainees at Camp Delta. His staff, and the JTF interrogators, had done the actually preparation of the summaries.

The reports were forwarded directly to the CIA, at the direction of the Joint Chiefs.

The 'Company' and the FBI felt that the tone of those reports appeared to support a "marked and unexplained decrease in the detainee's active resistance to the interrogations. And a corresponding unexplained increase in their level of cooperation with their JTF captors over the past six-weeks."

The general had privately acknowledged to himself that those concerns covered the full gamut of interaction between the guards and detainees. Including their responses to the occasionally absurd orders of the guards, the non-confrontational routine the detainees had surprisingly settled into, and the abrupt halt to the detainee's many previous attempts to commit suicide. Fortunately, the alert guards had interdicted each of the attempts, preventing any of them from being successful.

And overall, the usually hardnosed JTF guards had been passing on their educated observations to Command, that some previously closed-mouthed detainees, now sought out every opportunity to converse privately with the Muslim chaplains on-staff, and even the civilian-contracted Arabic translators during the near-daily two-hour interrogations.

Alarmingly, now that Montrose thought of it, a significant number of the Muslims detainees had come to display, in one way or another, a previously absent positive willingness to follow the guard's orders and directives. Even though a month ago it had been one big screaming session, day in and day out, to get the detainees to acquiesce to any mutual cooperation, even those that directly or indirectly benefited them personally.

One example of this, he mused, was that he noticed an increased number of the terrorist detainees had begun indicating with hand gestures that they wished to be permitted to visit Camp Delta's excellent sick bay facility.

Last month the detainees couldn't be dragged to the American doctors for treatment. Now they enthusiastically requested to visit the infirmary anytime they got a slight fever. Or suffered a minor sun burn from being exposed to the weather in those cells that were constructed out of chain link fencing, rather that solid walls.

On a further note, the general now admitted that he himself had begun to subconsciously notice that most of the detainees were now cleaning their meal plates—even of things the Muslim religion forbade them to eat. Something they had never done in the previous months since they had been captured by the Coalition, and transported to Guantánamo for incarceration.

He and his JTF Gitmo staff until this morning, and apparently foolishly, had been operating under an unsupported conclusion. The Americans had subconsciously convinced themselves that the previously militant terrorist cadre had finally begun to accept the austere life and restricted environment that was Camp Delta.

After all, as in every other penal facility in the world—good behavior could eventually bring prisoners some small degree of privilege and accommodation—but not as quickly as bad behavior would take it away from them.

General Montrose shook his head, and then acknowledged to himself if no one else, that his JTF troops must be getting complacent. Or perhaps he himself had come to be too sympathetic to the detainee's fears the interpreters had reported. The most predominant being that the Americans were only being truthful when they said the detainees would be kept in lifelong captivity here at Guantánamo. Members of the current administration in Washington D.C. had occasionally taken to threaten that action in possibly unwise and/or politically motivated press releases.

Montrose has personally seen to it that there were prohibitions against any and all action or behavior that could be, even remotely, considered by the media to be unnecessary physical and/or verbal harassment of the detainees.

But some of his less educated and less confident U.S. JTF

guards no doubt couldn't resist occasionally rubbing a little figurative salt in the psychological wounds of the terrorist detainees.

Like all other American troops assigned to JTF Guantánamo, the guards had excellent access to all informational media in their new quarters at Camp America. The 'lifetime of incarceration' threat certainly fell into the forbidden category, in the general's opinion. The newly constructed JTF troop's full-service barracks and compound was located on the Kittery Beach, below the Cuzco bluffs, on which perched Camp Delta.

With an involuntary shudder borne of twenty-plus years in the service of a country that often was not considered by her worldly peers to be the 'good guy,' he cleared his throat and addressed himself to Agent Davis. It seemed obvious that she was the nominal lead of the FBI investigation team seated across the oak desk from him. He began by sincerely apologizing for the nearly twenty-minute period he had keep them quietly sitting in his office, while he mentally organized his thoughts.

"Ok, Agents" he began. "In retrospect, I understand what the Bureau is saying here. The detainees, instead of getting less compliant due to their enforced restrictive surroundings and virtual incarceration, are suddenly putting on a front of being totally accepting and overtly cooperative. That despite being in what even I'll admit are not particularly pleasant surroundings."

"The CIA, the president, and at least the two of you, appear to believe there is no way that should be considered to be 'normal behavior' on their part. And now that I think about it, I agree that dog won't hunt here at Camp Delta."

"We have only to put ourselves in their shoes. What would happen if we Americans were forcibly confined on a bug infested/rodent overrun tropical hot-box island for the rest of our natural life. And during the entire time, we were held without access to our families, friends, mail, or what-have-you. Any of us with a shred of self-respect left, would be trying to tear out some guard's eyeballs. At least anytime the guard force became complacent or foolish enough to permit their attention to be distracted."

"Yes, Sir," Davis again spoke. "That is specifically what the Pshrinks think is completely wrong with the behavioral evolvement of the detainees incarcerated here at Camp Delta. Dr. Gordon's PBAU group has compared a normal detainee behavioral profile, developed over the past thirty years by the U.S. Bureau of Prisons, with what we are observing here. Their conclusion is that the current detainee's actions, excuse me in advance, Sir, for saying so, is just bogus and diversionary bullshit!"

Dr. Charlene Gordon, stepping into the dialog. "The detainee's behavior, actions, and what limited verbal intercourse some of the Arabic-speaking guards apparently have with them, is nothing but well-practiced drivel. A party line their leaders here have told them to parrot.

She continued, "The al-Qaeda and Taliban detainees being held here, aren't acting normally. They hate Americans worse than they hate Israel. Something major has recently come down the proverbial 'pike.' Information concerning some action, perhaps an escape or rescue, that the detainees believe has a high probability of success. Something so outrageous it has convinced even the most negative individuals among the detainees to go along. Something has brought them unexpected hope—when they had already given up hope for a miracle."

Davis returned to the conversation, excitedly, "What we need to determine, is in what form this 'perceived help' is anticipated. We have to know the basics—who, what, when and where. If we fail to determine that, we might just get our collective ass kicked here."

After checking her hand-written notes, Davis continued. "Logically, it has to be some variant of a well-planned, reasonable staffed and equipped, large-scale rescue assault on the base here, specifically on Camp Delta. And lets not forget they need to also incapacitate Camp America. Al-Qaeda can't have all those hot-blooded young American studs running around with automatic weapons, when they are attempting a 'sneak and peek' right under their noses."

The FBI agent proceeded, "The attackers would have to make arrangements to tie up the off-duty JTF guard force in their barrack's compound. The attack must be coming from al-Qaeda, or the hundreds of Cubans the CIA's Keyhole KH-11 satellite shows are camped just outside Guantanamo's perimeter security fencing. You know the Cubans wouldn't attempt an attack on Gitmo without the express orders of President Fidel Castro, or his damn perverted brother, Raul."

Agent Gordon interrupted politely, "You know, Sir, I assume you and I are on the same wave length and will stipulate that neither of us are big fans of the CIA. But all the intelligence intercepts, they and National Security Agency have made in the past two months, indicate something is going down. Something very, very big. And that Guantánamo is right in the middle of it."

"General, Sir, at the risk of being repetitive here," as Davis attempted to diplomatically segue her way back into the conversation, "let us review what we know up to this point. Realizing your time is valuable, I'm only going to cover the U. S. apprehensions of possible-enemy espionage agents who previously were directly or indirectly detailed to the JTF command."

"I'll restrict it to the three JTF staffers that TSA and U.S. law enforcement either detained or arrested during the month of September 2003. Will you permit me that time, Sir?" Davis inquired respectfully.

"Go ahead, Agent Davis, and you damn well better have your facts straight when you are accusing my people of capital crimes as serious as this," Montrose rumbled, ever the staunch protector of his troops, and his command's reputation.

Davis hurried to continue her carefully thought-out presentation. She felt it was important to get everything out on the table, before the general had any second thoughts about continuing this highly charged meeting with the FBI agents. A military commander is entitled to ask a member of his staff to sit in on any discussions of the type they were having. It was accepted practice and one the FBI never resisted.

"On or about 10 September 2003," Davis began, "U.S.

Customs personnel, acting on an educated hunch we understand, detained Army Chaplin Captain Yousef Yee as he was getting off a commercial aircraft that had just flown into Jacksonville, Florida. This accomplished former high school wrestler, immaculately clean shaven, wearing prescription wire-framed glasses, and a buzz cut, was summarily detained after certain classified, confidential, sensitive, secret and NOFORN-classification materials were found in his possession."

"Chaplin Yee, while cleared to read classified information, certainly had no authority to have detailed Camp Delta site layout cell arrangement sketches; name and home addresses of some JTF guards; or in fact any specific information on the detainees, in his possession. Yee's assignment here at Camp Delta, per the Pentagon's personnel assignments officer for Gitmo, was strictly as a Muslim chaplain. Captain Yee incidentally is one of only the seventeen such Muslim chaplains, out of the 3,100 or so chaplains currently in the U.S. military service. He has an otherwise-excellent service record."

"Chaplain Yee speaks Arabic, and reads it well enough to use the Koran. He currently has been detained without charge, and is being held at the Navy Brig in Charleston, SC."

"Does that about cover the detainment of Chaplain Yee, Sir?" asked Davis.

The general, as would any commander loyal to his subordinates, snapped back at the agent saying, "I supposed that is what the Feds are claiming but the Transportation Security Administration (TSA) better be damn certain that the Captain is guilty. And that Yee was afforded all his rights, Agent!"

"I'm trying to avoid prolonging this discussion unnecessarily," Davis said. "However I still have to do my duty. The FBI—Dr. Gordon, myself, and our superiors—feel it would be healthy to get some of the more germane details out on the table. It is important to insure that the three of us are all on the same page in the choir book. Do I have your concurrence with that, Sir?"

Major General Montrose, who had held the thankless JTF Camp Delta assignment for over two years, sighed. He gestured, indicating that Davis and Dr. Gordon could continue.

"Then, on to 23 September 2003," Davis proceeded. "Ahmed Fathy Mehalba, a naturalized U.S. Egyptian-American civilian, and a contact employee of Titan Corporation, a trusted government's supplier, was arrested when he deplaned a commercial flight in Boston. That flight originated in Egypt, with the eventual destination of Boston's Logan International Airport."

"Mehalba was forcibly detained when he was found to be in possession of 132 contraband computer disks, a U.S. Department of Defense I.D. card, and a JTF Gitmo security badge on his person. The latter he attempted to conceal, and initially refused to display, or turnover to the TSA security personnel."

Referring briefly to her notes, Davis persisted, "TSA's subsequent evaluation of the computer disks found in Mehalba's possession, revealed Classified, Sensitive, Confidential, and Secret information. Combined, the information on the disks ran almost 2,000 pages in length."

"The suspect Mehalba, age 31, was an Arabic linguist, assigned as a translator to this command. And as such, he had unrestricted access to both Camp Delta and other classified NOFORN information. Included in his possession was an electronic disk containing nearly 8,500 personal messages from detainees. Mehalba is currently being held under U.S. civilian jurisdiction in Boston. Is all of that correct, Sir?" Davis respectfully inquired of the JTF commander.

"Yes, Agent Davis," the general replied. "You appear to have all the FBI's ducks in a row, at least up to this point. However, you are going to be sadly disappointed if you expect me to stipulate to the accusation that Mehalba or any member of my command is guilty of anything," the general reminded her.

Davis reshuffled her reference pages, and continued. "Moving on General, to 30 September 2003. To Syrian-born, U.S. Air Force Senior Airman Ahmad I. Al-Halabi, permanently assigned to Travis Air Force Base in California, but tad'd here at Gitmo, as an Arabic translator."

"Al-Halabi was arrested for having prohibited U.S. maps, detainee names, cell location information, and other U.S. military secrets in his possession. For that reason, Airman Al-Halabi is currently being detained under military jurisdiction at Vandenburg AFB in California. Is that correct, also, Sir?" asked Davis.

"Again, Agent Davis, it appears the daunting FBI apparently knows the facts, however tenuous, questionable and unproven, in detail," muttered General Montrose. "Now, is that the end of this quaint dog-and-pony show? I know JTF Guantánamo has suffered serious security breeches lately. Or at least thanks to the FBI, I do now."

"I only can say that as fellow professionals, the FBI better have come here with a proposed solution, not just another God Damn list of unproven charges!" he said, slamming his hand to the desktop.

Now Agent (Dr.) Gordon verbally stepped into the breech, with the intent of giving both the General Montrose and Agent Davis a chance to cool off. "Sir, we are regrettably obligated to advise you, as the JTF commander, of the following. The DIA (Defense Intelligence Agency) has advised FBI Assistant Director of Counterterrorism, and through him, the FBI Director, that their intelligence spooks currently have their eye on one or more naval personnel. These individuals are currently assigned to here at Gitmo."

The general stood up, and gave the universal 'time-out' signal. It indicated he wanted to interrupt the discussion. "Great, Dr. Gordon. Does the FBI have any additional good news for JTF 160, today? Now, if we are we though, or at a convenient interruption point? I'd like to step outside for a brief smoke, and then make a head call. Ladies? Agents?" asked the general.

"Just one brief moment, if you will, Sir. Then perhaps all three of us can heed the call of nature, or grab a quick smoke, or whatever," Agent Davis doggedly continued.

"As you know, Sir, all of the JTF personnel who are suspects are being detained stateside. One or more of them may be charged under multiple counts of espionage. The JAG folks will throw in the fact that they also gave false and misleading information and testimony to the TSA."

Reading now from notes, Davis continued, "The Pentagon will insist on bringing charges of a violation of the General Orders;

illegally transporting U.S. classified military documents and giving information to the enemy; disobeying direct orders; lying to investigators; severe security breeches; bank fraud; and failure to report contact with an agent of another government. Add to that a multitude of other civilian, and/or military charges under the UCMJ (the Uniform Code of military Justice)."

"Each of the charges has a price tag running from five years of imprisonment and a $215,000 fine, to the death penalty by firing squad or legal injection." Davis paused, then said, "Now, with your permission, Sir. May I suggest we all take a fifteen-minute break. Then assemble back in here for the continuation of this discussion?"

The general grumbled his agreement. The three filed out of the general's office. Outside the door, someone had posted the two Marine guards apparently to insure the meeting wasn't interrupted.

Major General Montrose, displaying his West Point-ingrained courtesy, paused to point out the location of the closest woman's restroom to the two agents. Then he opened a side door, and stepped out onto a small roofless courtyard for a much-anticipated cigarette. Although neither smoked, a few minutes later, the two women joined him for a breath of tropically fragrant air.

Sixteen minutes later, they all were back in the general's office. Fresh coffee and some Cuban pastries had mysteriously appeared during their absence. After taking several sips, then setting down her cup, Davis continued. "The CIA's satellite reports that someone here has apparently managed to establish 'spot communications' with the al-Qaeda head shed, back in the caves of northern Afghanistan."

"Either bin-Laden, or the new guy who is replacing him, Abu Hazim al-Shar'ir." This caused General Montrose to raise his eyebrows in surprise. Davis had spoken the name, using the correct Arabic inflection. *That was a revealing fact, he thought. It certainly suggested that Davis had attended the government's foreign language school at Monterey, California. An administrative-assignment to the in-demand school almost never happened.*

It meant that she had been plunked down into one of the school's few seats, without having to go through the years-long waiting line. Arabic Language School was a unusually hard-to-obtain training billet. He'd himself had fought for a slot there for nearly three years before being accepted. That fact alone confirmed that Davis was indeed on the FBI's management fast track.

Davis continued. "General, I'm sure you have heard about al-Shar'ir—you know, that twenty-nine year old Yemenite wiz kid, who bin-Laden allegedly brought in to fill one of the empty slots in his management team. There must be a handful of available billets. Most of the senior al-Qaeda lieutenants have been killed or captured by the Coalition."

"The National Security Agency maintains that bin-Laden is no longer using his satellite phone, having learn his lesson from his previous screw-up. They believe he, along with select members of his personal staff, remain in deep hiding in Afghanistan or Pakistan."

"The National Security Agency (NSA) haven't been able to pull an intercept on his satellite phone for months," continued agent Davis. "So we've got to conclude bin-Laden is using foot couriers for his communications, with exception of whomever he is occasionally able to message here at Gitmo."

"Although it follows no logic I am aware off, the bad guys appear to be using some type of obscure text-messaging over an encrypted, instantaneous-burst-capable cell phone. Similar to what the Israelis have developed, and our own Delta Force guys use in the field. At least, that is the current intelligence community's theory of how al-Qaeda manages to communicate with their 'alleged' mole here."

Gordon added, "The CIA also reports that they have multiple confirmations, including some from fluent Arabic-speaking and appearing HUMINT (human intelligence) in the Saudi Arabia, that al-Shar'ir may have gone to ground there. At least those al-Qaeda terrorists that still haven't been exposed."

"The terrorists still in-residence in Saudi Arabia—for whatever reason—have been extremely successful, to date. They've been able to maintain whatever cover has made them successful deep-cover dormant agents. At least those 'sleepers' whose personal fear of bin-Laden and his discipline, has kept them from running around the world frantically trying to give birth to another terrorist atrocity." Dr. Gordon, returned her notes to her briefcase, and paused briefly.

"Ok," the general interrupted, "I understand what the problem is. What has to be accomplished immediately is to determine the complexity, scope, and timing of the threat. Let me share a secure phone call I received early this morning from the Joint Chiefs of Staff, via Southern Command."

"I understand your bosses in Washington, and perhaps even the president, feel that it would be best at this time, for you to continue to pursue a portion of the overall investigation. In other words, digging up the background on the three JTF suspects currently being detained stateside. It is also my understanding that the Powers-That-Be don't want to bringing Naval Intelligence or the CIA into that portion of the problem. I am assuming that is because the three, if proven to be spies, will be charged and tried under civilian law in the nation's courts. I admit bringing in the FBI will ensure the men get a fair airing of the matter at trial."

"But does this means that we here at JTF are effectively under an presidential gag order not to discuss this? Does that mean I can't provide requested feedback to my boss at U.S. Southern Command in Miami? What if I get a call from the Pentagon? Are my boss's orders and inquires superseded by the FBI's? The command of JTF 160 had placed me right in the middle of what we refer to as a situation around here. A major gray area—one that could well mean my job."

"Yes, Sir." Agent Davis quickly interjected. "I know it is putting you right into a firestorm that you don't deserve. But you'll admit it is at least possible that there may be a few more members of the JTF, or some additional civilian linguistics contractors, that are part of this plot."

"The president feels that we need to identify these people, and accumulate irrefutable evidence to pin these seditious bastards whatever their motivation to the wall with very sharp pins, before they catch wind of the investigation, and flee. Hell, it is possible that any additional yet-unidentified spies, have gotten cold feet, and left the island using the daily outbound C-130 air shuttle. Putting a news blackout on this, at least temporarily, is the only weapon the United States has available," Davis concluded.

"Well," the general began in a deceptively soft voice, "just how the hell do you plan on identifying them, let alone catch them? If the chickens have already flown the coop, where does that leave the security of this Command?"

"Sir." Davis said, "As I understand the process around here, everything including the detainee's visits to the first-aid dispensary, any chaplain visits or other counseling, and especially all interrogation sessions, are video and audio taped. Sometimes in duplicate, and mostly without either the detainee and interrogator's active knowledge."

The general attempted to interrupt Davis to defend Camp Delta's interrogation procedures. However, she plowed ahead, refusing him an opportunity to present his arguments. She knew there were valid reasons as to why things here, were procedurally, as they were.

"General, with all due respect, please hear me out here—it is important." Davis requested. "I am not being critical of Camp Delta's interrogation or security procedures. However, please consider the seriousness of what we are talking about here, Sir. Don't you agree, General that we've got to go the extra mile to ensure that we get all the 'doers'?

"I may not be proficient in military justice procedures, Sir," Davis admitted. "However, it is my understanding that the Geneva Convention's accepted rules of interrogation, include the practice of personnel isolation. Detainees, especially detainee's seen to be purposely resistant or non-cooperative, both with the interrogators assigned the job of debriefing them, as well as the entire interrogation process, are not permitted to converse with fellow detainees."

"That includes taking meals together, sleeping in common barracks, praying together, or participating in any group activity. The logic is that any failure to keep the combatants separated only serves to stiffen the detainee's personality. And that certainly is not in keeping with what Dr. Gordon here, would politely refer to, as maintaining custodial psychological control."

Dr. Gordon picked up where Agent Davis had left off. "It is my understanding that nearly seven-hundred terrorist suspects are being currently detained at this base. Most of whom are Muslims who do not speak English." Montrose leaned back in his chair, because it was obvious to him where these two FBI investigators were headed.

The president has dispatched this team of experts here to Gitmo, regardless of what it could do to my career, thought the general. I don't blame Command Authority for taking that position. If our responsibilities were reversed, I damn sure would be digging to get to the bottom of this SNAFU regardless of whose ass would be in the wind.

Dr. Gordon spoke up, "If I understand our orders from FBI Director Mueller, our assignment here is not to investigate the Camp's security procedures or even make recommendations. And certainly not to point fingers of blame. That isn't our job, no matter the dubious reputation, undeserved or not, the Bureau has earned in the past."

"What I suspect we have here is a potentially dangerous situation. It may directly involve any number of the detainees directly. Deep cover spies may have passed on the in-coming messages from al-Qaeda to the prisoner population. Perhaps the same individuals that TSA has already detained. They all served here as translators and/or Chaplains."

Gordon continued, "We know it is impossible to eliminate the practice of mouth-to-mouth passing of information, inbound or outbound. I suspect the 'word' got around to the entire terrorist detainee population in very short order."

Dr. Gordon sought the eye contact with the general, and continued. "The contraband information—all accessible to the JTF chaplains, guard force, Arabic translators, contract maintenance personnel—included the names and cell locations of every detainee incarcerated here. It also included illegally-taken photos and stolen maps of the base, classified details of civilian and military flights into and out of the bases' Leeward Air station—all of which would be of invaluable interest to anyone planning an assault on Guantánamo."

"The three JTF staffers who have apprehended and detained,

additionally had in their possession both written and electronic letters and messages, to and from detainees, families, friends or fellow—conspirators. Are we agreed on this, Sir?"

"Yes, completely, Agent Gordon. Please continue," General Montrose stated loud and clear. He knew the meeting was now getting down to the git-go. The general had not noticed any recording devices in the agent's possession. However, his military training made him aware that information of this nature, and at this level of seriousness, usually winded up on someone's detailed courtsmarshal charge sheet. Thus, it would be the height of foolishness for any military officer to think what was being said in this meeting, would not eventually end up being placed on-the-record.

Davis took over, "Then would we be also be safe in acknowledging, General, that Camp Delta, despite being considered to being administrated under humane conditions by a majority of the free world, it is considered by the Muslim faith to be nothing but a heavily-restrictive, inhumane, detention-and-interrogation operation? One where during the past twenty-four months, the United States has held nearly 700 terrorists without due-process of law, without charging them with criminal crimes, or granting them prisoner-of-war status?"

General Montrose again nodded his head, not bothering to attempt to explain the differences between what was necessary here, in dealing with the terrorists. Say as compared to interacting with car thieves and pickpockets back stateside, where confinement was the worst any prisoner could expect, in a politically correct confinement facility, in the contiguous United States.

Agent Davis, beginning to feel some professional sympathy for the general now, nevertheless continued to plow ahead. "A British court has called Camp Delta a 'legal black hole', or a 'rights-free zone.' Twenty of the detainees—some of them more than once—have attempted suicide. The world is calling this place a SuperMax prison. Some of the United States' spokespersons have alluded to the fact that the people here may be detained indefinitely, without access to attorneys or visits from family."

Grim faced, General Montrose took a deep breath, and urged the agent to continue, again knowing only too well where this conversation was going.

Dr. Gordon, attempting to soften what she considered an overly aggressive interrogation technique on the part of the young and aggressive Agent Davis, spoke up now. As a psychiatrist/psychologist she was committed to modifying the direction and scope of this conversation, to one that would elicit more cooperation. She intended to use more sugar, and less vinegar.

"General Montrose," Gordon continued, "what we specifically need from you at this point, is your permission to spend up to ten days here at Gitmo, roaming the base at-will. We'll require the services of a single bodyguard each, that individual to be of your choosing. Due to the gender sensitivity here, Diane and I will do our best to adopt the appearance of a couple of old maid Red-Cross inspectors."

"We'll not approach or attempt to speak with any detainee. However, we may interview one or more members of the JTF guard detail, always when they are off-duty. This is your advance notice that we do intend to visit the guard's quarters at Camp America. Such visits will not be cleared with your office in advance. They may or may not be conducted during normal business hours."

Referring to small black FBI notebook she had taken from her briefcase, Gordon went on, "Both of us will require secure housing in what ever passes for your BOQ here. We'll require a reliable civilian vehicle for transportation. We'll also require a totally secure audio-visual facility, available for our use 24/7, remote to the camp. We'll utilize those facilities to review copies of the previous intelligence reports which you have sent to Washington, and view the video and audio tapes covering detainee interrogations, and other interactions."

Taking breath, Dr. Gordon proceeded, "To assist us we'd appreciate you assigning two of base security's more-senior investigators, on call 24/7, to assist us in our inquiries. We'd appreciate you providing us necessary meals. Also any discrete clerical support we might require to help with the paperwork.

And access to you when we have an occasional question. Both Agent Davis and I are fluent in Arabic/Farsi/Pushtan. However we'll contact you if we find we need some help from the military Foreign Languages School in Monterey, California. It is conceivable that we could run into a dialect, in review of the audio and video tapes, that we are not familiar with."

Agent Davis again took over the conversation at that point. "General Montrose, we appreciate your understanding on this. We also would appreciate you keeping all this under your hat, which unfortunately must include members of your personal staff."

"For informational purposes only, we have been advised that the president's national security advisor, Dr. Rice, has assigned this inquiry the operational name 'Fallen Angel'." No one, with the exception of yourself, is cleared for any of the information we either have discussed here, will discuss in the future, or uncover in our subsequent research. Is that clear, Sir?"

Dr. Gordon, seeing the red flush raise again in the general's well sun-tanned face, hurriedly interjected, "That provision is to protect you and your command, Sir. That way, no media leak on anything uncovered or not uncovered here can be blamed on you, or your command staff. Unfortunately, at this time we can only hope that at the end of this investigation, the result will exonerate everyone on the JTF roster."

"But frankly, General, I have been in the FBI as a full-fledged investigator for fifteen years—and something tells me that won't be the case—which is why the FBI and the president are asking for your total cooperation, and an absolute total security blackout. Naturally the security blackout is just a request, Sir. Neither Agent Davis nor I can enforce that. Your obligation is first to the Pentagon, and we recognize that. But, if we are going to determine just how deep these three guys got into our shorts, we have to keep a lid on our investigation here. And as we have discussed, this team's target is strictly aimed at the past actions of the three JTF members that already have been taken into custody, stateside. Anyone else will be handled by the follow-up team."

"And just so it doesn't come as any surprise, Sir," Gordon went on, "NCIS has had TrueActive software remotely 'deployed' on all the PC and LANS terminals here at the base. This is the stuff the computer geeks call 'snoopware'. NCIS will be monitoring everything in-bound and out-bound the machine user does on the keyboard, without their knowledge. That information is obviously restricted to your ears only, Sir."

Special Agent Davis reentered the dialog with the general at that point. "Again, it is our understanding that right behind Charlene and myself, at the specific directive of the Chairmen of the U.S. Joints Chiefs of Staff, is a Air Force C-17 containing two dozen JAG/NCIS investigators and their equipment as requested by your Miami-based U.S. Southern Command, as well as armed security personnel to guard the aircraft."

"Let me reemphasize that this team is not associated with our investigation. You might also be thinking about where to house them. I imagine, if necessary, they could use the aircraft, but you are the best judge of that, Sir. Gitmo will also need to provide chow hall accommodations for them, Sir. When we were leaving the Washington D.C. office, our boss told us that he had heard 'scuttle butt' to the effect that an additional C-17 will land here later tonight. It will be bringing in some Humvees so that the transportation demands of the JAG/NCIS investigators doesn't deplete your motor pool."

"However, Sir, since Dr. Gordon and I are not cleared by the Marines to drive their precious humvees—go figure—we will continue to be dependant on your Command for assignment of a suitable civilian vehicle for our transportation."

General," Davis continued, "I certainly understand the negative feelings these two surprise outside investigations bring to you and your command. I apologize for that, but it really is beyond my control, Sir."

Dr. Gordon, jumped back in the briefing, "May I respectfully suggest, Sir, that relative to Agent Davis' and my specific assignment here at Gitmo, you are most certainly welcome to contact and verify our assignment with your boss, the Commanding Officer of the U.S. Southern Command."

"Your boss has his orders from the Chairmen of the Joint Chiefs, and is also aware of the president's independent assignment of the FBI. That team, at this time, consists mainly of yours truly, and Diane here. Again, rest assured we have only been assigned the background investigation of the three JTF staffers now in custody—nothing more, nothing less. And Sir, for what it is worth, Diane and I both wish you luck with the JAG/NCIS team—I'm told some of those folks should go back to charm school."

Agent Gordon, paused for a moment, then said, "When you contact your CO in Miami, he or she can and will verify that we are who we claim. They can verify that we have the authority to act independently here, as we have conveyed to you in this meeting. You also will be advised who our boss at the FBI is, our presidential authority, and everything he or she is willing to confirm about what we have told you here today."

"I can't imagine what Assistant Director Savage could say that would make what Agent Davis and I have had to share with you today any more palatable. "But at the very least, you'll know that we are here under the president's orders, and this is not just some weird CIA or FBI witch hunt—something I understand our agencies are accused of occasionally. Do you have any questions, at this time, Sir?" Dr. Gordon inquired.

General Montrose stood, shrugged emphatically, walked over and opened his office door, and beckoned one of his aides into the office. "Lieutenant Lewis, these International Red Cross inspectors, Ms. Davis and Dr. Gordon, are going to be with us for awhile."

"I'd like an appropriate security detail be assigned them 2400/7; one of our better civilian vehicles assigned for their use; and acceptable and appropriate quarters be assigned them in the BOQ. As you are aware, Red Cross inspectors hold the assimilated rank of full bull Colonel, 0-6, when on U.S. facilities. Also reserve the base's audio-visual facility for their exclusive use, until further notice."

"From this point on, it is to be under 2400/7 guard by the Marines, accountable only to the International Red Cross inspectors here. They'll need meals and passes to go wherever and whenever they wish in the performance of their assigned duties. Between us just now, we established what their access parameters are. Do you have any questions, Lieutenant?"

The young officer snapped to attention, and said "No, Sir.' But like a good West Point graduate, he still took the time to repeat back everything the general had said to him, to insure he had his orders correctly. Giving the young officer that acknowledgement, the general turned and thanked the FBI agents for their frankness. He told them to call him anytime, night-or-day, if they had questions, or otherwise found they were being prevented from accomplishing their mission. With that, he turned on his heel, and walked back into his spacious if aging office, closing the door behind him.

The young lieutenant was obviously invisibility scratching his head in response to the strange, curt orders of his general. He extracted a key from his pocket, closed and locked his desk. Then he went over and began to lock the eleven olive drab, four-drawer top-secret file cabinets with the case hardened steel security flaps. He slid the case hardened, one-inch steel rods down through the clasps, and closed the military padlocks, which had been painted high-visibility orange.

He then straightened, smiled politely at the two 'International Red Cross Inspectors,' and walked over and attempted to relive them of their luggage. As soon as he discovered that the women wanted to carry their own bags and briefcases, he straightened back up, and said "Well, Inspectors, lets get this show on the road, shall we?"

CHAPTER FIFTEEN

DAY 331—28 NOVEMBER

ABOARD A U.S. NAVAL WARSHIP
SOMEWHERE IN THE CARIBBEAN SEA
NORTHWEST OF HAITI

Commander Jethro Smith, the captain of the guided missile destroyer *USS Oscar Austin* looked with amazement as his ship smashed headlong into the seas. The waves were being sliced apart by the armored steel bow, one after another. All while he sat warm and dry, high above on the ship's air-conditioned bridge.

Short for a surface sailor at five foot, five inches in height, Smith was a farm boy from Western Kansas. A young man who only expected to get near water when he took his nightly shower.

The life of a farm boy in Kansas during his school years had been a hard one. He rose before dawn and didn't retire until long past dusk. His typical day included the operation of valuable farm machinery costing hundreds of thousands of dollars. It also extended to operating a pitchfork, mucking out the barn. Where his family's thirty head of milk cattle spent most of their day. Especially when the weather was too wet, too hot, or too anything.

No one outside his immediate family had ever asked him what he intended to do with his life, until his third year in high school. His answer probably would have been some inane comment about taking over the running of the family farm. The one thing he was sure of, is that it certainly wouldn't have included commanding an American Man-of-War on an exotic sea, a thousand miles from home.

Of course, all that changed when his local congressman, urged on by his loving but overly reserved father, lobbied for his appointment to the U.S. Naval Academy. Jethro Smith had a natural inclination for book learning. He had the highest GPA in his high school class. His father, the consummate farmer, had brought that fact to the attention of the area's U.S. Senator. The politician—always trying to prove his worth to his constituents—decided to take a shot at getting Jethro into the Academy. The only one more surprised than the Congressman when the appointment came through was the young man himself. His father's sole comment after the appointment was an aside when they had been pitching hay down from the barn's hayloft a week later. He had paused briefly, and looked at Jethro saying, "Know you have it in you. You do good now you hear, Boy?" The old man then went back to forking feed down to the cows.

Two weeks later, his father died of a massive heart attack, while attempting to birth a reluctant calf.

The Caribbean Sea is an electrifying monster in some ways and a pussycat in others. Located between Global Positioning Satellite (GPS) coordinates 9° to 22°N, and 60° to 89°W coordinates, the body of water is north of the countries of Venezuela, Columbia, and Panama. The countries to the sea's west include Nicaragua, Honduras, Guatemala, Belize, and the Yucatan Peninsula of Mexico. North lays the Greater Antilles Islands of Cuba, Hispaniola, Jamaica, and Puerto Rico. The land to the east consists of the Lesser Antilles Islands.

For a naïve farm boy raised on a one thousand acre spread, the Caribbean seemed huge and daring. The Caribbean covers over one million square miles. It contains the deepest known ocean depth in the world. The Cayman Trench runs between Jamaica and Cuba and is more than 26,000 feet deep. The latter fact, as it should have, raised the hair on the back of the neck of the surface sailor. Smith remembered that the trench's excessive depth was what made it the world's most favorable environment for attack/ killer, nuclear deep-diving submarines. Even with the defensive weapons on-board his ship, an attack from the depths was still frighteningly possible.

Sailors disliked speculating on the possibility of encountering an enemy submarine. It is a dangerous subject, and one that could rapidly drive a contemplative man out-of-his-mind.

It was now getting to be the latter part of 2003. The hurricane season in the Caribbean had folded its tent and theoretically was over for another year. This body of water gave birth to fewer hurricanes annually, than did either the Gulf of Mexico or the Western Pacific ocean. So in Jethro's logical mind—that made the Caribbean 'qualify' as a 'pussycat'.

The hard-charging hurricane season in this part of the world ran from June through October. However, the often unexpected and always terrifying storms were most commonly experienced in September. In an average year, these startlingly explosive storms could average as high as eight in number.

The Caribbean climate was considered to be 'tropical.' But that condition depends heavily on mountain altitude, water currents, and trade winds. Rainfall over the sea ran the gamut of ten inches a year off the Island of Bonaire on the coast of Venezuela, to a tremendous two hundred fifty inches a year in parts of Dominica.

The first European to enter this part of the world was Christopher Columbus. According to the geography and history classes at the Academy, Columbus first touched land in the Bahamas in 1492. Columbus was a vain man who proceeded to talk himself into the erroneous belief that he had discovered a new route to

Asia. That such was not the case, became glaringly obvious to Columbus as his flotilla continued south. There he and his crew came upon a Spanish colony on the island of Hispaniola.

Deep-water Atlantic Ocean sailors find the skies at night to be dark blue or pitch black, depending on the prevailing weather conditions. However the skies is this section of the world were yet unsullied by ambient light pollution. The nighttime Caribbean skies are blessed with a virtual cornucopia of stars. The sky was filled with planets, moons, space junk, shooting stars, meteors, and satellites. All of whose reflective images would be invisible were it not for the Earth's sun. The radiating light from the heavens was beautiful at night, thought the Captain. It was overpowering. The view was so much more impressive than he had ever viewed from his Western Kansas family home.

Years ago, his mother had followed his father to heaven. None of his eleven brothers and sisters wanted to be tied down by the farm, so they abandoned it. The farm was sold at auction and brought the expected pitiful price. The relatively small amount of money was equally divided up between he and his siblings. He figured he hadn't earned any share of the money and returned his check. He had been in his fourth year at the Naval Academy at the time. The financial needs of young men and women embarking on a naval career are taken care of by the Navy. He didn't need any of the blood money. So he sent it back to the trust officer, via an airmail letter.

The ship was generating most of the auditory sounds breaking the serendipity of the night. The powerful roar of the engines drove the sleek ship into the relatively moderate sea crests, with impunity. Which frankly made Captain Smith at times feel pretty insignificant. The constant throb and whine of the massive propellers pushed her through the night. She churned along in fulfillment of her pernicious mission to search out a yet undefined enemy.

From the jackstaff on the *Oscar Austin's* bow to the transom on her stern, she was a superb modern fighting machine. She was currently tasked to CNRSE (Commander—Navy Region Southeast.) At 509.5 feet in length, she was a marauding wolf of a ship. She had a 66.9-foot beam and a draught of 32.7-feet including the sonar head, which never ceased its search for the feared enemy submarine. The destroyer was currently blasting through the moderate sea conditions at close to her advertised top speed of thirty-two knots. She was capable of faster short-term 'dashes' than that. But as those timeless posters had said in the 1940's, 'Loose lips sink ships.'

The officers pulling bridge duty that night had lost all visual reference to land. An enemy ship unlucky enough to stumble across the *USS Oscar Austin's* patrol track tonight, would no doubt notice her high bow with sweeping maindeck tapering down to the flight deck. But most probably only seconds before DDG 79's compendium of death in the form of her SSM McDonald Douglas Harpoon missiles converted the unknown ship into just so much scrap metal. Destined to sink to the bottom of the Windward Passage.

The ship's orders from CNRSE were clear. She "was to eliminate any threat she could *not* otherwise exclude as being a critical threat to the security of Guantánamo Bay Naval Station. But only after the *USS Oscar Austin* was convinced that the enemy contact was steaming on that specific heading. Additionally the ROE required the target vessel had to have the capability of attacking NAS Gitmo. When those requirements were satisfied, the AEGIS destroyer was cleared to take action swiftly, silently, and without warning. There was no implied or stated requirement for the ship's captain to seek further orders. In fact, the ship was ordered to maintain radio silence unless attacked.

Following the attack, the *Oscar Austin* was to close on the site where the enemy vessel had been sent to the bottom. And collect whatever flotsam remained that would support the U.S. Navy's decision to destroy the intruder.

The modern guided-missile destroyer was more than up to the assignment. At 9,217 displacement tons she was fully outfitted for this mission with SLCM-56 GDC/Hughes Tomahawk missiles; eight Harpoon missiles in two quad launchers; and SAM-GDC standard SM-2MR, Block 4, Evolved Sea Sparrow (ESS) missiles.

For below surface undersea action, the AEGIS destroyer was outfitted with Loral ASROC VLA payload 46 Mod 5 Neartip torpedoes. For the Skipper who liked to get close and personal, she was outfitted with FMC/UDLP 5 (in 127 mm)/54 Mk 45 Mid 2 Vulcan Phalanx 6-barrel Mk 15's weapons.

But it wasn't necessary to close on an adversary or even be able to physically see her. The *Oscar Austin's* RCA SPY-1D (V) air search/fire control radar, and the Norton SPS-67 (V) 3 surface radar took care of those little details. The Ship's navigation department owned a Raytheon SPS-64 (V) 9 system. The fire control department was equipped with *three* Raytheon/RCA SPG-62 systems. And as for the ship's sonar department—the highest state-of-the-art system in the world today—the Gould/Raytheon/GE SQQ-89 (V)10.

The destroyer had airborne fangs as well in the form of a pair of Sikorsky SH-60F (LAMPS 111) (ASW) armed helicopters. To summarize, the *Oscar Austin* was prepared for bear. The outcome of any confrontation with any ship that fell into her mission's Rules of Engagement (ROE) on tonight's mission was a foregone conclusion.

The only obvious armament on the destroyer's forecastle was a five-inch gun mounting mid-way between the bow and bridge. If an enemy observer had time to look he might briefly spot the VLS missile tubes. They were situated between the forward gun mount and bridge just forward of the flight deck. The *Oscar Austin's* high-main superstructure was equipped with an aft-sloping pole mainmast atop.

There was only one other predominate identifying feature. Should an enemy observer have time before his enemy ship was sent to the bottom in very small pieces, he might briefly notice large twin funnels of unusual square section with black exhausts protruding at the top. The funnels are sited either side of midships. And gave the only clue that the warship which just blew his ship of the water, a Flight 11A version of the most deadly class of American destroyer—was the warship DDG 79.

The destroyer was teamed with the *USS Donald Cook*, DDG 75, a Flight II model. Both had been ordered by Navy-Southeast's command to steam an extended and accelerated race track-shaped patrol pattern in the Windward Passage. Their venomous hunting ground was located between Guantánamo Bay to the north, Jamaica to the southwest, and Haiti to the Southeast.

The extended oblong patrol pattern was one-hundred-three-miles long, by twenty-miles wide. It established the footprint necessary to permit electronic intelligence (ELINT) systems onboard the vessels to monitor surface traffic in the Windward Passage. The search pattern permitted the monitoring of thousands of square miles of water. The search area's boundaries were the port cities of Vieux Bourg de Jérémie in Haiti, and St. Ann's Bay in Jamaica.

The AEGIS intelligence-gathering systems were theoretically capable of detecting and classifying even the smallest wooden rowboat. Recent reports from Gitmo didn't support that claim. Wooden rowboats filled with Cuban mercenaries continued to land on Gitmo's Kittery Beach nightly. To date all their pitiful efforts to storm Camp Delta had been repulsed by JTF/GTMO.

The captains of the *Oscar Austin* and the *Donald Cook* lacked 'the need to know' further details regarding the attacks on Gitmo. The Naval Reserve Mobile Inshore Underseas Warfare unit 208 (NR-MIUWU) home-based out of Miami was responsible for the bases' coastal security at Gitmo. The inshore warfare units job was interdicting terrorist assault teams. Often the divers were identified as Cuban mercenaries when their bodies were recovered from the water. Some of the bodies still wore diving equipment. The hit-and-run attacks had been occurring haphazardly over the past two weeks. The introduction of two billion dollars worth of elite warships into the equation was intended to prevent the attacks from continuing. The question remained. Were the assault teams being dropped off? By perhaps a 'mother' ship disguised as a Cuban fishing boat? Or would that assumption prove to be incorrect?

MIUWU Unit 208, supported by Port Security Unit 307 (PSU) and other elements of the Joint Task Force 160, hadn't been able to stop the attacks. Nor determine from where they were originating.

The Navy's PSU 'guaranteed' the JTF that the 'hostiles were not using Cuban fishing or recreational vessels.

The U.S. Marines from JTF/GTMO 160 'guaranteed' the raiders were not coming from Camp Delta. It had been a ridiculous possibility anyway. Break out to break in?

Gitmo's on-water security, using nets and Navy Seals, were 'guaranteeing' the terrorists weren't swimming down from the Guantánamo's Upper Bay. The upper harbor was Cuban territory and the possibility not totally unlikely.

This left the waters off Windward Passage as the only other potential point of demarcation for the raiding terrorists.

Patrols in both Guantánamo Bay proper, and off Windward and Leeward Points by PSU 307's crews already were working 2400/7 (military's way of saying 24/7) hadn't been productive. Unfortunately not one of the attacking terrorists had been taken alive for questioning.

The failure to obtain enemy prisoners was simple. It came from a unique precaution being taken by the Cuban mercenaries. One they seemed to have ripped from some WWII Japanese playbook designed for the many fierce battles for the Pacific Islands.

The battle-bound terrorists were strapping a waterproof grenade to their chests before joining their attack. Apparently they were pulling the short-duration fuse if it became obvious that the defenders would interdict them before they reached Camp Delta. In fact, the American defenders were reporting more friendly casualties from grenade shrapnel, than terrorist gunfire.

Navy Region Southeast's motto is "Enabling Warfighter Readiness." CNRSE tasked the two AEGIS destroyers with ensuring that the "terrorists were not being dropped off by ships in Windward Passage." Something their ELINT equipment could guarantee or so the Navy claimed. All these guarantees from four separate elite American combat units. All the ranking officer of JTF/GTMO—Major General Geoffrey Montrose—knew, was that "the damn attacks had better stop forthwith."

The current shift's duty destroyer was the *Oscar Austin*. She steamed the designated patrol pattern with her eyes and ears wide open. The presence of the frightfully efficient warships almost established a 'cordon sanitaire.' Or a naval blockade off the mouth of Guantánamo Bay, while at least one warship remained in Windward Passage at all times.

The *Austin* and the *Donald Cook* were alternating twelve-hour patrols. But nothing untold had been detected to-date. There had been the occasional Cuban fishing boats and international yachts from time to time. In all cases, those vessels had been boarded. But nothing mission-suspicious had been discovered. Excepting the ritual bales of marijuana and a few kilos of cocaine powder. That cargo the U.S. Navy either burned or dumped overboard.

Once a day a couple Cuban destroyers (formerly Soviet) would steam down the coast to the mouth of the Outer Bay. They'd stand off a mile or so, and watch the Americans for a couple hours. Before returning to their base in time for Cervasa and Tequila happy hour.

Usually the arrival of the Cuban destroyers heralded the arrival of one or more tramp freighters en-route the Upper Bay at Guantánamo. The old freighters were covered with rust stains. Beat-up cargo containers were stacked two-to-six-high on the ship's main deck. The Cuban patrol vessels stood-by and just observed. The bedraggled vessels were shadowed by the American's PSU into and out of the treaty waters of the U.S. Naval Base. And up to the mouth of the Cuban waters of Inner Bay, to date without incident.

The two state-of-the-art AEGIS destroyers continued rigorously checking out all potential deep-water sources of the terrorist assault teams. However the raiders nevertheless would again materialize at night on the southern beaches of the Naval Base. The Cuban mercenaries would come ashore and attempt to scale the cliffs of the Cuzco Hills. Trying their level best to reach Camp Delta.

There death approached, as the invaders figuratively came face-to-face with the American defenders. But once again the mercenaries decided they couldn't reach their objective. So they committed suicide rather than surrender.

It had been a quiet evening on the bridge of the patrolling *Oscar Austin*. So quiet the captain had begun to consider going to his sea cabin. Leaving the ship under the command of the ship's Executive Officer (XO) Lt. Commander Jose Deliinez. Deliinez had volunteered to stand the evening's Officer of the Day (OD) duty. This occurred due to the illness of one of his junior officers.

Suddenly all his thoughts of a warm bunk fled the captain's mind as the clanging alarm from Command Plot began to pulsate. Captain Smith grabbed the 1MC ship-wide P.A. system microphone. He glanced at his watch to see it was nearly 0200 hours. Then he identified himself to the caller, and said "Speak!"

"Sir!" the caller began excitedly, "This is Stevens in Command Plot! Two 'fast movers' just launched from Camagüey Air Base! On an intersecting heading with *Oscar Austin's* course! ETA 'overhead'— twenty-seven minutes!"

"Slow down, Stevens," admonished the captain. "Now once again. What is the nature of the threat launched at this vessel? What is the threat's current altitude, heading, and time over overhead? And what is your best estimate as to threat type?"

The duty officer in Command Plot began again, in a more subdued tone of voice. "Yes, Sir. They are two MiG-29's. They are not currently 'in burner' at 37,000 feet MSL. Radar confirms they definitely are on an intersecting course with this ship. And they will arrive overhead in about twenty-six minutes."

The Captain twisted in his chair. He ordered the OD to "Bring the ship to general quarters." The loudly clanging bells began instantly alerting the ship's crew of the need to go to battle stations. The ship's pre-recorded announcement over the ship's 1MC verbally began informing everyone of the change in alert status.

The OD barked to the bridge crew. "You men get your battle gear on! Notify your designated relief that they're on-call! Get everything that's loose on this bridge secured right now!"

The captain in quieter voice informed the Helm, to "continue the ship's current speed and course. Be ready to execute emergency maneuvers on demand."

"Aye, Captain." acknowledged the officer in-charge of the ship's helm.

Captain Smith pulled his headset's microphone boom back to his mouth, and demanded, "Stevens, what the hell are those gomers doing now?" As he waited for Steven's report, the captain double-checked to make sure he had his helmet on, his flack vest buckled, and his command communications headset in-place.

Stevens, still struggling to bring the pitch of his voice under control, replied, "Captain, Sir. They are on the same heading. But are rapidly reducing altitude. Radar indicates they will be at less than 2,500 feet MSL when they first intersect with *Austin's* course. The bandits are actively 'painting' us with their offensive fire control systems."

The captain responded by quickly changing intercom frequencies. "Weaps?" He said into the microphone.

"Here, Captain," promptly replied Lt. Crissy Lockwood, the ship's weapons system officer (WSO).

"Okay, Weaps. I doubt these dudes are interested in anything except a little "You show me yours and I'll show you mine.' But lets get the Sea Sparrows awake and ready to go to work. Go ahead and lock-on to the inbound boogies with the VLS (Vertical Launch System) ASROC. And let's make damn sure the Phalanx Mod fifteens are slaved to the radar. And order-up a couple gunned-up interdiction birds out of GITMO most *ricky tick*."

"Aye, captain, already done," the Weapons Systems Officer, replied. "*Crusader One* and *Two* are currently en-route our posit in-burner. You don't think those MiG's are serious, do you, Sir?"

Captain Smith replied, "Doubt it, Weaps. But lets be safe rather than sorry, Okay? Light 'em up with all those expensive tracking systems the U.S. taxpayers bought you. If they come within *five minutes of this ship* we are going to sell them a couple of burial plots in the Havana Hero's Cemetery."

Captain Smith then again switched ship intercom frequencies. And called the air support currently enroute their location, direct. "This is the *Oscar Austin, Crusader One*. How does your garden grow?" using today's friend-or-foe identification phrase over the secure frequency to make sure he was talking with the 'good guys.'

"*Austin*, this is *Crusader One*. We are two Foxtrot 14s, en-route your posit. We're about five minutes out. Oh, and our garden is filled with all kinds of neat flowers to answer your question, Sir."

Captain Smith chuckled under his breath at the cocky way the attack pilots always blew off the day's 'friend or foe' identification phrase. Keying his microphone Smith asked, "What are your intentions, Gentlemen?"

"Well, Captain," *Crusader One* came back, "we'll be setting up a CAP over the *Oscar Austin's* current track, altering it for speed and direction. Once we are over your ship, again in less than 'five.' Unless you'd prefer something more exotic, we'll just stick with you until the MiGs go home. If they come ready want to play, we are ready for that also, Sir."

Crusader One continued, "From their radar emissions they appear to be the Fulcrum variant of the MiG-29. Not the MiG-31 enhancement. The Russians very rarely permit their newest toys to be checked out of the library. These are two-seater Fulcrums. Cuban MiG-29's have to be nearly eight years old. And I'd be willing to bet they haven't enjoyed an honest hour of aircraft maintenance in the past six months. Intelligence says the Cuban Air Force's maintenance is pretty hit-and-miss. At least it has been since the Russians got evicted from the Cuban's Lourdes Intelligence Base. And took most of their toys and went home. The most likely risk here would be if one of them has a catastrophic mechanical failure and falls on your ship. Things are going to get busy now, Sir. So I've got to go, Captain. *Crusader One* out," he said, terminating the transmission.

The captain changed the intercom frequency back to Command Plot. He felt much better knowing the two pilots and their WSOs were protecting his 'six.' Even if they were a couple of smart asses. He double-checked to made sure his coffee cup was empty. Should this confrontation get hairy—having to fight a warship with wet trousers always seemed to dim his natural competitive enthusiasm.

Meanwhile back in the Tomcats, *Crusader Two* heard his boss, *Crusader One* directing him to "stay on me." As *Crusader Two* looked out of his rain lashed canopy, he barely could see his leader due to the heavy storm clouds. He could see some bulky object out there all right. But it certainly didn't look like the sleek fighters they had just launched from Leeward Field less than eleven minutes ago. "*Two*," he replied acknowledging the command. Again looking over the cockpit 'rails' attempting to see the tumultuous gray sea he sensed was charging along ten thousand-feet below his aircraft.

Crusader Two's aircraft had always been slightly faster than that flown by *Crusader One*. This meant *Two* had to retard his throttles slightly to make sure he remained on *One's* wing without overrunning him. Having a 'mid-air' would ruin both of their days.

As his WSO in the rear seat verbally counted off the miles to target, *Crusader Two* checked his armament switches to insure every weapon was 'safed.' His 'heads-up' display was constantly updating the flight data. The flight control system churned out information by the bucket full.

The American fighters would pop-up to twenty thousand feet, once they arrived overhead the charging destroyer. Then all they could do was wait for the Cuban bandits to make an appearance to 'show the flag.' The lieutenant thought it surprising that the Cubans still attempted to fly the MiG-29 at night. In inclement weather such as they were experiencing. Most Cuban pilots have little chance to remain proficient in night flying. U.S. Navy Intelligence reported that Cuban pilots barely managed to get in two flight hours a month. *Hell*, thought *Crusader Two*. *I would refuse to fly with any pilot who didn't fly at least twenty Pilot-in-Command (PIC) hours per month just to prevent from getting dangerous rusty.* Of course, then he had to admit realistically, *with the Navy's current austerity program that is about all the saddle time we get these days.*

The Tomcat two-aircraft formation roared over the *Oscar Austin*. Then *Crusader One* radioed the ship. As ordered the Tomcats settled into a loose oval pattern at the highest flight level where they could still maintain a 'visual' on the surging destroyer. The F-14s didn't need to have visual contact with the destroyer. The Tomcat's electronic threat and attack systems were more than up to that task. But being typical Navy fighter pilots they felt an urgent need to keep a visual on any ship they had been assigned to protect. If for no other reason then to permit them the opportunity to employ the old *Mark One Eyeball*.

In the meantime, the *Oscar Austin's* bridge had been attempting to contact the inbound MiG Fulcrums on international military radio frequencies. But they had yet to make contact with the bandits. The warship had very exactingly messaged the Cuban pilots in English and Russian. The message, repeated time-and-time again, was that *"If you come inside a five-mile perimeter of this Man-of-War you will be immediately be classified as 'hostile.' The ship's weapons will then eliminate you without further warning. We have your course and speed data 'locked into' the ship's fire control system. You are 'history' unless you immediately come about, and depart this ship's Area of Operations (AO). We will assume your receipt of this warning without your response."*

Less than a minute later, the *Austin's* Command Plot reported the enemy fighters had just crossed into the destroyer's no man's land. The American captain prepared to order the WSO to fire her Sea Sparrow ship-to-air missiles.

Then, suddenly Stevens—the OD in the destroyer's Command Plot, again excitably came up on the intercom speaker net. He tersely announced, "Ship's radar shows that both descending MiG-29's have dropped their landing gear. Also have deployed their speed brakes."

Instantly, a million possibilities shot though the young captain's mind. He thought, *do I fire, or not? I'm within the ROE if I do. But how would I explain the fact that the MiGs were 'wheels down?'* And the bandits had deployed speed brakes, if not their flaps? Neither of which under international law is to be construed as a threatening move.

Then Smith demonstrated the reason the navy paid him all those big bucks. He decided to ignore his normal inclination to fight. Instead he maneuvered himself deeper into the upholstered captain's bridge chair and sighed. Only a handful of seconds later at 0225 hours the two Cuban 'Fulcrums' screamed over the *Austin* just above mast height. The Captain made himself note their GPS position at the time—of GPS 76°N, 19°E—in the ship's log. Just as the MiG's rapidly climbed back up into the dark tumultuous skies.

The inbound aircraft's radar profile told the *Oscar Austin's* captain that the two MiGs had retracted their landing gear and flaps. The American F-14s—in the process of executing a maneuver referred to as 'turn and burn'—at the same moment followed up with their report. The two MiGs had just turned on their running lights.

The bandits had executed a climbing turn, and appeared headed for the airfield of their apparent departure in Cuba. All this action occurred without a single communication with the *Oscar Austin*. Ordinarily a sure-fire recipe that can result in your ass getting smoked. As the young Lieutenant piloting *Crusader Two* would have said if asked—"weird in the extremis!" The night had been turning storm throughout the ordeal.

Fifteen minutes later the destroyer's Command Plot verified that both MiG's had left the area. Neither bandit was being currently considered a threat by the ships' fire control system. After mulling over that fact a few minutes longer, the captain ordered the OD "to stand the ship down from general quarters. But have Command Plot and the ship's defensive systems maintain a due-diligence watch until further notice."

With that order, the skipper dismounted his bridge's elevated captain's chair. As usual thinking *the damn thing had obviously been designed for much taller captains who formerly played in the NBA.* He walked back to the ship's communication shack with the XO where they hacked out an urgent heads-up message. It would be addressed to the U.S. Navy's Southwest Regional Command (CNRSE) and the U.S. Department of the Navy in Washington D.C.

The officers completed sending the required after-action signal at 0258 hours. The captain then turned to the XO. He dryly informed him that he wanted an after-action meeting in the officer's wardroom in thirty minutes. Smith then left the radio shack to go to his cabin to wash his face and replace his sweat-soaked uniform.

At approximately 0328 hours, the ship's Command Team including the senior non-commissioned officers (NCOs) met back in the wardroom. This meeting also drew some of the officers who had previously gone off duty. The wardroom almost wasn't large enough to accommodate include all the attendees.

The ship's galley crew had set out donuts, coffee, and soft drinks. All of which quickly disappeared as soon as the department heads and senior enlisted men grabbed the pastries and gobbled them down. The large stainless steel urn of coffee, and the soft drinks iced down in a high-sided plastic pan were the next target of opportunity. Senior crew assembled there—both those who had been on-duty—and those that had retired off-shift earlier but were awakened by the MiG fly over.

The Captain munched on a donut and drank a chilled can of Diet Coke. He waited for his team to finish their snacks. Everyone had either had settled into one of the chairs around the mess table or was holding up a bulkhead. The latecomers had taken seats on the wardroom's freshly buffed linoleum deck. When the crew saw the captain wipe the crumbs off his hands, they each pulled out a Navy memo pad and prepared to take notes.

Knowing what could only be coming next, Lt. Anton Stevens from Command Plot snapped to attention. And waited for the captain to fry him. Not wanting to disappoint the Lieutenant, Captain Smith jumped in with both feet.

"Lt. Stevens," he began, "How in the hell did those Cuban Go-fasts manage to get launched and well on their way? And noticeably before you decided to graciously bestow that critical information on the Bridge Duty Officer? Those two MiG-29 Fulcrums could have inflicted some serious damage to the *Oscar Austin.*"

The captain continued, "I don't remember requesting an escort from my friend El Castro. Or did it just slip my mind, Stevens? Tell me Stevens, do you think I am losing my mind? Would you please be so good to tell me how those God Damn MiGs *got so close to my damn ship!*"

At that point, Lieutenant Crissy Lockwood, the ship's WSO ('Weaps') stood up apparent with the intent of breaking into the skipper's castigation of Stevens. She had begun to say, "Sir, I don't think . . ."

The Skipper stopped talking and turned to her in amazement. The captain was unable to believe that Lockwood had interrupted his chewing out of Stevens. After nearly a full minute of silence, he finally spoke to her. "Obviously you *didn't think* 'Weaps' before you insubordinately interrupted me. Belay that and sit down, Lockwood. I'll have enough ass-chewing to go around for everyone. Unless you consider yourself to be too 'special' to be included in your peer group, Lieutenant."

Lockwood sensed she has really screwed up this time and shut her mouth. She plopped back down in the wardroom stack-chairs, after stammering "Aye, Sir—sorry Sir."

The captain turned back to Stevens and continued to talk in a deceptively soft voice. "Now, Lt. Stevens. Have your brought *additional* representation other than Lockwood here with you today to explain your foul-up? If not, would you mind telling everyone here why you decided to put everyone on this ship at-risk."

Stevens, quietly and warily began his explanation. "Well, Captain . . ."

"*Stop!*" yelled the captain. "I just ordered you to explain to *everyone* gathered in this room this morning—not just myself— why you failed to alert the bridge. Back when you *first* became aware of the possible attack by the MiGs. You do remember, do you not, the briefing Naval Intelligence gave us all last week? You remember the one, don't you, Stevens? The one about Presidente Castro making the Base Commander at Camagüey Air Base 'personally responsible' for making sure the American forces at Guantánamo Bay stay in-line?" Smith continued to rant.

"Don't you consider it important that Castro has assigned a high priority to anything happening at Gitmo, considering its latest counterterrorism function? Or is it that you have no idea of the importance that Premier Castro attaches to an order such as that? Where he makes one of his minions 'personally responsible' for anything? And the likely consequence should that individual fail in that mission?"

Lt. Stevens waited for the skipper to run down. Once he thought that moment had arrived, he re-squared his shoulders, opened his mouth and began to speak. "Sir, the routine sweeps we are doing on this leg of the patrol are designed to identify any vessel coming into, or leaving Gitmo. I made the decision to permit the electronic techs to trouble-shoot a persistent on-going problem we had been experiencing with the Air search/fire control radar, the RCA SPY-1D. While we continued to work tonight's mission using the Norden SPS-67 (V) 3 Surface search radar."

"The orders that were posted in the ship's wardroom," he continued, "didn't mention any threat of a possible air strike by the Cubans. So I assumed the temporary interruption of the Air Search scan, for the critical maintenance trouble-shooting, would be acceptable. I can see now, Sir, my assumption was dead wrong. I should have run it by the OD on the bridge. Before I authorized taking the Air search radar off-line. There is no excuse for my actions, Sir. I screwed up big time."

The captain continued to silently glare at Lt. Stevens for a full minute. Then told him to take his seat. Smith then turned to the Weapons Systems Officer, Lt. Crissy Lockwood. Again in a deceptively soft voice, he asked her "Lieutenant, do you have anything to contribute to this discussion?"

Lockwood stood up and came to attention, and carefully began her answer, "Yes Sir, Captain. I do have something to add. Although I can't say how germane you will feel it is. But here it is, warts and all. Lt. Stevens did discuss his problem with me. Before he permitted the SPY-1D to be taken briefly off-line for service."

"First," Lockwood continued, "That system is critically needed for the defense of this ship. The Air Search Radar had been failing regularly to 'plot' several incursions by Cuban aircraft over the past week. As they didn't trip any 'alert wires' and were either slow freight—DC 3s or crop dusters—I merely mentioned it to the Bridge OD at the time. Later I wrote it up in the Ship's Log—all per procedure. Perhaps that was wrong. But that is what I did and I will take my medicine for it. Stevens had come to me to discuss his problem. As WSO on this destroyer, it is my responsibility to defend her. Something I couldn't do relying on an undependable SPY-1D computer that had been routinely been going TU on us.

That worried me a lot. I take my job of protecting this ship, seriously."

Weaps continued, "At the time, both Stevens and myself knew that CNRSE's tasking was to keep our eyes open for surface craft of any type. That assignment was the ship's top priority. However, there had been no air attack threat alert notices posted here in the wardroom. Or sent down the chain-of-command by G-2 or anyone. Who could have suspected the Cubans would be this stupid? We would have totally within our ROE to blast those sorry ass MiG's out of the sky. If you had given me that command, those MiGs would have been 'toast.' I guarantee that, Sir!"

As an after thought, Lockwood said, "One further thing, Captain. Those MiGs possibly didn't take off from the Cuban air base at Camagüey. Admittedly they came from the direction of that base. And unless Castro has picked up some mid-air fueling capability lately, we just assume they did depart from there."

"The ship's radar tapes verify those Fulcrums came from that direction, all right. But aren't we are making an assumption the MiGs *had* to have launched from that base? Now, that might not seem important in this particular 'brinkmanship' incident. But let me tell you all it makes a big difference to the protection of all U.S. interests in the Caribbean. That includes this ship, the *Donald Cook*, and Gitmo as a whole."

"We are assuming that the Russian haven't provided the Cubans with in-flight refueling equipment. The Russian don't even utilize it for their air operations. Apparently thinking it is too dangerous, which isn't too far wrong."

'Weaps' went on, "But what if some nation, maybe one of our great 'coalition allies,' *has* sold Cuba mid-air refueling capability? Then CNRSE's current battle plan for the entire Region goes out the window." Lockwood finished her speaking, but continued standing at attention until the skipper motioned her to retake her seat.

"Okay," the captain began, "Learning from our mistakes is what this job is all about. What your jobs are all about, and mine also. So I think we have learned a good lesson here this morning."

"Now, any of you have an opinion as to why the Cubans took the potentially war-provoking risk they did earlier this morning? No one at the UN or on the Joint Chief of Staff (JCS) would have questioned us one iota, if we had taken those MiGs out for attempting a stupid stunt like that."

The ship's XO, Jose Deliinez, cleared his throat, glanced at the captain for permission and spoke. "Skipper, this entire SNAFU has my ears 'up.' Something just isn't right here. In theory the two MiGs came from Camagüey. Although Woodward feels that could be an assumption on our part. I tend to agree with her totally. But lets just assume that those are the facts."

"Camagüey is the home of the Castro's Eastern Army, if you still believe the CIA. It is about 374 Kilometers from Gitmo. Now we, the *Oscar Austin* at the time of the attack by the MiGs at 0225 hours, were just coming around to a north-by-northeast heading. That would permit us to resume the downwind leg of our specified 300-kilometer by 20-kilometer racetrack patrol pattern. The ships log shows our GPS posit at the time as being 19°N, by 76°E. At that time the *Oscar Austin* was 140 kilometers, or about 85 miles, southwest of Gitmo."

The XO continued, "Now per established procedure, when the fur began to fly we temporarily dumped the CNRSE assignment. We did that because the obligation to deal with threats to the ship, always comes first. And to accomplish that, we had to check the overall Area of Operations (AO) for hostile incoming traffic. Be it airborne or one of those Go-Fast Cuban hot rod patrol boats that are capable of sneaking up on us at ninety miles per hour."

"Okay," Deliinez continued, "So far everything per the book except for one interesting situation. From the minute Command Plot called out the threat, until, well, right now, we have had both the Air Search/fire control SPY-1D phased arrays, and the Norden SPS-67 (V) 3 surface search radars *off* the assigned mission. And if my calculations are accurate, that means the *Austin*, relative to patrolling for surface traffic in Windward Passage, has been blind for about forty-five minutes now."

The XO continued on excitedly, having now built up a head of steam. "Let's 'blue sky' for a minute. What if the Cubans only pulled this crap to get us to do just *that*? Just to force the ship to temporarily abandon our mission assignment? Cuban Intelligence would know standard operating procedure for American warships. They'd know the procedures governing the handling of a reported threat of harm to the vessel. And that the ship is to immediately drop everything else to protect the ship."

"Assuming that fact, then this is my question. What actions were the Cubans concealing—on one of the darkest and certainly the stormiest nights this month—off a U.S. Naval base for almost an hour?" Deliinez looked around the room, as if expecting someone there to have an answer to the question. Realizing that wasn't the case he sat down. But then bound quickly back to his feet, signaling to the captain he had one final announcement.

The XO said, "I forgot to pass on to you the contents of a medium-alert email the ship received from the Office Of Naval Intelligence (ONI). Reading from the memo, he began:

> "**The FBI warns an Al-Qaeda attack against U.S. interests abroad using chemical, biological or radiological weapons remains a possibility. The Bureau concluded that al-Qaeda and sympathetic terrorist groups continue to enhance their capabilities to conduct effective mass casualty attacks.**"

The Ship's Executive Officer set the memo aside, saying, "I know most of us tend to ignore these forwarded reports of potential threats. This is because we can feel pretty secure knowing we are on one of the most 'bad ass' warships in the U.S. Navy. But so were our shipmates in Yemen last year, when the *USS Cole* was attacked. Al-Qaeda is willing and able to bringing their attacks directly to the U.S. Navy's fighting fleet. Keep that in mind, folks." He said, before retaking his seat.

Captain Smith thanked the XO for giving them food for thought. He dismissed the now-thoughtful crew. Those who had been on-duty, returned to their duty stations. Those who had been off-duty would return to their bunks to in search of a few more minutes of sleep before morning roll call. The weather continued to deteriorate.

CHAPTER SIXTEEN

DAY 331—28 NOVEMBER

ABOARD A STOLEN RUSSIAN SUBMARINE SOMEWHERE IN THE CARIBBEAN SEA NORTHEAST OF JAMAICA

The Russian-built, 242 foot long, thirty-two foot beamed, diesel-electric submarine recently renamed the *Scorpion*, entered the Caribbean Sea from the northeast, at a submerged speed of fifteen-knots.

Her current top submerged speed was two-knots slower than the boat's original design speed. Just before al-Qaeda had managed to steal the boat from the Russian Federation, she had completed a retrofit, which now permitted her to serve as a delivery platform for several platoons of Special Operations Forces (SOF) troops.

At the same time, the engineers modified the boat's steering apparatus to enhance her stealth capabilities. The rework necessary to achieve both modifications, involved tweaking the submarine's exterior hull. Unfortunately, that modification had a negative consequence. Subsequent sea tests revealed the reformed, anechoic-coated hull somewhat slowed the passage of the otherwise sleek vessel through the water.

The sea-going killer's current GPS position was 20.5° N, 73.5° W. That is a location roughly midpoint between Barocoa, Cuba and Voûte l'Eglise, Haiti. The boat was taking advantage of her formidable submerged depth capability. The combination of the recent extensive upgrade, her SOF retrofit, and her captain adhering to strict 'stealth envelope' operating procedures by remaining the maximum distance possible south of the Windward Passage, was supposed to make the boat virtually undetectable.

The Russian engineers that al-Qaeda had bribed to learn of the retrofit, claimed the boat was now nearly invisible to the American's electronic searches, or ELINT. Including those being conducted by American warships currently patrolling the Caribbean Sea, due south of the island of Cuba.

The only serious threat of detection to the small but deadly diesel submarine could only come from one of the American Los Angeles-class, nuclear-powered SSN attack submarines, that dwarfed the Russian submarine. It was important to make sure the submarine would remain undetected. A tactical confrontation, intending to sow confusion, had being planned by bin-Laden's staff.

The proposed provocation required the approval of Castro's senior Air Force officials. Once received, it was to be put into action. The confrontation was intended to force the deadly American warships to look in the wrong place, at the wrong time, for the wrong type of threat.

The Russian man-of-war had been stolen along with a sister submarine on 04 May 2002. The renamed *Scorpion* attack submarine, which was quietly slipping her way through the depths of the Caribbean Sea in 2003, was under the command of one of al-Qaeda's proven mission leaders, Majed Moqed.

Moqed was the former executive officer of the stolen submarine. The al-Qaeda boat had returned to the Middle East following the previous year's Pacific Northwest terrorist attacks.

On the 2002 mission, the submarine had been under the

command of Captain Hani Hanjour. Following the attacks, Hanjour had used all his impressive skills to return the surviving boat to the secret al-Qaeda's submarine base in the Middle East. The second purloined submarine had been unceremoniously sunk. The hated infidels sent her to the bottom, off the coast of Washington State. It went down with all hands—the Americans had made no attempt to rescue any survivors.

However, despite Hanjour's efforts and the success of his assigned part of the mission, Osama Bin-Laden had executed him. Only later did the rumored 'reason' for the killing of the accomplished captain filter down al-Qaeda's four-level chain-of-commend. Allegedly, Captain Hanjour had been executed for the relatively minor infraction of failing to maintain radio communications, during the attacks, between the two stolen submarines.

His execution was meant to be an object lesson to the al-Qaeda cadre. The death of the otherwise successful al-Qaeda officer was intended to remind the 'faithful' of a basic rule. That rule being the fact that an order from bin-Laden was to be followed in its entirety, without regard to any and all obstacles encountered.

Islamic extremist officers on today's 2003 mission, augmenting the *Scorpion's* skeleton crew, included Zaid Samir Jarrah. Jarrah was a dark, balding skinny man whose physical appearance was deceptive. The man appeared to be near death's door. Marvan al-Shihhi, the always nervous, over-weight, shortsighted homicidal maniac, completed the SOF boat's leadership. Both men were the leaders of the al-Qaeda Commando team that was crammed into the any available space of the heavily modified submarine.

Heading up the boat's Engineering Department enlisted cadre was Abu Hof. He was Mauritanian, a medium height albino who trusted no one. He was also rumored to be mentally unbalanced. Reputedly, Hof had once executed a fellow al-Qaeda comrade for simply staring at him.

The Boat's Weapons System Chief was Saif al-Adil, an Egyptian. He appeared to be a jovial sort of man, if you did not know his background include the torturing of children, including some of his own.

The day-to-day operations of the boat fell to the new XO, a quiet, well-read, if slovenly kept devote Muslim, the crew had been ordered to address as 'Farouk al-Motasseded.'

The deadly *Scorpion* tiptoed, albeit with speed, into the Windward Passage. She was careful to remain at the maximum possible distance from the patrolling, hyper-vigilant, 362 foot-long American AEGIS Guided Missile Destroyer.

Once in Windward Passage, Captain Moqed ordered the submarine down to its maximum submerged depth. The boat hugged the Hispaniola coastline off the Port of La Plateforme with a death-like intensity, as her single brass propeller pushed the deadly boat westbound. Once Moqed determined that his submarine remained undetected by the Americans, he called for a heading change. The boat came southeast to a revised heading, which would take the boat to a point off the Port of Gonaïves.

Upon reaching that waypoint, the boat turned onto a southwestern course. In sixteen-hours time, the new heading would bring the stolen submarine to its planned night 'lager' position on the sea bottom. The submarine's RON (remain-overnight) position was less than five kilometers from the port City of Anse d'Hainault, in war-torn Haiti.

It was after midnight when the submarine's Muslim crew carefully maneuvered the 3,076-ton boat down onto the sandy bottom. Anse d'Hainault was one hundred, three kilometers due west of infamous revolution-torn Port-au-Prince, Haiti. With the exception of those required on-duty, the crew, in addition to the thirty al-Qaeda commandos, managed to gulp down an atrocious-tasting American MRE (meals, ready-to-eat). They also gulped down all the life-sustaining, fresh water the submarine's galley stores could spare. Then, they said their prayers, without much regard to which direction Mecca lay. Following which they all fell into a exhausted sleep. Due to the crowded conditions of the submarine, sleeping men were found in bunks, on the deck, in the galley, in the passageways, in the filthy heads, sandwiched into the torpedo spaces immediately under the deadly hanging mechanical 'fish,' and at their workstations.

Even with a skeleton al-Qaeda operating crew, the additional commandos and their gear crammed the narrow confining spaces of the submarine to overflowing. The lack of privacy would have driven the men to the point where mutiny certainly would have broken out. But each of the team members had seen at least one example of bin-Laden's cruelty towards troublemakers. The fear of bin-Laden was instilled deep into each one of the terrorist's souls, stronger than the sum of all their phobias.

At Guantánamo, almost nightly incursions by freed Cuban criminals continued their assault landings onto the southern shores of the Gitmo. From the beach, the mercenaries attempted to scale the rugged 485 foot tall bluffs of Cuzco Hills, attempting to reach the imprisoned detainees at Camp Delta. The brand spanking new facility was located on the remote American base where the nearly seven hundred al-Qaeda and Taliban terrorists were being detained.

The mercenaries usually came in small groups, two to three to a hardscrapple assault team. They were generally lightly armed. Some only carried rusty handguns or beat-up old AK-47s with a single, partially full, magazine of moldy ammunition. The ill-equipped assault teams neither wore, nor possessed, body armor. The men often carried little but the clothing on their backs, a joint or two of crappy of Cuban marijuana, and the obligatory symbols representing their faith around their scrawny necks.

The far superior American troops were armed with fully automatic weapons. Those weapons were equipped with infrared night sights. The Marines and JTF guards, wearing full body armor, once alerted, would drop dozens of fragmentation grenades over the bluff's crest, easily eliminating the infiltrators.

Per the orders of their Cuban leaders, the infiltrators chose suicide. The alternative was capture, interrogation, and incarceration for the rest of their normal lives.

Following the nightly infiltration attempts, and closer to daybreak, the environment on the bluff at Camp Delta began to reflect the chilly, damp breezes blowing in off Windward Passage. However by midday, the sun was again warming the velvet breezes that blew in off the Caribbean Sea.

The almost-nightly attempts to infiltrate Gitmo, were of course being reported in the worldwide press. But the information available to the media was minimal. For instance, neither the Americans or the pesky world media knew that while these small groups of infiltrators were al-Qaeda-believers, they were Cuban, not Arabic.

Cuban criminals, released from Castor's prisons and scoured from barrios across Cuba, were being covertly bivouacked in a small well-concealed military base called *Juanco*, twenty-four kilometers east of Gitmo. There, they had been fed food high in fat content, and in much abundance. In fact, much more than any of them had experienced in their wildest dreams during the last five long years of Castro's failed economy.

The starving Cuban criminals had been released from notorious jails all over Cuba, with the knowledge of a slightly demented and aging Castro, and taken to *Juanco* by army truck under the cover of darkness. There they received food, adequate accommodations, and reasonable quantities of their drug of choice. One day they would ordered to transport themselves from *Juanco*, to the southern beaches of the American base in small rickety wooden boats. Some would survive the short voyage, and would manage to beach their boats at the base of the Cuzco Hills, under the radar screens of Guantánamo's perimeter security forces. In any case, the craft the men used would not have showed up as anything but ground clutter on the radar. So cheap was the non-reflective material the ragged throwaway boats had been hurriedly constructed from.

The conscripted Cuban criminals did not know that the beach they had specifically had been ordered to land on, was a few hundred yards west of the newly-constructed Camp America. The American camp contained stand-alone and guarded housing facilities for potentially two thousand of heavily armed guards. The camp provided housing for JTF 160, NRMIUWU 208 out of Miami, and PSU 307, also out of Florida.

Camp America had been built between 'Windmill' and 'Kittery' beaches. Engineers prudently sited Camp America on the beach only a few hundred yards east of the heavily guarded

Camp Delta. The Delta facility was located some 485 feet above the beaches, on the crest of the bluff of Cuzco Hills.

For a lightly armed small force of untrained and ill-equipped infiltrators to even attempt to make an assault on an unknown beach in the dark, was pure folly. Let alone, when the untrained men had to scale 485 feet of dangerous cliffs, toting rifles and pistols. Any such attempt was terminally doomed to failure.

If the Cubans didn't slip and fall to their death, once alerted, the Americans showered dozens of fragmentation grenades down on the climbers. In the remote chance that any the Cubans managed to survive the explosive death raining down on them, they quickly would become isolated. Before the mercenaries had departed *Jaunco* only hours before, they had once again been ordered to kill themselves, rather than surrender and undergo that they had been told was the "American's inhuman torture."

Knowing the absolute penalty of disregarding such any order in Castro's Cuba, the Cubans always choose death before dishonor, capture and confinement. Even if the dishonor was only in the eyes of the Presidente-for-Life, and his homicidal brother Raúl Castro Ruz, the demented head of Castro's Secret Police.

The seemingly on-going ineffective infiltration attempts actually serviced a purpose. Albeit one, which only Presidente Fidel Castro Ruz held to be for the good of Cuba. Every month the world read in the print media of the dozen of failed attempts by Al-Qaeda to rescue the detainees. They sadly shook their heads, and thought *"what a pitifully brave, if misguided, revolutionary force."* However, al-Qaeda and Castro had a plan.

Fidel and bin-Laden felt that eventually these half-assed, underfunded, and poorly equipped attempts to rescue the terrorist detainees would eventually lull a portion of the hundreds of Joint Task Force guards, into complacency. And complacency was always something that could be exploited.

Within a week or two, America's two enemies expected the JTF guards to mentally degrade their concern for the rescue attempts. Perhaps down to such a low level of concern, that the guards would begin to consider the infiltration attempts only an irritant, a minor irritant at that.

Knowing the historical thought processes of Castro well, and al-Qaeda only somewhat slightly less, the commanders of Joint Task Force 160 re-doubled their efforts to keep the morale and alertness of the American troops high. They scheduled twice-weekly briefings inviting all JTF personnel, where CIA operatives gave heretofore-secret tactical briefings. The JTF Command team expressed an absolute commitment on to 'what iff-ing' every hypothetical attack, as well as providing constructive criticism on every after-action report.

Despite these motivational efforts by the dedicated JTF command, a few troops, as will troops in any army no matter how well they are led, began to downplay the possibility of a more formidable attack. The concept of a large group of heavily armed, well-trained and equipped enemy commandos, launching a massive infiltration intended to overrun the south end of the base, seemed to be beyond their comprehension. These naysayers would soon learn that they had been wrong.

Top strategists in the Pentagon knew only too well the risk to Gitmo was "significant and possible." Compared to the frail Cuban infiltration efforts in the past, such an dedicated attack would come from a committed force of al-Qaeda terrorists. Hardened terrorists who knew it was impossible to fail. Knew that if they did, they would be violating their unbreakable vows to bin-Laden, Islam and their brothers in al-Qaeda who had 'gone before them.' The terrorists had all the historical lessons of modern guerilla warfare to draw on. They could conceivably come out victorious; at least in the initial two-hour period following the beginning of the gore-laden attacks.

With nearly one thousand troops off-duty at Camp America, five hundred more on-duty either at Camp Delta or elsewhere at the Guantánamo base on other guard details, bin-Laden himself had to acknowledge it wouldn't be a cakewalk. The terrorists needed a loud, instantaneous, all-hands diversion exactly an hour before the thirty al-Qaeda commandos landed. The success of the attack required that a majority of the JTF troops be lured away from the base's southern shoreline and the camps. A red herring would be required to drawn the JTF to emergency duty elsewhere on the massive forty-five square mile base. Ayman al-Zawahiri, al-Qaeda's master planner and Bin-Laden's chief deputy, quickly came up with an unbelievably simple plan.

The diversion had to be timed to permit al-Qaeda's commandos the time to infiltrate and begin releasing the al-Qaeda detainees from incarceration. It must also misdirect and tie up the balance of the JTF 160 off-duty and on-duty troops, along with all the Navy base's security personnel, Port Security Unit 307, and US Marines, elsewhere.

An excellent 'elsewhere' would be for the Americans to have to deal with the detonation and massive destruction of the base's life-sustaining electric-generation and water-purification facility at Fisherman's Point. The physical plant was located several miles away on the base's shoreline of the Inner Harbor.

Earlier surveillance by the Cubans reportedly had indicated the critical facility was considered by the Americans to be impregnable and unassailable. Despite the fact that losing its hypercritical services would make the U.S. Guantánamo Naval Facility totally uninhabitable and indefensible in about one-week's time.

CHAPTER SEVENTEEN

DAY 332—29 NOVEMBER

JOINT TASK FORCE 160 HQ
THE INFILTRATION DISCOVERY
GUANTÁNAMO BAY
CUBA

Major General Geoffrey Montrose was commander of JTF 160. The JTF was the multi-service taskforce chartered with the assignment of looking out for the well being and security of nearly 700 Taliban and al-Qaeda detainees, on the U.S. Guantánamo Naval Station.

The general was out at 0600 hours for his daily five-mile run. General Montrose often referred to the run as 'his pact with the citizens'. The general felt that it was his obligation to the American taxpayers, to stay fit and ready for anything that fell into his job classification. The definition of 'anything' was the purview of the Joint Chiefs of Staff (JCS) at the Pentagon, and his direct superior in Southern Command, in Florida.

The general's eight man-security detail (America was in a state of war, and as such, extended an unusual level of protection to its general officers) could have easily outpaced the officer. But early in their respective careers, they had learned a very important military rule—never, ever make a general look bad.

So two of the Marines, their Uzi's concealed beneath they sweatshirts, and chosen largely for their athletic prowess, ran five paces in front of General Montrose. Two more brought up the general's rear. And one paced alongside the general, on either side, being careful to keep their bodies between the man and the roadside ditches.

Two additional heavily armed marines followed the jogging group. They drove an olive drab ambulance. The Navy Corpsmen relaxing in the vehicle's rear, reading the morning paper that was flown in from Miami daily. But only after double-checking their fully stocked emergency medicine supply kits, and the state of the stored electrical charge on-demand in the vehicle's two defibulators.

The final Marine, formerly a Busch-level, race winning, NASCAR driver, drove the Humvee, in front of the ambulance but behind the jogging U.S. Army general. Although equipped with dual-hydraulic assisted power steering, the armored Humvee was still difficult to maneuver with any finesse in close quarters.

The Humvee driver's main concern at the moment, was retaining his grip on the large steering wheel, while at the same time attempting to drink this morning's third cup of coffee. Perched on a piece of toilet paper on the passenger-side seat alongside him, were the two donuts he had managed to smuggle out of the mess hall under the general's copy of the newspaper. The driver felt he was demonstrating his professionalism by accomplished all those simultaneous functions without getting crumbs on his immaculate starched and pressed fatigues.

The entire security detail respected General Montrose. They had often voiced their personal opinions that they thought he was accepting far too much responsibility for the recent al-Qaeda spy revelations. That discovery had resulted in the deployment of several dozen JAG/NCIS investigators to Gitmo, who were poking their noses into every nook and cranny.

The general's security contingent realized that the disruption the investigators brought to day-to-day operations at Camp Delta and Camp America was unavoidable. A number of spies had already been discovered, and their prosecution was rumored to be a 'slam dunk' for the JAG Corps.

The spies already uncovered but not yet convicted, had been in-place at the JTF, either as civilians under American employment contracts, or even in some cases, on active duty in U.S. military service. After the men were caught, and the men's credentials reviewed, the investigators had been astonished. Without any review of the men's backgrounds and service records, they somehow had managed to obtain employment in the super-sensitive ranks of the Joint Taskforce. Often these hiring decisions were based on nothing more than a recommendation from a ranking officer at the Pentagon, or a civilian with political clout.

General Montrose, and his West Point 'not on my watch' management style, seemed to be taking all the heat as these revelations fell onto his shoulders. The American Government had, to this point, only brought charges against two of the espionage agents. It was unknown how many more were embedded deep inside the JTF command structure.

But the 'Word,' a living, breathing organism present on all military bases throughout the world, said the U.S. investigators were "building strong cases against at least a dozen more persons." The already detained spies had once been the roommates of Camp Delta's guard force. The spies had shared the same complex of Sea Huts with the guards at Camp America.

To avoid possible contamination of his immediate staff, the general had abruptly relocated his personal security teams into other quarters on the forty-five square mile base. The general hoped to protect his troops from 'guilt by association.' Unfortunately, the 'broad brush' approach often turns out to be the preferred investigation method of the U.S. military intelligence community.

On that day, General Montrose and his security contingent once again completed their daily five-mile run, without incident. The team had turned the general over to four fresh members of the security team, at his office. The new team waited while the general showered, and changed into a Class-A uniform for the routine day's busy schedule. The selection of the more formal uniform, over his usual starch fatigues, signaled that the general was expecting visitors.

The guards who had been on the morning run, parked the ambulance and armored Humvee in a 2400/7 guarded, covered parking lot alongside JTF headquarters. Then they grabbed two of the half dozen newer Humvees that always were available for use by the general's private staff. The men returned to their barracks for showers, and a clean uniform.

Once they had completed their ablutions, they met in the reception area of their renovated barracks. They piled into the Humvees, and drove to the mess hall at Camp America for a late breakfast. After breakfast, there would be the requisite hour-long, physical training session in the camp's well-equipped gym.

Following that, the team would return to the general's HQ where they would spend the remainder of the morning in their dayroom. There, they would assist the general's clerical staff with paperwork, when directed, or study for promotional exams.

Unless the security team was called to transport the general somewhere on base, they were free to watch satellite television, or read. When it came time for the general to return to his base housing, a second somewhat smaller security team took over responsibility for the general's safekeeping until the following morning. Then the eight-man day shift would relieve the night team at 0500 hours. And they, once again, would accompany the general on his daily five-mile run.

To a civilian, the level of protection afforded a general on a U.S. Naval Base might seem excessive. However, those who were informed knew that al-Qaeda and the Taliban had offered a million U.S. dollars to capture or kill the general. In their mind, he was responsible for the fact that six hundred, seventy-five of their countrymen were currently being detained at Camp Delta.

Under the current administration's interpretation of the law, the terrorists were being without any contact from their families, friends, and in most cases, legal representation. General Montrose, if he would have admitted it, knew he was a wanted man in extremist Muslim circles. Protecting General Montrose, or any U.S. commanding officer, was of supreme importance to the president of the United States.

The general's business day began at 0800, or 8:00 a.m. local time, each morning. This workday cycle was repeated at least six days a week. His office staff knew they had better be at their desks, well prepared, and ready to roll, at 0745 hours. A U.S. Army master sergeant, with thirty-years-worth of time-in-service hash marks on his left forearm, ran the general's daily calendar and managed the office.

The master sergeant was as important, if not more so, than the JTF commander's commissioned staff officers. Naturally that fact was not lost on those fine gentlemen and ladies. Lieutenant Jason Johnson, one the general's two aides, fell into that classification.

The first order of the morning would be a pre-arranged secure, encrypted conference call between General Montrose, FBI Headquarters in Washington, D.C., and the JAG officer assigned to General Montrose's boss, at U.S. Southern Command, which was headquartered out of Miami.

The military lawyer assigned the C.O. of Southern Command was only on the call to make sure his boss was protected—legally and politically—in the cover-your-ass environment that is today's U.S. military. The JAG lawyer mostly just listened on the calls. No one could remember a situation when he or she had voiced an opinion or asked a question, during any of the frequent calls.

General Montrose's prime purpose for today's conference call with the Justice Department was to learn what action would be taken, as a result of the reports of the two FBI investigators who had arrived virtually unannounced in front of his desk, nearly a month ago.

In retrospect, the general knew he had been thoroughly pissed at the time, for what he viewed as a slight by his higher command. At first blush, the general had assumed the FBI was questioning his proven ability to operate a U.S. military installation. After further investigation into the actual facts, the general had revised his initial faulty opinion.

A month previous, the general had not been privy to the circumstances under which the FBI agents being sent down to Guantánamo to interview him. Additionally, the polite, respectful, and business-like manner in which they had interfaced with his command for nearly two weeks, had also served to temper his earlier opinion. He now admitted that he had been guilty of jumping to conclusions.

The general thought the two FBI female agents had been exceptionally courageous to accept the assignment in what could have been a very dangerous environment, for them.

One of the agents was a tough but diplomatic long-term FBI supervisor by the name of Gordon. Her specialty was developing serial murderer and violent sex offender personality profiles.

The other was a young, and determined special agent, who had earned her spurs up in Washington State, during the terrorist attacks of 2002 that had killed over a thousand persons. Terrorists had destroyed a billion U.S. dollar's worth of infrastructure in the Pacific Northwest, before the multi-agency federal task force, under the young agent's command, managed to interdict the terrorist's efforts. The taskforce's exceptional results had the collateral effect of running the bad guys, at last temporarily, out of the Pacific Northwest.

The young agent, Diane Davis, was a qualified member of FBI's fabled HRT team. Her team had prevented a 747-400 hijacking on Paine field, in Everett, Washington.

Davis and the HRT team had been credited by President George W. Bush as the primary reason that the brand new $100 billion-dollar aircraft carrier, the *USS Ronald Regan*, wasn't just so much scrap iron resting on the bottom of the bay at the Bremerton Naval shipyard. The mammoth brand-spanking new aircraft carrier had been moored at the shipyard at the time for some critical electronic adjustments, following her sea trial shakedown cruise, before the state-of-the-art ship could be accepted into the U.S. Navy.

The general's intercom quietly buzzed. It was Lieutenant Johnson informed him both the FBI and the Southern Command were on the line. Pushing a red button on his secure STU-III tamper-proof telephone, the general picked up the line, first greeting his boss's JAG lawyer to make sure he was on the call. Then he greeted the FBI.

The general began the call, with a comment directed at the FBI agents. "Well, how are the hardest working 'Red Cross Inspectors' that have ever visited Gitmo? Do you know that some of the detainees are still asking to talk with you?"

Special Agent Davis chuckled, and acknowledged General Montrose's comment by responding, "Hell, General, the next representatives from the IRC (the International Red Cross, referred to in the Muslim world as the Red Crescent) ought to be briefed in advance. Those so-called virtuous brothers of Islam you are graciously providing accommodations for down there, are not above pinching a lady's tush. My boyfriend wouldn't talk with me for a week. Until I finally got tired of the inattention, and explained to him just how I had gotten the bruises on my backside."

General Montrose could hear Davis, another female he assumed was Dr. Gordon, and their boss—FBI ADC/Counterterrorism, Bill Savage, having a good laugh at his expense.

"General Montrose," Director Savage began. "I understand you would like a advance confidential briefing as to what our agents uncovered, regarding the three suspects they were sent down there by the president to investigate. And what the FBI's intentions are, concerning your staff, in the matter. Both Davis and Dr. Gordon have told me they gave you an unofficial briefing before they returned to the mainland. But since that was contrary to FBI procedure, lets forget it happened, and start over."

"Evidence on these three subjects, formerly attached to your command, is being handled separately from anything dug up by the U.S. Southern Command out of Miami. I understand that Southern Command still has a couple of dozen JAG/NCIS teams operating on your soil right now. Director Mueller here at the FBI had received a request from the Pentagon with regards to any further interaction between them, and our people here at the bureau. At the order of the president, the FBI will refrain for getting involved in the investigations of any additional espionage suspects that fall under the JTF command umbrella at this time."

"If you don't mind, General, I'd like to let Agent Davis and Dr. Gordon take over the briefing from here," concluded Assistant Director Savage.

The general replied, "No, that is fine, Bill. I assume you have more things on the FBI's counterterrorism plate, than sitting through another conference call from the JTF, anyway," he joked.

Savage laughed, and told the general not to hesitate to call any of them 24/7 if he had any questions. After receiving the general's assurance that "the FBI can count on that," Savage terminated connection to the secure STU-III phone network. Then the ADC picked up his unsecured FBI phone, and called the FBI's new 155 million dollar laboratory at Quantico on another matter.

"General, Sir, if you don't mind, I'll be the 'primary' on this briefing, but Charlene Gorton had agreed to stick around in case you have any questions that fall into her area of expertise," Agent Davis began.

Davis continued, without waiting for General Montrose's reply, "First, the case against the civilian Arabic-language translator, Ahmed F. Mehalba, has been turned over to the civilian prosecutors. He has been charged by the Grand Jury with 'Improperly gathering of military information' and 'Lying to the FBI.' We wouldn't normally expect to have any further input into that case, unless specifically requested by the U.S. Justice Department."

Considering the current political climate, he stands to receive a sentence on those charges, of up to a maximum of ten years in prison, and a $250,000 fine. Typically, his attorney will plead him *Not Guilty*, and the show will go on from there."

Davis explained, "The other two suspects will be tried under military law, unfortunately for them. Ahmad Al Halabi, the Air Force translator, is being charged with 'Spying' and 'Aiding the enemy.' Either or both charges can result in the death penalty, especially in the time of war. Al Halabi has a steep road of solid evidence to overcome if he ever is going to walk away from this. Most of the JAG people I've talked to, since Dr. Gorton and I had to leave your balmy Caribbean Island, have strongly recommended that one shouldn't risk their 40lK by betting against JAG on this one."

"It is my personal opinion, that the evidence on the Muslim chaplain—Captain James Yee—may be a lot less substantial. We've been told that as a result of the NCIS/JAG investigation, he is only going to be reprimanded on two violations of military law: 'Adultery' and 'Improperly downloading pornography onto a Army computer.' Apparently, there wasn't enough evidence to substantiate the original charge of 'Mishandling Classified Information.' Whether he is going to plead 'simple carelessness' is unknown at the current time. To top that off, despite the fact that he was found guilty of the minor charges, I understand he is demanding an apology from the Army. Go figure. For some reason JAG appears disappointed this case didn't get thrown into the civilian courts. But they knew that was not possible because Captain Yee is active military. The word is that Yee is going to be returned to full duty at the Army base at Fort Lewis, Washington."

Davis continued, "It is my understanding that Yee was recommended for the Muslim Chaplain's billet at Gitmo by a high-ranking American Muslim cleric. Rumor has it that the recommending party is a large political contributor to both parties. And, he is no stranger to being asked for Islamic advice by the 'star-pilots' at the Pentagon."

Dr. Gordon, apparently bored with sitting on her hands, broke into the briefing, "General, Diane and I are essentially out of those investigations at this time. In Mehalba's case, it is because he has been formally charged. In both the remaining cases, Halabi and Yee, the Pentagon has been quite clear in advising FBI Director Mueller that they no longer require our services in the handling of these specific cases."

"It is my impression that the military has complete faith in the JAG/NCIS investigation teams that U.S. Southern Command brought in. Diane and I followed our boss's task assignment to the letter when we were your guests." Dr. Gordon paused for a moment, before continuing. "So neither of us knows if the 'dozen or so additional persons under investigation' news release that someone has been leaking to the media, is fact or fantasy. I'm sure you are hoping for the later."

"Is there anything else we can do for you today, General? Again, Diane and I would like to restate our appreciation for the courtesy you showed us when we arrived on your doorstep, unannounced, last month. It was a difficult situation, in difficult times, and we both thank you for making it less dangerous and productive for us, than it obviously could have been," Dr. Gordon concluded.

General Montrose concluded, "Thank you both for taking the time for my call today. I want you both to know that I have passed on my appreciation of the professionalism you both demonstrated here, under most difficult conditions. I copied my boss in Miami, and Director Mueller. You two can come visit this old warhorse anytime the Bureau gives you some well-earned vacation time. Hell, I'll even ask PSA 307 to take you both out water skiing," he laughed.

Davis response, "Why, General, what makes think a couple of FBI agents, who are after all just girls, can swim? And don't think we haven't heard about the armada of sharks that troll for Americans foolish enough to swim in the Caribbean's Windward Passage," Diane quipped. Laughing, Major General Montrose hung up, breaking the secure conference call connection.

After going into the courtyard at his headquarters to have a cigarette, again forgetting to remind himself that he had given up smoking a year ago, Montrose returned to his office to meet with the ranking head of the JAG/NCIS team that currently was roaming his turf at Guantánamo. The team was comprised of investigators and lawyers that U.S. Southern Command had flown into Guantánamo BAY NAS, almost a month ago.

The team's mission, he had been told, was to root out any additional al-Qaeda or Taliban deep-cover spies embedded in his JTF force. This would be the team leader's first meeting with the general. The lawyers in the group tended to hold all the information they had collected close to their chests. Apparently they were concerned that he or his staff was going to the leak the information all over the base, to the media, or possibly even around the world.

Lt. Johnson escorted U.S. Marine Colonel Marvin Lokkesmoe, the team-supervising JAG lawyer into the general's office. The colonel, still wearing his lid, had come to attention in front of the general's oak desk and saluted him. General Montrose, being uncovered, didn't bother to return the salute.

Instead, Montrose indicated for the Marine to take a chair across his desk. As the colonel was seated, Lt. Johnson walked into the office with a pot of coffee, to refill the colonel's loaned cup.

Once the colonel and general were both settled in with a fresh cup of Cuban coffee, the JTF general asked the JAG/NCIS taskforce leader why someone in the colonel's organization had seen fit to leak the 'other suspects' rumor to the media? The one that claimed that Montrose's command still harbored "up to a dozen or more spies." Where was the evidence to support the allegation?

The colonel took another sip of the overly hot coffee the general had specifically instructed his aide to prepare and have on hand for this specific meeting. Then he set his cup down on the napkin Johnson had provided him on the general's well-worn oak desk.

The colonel began, "General, Sir, perhaps you have been misinformed—no one in my team leaks anything to the media, other than I."

"Ok, then Colonel, why are *you* leaking unsubstantiated drivel such as this to the media, then?"

"Oh, I'm not, General, I'm not," the colonel coolly said. "In fact, our public relation nerds back at JAG Headquarters in Falls Church have been snooping around trying to identify the leaker, whether on your team or mine. Only one confidential source has been forthcoming. Mainly because we promised that particular news network the jump on their competitors, when and if this story does break."

"As I said," continued the colonel. "our source claims that the leaks are coming from a permanent party member of JTF 160, currently assigned here. In other words, the 'leaker' is in your house, General. Our computer geek at JAG/HQ in Falls Church has been tracing back which terminal here at Guantánamo the emails are originating from, using the FBI's *Carnivore* software. She has narrowed it down to two of the Internet terminals provided for troop use up at Camp America.

"Computer internet mail access here at Gitmo requires a password," said the Marine. "Each password is individually assigned to the JTF employee requesting time on the net. However this 'leaker,' for the lack of a better term, seems to have access to a whole pocket full of passwords. They were initially issued to troops that have since rotated back stateside, or are sans any terminal access, over at the base hospital center on Hospital Cay with complications from the flu or food poisoning."

"We briefly considered canceling password-access for all service and civilian personnel stationed here at Gitmo. At the time we reasoned we could then reissue them a 'tagged' replacement. But we decided to run that idea by the head shrink in your base medical department. Now that was a calculated a risk, I agree. But we had to take a chance on the possibility that *he* wasn't involved in this leaking. So we went ahead. And, surprise, the doctor recommended against it."

Without a break, the colonel continued, "His reasoning, which frankly makes sense to me, was that morale in the JTF is already marginal due to the damn media leaks. Also, he was concerned about the level of suspicion an investigation like this, out of necessity, throws on the base's command structure. Meaning you and your staff. And also, quite honestly, because my boss told me I was freaking nuts to even suggest it," Colonel Lokkesmoe finished. He reached over, picked up his borrowed cup, and drained it in a single gulp.

General Montrose toggled the intercom, and asked his aide to bring the colonel some fresh coffee. The general jotted down a few notes covering what the colonel had said, as they waited for Johnson to brew up the new batch. After a few minutes, Johnson burst in the office with a fresh pot of coffee, almost tripping over himself in his eagerness. He poured both the general and the colonel fresh cups, set the new pot on a insulated stainless steel platter on the corner of the general's desk, and left the room quietly closing the door behind him.

Both men remained silent, sipping their coffee, for almost a minute before the Marine, unable to restrain himself any longer, broke out laughing, shortly to be sheepishly joined by General Montrose. After they both had a good laugh, Colonel Lokkesmoe, wiping the tears from his eyes, said "Whatever idiot decided years ago, that a U.S. command-rank officer must have the services of a wet-behind-the-ears commissioned officer as an aide, instead of an experience combat-tested senior non-com whom he could bounce ideas off of, was surely a member of the freaking U.S. Air Farce."

That brought additional, if more restrained laugher, as they both remembered the vision of the general's aide, Lieutenant Johnson tripping, almost falling into the colonel's lap with a hot pot of coffee.

The general was the first to regain his composure. *Probably*, the colonel thought, *because the God Damn pot of coffee wouldn't have ended up in his God Damn lap.*

"Lokkesmoe," said the general, "regardless of what Washington thinks, if there are additional spies in the JTF, I want them identified, hung by the balls or shot almost much more than I want to get back to my understanding wife's warm bed in Florida. But this damn leaking is destroying my men's faith in me. In fact, in the entire multi-service JTF force concept. It has even caused several serious fistfights up at Camp America when some of my guys noticed their SeaHut roommates had Arabic-sounding surnames. Or when the fact that one of my non-translator troops speaks fluent Arabic, suddenly became common knowledge."

"I've got a half-dozen of the JTF guard detachment over on Hospital Cay in quarantine. We are trying to conceal from the media, and the International Red Cross, that a few of our guards have flipped out, and tried to kill each other, often for no discernable reason."

General Montrose continued, "If this kind of behavior continues for another six months, I won't have enough people left, alive and not placed under protective custody in the Navy hospital's mental ward, to guard the detainees. Bearing that in mind, Congress and the president are going to be forced to make a hard decision very soon."

"Do we continue to incarcerate the some six hundred plus terrorists? Or do we turn them loose, when we all know they'll just return home and rejoin the Jihad? The majority will return to the commission of whatever atrocity they were in the middle of, when coalition forces arrested them the first time. I understand your JAG/NCIS task force has been charged with rooting out any remaining spies. Especially, if those bastards are on staff here. I support that."

Expanding on the subject, the general said, "But I am asking, one officer to another, for your immediate help in identifying the source of these on-going media leaks. So I can put my foot up someone's ass, and get them stopped. Can I expect your help on this matter, Colonel?"

"Yes, General," the Colonel replied. "Now I've got to get back to my young lawyers before they all run off and try to get one of the patrol boats to take them water skiing. Oh, would you like me to take your aide with me, General, and arrange for him to get a little valuable field experience?" he asked with laughing eyes.

Trying to keep himself from smiling, Montrose replied, "Colonel, I'll let you answer that question yourself. But I think it only fair to tell you that his daddy is the Chairman of the U.S. Senate Armed Forces Committee."

The Marine, in a very non-military manner, said "Opps!" Then he stood up, replaced his lid squarely on his head, performed an about-face maneuver, walked to the office door, opened it, and left the general's office, making sure to politely thank Lt. Johnson for "the excellent coffee—best I've ever had, Son!"

Following his morning meetings, General Montrose took lunch with his aide at the Base Officers Club. Then he returned to his office, and spent a couple of hours processing what Navy Regulations classified as "absolutely mandatory command paperwork." It was mostly personnel-related in nature. Reenlistment recommendations, disciplinary action concurrences, promotions, demotions, over-turning excessively stiff sentences from UCMJ Article 32 hearings, and alike. *All things a chimpanzee could be easily trained to do*, thought the general.

Then, seizing on an innocuous security report he had just come across as justification, the general decided he needed a break. He had his security team drive him to the base's east end ferry terminal. There they parked the Humvees in a secured lot, which was guarded by an base security officer. The general and his four bodyguards walked onto the ferry, grabbed a cup of watered-down coffee, and sat down on the rough canvas-wrapped benches provided. The ancient boat pulled away from the dock, and struggled its way up stream to Hospital Cay, the site of the base's small hospital. Although both Camp Delta and Camp America had fully equipped, advanced first-aid facilities—the military version of a civilian ER—the old hospital was still used by the base's permanent party.

In theory, the Joint Taskforce only needed the new medical dispensaries to treat day-to-day health needs. This included minor injuries, medical emergencies such as heart attacks, occasional heat stroke, minor illnesses, and other maladies.

Of course, due to the interactions between the detainees and the JTF guard force, injuries to both guards and detainees, while not infrequent, were not considered to be business-as-usual. Until several months ago, most of detainees would risk the punishment of being locked into solitary confinement, if it meant they might get a chance to bit, kick, spit, urinate on, or inflict some other minor injury on their American captors. Officially, the only penal action the JTF could dish out at Camp Delta, consisted of placing the offending prisoner into a one-man chain-link cell, which was isolated from the general camp population.

The JTF commander had quickly moved to stop the majority of those incidents. The detainees, when being transported, were now shackled at the ankle, handcuffed behind their back, blindfolded, with the additional precaution of a lightweight but opaque hood being placed over their heads. The detainee, thus restrained, still was not transported unless accompanied by two JTF guards, who were to have physical hands-on control of the prisoner at all times.

The procedure may have seemed excessive to a civilian. Admittedly it was one of the frequent complaints of the IRC, the International Red Cross inspectors. Their inspectors were permitted limited and escorted access to the non-occupied confinement areas at Camp Delta. But, the general mused, *neither were the IRC drones getting spit on by detainees who never bothered to utilize the dental hygiene supplies each man had been given. Nor, in the nearly unheard of instance when a foolish IRC inspector had chosen to venture into areas from which they were prohibited, had a prisoner ever attacked them,* the general thought.

To date, knock on wood, General Montrose thought, *there hadn't been a single instance of one of the JTF guards being inflected with one of the many communicable diseases, which were documented in most of the detainee's extensive medical histories. Ninety-five percent of the detainees, despite being permitted access twice daily to toothbrush/toothpaste/floss, ever bothered to brush their teeth. Due to past and perhaps present sexual preferences, a great number of the detainees were HIV-positive. That fact alone didn't endear them to the young homophobic American guards.*

In any case, there were always more serious injuries. Most occurred at the guard force barracks at the JTF's Camp America, and at other barracks across the forty-five square-mile base not directly affiliated with detainee confinement. There was the occasional Humvee accident. An occasional staff member drowned during the recreational activities the base's Special Services office offered. And a few soldiers still managed to gain access to illegally-manufactured moonshine, take illegal drugs, or attempt suicide, to name but a few.

The Pentagon realized that despite the new 'band aid' facilities at the two camps, access to medical care for the base's permanent party' would continue to be a U.S. Navy priority at Guantánamo.

The recently renovated Naval Hospital, located on the most eastern end of the Guantánamo Bay's lower basin, had been designated to handle non-ambulatory special medical needs. Those situations were well-defined by the Pentagon: They included "Incidents where a member of the permanent party attempted suicide; had acquired a communicable disease; were seriously injured and required more than two day's worth of hospitalization as ordered by competent medical authority; or had nearly OD'd on drugs, and therefore by Navy regulations must be confined, until evaluated by the appropriate U.S. Navy medical doctor."

However, as soon as the offending soldier or sailor who had ingested the drugs, was cleared for discharge, the base commander promptly made arrangements to have the offender flown back to the U.S. mainland, under guard, for disciplinary action. Nine times out of ten, that meant an extended sentence in a stateside Marine Corps brig.

But that wasn't the reason General Montrose had left his overflowing desk of must-do paperwork, today. Today, to break up the monotony of the never-ending paperwork, he had decided to take a brief break to play *let's solve a mystery*. The general knew he should be back at his desk, working with his clerical staff. Somehow, the huge pile of requests and approval paperwork, necessary to the orderly running of a U.S. high security detainment facility, must get processed.

Montrose had completed this morning's conference call with the FBI. Then he had met with the Marine colonel, who claimed to be out rigorously looking for imbedded spies in the general's JTF command. After completing these two scheduled activities, the general had dived into the waiting piles of paperwork, like the dedicated commanding officer he was.

But no matter how many piles the general worked himself through, duly reading, then evaluating, and finally either initially or signing each page, a member of his staff would carry in yet another stack of paper, guiltily mumble "sorry," and nearly bolt out of his office, always quietly closing the door behind them.

After several hours of this grunt work, the general was almost ready to throw the tantrum his rank afforded him. He was also giving additional consideration to taking Colonel Lokkesmoe up on his offer to have Lt. Johnson, his pain-in-the-ass aide, transferred to a Marine rifle company for 'seasoning.' That was when he happened to notice a piece of paper laying on the office floor under his desk.

Apparently the errant report on the floor had fallen off the top of the last load of documents his aide carried into his office for processing. Feeling that at the very least, this unique discovery, gave him a due cause to summon Lt. Johnson into his office. And to subject him to a tongue lashing, relative to the Lt's carelessness in the safekeeping of official government documents, that Johnson would not soon forget.

But, after some additional thought, the general hesitated. After all, Johnson's daddy was a powerful U.S. Senator. Major General Montrose decided he ought to at least read the mislaid piece of paper he'd discovered on his floor. If for no other reason than it would supply him with additional facts with which to really ream out his aide. Thus giving the general some badly needed stress-reliving therapy.

The general reached over to pick up the report off the floor, replaced his reading glasses, and began to speed read the document. By the time he was into the second paragraph, he had begun to sit up a little straighter in what his five-year old granddaughter called his 'high-chair.'

The report had the current date, and had been prepared by the GS-15 civilian, Ollie Kellogg, who was responsible for maintaining the base's critical Desalinization and Power Generation plant over on Fisherman's Point.

Kellogg's yeoman had typed:

GUANTÁNAMO BAY NAVAL STATION
UNUSUAL INCIDENT REPORT

"At shift change this morning, out of the six mechanic/guards assigned to monitor the operation and safe keeping of this multi-billion-dollar stand-alone utility on the graveyard shift, only four had been present when it came time for shift change at 0800 hours this morning. Due to the fact that the base's DSPG plant has a great deal of dangerous moving equipment, where a person not exercising due care might inadvertently suffer severe injury, a full-scale search of the areas those individuals were expected to patrol, was launched.

At nearly 1100 hours Local, one of the searchers, on the way back from relieving himself of one of the latrines situated throughout the plant, having taken a little-used route back to his search assignment. In doing so, he came across the body of one of the missing men. The man's body lay in plain sight, close to the M-16A shoulder weapon he apparently had dropped, under a series of ladders whose purpose was to permit access to the top of one of the desalinization tanks, which is over fifty-feet in height.

The condition of the body, which appeared to have slipped or tumbled off the highest of the catwalks, landing on his head, left no doubt to the searcher that the victim was dead. Without stopping to check for a pulse, the search team member called dispatch to report the dead body. The civilian employee then waited approximately five minutes until the rest of the search team arrived at the apparent accident scene.

The first supervisor on the scene, remembering the training he had received when he had been in the military and a member of NCIS, Naval Criminal Investigative Service, secured the scene and directed one of the members of the search team to start a Accident/Crime scene log, taking note of the names of all the on-scene personnel, their time in and time out, et cetera, and other details.

The former NCIS employee was improperly

instructed by a new supervisor that the location of the 'found' body was not a crime scene. Hence traditional crime scene booties and latex surgical gloves were not used, which had the effect of contaminating the scene further. However, another civilian employee did have the forethought to obtain a clean, empty trashcan from an adjacent operational area, as a receptacle for the depositing any trash generated by anyone who entered the formerly secure area. The other man's assignment, until he was relieved by Base Security, was to prevent *anyone* from trespassing inside the unofficial accident scene area, that his higher-graded co-worker, the ex-NCIS investigator team member, had prudently roped off.

Within ten-minutes, both Base Security in the person of Lt. David Hasseldorf, USN, and an base ambulance driven by USN—HN 3rd class petty officer, Joan Gunderson, and staffed by USN Hospital Corpsman, HN Billy Joe Hargasy, had arrived.

The Base Security officer also had his men secure the beach area outside, and behind the large utility plant, that extends approximately 100-yards to the shoreline of the Guantánamo Bay Naval Base, lower basin. The beach directly next to the building is overgrown with Jaguey, a short, fat trunk tree with stocky branches that grows on portions of the Naval base.

The responding medical team unloaded a collapsible aluminum stretcher, walked it with some difficulty through the maze of desalinization equipment to get to the place where the DB lay.

Lt. Hasseldorf, acting OD, Officer of the Day—for Base Security, believing the death was caused by carelessness, accident, or misadventure; authorized the Medical Corpsmen to move the body, and transport it to the closest Medical Aid station, where the victim could be declared legally dead, and then transported out to morgue located on Hospital Cay. At that point, as the body was leaving by ambulance to be transported as directed, the second missing mechanic/guard had not yet been located.

However, one of the members of the co-joined search team, did indicate that the missing civilian individual had been a disciplinary problem in the past. His co-worker also reported that the missing man occasionally left his assigned post exactly on the hour he was to be relieved, but prior to actually being relieved, when his relief was unavoidably a few minutes late.

The missing mechanic/guard is reportedly believed to be cohabitating (this a unsubstantiated claim) with, and in the quarters of, an unknown female management employee of one of the bases' service vendors. Inquires are continuing to determine the name of the employee, her domicile location on base, and the missing mechanic/guard's current whereabouts.

A couple members of the plant's on-duty general maintenance staff, although not being instructed to, misunderstood their supervisor's orders and had subsequently swabbed and power washed the victim's blood off the expanded metal flooring, and removed the yellow four-inch tape, imprinted with Accident Scene—Do not Disturb.

General Montrose, when he arrived at that section of the report, cursed under his breath, and read on.

When the body arrived at the ER on Naval Hospital, the on-duty physicians, Naval Ltjg. Susan Rickmore, and Lt. David Hightower, performed an routine triage inspection of the body. After a detailed medical examination, the two medical doctors briefly conferred, and then placed a call to inform the Base Security OD, Naval Lt. David Hasseldorf, that while they "would have to wait for an autopsy to make sure, their preliminary finding was that body was a victim of apparent foul play."

Submitted,

Ollie Kellogg,
DSPG Manager—GS 15

This is exactly what I need to get away from this paperwork for a while, the general had thought—a genuine who-dun-it. He picked up his phone and summoned the head of his security detail. That phone call unknowingly forced the JTF duty Sergeant, Cheryl Johnson, currently down $20 in a cut-throat poker game, which was being played against military regulations in the guard's dayroom, to regretfully fold her hand. Johnson was responsible for supervising the security team, whose mission it was to guarantee that the general reached the U.S. Naval medical facility located over on Hospital Cay without incident.

That requirement forced Johnson to leave the poker game, which prevented her from blowing the remainder of her paycheck on the card game. The very same card game in which it seemed only she had been unaware, that the cards in play were 'marked.'

General Montrose arrived in the ER and was met by the two USN medical doctors. They escorted him without delay to a private room, which by Naval Standards seemed a little too pretentious.

Unknown to the general who was said to have a phobia for hospitals, having spent nearly a year in one recovering from combat injuries after the first Gulf war, the room he had just entered normally if covertly served as a recreation lounge for the Navy's duty ER physicians. The medical officers consider it their due, as partial and unofficial compensation for their long, boring shifts. Often was the case when a complete shift would go by without seeing a patient having a valid medical complaint. Not even a patient complaining of a hangnail.

Yes, the doctors thought, fantasizing about the big paychecks they were going to be drawing down one day in private practice. Once they had completed the inconvenient military service they had obligated themselves to serve, for which the Navy had paid for their expensive medical educations. Yes, the doctors thought, a recreational lounge was their due.

However, once the ER's acting head nurse, a newly minted U.S. Naval Ensign full of herself, heard through the grapevine that the JTF commanding officer was en-route the ER, the regular rules went out the window. Suddenly all the unauthorized equipment in the misappropriated room, such as the big screen television, several recliners, a Play station.2 machine, and DVD-player, all vanished, as if into thin air. Actually the unauthorized entertainment equipment had been frantically shoved down the hall. The doctors shoved it all into the hospital's morgue, and covered it with white autopsy table drapes.

The unsanctioned recreational lounge had been hurriedly vacated, and returned to some semblance of the Navy's original designated use for the space—as isolation room for patients discovered to have a highly communicable disease.

And immediately, once the decedent's cause of death status had unexpectedly changed from 'Accidental,' to 'Death—Foul play suspected', the bed containing the mechanic/guard's shattered body, had been hurriedly rolled on its casters from the small cloth-screened cubicle in which it had been originally been placed in upon arrival, to the now-available two-bed, hard-walled, isolation room.

The ER staff, especially the doctors, were silently praying that the general didn't notice that Navy physicians over the years, had managed to con some maintenance guy into tearing up the room's original lowest-bidder-installed linoleum floor tiles. And replace it with some far more expensive carpet that one of the doctors had stolen one evening from a base construction shed. It was being temporarily stored there for its scheduled installation in the multi-denominational base chapel.

The two ER doctors, the general, and Lt. Johnson, the general officer's aide, all donned contamination-prevention surgical facemasks, and entered the room which now was occupied by the sheet-wrapped body of the dead DSPG mechanic/guard. One of the doctors snapped up couple x-rays up on the viewing screens, that only minutes before had been recovered from some remote closet. Then using a Navy pen, he pointed out the trauma damage to the body's cervical spine, including the dislodged first and second vertebrate, and the severed spinal cord in between.

The younger of the two doctors approached the body which was now laying on one of the over-sized room's two hospital beds. He unwrapped the sheet from the head and neck of the deceased. Lt. Hightower, the ranking ER physician on duty that afternoon, log-rolled the body over to point out the entrance wound on the rear of the cervical spine, and ventured his professional opinion how the young man had received the injury. Dr. Rickmore nodded her concurrence with the opinion being expressed by Dr. Hightower.

Dr. Hightower added that the reason the first responders apparently had missed the entry wound, was that the head, neck, and shoulders of the victim had gross injures. And that those injuries were consistent with an individual falling from a significant height, striking his upper torso and cranium numerous times on immovable metal structure, as the body fell to the expanded metal floor, landing on its head.

Dr. Rickmore volunteered that pre-mortem bruising was present on the victim's forehead, and she felt that the post-mortem autopsy would show that the anterior muscles and esophagus in the neck were torn. Rickmore, from the experience she had received during her internship with the Navy Medical Examiner's Office, said she'd seen bruising like that before. And based on that experience, she felt the autopsy would show that the victim had been murdered. She ventured the death likely was at the hands of someone who had been trained in hand-to-hand combat.

General Montrose, who up until that point, had been hoping

the doctor would just move on and reapply the sheet wrap to the victim's head, hesitated, and took another look at the extensive damage to the head and neck of the guard. He thought, *damn— here we have an apparent murder victim. The other missing mechanic/ guard still has not been located, according to the latest report he'd receive from the base security officer of the Day, despite a full-base BOLO, be-on-the-lookout.*

The civilian G-15 over at the Desalinization and Power Generation plant, apparently had written the guy who was still missing, off as a long-term discipline problem and had driven on—just business as usual.

The general thought, *this entire situation just doesn't seem right. The investigators at base security seemed content to close this out as an accident until the cause of death was changed from 'accidental' to 'death by foul play.'*

We're making this far too simple, and not bothering to take the time to dig up all the pertinent details. If the still-missing guard was a chronic discipline problem, why haven't I heard his name before? According to the security briefing, the manager claimed the missing man had been living with a female manager who was employed by one of the base's civilian contractors. Why hadn't I heard that? Christ knows I hear all other kinds of bullshit rumors on this damn base, most of them from the clerical staff in my own office. If one of the master sergeant's office specialists hears this stuff, why haven't I?

Well, I damn well am going to get to the bottom of this. Without the base's Desalinization and Power Generation Plant, we'd have to pack up Guantánamo and head home, with our tail between our legs. Probably dragging the nearly seven hundred Taliban and al-Qaeda terrorist suspects with us. The only other option would be to turn them loose—which you can bet your last dollar, this president of the United States isn't going to approve. Not after over six hundred American body bags that have already been flown home from Iraq, Afghanistan, and Pakistan.

The general turned to his aide and said, "Lt. Johnson, you get on the horn and alert the base security OD and Lieutenant Commander Murphy. Tell them I said he is to form a search team immediately, and get them over to the base's power plant, most *ricky tick*. We'll meet him there. I want to see every counterterrorism-trained soldier, and bomb-squad trained expert assigned this command, on-scene when we arrive. And, should those two MOSs be currently understaffed, tell the base security duty officer I said to go ahead and temporarily release anyone with that military occupational specialty code, who might be in the brig over there. In other words, those individuals who are being held for trial, but not yet convicted of, minor UCMJ Article 32 infractions and the usual misdemeanor crap."

"I expect the counterterrorism guys and the bomb squad guys to check out, and arrive with, their authorized load-out of explosive disarming equipment. I expect to see no less than ten CT/BS specialists, with their bomb wagons, waiting for us at the plant, ready to roll, in less than forty-five minutes. Now do you have any questions, lieutenant?"

To his credit, Johnson recovered quickly to the unanticipated flurry of commands. He wisely decided to use his military-encrypted cell phone, instead of the bases' hard-line system, that base security recently had announced could be 'tapped' by the Cubans.

The general noted that his young aide, when speaking for Montrose, spoke carefully in an authoritative tone. He also had refused to accept any argument from the officer on the other end of the conversation, who out-ranked the lieutenant by several pay grades.

Montrose thought, *maybe this kid has what it takes after all—maybe I haven't given him much chance to show what he is capable of. After all, an aide billet to a general officer is only assigned after that junior officer has been judged by his superiors to be worthy of being put on the fast track. Aides are supposed to not only support the general in performance of his duties, but also to learn from the superior officer he is serving. The desired end result being that the aide will be a better, more effective officer, once he has gained enough experience and time-in-grade to be given a shot at additional command responsibility himself.*

Of course, these were unvoiced thoughts of General Montrose, and not spoken words. So he continued to glare at the lieutenant, and asked "Are you about ready to get to work, Johnson, now that you have had a nice little conversation with the security commander concerning your weekend golf date?" All Johnson said in reply, was "Yes, Sir."

The aide signaled the general's security team to mount up, and assume their assigned protective positions for twenty-minute drive over to the base's DSPG plant located on Fisherman Point.

When the Gitmo JTF commander and his retinue arrived at the 100,000 square-foot Desalinization and Power Generation plant, Lt. Commander Murphy of base security was already there, with no less than fifteen fatigue-clad U.S. Navy demolition specialists. Each man was busily inspecting the tools and equipment of their chosen military trade.

The base's three, boiled-egg-shaped blast suppression trailers, each being pulled by a Humvee, were lined up immediately adjacent to each of the utility building's main overhead access doors. The civilian plant superintendent, Otto Kellogg, was also present with a dozen or so of the plant's journeymen operators.

Lt. Johnson, the general's ever-surprising young aide, who now appeared to have the makings of a future 'dog robber', also had the foresight to obtain four, fully-staffed Army ambulances from various command's around the forty-five square mile base. Lt. Johnson dismounted ahead of the general from the command Humvee. He walked over to the ranking base security officer present, Lt. Commander Murphy.

Lt. Johnson, unceremoniously, instructed Murphy to reach out for his noncoms and junior officers, and have them report to the general's Humvee for a briefing in five minutes. Without taking any time to acknowledge the order delivered by the junior officer, Murphy turned, jogged back to his men, and started giving orders.

Inside five minutes, Johnson had returned to the command Humvee, and briefed the general. The lieutenant instructed the driver to "get the Mobile Command Center," each of the designated Humvees carried, "out and set up. Then verify we have established encrypted radio contact with the base's subordinate commands."

Inside the same five minutes, General Montrose had completed jotting down a few notes for his briefing. He climbed up on the hood of the Humvee to address the soldiers, civilians, and one USNR Medical Doctor, assembled there. Once the men had 'taken a knee,' Montrose sat down on the Humvee hood, and began his briefing.

"Ok, troops, here is what we have. Sometime during the early morning hours today, two of the six mechanic/guards assigned the night watch here at the DSPG plant, went missing. Apparently, and I'm sure that Commander Murphy will dig out all the facts on this later, the radio procedure intended to insure the integrity of the watch was either not activated, or simply sloppily maintained. Either way, it will be someone's ass—and I hope it isn't the butt of anyone assembled here."

Montrose continued, "At the DSPG plant's shift change this morning, the disappearance was noted—hell, I should hope so! Thirty-three percent of the night shift's mechanic/guard contingent was missing. Ray Charles could have seen that! Ok, when the base security's 'flying squad' arrived to search the place, they found one of the missing men, dead. He apparently was the victim of an accidental fall off one of the desalinization holding tanks. The body was pretty beat up, what with the presumed damage suffered from falling over fifty-feet down through the steel catwalks, railings, and support structures."

"The search team from base security didn't find the second missing guard, but did obtain some history from his fellow co-workers. The guy reportedly had some disciplinary problems in the past, by way of unacceptable behavior, and failure to follow orders. The man had abruptly walked off his assigned duty station before, when his relief had unavoidably been a few minutes late in relieving him. The still-missing second man is now classified as being administratively AWOL, and the base's security command has issued a base-wide BOLO."

"According to some of his co-workers," the general went on, "the missing guard had recently bragged that he was shacking up with some currently unidentified female civilian employee on base, and was no longer staying in his assigned barracks. Yet another charge for his arraignment sheet, once Commander Murphy's troops run him down."

Montrose continued, "The body of the mechanic/guard that the security team discovered this morning, was transported first to the nearest medical facility for formal death declaration, and then to the ER over on Hospital Cay for preliminary certification of cause of death and a official post-mortem autopsy later today."

At that point, the general paused, referred briefly to his notes, and went on, "When the body of the night shift mechanic/guard finally did reach the ER at the Naval Hospital, two of the Navy doctors over there decided that despite the massive injuries to the upper torso and head of the deceased, they didn't believe the death to be accidental, as everyone else had assumed. Especially after post-mortem x-rays revealed two shattered cervical vertebrates, a severed spinal cord, unexplained facial bruising, all incidental to a entrance wound apparently from some type of thin-bladed knife to the victim's neck."

"Base security is looking for the AWOL guard. I am told they have a base-wide dragnet deployed, and hopefully it will be successful before military twilight, tonight."

General Montrose stretched his shoulders, and slid off the Humvee hood to continue. "Ok, this is what this says to me—I'm assuming some of you more experienced troops and senior investigators also are having some doubts."

"So I'll just open the briefing for discussion. First assume, even though the medicos will have to complete their port-mortem autopsy, and get their toxicology reports back before issuing a written cause of death finding, that the first guard was murdered."

"Ok, why? Each of the civilian mechanic/guards, on night shift here, have the primarily responsibility to make sure none of the desalinization and power generation equipment 'breaks' on his or her watch. Secondarily, they are to protect the plant's safekeeping, due to the criticality of the plant itself to United States interests here at Gitmo. Ergo, why was this non-combatant killed, and what makes the ER docs think it was at the hands of a experienced professional killer?"

"The dead guy, a Staff Sergeant Billy Masters, had been in the army for nearly ten years. He had a spotless military record. A couple years ago, he decided to try civilian life for a while. Didn't like it. He planned to reenlist, and go for the gold butter bars. He was committed to making a little-late-in-life bid for OCS (Officers Candidate School). He had no civilian yellow sheet we could find, and was a master mechanic. Meaning he could stayed out of the military and earned big bucks on the outside. Masters had excellent performance reports from his superiors, dating all the way back to his enlistment."

The JTF commander proceeded, somewhat sarcastically, saying "I guess it is no secret anymore that Gitmo, specifically Camp Delta and Camp America, and the new expansion camp called America—North, have been infiltrated to one degree or another, by a few spies who were drawing paychecks from the JTF, but loyal to al-Qaeda. I just got off the phone with the FBI this morning, and they advise that two of the three suspects have already been charged. At least one of them may get the death penalty, which in my opinion, is too good for him. The JAG/NCIS teams from Southern Command you see poking around the base, tell me off the record, that they at this point suspect nearly a dozen more military and civilian persons may be spying for al-Qaeda. I, personally, can't in my wildest dreams believe that figure is factual, but that's just me."

"My question still is, why would anyone go to all the trouble of infiltrating a well-fortified American base, be they Cubans or whomever, just to kill a mechanic or two? It doesn't make any sense to me—anyone here have an ideas?"

Both Lt. Johnson, and Lieutenant Commander Murphy, spoke up at the same time. The aide turned to the superior officer, and said "Rank has its privileges. Sir. Go ahead"

Murphy tugged his ear lobe, and began, "As you know, this multi-million dollar desalinization plant and power generation plant was built in the 1960's, after Castro kept flipping the utilities switches to the base, every time he got a little heated over anything. In two of these instances, the United States had no choice other than uproot hundreds of military and civilian dependants, and send them back to the U.S. mainland."

"Back on the mainland, our families would spend up to a year settling in, then be uprooted to return to Guantánamo when some politician judged the crisis was over. This occurred at least two times, until Congress told the Navy to build a desalinization plant, and stand-alone power generation facility, sized to sustain the base without any reliance on Cuban supplies, equipment, or utilities."

Holding up his hand, General Montrose broke into the monolog, and said "Commander, each of us had to go through the standard briefing on base history, and customs and culture of the Cuban people, before we were assigned to this hardship duty station. Let's forego the Chamber of Commerce speech, if you would, and get to the answer for the questions I asked."

Commander Murphy nodded to the general, and said respectfully, "Well, Sir, you know an Irishman is never permitted to use a few words, when a couple of dozen will due."

"Not on my dime, Commander," the general said with a slight smile on his face for his old West Point classmate.

"General, men," Murphy began again, "I've got a gut feeling here, and I'll wager a month's paycheck check that the general does too. But he is practicing one of the those management styles that generals all learn at Command and General Staff school at Fort Leavenworth, before they put on the stars. My gut tells me this plant may have been mined to the fair-thee-well. Taking this facility out of commission would effectively return Guantánamo back to the early 1960's. It would force either the relocation, or the release of, nearly seven hundred Taliban and/or al-Qaeda terrorist suspect detainees. Which, if nothing else, would cause America to lose face. That would negatively impact our leadership role in the War-on-Terror Coalition, as well as throughout the world. Any in disagreement with that statement?" the commander inquired.

Lt. Johnson, invited by the commander's hand gesture to speak began, "General, Commander, men—that is pretty much chapter and verse what also has been running through my mind today. Except, I had one additional thought—if this plant is mined, are the detonators on timers, or are they to be manually activated by one of al-Qaeda's spies? Either way, I suspect we ought to stop pontificating here, and get into the plant in systematic teams.

Each team ought to be accompanied by a civilian mechanic. That is, if they are willing to confront the risk factor. We have to check this place out, carefully but expediently, from deck to overhead."

The general, thinking both of these relatively junior officers were pretty damn smart, turned and told Lt. Commander Murphy, "Get with Superintendent Kellogg here, Commander, and make this happen. In the next fifteen minutes, I want to see nothing but assholes and elbows, swarming all over this plant."

"To get Lt. Johnson and his boyish enthusiasm out of your hair, I'll take him with me into the plant's employee training room. We'll set up a command post there, and be prepared to receive for the reports I want from your people on the half-hour. Are there any questions?" The general asked, looking around at each man assembled in front of the Humvee.

Lt. Johnson spoke up again, "Er, Sir, wouldn't I be more effective, out on the plant floor, working with one of the investigation teams?" Proving to himself that he still the game face he had spent hours in front of the mirror developing when he was a rookie Army linebacker at West Point, the general only had to glare at his aide to answer that question. Without any further discussion, Johnson and the general's security contingent began to rapidly remove the portable MCC systems from the Humvees, and carry them into the plant's large training room.

Johnson didn't have to be told that the general expected the command systems to be on-line, and fully operational within thirty minutes, or less.

Several hours later that afternoon, the general would admit to himself that the entire exercise, while critically important to Gitmo and the United States, had rapidly turned anti-climatic.

Within the first hour, the searchers had located the remaining missing guard's body, jammed headfirst into an empty 55-gal drum that originally has contained grease-sweep. Then, one after another, five large caches of weaponized Semtex explosives were detected. Each hiding place had been brilliantly selected, but poorly concealed, in floor-level nooks and crannies, instead of much more difficult to inspect locations high on top of the plant's tall operating equipment.

In the instance of the concealed mechanic/guard's body, it clearly was a case of the doer having too little imagination, or more likely, too little time and/or patience. The hiding place the doer had selected would only have concealed the body for as long as the smell of decay had permitted. In the tropics, that limiting factor would have been hours, not days.

To root out the explosive caches, a half dozen bomb sniffing dogs had been brought in. Within fifteen minutes of the K-9 teams hitting the utility plant's floor, the dogs had alerted on the explosives. The six canines seemed greatly disappointed at only finding five emplacements of the deadly Semtex. The dogs, their naval handlers, and Murphy's search teams, went over every cubic foot of the 100,000 square foot plant. This including crawling to the top of each of the steep, steel cat walks that provided access to roofs of the huge fifty-foot tall, 'holding tanks.'

The general gathered the team's noncoms, officers, and enlisted dog handlers in the training room a couple hours later, and demanded, "Tell me you are absolutely sure there are no more explosives in this facilities."

One of the Navy chiefs, a former SEAL, with thirty years of experience and an attitude to match, shook his head before standing up to address the general. Somewhat flippantly, the old chief told the general to have the chief's wife, and eight-year-old son, flown in from Florida on a fast jet (he'd love the flight, sir!). The family would bring a small portable television set, so the chief could watch football. Then the entire family would camp out in the plant, as long as it took to convince the general that the place was now danger-free."

After the chuckles subsided, the general posed one question directly to the ex-SEAL. "Why did the guys who placed this stuff use expensive digital timers, instead of much cheaper and far more available Casio detonators on the Semtex bombs? And in your opinion, chief, you old sea dog, is there any significance in the fact that all the charges were apparently set to detonate at midnight, but the specific day timers, were not even activated?"

"Well," the old chief drawled, "First, General, who knows how terrorists think? And how much training do you think they have? Are they terrified to be anywhere around the unstable Semtex—I know I am. More importantly, did their bosses expect and want them to survive the explosion? It took me six months to learn all facets and complicated methodology necessary to intelligently use explosives in the advanced BUD/S course at Miramar, Sir. And I still learn something new, everyday."

"If the bad guys only wanted something to go boom, to shake up the natives, and didn't really want the person who placed the bomb to survive, to be available for interrogation, he may purposely have decided to sacrifice the expendable, low-level, operative."

The chief continued, "One further fact that I called and verified with SEAL Team Four, was that this particular brand of timer is shipped by the manufacturer in Poland, through a third country. It is calibrated and set at the factory with the default of midnight on the 'hours' circuit, and no setting on the seven-day 'date' circuit. Supposedly, this gives the recipient a 'marker' by which to ensure the device hasn't been removed from the packing, or altered, on the way from the factory. Of course, Sir, someone could have reset the device to the settings they were on when we found them, sir. But then, that is above my paygrade."

"The only thing we know as certain as death and taxes, is that those explosives are not going to detonate now. SEAL Team Four's recommendation is that base security should make sure the unstable shit is burned up immediately, as in ASAP. And not retained for future use, such as the base's annual barbeque. Modified Semtex, as highly enhanced as this stuff is, is already very unstable. That is why the SEALS, the Green Bennies, the Rangers, and Delta Force only use composition four, or C-4. Its a lot more stable. Semtex, which is unstable to start with, becomes brittle and sensitive over time. And we have no idea how old this particular batch is. Its not a problem today, but an old Navy Bosuns' mate on my first carrier, the Enterprise, told me once—It never hurts to keep a deck swabbed clean, even when it ain't fouled, sir."

The next day, the general would find himself wishing he had spent more time with the old Navy chief. Perhaps the chief could have provided some foresight into the deadly hell storm that had assaulted the Guantánamo Bay Naval base, at midnight, that same day. When the hands of time both raced to reach the numeral 12, and his command had exploded!

NEWS BULLETIN (Excepts from)
Associated Press
01 February 2004

U.S. TROOPS TAKE
POSSIBILITY OF
AL-QAIDA ATTACK
ON GUANTÁNAMO
BAY SERIOUSLY!
By Ian James
Associated Press Writer

GUANTÁNAMO BAY NAVAL BASE, Cuba—Firing heavy machine-guns and mortars, U.S. soldiers practiced repulsing a commando attack Saturday at the maximum-security prison for terror suspects at Guantánamo Bay.

While the possibility of terrorists trying to break out prisoners seems remote, its critical for the soldiers to be prepared, said Capt. Gregg Langevin, a 33-year-old from the Massachusetts Army National Guard.

"There have been reports that the al-Qaida are out there actively trying to buy small crafts," Langevin said, suggesting a stealthy approach from the coast.

Some 650 men from more than 40 countries are detained at the remote camp in eastern Cuba, suspected of fighting for Osama bin-Laden or the ousted afghan Taliban regime that sheltered his insurgents.

Major General (NAME REDACTED BY SECURITY PERSONNEL), commander of the detention mission, said guards warned detainees that they would hear blasts that were a part of a training exercise.

Guantánamo is about 110 miles from Haiti, 150 miles from Jamaica and 230 miles from the U.S. coast around Miami.

Saturday's drills ended four days of exercises involving about 1,200 soldiers. Such training has taken place every four to six weeks since the prison camp was established in January 2002, in the wake of the Sept. 11, 2001 terrorist attacks and the war in Afghanistan.

Because escape from the base is an "enormously remote" possibility, that scenario isn't a training priority, (NAME REDACTED BY SECURITY PERSONNEL) said.

30—END OF BULLETIN

CHAPTER EIGHTEEN

DAY 332—29 NOVEMBER

MOHAVE COUNTY—0900 HOURS

THE SABOTEURS

LAKE HAVASU CITY

ARIZONA

Mohammed, the leader of the planned Lake Havasu City attack had received Osama bin-Laden's coded 'be-prepare-to-attack' message a week earlier. It had been received over the expensive Zenith short wave radio he had purchased from the Radio Shack store in Lake Havasu City. Bin-Laden's plan was that the two al-Qaeda diversionary attacks were to occur at the same moment. One of the targets was destruction of the water intake towers above Hoover Dam. Occurring concurrently would be the attack on infrastructure some one hundred twenty miles away in Lake Havasu City, Arizona. The latter attack was Mohammed's responsibility. Both had been planned in great detail by Ayman al-Zawahiri, al-Qaeda's chief planner and bin-Laden's chief deputy.

The resulting region-wide disruption wrought by the attacks, would cause American law enforcement agencies to focus on the southwestern portion of the United States. Only then could the final execution for the assault on the U.S. Guantánamo Naval Station in Cuba begin. The goal of the Guantánamo mission was to rescue as many of the detainees now being incarcerated at Camp Delta as possible.

Osama bin-Laden intended to send a clear message to the American's hated 'Coalition.' That being that "there was no safe haven in the world that al-Qaeda couldn't penetrate, breach and destroy."

If Mohammed had been operating in Saudi Arabia, permission for the acquisition of the hi-power short-wave radio would of required that he complete dozen of forms, in triplicate. He would also have to endure several, possibly physically unpleasant interviews, with officials at the Saud Government's State Security offices in Riyadh. They would have insisted on a complete background check of himself and his family going back three generations. The investigation would have taken at least six months to complete.

He never would have passed background check. Despite having been told that 'approval' would be forthcoming once he had proven his worthiness by making "a suitable monetary gift" to Saudi government officials.

The authorization to proceed with the current phase of al-Qaeda's planned diversionary attacks had been concealed in a minor news story regarding the OIL-FOR-FOOD program. The Americans had been pushing the program in the United Nations Security Council for post-war Iraq following the infidel president's declaration that "The time of hostilities are over in Iraq."

Mohammed, knowing that hundreds of American soldiers had died since that announcement, could only wonder if all the American infidels were that naïve.

The messages had been broadcast through an al-Qaeda arrangement with *Al-Jezeera*. The message that Mohammed had received was intended for the two of al-Qaeda's assault teams, albeit with separate missions. The individual team leaders were expected to go to a local American public library to obtain access to the Internet. Each team leader would log into a secretly funded al-Qaeda website to obtain his team's unique set of instructions.

The message *Al-Jezeera* had aired was repeated in the same time slot over three consecutive nights. Al-Qaeda always compartmentalized such information on a strict need-to-know basis for reasons of operational security.

The al-Qaeda 'notice-to-proceed' message, that *Al-Jezeera* broadcast had been scripted in a cave deep in Afghanistan. The message would eventually bring death to hundreds if not thousands of the infidels. It had been hand-carried by a trusted courier from bin-Laden's immediate family. Its route had extended from the mountainous lair where the surviving members of al-Qaeda's upper command were hiding, to the terrorist's contact at *Al-Jezeera*.

Al-Jezeera was headquartered in Riyadh, Saudi Arabia's capital city, which is located in the southeast section of the country. The Arabic-language, multimedia conglomerate, consisted of a regional newspaper with a daily circulation of over fifty million readers. It also included a high-power satellite TV channel, and several radio stations, and frequently had served as a communications link for al-Qaeda. For Osama bin-Laden, more specifically. Most Arabs incorrectly assumed that the bin-Laden fortune financed, and controlled the media giant.

The tactic of using hand-to-hand couriers was a method taken from the Arabic centuries-old history in waging warfare. Osama Bin-Laden had been forced to return to the low-tech method almost a year earlier.

Al-Qaeda had discovered that the American's National Security Agency, NSA, had managed to tap into bin-Laden's satellite telephone transmissions. The Al-Qaeda leader reasoned correctly, that the Americans could have used the logistical GPS information from the cyber tap on his sat-phone, to launch a cruise missile attack on the subterranean hideout of al-Qaeda's top commander.

However, the Americans had failed to take advantage of the eavesdrop-obtained GPS information. Bin-Laden had no doubt that NSA and the Pentagon had briefly known his exact location. The location where he placed or received the calls. Fortunately, or unfortunately depending on whose side one was on, the charismatic leader of al-Qaeda never stayed in one location for more than a few hours.

Someone in the American intelligence community, or higher, apparently elected to pass on the opportunity to seize the moment and act. The GPS fix from the satellite phone would have easily pinpointed the user's exact location, plus or minus six feet. To Al-Qaeda, and the rest of the world's extremist Muslim community, the infidels had once again demonstrated their unwillingness or inability to risk the condemnation of the world community.

The resulting cruise missile attack would have no doubt resulted in unavoidable collateral civilian deaths, and casualties. That consideration apparently was of greater worry to the American politicians, than the existence of one militant terrorist. Despite the fact that particular Arab had massacred in excess of 3,000 of their countrymen on 9/11/01.

This perceived lack of commitment, as the many enemies of the United States have construed that hesitation, demonstrated to the Arab world once again why the extremist Muslim community people should never fear the Americans as an enemy. The infidels were perceived by Arab community, and occasionally also their Coalition partners, as lacking the resolve to protect their nation from a declared and committed enemy.

In the Muslim world, that was considered a sign of weakness. According to the Arabic elders, Americans had yet to mature to the point where they understood that unflagging resolve and commitment to purpose was required before any nation-state could achieve greatness from, through, and by her people.

That perceived character fault had first brought the Americans defeat on the battlefields of Vietnam. Then some years later, through the medium of a commercially distributed Hollywood action movie, entitled 'Blackhawk Down,' the wealthy nation had accepted the glamorization of the deaths of its brave warriors at the hands of an insignificant tin pot warlord. The movie even documented the

American's retreat from Somalia. Even now, al-Qaeda's strategists were telling bin-Laden that the American's lack of resolve would defeat them in post-war Iraq.

The weakness was perceived to come from the American's lukewarm support of her military endeavors. The public was usually in favor of the Americans moving into a small country under arms, until the first battlefield death. The American military measured the successful pursuit of the country's seemingly endless cyclical conflicts, by units of years, months, weeks, hours, real estate won, and enemy body counts on the battlefield. Her citizens measured it by the number of her young people who returned home in body bags.

The Americans had enjoyed unqualified success in developing high technology, and marketing it around the planet. However those same accomplishments contributed to their leader's inability to accept the fact that terrorists were still willing to utilize 'hand-to-hand couriers' as a viable method for warfare in the new millennium. It just didn't fit into the Pentagon's flexibility-restricted method of conducting today's warfare. In the eyes of their highest military leaders, it simply wasn't the way one did the warfare business these days.

This despite the fact that alumni of America's finest military colleges would attest to the fact that an ancient Chinese General's motto had long occupied a spot on the classroom walls at West Point, the Colorado Spring U.S. Air Force Academy, and the U.S. Naval Academy. The framed motto was each student's mandatory first stop upon enrolling at the US Army's Staff and General Officer College in Fort Leavenworth, Kansas. It read, "In peace prepare for War, and in war prepare for Peace. The art of war is of vital importance to the state. It is a matter of life and death, a road either to safety or to ruin. Hence under no circumstances can it be neglected . . ."

Osama bin-Laden, absent his radical extremist mindset, might have been much in demand on the speaker circuit at the military academies of the world. He had come to accept the same time-measurement methodology, as did Napoleon and Genghis Khan. And later General Sun Tzu's composition entitled "The Art of War" written some 2,500 years before by the Chinese commander-in-chief. Bin-Laden closely followed the teachings of history of which he was a devout student.

Al-Qaeda planned operations, using the time-proven method of transporting hand-carried documents and/or messages via a hand-to-hand courier, must be measured by the achievement of carefully defined packages of 'work.' And only after the necessary supporting infrastructure is in-place to permit the activity. Or, in other words, the courier will deliver the message into the terrorist operator's hands, *once* and only *once* he/or she reached the city, airport, and contact locations, specified is the courier's orders for this particular transaction.

Hopefully, this explanation allows us to understand the immense challenge that the U.S. Homeland Security Department, the FBI, or the CIA, have to overcome and deal with in order to propose any change in terrorist alert status to the president of the United States.

The part of the equation that often is confusing to the average American is the time required for escalating from a yellow status alert, to a far more serious red status. It involves literally ten of thousands of intelligence man-hours. NSA must first eavesdrop on hundreds of thousands of otherwise private telephone and email conversations.

Then it takes from eight to sixteen hours of dreadfully expensive Cray supercomputer time to process all the data the NSA collects. These mysterious Cray's are located in well-guarded basements at the National Security Agency, the CIA headquarters out in Virginia, and at the Pentagon. Also through exorbitantly expensive, time-share contracts the government maintains with the Los Alamos National Laboratory in New Mexico, and privately owned supercomputers located in Arizona, Illinois, Virginia, and in Washington State.

The Jihad targets that the al-Qaeda planners select often don't make much sense to a trained military officer. Nor would the ones al-Qaeda planned for Lake Havasu City. A number of soft targets had been selected, and only two, hard targets—the airport and a critical cell tower. However, each of the six target's explosives charges was to detonate at the same time. The purpose was to cause maximum disruption and diversion.

The targets had been selected for their ability to 'shock and awe' American attention away from what bin-Laden felt were ones of higher value. Or at least those that were of greater benefit to the furthering of al-Qaeda's long-held commitment to bring the terrorist attacks back onto U.S. soil.

Bin-Laden meant to force the Americans to abandon the support of the ruling Saud family in Saudi Arabia, which would hasten its downfall. And stand idly by during a coup by fanatic Muslim idealists, who were only beholden to the extremisms established by Allah's messenger, the Prophet Muhammed.

The first target that had been selected, back in that drafty Afghanistan cave, was the destruction of the world-famous London Bridge. Only reassembled in 1971, its 100,000 tons had been shipped as ship's ballast from England by the late Robert McCulloch, founder of Lake Havasu City, three decades earlier. The island was created by the cutting of a channel through a existing peninsula.

The island, which juts out into Lake Havasu, is part of the city. It was on the island that the area's first airport was built. The tarmac provided self-made real estate and chainsaw manufacturing mogul, Robert McCulloch, a landing strip for the hundreds of prospective buyers, he regularly flew from California to Lake Havasu to purchase lots in his new city.

Today, isleside remains a vital part of the community. It generates more sales and bed tax revenues, than does the city proper. Over the years, the rustic old island airfield has been abandoned, and the function relocated.

The new Lake Havasu airport is capable of handling narrow-body commercial jet aircraft. The tourist trade supports limited passenger operations, which are provided by a regional air carrier. The airport is located north of the city proper, across from the

New Home Depot store—along Highway 95 North, nineteen miles south of Interstate Highway 40.

The island's only connection with the 'mainland' is the bridge that developer Robert McCulloch brought to Lake Havasu in the late 1960's. Real estate developers hope that the island will be developed in a manner reminiscent of that highly conservative bastion, Balboa Island. Balboa is located in the City of Newport Beach, Orange County, California.

Both permanent residents and snowbirds call Isleside their home. Modern hotels, trailer parks, campgrounds, a golf course, marinas, and dozens of service-oriented commercial businesses, have been developed. The Lake Havasu tourist trade frequents the island for its excellent restaurants, recreational opportunities and enthusiastic nightlife. The sole commercial means of traveling by boat between the lake's California and Arizona shorelines is the large passenger shuttle *The Dreamcatcher* that travels cross-lake between Havasu and the Chemehuevi Indian tribe's casino at Havasu Landing on the California shoreline.

One of the current arguments supporting the construction of a second bridge between the island and city proper is one of logistics. Any serious structural failure of the old London Bridge would result in the island's tourists and residents being marooned on one side of the incapacitated bridge, or the other. Realistically, that would be disruptive and negatively impact up to ninety percent of the city's economy, until repairs could be accomplished.

The terrorists that had been assigned London Bridge as a target managed to secret their plastic explosives. They had crudely molded the composition four (C-4) to resemble the large lighting fixtures that were mounted under each of the historic bridges' three arches.

For whatever reason, those fixtures seem to burn out frequently. Thus the saboteurs felt another 'burned out' fixture or two likely wouldn't generate an emergency callout for a repairman to come inspect and replace the lights.

One of the more electrically skilled members of Mohammed's team, had donned a pair of city maintenance coveralls he had stolen from the back of a city-owned pickup truck. He had managed to run a two hundred-foot length of shielded electrical cable between the disguised packages of explosives, and wired it to the transmitter of a remote hand detonator.

The detonator was basically just a blasting cap—which contained a core of fulminate of mercury. When activated it would cause the wires to heat up, sending an electrical charge through the cable, setting off the primary explosive, which in turn would set off the main C-4 charge. Mohammed's timetable called for the explosives to be detonated exactly at dusk on the designated evening, as were all other planned explosive devices on the island.

Target number two had required a greater amount of planning, and a goodly bit more of engineering skill. The mission involved the sinking of the Chemehuevi Indian Tribes gambler's shuttle the *Dreamcatcher* near the end of her voyage returning from the tribe's Havasu Landing Resort.

The profitable Indian owned and operated casino was located on the California side of the lake. Al-Qaeda planned the attack to come as the vessel passed northwest of the site of a flooded former mining camp, en-route the vessels' home terminal. The vessel, when not on her routine periodic trips across the lake, was moored below Shugrue's and Barley Brothers restaurants. The island dock was located in the dredged channel on the Arizona side of the lake.

No explanation for the selection of that specific target was given Mohammed. Again, its scheduled time of detonation, as was at dusk on the designated evening.

At that time of day, it was reasonable to assume that the shuttle would be filled with gambling passengers, anxious to return to Lake Havasu City and the island's popular cocktail bars before nightfall.

The explosive device destined for the sinking of the *Dreamcatcher* was fashioned much like one of the bottom-secured magnetic mines used during WWII. The huge cylinder has been wrestled overboard. from a small rental boat by the terrorists after dark, on a prior evening.

After it sank, the team's scuba divers had secured it to an old long-discarded marine engine they found lying on the bottom of the channel. After it had been secured, the terrorists activated its radio-controlled clamping harness. That was the only thing now holding the huge bomb to the bottom, as they had inflated its airbag bladders. The explosive charge would remain on the sandy bottom of the lake, until it was summoned electronically.

The tethered mine lay directly under the regular scheduled route the *Dreamcatcher* had to follow to reach her isleside pier. Once the shuttle was almost to the point where the mine was moored, one of the terrorists on the shoreline at Crazy Horse Campground would send it an electronic command, via a radio-communicator.

The explosive device's receipt of the electronic command would cause it to generate a small electrical charge, which in turn would blow eight explosive bolts. That would permit the bomb to separate from the restraining harness that had held it anchored to the bottom. Once free, the air bladders cradling the bomb would provide the necessary buoyancy carrying the device closer to the surface, where it would be command detonated, just under the hull of the *Dreamcatcher*.

The lake's depth in the dredged channel was less than thirty feet. The two hundred pounds of weaponized C-4 had been carefully calculated to only capsize the boat. Not blow the passengers to smatterings, despite the suggestion of one of the terrorist team's youngest cadre.

The strength and placement of the charge would be sufficient to cause the boat to sink within thirty seconds, ejecting the passengers into the water as the hull capsized. The crew and passengers would suddenly be immersed in the now-opaque dark, sixty-three degree water. It was doubtful many would be spared the panic of drowning by first going into shock.

Mohammed expected death would be faster for those who were intoxicated, having over-imbibed at the California-side casino. Here, the intent of the al-Qaeda planning council was more obvious to the team's leader. His intelligent mind approved of the method that al-Qaeda's planning council had selected for the destruction of the *Dreamcatcher*.

It was a well-known fact that Lake Havasu had been a training ground for student military pilots during WWII. Thus the actual cause of the explosion might be forever cloaked in history. The sinking of the shuttlecraft might forever be blamed on the wartime ordnance those brave wartime trainees carried under the wings of their aircraft.

It was rumored that a P-48 aircraft sat on the bottom a few hundred yards upstream from the water shuttle route. Had ancient, unexploded wartime munitions, such as an old unstable torpedo, suddenly without any explainable reason, broke free of the bottom's grip, and floated to the surface to seal the *Dreamcatcher's* fate?

Had that caused the sinking of the Havasu Landing pedestrian shuttle, resulting in a heavy loss of life? Had previous searches of the lake bottom failed to reveal the existence of other live ordnance dropped by the WWII single-engine fighter-bombers, due to engine failure, or pilot error? How many of the training aircraft, especially those armed with yet unexploded bombs, had failed to make it back to the training base? How much deadly WWII munitions was still embedded in the lake's bottom silt, not *unlike* the millions of land mines in Kosovo, just waiting to detonate?

Occasionally rumors of 'discovered' jettisoned underwater bombs, rockets, and other explosives surfaced, and traveled by word of mouth around the small recreational community. Despite the best efforts of the city's tourism bureau, public safety officers, the U.S. Coast Guard, and U.S. Bureau of Land Management public information officers, to squelch them.

Some of these unfounded rumors still managed to find the ears of the owners of the $300,000 to $1,3000,000 high-end 'off-shore' boating toys. The expensive boats could be observed on any weekend, wildly churning the surface of Lake Havasu throughout the boating season. Mohammed, although not trained in business, could well imagine how such a rumor, true or not, would serve to deflate the region's $60,000,000 million dollar, tourist industry, overnight.

The third target, located on the west side of the island, involved the destruction to the DAR historical American war monuments at 'Site Six.'

The now-long-abandoned runways at Site Six, as had those at Site Five and Site Seven, were emergency landing strips for B-17 crew's who had been unable to make it back to their main training base in World War II. The main training base had been located at Kingman, Arizona. Site Six, then called Pittsburg Point during the war, had hosted a U.S. Army Air Corps barracks, and a rest camp capable of accommodating up to one hundred—fifty soldiers at a time.

In November of 2003, the Daughters of the American Revolution had established a memorial at Site Six, commemorating the 10,000 servicemen that had pashed through the area during the war.

The value of such a target made no sense to Mohammed. But he admitted his extremely limited understanding of what al-Qaeda's planners, educated to a man in expensive universities in the West, called the 'big picture.'

That portion of the overall mission itself would be simple enough to accomplish. The team went to the site, and feigning having a disabled vehicle, buried enough explosives at the base of the infidel's memorial to accomplish the mission. Again, the explosive detonation was scheduled for dusk. There was little likelihood that any tourists would be collaterally injured by the Site Six explosion. Thus, Mohammed assumed the al-Qaeda's intent was accumulative in nature. In other words, the explosion would serve to reinforce the message that bin-Laden was sending to the infidels. Once again demonstrating to the hated Americans, that nothing was safe from the unleashed fury of al-Qaeda, not even the monuments she had built, dedicated in honor, to the servicemen of a war long past.

The number of al-Qaeda team cadre still available to fulfill the remaining missions that Mohammed had been tasked with, had by now been significantly reduced. Two major targets remained, both off the island. Both were located in areas easily available to the infidel's well-equipped, and well-trained local police.

Any increased risk of interdiction by the infidel's police forces, preventing the completion of the remaining two missions, was unacceptable. Failure would mean Mohammed and every living member of his strike team would be unwelcome anywhere in the land of Islam.

In fact if historical indicators were any guideline, Mohammed himself, for his failure to successfully bring all of the missions to a successful conclusion, would be put to a painful death. And his entire immediate family forced to live like animals for the rest of their pitifully few remaining years of their lives.

Target number four was the destruction of a large cellular transmission tower located in the city. Although the al-Qaeda operatives had successfully managed to plant small charges at the base of other cell towers throughout the area, they had been unable to gain access to the one located near the intersection of Lake Havasu and Mesquite avenues. The al-Qaeda planning council had emphasized that particular tower's importance.

Target number five involved the placing of explosives charges on every flight control management device at Lake Havasu's municipal airport. The airport, a small, modern facility, was located several miles north of the center of the city.

A portion of the airport-based mission, due its apparent importance, had been designated as mission number six. The mission involved locating the regional air carrier's Beechcraft

1900D, nineteen-passenger remain-over-night (RON) tie-down position on the airport tarmac. Once identified, the saboteurs would attempt to approach the parked aircraft. According to the planners, the aircraft was valued upward of two million dollars.

The saboteur's orders were secrete explosives in the wheel wells of that aircraft, wired to explode when the plane lifted off the runway on its next flight. The gear would begin to retract, after which the aircraft's wheel well doors would begin to close.

Again, Mohammed had been unable to satisfactorily explain the planner's reasoning to his men. However, the obvious assumption of the team had been that the explosion during takeoff it would accomplish the goal of shutting down the entire operational ability of the facility to operate, until the debris could be removed.

Mohammed also thought a secondary goal of mission number six would serve to prevent the FBI's fast-reacting Hostage Rescue Teams (HRT), once alerted to what was happening in Lake Havasu, from using the field to land quick-responding, troop-carrying aircraft.

The al-Qaeda team commander during his training in the flea-bitten, scorpion-infested, training camp in Saudi Arabia had been warned of the danger presented by the infidel's infamous HRT. He had been told that on as little as four hours notice, the FBI's large C-130 olive-drab aircraft would begin landing at Lake Havasu's airport if the runways were still operational.

Mohammed only had seven remaining unassigned operatives. Three of them were women, brave and loyal, but untrained. Their lack of training was due to the Muslim religion's unbending beliefs on the education of females. The women had been included with the work force brought in for the mission, solely for diversity, which would serve to divert unwanted attention away from the group. The al-Qaeda planners had told Mohammed, that since 9/11/01 the American law enforcement forces were only looking for groups made up solely of young men who had Arabic features.

The women, eager to assist in the cause, and both brave and

intelligent, had no problems finding jobs as construction flag persons on the Highway 95 remodeling project.

Mohammed had been given explicit orders that he was not to become a participating member in any of the six mission teams. His only function was to supervise and guarantee the success of the overall mission. He was to provide on-the-ground guidance to each of the six teams, and to be both commander and disciplinarian for the overall team. Mohammed was reminded, repeatedly, that the responsibility for the success of the overall mission rested solely on his shoulders. His future, and that of his immediate family, rested on his shoulders.

The Muslim team leader was to take whatever actions were necessary to assure total success of all mission goals. Bin-Laden demanded a one hundred percent return on al-Qaeda's investment. Only successful achievement of all of bin-Laden's goals would justify al-Qaeda's faith in him. Two million dollars, each dollar difficult to come by since the infidels had started cutting off funds from Islamic charities, had been entrusted in his leadership of the Lake Havasu City operation.

Mohammed had been given the responsibility for the lives of the two-dozen loyal al-Qaeda irregular soldiers. To justify the faith that had been entrusted him, he was expected to fight the infidels to the death, if necessary. The responsibility for two million U.S. dollars, to a man who had never had the equivalent of more than $5.00 U.S. dollars in his pocket at any one time, was far beyond his comprehension. But he had accepted the responsibility, it being a mandatory requirement of his being selected to assume command of the Arizona mission.

However, Mohammed knew that unless he set aside, and subordinated his fiduciary responsibility as team commander, to personally provide two extra hands on the cell tower or airport missions, there was a better than average chance both of those attacks would be compromised.

No matter however successful the island missions turned out, the failure of the last two missions on the mainland side of the city, would doom his two-dozen loyal followers to what in the Muslim world was a fate worst than death—dishonor.

In all likelihood, by diverting from the planner's specific orders, he had just sacrificed the remainder of his young life in trade for those of his two-dozen team members. Having made the first major independent decision he had ever made in his life, Mohammed was determined to do his best to insure the last two missions were accomplished as Osama bin-Laden demanded. Not even in the most optimistic recesses of his young mind was there any hope, in the instance of operational failure, that any of them could expect any mercy.

On the day al-Qaeda had designated for execution of the six missions, the terrorist operatives began to drift into town, midday, in groups of two or three. All were dressed casually in resort or water sports outfits, with two of the younger women even wearing two-piece bikinis.

Those women over the abbreviated beachwear they wore, that if worn in their home country of Saudi Arabia would have resulted in them being stoned to death, wore skimpy cover-ups over their upper torsos. This dress was typical of the female tourists from Southern California that flocked to the City, year round.

The male saboteurs, as instructed, wore simple single-colored bathing suits, ragged t-shirts, faux tattoos, multiple strings of river beads, and sunglasses. If there was any noticeably anomaly of dress among the masquerading terrorists, it was that each of them wore lace-type, rubber-soled shoes. They had left their large multi-color gym bags in the cars.

One of the absolute, most inviolate rules of al-Qaeda doctrine was that nothing was to be included in the planning of an attack, without first being subjected to exhaustive scrutiny, testing, and surveillance. Mohammed had fudged on this one aspect of his plan. He had randomly selected Tri-M Mini Market, as the team's initial assembly point for the day of the mission, prior to being dispatched to their operational targets.

The Tri-M, a combination mini-mart, deli, and gasoline station, belonged to Alan Dodd, one of Lake Havasu's long-term businessmen. The business was located just off Highway 95 at Smoketree Avenue.

Mohammed's mistake would be costly. It jeopardized the total effectiveness of al-Qaeda's mission in this young, vibrant northern Arizona community.

A small sampling of Tri-M's daily walk-in customers, unknown to Mohammed, included a couple appointed Officers of the Court, both former flat-badge police officers; a handful of relatively conservative contractors; an occasional off-duty civilian-clothed police officer; a Doctor of Optometry; a amicable real estate broker; the retired owner of several of the community's largest automobile dealerships; a long-haired female bank supervisor; a retired Washington State Chief of Police turned author, and during the winter months, even a retired FBI agent or two.

Mohammed hadn't been born into a family of wealthy retail businessmen. Therefore, he had never learned that there exists no sharper pair of eyes and superior people-judging instincts, than those of a small merchant. These skills come from the day-to-day life experience of having to detect shoplifters, and identify and deal with potential cheats, in today's environment of tumbling personal values. Just such a person was the owner of Tri-M Deli.

The small groups of tanned, hardened beyond their years, al-Qaeda operatives entered the store, made their minor purchases, which were rang up the verbose, if stoic cashier. The young people without uttering a single word would loiter to consume their purchases, then leave the premises and return to their vehicles.

Almost simultaneously a germ of suspicion began to grow in the fertile minds of some of the store's newspaper-reading regular patrons. They, at the time, were seated at six small café-like tables, some of which rocked to and fro due to the microscopic unevenness of the tiled floor.

The customer sitting area was located next to large plate glass windows, which make up the entire southern exposure of the well-maintained 2,000 square foot retail store. The customers noticed the nearly identical small groups of like-dressed men and women, walking with almost militaristically-correct postures and gaits, all driving nearly identical small rental cars and pickups, and who appeared extremely quiet and well-behaved. This latter behavior alone drew attention. After all, this was Lake Havasu City, where most of the tourists came from the rowdy communities of Southern California. Some of the young tourists the locals normally encountered, seemed incapable of displaying any manners or decorum.

At the young people began to ebb and flow at the Deli's cash register, the regular male customers, not-so-quietly reading the newspapers they rarely purchased—began to take heightened notice. Although perhaps not a quickly as they would have if Brittany Spears, Janet Jackson or Paris Hilton had suddenly sashayed into the store.

Mohammed was outside, slouched down in the driver's seat of an older gray Ford Series 150 pickup truck with camper shell parked on the far side of Smoketree Avenue. He appeared to be reading the *Havasu News-Herald* newspaper, and drinking the coffee he had bought earlier from the Tri-M Deli store. But in reality, he was mentally checking off his team members as they arrived.

Two days earlier, in the late afternoon, Mohammed sent six of the team members to rent a twenty-five foot, wooden-hulled boat with an enclosed cabin, from the Lake Havasu Marina on isleside. The men, outfitted with fishing and scuba gear, were to take the boat out into the lake and drop in a couple of lines. Once it got dark, they would go to the where the men had, using scuba gear, hidden the explosives in an underwater cave, weeks previously.

There, once it was pitch black, using night vision goggles, they would retrieve the cases of waterproof explosives, secreted twenty-five feet under the lake surface, from an flooded copper mine on the California side of the Colorado River, before the dawn arrived along the Colorado River. The mine had been inundated with water when Lake Havasu was formed.

Maneuvering in the early morning darkness, they had offloaded the heavy crates of explosives from the boat's cabin, into the bed of the camper-shell-covered Series 150 ford pickup truck. Then they had pushed the boat out into the river, after kicking a large hole in its bottom. It had sunk rapidly below the surface of the Colorado River, which established Lake Havasu when the Parker Dam was constructed.

The boat had been rented for a four-day period, using the guise of a group of inexperienced striped bass fishermen. Therefore it wouldn't be missed until the terrorists either had completed, or failed at, the multi-task mission al-Qaeda had assigned Mohammed and his team.

Apparently Allah had been elsewhere on the night the six-man team was unloading the critical crates containing the explosives, as one container, the one which held all the timers for the detonators, unexplainably came apart. This permitted the devices to fall into the deep water off the cove's launch ramp, beyond recovery, and lost from their intended use in the operation.

For the following twelve hours, Mohammed had frantically crisscrossed the county attempting to find replacements for the lost timers. But Mohave County, although large in relatively size, didn't have much need for detonator timers any longer. The local mining industry had ceased to exist in the early 1930's.

The end result of this avoidable mishap was that each of the explosives, after they had been placed, would have to be then detonated manually. A much more dangerous undertaking than had been the Al-Qaeda plan.

Of course, secretly Mohammed mused, that was assuming that bin-Laden hadn't somehow 'arranged' the accident to insure a closed-loop was maintained to protect the mission's operational security.

Setting off the explosives manually, especially on a island that is only served by a single bridge, meant that a quick-response by authorities could bottle up his mission teams, with the exception of the of those assigned the airport and cellular tower attacks.

Mohammed had not followed al-Qaeda procedures. He had

instead made an impulsive off-the-cuff decision to use the popular Tri-M Deli in Lake Havasu City as the pre-assembly point for the members of his team. This action had logarithmically decreased the odds that some members of his team would ever live to see another dawn.

Or that they could avoid spending the rest of their lives behind steel bars in a bug-infested steel cage. Foreign terrorists were seen as fresh meat for the surprisingly number of patriotic 'lifer' inmates found in America's SuperMax federal prisons. The worst of these facilities lack air conditioning, despite being located in the hot, humid southern United States.

Mohammed had been told that bin-Laden has personally chosen him for the mission. The young man considered it an once-in-a-lifetime opportunity to serve Allah. He had been chosen for his dedication to the cause, his fearlessness, and commitment to do whatever was necessary to get the job done. He must be willing to give the life of himself, and those of his fellow saboteur conspirators, to successfully accomplish what the fanatic Islamic scholar demanded. Al-Qaeda's eventual goal was that the culmination of all their attacks would force the Great Satan to her knees, and out of all Muslim lands.

Reminding himself constantly that the end justified the means, Mohammed kept these facts and his suspicions to himself. He started the old Ford pickup, then pulled out and crossed Highway 95 for the short drive across London Bridge. Once on the island, he took the road to the Site Six boat launching facility.

Site Six had been a military training camp during WWII. However, it had long ago been converted into a multi-lane boat launch facility. The number of boating enthusiasts using the ramps was small during early dawning hours on weekdays. The quasi-remote location had been selected by Mohammed as an early morning out-of-the-way place to meet his teams, to trans-load the delicate crates of explosives from his pickup truck, into the team's small rental cars. The team commander had surmised that the American tourists would sleep-in until noon, while on vacation.

This would permit the al-Qaeda strike team to continue unfettered in their preparation for the approaching dusk's deadly missions.

Al-Qaeda's planning directorate was a micro-managing group of highly educated individuals, who never got their hands dirty in the missions they planned and assigned. They left that to the less-educated, and less-well-connected believers on the action teams. But the planners months earlier, had selected the targets for the Lake Havasu City mission.

The actual target determination had been set in concrete, months before Mohammed had been encouraged to apply for consideration as the commander of the planned terrorist operation. He had no opportunity for input into the selection of the targets by the planners. Ayman Al-Jawahiri had never seen the area, and had used nothing but al-Qaeda's file of obsolete maps of the area, by which to do his planning.

Despite this, Mohammed's input had not been solicited, nor would it have been welcome. He only had the option of accomplishing the mission, or dying—or perhaps in the current situation, both.

CHAPTER NINETEEN

DAY 332—29 NOVEMBER

MOHAVE COUNTY—1100 HOURS

DAY OF ATONEMENT

LAKE HAVASU CITY

ARIZONA

Today would be another day of atonement for the Americans. The team leader, Mohammed, began to deploy the al-Qaeda strike teams.

The first team of terrorists had found concealment in a small, temporarily vacant, retail building under the arches of the famed London Bridge.

The second team sat in an unremarkable rental car, parked just west of Crazy Horse Campground. They had an unobstructed view of the on-water route used by the Havasu Landing's shuttle, the *Dreamcatcher*.

Members of the third team were attempting to remain unseen. They were parked behind a stand-alone restroom facility surrounded on three sides by scrub brush, at Havasu's Site Six boat launch ramp facility.

The fourth team had already entered the Lake Havasu's Midtown Storage Facility compound, using a key card stolen from one of the business's office employees. The young woman had carelessly left her purse on the front seat of the company pickup truck when she had gone to Havasu City's post office to collect the mail, a couple of days earlier. The two al-Qaeda men had been following her, hoping for just such an opportunity. When she parked, they had pulled into a nearby empty parking slot.

As soon as the woman had walked through the storefront doors of the brick post office, one the men had vaulted out of their vehicle. He darted over to the driver's side of the truck, and opened the driver's door. He briefly rummaged through the woman's purse, which was lying on the well-worn seat. In less than three seconds he had found what they had been looking for—a plastic pass card for the storage facility gate.

He had quickly grabbed the key card, tossed the purse back on the driver's seat, shut the door, and sprinted the few steps back to his vehicle, and got in. No sooner than the car door was closed, the driver had reversed the car out the parking slot. They were driving out of the lot at a moderate speed, when the woman reappeared out of the post office and headed back to her truck.

The woman had returned to the pickup truck with her arms full of mail for the storage business. With some difficulty, she managed to open the driver's door without losing her load. She never noticed that her purse was in a slightly different position, than when she had left the vehicle. Tossing the mail across onto the passenger's side, she got into the truck, slammed the door, started it, and drove out of the lot. After stopping at the stop light for McCulloch Boulevard, she headed back for work.

As she pulled up to the gate at the storage facility, a vehicle had just passed through the gate. That enabled her to follow it though, without having to dig through her purse for the keycard she frequently misplaced.

Glancing at her watch, she thought about the luncheon date

she had with one of the town's more available young men, up at the Big Salad Restaurant, less than a block away.

She thought the planned lunch date would be productive in getting the guy to ask her out for the coming weekend. She had purposely gone without a bra under her t-shirt that morning, hoping her size-D assets would motivate the quiet guy to ask her out. A little extra time had been spent before she left her apartment, in making sure her makeup was a little 'vampy.' She figured the rest was up to biology and hormones.

Once into the storage yard, the saboteurs had parked their vehicle against the compound's inner chainlink fence. The barrier separated the business from the adjacent Mesquite 'wash' as drainage ditches are called in Arizona. The men only needed to breech the fence to gain access to the base of the cell tower. Then they would place the several explosive satchel charges they had brought in with them, and conceal them with rocks obtained from the nearby wash. At that time, they still had to decide how to detonate the explosives, once dusk came to the desert city.

Mohammed had reminded team four that their stealth in planting the explosives was critical. The cell tower was located one hundred yards, north by northeast, of the American flag that flew eighty feet over the Terrible Herbst gasoline station. The service station was located at the intersections of Mesquite and Lake Havasu avenues, in Lake Havasu City.

The base of the cell tower was concealed from the homes, which bordered the north side of Mesquite wash. However, as it was directly under the southern runway approach to the municipal airport, it was visible from the air. The flagpole and cell tower were on a relatively short list of structures that made up Lake Havasu's skyline.

The fifth team, now inclusive of the leader Mohammed, had managed to finally ditch the American police car that had kept them under surveillance for the past ninety minutes. They had cut the gate chain at the Ultra Light Aircraft dealership south of the airport that currently was closed. They drove into the parking lot. The men slipped under the airport's seven-foot chainlink fence, using one of the dozens of natural rock gullies eroded over the eons by torrents of draining storm water. During rare periods of heavy rainfall, the mini-rivers formed by the cascading rainwater drained down from the area's modest hills, across the desert floor, and ultimately into the Colorado River.

Using camouflaged ground sheets that had been purchased from a local military surplus store, the three men cautiously belly-crawled nearly five hundred feet across the rocky terrain. Their destination was a small building housing the remote back-up electrical panels for the airport's runway lighting. Popping the cheap padlock off the door, the men entered the building. Then using tools the American's had carelessly left in the structure, they began to destroy the emergency back-up circuits.

Once they had completed that task, the men again put the camouflaged ground sheets to their intended use. The three men covertly crossed another open area to gain access to other equipment huts, which were closer to the passenger terminal. These smaller buildings housed the electronic support equipment associated with the airport's radio antennae, which they would attempt to disable.

An aircraft mechanical problem in Phoenix that afternoon cancelled the scheduled in-bound flight of Havasu's regional passenger flight. That unplanned delay would serve to save the airline nearly $2,000,000 in replacement costs for the nineteen passenger, Beechcraft 1900D turbocharged aircraft, that day. It would do nothing to save the City of Lake Havasu the $323,000 replacement cost of the vital FAA-mandated back-up equipment the terrorists would destroy to disable the airport.

Nor would it serve to repay the heroism demonstrated by the airport's sole on-shift watchman. He was destined to stumble upon three armed terrorists in a maintenance hanger. The saboteur's normal operational awareness had been overshadowed by their feverish attempts to tear out electrical cabling and smash the navigational aid circuits. The expensive equipment was required for the operation of the FAA-supervised municipal airport.

The 68-year old, retired U.S. Marine Gunnery Sergeant had never before fired the heavy, .45 caliber Colt Peacemaker pistol he carried with its ten-inch barrel. The pistol had come with a fancy holster and a box of steel-jacketed slugs. The need to supplement his meager military retirement income had forced the 'Gunny' to borrow $500 from his brother-in-law and purchase the weapon three months previously. Unlike the majority of both retired and active duty marines, the sergeant, all too familiar with the high frequency of accidental shootings in the home, hadn't owned a handgun.

However, the advertised TSA job requirements to qualify for the near-minimum-wage watchmen's job stated he would need a handgun. The sergeant who considered himself lucky to have had landed the security job, had no choice but make an exception in the current situation.

The Vietnam-era veteran had twenty-five years previously earned a Bronze Star and Purple Heart in the 1968 battle of Hue. That afternoon he had walked in unannounced on the three terrorists. He had drawn the heavy weapon out of his spanking new holster, and hoarsely challenged the three men, who were forty-five feet away, to "raise your hands!" The surprised terrorists gave no indication that they were going to comply with the old Marine's command. Instead, all three sought cover behind several acetylene tanks that were chained to a nearby wall.

In the same instant, the three young terrorists had grabbed up the semi-automatic weapons they had carelessly set down on the concrete floor to free their hands for the work at hand.

At that particular instant, the new employee of the Transportation Security Administration—that same employee the penny-pinching agency had tried to save money on, by never sending him through the required security training—decided his life was in extreme danger of immediately becoming yet another dead 'gyrene' unless he took some immediate defensive action.

Not even a nanosecond passed, before that thought had been converted to a sensory signal that traveled from his combat-trained mind, down to the trigger finger on his right hand. As the watchmen himself sought cover, he aimed in the general direction of the three men, and pulled the trigger of the bulky old revolver a single time. The one ounce, .45 caliber steel-jacketed projectile, spiraled out of the 10-inch barrel, and penetrated one of the recently filled acetylene tanks, which immediately exploded. The resulting detonation, caused the heavy schedule-80 steel that had formed the tank container, to fragment easily shredding the upper torsos of two of the terrorists, and decapitated the third, instantly killing them all.

Occurring previously the morning of that day, the day the al-Qaeda terrorists elected to launch their attack on Lake Havasu, was a demonstration of the initiative and acceptance of responsibility that lives in the souls of all Americans today, post 9/11/01.

An intangible gut feeling of the patrons who routinely were consuming their morning wake-up coffee at Union 76/Tri-M Deli nearly half day earlier, had resulted in a heads-up call to the Lake Havasu Police Department. Alan Dodd, the business owner, made the initial call.

Dodd's call to the authorities was soon replicated by several other cell phone calls to the PD a few minutes later by three of the store's six customers—Frank Skuse, Bill Tracey, and Dr. Stuart Adams.

The three men had been sitting in the deli's seating area, each reading the newspaper. They had been engaging in the practice in which they all were so proficient—the time-honed skill of bullshiting. They were accomplishing that by commenting on the current political situation in one manner or another. They also were dissecting some of the more lurid rumors that were circulating that day throughout the 50,000-resident resort community.

As is typical in situations of male bonding, they were also 'ragging' on the deli's temporarily absent owner. He, without explanation, had left the group to return to his small office on the north side of the store to make a 'heads-up' call to the city's police department.

As was more frequent than not, the subject of that day's light-hearted badgering centered around the 'market-driven' gasoline prices that Dodd claimed had forced him to again post price increases to the station's reader board sign, located in the far eastern corner of the station's parking lot.

Six of the store's regular patrons, the deli owner, and the cashier had been present. Five groups of silent young men, suspicious due to the nervousness they attempt to conceal, their otherwise exemplary behavior, stiff military-like postures, and their apparent choice of nearly identical rental cars, had separately entered the deli. The men made small food purchases, which they promptly consumed while still remaining on their feet, all without making a single comment to anyone.

Five to ten minutes went by as the coffee-drinking patrons covertly watched the young men around the edges of their borrowed newspapers. The patrons, at that point, were unaware that the deli storeowner had quietly walked back to the rear of the store and had placed the initial heads-up call to the police. His intuition was based on the many times his gut feeling had proven to be correct in the past.

Apparently based on the old saw that great minds think alike, three of the patrons also decided to make a call to report the strange behavior to the PD, themselves. But they did so without informing one another of their intentions.

Bill Tracey, a local drywall contractor, stood up, left his chair, and walked back to the currently unoccupied unisex restroom to use his cell-phone.

Dr. Stuart Adams returned his coffee cup to the tabletop, stood, and walked outside the Deli. In the parking lot, he opened the door of, and sat down in, the privacy of his latest toy—a 1968 classic, fully restored, red chevy Camaro chick magnet—to make the cell-phone call reporting his suspicions to the city authorities.

Frank Skuse, a locally well-known house builder and Harley Davidson motorcycle aficionado, crossed the room from the seating area to the store's soft drink dispensers to make his call to the police department' non-emergency operator. He spoke softly into the phone's mouthpiece to avoid being overheard by the suspects who now stood at the rear of the deli's seating area.

The three local men had not discussed their intent to make the calls, before the fact, with each other. They were always hesitant to give their long-time acquaintances fresh ammunition on yet another topic on which they could be ridiculed, should the situation turn out to be unfounded, and just some much paranoid hogwash.

Each man who took the potential risk to make the call, considered the act just another of the many personal responsibilities a resident owes his community. The men felt it was their personal duty to place the call, and at least bring it to the attention to the city constabulary, even if such an action put their own lives at risk.

Following the call each man made, all then returned to store's customer seating area, and took up where they had left off—solving the problems of the world.

The long-term, long-established credibility of the four citizens who made the heads-up calls—the long-time business owner and his three customers—was undoubtedly directly responsible for the police department immediately dispatching four plain clothes detectives to investigate the situation further. Stuffing the criminal cases folders they had been working into a secure desk drawer, then pausing to retrieve their personal weapons and holster them, before briskly walking out to their unmarked 'slick-backs' in the police department's parking lot.

The detectives, each using a separate arterial route, all rolled on the reported complaint running a silent Code-3 callout towards the Tri-M Deli, which was located less than thirteen minutes away.

As the four responding detectives approached to within a block of the Tri-M Deli, they had already agreed on a stakeout set-up over one of the department's secure tactical frequencies. Each drove to the location the senior detective among them had assigned.

The officers parked their unmarked cars, once again checked their personal weapons, and slid down in their seats behind a newspaper, a convenient paperback book or magazine. The surveillance plan called for them to maintain the stakeout until they could determine what was going down, if anything, inside the busy store.

Based on experience, the detectives knew the subjects could be casing the mostly-cash business for a future robbery. It was also possible that the seemingly strange actions of the young men, which the four phone calls had described in detail, would amount to *nothing*. Such as the continuing claim of a famous pop star entertainer, the owner of Neverland Ranch, Santa Barbara County, in California.

The four police officers were following established threat-response procedure. Thus the department could defend the action of deploying its detectives on the sole basis of telephonic citizen reports, on the grounds the department was just taking routine pro-active crime prevention/deterrent measures.

If necessary, the department's actions could later be justified, based on the city's long-standing policy of responding to any reasonable citizen complaint. Each of the calls had come from reputable citizens; representing a curious set of perhaps random circumstances that either could, or could not, rule out the potential of a felony crime-in-progress.

With today's budget constraints that the majority of local police departments across America had to shoulder, the citizens of a community had become its first line of defense. Communities such as Lake Havasu City relied increasingly on concerned citizens to be its eyes and ears.

Part of the trust that paradigm between customer and service provider created, meant that a police department never failed to respond in some manner to a tip called in by one of her citizens. The policing philosophy behind the policy was that even if the complaint turned out to be without merit, both parties benefited from strengthening of the trust bond their interaction generated.

The four unmarked police cars had taken up positions that permitted them to monitor both the front door, and supplier's only door at the east side of the building.

One slick-back cruiser parked in the alley at the rear of Movies Havasu. Another had taken up position where the unmarked cruiser was concealed in a lot under construction, due west of the Tri-M Deli behind an unattended large white, Chevy 7500 diesel dump truck towing a double-axle flatbed trailer. On the trailer was chained a piece of light construction equipment called a Bobcat painted John Deere green and yellow.

A third unmarked unit had taken up station inside the exit leading out of the Lake Shore Village Condos development, directly across from the main entrance to the deli.

The fourth cruiser, an older model that probably should have been auctioned off years earlier, was parked off the highway in the breakdown lane. It sat just south of the intersection of Highway 95 and Smoketree Boulevard, with its hood up. The detective, playing the role of a cursing driver, smoked what appeared from the distance to be a roll-your-own cigarette. He was wearing a ragged baseball cap, turned around backwards, a just-soiled white t-shirt, newly torn blue jeans, and well-abused engineering boots with the run down heels, he carried in the trunk of his unmarked cruiser.

But perhaps the most unique, if late-arriving, surveillance vehicle dispatched by the PD, was a $58,000 yellow H-2 Hummer, with Florida license plates. The yellow and green, over white, license plate logo, read "The Sunshine State." The conspicuous 6,000-pound SUV sported four, after-market 25-inch chrome wheels, on which were mounted Toyo A/T Open Country off-road knobby tires. To top off the impressive vehicular package, a flat-black front brush guard, and chrome luggage roof rack, had been added by the original owner.

One of the police department's senior shift supervisors, a duty sergeant, had grabbed the H-2's keys off the dispatch pegboard, when the detectives were hurriedly dispatched. He'd run out to the vehicle, which had been concealed under a large opaque tarp in the department's 'drug-bust/vehicle confiscation' yard.

After first stripping his uniform blouse and SafariLand bullet-resistant vest off—neatly folding the shirt, and putting both in the H-2's rear seat, the sergeant had followed his detectives out of the station parking lot, driving the confiscated high-end monster SUV.

The sergeant's intent was to oversee the budding situation, in his supervisory capacity. He was along in case the complaint's suspicions proved valid, and something untold was about to go down at the Tri-M Deli. Something, that if a felony by definition, would require the services of a shift supervisor.

Without any notice, the duty sergeant who per LHCPD policy was a uniformed officer, had to attempted to undergo a rapid transformation into Joe citizen. A stakeout, such as the one currently in-progress, required the on-scene sergeant, now attired in uniform trousers and a t-shirt, drive an unmarked vehicle.

The sergeant assumed due to the out-of-state license plates on the suspect's rentals cars, that none of the subjects were local. Logic followed then that it was unlikely any of the possible perpetrators would suspect that the flashy 6,000-pound yellow canary, was a 'seized vehicle.' And now assigned for special operations-use to the Lake Havasu City Police Department.

This being the case, the duty supervisor made the conscious decision to park in what amounted to be 'in plain sight' in the Arby's Roast Beef parking lot, located behind the Tri-M Deli.

Each of the five, experienced, law enforcement officers now on-scene would readily admit that situations like this were the reason they each, years ago, had made the unselfish personal decision and sacrifice to become a police officer. Each had numerous citations for bravery and above-the-call-of-duty job performance in their personnel folders. They all felt the calling to be on-point, out on the front lines of the battle against crime, with their hearts pumping pure adrenaline, manning that thin blue line in defense of the citizens of their community.

As the clock continued to tick, the police officers patiently continued to 'sit on' the situation. As each small group of subjects eventually walked out of the store, got into their cars and drove off—one of the detectives would follow keep the individuals under surveillance. Based on their law enforcement experience, the cops instinctively knew they'd better stick reasonably close to these folks until they determined what their intentions were.

The proactive action by the police in establishing an invisible cordon around the Tri-M Deli was being further evaluated by higher command. Finally the chief made the decision to bring even more unmarked units into the surveillance.

The highly regarded Lake Havasu City Police Chief made a request to other nearby law enforcements agencies, such as Arizona Department of Public Safety (DPS), and the Mohave County Sheriffs. Operating under the provisions of mutual assistance, he asked them to supply a couple of unmarked cruisers and plainclothes officers if they could afford to temporarily loan them to the fledging surveillance operation.

Ten of the persons the police department had under surveillance, by then, had left the deli. Without a single glance around at their surroundings, the individuals who had already left the store, had piled into rental cars in seemingly small pre-arranged groupings, and had headed towards London Bridge. The rentals were hung with loose tails by the unmarked police cars. Two of cars under surveillance had continued across the bridge, and onto the island.

The last vehicle, instead of following the other rental vehicles across London Bridge, had separated from the 'island' group. It had turned back down Swanson Avenue. There, across the street from the local Mickey D's, the car had turned into and parked at the London Bridge Resort.

The young dark-haired individuals had exited the parked car. Each carried a bulky gym bag, and one even had a fishing pole. All three headed for the tourist shops located in the retail area under London Bridge. Southern California acronym-addicts referred to the area as the UTB—Under The Bridge.

UTB was the area physically located beneath the arches of the regionally famous London Bridge. The small stores there cater to the desires of the tens of thousands of tourists that flock to Havasu annually.

The type businesses represented by shops were varied, and in many cases, duplicative. Included were swimsuit shops, candle factories, cocktail bars, eateries, watercraft rentals, and other vendors that were totally reliant on the tourist trade.

The police officers that had followed the terrorist group into the resort's parking lot, hurriedly attempted to modify their appearance with whatever means was at hand. Their cover would be blown unless they modified their appearance to better fit in amongst the meandering tourists.

Soon the cops had exhausted their imaginations and resorted to just 'dumbing down' their normal casual work attire. Then they each grabbed a handheld transceiver, switched it from 'audio' to 'vibration' mode, crammed it into their trousers in the small of their back, and followed the suspects into the tourist areas under the bridge.

The remaining two cars of suspects had continued across London Bridge onto the island, and then split up. One car continued straight ahead in the direction of the Site Six launch ramp, which was located on the west side of the island.

The other car turned right towards Crazy Horse Campground, located on the island's north shore. The drivers of both rental cars obviously were exercising extra caution to make sure they stayed within the legal speed limit, followed all traffic regulations, and drew no attention to themselves.

The unmarked police cruisers kept their distance while trailing the suspects. The shift sergeant and his yellow H-2 Hummer remained on stakeout at Tri-M Deli. A factor aiding the surveillance was the limited road infrastructure on the island. Once on the island, there were only two roadways the suspects could select. And both those roads eventually joined back up, forming the island's perimeter loop.

As the unmarked units drove past Site Six, and Crazy Horse Campground the surveillance officers noted that the suspect's rental cars were parked in the outer-most lots of those facilities. Their chosen parking location would require the occupants to hike some distance to reach the shoreline.

Further observation by the officers using the department's high-power binoculars, revealed the suspects each shouldering gym bags and fishing gear, making the trek down to the lake.

The two remaining vehicles under surveillance, the ones who had not earlier left the store and accompanied their fellow associates either onto the island, or into London Bridge Resort, finally did depart the parking lot of Tri-M Deli. As the cars left the lot, they acquired a loose tail, provided by unmarked two-man DPS and Mohave Country units. The LHCPD sergeant in the highly noticeable H-2 hung back several blocks to avoid burning the surveillance.

The suspects in the remaining car, tagged as team four, seemingly were trying to give the impression they were sightseeing. Their vehicle had been traveling northbound on Lake Havasu Boulevard. Then they turned right, directly across from the Terrible Herbst service station. The vehicle drove eastbound on Mesquite Avenue at the 35-mile-per-hour posted speed limit.

Apparently in an attempt to appear 'lost' the subjects took a number of exploratory left-hand turns. They would drive northbound using the short streets that connected the busy arterial with the wide-paved alley, and a municipal parking lot located beyond.

The Mohave County sheriffs were well familiar with the street arrangement, and had no difficulty in maintaining a parallel-street surveillance. This relieved them of the necessity of constantly being on the subject's tail. Therefore, the county officers had no difficulty in avoiding the trap the other driver appeared to be baiting, in an amateurish attempt to determine if he were being followed.

After twenty minutes of the tail-shedding maneuvers, the suspect's car abruptly pulled up the gated entrance of Midtown Storage. It was large modern facility located at 146 North Lake

Havasu Avenue. The driver of the car the officers were tailing, came to a sudden stop at the access gate's keypad. He apparently used a key card to gain access. As it slid open, the driver rapidly drove through the twenty-four foot wide opening. Then he suddenly slammed on his brakes, on the far side of the seven-foot tall, barbed wire topped, rapidly closing chainlink gate.

The sheriffs in the unmarked police cruiser had been attempting to maintain a low-key surveillance in order to not spook the subjects. However they were left frustrated and stranded outside the commercial gated facility, when the gate finished closing, sliding back into its heavy-duty locking mechanism.

The plainclothes officers couldn't continue to follow the subjects until someone in authority either opened the gate or radioed the sheriffs the gate's entry code. Normally, the code was available to both the Havasu police and fire departments. But the Mohave Sheriff's rarely needed access to the gated storage yards in Lake Havasu City.

Only the Lake Havasu's uniformed patrol units and the city's fire department carried the access codes in their vehicles. They were normally the first responders on any complaint scene, in any case.

The two sheriffs sat there frustrated in front of the closed gate. Each wanted to pound the dashboard but was careful not to. The suspects they were following may be watching what transpired behind them in their rear view mirrors, as they drove into the facility. The suspect's car continued in a northerly direction, deeper into the ill-regularly shaped complex of small storage units, until the small car had vanished from their sight.

A DPS unmarked cruiser had been maintaining a loose tail on the team five, who had been headed north on Highway 95. However, the patrol officers had gotten stuck in the construction traffic. A female flagperson wearing a shiny new yellow hardhat that appeared two sizes too large for her small head, frantically waved a yellow sign that said STOP. She also appeared to have a serious death wish, as she had abruptly stepped out onto the pavement without warning. Directly in front of the moving unmarked unit, which forced the officer to slam on his brakes to avoid running over her.

Once the officers did manage to free themselves from the gridlock, the suspect's car was no longer in sight. Having no idea of the intended destination of the individuals they had been following, the officer in the observer's seat got on to his Motorola handheld portable, and gave LHCPD dispatch the bad news.

Dispatch came back with a response less thirty seconds later. The prompt response indicated that someone of authority had been sitting in the quiet McCulloch Avenue suite occupied by the department's dispatch operators, not-so-patiently waiting for the two DPS officer's report.

The city police dispatcher came back up on the tactical frequency, and notified the officers that they were to continue northbound on Highway 95 in hopes they would happen onto the suspect's vehicle. It was possible that team five had already reached the Pilot Truckstop. It was located where the Highway 95 intersected with the east-west running, Interstate Highway 40.

In the event that the DPS officers reached the truck stop, but still hadn't come across the car they had been following, they would initiate a perimeter search of the facility's lot. The officers would make sure that the suspect's vehicle wasn't concealed behind one of eighteen-wheelers parked there, or in a second gasoline station located just south of the truckstop.

The state police officers demonstrated initiative by parking their patrol unit, and performing a walk-through of both facilities. Their bodies were spiked by the adrenaline of the chase. So the walk-through turned out to be an excellent opportunity for both officers to take a leak. Of course, they reasoned, all while continuing their mission by checking the rest rooms for any suspicious characters.

Both seasoned officers knew their foot patrol of the premises would likely be for naught. After all, they hadn't seen enough of the suspects to permit them to make a positive identification even if the perps had walked right past them.

Failing to locate the subjects in their search of the two commercial facilities, the officers returned to their patrol unit, and reported that fact back to LHCPD dispatch.

What the two DPS officers would not learn until later that day was that the suspects, after managing to break free of the construction gridlock, had turned right off Highway 95 north. They selected the driveway of a currently closed Ultra Light Aircraft business, located across from the Home Depot store, just south of the airport.

One of the saboteurs had pulled a pair of previously acquired commercial bolt cutters, from under the vehicle's front seat. He severed the lightweight chain that had been holding the two opposing gate frames together. The three men then drove through the gate, pausing to wrap pieces of the chain around the gate frame, to make it appear secure.

Once inside, they drove around back of one of the small storage sheds on the property. From there, they gained access to the municipal airport, which was located to the north, by crawling through a flood-created gully under the chainlink perimeter fencing.

The small terrorist unit of two operatives had been fleshed out by the addition of Mohammed, the group's leader. Mohammed decided to ignore one of the unbreakable rules that he had been trained to obey in the training camp in Saudi Arabia. Mohammed made that decision—to get personally involved operationally—only after a period of deep meditation. And following an evening listening to his young charges speak with loving devotion about their families which they had left behind in the 'Land of the two Mosques,' as devout Muslims referred to Saudi Arabia.

Mohammed knew that only the total success of all six missions, here in Arizona, would guarantee that the dozen believers on his team would be permitted to return home to their families. Never mentioned, was the fact that their immediate families were currently being held hostage, under what Osama bin-Laden called "my family's personal protection."

Mohammed believed his personal involvement with the understaffed airport assault team four would increase its chances for success.

Team five, of which Mohammed was now an operative member, had been tasked with blowing up the runway lighting and destroying the airport's intercom flight control radio antenna. They also were to incapacitate other critical machinery, required to operate the facility.

And, if the opportunity presented itself, the terrorists were to double as team six, who were ordered to destroy the regional air carrier's nineteen passenger aircraft. Except for two sparsely ticketed flights daily, the expensive turboprop sat idle and largely unguarded on the tarmac, waiting for its next schedule flight back to Phoenix.

The Lake Havasu City authorities were now convinced that the actions of the subjects they had under surveillance, presented 'a clear and present danger to the community.' Therefore, the local police department's contingency plans kicked in.

Contact had been lost with what the police now referred to as team five's vehicle. It had appeared to contain three subjects and had escaped surveillance in the construction snarl on Highway 95 North. Closing in to interdict the remaining teams, all of which it had been determined to be significant threats to the community, put the Lake Havasu City police under heightened alert.

Uniformed patrol officers and plainclothes detectives from several departments swarmed into the retail shop area, under London Bridge. Unusually cool weather, and the fact that the tourist season was almost over, combined to keep the number of shoppers in the area down to a few hundred.

The plainclothes detectives, who had originally followed the terrorist team into the retail area, had lost contact with the individuals when they split up. The officers mingled with the lighter-than-normal crowds of tourists, who were going from shop to shop, mostly window-shopping.

The now-redressed shift sergeant driving the seized yellow Humvee had arrived, parking in London Bridge Resort's upper north parking lot. He got out of the car, not locking the vehicle in his haste, and raced down the steep concrete stairway to the retail area carrying two-large, brushed aluminum Halliburton cases.

The physically-fit, compactly-built sergeant also carried a bag containing Velcro-secure eXoskeleton holsters®, nylon model #44840 waist packs that looked like a tourist's fanny pak, and the model #44830 (right handed) and model #44835 (left handed) ballistic nylon thigh holsters. The cases contained two-each of the new X/M26 Advanced Tasers®. The LHCPD had purchased them from TASER for handling situations where non-legal alternatives were the degree of deterrent that was most prudent. The LHCPD uniformed officers carried the new non-lethal weapons, however the officers currently in plainclothes, did not.

Stopping in the shadow of a real estate office's roof overhang, the sergeant called the plainclothes officers that had already dispersed on his handheld radio. He ordered all non-uniformed officers who did not currently having the subjects physically in sight, to report to him behind the retail shops. As four officers responded, the sergeant issued each one of the new model #44005, 50,000-volt, 26-watt yellow polymer Tasers.

Every officer on the Lake Havasu City police department had previously been thoroughly trained in the safe and efficient operation of the high-tech devices. However, the sergeant reminded the men, who might conceivably forget details in the stress of the moment, that the 'fin and blade' sights of the weapons were optimized at twenty-one feet. Any shot taken at a range further away than that, "was pissing into the wind," as he described it. He told them to keep the ambidextrous safeties engaged, until they had a confirmed target within the weapon's optimized range.

Due to the number of tourists in the area, even on that cool day, he reminded the officers that unless their lives, or the lives of citizens were at-risk, they were not to employ lethal force against the subjects unless there was no other option.

He didn't intend to open a shooting galley there, regardless of the circumstances, with so many innocent civilians present. Although he didn't feel he needed to do so, the sergeant also reminded his men that their subjects were now dressed identically to many of the tourists. The officers would have to determine which was which before taking any action.

The explosives placed by the terrorist were already in-place. That was something the responding police officers could not have known. The terrorist team's sole assignment was to get close to the fake lighting fixtures they earlier had installed under the bridge arches. Close enough to permit the detonators to receive signals from the low-power electrical transmitters the al-Qaeda strike team had been forced to employ.

Back in Saudi Arabia, al-Qaeda couldn't have predicted that the individuals assigned the task of retrieving the explosive materials from their interim place of concealment, would be so clumsy. This ineptness had caused the Casio timers, long used by Muslim extremist groups, to fall overboard into the fast-flowing Colorado River. The accident had occurred when transferring the crates from their underwater storage location to the rental boat, and then to the group's pickup truck off a remote Colorado River beach in the blackness of an overcast night.

The mission's only fall-back had been the cheap Japanese electronic low-power remote transmitters someone back in Saudi Arabia had thought to toss into the mission's load-out, just-in-case. Due to the unforeseen loss of the Casio timers, the unsophisticated limited-range electronic transmitters were the only reason any of the terrorist team's targets remained at-risk.

The six police officers, all now equipped with the yellow Tasers, began their walk-around scrutinizing everyone of adult age in the crowd. The tourists, even on a mildly cool day, were enjoying the sunshine, and excitedly looking in all the retail shop windows, trying to decide what they could afford to purchase. The kids as usual were running around yelling, some acting rowdy, which generally was expected in this resort area. The prevailing ambiance London Bridge created for the children, approached that of the much more-costly Disney World, in Anaheim, California.

A fistfight between several young teenagers broke out in front of one of the numerous bikini shops. The uniformed officers and sergeant, to the obvious confusion of the parents in the area, refrained from responding to break up the fight. The department's community policing officers would have to hold a meeting in the area later, to explain their current inability to get involved in stopping the fight.

The community based policing officer would explain that the officers had been detailed there specifically today to apprehend far more dangerous criminals. The parents would have to deal with the situation—which consisted of a couple of skinny kids, risking juvenile hall, and scraping their knuckles, showing off for a couple of impressionable, under-supervised teenage girls.

The policemen filtered through the crowds, looking for anyone who appeared appropriately attired, but otherwise out of place. Normally mouthy teenagers took one glance at the officers, then selected discretion over valor, and held their tongues. The teenagers were careful to step off the narrow sidewalks to permit the police officers unrestricted access. All it took the kids was a single glance at the dead-serious game face each officer was wearing.

Some parents, sensing danger, grabbed their kids and pulled them—loudly protesting—to the nearest exit. Another set of concerns to be addressed by the department's community policing officers, at a later date.

One of the younger officers had been keeping his eyes on a couple of suspicious youths that appeared to be in their mid-twenties. They were dressed in attire appropriate for a resort, with exception of gym bags slung over their shoulders. That appeared out of character, considering the surroundings.

The officer and his partner decided to check out the hard-looking, young adult males. But as the police cut across the lawn toward the two, both youths broke and ran. The youths frantically reached inside their gym bags. And both came out gripping a 9 mm semi-automatic handgun in one hand, and a device that appeared to be television remote in the other. Suddenly they stopped their flight, turned and pointed the device at the underside of the bridge.

Both police officers, in seemingly a single voice, began to yell at the crowd. *"Get down! Everyone get down! Now-now-now!"* Just as a loud clap of sound not unlike a thunderbolt, magnified by the underside of the bridge's curved arches, assaulted the crowd's eardrums.

The crowd suddenly found themselves on the ground, in some cases hemorrhaging from their ears and eyes. In the initial seconds following the explosion, the tourists had been shocked silent. Debris from the underside of the bridge cascaded down on them. In less than a dozen seconds, the unnatural silence ended. The breezy summer air was then filled with the screams of dozens of frightened tourists.

The two police officers, both former U.S. Marines with recent combat experience although also deafened, had the presence of mind to remain on their feet. They charged after the two perpetrators who now had discarded their transmitters. The fleeing young men were sticking the handguns down inside their waistbands and unsuccessfully attempting to blend into the crowd who were all racing for the exits.

The officers had managed to close within ten feet of the fleeing men. It was then the cops realized that the significantly younger if not better conditioned men, were fleeter on their feet than the officers, and therefore possibly could be maintain their frantic pace longer, and possibly even escape.

Both cops unholstered the yellow Tasers and fired a single dart into the fleeing man's back immediately in front of him. The projectile instantly transformed the saboteurs from sprinting athletes, into withering hunks of humanity, spasming at the officer's feet.

After some difficulty in handcuffing the flailing hands of the two suspects behind their backs, both officers yanked the darts at the end of the wire leads from the captive's backs. The cops straighten up, and looked up at the underside of the bridge arch directly over their heads. A small piece of granite facing had been torn off, and fell either into the channel, or onto the retail area.

The officers could see the blast had dislodged some gray, modeling clay the terrorists had used to conceal and disguise the remaining two large improvised explosive devices. The disguised packages of explosives had been shaped to resemble high-powered exterior lighting fixtures. Two of them continued to dangle from the arches.

After asking a couple of nearby athletic Hispanic men they knew, apparently only minimally impacted by the deafening explosion, to temporarily hold their disoriented prisoners, the officers ran back to assist the other officers. Despite their injuries, the officers were ground wrestling with two subjects that had been observed trying to flee the scene, *before* the blast detonated.

The young men, who were shouting insults to the American police officers in guttural Arabic and Farsi, had just been brought under police control. Their hands were cuffed behind their backs. Then two shots rang out from the direction of one of the moored tour boats.

The confused wails of the tourists and employees of the retail shops, which now stood with only remnants of glass shards left in their supposedly shatter proof display windows, now reached a feverish pitch! However, the well-trained Havasu police officers had no trouble differentiating the sound of the injured, from that of the gunfire. The two shots appeared to have come from inside one of the now-windowless tour boats. It had been moored to the pier alongside the retail shops when the explosion had detonated.

Paramedics from Havasu Fire Department and River Medical began to flood the area and attend to the injured. A couple of off-duty Game Wardens took temporary custody of the handcuffed prisoners.

The gutsy police officers formed a rough skirmish line. Then they cautiously advanced, utilizing what sparse cover was available. The Havasu line-of-blue and mufti advanced towards the tour boat that the shots came from. The boat appeared to be unoccupied. Because of its height, the double-decker tour boat had suffered a significant amount of superficial damage to its superstructure.

The sergeant, who was leading the advance on the boat, had commandeered a loud hailer. He was repeatedly hailing the tour craft, demanding that whomever was on-board, "come out with your hands in the air." The officers who had been holding their positions as directed by the Sergeant, continued to exercise the safer option of remaining behind cover, waiting for the occupants of the multi-decked boat to show themselves as ordered. Fifteen long minutes expired without any response from the boat. No on-board movement had been observed. The police officer's job wasn't going to be that simple, or that safe.

By this time, the Mohave County Sheriff and the California Riverside Sheriff had dispatched armed officers outfitted with full-body armor and Colt AR-15 semi-automatic rifles to the scene in patrol boats. Those patrol boats took up a protected position behind the unoccupied tour boats that were moored on the west side of the channel. The county deputies were responsible for maintaining custodial control over anyone they observed on the channel-side of the craft, whether or not that individual was attempting to flee the vessel by jumping into the shallow channel.

The Havasu police department only permits shift supervisors to carry semi-automatic shoulder weapons in their cars. And with the chaos that had gone on under the bridge, no officer had the opportunity to have to drag out the department's bulky full-body armor. The officers felt a little under equipped in the current situation. They wore their lightweight bullet-resistant vests, as they cautiously resumed the approach to the moderately damaged vessel.

The police officers reached the tour boat gangplank. Havasu's shift sergeant indicated he would go aboard, and clear the vessel. The remaining officers would avail themselves of any existing cover, and follow his movement throughout the vessel with their handguns. The SWAT-equipped Mohave county officers were carefully briefed on the details of city police plan, using the handheld radios. The sergeant wanted to ensure no one got an itchy trigger finger, especially since the location was a rich environment for potential blue-on-blue crossfire accidents.

With the paramedics arrival the sounds from the frightened and injured in the background, with exception of what seemed like continuous sirens of ambulances departing the scene for the Havasu Regional Medical Center, began to steadily diminish as emergency medical care was dispensed. In fact, at the tour boat, an almost eerie heightened silence seemed to have settled in, no doubt the post-result of the burst of adrenaline that had originally enhanced the hearing of the officers involved.

The silence continued as the officers moved to provide cover for the sergeant searching the damaged boat. The men could hear the heavy soles of the combat boots the sergeant wore, making his way cautiously around the boat. The steps were heard from the below-decks engine room, moving up to the upper observation decks, occasionally briefly pausing when he came across something of interest.

After twenty-tension filled minutes, he reappeared and instructed one of the officers to release the county patrol boats back into service. Shaking his head, the sergeant summoned the on-scene Havasu's crime scene unit, who in their careers thought they had seen it all.

The equipment-laden CSI team had been patiently waiting inside one of the now-abandoned storefronts, drinking the hot coffee they always managed to scavenge from somewhere or someone at every crime scene.

The sergeant apologized to the waiting police assault team that had been covering him. He said he wouldn't be able to permit them onto the boat, as it was now a primary crime scene. The CSI techs began to wrap the boat in the four-inch high, bright yellow tape, continuously printed with the warning of POLICE CRIME SCENE—DO NOT ENTER.

The shift supervisor described to his waiting officers that he had found two deceased adult Arab-appearing males on the upper deck of the boat. Loaded handguns lay by both bodies, and another one of the small television remote-like devices had spilled out of one of their pockets.

Based on his experience, the sergeant said unofficially that he expected it to end up being classified a Murder—Suicide. The initial evidence pointed to the fact that the two remaining subjects had taken refuge on the unoccupied boat, when their fellow team members began to scatter in front of the advancing police skirmish line.

It was obvious the saboteurs had not anticipated the significant numbers of police that responded. And then the commandos had observed two of their men easily taken down by the Tasers. That was a weapon they never had been briefed about. The now deceased males had apparently come to the conclusion that if they survived the next hour, they would only end up at the American's insect-infested prison at Guantánamo Bay. Apparently, both felt that going to meet Allah immediately was a preferred alternative to that lifetime sentence.

As the officers slowly walked through the ground zero site of the explosion, it was easily to see that the carnage could have been far worse. Only one of the three improvised explosive devices had detonated. There were a large number of ruptured eardrums and abraded eyes from the explosion among the casualties.

An older male tourist had died from an apparent heart attack. Injuries to other tourists and first responders had been limited to broken bones, flash burns, lacerations and bruises from the falling bridge mortar, and a severed retina. A middle-aged pregnant woman had been rushed into delivery at the Havasu Regional Medical Center hospital, already in labor.

The entire UTB area, and one hundred yards beyond the retail shops, had been roped off. CSI was still gathering evidence, and that activity would likely continue into the following day.

The area would be secured by the posting of just-arriving state and federal officers. The officers had come from National Parks, and Fish and Game. They would remain on-station until the local police officers had dealt with the continuing terrorist attacks, completed their reports, been debriefed, gotten a good night's sleep, and were ready to return to work. ATF was currently en-route to Havasu from Vegas in a Blackhawk helicopter, to deal with the remaining two improvised explosive devices, still hanging from the bridge arches.

The local Coast Guard Auxiliary had been called into service. Their boats would block both ends of the channel leading to the London Bridge. They and the federal officers would keep the sightseers out of the area until the remaining bombs were disarmed and removed and the crime scene investigation was completed. After the CSI tape came down, the area would be thoroughly cleaned by city crews, and the city engineer would inspect the surviving structures to guarantee their safety.

Four of the Havasu's police officers had to seek medical attention at the hospital's emergency room. Two for ruptured eardrums, and two more with possible infectious bites received in their scuffle with the captives. Those lacerations were carefully cleansed, and the officers admitted and held over night. They would be released, once the lab results of their toxicity scans became available, and the doctor's signed off on their discharge.

CHAPTER TWENTY

DAY 332—29 NOVEMBER

MOHAVE COUNTY—1200 HOURS

THREAT ERADICATION

LAKE HAVASU CITY

ARIZONA

The Lake Havasu Chief of Police mulled over the two remaining terrorist teams known to be on the island. He speculated about their targets and how best to apprehend and/or interdict them. The department's paramount goal was to accomplish that without any loss of life to his police officers or the citizenry. He was equally committed to avoiding further property damage. He thought, *even with all the federal resources at our beck and call, we still haven't gotten a handle on what the terrorists are up to.*

An hour ago, he and one of his lieutenants had put on civvies. He had borrowed a 'beater car' from one of his officer's kids. Then he and the duty lieutenant had driven onto the island and past the locations where the remaining subjects had been observed.

Hell, he speculated, *the perps probably weren't even aware that they could no longer get off the island. Or at least not do so without swimming the channel, stealing a boat, or both, which I have to admit is possible.*

One of his men was known as a deep thinker. The officer was usually correct in his predictions. The man had voiced the opinion that the only target the scumbags at the campground could conceivably be after was something that traveled on water past that location.

At first I had simply written it off as another wild ass guess, thought Chief Lion. *SWAGS had been flying around the department today like locusts. Then, I remembered that this particular officer's predictions had proven to be more right than wrong over the years.*

The officer had successfully predicted the Superbowl winner, every year for the past decade. Which, the Chief had heard, won the man many friends among the wagering rank and file.

Speaking of gamblers, the Chief thought, *perhaps the next time that Superbowl came around, I will jump on Havasu Landing's shuttle boat. And zip over to the casino on the California side and place a little bet. But of course, I'll have to make sure my wager isn't known to anyone on the department.*

The Chief picked up his office phone and dialed the Havasu Landing Resort Casino, on the other side of the lake. When the phone was answered, he asked for Ms. Farris, the casino manager. Beth Farris came on the line, and the two followed the ritual routine of exchanging small talk. Then the Chief asked "Beth, does the *Dreamcatcher* still run directly from the casino to the pier below Shugrue's?"

"Chief Lion," the contralto-voiced woman replied, "if you visited us once in awhile, you might know that information without having to ask the question."

"Beth, I'm serious here—please hear me out. We have a situation today over on this side—you might have heard about it on the radio." said the Chief.

Beth laughed and replied, "Chief, do you honestly think that I can run this business like you run yours? Sitting at a desk with my feet up on it? And fail to make my hourly Harvard MBA management-by-walking-around treks? Hell, if I did that, my customers would steal the gold fillings out of my teeth. And perhaps even manage to grab that mythical uplift bra you cops claim I wear, right off my boobs."

"Beth, this is the situation," the Chief said. "I'm going to ask you to go along with me on this. I know it will temporarily upset your apple cart over there. Maybe you can give out free drinks to placate the gamblers from the Arizona side."

"Chief, this better be good. You should know we already give them free drinks. You have to know that. Because your officers seem to have nothing better to do, than arrest my 'whales' for DUI after they have returned to your fair city. And consumed a pop or three at Shugrue's or Barley Brothers, before getting in their cars to head for home."

"Beth, please just shut up and listen to what I am going to tell you. Today, we've had contact with at least five terrorist teams right here in beautiful Lake Havasu City. Only two of which have been neutralized as of this minute. The three remaining teams of 'alpha hotels—that means" . . .

Beth broke in, "I know what it means, Chief. I was in Army Intelligence if you'll remember."

"Oh, yeah, sorry I forgot, Beth," continued Chief Lion. "Anyway, three of the terrorists were killed when a old Marine Gunny working armed security for TSA at the airport stumbled upon them committing some mischief. He told them to freeze, which the idiots ignored."

"So he drew down on them and fired one shot. The single bullet he fired hit a compressed air bottle filled with acetylene gas. It exploded, punching all of the bad guy's tickets big time. My guys also just interdicted another team of bin-Laden's finest, but only after they had blew up a portion of London Bridge."

After a pregnant pause, Beth spoke, "Ok, Chief, what can I do for the Lake Havasu City Police Department?"

"Beth, we have identified at least three more teams. My guys are currently sitting on two of them, on the island. One of the teams was observed hanging around Crazy Horse Campground. Each of the perps is carrying a bulky gym bag. The beach at Crazy Horse would be a perfect location to take a shot at the *Dreamcatcher* the next time she trolls by."

Chief Lion continued, "What I'd like you to do is temporarily suspend your shuttle service between the casino and Lake Havasu. For at least for the next couple of hours, until we can take these guys down. You could tell the shuttle passengers that the damn boat broke, or something. If necessary, I could get a charter bus, looping around I-40 towards the casino, to pickup anyone that becomes real nasty about waiting. Can you help me out here, Beth?"

A now somber Beth responded, "Better than that, Chief. You take care of those alpha hotels. I'll make sure everyone stays happy here until we can get the shuttle 'crossing the pond' again. Forget the bus. If we have a medical emergency, I can always call in the *Life Flight* helicopter. They owe me a couple favors you wouldn't want to know about, anyway. Keep me advised." And the casino phone line went dead.

Forty minutes later, two unmarked Lake Havasu City PD patrol units, loosely backed-up by two boats from Sheriff Tom Sheahan's Mohave Country Sheriff's office, rolled into Crazy Horse Campground. The male suspects were currently sitting on a wooden picnic table, watching the boats pass by on the channel.

The officer's approach was intended to appear to be nothing more than a random spot check for underage drinkers. The officers had left the marked cruisers and were calmly strolling over to confront the subjects, when one of the perps flipped out. He reached into an open gym bag sitting on the table alongside him, and tried to snake an AK47 semi-automatic assault rifle out of it. But the gun's front sight snagged on the bag's zipper.

The other terrorists then drew semi-automatic handguns and began to fire at the officers. The officers dropped to the ground, and ate sand, as they sought cover. The county deputies on the patrol boats, who were wearing full-body armor, appeared from the distance to secretly smile. Then they began to direct withering semi-automatic weapons fire from their assault rifles at the subjects. The metal-jacketed rounds, *thwack-thwack-thwack-thwack*, hit the bodies, drawing flecks of smoke as they burned through the subject's clothing!

One of the terrorists, just before he took a round in the head and had his gray matter rearranged across the campsite, managed to pull a small television-like remote from his pocket. He pointed it towards the shoreline, and frantically pushed the device's actuation button. Nine seconds later, a 55-gallon barrel ringed with a floatation collar, broached the lake's surface. When the radiating wave action the broaching had created began to subside, the barrel settled back under, and began to bob about, just under the surface of the water.

The three terrorists, as a direct consequence of the rifle fire from the two patrol boats, were dead on-scene. The uniformed Havasu officers, who had arrived in the patrol cruisers, had never gotten off a shot. Both departments, without even bothering to check the torn, chewed-up bodies for a pulse, keyed their hand-held radios. They reported the officer-involved shootings to their respective headquarters.

One of the Havasu officers also notified his department's CSI unit. It had been waiting a mile down the island's perimeter road. The other Havasu policeman grabbed a roll of crime scene tape from his cruiser's trunk. He began to drape it from small shrubs and picnic tables around the kill zone. As he carefully accomplished that task, he once again thought he should have long ago invested money in the stock of the company that made the tape.

Havasu's Police Chief Lion caught the radio call concerning the bloody interdiction, and winced. He was at the Havasu City police department's headquarters off McCulloch Avenue. After a brief moment to think, he picked up the phone and called Beth Farris at the casino. The chief gave her a status report, and thanked her for the cooperation. He promised he'd personally call her back, once the ATF had disarmed the floating bomb. The ATF would also send divers down to the bottom of the channel. They wanted to make sure the apparent bomb didn't have any brothers or sisters sitting down there, waiting to be activated on the channel's dredged bottom.

Beth thanked the chief, and laughed when he promised that he'd be over to the casino to place a bet the next time that the Superbowl rolled around.

Later that day, ATF called the chief to report that the bottom was clear of unexploded ordnance, at least in that location. The ATF officer hypothesized that one possible reason that the bomb had failed to detonate when the dying terrorist had toggled its release, was because it was a 'contact bomb.' Something similar to what the Navy called a magnetically activated, just-sitting-here-waiting, bottom-moored mine.

Another possibility that ATF surmised was that the low-power transmitter the terrorist had used to release the mine from where it had been moored on the bottom, didn't then have enough residual battery strength left to trigger the actual detonation.

The fifty-five sworn officer Lake Havasu City Police Department was fast running out of resources that day. Securing the crime scenes at London Bridge and the Crazy Horse Campground was easily tying up nearly one half that number.

The intent behind the Northwestern Arizona Mutual Aid Pact, of which most regional agencies were signatories, was that in the time of need, other law enforcement agencies could be called on to provide temporary assistance and support. On that basis, the manpower-depleted Lake Havasu City police department asked the Arizona State Department of Public Safety (DPS) to go in, and roll up the three suspected terrorists who had been observed in the vicinity of the Site Six boat launch facility. At the time, the assignment seemed like a no-brainer, as no one expected any resistance from the terrorists—no civilians were around, and what could the bad guys possibly feel was worth sacrificing their lives for at that remote location?

Additionally, three resident FBI special agents, that had until just recently been operating out of borrowed space owned by the Havasu Police Department, also volunteered their services. The senior resident agent agreed to contribute manpower in whatever manner Chief Lion deemed most useful. The chief decided to hold the FBI agents in reserve, for use as a 11th hour rapid response squad, which the RA concurred with.

The Havasu police department had also run out of available certified crime scene investigation (CSI) teams. So the Chief placed a call to the Las Vegas metro police, who unfortunately was not a signatory to the region's Mutual Aid Pact. Nevertheless, he asked for and was granted the loan of a couple of their crime scene investigation teams. The multi-fatality crime scene out at the airport had been locked down, until the borrowed Las Vegas crime scene personnel and their equipment were airlifted into town by two military Blackhawk helicopters.

The DPS assault on the remaining 'isleside' al-Qaeda team at Site Six, began less than an hour later. The highway patrol team, four officers divided between two marked patrol cruisers, cautiously drove into the Site Six boat launch facility.

The area was deserted that day, apparently due to the unseasonably cool, breezy weather out on the lake. The outermost parking lot was barren except for the rental vehicle the terrorists had driven to the site. The DPS officers, after a brief visual glance around, drove up to within fifty yards of the suspect's car. It was parked near the Daughters of the American Revolution monument, which had been erected in 2003 in memory of Site Six's use in WWII as a training and troop rest area.

The officers were relieved to find that no innocent bystanders were present in the lot. That meant no threat of collateral civilian casualties, in case the police confrontation turned ugly.

The fact that the officers unexpectedly found the parking lot empty, coupled with the adrenaline rush any police confrontation generates, resulted in a little over confidence which inadvertently gave birth to what came next.

Havasu officers had previously confirmed the identification of the sole car occupying the outer parking lot at Site Six. It was definitely the one being driven by the suspects. The FBI had by now also officially classified the occupants as 'terrorists at-large' meaning that provisions of the Patriot Act came into play. The officers began a cursory visual scan of the area, once their cruisers came to dusty stop a short distance front of the suspect's vehicle. No one was observed either in, or around the seemingly abandoned vehicle.

Believing the vehicle to be empty and therefore not a threat, the DPS team had not bothered to inspect the car, before driving both patrol units into close proximity with the suspect's vehicle.

All four highway patrol officers wore Safariland light body armor. They carried locked and loaded 12-gauge shotguns held at the ready. The three male and one female officer got out of the cruisers. They formed a rough skirmish line, and began to cautiously approach the vehicle.

The dispatched DPS officers were equipped with handheld Motorola radios. Therefore it was not procedurally necessary for one of them to remain behind with the cruisers, in case the developing situation required immediate radio communications with their 'higher authority.'

If the officers had not been equipped with handheld radios, standard DPS procedure required one of the police officers standby the patrol car radio when technically making a felony vehicle stop, such as what was occurring.

As the apprehensive young officers drew within twenty feet of the apparently abandoned car, it exploded. The blast blew dozens of pieces of glass and metal shrapnel at them, horizontally. The flying debris lacerated their uniforms and skin. The car's doors, hood, trunk, and roof were torn from the vehicle, thrown into the air, and accompanied the fireball that rose at least fifty feet straight up into the partial overcast. The fire, overwhelming noise, super-heated air, and a rippling shock wave assaulted the patrolmen.

As gravity overcame the effects of the explosion, the airborne pieces of tortured sheet metal and safety glass ceased to rise on the heat thermals. They rotated as in an aerial ballet, and began their fall back to earth. The four stunned DPS officers dove to the ground and began to eat sand, as they each instinctively attempted to find cover in the sun-baked parking lot. Finding none, they began to belly crawl away from the fiery conflagration.

As the still shocked officers slithered away from the heat, each mentally attempted to organize his or her thoughts. They had not been expecting the predicament they now found themselves in.

Suddenly without warning, deadly fire from several weapons, sounding like AK47 assault rifles, began to slam into the fiery hulk burning behind them as they crawled away. The metal-jacketed rounds also punctured the hard sandy surface of the unpaved parking lot, each round seemingly searching for the officers.

Explosions from the still-burning terrorist's car continued, first the gas tank and then the tires. So did the automatic weapons fire which now seemed to be coming from multiple locations. Most of the in-coming bullets were being fired from a football-field's length or more away. The shooters were well concealed in the low scrub brush that encircled the parking area.

The fact that the in-coming rounds came from three specific directions, indicated they had been taken under fire by trained combatants.

The terrorists had taken the time to stakeout their intended fields of fire, before they had fired the first shot. Combat-trained soldiers and police officers all knew that nothing is more dangerous than a situation when multiple individuals all fire towards a single common target. The shooters were as at-risk of catching one of their own rounds from a blue-on-blue crossfire incident, as were the individuals they were targeting.

This also meant that it was impossible for the officers to use the wreckage of the terrorist's car as cover and concealment.

The senior DPS officer on-scene also happened to be their detachment's most accomplished marksman. He began to belly crawl rapidly back towards the patrol cruisers, in an attempt to reach the M-16A1 assault rifle each cruiser carried in its trunk.

While the brave officer exposed himself to get to one of the patrol units, the other two men laid down covering fire, using their Winchester Model 12 shotguns. However, the patrolmen's covering fire was of little consequence. The terrorists were beyond accurate range of the 18.5 inch-long barrels of their police-issue riot guns.

The remaining DPS officer crouched near the burning wreck. Only by inserting her index finger in her ear, could the officer block out the nearly continuous sound of in-coming heavy-caliber rounds. Thwack-thwack-thwack-thwack! She had first been deafened by explosion of the car's gasoline tank. Then by the much louder detonations of the tires cooking off as the vehicle continued to burn.

In her right hand she held a tactical handheld radio. Over which she was shouting repeatedly, "*Officers under automatic weapons fire! Officer down! Request emergency medical assistance, and backup, now!*"

Before the crawling officer had managed to reach the either of the cruisers, a dozen or more puffs of sand, thrown up by the heavy assault rounds hitting the packed sand in front of the crawling officer's head, stopping his forward movement.

The other DPS officers yelled to the motionless form, to *"Keep going, man! Go! Go! Go! Don't lay just there—you are giving the assholes a fixed target!"* But the supine form made no further movement. The air was filled with gunshots, explosions, ricochets, yelling and the shrill sound of steam venting from their cruiser's punctured radiators.

The DPS officers who had been first on-scene, had come with limited firepower. Each of their four shotguns—the patrolman, who had been attempting to reach the cruisers, had left his shoulder weapon behind when he began the heroic attempt to reach the cars—only had five shells up-the-snout. Six more rounds were fitted in the slab-sided shell holder, elastically adhered to the shotgun's butt. That meant they only had a total of forty-four rounds of buckshot between them when they had first been ambushed.

By this time, all of the officers had already emptied their shotguns of the initial loadout, attempting to cover the now-fallen officer. The damn shotguns were useless at that range anyway. But the earsplitting reports when the twelve gauges were fired monetarily served to provide some needed courage to the trapped officers. The three remaining DPS highway patrol officers were attempting to find any safe haven in the concrete-like packed sand surface of the parking lot, until backup arrived.

Each of the three officers remaining in the shootout coincidently carried stainless steel, Smith and Wesson .357 magnum pistols. As with most law officers in the world today, they didn't bother to leave one empty chamber under the hammer, despite departmental safety procedures to the contrary.

Each officer carried six shells in his pistol, and two—six-shot 'speed loaders' on their gunbelt. That meant that between them—the fallen officer's handgun was out of reach—remained a total of twenty-four shotgun rounds of buckshot in the slab sides, and fifty-four rounds of .357 Hi-Power ammunition. That would have to suffice until help reached them. Further firing for effect was out; ammunition conservation was in.

The three officers continued their frantic attempts to burrow into firmly packed sand of the parking area. They maintained fire discipline as they had been trained. They forced themselves to refrain from taking a shot, unless one of the terrorists stupidly showed themselves—which none did. The perps had apparently had come prepared to rumble. They had pumped over seventy-five steel-jacketed rounds into each of the Crown Victoria police cruisers, turning them into Swiss cheese.

The terrorists didn't turn their fire back onto the trapped officers until the gasoline tanks in both cruisers had exploded. So much for the new improved self-sealing NASCAR-proven, gas tanks. DPS and other Arizona police departments had only recently bullied the Ford Motor Company into retrofitting the gasoline tanks in the patrol cars. FORD was attempting to mollify the law enforcement community's litany of complaints about the Crown Victoria's original equipment (OEM) fuel tanks. They tended to explode, posing a serious hazard to officers in instances when the police vehicles were stopped, occupied, and were struck from behind by another vehicle.

The terrorists had apparently lost interest in the target represented by the body of the fallen officer. However, respecting the patrolmen's range skills, they were being extremely careful not to expose themselves to the other trapped officer's shots.

Then, with no discernable signal, the saboteurs began to fall back while continuing to fire their shoulder weapons to keep the patrolman's heads down. One DPS officer after another exhausted his or her meager supply of handgun ammunition.

That left them with the sole option of reluctantly returning to the short-range 12-gauge shotguns. It wasn't much of an option. Each of the riot guns was down to a five rounds of buckshot, up the snouts. The air stunk of the smell of cordite, burning tires, blistering paint, inadvertently released sphincters, and the acrid copper smell of spilled blood.

At that moment, someone up there in Heaven must have looked down on the brave officers, and said "Enough of this crap!" The three DPS officers, without rising to their knees, yelled in relief! Six fast-moving marked and unmarked two-man patrol cruisers had just slid sideways into the Site Six parking lot. Each raced towards the position where the DPS patrolmen were pinned down.

Failing to immediately locate the positions of the concealed terrorists, the rescuers stopped their cars. They piled out and took up defensive positions, but only after maneuvering their cruisers to shield the embattled DPS officer from further gunfire.

The terrorists quickly came to the conclusion they had worn out their welcome at Site Six. The three men, wearing nothing but thongs, river beads, colored muscle shirts, cheap wrist watches, sunglasses and bathing suits whose elastic waistbands were stuffed with black, thirty-round banana clips for their AK47s, jumped up and ran towards the two cruisers.

The saboteurs had forgotten they had previously turned the cruisers into steaming hunks of creaking and popping metal, that now were only good for establishing underwater reefs in the on-going development of Lake Havasu's fish habitat.

The dozen rescuing police officers and surviving highway officers watched in amazement as the flight of three perps continued. In a manner not unlike that of the Cardinals Pro-Bowler, Emmitt Smith, the gunmen ran headlong towards the two junkers keeping their eyes on the rough sand in front of then.

They seemed oblivious to the fact that their intended 'getaway' cars now sat flat on the sand, smoking, on tireless steel wheels which had warped from the heat and firestorm of the explosions.

As the three perps came to within ten feet of the cars, they suddenly realized their error. And apparently desiring an immediate opportunity to meet Allah, the fleeing Arabs all turned their assault weapons back on the pursuing police officers. The responding officers, by now well into the adrenalin moment, had left the safety provided by the sheer bulk of their cruisers, to stalk the men on foot.

The terrorists began firing their banana-clipped AK47 assault rifles towards the law enforcements officers closing in on them. Then, a bloodied caricature of a man materialized from behind one the first cruisers disabled in the firefight. The apparition was clutching a .357 revolver in both hands with obvious difficulty. It rested its elbows on one of the still smoldering hoods, and methodically proceeded to squeeze off three single shots. Each round took a terrorist at the base of his skull, sending blood spatter and gray matter out in a cone-shaped pattern. Then the battered figure crumbled back to the parking lot surface.

The crowd of exuberant police officers was finally moved out of the way, permitting their injured colleague to depart in a River Medical ambulance. It would no doubt be running balls-to-the-wall Code 3. The rig was en-route Havasu Regional Medical Center. After a detailed examination of the injured officer, the on-scene paramedics reported that the DPS patrolman would have to undergo emergency surgery.

That was necessary, they told the nearly two-dozen, now-assembled police officers to remove the sandy grit and metal fragments the terrorist's high-powered metal—jacketed slugs, ricocheting off the densely packed sand of the parking lot, had driven into the officer's torso, face and eyes.

The wounded officer also had superficial lacerations and burns, primarily on his back, his butt and arms. The EMTs ventured the guess that the shrapnel came from the police cruisers the officer had so valiantly been attempting to reach, when their gasoline tanks exploded.

Considering the severity of officer's wounds, no one could believe that he had the strength to force himself to stand. Then summon the intense concentration required to make the three head shots. Especially since at the time, the paramedics claimed his eyes would have been awash in blood.

Other ambulances had taken each of the other three surviving DPS officers to the hospital's emergency room. There, they were treated for lacerations and abrasions, second degree burns, eardrum injuries, and trauma-related exhaustion.

The DPS officer's families had been notified by the Police Chief Lion, as to the extent of their loved one's injuries. The heroic DPS officer's injuries had been classified by the hospital's medical spokesperson as being "serious, but not life threatening or permanently disabling."

The Arizona Department of Public Safety—Phoenix detachment—had assigned four sergeants, each driving a DPS-rented full-size van, to pick up each officer's immediate family members and their hand luggage. They were driven directly to an American West charter flight, which was holding at a gate at Sky Harbor Airport.

Once all the families had arrived and were on-board with their overnight luggage, the aircraft would depart for northern Arizona. The families would be flown to Lake Havasu's municipal airport. When they landed they were to be met personally by Lake Havasu City's Mayor, Bob Whelan.

The mayor's office had made arrangements for the families to be put up in rooms at the local Ramada Inn. After the family members had freshened up, they would be driven to the local hospital to see their loved ones. The injured hopefully would be out of surgery, released from recovery, and back resting comfortably in their hospital rooms by that time.

The ATF bomb squad arrived to disarm the explosives the terrorists had planted on the DAR monument at Site Six. The bomb techs noted that the terrorists had originally buried all of the explosives at the base of the monument.

However, there was also evidence that a significant portion of the improvised explosives had later been hurried dug up. And instead wired into the engine compartment of the vehicle the al-Qaeda team had driven to Site Six.

The saboteur's vehicle had been totally destroyed by the resulting explosion. However, there were a few pieces of still-identifiable hardware lying around the scene. They were gathered up by ATF crime scene investigators, and scrutinized. Microscopic inspection indicated that the detonator used in the vehicle had been makeshift, and unconventional. But the device used for the detonation of the explosives still under the DAR monument, had been a commercially available model.

It appeared the terrorist team had never planned to destroy anything other than the monument. The crime scene evidence seemed to indicate the terrorists had changed their mind at the last minute. Then they had to call upon the mother of invention by which to detonate the explosives, which had only then been placed in the vehicle's engine compartment.

ATF suggested this finding be reviewed in further depth, in an attempt to isolate the reason behind the sudden change in plans. In historical situations involving Al-Qaeda 'sapper' squads, it had been noted time and time again that the terrorists rarely deviated from the use of proven methods and materials to make and detonate their bombs.

It was believed the young Arab's lack of technical expertise was behind their reluctance to abandon classic, time-proven methods, in favor of anything potentially seen as being experimental.

Determining why the terrorists had failed to follow their original plan, in the current situation, could provide valuable insight into dealings with future terrorist threats.

In the meantime, Lake Havasu City police officers still had one known remaining group of terrorists to deal with. The two subjects had gone-to-ground in a commercial storage unit facility, which was located less than one block from a residential area.

The sheriffs tailing the men, had reported back to their supervisor, via radio, that they were about fifty percent sure that their loose surveillance hadn't been detected by the two suspects. While the suspects had executed numerous maneuvers designed to reveal the presence of a tail, that could just be a routine part of their training. And not necessarily an indication they actually thought they were being followed.

Also under discussion were the suspect's actions immediately upon clearing the sliding security gate at the storage facility. They had abruptly stopped their vehicle on the far side of the sliding gate, as if to make sure no one else got through, while the gate slid closed.

That action served to block the sheriff's unmarked cruiser from following them into the gated storage yard, thus curtailing the surveillance. The cruiser had been about fifty yards behind the subject's vehicle. But the blocking action could once again simply be another example of al-Qaeda's obsessive concern with operational security.

Information reported by highly paid Arab informants, indicated that any mistake or lack of discipline while attending the desert training camps in Saudi Arabia, invariably earned the lax and inattentive Muslim student a severe beating, or worse. This no doubt led to the field operator's obsession with following al-Qaeda procedures to the letter.

The on-scene law enforcement commanders had set up a temporary command post in the old fire station located kitty-corner from the Diamond Car Wash, on Lake Havasu Avenue North. The current atmosphere or mood in the building was quiet, thoughtful, and contemplative. The influx of all the persons attending today's meeting, stretched the old municipal building beyond its rated capacity.

Present were members of local, county, state and federal law enforcement agencies. The attendees included Lake Havasu's Police Chief Lion; Mohave County Sheriff Tom Sheahan; Fire Chief Hazard; Mayor Bob Whelan, and the county's three resident FBI special agents.

Also in attendance was an attractive Afro-American woman who had been introduced as FBI Supervising Special Agent, Diane Davis of the FBI. She had arrived with two male special agent assistants in tow. The three headquarters' agents represented the Bureau's Counterterrorism directorate in Washington D.C. They had flown into Havasu regional airport in a government-leased Lear 35, an hour earlier.

Reportedly the headquarters agents were on-scene in an advisory capacity for the Bureau. And according to the scuttlebutt, Davis also had the ear of the president of the United States in matters relating to her proven expertise—mainly counterterrorism.

Parked in the covering parking stalls and open lot at the rear of the building, waited four ambulances. Also filling the lot were the unmarked cars that brought the police chief; the fire chief; 6'10" Mayor Whelan; two of Havasu's City Council members; and Buster Johnson, the most vocal of Mohave County's three supervisors; and the various vehicles that had carried the FBI and other agencies to the afternoon's pre-assault briefing.

The seemingly fugue state being displayed by most of the operational attendees present, was easily explainable. It was inevitable, when one considered the amount of death, collateral casualties, and destruction that the terrorists had already wrought on this small community that day. And everyone present knew the crisis wasn't over yet.

If that wasn't enough, factor in the community's concern for a number of law enforcement officers who already were hospitalized at Havasu Regional Medical Center. They had been admitted there, after suffering serious wounds received in confrontations with the terrorists earlier in the day. Add to that the torn bodies of the deceased terrorists, who already overflowed out into the hallway, at Havasu's small morgue.

One could additionally factor into the equation, officers, bomb squad members, and paramedics who had been actively involved in life-threatening combat from early that morning. Being only human, their mental acuity was rapidly deteriorating as they began to crash, having exhausted the benefits of the adrenaline highs that blanked out normal human fear. The natural chemical high that had driven them to aggressively perform incredible acts of heroism, earlier in the day.

And those that were able to maintain their cutting edge, despite these factors, quickly sobered when they considered the two terrorists they now sought. Extrapolating off the large quantities of deadly plastique their now-neutralized cohorts had in their possession, taking these men down wasn't going to be any cakewalk.

The sheriff's men had tailed the suspects, now being referred to as team four, to the storage yard. The thought of the detonation of high explosives at that location, chilled the men and women assembled there to the bone. The storage facility was less than one city block from a residential area.

And no one wanted to voice the fact that the surrounded suspect's current location, was less than a couple of city blocks away from Havasu's only medical hospital. Nor that the building the taskforce was currently occupying for this meeting, was located just across the street from that storage facility.

Police Chief Lion stepped up to the makeshift podium. Because of the limited available room, he was easily able to address the group without the necessity of a sound system. The man looked tired, but not yet totally exhausted. He appeared resigned, but not willing to cede a single victory to the terrorists. And, thought Special Agent Davis, *he really looks pissed!*

"Look," the chief began. "to the best of our current knowledge, the two scumbags who entered the yard at Midtown Storage an hour or so ago, are the last of these guys. Or at least that is my most fervent wish. We currently have no idea what the terrorists hoped to accomplish today by attacking the Lake Havasu community, let alone whatever they are planning over in that storage yard."

"The manager of the facility has agreed to lock down the facility, claiming one of the exiting customers had reported smelling chlorine fumes. He also, even as we speak, is assisting his wife and daughter handpull all the paperwork associated each of the rental units in his facility."

"But," the chief continued, "the magnitude of the job means they won't be finished for at least a couple more hours. Luckily, the guy has one of those photographic memories. His wife claims the guy is pretty proud of the ability, even though his recall ability occasionally drives her nuts. He says none of the facility's units are short-term rentals. Each of the tenants has rented their particular unit for no less than two consecutive years. You know, snowbirds stashing their wave runners, four-wheelers, and boats and the like, between winter seasons."

Chief Lion continued, "There is no way to check what is going on in the yard from the office, as the facility's CCTV security cameras have been on the blink all week. The manager says he hasn't been able to get the security company repairman off his duff, and up from Phoenix, to fix them. The layout is so odd-shaped, and so cluttered with small buildings, that it is literally impossible to check the interior grounds from outside the perimeter fence, and remain undetected."

"Based on this group's history of shooting first, we can't put a chopper in the air over the facility to get some real-time observations. If they got off a lucky shot and hit the bird, it could come crashing down onto one of the $300,000 homes on the north side of Mesquite wash."

"Our resident FBI friends went over to Willow Street. They attempted to take a sneak-and-peek look into the rear of the storage facility. But the housing developer constructed a high berm to shield the homes, from having to view the stalag-like perimeter fencing of the storage facility."

"Anyone who pokes their heads over that berm," the chief explained, "risks getting shot. We base that assumption on the terrorist's total lack of hesitancy to deluge the surrounding area with automatic weapons fire, as those guys have demonstrated all day long."

The chief took a sip of water from a water bottle, and continued, "We really don't want to go into the storage yard after these guys, until we get some idea of their intended target. Based on the information the facility manager gave us, or rather based on his memory, we don't think it is too likely the perps have managed to previously secret any explosives in one of the storage lockers. Even temporarily empty units are kept securely locked. The manager says he does a walk-through of the entire facility, twice daily, and he has never had any indication that any of the padlocks have been jimmied, left unlocked, or otherwise disturbed."

Taking another drink, Chief Lion went on, "That would indicate any mischief they intend to get into will be accomplished with explosives they brought into the facility with them, earlier today. If the other assholes we have rolled up today are any indication, we have two heavily-armed guys, neither of which probably has any fear of dying."

"Explosives must figure into their plans. We have to assume that they will, as they have at each of the other targets they've hit today. Oh, with exception of the airport, where the watchman got off a lucky shot. The collateral results of which blew all three of the bad guys to Allah, or whatever they call Heaven."

"We can't permit them to detonate those explosives, or fire their weapons. Mayor Whelan, members of the City council, and the County Supervisor Johnson have been very, very helpful by *continually* reminding me of that. There are several hundred residents within the range of a steel-jacketed assault rifle round."

"Luckily," the chief reflected, "the relative remoteness of the storage facility along its south side; and the tall berm and Mesquite wash on the north side, will channel any explosive blast more or less straight up in the air. Therefore, my primary concern right now is the assault weapons, rather than their explosives. I'd still like to identify their target in advance. Before we storm in there like a wild-ass gorilla and have to say 'Opps, we weren't planning on you doing *that*!"

Then Supervising FBI Agent from Washington, Diane Davis stood up, asking the police chief if she might speak. The chief nodded and took another long drink of water, before stepping back and relinquishing the podium to the Fed.

"Chief," Davis began, "I think we might have an idea as to what their target may be. The National Security Agency has been downloading telephonic messages from this area for the past several months. We suspected they might be coming from a newly activated, deep-cover terrorist cell. But up until now, we couldn't get enough of a handle on it, to sell an affidavit for a preemptive warrant to the U.S. Attorney General."

Davis went on, "Just last week, one of NSA's Cray supercomputers broke this particular group's code. Our counterterrorism analysts managed to isolate several words, that were repeated more often than others. Among them were 'bridge, casino, launch, airport, and cell tower."

"Chief, I happened to be absently looking over your shoulder a few minutes ago, when my eyes fell at the notes you have been taking today." The special agent continued, "After giving it more thought, and after knocking it around with the resident agents, we've come to the conclusion that your men have already interdicted the terrorist's assaults on four of the five targets that NSA has alerted us to."

"Isn't there a cell-phone transmission tower just outside the storage yard's perimeter fencing, at the rear of the facility? The satellite shot shows a metal communications tower, about one hundred yards north by northeast of that huge American flag flying from the flagpole at the Terrible Herbst gasoline station. The flagpole is located on the corner of Lake Havasu Avenue North, and Mesquite Avenue," the agent stated.

The room immediately broke out in low roar. Everyone's adrenaline began to pump again. Comments such as 'Shit, yes", and "Why didn't we think of that," were made. Along with at least one comment spoken under someone's breath, to the effect of "That damn broad is trying to make us look bad, Charlie." The men and women in the room began to nod their heads up and down, until they looked like a herd of bobble-head dolls.

The police chief smiled and looked over Agent Davis, who by now had retaken her seat. He said, "Hell, Diane, now I have to take back all of the mean, politically-incorrect things I have been saying about the FBI all my life. I think you might have it. Now here is what I propose we do about it."

The police chief looked over at the Havasu fire chief, and said, "Chief Hazard, how would you and your men like to play cops-and-robbers for awhile?"

The fire chief looked back at his friend of long-standing, who after the current hectic day fighting the terrorist hoard, looked like he had been ridden hard and put away wet. Chief Hazard said, "Well, buddy, I'd sure like to help you. But my guys would have to dumb down our skills, and take a cut in pay, and we just can't do that. I hope you understand our position!" he jokingly responded.

After the eruption of the interdepartmental humor that no one in the room had ever expected to hear again after the infamy they all been subjected to that day subsided, the police chief shook his head. "Funny, very funny—you know they name streets after you and your fire department, buddy—dead ends!"

When the laughter had again quieted down, the police chief began to describe a plan that would almost guarantee that they could neutralize the two terrorists in the storage yard, without collateral damage. Possibly even without firing a single shot. Or allowing the demented scumbags to detonate any explosives that would bring down the expensive communications tower.

But to accomplish that, Chief Lion knew everyone in the room would have to be prepared to take immediate overwhelming action, with the appropriate manpower to achieve that goal.

The men from the various agencies in the room took a knee, and began to listen intently to the police chief's plan. "First," the chief began, "I want a dozen of your firemen to accompany my officers to the homes on Willows Street. Those that are directly north of the high berm and the storm water runoff wash, that separates the Willow street residential area, from the storage facility."

"Secondly, your guys will execute a Class-A mandatory emergency evacuation of all the homes on that block. You know the drill, a gas leak, or something like that. The pets will also have to be evacuated to make this believable to the residents."

"The terrorists won't be able to see the commotion," explained Chief Lion, "due to the 20-foot high berm. But they will hear the sound of all those residents getting into their vehicles, and sprinting down Willow Street. That is the distraction I want."

"Advise the temporary-displaced residents that they may hear some minor explosions, and see some smoke. Tell them not get concerned. Inform them that we are just using the actual emergency evacuation justified by the gas leak, as a no-cost chance to practice some of our Homeland Security procedures. They've heard enough about that happening down in Phoenix, Seattle, New York, and Miami. So they'll probably feel honored that you selected their neighborhood for the exercise."

"Thirdly," the police Chief continued, "your men will take up position wearing smoke inhalation masks, about twenty feet below the crest of the berm. Low enough so you are still invisible from the rear of the storage yard. My men will begin detonating flash-bangs consecutively, say one every fifteen-to-twenty seconds or so. And at the same time I want your men to pull the pins on about a dozen smoke grenades, and just toss them somewhere they won't start a brush fire."

"Three minutes after that," he continued, "I want two of your fire trucks, ringing all their bells and whistles, to pull up in front of the now-vacated homes. Remember the terrorists won't be able to see you, but will assume that one or more of the houses is engulfed in flames."

"By that time, I'll have two of my officers in full body armor belly-crawl up to the sliding gate at the storage yard's entrance, activate it, and jamb it into the open position."

"Now," the police chief cautioned. "I'm relying heavily here on the perps being so distracted by the racket and smoke billowing in the air just across the wash from them, to not question our next move. As soon as the sneak-and-peak guys get the sliding gate open, I want that humongous 'pumper' fire truck of yours, the one with the aerial water cannon, to enter the storage yard making as much noise as possible. Instruct them to weave their way through the storage buildings, until they get to the rear of the property. I am betting that the terrorists will temporarily stop whatever they are doing, and began to look around their immediate area for visual evidence of a structure fire."

"As soon as your truck reaches the rear of the storage yard, pull as close as possible to the perps. Then have your best operator train the water cannon directly on the bad guys, and blast the hell out of them. Don't stop until you are sure they are either incapacitated or have drowned."

Lion resumed, "My guys, wearing firefighter turnouts coats, are going to be standing right alongside your pump operator in case he or she needs some lethal protection. The cops will be carrying M-16s. But I hope to hell they don't have to use them. But if they do, they do. After all, we will have already proactively evacuated all the residents that would have conceivably been in the line of fire, anyway."

"And if the perps really want to join Allah, well I suppose we'll reluctantly have to accommodate them. But I'd rather we pull off the entire interdiction without a shot being fired. As soon as the on-scene fire commander gives the word, the ATF bomb squad will move in and secure whatever explosives are still a threat. Anyone have any questions? No? Well then, let roll!"

The assault on the two remaining terrorists that late afternoon went off like clockwork. Only one shot was fired, and that by a young inexperienced police officer from another jurisdiction. He had failed to keep his semi-automatic pistol's safety engaged, discharging it harmlessly when he tripped.

The excited young officer had been running towards the rear of the storage facility to reinforce the Havasu police officers and firemen. The police officers, wearing full body armor under the turnouts coats, were standing guard over the brave water cannon operator. The fireman had held his ground, standing behind the powerful water cannon, directing massive streams of water from the fire truck's internal storage tanks directly into the two terrorist's faces.

Unfortunately, the police chief's desire to capture one or both of the terrorists alive for questioning was not to be. The powerful streams of water, as they smashed into the surprised terrorist's faces, had fractured the portion of the cervical spine that controlled the human body's ability to breath. In effect, both terrorists died by suffocation.

Before the water in the fire truck's tanks ran dry, the cannon had also torn away and completely inundated the improvised explosives that the two saboteurs had managed to plant in a hole, they had laboriously excavated at the base of the tall cellular transmission tower.

Cellular calls in Lake Havasu were therefore not affected by al-Qaeda's attempt to bring down the transmission tower.

CHAPTER TWENTY-ONE

DAY 333—30 NOVEMBER

THE AMERICAN NAVAL BASE

THE INFILTRATION

GUANTÁNAMO BAY

CUBA

The time of day was what old Marines refer to as O' dark-thirty hours. The night had been hot, muggy, and oppressive. Those conditions had continued over into the early morning hours. The heat from the day hadn't lessened appreciably as night had fallen. Compounding the discomfort, the brisk breeze blowing on-shore from the Windward Passage during the daylight hours, seemed to have vanished abruptly as soon as dusk came to the Caribbean.

The night was unusually dark for this time of year. The opaque conditions were mainly due to a tropical storm front that had stalled over the area earlier in the afternoon. The rain-filled clouds the storm had brought with it, hung low over the U.S. Naval Base.

NAS Guantánamo was forty-five square miles in size. Created

by treaty, the base was diplomatically considered to be U.S. territory. And it had been so, ever since the first leasehold signing back in 1903. The lease had been renewed in 1934, in admittedly more peaceful and less antagonistic times. The annual rent paid the Cubans for the leasehold, was a paltry sum of less that $5,000. The rental fee was frozen by treaty.

The humid night air was filled with sounds common and non-threatening to residents of a rural tropical environment. Here, indigenous animals including its humans came out at night to hunt, scavenge, procreate, and occasionally commit murder.

The isolated U.S. base, called Gitmo by almost everyone that has ever had occasion to refer to it, is located in a sheltered Caribbean Sea inlet. The American base is eight miles south of the Cuban city of Guantánamo. The fact that the U.S. leasehold and the Cuban City both carry the name 'Guantánamo,' often creates confusion, among westerners in particular.

Presidente-for-Life Fidel Castro Ruz is only interested in the number of occupants in the agricultural and commercial community of Guantánamo for the purpose of taxation. He feels no obligation to keep his unwelcome lessee advised of the current population statistics of the Cuban municipality.

However, a decade or two ago, the last time the Cuban government initiated a census, the CIA reported that about 190,000 Spanish-speaking Cubans called the area home. Guantánamo City is supplied by two ocean ports-of-call; Caimanera on the west, and Boquerón on the east. The ports are located across from one another, on the central inlet narrows. Guantánamo City could not exist without at least one of the two seaports.

Logistically, the two Cuban ports are landlocked. The only access is passage through Guantánamo Bay's inner basin, which transits the American base. Both shorelines adjoining that body of water, fall under the purview of the U.S. Navy.

The U.S. Naval base includes two airfields. Both have related facilities and a heavily fortified infrastructure. Recently the base was joined by the addition of Camp Delta. Delta currently is home for approximately seven hundred terrorist detainees.

Also located on the southern end of Gitmo, not far from the detainee camp, is another new addition, Camp America. This new, high-tech facility provides housing, feeding, recreation, and medical care for over two thousand U.S. troops who are assigned to Joint Task Force 160. The JTF is a multiservice command. It is in-charge of custodial operations, which provide for the protection, safekeeping, and welfare of the Taliban and al-Qaeda detainees.

This vulnerable U.S. Naval base is located well over a hundred of miles south of the U.S. mainland. The base is integral to our country's pursuit of the War-On-Terrorism. Base security at Guantánamo Bay is not just *one* of the duties of the troops assigned there, it is figuratively their *only* duty.

Differing from most U.S. Naval facilities, Gitmo is bordered by water and the enemy. It is reminiscent of a former U.S. foreign facility, Cam Ranh Bay back in the Vietnam era. Despite its vulnerability, Guantánamo Naval Station has again been assigned an important mission. That meant the base's remoteness must be dealt with, and the mission accomplished, regardless of degree of difficulty and other hardships.

U.S. Port Security Unit (PSU) 307 is a Coast Guard unit consisting of specialists in port security and harbor defense. It had been assigned the responsibility for providing the Guantánamo base with water-borne surveillance and interdiction capability. PSU was also responsible for monitoring all activities on the bodies of water inside the base. This includes waters inside the southern inner basin, and along the base's perimeter shorelines, which border on the Caribbean Sea's Windward Passage.

PSU 307 is home-based out of St. Petersburg, Florida. The unit consists of reservists who had previously been assigned to Boston, following the 9/11/01 attacks on the World Trade Center and the Pentagon.

If something suspicious is detected, PSU 307 investigates it and takes appropriate action. PSU 307 is also charged with monitoring the movement of all foreign ships inside the base. This includes those who transit Guantánamo Bay, to and from the Cuban commercial shipping ports on the far side of the U.S. naval facility.

PSU bird-dogs these ships, and makes certain they proceed with all due dispatch to and from their destination ports. The unit also ensures the ships neither off-load, or take aboard, anything or anybody inside the U.S. leasehold's boundaries. The units mission includes maintaining constant surveillance on the recreational boaters and fishermen who use the southern inner basin.

PSU 307 was involved in routine patrol activities that dark morning. The two most prevailing conditions in the harbor, at that early hour, were darkness and dampness. Two of PSU's armed twenty-five-foot patrol boats, equipped with blindingly bright spotlights, were extremely active in the basin that morning, darting to and fro. This haphazard 'jinking' was intended to confuse anyone that might be observing them, trying to determine their procedures, methods, search patterns, and operational routines.

To insure that PSU provided the widest coverage possible in the inner basin, the two patrol craft didn't 'partner-up' unless their headquarters sounded an alert of a specific nature. The two boats, operating separately, flitted up and down the basin, in and amongst the vessels moored in the bay's designated general anchorage. An unintentional collateral effect of the noisy patrol boats operating in such an erratic manner was that it served to keep the 'watch' personnel awake on-board those ships. And their eyes focused on their assigned area of responsibility.

Both of the patrol boats idled along in the basin at between five to seven knots. They were passing within one hundred yards of one another, at about 2:55 a.m.—one northbound, the other southbound. Suddenly the oppressive night was shattered like a piece of cheap, single pane glass. A loud screeching raced up through a many as four octaves. It was accompanied by several bright lights, which rapidly disappeared into the low overhanging scud. The patrol boat crews judged that the rockets had been launched from Windward's McCalla Airfield. That facility was classified as being inactive, due to unacceptable runway conditions.

The rockets were now out of sight, well above the clouds. The personnel on the patrol boats heard them detonate, and noted that it sounded like fireworks. The Chief Petty Officer in command of each boat, ordered their crews to action stations. The crew tossed their cigarettes into the oily water, and hurriedly removed and stowed the tarps that served as rainproof dew-covers for the three large machine guns that were mounted on each vessel.

The crews checked the ammunition belts for the machine guns, making sure they had the proper mix of high explosive, and tracer rounds. Stacks of forty mike-mike high explosive and illumination rounds were cradled alongside each boat's M79 grenade launcher. The patrol boat's spotlights had been tested before PSU went on-shift at 2300 hours, almost four hours previously.

The boats were ready to get underway, once their captains had contacted the PSU Command Center to advise them of the incident. Their head shed was located in the heavily fortified, Guantánamo Base Security complex.

After a few seconds, the PSU 307 duty officer came back up on the radio. She ordered the two boat captains to proceed at full-military speed, down the shoreline, to a point just off the inactive airfield. PSU was 'fragged' with the mission of obtaining identification of the persons responsible for the detonation of the fireworks. The duty officer seemed royally pissed that someone had interrupted what to that moment, had been an uneventful dawn patrol.

The OD advised she was also dispatching a pair of Humvees, with a detachment of base security officers to the old airfield. The duty officer passed on the message from the JTF commander, that "he hoped the boats and Humvees would apprehend the guys responsible, *this time*!" Then they could finally roll these 'alpha hotels' up.

The base commander wanted those responsible, charged, convicted and sentenced in an UCMJ Article 32 Summary Courts Martial. Once sentenced, the convicted would be escorted under guard, back to the U.S. mainland for a little vacation in a very unpleasant U.S. Naval Brig. The PSU duty officer almost couldn't contain her glee, in anticipation of that day.

During the past two months, a handful of the U.S. base's troops had come under suspicion of the illegal manufacture of moonshine, somewhere on the large base. Drinking hard alcohol was no longer permitted on base. The only exception to the 'no alcohol' prohibition was a 3.2 beer, available only at the base's Enlisted, Noncom, and Officer's clubs.

Since the transfer of the terrorist detainees to their isolated base several years ago, Guantánamo had been held at an advanced stage of alert—Red—by order of President George W. Bush. All the president's men were painfully aware of how understaffed the huge facility was. The Joint Task Force was still staffing up to fill the guard billets for Camp Delta.

JTF 160 had only marginally enough men available for duty-rotation. There simply wasn't any additional staffing available, to offset any alcohol-generated sick bay absences. From historical experience, the Navy knew that the unmonitored availability of alcohol could lead to lax duty-standing, hung over personnel, and inattentive custodial performance. This was especially true among the very, very small number of JTF guards who seemed resentful of the existence of the detainees in the first place. Resentful guards make mistakes. Mistakes were dangerous, and could not be tolerated in the high-stress environment of Camp Delta.

A handful of the base's malcontents were making their displeasure known regarding the 'no alcohol order.' At least once a week, they staged some stupid stunt to demonstrate their total disregard for authority. Most appeared to have had long forgotten that Guantánamo was on the front lines of a country that was very much at war.

In the recent past, this resentment of authority had included some of the men sneaking around the huge base after dark. They would occasionally stop to shoot off homemade bottle rockets, misappropriated 'very pistols,' or rudimentary aerial rockets.

The rockets were being produced using the powder from Navy-issue shotgun shells. Invariably, these acts necessitated calling out the base's shore patrol. It also drew on-duty PSU security officers away from their critical assigned duty stations, to investigate and attempt to apprehend the perpetrators.

The Commanding General at JTF, only last week, had declared "Enough is enough!" On a quiet Sunday, following church services, General Montrose had issued an order to all commands on the base. His order, as one might expect, was short and to the point.

The general wanted anyone and everyone, regardless of criticality of assignment or rank, who were apprehended taking part in the prohibited activities, charged with 'providing aid and comfort to the enemy.' In wartime, individuals convicted of that serious offense could expect to go before a firing squad. In this instance, General Montrose said he was going to be compassionate. His definition for that term was that following sentencing, those convicted were going to a U.S. military prison to serve hard time for a very long time.

The general also sent a scathing communication, copy to the Joint Chiefs of Staff, to the command officer of the U.S. Air Force unit responsible for flying the C-17 transports into Gitmo. In the memo, the general informed his counterpart that in the future, he would hold *him* personally responsible for violations of Gitmo's contraband regulations.

The general said that he fully expected the Air Force to do its duty. He expected them to immediately implement a rigid set of inspection criteria for anyone boarding one of their aircraft, en-route Gitmo. General Montrose said he didn't want even one 'ladyfinger firecracker' found on personnel, their luggage, or incoming base supplies for Gitmo. His Marine guards on the Leeward airfield would enforce the order.

The JTF commanding officer followed up this threat. He held a surprise inspection of the next arriving C-17 that landed on Leeward Point Field, the following morning. The Marines searched everyone coming off the aircraft. One of the privates was unlucky enough to have a dozen M-80 firecrackers concealed in his luggage. The Marines found them, promptly arrested, handcuffed, and strip-searched the private, before throwing him in the back of a Humvee, and delivering the unfortunate soul to the base's Marine-run brig.

The pilot of that particular C-17 flight was a popular Air Force major. However, thanks to the influence the JTF commander enjoyed in the Pentagon, as partial payment for accepting the thankless JTF command in the first place, the C-17 pilot soon would be wearing the bright new rank insignia of an Air Force Captain.

After word of the highly unusual example of military disciplinary circulated in Air Force circles, unsubstantiated rumors began to circulate. One of the most frequently heard was that all troops flying to Gitmo were physically being strip-searched by the aircraft's crew without regard to rank or gender. This was allegedly happening *before* the troops were permitted to board the C-17, for their flight to Gitmo.

The PSU duty officer knew that the JTF general was 'ichi bon, numba one' pissed. The drunken troops were disrupting his responsibility for the protection of the detainees. So the young OD didn't hesitate to pull both patrol boats out of their assigned duty patrol area. Even though normally this type assignment would routinely be handled by base security. Within less than twenty-four hours, she would come to regret her decision.

The two powerful PSU boats turned downstream, and accelerated to forty knots to take up position off McCalla Field. Their engines screamed a high-pitched scream. The wakes the boat hulls created as they cut through the dark waters, curled outward to eventually slap up against the nearby shorelines.

The two patrol boats had only just departed their assigned patrol area when twenty figures cautiously emerged from the thick brush on the bay's north shoreline. Prolific indigenous plants grew all along the swampy north shoreline. The 'sticker bush' grows wild in Cuba, and can get taller than a man. The brush was heavy, and typically grew together almost like a shrub, despite the best efforts by base security to keep it defoliated.

The Cuban commandos were clad head-to-toe in old, but still serviceable Soviet-era black neoprene diving suits. Each man was laden with multiple diving tanks, all of which had been painted black. All wore a full-face mask with an internal communicator, a diving belt with weights, a buoyancy vest, underwater gauges, gloves, fins, an underwater flashlight, a state-of-the-art air regulator, a Swedish underwater diving watch, and a wicked-looking sheathed flat-black K-Bar or stiletto knife. Hanging from black harnesses were small sealed packages of Skoda explosive detonators, a compass, and other equipment of their vocation.

Fourteen of the divers tugged black, high-tech, aluminum rafts into the water with them. The neutral-buoyancy assault rafts had been designed then quietly abandoned without explanation, by the U.S. Navy Seals nearly a decade earlier. They were designed to submerge with their loads, until they were concealed just under the surface of the water. On moonless nights, such as the present one, their awash profile prevented them being spotted, as they were towed by the submerged commandos along the dark shoreline. Their buoyancy, even when loaded, made them relatively easy to tow through the water.

Additional divers, charged with transporting much heavier loads, were equipped with two black motorized submersibles. They were steerable underwater sleds, propelled by motors similar to some of the early chemically fueled torpedo designs. Three divers muscled each of the two motorized sleds out of the dense brush and into the bay's shallow water.

The fierce-appearing black-clad divers, operating under the cover of darkness, slipped into the murky, oily water along the American base's 4,500-yard-long north inner bay shoreline. Because the water adjacent to that shoreline was extremely shallow, the Americans had found it nearly impossible to patrol by boat offshore, or by vehicle on land.

Each of the commandos mucked their way through the shoreline's swampy bottom, dragging their equipment, until they were finally able to fully immerse themselves underwater. The members of assault team were all heavily burdened. Not just by the heavy motorized sleds, and less-laden tow-rafts, but also by the weight of their harnessed triple-tank air supply.

Special Forces divers wouldn't normally have considered using the cumbersome triple, seventy-two cubic inch tank set-ups. In short, they were heavy as hell. However, their Cuban bosses had demanded they do so to obtain maximum duration for this operationally critical mission.

Once the black-clad divers were buoyant and beyond the influence of the sucking bottom, they separated as planned. After checking their Soviet-made wrist compasses, they began the long swim to their planned targets.

The two crack Cuban Underwater Demolition (UDT) two-man teams were led by Master Chiefs Manuel Garcia, and Jorge Jaminez, respectfully. Those teams laboriously swam upstream against a killer four-knot current, towing the submerged rafts. Their assignment was to plant Semtex plastic explosives under the base's dining facility located on Deer Point's south shoreline. That large complex housed the base's Officers, NonCom, and Enlisted Men's clubs; the dirty-shirt mess; the Officer's dining room; the base theatre and recreation center; and the base's mail facility.

The terrorists hoped their bombs would catch at least some of the base security personnel that night in the 'dirty shirt mess' having meals. The casualties from the explosions weren't expected to net any JTF personnel. Al-Qaeda's spies had infiltrated the JTF. They were working as translators and chaplains inside the Joint Task Force. Recently, one of them had passed on the information that the multiservice JTF guard detachment was restricted to only using the secure and well-guarded mess hall at Camp America. This proactive measure was part of the JTF commander's overall security plan.

The detonation of the mines Manuel and Jorge's crews were emplacing, would be were controlled by timers. This would permit coordinating their detonation, with those bombs being placed by the other UDT teams. The explosions were all timed to occur late the evening of the current day, or about twenty hours later, at midnight.

Two additional two-man dive teams, these commanded by Cuban Navy Underwater Specialists 'Perky' Hernandez and Hector Lopez, had swam downstream with little difficulty sticking close to the north shoreline. The water there was too shallow for anything other than flat-bottom rowboats.

Those teams were to place mines under the terminal that served the American's vehicle/passenger ferryboats. Those ferryboats and modified LSTs (Landing Ship, Tank) provided the only significant water-borne means of crossing the 3,000-foot wide Guantánamo Bay navigational channel. The timers on the bombs they placed were set to detonate at the same time as those placed else where by their fellow saboteurs.

Nothing said the U.S. Navy ferries couldn't access other docks up and down the narrow Guantánamo lower basin waterway. But ninety-eight percent of the base's considerable cross-water traffic was between the Leeward airfield and the main base, on what was referred to as the Windward side.

When the ferry shuttle went down for any reason, for any appreciable length of time, the base's CH-46 troop helicopters were always pressed into service. That was done to maintain the critical thread of logistics that was required to keep a multi-section military base operational, and capable of defending itself. In the terms of combat air support, being the recipient of prompt airborne help from the American mainland had until two years always been the preferred contingency plan. However, Mr. Murphy often had a voice in those circumstances. So other stand-alone contingencies had been put into place and implemented. Stand-alone close air support was now available.

If the terminal was ever heavily damaged, the passenger ferries could be kept in-use on a limited basis. However, they would have to use a nearby beach, on the Leeward side for on and off-loading of personnel only. Heavy equipment could not be ferried across the bay until the terminal was returned to full service, to accommodate the LSTs.

Guantánamo Bay, over the years, had silted up until it was a relatively narrow, if well maintained, nautical waterway. It ran from the inlet's entrance from the Caribbean's Windward Passage, up the inner waterway, to the U.S. Naval Station's seven designated general anchorage 'swing' moorages. The waterway continued north to the far end of the U.S. leasehold at Palma Point.

All the minor channels branching off the bay had silted up

years earlier. Only continuous dredging by the Navy's contractors kept the main bay open for navigation. The annual dredging contracts were a major part of the cost of keeping the Guantánamo base in-operation. That the American's picked up the lower bay's dredging cost, naturally pleased the harbormasters of the two upstream Cuban territory ports, in the extremis.

The remaining twelve Cuban saboteurs consolidated into two-six man teams. Each team would take one of the two underwater, motorized sleds. The sled would be used to transport the olive-drab-colored waterproof explosive Semtex bricks to their designated targets.

One of the six-man teams, under Cuban Lieutenant Jesus Martinez, would head upstream to the American base's designated general anchorage area. The huge mooring buoys anchored there, were used by U.S. naval vessels, civilian tankers and freighters. On that particular pre-dawn morning, only three of the base's seven 'swing' anchorages were occupied.

The Cuban commandos eventually reached the general anchorage. Having fallen behind schedule due to the stiff current they were fighting, the lieutenant immediately directed his men to work as a single team. They would visit each of the three moored hulls, consecutively. The divers would attach the self-adhering explosive limpet mines to the mooring buoy's anchor chain, the ship's propeller shafts, and rudder stakes of the vessels. The deadly charges, when they detonated nearly twenty hours hence, were designed to break the massive vessels free from their moorings.

The commandos had no doubt that a couple of watch standers would be on-duty aboard each of three vessels, when the bombs detonated. To provide power for the ship's operating systems, at least one of the engines on each vessel would be kept turning to generate electricity.

However, at midnight, it was doubtful that the ship's bridge would be occupied by anything but a standing watch consisting of junior-grade duty officers, and their enlisted staffs. The terrorists reasoned that the vessel's major decision-makers would have long ago retired for the evening. And the junior officers certainly didn't have the authority to crank up the vessel's massive engines, without higher approval.

The saboteur's prayer was that each of the now-adrift vessels would float down the narrow bay on the outgoing tide. Unless they managed to bring their propulsion systems on-line, all eventually would come together, in-collision, mid-channel.

That act of metal-on-metal savagery, would serve to block the narrow access/egress to the bay. The timers on the limpet mines attached to the three ships, were set to detonate simultaneously with those set by the other teams. The mid-channel collision of three large capital ships, if nothing else would result in immense confusion, bedlam, and disruption to the American base commander's security plan.

The remaining UDT team, under the command of Cuban Naval Lieutenant Luis Hernando Barbosa, had the most critical mission of the assault. His team would swim cross-current/cross-channel, south across the bay's dredged channel. The anticipated four-knot current would make each of the divers wish they were able to hitch a short-duration tow from the motorized sled. However, it would already be critically over-laden.

Under the cover of the early morning 's tropical coastal cloud cover, the Cuban Navy divers would quietly leave the water at the base's south shoreline. Once on dry land, they would crawl underneath the camouflage ground sheets they had brought with them and take a five-minute break.

If the sky remained overcast and pitch black, they would carry the camouflage sheets to the utility plant with them, rather than use them for cover. However, the approach of dawn practically guaranteed they'd have to employ them for their intended use, on the return trip to the shoreline.

Once the divers had caught their collective breaths, they would divide up the five hundred pounds of enhanced Semtex explosive, they carried with them across the bay. The explosive had been previously waterproofed. It would now be repackaged in 250 gram, olive-drab rectangular bricks. Each brick, or more likely, cluster of bricks, required a Skoda detonator which must be inserted into the explosive, before arming.

The six young and fit men, lugging their loads, would painstakingly crawl across the one hundred yards of beach from the water, to the foot of the base's combination desalinization plant and power house.

Before the commandos left their training base earlier that afternoon, General Raúl Castro Ruz himself had arrived with great fanfare, to emphasize the importance of this particular mission. Fidel's brother was not as verbose as Cuba's president, but nevertheless on this subject, he spoke at length. Before Raúl's arrival, Barbosa' small team had been carefully briefed on the placement of each brick of the plastic explosive, at the American's power plant.

When Raúl and his heavily armed entourage arrived, Lieutenant Barbosa's team had been given yet another briefing stressing the importance to Cuba of them achieving their specific portion of coming mission.

The head of Fidel's Secret Police explained the Presidente's every expectation. Raúl, no less than three times, repeated Fidel's minimal expectations for the successful detonation of the massive cluster bricks of plastic explosives they would be emplacing at the plant. Al-Qaeda had provided the impoverished Cuban Navy with an ample supply of Semtex. The Arab engineers claimed the Cubans only needed a small portion of that amount to do the job. The technocrats explained that if Semtex were used in a coordinated detonation, most of the American's hundred million dollar, state-of-the-art, desalinization and power generation plant would be put out of business for years.

Years ago, the Americans had installed the high-technology plant at Guantánamo Bay to make the remote base totally independent of the Cubans. The communist country's utility systems were worn-out, marginally maintained, undependable, and technically archaic. In those days, Fidel had enjoyed yanking the American's chain by figuratively manipulating the utility systems controls, on and off, depending on his unpredictable moods.

Consumption at the U.S. Naval base at Guantánamo Bay required an average of 2.4 million gallons of drinkable water, and 800-kilowatt hours of electricity, daily. After Castro's disruption of the base's water and power supplies became the rule rather than the exception, Congress finally decided that Gitmo must have stand-alone capability, relative to its need for life-sustaining utilities. The new plant the American's built greatly distressed Presidente Castro. His frequent cutting-off of utilities to the base over the years had always been accompanied by Castro's sincere explanation that his country's struggling infrastructure had unavoidably again broken down.

Fidel was aware that Cuba's utility systems had long ago fallen into a state of unrecoverable disrepair. The Cuban system was far beyond the point where Castro's meager treasury could afford to repair it. Fidel had long ago bled the Cuban economy dry of available tax revenue. Castro either didn't understand, or professed not to, the relationship between preventative maintenance, and the reliable operation of his country's infrastructure.

Years previously, Castro had approached the Soviets, asking that they bankroll the replacement of his country's utility infrastructure. The Russians, in dire financial straits themselves in those days, only provided him with lip service. Next Castro decided to blackmail the Americans into rebuilding Cuba's utility infrastructure, if they wanted continue receiving supplies of potable drinking water and electricity for the Guantánamo Bay base.

The Cuban Presidente used the frequent interruptions of utility service to Gitmo, as a club. He felt it would soon force the Americans to come around to his way of thinking. After all, America was rich. And although Castro would never admit it, his policies had driven down the Cuban economy into the toilet, until the country was considered 'dirt poor' even by Caribbean standards.

Castro never had taken into consideration that the Americans might someday call his bluff, and decide to build a stand-alone, on-base utility plant. He had great faith in his mastery of third-world revolutionary tactics. After all, any alternative proposal, to the Americans continuing their dependence on Cuba's haphazard utility systems, would have to be 'sized' to exceed the base's needs. Only then could it be expected to provide stand-alone capability that would permit the base to operate autonomously. He had never envisioned that one day Congress would tire of him and his childish games, and get firmly behind the project.

Today, if a small portion of the plant's massive petroleum-fired, utility-generating ability is temporarily out-of-service, the Gitmo base commander barely even noticed. If he did notice, he or she would find it a matter of slight concern. Contingencies had been developed for up to, and including, a hypothetical 48-hour outage.

But these contingency plans were predicated on the existence and ready availability of an uninterruptible power source (UPS). If the UPS couldn't be brought on-line to back up the main plant during a long-term outage, the base's personnel, detainees, and civilian support personnel would have to be evacuated.

Such an evacuation, considering the United States' dwindling number of nation-state friends in the region, would require the entire Gitmo operation be transported to the U.S. mainland well over a hundred miles away. It would be an operation that would be significant and costly, even if it didn't make Dunkirk appear to have been a minor reduction-in-force.

The U.S. Navy had years ago, stolen a page from the technocrats over at Freight International Express' huge modern freight hub in Memphis, Tennessee. FiEX had installed a series of tethered 727 jet engines to create a reliable UPS facility for their hub and headquarters operations.

The Navy applied the same technology to the new utility plant they had designed and built in Guantánamo Bay. In the event of a power failure, the UPS system would be spooled up. The backup system then would temporarily supply the base for the duration of the not-infrequent periods of disabling hurricanes and tropical storms. The UPS system was also capable of covering for scheduled generating plant shutdowns, to accomplish planned maintenance.

However, the tethered 727 turbine engines that generated all that critical temporary electricity and water, required substantial quantities of aviation fuel to operate. And the U.S. Congress, for various reasons, had never seen fit to fund the 'supersizing' of the base's underground fuel storage capacity. Once the fuel for the UPS system was consumed, the base would essentially and literally go dark and dry.

The team leader of the primary Cuban UDT unit charged with destroying the American utility plant, Lieutenant Barbosa, was personally aware of the importance of his team's mission. Success of his mission was not only important to Cuba, but also to himself and his family.

His wife, and their four young children, without explanation, had been taken into 'protective custody' by one of Castro's elite army Special Forces units. This activity had occurred at the exact moment Barbosa's team had been boarding the trucks, which carried them tonight to the American base's perimeter fenceline.

It was not unheard of for Castro to kidnap a Cuban military officer's family. If for nothing else than to ensure the man/woman did whatever the mission required. This included giving their lives if necessary, on any mission critical to the Cuban Revolution, as determined by El Presidente. Generally, the family was treated well during the period of detainment. And they were promptly returned home carrying cheap trinkets at the end of the assignment, assuming their breadwinner's mission was accomplished within Castro's expectations.

Lt. Barbosa, after carefully stepping through a hole others had previously cut through the heavy gauge chain-link perimeter fenceline, urged his crawling men towards the inner bay shoreline.

When the Americans patrol boats had roared away, he and the other nineteen Cubans crept from the heavy sticker brush, and slipped into the pleasantly warm water. They pulled the neutral buoyancy rafts, and tugged on the motorized sleds. The fully laden sled weighed nearly two hundred pounds when out of water. But the weight was significantly less once it got settled below the waterline.

Barbosa's leadership style was to lead-by-example. That insured each of his men would perform as they had exhaustingly been trained. Russia's elite Spetnez instructors had trained almost every active senior Cuban Navy diver. They were the best. Even the egotistical Americans grudgingly admitted that the Spetnez "were good." The training had occurred before the Soviet Union had decided it could no longer financially afford to be a participating friend of the Cuban Revolution.

Each member of tonight's team fought to remain motivated. In addition to their personal underwater loads, each diver had eight-five pounds of aluminum air bottles, and other miscellaneous equipment on his back.

Each of the Cuban commandos carried wire cutters, clips, a first-aid kit, night vision goggles, their personal weapon and ammunition, three small but deadly Russian-manufacturer assault grenades, and of course the plastic ties, fusing wire, timers, and detonators that would make the water-proofed Semtex explosive, when properly placed, go 'bang!' Two of the more athletic men also carried a lightweight shovel, in case the team had to bury, or trench, any of the fusing wire beneath the hard dirt of American's utility plant.

Trudging through the boggy, soft bottom of the lower basin's northern shoreline was a physically demanding task. Each step the divers took was like walking in quicksand. Forward movement required a mechanized shuffle only developed through extensive practice. The diver would slide his foot forward, then lift it, all in the same combined motion, to reduce the strong suction of the bottom.

Weeks before, the twenty Cuban divers had been ordered into the mission's sequestered isolation area. This was a practice long adapted by each one of the world's elite SOF teams, before they undertook a difficult mission. There, the instructors had the divers make runs of an hour in duration, three times a day, through the boggy shallows of a nearby swamp bed. During these initial exercises, each man carried a rucksack full of nearly twenty-three kilograms (fifty pounds) of rocks. In two weeks, the duration times had doubled, then tripled. And the rucksack weight increased until the canvas deteriorated and began to split.

While the exercise didn't turn them into supermen, it did provide a preview of the difficulty they could expect on the upcoming Guantánamo Bay mission.

Once the team finally arrived at mid-channel in Guantánamo Bay, the constant dredging the Americans had to maintain to insure a viable harbor, insured there was at least ninety-five feet of depth to guarantee their invisibility during the hours of darkness.

However, as the Cubans swam closer to the south shoreline of the inner bay, the water would begin to shallow appreciably. In areas, such as the American base's designated general anchorage, and off the location of the power plant, the water there was only about sixty-feet deep. Fortunately it was forecasted to be a very dark night, followed by an equally a dark pre-dawn morning.

The assault team moved slowly and carefully, least they be discovered before they reached the inner base's southern shoreline. The American's power and desalinization plant water lay one hundred yards inland, from the shoreline.

Cuban and al-Qaeda spies, already inside the Guantánamo Naval facility, had arranged to eliminate the utility plant's waterside, exterior lighting fixtures. Through the use of low technology weapons such slingshots, one after another of the pole-mounted floodlights, which were intended to light up the beach between the shoreline and the utility plant proper, were broken. Any lens that survived the slingshot, likely had been allowed to accumulate so much air-borne dirt over the years that they essentially were ineffective for the purpose for which they were intended.

This didn't mean that once the Cuban divers reached the southern shoreline beneath the plant, they could just stand up and stroll into the desalinization and power plant. The Cuba divers would still have to slowly crawl across the narrow beach, possibly even using the camouflaged groundsheets provided them for that specific purpose.

CHAPTER TWENTY-TWO

DAY 333—30 NOVEMBER

THE AMERICAN NAVAL BASE

SABOTEURS PLANT SEMTEX

GUANTÁNAMO BAY

CUBA

The infiltration of the American base at Guantánamo Bay continued. Lieutenant Barbosa was the leader of this particular team of Cuban saboteurs. He had paused to speak with each of his men. He wanted to make sure there were no questions before they started out on the dangerous trek across the beach, to the American power plant. It was his manner to solicit input from each man on his team. Of the years, he had found this enhanced team-unity. And increased their overall performance. Only Jose had a question. He was the youngest, most in-experienced man on Barbosa's commando team.

"Jefe," the quintessential newbie had whispered. "I understand that we needed the motorized sled to carry the heavy explosives across the channel to the target. But why not just leave it here? After we get everything placed, wired, and timed? It will just slow us down, when we are hurrying to get the hell out of there and back across the channel. If not, we'll have to haul the damn thing through the heavy brush again on the north shoreline of the channel. And how do you plan on getting it back through the American's perimeter fencing, all before dawn?"

Lt. Barbosa understood the intelligent if undisciplined young man. And the officer felt he had possibilities of becoming one of his strongest team members. But Barbosa also knew the kid was a 'slacker.' Most teenage conscripts in the Revolutionary Cuban military were these days.

So the lieutenant had responded, "Jose, normally that would be an excellent idea. But we don't want to leave anything for the American sentries who patrol the beach to discover, now do we?"

Jose, thinking perhaps his leader was getting a little forgetful had whispered, "We have a couple shovels, Sir. We could bury the sled in the sand. Before we swim back across the channel."

Barbosa, thinking "*Why me, Jefe?*" had just patted the young diver on the arm. He then whispered, "Jose, think back to the Commandant's briefing. The two Cuban ports that serve Guantánamo City, up in the upper basin, use this waterway. And the large ships that service the ports, produce a great deal of 'wake.' That wake splashes up on the adjacent shoreline. This is true regardless of which way the big ships are headed. Going into, or out of the upper bay. That keeps the beaches in the channel very wet."

"So if you dug a hole, and buried the sled, wouldn't the sand on the new top surface be dry, thus alerting the American sentries? And then wouldn't the American sentries alert their base security troops? They would in turn search the plant, and find our explosives. Before the Semtex could detonate?"

Jose gave this idea a few more moments of thought, before deciding the lieutenant was correct. The young man silently chastised himself for not thinking the idea out, before he voiced it. He thought *I just made an ass of myself in front of the L.T. and more-experienced divers.*

The young man was ambitious. He knew his lieutenant understood and accepted that. But Jose would never go on to be the team's leader, if he continued to make mistakes like the one he just had. He hung his head, and Barbosa, a compassionate leader of men, again patted him again on the arm, as if to say, *I understand, Jose. I once was a young, ambitious young man like you.* Then Barbosa rose, and entered the water to lead the team to their objective.

The team finally cleared the sucking bottom of the shallow north beach. They all followed the specially trained navigator/operator, who was steering the motorized sled along the bottom of the channel. The men were thankful for the aging Russian wet suits, hoods, full-face masks, and fins. And they felt assured of their own invulnerability, by the awesome weapons they carried.

As team leader, Barbosa was the only one who carried a Soviet-style attack board, and compass. It was his responsibility to double check the underwater progress and navigation of the motorized sled operator. Currently, the large, faintly illuminated digital readouts on the board showed the sled driver to be on-course. They were headed for a waypoint one hundred yards short of the opposite channel bank.

The current at the bottom of the dredged trough seemed weaker than it would have on the surface. However, it still tugged mightily at each heavily laden diver. Barbosa checked around the immediate vicinity to make sure his men were maintaining their assigned positions. However, water in the channel was very oily and murky. So much so, that he could only make out the man swimming on either side of him.

The lieutenant had ordered the team to proceed in a tactical assault-line formation. They were to maintain a thirty-foot separation between each other. Considering all the sediment in the water, his inability to see his entire team didn't surprise him. He was sure everyone was struggling under the burdensome loads. And he had faith they were doing their level best. Just as they had been trained by the Soviet instructors.

A few minutes later, the diver who had been swimming 'point' immediately in front of the heavily laden sled, suddenly stopped.

He shot up an open-palmed right hand, signaling for them to stop. This caused the sled's operator to frantically adjust a number of valves on his control panel. The buoyancy adjustment was necessary to prevent the sled from sinking to the bottom as it lost forward momentum.

Lt. Barbosa glanced around to make certain that the entire team had halted and were treading water to maintain position. Then he knifed to the side of the diver who was swimming 'point.' The diver, non-too-gently, grabbed the underwater writing stylus off the attack board the officer gripped. He hastily scribbled a note to the officer. The man reported that he had just seen the vague outline of a thick sensor cable, on the bottom of the channel in front of him. The man apparently was afraid to use his communicator, least the signal be picked up by the sensor cable.

Happening onto the sensor cable was alarming to both men. Their supervisors had told them that the Americans, in their normal over-confident manner, never bothered to lay sensor cables in the ship passage channel. After all, continuous dredging was required to keep it free of silt accumulation and navigatable.

The cable, his best diver had just reported, supposedly did not exist. Or at least not according to the double agents al-Qaeda managed to get assigned to Camp Delta to spy on the American security defenses.

The officer didn't bother to take time to process this new bit of information. His entire immediate family's future, and the lives of each one of his loyal men, rested on the successful accomplishment of this mission. So, dropping all caution, he uttered a terse command over his underwater communicator. The team was to back off about one hundred yards, and take up station a couple of yards over the channel bottom.

In less than ten-minutes, but ten minutes out of his already tight schedule, fate smiled on he and his men. The hull of a small Cuban tug towing a garbage scow down the channel from the upper basin became visible out of the swirling sediment, as it churned its way on its run out towards the Windward Passage. There the city's trash would unceremoniously be dumped into one of the passage's many undersea canyons. The deep natural ravines proliferated between Cuba and Jamaica coasts, reportedly one of the deepest points on the planet Earth.

Barbosa firmly grasped the point diver's air tank regulator to regain his attention. He indicated to him that just as the tug crossed less than sixty feet overhead, the team would make a sprint past the sensor cable, and on towards the south shoreline. The officer was betting that the complacent Americans routinely ignored alarms from the sensor cable. Especially during the anticipated times when the unescorted Cuban garbage scows were permitted to pass through the lower basin, en-route the dumping grounds out in Windward Passage.

Rapidly, the sled operator got his equipment moving, and the remainder of the diving team proceeded in its sediment-churning wake. They followed the point diver across the sensor cable, and on towards the approaching shoreline.

Crossing back over the sensitive sensor cable, on the return trip, was obviously going to be a problem. The team would then be racing the Caribbean dawn. They would not be able to wait for other randomly transiting vessel to mask their crossing.

Lt. Barbosa, upon reaching the far shoreline's shallows, pivoted around in the water. He motioned the sled operator to ground the sled in the bottom muck. The team was now about three hundred feet short of the shoreline, under the still-dark pre-dawn sky.

The six-man crew put their shoulders into removing the explosives off the sled. Then they swam the waterproof packages towards the shoreline. Where they gently set them down on the silt-covered bottom in a foot of oily, opaque water.

All of the men, despite the nearly one-mile swim, a vicious crosscurrent, and the mini-crisis en-route, were still breathing normally. None of them appeared to be dangerously fatigued, to the point of unrecoverable exhaustion.

After taking a few minutes to reclaim their strength, they all turned to Lt. Barbosa with questioning looks. Using the Russian hand-signals they had all been taught, he instructed them to pickup the explosive devices off the bottom. The dark moonless overcast still concealed their presence adequately.

The lieutenant elected to make up a few of the previously lost minutes by not deploying the camouflage groundsheets. He knew, however, they would need them on the return. So the team would have to carry them with them, as they slowly and silently crawled across the flat sand beach.

The decision to carry the groundsheets, instead of putting them to their intended purpose, bothered the team. True enough the Cuban night was still dark enough to not yet force the use of the cumbersome devices. Their leader had similar misgivings.

The lieutenant thought, *it is possible that one of those damn American CIA Keyhole KH-11 surveillance satellites, that collect sharp imagery even through clouds, rain, and darkness, happens to be overhead at this specific moment.*

The officer reasoned he couldn't do anything about that remote possibility now. If their luck turned out to be bad, then they would have to fight the plant's security personnel. They had been exhaustively coached by their bosses that they were not to surrender under *any* circumstances. So any attempted interdiction by the Americans meant a firefight. And a firefight realistically meant they never would see their families again.

Thinking ahead, the lieutenant carefully reviewed the plan's next steps in his mind. The team would laboriously, dragging the explosives and pushing the other equipment in front of them, crawl the one hundred yards across the beach from the water's edge, to the base of the American's utility plant.

Then he supervised to ensure that all the explosives were properly placed. Each pre-prepared package had to be attached to a specific operating mechanism in the huge utility plant. And then timed to explode exactly at midnight, some nineteen hours later.

When they finished attaching the mines, it would then be less than a half hour away from what the Russian military refers to as BDND (Beginning of Day, Nautical Dawn.) In other words when it is light enough to strike camp, but not yet light enough to proceed on to next objective, safely.

In order to not invite attention on the egress back across the sand beach, the commandos would have to crawl very slowly. This time there would be no question about using the camouflage groundsheets. They would have to be used if the team was to return to the presumed safety of the channel, without being seen by a passing beach patrol.

Holding that thought, Barbosa lead his centipede-like procession slowly out onto one hundred yard-wide section of nearly flat beach. The beach ran from the lower basin's south shoreline, to the green-painted, pre-engineered metal buildings. The taller structures housed the desalinization towers. The shorter buildings contained the all-important power generators.

The al-Qaeda spies working for the gringos at Gitmo, had assured the Cubans that only six Americans were assigned the night shift at the utility complex. Each of those individuals were active or retired U.S. Navy Petty Officers, enlisted mechanics, primarily trained for emergency maintenance needs, and only secondarily for defense of the critical facility.

According to the reports of the al-Qaeda's spies, the Americans often got lazy and careless. Occasionally they blatantly left the security-access walk doors leading into the plant off the adjacent beach, open for ventilation. This practice was contrary to the express orders of their superiors. Hopefully, tonight would prove to be no exception.

Barbosa led his men, quietly slithering on their stomachs, towards a conveniently open, four-foot wide, green-painted metal walk door. Immediately in front of him, facing away from the beach and into the innards of the plant, sat a large t-shirt and shorts-clad white man, furtively smoking a Cuban leaf cigar, wearing well-scuffled combat boots. The sentry's M-16A assault rifle leaned uselessly more than five-feet away, leaning against a 30-gallon, royal-blue-painted garbage can. The can was located under a large sign, which both in English and Spanish, proclaimed NO SMOKING!

Barbosa came silently to his feet. He stealthily approached the smoking man from the rear. Then he reached a powerful left hand forward over the man's shoulder, and gripped the man's jaw. The lieutenant simultaneously put his other hand flat against the guard's head, while his left wrenched the guard's jaw hard to the right. At the same time, he shoved the man's head downward to the left, breaking the neck with a loud snap at the fourth vertebra.

Barbosa held the guard's torso tight to his own chest, until the death throes had expired. Then he almost gently lowered the body soundless to the expanded metal floor decking. Grabbing the man's booted feet, he dragged the body under a nearby, elevated walkway. The place he selected, was one the building's sparse lighting never properly illuminated. Barbosa hoped the remote location would conceal the body, at least until nineteen hours later, when the explosives detonated at midnight.

The lead saboteur slowly swiveled his head from side to side. He was making a visual check of the immediate area for the presence of additional guards. The lieutenant permitted a valuable, non-recoverable, minute to elapse, as he intensely listened for any man-made sounds, other than the plant's operating machinery.

Finally satisfied he was alone; he raised his arm over his right shoulder, and beckoned his men past him, into the large metal, high-bay building. Then, using only hand signals, he directed them off in separate directions. He stopped them momentarily to whisper a final warning to each of them. They were not to permit themselves to be seen by any of the remaining American mechanic/ guards. One missing guard might be missed at shift change, but more—never. Each man then moved forward. Using a crouched stance, they sought out their pre-assigned targets.

However, the fates were not smiling on the commandos in the pre-dawn hours. Only a few minutes later, another of his men was cautiously rounding a piece of large machinery, on the way to his assigned target location. Then he sensed something which made him freeze, and would have driven a normal man to heart palpitations.

Right in front of him was another sentry. This one was also looking the opposite direction, hunched over, intently studying some type of knee-level, wall-mounted gauge.

Acting on instinct, the commando reached over the man's stooped shoulder with his left hand, and grasped the sentry's forehead in a vice-like grip. The commando had used his right hand, to draw his stiletto knife in the same motion. After knotting his abdominal muscles, he plunged the sharp blade into the back of the engineer's neck. The knife's tip entered between the first and second vertebrate, just below the skull. He then pulled the man's head back sharply with his left hand, easing the passage of the sharp knife into the man's spinal cord, severing it completely.

The saboteur dropped the bloody corpse. Then he calmly but immediately spoke into the waterproof mouthpiece of his low-frequency encrypted communicator. He quietly explained to Barbosa what had happened. The Lieutenant told him to continue on his mission. The Cuban officer would come to his location to handle disposal of the team's latest body.

Before moving out to locate the second body, Barbosa contacted each of the members of his team on the communicator. All had already reached their assigned targets, and were planting their mines. He quietly reminded them, "there are still four armed guards in the facility. You must avoid them at all costs. Abort your mission, if it cannot be accomplished without having to confront another guard."

The team's Master Sergeant, Julio Gonzalas promptly came back up on the small Russian transceiver. He reported to the lieutenant that perhaps that wouldn't be necessary. The sergeant had observed the remaining four Americans, lounging comfortably in a soundproof, air-conditioned lunchroom, watching an American NFL, same-day taped football game on a large plasma screen television. Barbosa took that as a promising omen.

When the Lt. reached the second body, he grabbed it under the lifeless arms pits, and with a great deal of effort, dragged the body up two-stories-worth of steep metal access ladders. Then he dumped it over the railing. The sentry's body fell forty feet, impacting on the back of the corpse's head.

Hopefully, he reasoned, when the body was found the initial assumption would be that the guard had simply been careless. And that the dead man's co-workers would buy into the fallacy that carelessness had caused the American to slip on the greasy expanded metal grate flooring. Resulting in the subsequent fall over the railing, to an unfortunate death.

In the next thirty stress-filled minutes, the Cubans completed attaching the Semtex charges without further detection. The olive-drab bricks of Semtex had been poked into as many out of the way places, as humanly possible. The commandos had calibrated and set their timers, as their leader had instructed. Then they retraced their steps out of the building complex, to assemble outside, using the Jaguey trees for cover.

There, the men unfurled the groundsheets. Then they proceeded to lie down on the cold, damp sand, and pulled the tarps over themselves, after inserting their gloved hands into the built-in mitts the manufacturer had built in the heavy cloth. They began the slow crawl back across the vulnerable beach to the shoreline. Their progress across the beach was increasing visible in the light of the fast-approaching dawn. The commando bringing up the rear of the procession was crawling backwards with difficulty. He used a small hand broom to brush away the scuffmarks the men were making, as they elbow-crawled along the sand.

The sabotage team finally reached the southern shoreline some twenty-three minutes later. The divers carefully stood up, and taking everything they had carried in with them, walked into the murky water. Once the water closed over their facemasks, they swam back out to the anchored motorized sled, which had been grounded in the muck just off the beach nearly four hours earlier.

The motorized sled was again made buoyant. Then the team proceeded to tie the purely offensive weapons to the sled. Any equipment that would not be needed in the team's extraction was also hog-tied to the sled's cargo rails. All of the equipment the

Cubans had carried in with them had been sanitized beforehand, to remove all possible means of identification. They put their swim fins and diving masks on, and tested the air regulators and the circuits of the multi-channel communicators.

On the return trip, the lieutenant planned to avoid the American's sensor cable. He and his men would cross it at a point where the water movement, both from tidal action and frequent ship movements, had caused the bottom silt to mound over it. He prayed on his Mother's grave that the thin layer of sand would reduce the device's sensitivity.

Once over the cable, Barbosa also planned to sink the heavy motorized sled in the deepest point of the dredged channel. To it, the divers had secured any of the equipment they absolutely wouldn't need on their planned egress off the American base.

Approximately forty-five minutes later, the nearly exhausted Cubans emerged from the water on the channel's swampy north shoreline. It was straight-up 6:00 a.m. The individual teams morphed back into the original twenty-man infiltration squad.

After a brief rest to collect their senses, the team guide sought out the infiltration route they had followed earlier that morning. Once it was located, the men hurriedly crawled into the dense brush, concealing themselves from the fast approaching dawn.

The team was on its way to the planned rendezvous with a Cuban Special forces exfiltration unit. Lieutenant Martinez had memorized the designated rendezvous point, which lay along the American base's seventeen-mile-long perimeter fenceline. Once they reached the designated point along the electrified chain-link fenceline, the squad would be exfiltrated by members of Raul Castro's elite security forces.

The Cubans anticipated that the Americans would have already discovered the 'shunted' hole that had been cut in the perimeter fence for the infiltration. So a single-use tunnel, one that had been dug under the American's elaborate perimeter security fencing and through the Cuban's own landmines fields, was activated for the exfiltration.

Once outside that perimeter fencing, the exhausted men walked nearly five kilometers. But then, they had been picked up. The late-arriving convoy consisted of four military two-by trucks. The twenty-man squad was then trucked to an abandoned Cuban Army base some sixty-five kilometers away.

The men were relieved of their personal firearms and equipment, and offered showers, hot food, cigars, and clean fatigues. More importantly, they were offered rum by the gallon. Raúl Castro again was present. He urged the men to celebrate their victorious mission. Each man was promised a field promotion, and other untold rewards, based on the personal orders of Fidel, himself.

The commandos had progressed into the celebration's liquor-fueled second hour. Suddenly, at an obscure signal from the always-paranoid brother of Fidel, the Secret Police surrounded the commandos. The divers fought bravely, but soon were clubbed into submission.

Once they were unconscious, the security troops slit their throats. Their mutilated bodies were dragged in a large pit, which had been concealed to look like a concrete foundation for a new building.

Then the bodies were covered with a six-inch thick layer of lye. Once that was accomplished, the Secret Police covered over and compacted the pit, using a backhoe and bulldozer that had been waiting nearby, concealed with tarps, on an Army lowboy truck.

For a number of weeks, until the Cuban Army rumor mill got around to it, the men's families would have no idea what become of their loved one. Or who was responsible for the atrocity. The massacre had taken place on the orders of Fidel Castro. But the grievous act was at the hands of Raúl, his mentally deranged brother.

Back at Guantánamo the JTF was momentarily unaware that a well-planned attack would descend on the base, in less that fifteen hours time. For the present, the soldiers at American Naval Station went about their routine duties, defending America interests, and as the base motto stated, "Enabling Warfighter Readiness."

CHAPTER TWENTY-THREE

DAY 333—30 NOVEMBER

THE AMERICAN NAVAL BASE

ASSAULT ON CAMP DELTA

GUANTÁNAMO BAY

CUBA

> NEWS BULLETIN
> Associated Press
>
> *PENTAGON: GUANTÁNAMO HAS A SENSE OF URGENCY!*
> By Robert Burns
> AP Military Writer
> 25 November 2003
>
> WASHINGTON—The United States is fighting a "raging intelligence war" with suspected terrorists held at a high-

security prison at Guantanamo Bay, Cuba, a senior Pentagon official says.

"Its being conducted with a great sense of urgency," Thomas O'Connell, who oversees Pentagon policy on the holding, interrogation and release of suspects at Guantanamo, said in an interview Monday.

Interrogations and related work are conducted 24 hours a day, seven days a week, O'Donnell said. He asserted that satisfactory progress is being made in extracting useful information, despite the wall of hatred and defiance the prisoners throw daily at their questioners.

Several of the approximately 660 suspects being detained have provided timely information that has helped avert terrorist attacks and led to additional arrests, he said. But others refuse to cooperate and in some other cases, U.S. officials have been unable to obtain basic information to determine whether prisoners are in a position to know much of value.

Intelligence gleaned from the interrogations there and from arrests in Europe is believed to have helped thwart several attacks planned against U.S. targets in Italy, Britain and Singapore. Last February, the FBI said it based a public warning of a possible terrorist attack against U.S. interests in Yemen on information from detainees at Guantanamo and in Afghanistan.

Out of the 88 released so far—including 20 last Friday—the United States has agreed that 84 could be freed once they arrived in their home countries. The other four were repatriated to Saudi Arabia several months ago, to continue in detention there under a U.S.-Saudi agreement.

Officials say there are plans to send dozens more home soon. They likely will get out of the Guantanamo Bay (author's note—I.E. *Camp Delta*) only on condition that their governments continue to investigate and imprison them upon repatriation, two senior U.S. officials said.

30—END OF BULLETIN

2305 hours: The 3,076-ton Soviet-made, Kilo SSK class submarine, the *Scorpion,* arrived submerged at her troop deployment position, two miles off the American Naval Station, Guantánamo Bay, Cuba.

The *Scorpion* originally had been known as 'Kilo-2.' However, bin-Laden had renamed her for the current mission. The Russians had modified the diesel-powered, cold war-era submarine to carry thirty special operations (SOF) troops and their equipment. Of necessity, this resulted in having to drastically downsize the boat's operating crew to provide space for the shock teams.

Following the boat's remodel, al-Qaeda had stolen it from the Russians. They had utilized guile, and a significant amount of US dollars, deposited to the Swiss Bank account of the Russian base commander. The officer was responsible for guarding Russia's warships at that particular northern base.

Seven nerve-racking hours before, the *Scorpion* had blown her ballast tanks. She had risen off the sandy bottom of Windward Passage, some 183 miles west of Port-au-Prince, Haiti. The silent-running diesel had sprinted at her maximum 'submerged' speed of seventeen knots on the lengthily voyage to her designated deployment position. That GPS-established position was off Kittery beach, 485 feet below a steep bluff on which the infidel's infamous Camp Delta was located.

Just after 0030 hours, the waiting submarine had partially rose to the surface. Only the boat's conning tower and forward crew hatch were permitted to peek above the water line. Once the hatch had been opened, the submarine hastily deployed two, fifteen-man special operations teams and their equipment.

The al-Qaeda shock troops finished exiting the boat. They inflated their black rubber Zodiacs, and attached the heavily muffled, 300 h.p. Mercury, outboard engines. As soon as the submarine's decks were clear of the men and equipment, she again began to take on ballast.

The silent black killer slowly sank back under the azure-colored waters of the Caribbean. The crew stopped the descent at a predetermined tactical depth, deep enough to obscure the boat's outline from the surface, meaning the American's satellite surveillance. But she could not go so deep, that the boat would not be promptly recallable for the returning special operators, several hours later.

Out of necessity, the *Scorpion* had made the underwater crossing by sneaking beneath under patrol pattern of a American's Arleigh Burke class, AEGIS destroyer. The pattern specified by the U.S. Southern Command was a rather ambitious oval, 130-miles long by 30-miles wide.

Two American warships were alternating the patrol duty in twelve-hour shifts, 24/7. The ship going off-duty had just dropped anchor just inside Guantánamo Bay's inner basin.

The anchorage chosen by the skipper of the off-duty destroyer was not an acceptable location to *drop the hook* by U.S. Naval standards. However, the site's proximity to the Windward Passage permitted the sleek man-of-war to rapidly get underway, in case she was called upon to provide emergency backup. The off-duty destroyer could then steam at thirty-two knots to rendezvous with the patrolling destroyer, in the event of attack. The off-duty destroyer anchored approximately one mile south of the base's recommended anchorage area, off Deer Point.

The captain of the *Scorpion* made sure the infidel's destroyer was at the far eastern end of her assigned patrol pattern, before the submarine had passed underneath the patrol pattern at a depth of 200-meters, nearly five hours previously.

This turned out to be over-caution on the part of the al-Qaeda captain. Shortly before the submarine's underwater passage, the *USS Oscar Austin*—the destroyer on-duty at the time—had been forced to temporarily put her priority assignment on-hold. The

American's mission was simplistic. The destroyers were to ensure no vessel, capable of off-loading assault troops, was permitted to steam to within ten miles of either Windmill or Kittery beaches. Both beaches were located at the base of the near-vertical bluff, on which Camp Delta had been constructed.

A short time earlier, two Cuban MiG-29s had launched from the direction of Cuba's Camagüey Air Base. They had headed directly for the patrolling destroyer. This had initiated a confrontation between the Cuban Air Force and the U.S. Navy. Permission for the highly unorthodox action had come directly from Fidel Castro Ruz. The Cuban President had formed a temporarily alliance with al-Qaeda.

Castro's unusual concurrence was based on a secret agreement between Fidel's brother, Raúl, and one of bin-Laden's elder sons in Havana earlier that year. The young bin-Laden said his father would force the infidels to evacuate the Guantánamo Naval Base. All Castro had to do was lend al-Qaeda the services of several of Cuba's crack commando teams to infiltrate the base, and plant some explosives. Al-Qaeda would also provide the explosives for the covert assault.

Fidel's willingness to participate in the action resulted in the launch of two Soviet-built, advanced fast-movers that approached the *USS Oscar Austin* in what only can be described as a threatening manner. At the time, an unexpected tropical storm with reported winds in excess of one hundred m.p.h. was rapidly moving across Windward Passage towards Cuba. This made the impending confrontation even more hairy. The American AEGIS destroyer and the two Cuban M-29s were caught up in the storm's fury. Despite the combatant's relative difference in size and weight, the storm was tossing them all around like ping pong balls!

The guided missile destroyer's captain, whose prime responsibility was the safety of his ship and crew, had no choice other than to break off the patrol pattern, to take evasive action. As the vicious winds battered the potential combatants, the situation was fast getting out of hand.

Only in the final thirty seconds of the Cuban's approach, long after the Americans had given both Cuban combat aircraft their final '*cease and desist or else*' command, did the fighter pilots turn off their attack radars, drop their gear, and deploy their speed brakes. Their action was the internationally-accepted signal for non-hostile intent.

Both the MiGs had then come smartly about, and run from the storm and the scene of the confrontation they had so recklessly created. Per procedure, the destroyer captain continued to keep his ship's 'eyes and ears' activated. That guaranteed the ship would be ready in case the Cubans decided to 'turn and burn,' escalating the confrontation to round two. Due to the manpower limitations in today's all-volunteer U.S. Navy, that realistically meant that everyone in the on-board AEGIS suite was watching the above-surface radar. And giving little attention to either the surface, or below surface, threat recognition systems.

Al-Qaeda's planned assault on Camp Delta was imaginative, ingenious, and costly, but failed to take one important possibility into consideration.

Timers on the explosive mines that the infiltrating Cuban commandos had planted at four on-base locations, were synchronized to detonate at midnight, that very night. However, unknown to al-Qaeda or their Cuba accomplices, at one of the target locations—the base's Desalinization/Power Generation Plant—the explosives had already been discovered by the Americans. The discovery of the explosives at that location would minimize any possibility of success in the coming attack.

The Cuban Underwater demolition divers had been in the process of placing the explosives at the plant, when they had run into American security guards. The battle-trained Cuban divers had easily eliminated two guards. But the infiltrators had failed to properly conceal the bodies, when they finished their mission, and exfiltrated the utility plant. The explosive devices the Cuban divers had planted in the all-important Desalinization /Power Generation plant, subsequently were discovered, disarmed and removed.

The explosives at the three remaining target locations on the base, detonated at midnight, as planned. However the U.S. base's commanding officer had elected to defer calling out the off-duty force of JTF guards, until the cause of the three explosions could be identified. Guantánamo was, after all, a decades-old base, subject to the deterioration and rot found in all tropical climates. Frankly, occasional mechanical and electrical failures were not all that uncommon, and sometime they even sounded like explosions.

The American commander's decision to postpone the decision on whether the JTF reserve should be called out would prove to be prudent. It greatly decreased the likelihood the terrorists would fully achieve al-Qaeda's primary objective.

The al-Qaeda plan had been predicated on the assumption that no less than fifty percent of the off-duty guards at Camp America, and a goodly number of the on-duty guards at Camp Delta, would be called out to respond to the simultaneous, on-base explosions.

One of the other al-Qaeda targets, after the Americans disarmed the mines placed at the base's Desalinization/Power Generation plant, had included three commercial ocean freighters. The vessels were contracted out to the U.S. government and had been in the base's general anchorage harbor.

Explosions also had caused the unplanned shutdown of the cross-bay ferry terminal on the base's Leeward side.

And on the Windward side, explosives had detonated under the dining areas of the base's 'dirty shirt' mess hall. The latter targeted U.S. senior-level naval officers and Petty Officers, who had been assigned OD duty over their organization's graveyard shift. Those men, out of necessity wearing their working uniforms and fatigues, were thus required to use the less formal late-hour dining area.

Structural fires, collateral to the detonation of the explosives planted at the Leeside Ferry Terminal, and the dining areas at the base O-Club, were initially attributed to electrical shorts in the base's multi-decades-old wiring. For that reason, the base fire department, HazMat Team, and on-duty electrical engineers from the base facilities department, responded to those 'less threatening' incident call-outs.

The explosions from the limpet mines the Cuban's commandos had placed, severed the anchor chains, and damaged the propeller shafts and rudder stakes of the three freighters in the base's general anchorage. Those particular explosions for a brief time were attributed to the sympathetic detonation of some old, unstable Vietnam-era, 1,000-pound blockbuster bombs, long-buried under the silt bottom of the harbor.

A cursory review of some brittle and yellowed 30-year-old incident reports found in the archives, documented that several pallets of the deadly bombs had fallen overboard. The decades-old reports said the accident happened when lifting straps had parted as barge cranes were loading a supply transport headed for Vietnam, back in the early 1970's.

The United States was at war at the time, and the operational mood in those hectic times was 'do the best you can, and drive on!' The files noted that at the time, damage control crews had been unable to pinpoint the actual location of the sunken explosives. The 'experts' the Navy had brought in, thirty years previously, had pontificated on the question for a short time. Then they wrote their report, which said, "The missing bombs in question are now inert, due the amount of water that no doubt has seeped in and diluted the explosive chemicals, through the non-waterproofed casings."

The base's ever-rotating command bureaucracy had long ago come to the conclusion that the missing bombs were now safely covered by a dozen of feet of silt. That muck had accumulated on the floor of the general anchorage over the past three decades. Since no one knew the exact location of the missing ordnance, it wasn't a stretch of the imagination for today's investigators to blame the mysterious explosions on the lost-lost bombs.

Having taken the initial if erroneous causal reports of the explosions at face value, the base security OD had decided that the three incidents did not require the emergency call-out of any supplemental forces. The decision meant the JTF guard shift up at

Camp Delta, was staffed at normal levels, and not 'drawn down' as the al-Qaeda planners had projected. The camp was fully staffed, when the al-Qaeda shock force off the *Scorpion* assaulted Camp Delta.

The al-Qaeda planners, specifically Bin-Laden's deputy Ayman Al-Zawahiri, had been gambling that the destruction of the base's Desalinization/Power Generating Plant, would serve to destroy the overall naval facility's ability to function. Without electricity and potable water, the plant's loss would have been the death rattle for the continued operation of the remote American base.

But even if that had been the case, the base's 727-UPS backup system would of provided an alternative, albeit temporary, source of power. It would permit the Naval Station to remain operational for a limited time. Potable water could always be airlifted in to supply the base's needs.

There was little doubt that al-Qaeda would have been cancelled their assault plans, had they become aware that the Americans had discovered and disabled the explosives that their allies-of-convenience had placed at the utility plant.

NCIS investigators would pursue dozens of leads for months, trying to determine why the embedded al-Qaeda spies in JTF 160, hadn't attempted to seize a marine radio for the few seconds it would have taken to broadcast this information to the *Scorpion*.

Bin-Laden had negotiated a deal with Fidel Castro months ago. If Castro would assist al-Qaeda in distracting the Americans, permitting bin-Laden's troops to free some of the currently detained VIPs from Camp Delta, his *quid pro quo* would be providing the explosives by which the Cuban's could destroy key operating equipment at the base.

As far as Castro was concerned, the cornerstone of that agreement was that Cuban commandos, using explosives provided by al-Qaeda, would destroy the desalinization/power generation plant that made it possible for the hated and unwanted Americans to smugly continue to occupy the Guantánamo Naval Station.

"The loss of this critical equipment," bin-Laden's son, Saad, had promised, "will within the month, force the United States to vacate the Guantánamo Bay base. This would mean the removal of all American occupants and their belongings, including transferring the remaining Camp Delta detainees back to the U.S. mainland."

Young bin-Laden had speculated, "The forced transfer of the detainees back into the CONUS (the Continental United States) will raise a renewed onslaught of challenges to the questionable legality of the American's 'incarcerating captured al-Qaeda and Taliban warriors, without legal representation' position, held by the Bush administration."

Saad persisted, "Rather than having to fight each detainee's situation through the courts for years, the administration may elect to release all the prisoners back to their own countries, of birth. The Americans have already quietly repatriated over eighty of the detainees back to their home countries since the beginning of October 2003. And, the Americans have continued this practice, albeit piecemeal, ever since."

The amount of explosives al-Qaeda asked the Cuban special operations infiltrators to place in the base's Desalinization/Power Generating plant, was calculated to damage it beyond cost-effective repair.

"Our engineers tell me," said young bin-Laden, "that when the base's main generation plant is taken out," bin-Laden postulated, "the combined electrical demand, represented by the needs of the base proper, and all the ancillary electrical loads associated with camps Delta and America, will require an alternative source of energy be brought on-line, immediately. It will have to remain operational until the damaged plant, if found to be not repairable, can be replaced."

"When the base's power generation plant is destroyed," Saad persevered, "the Americans will need an alternative source of electrical power. It can be provided in the short term by the tethered 727-UPS backup system. However, the electricity provided by the alternative system will be fleeting," predicted the younger bin-Laden.

"Generation of the alternative electrical power will cease

immediately, if the backup system suffers a inevitable mechanical breakdown. Or when it runs out of the limited stores of JP-4 fuel, the Americans keep in underground storage tanks to power the jet engines."

"And even better," had sneered the Al-Qaeda leader's arrogant son, "destroying or even seriously disabling the American base's main desalinization system, means that in less than ninety-six hours time, all drinking water reserves on Guantánamo Naval Station will have been fully consumed. The entire base will be thrown into chaos. Everyone, including my father's imprisoned freedom fighters, will then be totally dependent on bottled water that must be flown to the base on the American's C-17 air freighters."

Castro, accepting bin-Laden's promise at face value, had given orders to his brother Raúl for the future infiltration of the American base. Many months later, Soviet-trained, Cuban special operations troops would infiltrate the American base and plant the explosive charges, exactly as al-Qaeda had requested.

Saad had insisted, "All of the explosives must be set to explode at midnight that night, an hour before my father's planned assault on Camp Delta commences. If your commandos, Raúl, achieve the destruction of all four targets, the entire base will 'go dark' until the American's back-up power generation system can be spooled up, and brought on-line."

Anticipating the expected disruption and confusion caused by losing the base's critical Desalinization/Power Generation plant, the al-Qaeda planners thought it not beyond reason that all the JTF 160's off-duty guard force would be rolled-out, and temporarily deployed to duty (TAD'd) with base security, to secure and protect other critical infrastructure on the base.

Those same Islamic planning experts, from the relatively safety of their deep Afghanistan caves, postulated that it was also reasonable to assume that the base's leadership would error on the side of caution. The commanding officer's orders would likely entail stripping every third JTF 160 guard, from the contingent currently on-duty at Camp Delta.

"That emergency deployment," Ayman Al-Jawahiri stated, "will be undertaken by the Americans to provide the base with the option of forming a rapid response force. As an example, if that became necessary in the instance when the thousands of starving Cubans outside the base, may exacerbate the situation by breaching the base's seventeen-mile long perimeter fence, and attempting to overrun the now-vulnerable U.S. Naval station."

"The around-the-clock operation of the remote bases' all-important ferry system, will temporarily be disrupted by the explosions. At least until such time as an alternative means of cross-water transportation again became available. However, the suspension of ferry service would normally have no effect on the base's CH-47 Chinook helicopters, which were each capable of quick-lifting fifty-five fully-armed and equipped troops."

Back in the real world, it is interesting to note that Guantánamo is not considered to be part of the CONUS. Thus the US Navy and the JTF feels they are exempt from the Pentagon's no-weapons mandate for military helicopters billeted stateside. Thus, each of the CH-47s at Guantánamo is outfitted with multiple, bungee-hung, M-60 machine guns.

And a recent shipment of six USMC, AV8BII Harrier jump jets, had arrived by C-130 earlier in the week. They already had been reassembled, flight-tested, and were now certified for combat.

But losing the vital cross-bay ferry service, even temporarily, cleaved the forty-five square mile Naval base, into two logistical elements. The Leeward side, where the U.S. Navy's heavily guarded, 24/7 air base is located. And the Windward side, where the remainder of the naval base was located, including Camp Delta, and the JTF guard barracks, Camp America.

The two elements of the base, located on opposite sides of Guantánamo Bay's inner basin, were adequately defended individually. But losing the synergy that was achieved by the coordination of their defensive efforts would be a significant blow to the American base's security capabilities.

Explosions at the 'dirty shirt' mess could be expected to catch a number of senior-level commanders and petty officers in the resulting conflagration. Even in the best-case scenario, the disruption would delay them from responding to their assigned battle stations on the base.

The concurrent limpet mine explosions in the base's general anchorage, would catch the civilian watch-standers on the three ships anchored there, at the beginning of their shifts. That is acknowledged as a warship's most vulnerable moment, before the sentry's eyes have time to become acclimated to the darkness of the Caribbean night.

Due either to the luck-of-the-draw, but more likely to some obscure decades-old, harbor-defense tactic of the U.S. Navy, the three freighters had been ordered by Harbor Command to *drop the hook* in the southwestern end of the approved anchorages, which bisected the nearly one mile-wide waterway.

There were seven designated approved zone-A anchorages, all sited mid-channel. They extended from position #1—located off Fisherman's Point, northwest to #7—which was located at the relatively shallow south end of Granadillo Bay.

All of the designated zone-A anchorages had been planned to provide ample room for a large ship to swing 360 degrees on her anchor chain, as the tides and harbor current moved her. And due to the relative abundance of lateral clearance in the navigation channel, it also permitted the passage of any of the merchant marine's larger vessels, in the remaining room between the anchorages and the bay's northern shoreline.

Three freighters currently occupied zone-A anchorages #2 through #4. Anchorage #2 was offshore of Corinaso Point on the Windward shoreline. Anchorage #3 was located off Deer Point, also on the Windward shoreline. The freighter in anchorage #4 was located offshore of Caracoles Point, off the swampy Leeward shoreline.

Al-Qaeda's planners calculated that the limpet mines the Cuban special operation's divers had planted, would easily sever each ship's anchor chain. The explosions would also result in disabling damage to the ship's propeller shafts and rudder stakes.

Suddenly cast adrift, the large freighters would be totally without any semblance of navigational control. Or at least, until the base's harbor tugs could be called out. Adrift, the heavy ships would helplessly float down the bay's inner channel, until they were able to bring their propulsion engines back on line.

They could damage critical infrastructure on-shore as the vessels drifted down the waterway, banging into this and that. Or, just as likely, they might float down the harbor, until one or more of them eventually smashing into the anchored multi-billion dollar, off-duty *Arleigh Burke* class AEGIS destroyer.

However, by then the destroyer would likely have raised anchor and steamed out of the harbor, having been alerted to the impending danger by the Navy's harbor controllers, as their control tower is manned 24/7.

This meant the 8,400-ton, 510-foot long Guided Missile destroyer would have to get underway, and exit the harbor, in under twenty-two minutes.

It was the expectation of the terrorists, that even with the relatively limited number of al-Qaeda shock troops from the *Scorpion*, they could overcome the remaining JTF guards left on-duty at Camp Delta. Al-Qaeda was betting heavily that the camp's normally scheduled guard strength would have been decimated by that time, by the base's aver-reaction to the explosions.

Al-Qaeda's embedded spies in JTF 160, had made the guess-based prediction that the American's moderately-staffed base security units, would find it impossible to deal with the resulting chaos, if all of the four-planned explosive attacks, concurrently detonated across the forty-five square mile base.

Especially, they reasoned, when the Guantánamo JTF commander discovered that his formerly monolithically structured base, had now been cut into two isolated elements.

Al-Qaeda strategists maintained that this severing of the base into two more-difficult-to-defend elements would the base to lose the vital synergy, on which the Navy's contingency plans had been predicated. At least it would, should it ever become necessary to repel an assault, such as al-Qaeda was planning on the remote American base. The elaborate war-gamed plans of the U.S. Navy went out the window, once the terrorists isolated the base into two separate, stand-alone defensive bastions.

The two, fifteen-man teams of al-Qaeda shock troops, would land on Kittery/Windmill beach, scale the 485-foot tall bluff and assault Camp Delta's perimeter defenses. Due to the difficulty of the climb up the bluff, most of the tactical body armor they would require at the crest was tied to the ALICE weight-bearing harness frames they wore on their backs. Of course, al-Qaeda's plan had not taken into consideration the violent tropical storm, currently raging across the American base

The encountering of a skeleton force of JTF guards, those remaining at Camp Delta, was what al-Qaeda planner, Al-Jawahiri, had instructed the SOF troops, to expect. The planners assumed that the American defenders would follow traditional battle theory. They would divert a significant number of the on-duty JTF guards, to provide manning for a base's emergency, quick-response team. The al-Qaeda SOF troops intended to engage and quickly dispose of the remaining Camp Delta guards.

Al-Qaeda's plan then called for its shock troops to spread out, and locate the detainees on bin-Laden's VIP short-list. The list was restricted in number, not because of family connections, but rather due to the extremely few billets aboard the catastrophic confines of the submarine. Once located, the selected few would be promptly rounded up, spirited back to the submarine, and back into the indentured service of bin-Laden.

The great majority of detainees would not be on bin-Laden's VIP list. However, the shock troops had been instructed to be positive. They had been told to encourage the remaining terrorist detainees to arm themselves with discarded weapons, food and water, and flee towards the bases' closest perimeter fence line. Cuban forces would be waiting there, to provide them whatever assistance was needed in make good on their escape over the multistage barrier, and into the Cuban countryside.

Meanwhile, the weather had grown progressively worse. One hundred and seven m.p.h. rain-saturated, gusting winds were now blowing horizontally in a northern direction, directly across the Caribbean Sea towards Cuba. The repetitive and ever stronger gusts, smashed into the bluff, and on the beaches just below Camp Delta. There, the budding hurricane changed directions, and bounded up the 485-foot bluff, before again changing directions, and resuming its northward dash inland into south central Cuba.

Guantánamo Bay's C-47 troop helicopters, and the heavily armed Marine jump jets, were still in their hangers, grounded by the storm. As a result, all stand-alone close air support need in the defense of the remote U.S. naval base, had temporarily been defanged.

Bin-Laden had made sure that the al-Qaeda commandos had been rigorously trained back in the desert, fly-infested terrorist camps in Saudi Arabia. It had been hammered into one and all that the schedule, was the schedule, was the schedule—regardless.

Thus, despite the near inhuman conditions caused by the raging summer storm, the assault on Camp Delta began shortly after 0100 hours. The terrorist's climb up the bluff was tedious, dangerous and slow. Even if it hadn't been for the deadly land mines, which the Americans had somehow managed to bury into the near vertical face of the bluff. Somehow, the Americans had also managed to piggyback the mines, with jellied napalm that turned the vertical cliff into Dante's inferno.

For some unknown reason this significant improvement in the camp's defensive capabilities, had not been reported to al-Qaeda, by the JTF-embedded spies. Perhaps they were now overly cautious, after several of their number had been exposed, and were being detained, stateside.

A number of well-placed al-Qaeda spies and sympathizers, those who hadn't yet been exposed by the America's intelligence apparatus, still continued to work unrestricted inside the JTF organization. A rumor put out by a disreputable member of the media, claimed the number of such agents still in-place, numbered close to a dozen. Investigative officers from the JAG/NCIS taskforce would not comment on the unsupported news story.

The land mines killed, incinerated or maimed fifty percent of the al-Qaeda shock troops the *Scorpion* had delivered to the Caribbean. Collaterally, that meant more available billets for rescued detainees. But tactically, it meant that the shock force was reduced by fifteen troops. That number was dangerously approaching the break-even point that would determine the failure or success for the al-Qaeda mission.

Less than sixteen of the bin-Laden's elite special operations troops reached the detention camp's perimeter fence line. The al-Qaeda assault team had been expecting moderate-to-light resistance from the JTF guards. But that was not the bat that the Americans brought to the plate.

Al-Qaeda's assumption was that only a couple handfuls of JTF troops would be been left to guard the detainees at Camp Delta. That supposition was based on bin-Laden's chief planner's belief that the massive, timed detonation of multi-location explosive mines throughout the base, would force the Americans to strip Camp Delta of a significant portion of its assigned guards.

The surviving al-Qaeda shock troops began to physically attack Camp Delta shortly after 0200 hours. The surviving commandos, once they reached the bluff crest, sought cover and concealment to give them a moment to catch their breath after the long climb.

They donned their body armor. As a few of the remaining al-Qaeda troops circled around and cut through the camp's perimeter fencing, the other shock troops began a frontal assault on the camp's main gate. Immediately both al-Qaeda groups ran into massive resistance, that neither had expected. Doggedly, the commandos poured AK47 fire into the American positions—BLAPBLAPBLAPBLAPBLAP.

Al-Qaeda planners had made a tactical decision not to inform their men about the half dozen Browning fifty caliber heavy machineguns, installed in thick reinforced-concrete bunkers that were positioned between the camp and the bluff they had just scaled. The planners figured no good and a lot of potential harm could come from releasing the need-to-know information to the operators. Neither did they inform the SOF troops about the clusters of claymore personnel mines that had been emplaced 'THIS SIDE TOWARDS THE ENEMY' to takeout members of the assault teams, who *had* thus far been successful in reaching the top of the bluff, after the long climb from the beach below.

No one had warned them about the buried canisters of nitrogelatin, that when detonated, incinerated anyone within ten feet of the blast, sticking to their skin like adhesive homemade jellied gasoline.

Or the white phosphorous 'Willy Peter' grenades the Americans were using for tactical illumination. Once the chemical landed on you skin, it never stopped burning until it could be surgically excised, and then only while the body part was immersed under water to retard its ability to burn.

The big bat the Americans brought to the plate in this firefight was that the JTF command had *not* diluted Camp Delta's on-duty guard force. The al-Qaeda assault force, due primarily to the extremely limited space available aboard the *Scorpion* was far too undermanned to mount the contested assault they presently were attempting.

Over the past week aboard the submarine, al-Qaeda political leaders had spurred them on by continually repeating that the combined shocks caused by the explosion of all *four* explosive devices would force the Americans to strip troops away from Camp Delta.

The al-Qaeda assault team had already been reduced to a mere fifteen commandos by the American's land mines and other weapons. However, the fanatic terrorists were still able to breach the perimeter defenses in isolated places with their satchel charges. They entered the camp, but only with great effort and even greater luck. Then a small group split off. But the commandos all too soon found themselves under withering automatic weapons fire, as they attempted to locate the specified VIP detainees for extraction.

The list of VIP detainee's names for al-Qaeda extraction was complete with maps and locations within the compound, where they could be located. Some said the beautifully detailed maps had been drawn up by bin-Laden personally. If he had, they were based on the periodic intelligence reports of spies and sympathizers that the Americans had not yet detected. The deep-cover insurgents had been instructed to continue to report to work inside Camp Delta, even after several of them had been discovered and apprehended by the infidels.

The al-Qaeda shock troops, now all wearing full body armor, each a veteran of countless firefights such as this, took hit after hit on the ceramic wrap-around shok-plates that were an integral part of their unique protective equipment. Despite the armor, every time an assault rifle round impacted with their torsos, they were knocked down. Then they had to struggle back to their feet, as they fought to penetrate ever deeper into the camp, to locate the detainees that bin-Laden ordered rescued.

More frequently now, the 'THUNK-THUNK-THUNK-THUNK' of American M79 grenade launchers was heard over the AK47 and M16 firefight. Each 'thunk' was followed by a earsplitting explosion when the .40 mm shell impacted, and then by a high-pitched scream. Another terrorist had been the recipient of blazingly hot shrapnel that not even al-Qaeda's cumbersome body armor could deflect.

The defending fire of the Americans had unavoidably taken down a handful of detainees who had nothing to protect them from the bullets, but the orange coveralls that merely served to highlight the target. Blood spatters tinted the chain link perimeter fencing a bright red, and formed scarlet halos around the lamps of the camp's pole-mounted lighting fixtures.

The al-Qaeda assault team was firing indiscriminately into the camp with their AK47's. The detainees were taking hit after hit from their assault rifles. THWACK-THWACK-THWACK-THWACK. As the prisoners went down, their falling bodies seemed surrounded with minute puffs of smoke, every time a tracer round burned though the detainee's orange coveralls, into their flesh.

Sphincters had been released in death and fear, which tainted the entire compounded with the stench of a charnel house. The entire area smelled like the pit of an outhouse.

The JTF guards were not intentionally firing at the detainees—even the hardened American troops weren't capable of that. But the compound was heavily layered in smoke—from the commandos' smoke generating satchels, the American's forty mm high-explosive grenades, and both side's tracer rounds. It was difficult to make out individual shapes. And when you did, it invariably fired at you, because the man represented by the vague shape had no idea who you were, either. Each combatant, by now, was deaf and nearly flash-blinded by the unrelenting gunfire and grenade explosions.

The acrid gunpowder was singeing unprotected eyes. The malignant smoke, even in the gusty, swirling winds of the raging storm, was making the men nauseatingly ill, causing some to throw up on themselves, right in the middle of firing their weapons. The smell of spilled blood, urine and feces, was everywhere. It smelled like an abattoir.

Despite the murky brilliance of the prison camp lighting, everything in the camp came to an abrupt halt as a stray round hit a main breaker, and the compound was plunged into darkness.

In less than thirty seconds, the emergency lighting had come on, and the constant firing began once again. The brief period of darkness had not bothered the Americans. They routinely wore their night vision goggles (NVGs) on the top of their helmets at all times, and only had to flip them down. But the al-Qaeda commandos, those remaining alive and operational, had been quick to grab theirs from under their chest shok plates, were they had been ordered to carry the prohibitively expensive devices. Red and green tracers burned through the smoky air from all directions. The American's prolific use of forty mm grenade launchers served to further blind combatants on both sides.

The intense automatic weapons battle had been going on for a period of less than ten minutes overall, but fighters on both sides felt as if days had passed.

The small handful of al-Qaeda commandos, assigned to find and assemble the VIPS, began to push them through the holes their comrades had cut earlier in the multi-layer perimeter fencing.

Surviving members of the al-Qaeda blocking force, numbered less than seven men now. However, they never hesitated to brazenly expose themselves in the deafening hell storm, and took to burning off entire thirty-round, lead-core ammo, banana clip magazines into the heavily fortified American positions.

The shock troops' objective was to prevent the infidels from making the end run around their position, as they were now attempting. At least a dozen Americans were attempting to establish a blockade-by-fire, between the al-Qaeda shock troops, and the camp's already breached perimeter fence.

The now nearly-rabid, adrenaline-crazed American guards, some having picked up the now-silent weapons of their fallen comrades, advanced on the terrorist positions awkwardly firing automatic weapons in both hands. With facial expressions straight from hell, the JTF guards still standing, holding thirty-round replacement clips of ammunition at-the-ready in their teeth, were attempting to follow the escaping al-Qaeda shock troops out of the camp. The al-Qaeda commandos had roughly buckled bullet-resistant Kevlar vests they had stripped off dead Americans, onto the six VIP detainees, physically dragged them through the fence and out of Camp Delta, and over to the bluff's crest.

Orders, detailing the minimal physical abilities bin-Laden expected these few men to acquire, through daily physical exercises and restriction of diet, prior to the rescue attempt, had been smuggled into Camp Delta to these specific VIP's months ago. Bin-Laden's messages had been transmitted to the detainees by two JTF-employed Arabic translators. The two men only recently had been revealed as American traitors. They were al-Qaeda spies, arrested by TSA, and now were being investigated by both the U.S. Naval Criminal Investigative Service (NCIS) and the FBI.

The physically fit, but untrained detainees, each securely harnessed to one of their rescuers, buddy-rappelled down the near vertical bluff. There three, flat-black inflatables waited under camouflaged ground cloths on the beach below. The fast boats would transport the surviving shock troops and the six rescued detainees back to the *Scorpion*. The submarine, whose captain heard the commando's pessimistic reports over the battle frequency of his radio, had violated orders and steamed towards the fight, until he now impatiently waited less than one-half mile, offshore.

The surviving rescuers and the rescued alike, dove into one of the inflatables. As all combat manpower carried by the *Scorpion* had been one hundred percent committed to making the rescue assault, al-Qaeda had foregone providing each inflatable with the customary coxswain.

Thus, it fell to an exhausted and badly wounded al-Qaeda commando, to push the inflatable off the beach into the water. The man then struggled over the low gunnels into the raft, and started the notoriously balky, high-powered outboard motor. Once the engine started, he would guide the heavily laden, rigid-decked craft south out into Windward Passage, to the nearly submerged submarine.

Due to the unexpected loss of eighty percent of the al-Qaeda's special operation troops, only one of the inflatables was required for the return trip to the Kilo-class attack submarine. The other two powered craft were abandoned on the beach. No one had the energy required to destroy the remaining zodiacs. They would be left behind, intact.

Also being left behind, were twenty-four dead or maimed members of the al-Qaeda shock team. This number included Zaid Samir Jarrach, the leader who had been killed in the first five deadly minutes of the assault on Camp Delta.

Once on-board the submarine, the single returning inflatable would be slashed to ribbons. All the equipment and weapons were tossed overboard.

The six rescued detainees, and the small handful of surviving al-Qaeda shock troops, were each welcomed aboard by the submarine commander, Majed Moqed, and the boat's XO, Faroauk al-Motasseded. The weary men struggled to find the energy to climb down the ladder from the crew hatch, into the boats' command center.

Brief congratulatory messages from bin-Laden, were verbally passed to each man. Then the rescued detainees were whisked below to the submarine's sickbay for a brief physical.

Osama bin-Laden couldn't afford to permit even one of his rescued men, should he be found to have acquired a communicable disease while incarcerated at Camp Delta, to roam the boat.

The risk of infecting even one of the skilled members of the boat's skeleton crew, each critical to the operation of the valued submarine, could not be chanced. Bin-Laden had been emphatic when he talked with the boat's commanding officer, Majed Moqed, before they had sailed for Cuba. He had said, "This magnificent boat has proven herself in the 2002 battle in the American's Pacific Northwest. It is critically necessary to the future achievement of al-Qaeda's goals and objectives. If you are unable to return her undamaged to me, do not bother to return home yourself."

The sickbay's laboratory tests revealed two of the detainees had acquired a highly virulent, communicable form of HIV. It had mutated into fully developed AIDS. In bin-Laden's fundamentalist mind, the only way of becoming infected with the disease was from relationships with one or more of their fellow detainees in the camp.

Here, aboard a small densely-packed submarine, the crew was looking at a largely submerged journey that would last nearly three weeks. The boat would only be permitted to be surface after dark. Only then would fresh air be circulated below decks. It would not be possible to maintain any but extremely basic hygiene standards in the sharing of food, cleansing of eating utensils, and dispensing the limited water supplies. Therefore, any risk of cross contamination was unacceptable.

The two VIPS, without being informed of the results of their lab tests, were each administered a lethal full-grain dose of morphine, intramuscularly. They were told it was a tetanus inoculation. The heavily overdosed men first became euphoric, then drowsy. They were each led over to lie down in one of the sickbay bunks, which had been shrink-wrapped in thick plastic.

Once comfortable on the bunks, the corpsmen had suggested, "Why not close your eyes and take a little nap? We'll finish examining these other brave true believers, who were fortunate to escape with you."

The charade continued. The four remaining freed detainees were tested, found to be reasonably healthy, and sent on their way. They were provided with oral antibiotics, a sedative, vitamins, a rich snack, two quart-bottles of mineral water, and most importantly, a prayer rug.

Once the sickbay had emptied out, the corpsmen quickly donned bio-hazard contamination suits, and cotton facemasks. Then they swaddled the two deceased men in several layers of sheets, being extremely careful to seal each makeshift body bag with heavy packing tape.

Finished with the grisly task, the two corpsmen lay down on other unoccupied bunks to wait. Wait until the rest of the freed detainees, who had been taken back into isolated quarters in the rear of the boat, had grown tired of their conversations and fallen into the deep sleep of total exhaustion.

Then the corpsmen individually manhandled the awkward bundles out of the small dispensary. And down a short passageway into the torpedo department. There the captain, and the sole torpedo officer aboard the submarine, awaited them.

Each of the long, tightly wrapped bundles was inserted into one of the six—unoccupied twenty-one inch torpedo tubes. The tube's inner-pressure doors were secured, and the outer doors opened. Then, by manipulating a lever, the torpedo officer ejected the bodies into the sea with a blast of compressed air.

The two corpsmen, who had performed this gruesome task many times before, returned to the sick bay. Once the door was closed and locked, they laid their prayers rugs on the floor, not bothering to determine the direction of *Mecca*, knelt, and prayed.

The two men asked Allah for his forgiveness. For sending two of his most dedicated believers to him early, solely as a consequence of a weakness of the flesh over the many months they had been imprisoned.

The skeleton operating crew of the *Scorpion* had long ago given up trying to conceal their uncontrollable fear of being captured by the American Navy, primarily due to the numbers of the brave American sailors that al-Qaeda had massacred, in the Pacific

Northwest in 2002. So they hurried to act on the captain's orders to dive the boat to a depth of 200-meters and get underway. The boat began the fourteen-hour, 241-kilometer dash, east though the azure Caribbean Sea, for the perceived safety represented by the depths of the Atlantic Ocean.

CHAPTER TWENTY-FOUR

DAY 334—01 DECEMBER

THE AMERICAN NAVAL BASE

DAMAGE CONTROL

GUANTÁNAMO BAY

CUBA

As the al-Qaeda submarine *Scorpion* dashed east to their illusion of safety, the situation in *real time* at Camp Delta and Camp America was one of near-chaos.

The base commander felt the post-attack chaos was controllable. The Americans had prevented the destruction of the base's Desalinization/Power Generation and 727-UPS systems. If those facilities had been permanently taken out of commission, Guantánamo would have been forced to evacuate within weeks. The closure of the base had been one of the al-Qaeda's objectives.

At the United States Military Academy at WestPoint many years ago, now-Major General Montrose had been taught that only through use of excellent organizational skills, a realistic appreciation for priorities, and good pre-planning, could a commanding officer deal with a post-attack scenario that threatened the future survival of his command.

The emergency post-attack damage control meeting was just getting underway. Sitting at the head of the large rectangle oak table in the base's situation room, with his staff and authorized visitors overflowing the supply of available chairs, General Montrose paused before beginning to speak. He thought, "*Well, as Steve McQueen once said in the movie 'Hud' years ago, 'What we have here is a lack of communication. Everyone here seems to think we just achieved a victory. Well, the first thing I have to do is correct that error in thinking. So I'll begin with that as point number one on the agenda.*

The al-Qaeda commandos almost took us to the cleaners. We never thought those Alpha Hotel's would be brazen enough to risk taking on the U.S. government military, face-to-face. If so, we'd never thought they'd attack a fortified U.S. Naval facility. None of the contingency scenarios the 'stars' in the Puzzle Palace developed, addressed that possibility. It will definitely be someone's ass when the results of the upcoming inquiry are released.

But right now, we have to accept that we just got an ass kicking. We've got to regroup, and attempt to resolve this situation, without any additional loss of life and dilution of our mission. All we have to fall back on is the organization in this crisis, and hope we can pull our chestnuts out of the fire.

Without further ado, Major General Montrose, the current commander of the Joint Task Force 160, began to speak. Each of them had been up all night long. None of them, including himself was looking particularly bright-eye and bushy-tailed at 0800 hours. Even the non-coffee drinkers appeared to have broken their no-caffeine taboo, this morning. Everyone was consuming cups of vile stuff his aide had been brewing up all morning.

The general's staff had been fielding calls on the base's secure command phones, every few minutes since the attack. The president, the JCS, every sitting politician on the Congress's Military Appropriation Committee, and every 'star-wearing' ego in the Pentagon, was calling to demand a personal after-action report. Then they'd throw in a snide remark, "How could this have happened on your general's watch?"

Normally not being one to duck responsibility, the general nevertheless managed to 'not be available' to accept those calls. He believed that his first responsibility was out in the field, visiting each of the attack sites. He and his staff were busy making assessments of the damage Guantánamo Bay Naval Station had suffered, in this morning's attack.

The NCIS investigators, who had just yesterday been criticizing the base's security procedures, had hurriedly shifted gears. They now were doing their utmost to provide General Stark with hourly reports covering every scrap of information they collected. The Marine colonel in-charge of the investigation, said "Look no further, General—it God-damned straight was al-Qaeda, perhaps with a lot of help on the front end from President-for-life Castro."

Montrose's mind returned to the staff assembled before him. He turned to a rugged U.S. Army Brigadier General to his right, and said, "Dave, NCIS says with one hundred percent certainty that Camp Delta was the primary target this morning, as was the base's power plant. That is the part of the information we need to deal with first. Then you'll generate a formal report to Southern Command in Miami."

"Then hopefully, Southern Command will take some of the heat off us here, permitting us to get on with our jobs, instead of responding to these *immediate priority* demands for information."

General Stark, Montrose's subordinate, ran the day-to-day operations of Joint Task Force 160. He arranged his notes in orderly piles, and began to address the meeting.

"General Montrose, people, visitors, all bullshit aside—we just got our ass kicked. Somehow, unknown parties we expect were Cuban special operations troops with the approval of Comrade Castro infiltrated our base. They planted explosives at four specific locations."

Stark continued, "Our subsequent fact finding over past several hours, has modified our initial thinking. We have dismissed our previous assumption that the concurrent explosions at the dirty-shirt mess at the O-Club, in the bases' general anchorage, and at the Leeside ferry terminal, were accidents. While we originally couldn't believe all those separate incidents were enemy-attributable, our preliminary crime scene investigations indicate that each of those explosions were just that. They were timed to detonate concurrently."

"The trace evidence indicates that the improvised Semtex explosives discovered and deactivated at the Desalinization/Power Generation plant yesterday afternoon, were of the same type and probable batch number at those used in the three other explosions."

"Approximately two hours following the explosions, or 0200 hours, a total of thirty, well-armed and equipped special forces troops—all the corpses appeared to be Arabic—landed on the Kittery Beach. That, as you know, is one of the two beaches at the base of the bluff, on which Camp Delta is located."

"We know," Stark continued, "from what they left behind, that they landed on the beach in at least three inflatables. Each was powered by an American-brand outboard motor. The motors are available on the open market throughout the world, so that in itself doesn't point back to our shores relative to source acquisition."

General Stark glanced briefly again at his notes, and continued, "The NCIS crime scene investigators were still here pursuing the on-gong inquires as to how many, if any, additional al-Qaeda spies and sympathizers, are embedded in the JTF. So we put them to work on the Kittery Beach landing site, as Gitmo's base security crime scene specialists already had their hands full elsewhere, all over the base."

"It didn't take the NCIS specialists long to gather up the evidence. They've come to the conclusion that two-dozen-plus troops attempted to use those North Korean rocket-propelled grappling hooks to scale the bluff."

"The only surprise," General Stark paused to consult his notes, "was that their spies had forgotten to tell them about the new 'phosgas' land-mines the Marines drilled into the vertical face of the bluff, last week. These mines cost the assault team at least fifteen troops. We've come up with that figure, by comparing the numbers of whole bodies, and partial body parts, found at base of the bluff following the attacks."

"The rest of this scenario comes from eye witnesses. The on-duty JTF guards at Camp Delta, after hearing the cliff-side mines detonating, formed a quick-reaction team. As the new concrete bunkers were already in-place, they didn't need to dig defensive positions into the rocky surface, between the crest of the bluff, and the camp's perimeter fence."

Brigadier Stark looked over at General Montrose, and added as an apparently after thought, "Those guys need to get some serious recognition—without their proactive actions, everything would have gone to hell in a handbag. Costing more lives of not only the JTF troops, but also the detainees. The prisoners were locked down in their enclosures during the ensuing firefight, with nowhere to run or hide."

General Montrose, thought briefly, then nodded his head, and said "Go on, General—you write them up, and I'll get them approved. Please continue."

Shark resumed his briefing, "As soon as the remaining gomers came up over the bluff crest, they sought out what cover was available. There they donned the body armor their ALICE frames had carried up for them. As soon as they got it all in place, they began to advance on the JTF troops."

"Our .50 cal machineguns were cutting most of them down as fast as they came showed their faces. However, the survivors among those on the camp's self-formed quick-reaction force, told me later that the enemy's body armor seemed to be nearly impossible to penetrate," General Stark said.

"Our guys said they threw everything at the gomers, but the kitchen sink, and still nothing seemed to penetrate. When their body armor took one or more assault rounds, the gomer naturally was knocked down. But our guys said that in almost every instance, the enemy trooper promptly returned to his feet, apparently none-the-worse-for-wear, and continued to advance on the our positions."

After taking a swallow of water from the glass that had been placed in front of each staff member, Brigadier Stark continued. "I have the gunny doing a port-mortem on the gear the assault team was wearing. We couldn't identify the armor-pak they were wearing on their legs, and arms—it is either R&D stuff, and has not yet been circulated for sale on the open market, or it is home-grown."

"If the latter, and the manufacturer turns out to be a U.S. firm, their ass will be grass if we can tie this stuff back to them. What we do know, is that the stuff is fully combat-capable of stopping or deflecting rounds from our M16s. As I said, our witnesses say these guys were absorbing a hell of a lot of incoming fire. And although they got knocked down repeatedly, they always seemed able to get back to their feet, and continue the assault."

Stark, paused to turn to one of the staff members, a short, trim and blond USMC Lt. Colonel, who like the other staffers, was occupying a chair along the situation room's outer wall. He asked her several questions, quietly. Apparently he was satisfied with her answers, as he began speaking again, upon turning back to the oak table. "Ok, Colonel Stinson has verified that the remainder of the combatant's body armor is also of U.S. manufacture, but with a twist. The assault helmets are easily recognizable as those issued to the Green Bennies, back when their headgear was indeed green."

Several years ago, the U.S. Army in all its collective wisdom, had decided that all its members, not just the most elite, would be permitted to wear the coveted Green Beret. Naturally, this didn't sit well with Army Special Forces, whose training and qualification requirements far exceeded that of the regular army unit. And as such, they felt they merited special recognition. The U.S. Army command at the Pentagon, never comfortable with the concept of elite units, didn't agree.

In the end, the Special Force cadre bit the bullet, and changed to black berets. However, now years later, the issue still hadn't lost its sensitivity. It was well known that some of less political-motivated rogue commanders in SOF were lobbying Congress, for a return to the old headgear's qualifications criteria.

"The helmets the commandos were wearing, were part of a shipment of helmets initially designed exclusively for the Army. Each of the Army's SOF troops, including the Delta Force boys training out of 'Wally's World' at Quantico, are equipped with the same model helmet we found this morning. It is part of their standard issue. So we aren't going to get too far trying to reverse-track how they acquired the assault helmets."

"But the vests are a different matter entirely. Those definitely are based on American 'milspec'—military specifications. The vests are standard U.S. Army issue, designed to be worn over normal fatigues. It is strong enough to stop most jacketed ammunition from assault rifles."

BG Stark went on, "A typical U.S. Army bullet-resistant vest consists of a throat protector, the vest proper, and a groin protector. The vest and other pieces are made of Cordura and Kevlar."

"That is strong enough, all by itself, to protect the soldier from shrapnel fragments and 9 mm rounds. Normal U.S. Army vests of this type and model have a front-and-back removable composite ceramic plate. They are manufactured by bonding a layer of ceramic materials to a hard panel of Spectra Shield, then wrapping it all in fabric covering."

General Stark continued, "That being said, here is where each of the vests we found on the bodies of the gomers, differs. The vest manufactured for the U.S. Army, as I said previously, has a removable twelve inch by fourteen inch shok plate, front and rear."

"But the vest we found on the Arab's bodies is unique. While the shok plates on the U.S. Army version are removable for weight considerations, the vest we found had been heavily modified to include another layer of Spectra Shield shok plate. This additional layer is flexible, and wraps all of the way around the width of the vest."

"My question is not who made this stuff, but rather how in the Sam Hell did these guys manage to lug all that weight around with them. The standard U.S. Army version weighs 16.4 pounds. One of the gunnys stripped one of the special vests off a body that had received a headshot. He took it to the nearest scale he could find. It weighed in excess of thirty pounds, for Christ Sake. No wonder they elected to tie the vests to their ALICE frames, when they were scaling the bluff. This thing is like carrying a kitchen sink with you."

"But as the JTF guards will attest, it makes the average 'Mohammed' nearly bulletproof. Gunny thought the vest had probably been designed for specialty troops, trained solely to serve as a blocking element. In other words, troops that are expendable, and are willing to stand in place and trade round after round with an objective's defenders," Stark mused.

"American battle philosophy doesn't support using those tactics. Our men are our most important assets. We damn sure aren't going to throw them away as cannon fodder. But that is exactly what these vests were designed for. To me, that sounds a lot like the crap the uneducated trainees in those al-Qaeda desert training camps, in Saudi Arabia, are brain washed into believing. Questions?" Asked the general, looking around the room.

Stark shuffled some more papers, and turned to indicate a huge Afro-American USMC Master Sergeant, who was sitting off to one side behind him. The general introduced him as Master Sergeant John Battle, and indicated he would take over the briefing.

Battle stood up, all six foot, eight inches of him, and began to address the meeting. As with most Army Master Sergeants around the world, he ignored the normal pleasantries and simply said, "Ok, listen up people."

"Here is the casualty count from the Camp Delta assault. The gomer's assault team lost a total of twenty-four of its troops, all killed-in-action, KIA. Whether or not there was a reason behind none of them merely being wounded-in-action, or WIA, is for someone above my paygrade to determine."

"On our side, JTF lost a total of six KIAs, mostly consisting of those guys that set up a blocking force between the advancing terrorists, and the outer fence perimeter. Inside the camp, we suffered no KIAs, but a hell of a lot of wounded, twenty-three to be exact."

"Obviously the reason behind the KIAs ratio, as compared to the number of our wounded, was the fact that Camp Delta has a 2400/7 first rate, fully-equipped-and-staffed medical facility. The aid stations have very competent medics on-duty around the clock."

The MSgt continued, "Most of these young Corpsmen must have grown up watching MASH 1077th on television, because they certainly performed well under-fire. My hat is off to them. I would welcome any of them in protecting my backside in a combat situation, believe you me."

Master Sergeant Battle resumed, "Ok, we have a hell of a big loss of life among the detainees. That shouldn't surprise 'higher command.' They know that these guys are locked up 2400/7. There was simply no way for any of them to avoid the gunfire. No doubt, their deaths will turn this into a political arena. There are plenty who disagree with the current administration, relative to the detaining of the terrorist suspects here, without a trial."

"Ain't no nice way to say this—but here it is—eighty-seven of the detainees were killed, either by gunfire or shrapnel. Seventy-five of the dead were Taliban prisoners. The remaining twelve, al-Qaeda troops that were captured actively fighting in skirmishes with Coalition forces."

"Only an autopsy will determine if the rounds that killed them came from M16s or the AK47s. As you know, the al-Qaeda commandos that escaped did so by repelling down the face of the bluff to the beach. In addition to the eighty-seven detainee KIAs, there were also forty-eight detainee WIAs. The nationality ratio of the WIA injured, Taliban versus al-Qaeda, is expected to be the same as it was for their KIAs."

"And if we already weren't going to get enough crap on this from higher command. A physical roll call of surviving detainees an hour ago, revealed that the terrorist assault team managed to spirit away six of the highest-ranking al-Qaeda suspects we were detaining here. I believe they are part of what is known in the camp as the Skagit Eight. They managed to get them out of the camp, down to the beach, and into one of the inflatables the assault troops arrived in," said the Master Sergeant.

"We don't know where the escapees went from here. But we damn straight know that the one inflatable they took, was filled with no less than twelve occupants. Six were the freed detainees, who only had their orange coveralls on their back, and surviving six members of the al-Qaeda SOF assault team."

"With that weight, there is no way the inflatable could have been carrying enough fuel to reach Haiti or Jamaica. So we figure there was a larger mother boat of some type involved. Which is exactly what the one-billion-dollar-per-each AEGIS destroyers were supposed to prevent, but that is another story. Any questions before I toss this back to General Stark?" he asked. After glancing around the room, and finding no raised hands, the Master Sergeant returned to his chair.

General Stark took up where he had left off, "Thanks, Master Sergeant. Let's hope the post-mortem autopsies prove that most of the detainees died from bullets the AK47s."

"I agree that the Desalinization/Power Generation Plant was both the terrorist's main diversionary ruse, and a secondary target. The explosions were intended to draw troops and our attention away from the assault on Camp Delta. The Cubans killed two of the plant's nightshift Engineer/Guards. Their bodies are being held in the hospital morgue, for transportation stateside. Lets discuss the other attacks at the three sites, where the Cuban's explosives did detonate."

"It is reasonable to assume there was lesser strategic value in the terrorists hitting the ferry terminal, and the 'dirty shirt mess' at the O-Club."

General Stark referred to his notes, and continued. "No one was killed at the terminal. The only wounded were a couple of aircraft mechanics, and the two security guards, all of which received 2nd degree burns. They are currently being sedated over at the naval hospital. In a few hours, if seriously injured enough, they will be airlifted back to the mainland on an Air Force C-130 hospital flight. I called Southern Command less than thirty minutes ago to verify that flight is on-schedule."

"The casualties at the dirty-shirt mess hall, over at the O-Club, were significantly greater. A total of four naval officers—a Commander, two Lt. Commanders, and a Chief Warrant Officer waiting for daylight to fly a CH-47 back stateside for a major engine refit, were killed. Those bodies temporarily have been sent to the base hospital's morgue."

"Additionally, four enlisted cooks, and the dining room's enlisted protocol Officer, a 1st class Petty Officer, received injuries serious enough that our burn unit here on base can't properly provided them the required level of trauma care. The more seriously injured of these men, will also go out on the Air Force C-130, later this morning."

"Now to the *fiasco* in the bases' general anchorage, and I only refer to it as that because the Cuban or Al-Qaeda planners must have never heard of tide charts. It caused a hell of a lot of expensive damage, but no loss of life, or serious injures. If the Cubans would have read their chart books, it would have been obvious to them that on the ebb tide, any vessel that comes loose of her anchor in zone-A, can only drift south on the tide until they run aground on the sandbar off Fisherman's point," BG Stark explained.

"Currently, I have three very pissed off civilian captains screaming for the Navy's tugs to tow them out of the mud, and back out into the channel. There they can drop and set an auxiliary anchor, until salvage vessels arrive to tow them back into Miami for repairs," grimaced the BG.

"We'll have the harbor control tugs, either maneuver some crane-bearing barges over to the damaged freighters, or drag them over to the deep-water pier, so we can off-load their cargo before they are towed back to Florida. The replacement of the anchor chains is no big deal. It could have been accomplished here, on-base."

"But the replacement of the propeller shafts and rudders, ever since Gitmo lost the Naval Maintenance Yard as a tenant, is out of the question." General Stark went on, "Those freighters are going to be tied up for the better part of six months to a year, before they are seaworthy again. You can bet the Government Accounting Office is going to be thrilled to receive that claim."

The general referred to his notes again, and continued, "Getting back to the Desalinization/Power Generation Plant incident. Two Engineer/Guards were killed. Assumedly by the Cuban saboteurs. The men must have interrupted the Cubans, while they were planting the explosives. The mechanic's bodies, and the bodies of all other Americans who lost their lives in this morning's attacks, go onto a second C-130 medical airlift being sent here today."

"The on-load for a third C-130 will include the deceased JTF guards from Camp Delta, the officers from the dirty-shirt mess, and any of the casualties from the ferry terminal explosion, who expire before that C-130 touches down here at Leeward Point field, in a couple of hours. That aircraft will go direct to Wright-Patterson Airfield, and be met, I understand, by Forensic Medical Teams."

The general, checking off each point on his to-do list as he spoke, continued, "Now with reference to the detainee dead and wounded. The U.S. State Department has made a recommendation to the president and the Pentagon. In order that the chain-of-evidence is maintained, all the autopsies of the dead detainees will be accomplished here, outside CONUS, at Guantánamo. The less seriously wounded casualties also stay here."

General Stark explained, "Southern Command responded by reminding the Pentagon, that if the equal-treatment policy requires they place the forty-eight wounded detainees into beds at the U.S. Naval Hospital here, it will mean having to kick the wounded JTF guards out of the hospital beds they currently occupy."

"The SC certainly didn't win any friends at the Puzzle Palace with that observation, but here is how it worked out. The JTF doctors will treat the less-seriously wounded detainees over at the medical facility at Camp Delta. All major wounds suffered by anyone will be treated here at the naval facility on Hospital Cay. Then detainee patients will be returned to the first aid stations at Camp Delta, for observation and follow-up treatment."

BG Stark resumed, "In the meantime, the U.S. Army is going to fly two complete Army MASH units in here this afternoon. They will set up shop just outside the perimeter fencing of Camp Delta. To provide extra hospital beds, one of the large, fully equipped hospital ships the Pentagon recently pulled back stateside, will steam into the bay here in less than forth-eight hours. Any questions on that, Staff?" asked General Stark.

At this point, one of meeting's visitors, with a gesture of approval from both generals, stood up and introduced himself. Them he turned and redirected his introduction to the visitors from the FBI and Coast Guard that also were attending this post-action meeting, as 'U.S. Army Colonel, Timothy Riley.'

Colonel Riley stated "Three hundred construction workers, and their equipment, under contract to the U.S. Corps of Engineers, will begin arriving here by air and ship in the next forty-eight hours.

Their orders are to do whatever it takes to reconstruct the facilities that had been damaged by the terrorist's bombs. Beginning with any facility damage up at Camp Delta." The Colonel completed his announcement, and asked if there were any questions? He was told to keep himself available at the end of today's session for a meeting with Generals Montrose and Stark. Colonel Riley acknowledged the order, and returned to his seat, as did General Stark.

"Ok," General Montrose continued, "this is only a preliminary damage assessment meeting. We just had a quick run down of the human losses this morning's terrorist attack cost us. It would appear that the right wheels are in motion to bring the facility side of the base, at least, back to its pre-attack condition."

"There is one thing that I want emphasize before we go any further. I can understand our collective feelings about the terrorists that have been detained here, in general. They are, after all, our declared enemy. However, every responsibility has a down side, and this situation is no different."

The Commanding Officer of Joint Taskforce 160, continued, "By restricting the freedom of movement of the detainees, by incarcerating them here at Camp Delta, the United States at the same time has assumed a undeniable obligation to provide care and protection for them, and do so in a humanitarian manner. Several hours ago, the president of the United States reminded the Pentagon of this obligation, and now I am reminding you."

"Regardless of our feelings, or lack of same, regarding these people, their wounded and dead are to be treated in the same manner as we treat our own casualties. That is one of the reasons the president has ordered the hospital ship to Guantánamo. It is equipped to provide the detainees with quality care, equal to that shown our own troops. Their dead are to be treated with respect, and in a manner consistent with their religion. In this case, that means that once the autopsies of both the detainees, and the enemy assault troops have been completed, and forensic post-mortem reports have been issued, and signed off by at least two U.S. Navy 0-6 grade medical officers, we need to get them buried immediately as is their custom."

"I know there are huge potential political hazards in following that action. Members of the world community, including some of our lesser allies I imagine, are going to ask for proof that the detainees weren't executed by the JTF troops."

"They'd love to be able to prove to the world community that the American Joint Taskforce gunned down their helpless, unarmed countrymen. That is the reason that the Navy's forensic teams being flown in here, later today. They are going to be documenting-documenting-and-documenting once again, all aspects of each body's post-mortem findings."

"The medical staff working on detainee autopsies will work in pairs. Complete photographic evidence, exhaustive laboratory workups, and a formal chain-of-evidence will be maintained, just as if it was a criminal investigation. Everything will be processed according to the NCIS chain-of-evidence procedures," General Montrose concluded, also checking off that item from his list. "Any questions? If so, lets get them on the table now. The president has reportedly told the Joint Chiefs that there better not be any slipups, or sloppiness in this accountability process. World opinion and the United States' reputation for fairness are at stake here."

General Montrose checked his watch, and called for a twenty-minute recess. He told the FBI and other present that they would have an opportunity to speak, following the recess.

Colonel Riley was asked to come forward to meet with he and General Stark, to briefly discuss the reconstruction phase, during the recess.

CHAPTER TWENTY-FIVE

DAY 335—02 DECEMBER

THE AMERICAN NAVAL BASE

PURSUIT OF THE *SCORPION* OFF THE BAHAMAS

THE SOUTHERN ATLANTIC OCEAN

> NEWS BULLETIN
> *NAVY TO LIMIT USE OF SONAR!*
> *Noise a threat to marine life*
> By Angela Watercutter
> Associated Press
> 01 December 2003
>
> SANTA MONICA, Calif.—The Navy has agreed to limit its peacetime use of a new sonar system designed to detect enemy submarines but which may also harm marine mammals and fish, an environmentalist group said.
> The Natural Resources Defense Council, which sued the military on the issue, and the Navy reached a settlement last week in which the Navy agreed to use the new system

only in specific areas along the eastern seaboard of Asia, according to documents provided by the environmental group.

The agreement must be approved by a federal magistrate to become permanent, but if implemented, the deal would greatly restrict the Navy's original plan for the sonar system, which once was slated to be tested in most of the world's oceans.

(Partial Text)
30—END OF BULLETIN

The post-attack damage control meeting reconvened at 1000 hours. Major General Montrose took up where it had left off, after refilling his coffee cup—the fourth such refill in half as many hours. "We still have a lot to do this morning. That isn't taking into account that most of you haven't even been to bed yet. But we have a final matter for discussion here. Where in the hell did the terrorists, who managed to get off the base, escape to? This is a major unresolved concern of the president and Homeland Security."

"I'd like to introduce FBI Special Agent Diane Davis. On her right is Commander Jennifer Stalwart of the Coast Guard. Commander Stalwart flew herself and Agent Davis in here a few hours ago in a F-14 to brief us on this last issue."

"The tactical questions still remaining unanswered, are first, by what method did the surviving terrorists manage to extract the six liberated detainees, who apparently are important to bin-Laden?"

"Secondly, how does the United States plan to obtain the answer to question number one? Ladies, the floor is yours," General Montrose said, taking his chair.

Agent Davis stood to address the assembled base staff. Those who read American newspapers with any regularity, knew that Davis was a fast-track member of the president's new counterterrorism intelligence clearinghouse directorate. She had been assigned there after leading a reasonably successful response, to al-Qaeda's attacks on the Pacific Northwest in 2002. While on paper, she still reported to the head of the FBI's Counterterrorism unit, her dotted line reporting relationship was directly to the president's Nation Security Advisor.

"Ladies and Gentlemen, I'm FBI Special Agent Diane Davis. I've been with the FBI for a little more than seven years now. I am currently assigned as the Acting Director of the National Terrorism Intelligence Clearinghouse. The president established the TTIC in 2003, following 9/11 and the al-Qaeda attacks on the Western U.S. in 2002. Both Commander Stalwart and I have been more or less up to our respective asses in alligators for the past three years."

A pregnant thirty seconds of shocked silence followed the agent's comment. It was followed by laughter. The military personnel assembled in the room, then realized what the FBI agent had been trying to accomplish by her use of the gutter expression. She was putting them on notice that she and Commander Stalwart were operational 'players,' and not window dressing, in President Bush's War on Terrorism.

Agent Davis continued, "It is the FBI's belief, and therefore my belief," which again drew a chuckle for those listening, "that a submarine was used in yesterday's mission. The boat, we believe, was used to transport the assault team from somewhere in the Middle East, here to Gitmo. It was also used to extract the six surviving terrorists and a handful of rescued VIP's. We know that bin-Laden had two Soviet-made Kilo class submarines in his weapon's arsenal in 2002. He stole those from the Russians."

"Command Stalwart's people caused one of those boats to perish with all hands aboard in 2002. Remnants of it are submerged under the silt at the bottom of the Strait of Juan de Fuca, off Washington State. That left al-Qaeda one of the diesel submarines, which prior to the vessel's theft from the Russians, had been extensively modified to include spare accommodations for up to thirty special operations troops. The downside of the refitting was that the submarine no longer had space for anything other than a skeleton operating crew."

Davis continued, "I'm going to turn this over to Commander Stalwart at this point. She is the U.S. Coast Guard's expert, on-loan to the FBI, on all sorts of fast mover aircraft, warships, and tactics. She is certified in the operation of nearly every one of the airborne weapons available to the U.S. Armed forces today. Jennifer . . . ," Davis concluded as she retook her seat.

Commander Davis, a magnificent-looking, highly decorated officer wearing her service's class "A" uniform, the jacket covered with combat medals and certification devices, stood and addressed the group in a firm, authoritative contralto voice. She had no need for the podium microphone. "Good morning. The Pentagon thought their security at Guantánamo was sufficient, relative to the safety, protection, and welfare of the nearly seven hundred detainees incarcerated here at Camp Delta."

She continued, "That security included the assignment of two of the U.S. Navy's most expensive, non-carrier warships—the Arleigh Burke class AEGIS, guided missile destroyers #DDG 79— the *USS Oscar Austin* and #DDG 75—the *USS Donald Cook*."

"The destroyer with the 'duty' was to patrol a oval search pattern alert area, 130-miles long by 30-miles wide, right down the middle of the Windward Passage. That body of water, incidentally, contains one of the world's deepest submarine canyons, the Cayman trench, at 7,535 meters."

"CNO, the U.S. Chief of Naval Operations, directed that the two destroyers should work rotating twelve hour shifts. Their mission was to ensure that no unknown surface vessel, capable of landing troops at the base of Camp Delta, be permitted within ten miles of Windmill or Kittery beaches. These two beaches lay at the base of the tall bluff on which the camp is located, as you know."

The commander proceeded, "Yesterday, two Cuban MiG-29's loaded for bear, with the apparent approval of the Cuban Presidente, launched a harassment sortie out of a southeastern Cuban airfield, directly at the on-duty patrolling AEGIS destroyer, the *Oscar Austin*. The two Cuban fighters ignored all challenges and warnings from the bridge of the *Austin* to cease and desist. Per wartime ROE procedures, the destroyer broke off her patrolling mission, and prepared to engage the MiGs. The Pentagon says that America was as close to going to war with the Cubans, than at anytime since the Soviet ballistic missile crisis back in the early 1960's"

"The ship's SSM-8 Harpoon missiles and the evolved Sea Sparrow missiles, were all on their final count downs, prior to actual launch. The Vulcan Phalanx 6-barrel MK-15 cannon was locked onto the radar coordinates of the approaching MiGs. But suddenly the bandit aircraft abruptly shut down their attack radar, dropped their landing gear, and extended their wing flaps, the international signal for non-hostile intent."

"As soon as the two aircraft blew over the destroyer at mast height, they retracted their gear and wing flaps, and went to zone five afterburner in a vertical climb. At the top of that climb, they came about and eventually segued into a course on a reciprocal heading, which took them back to their base in Cuba," the Coast Guard officer reported.

"This confrontation served to disrupt the destroyer's mission. The destroyer's captain radioed Southern Command in Florida; who in-turn notified the Chief of Naval Operations (CNO); and I imagine, he notified the Secretary of Defense; who per procedure would notify the National Command Authority (NCA), the president. The order came back down the chain of command that the destroyer was to return to her mission, but was to only do so, once the captain was fully convinced that the MiG's were back in their nests."

"The Pentagon advises that weighty command determination took another four hours, as the destroyer's bridge delayed any action until intelligence from an 'sneak-and-peek' over flight by the CIA's KH-11 satellite, verified that the two MiG's were back in their revetments at Cuba's Camagüey Air Base."

The Commander referred to her notes, before continuing. "Now, the submarine had been careful to make its move during the period when the duty destroyer was at the far end of the patrol pattern. This meant that the warship would have been no less than sixty-five miles away, from bisecting the point the submerged submarine had to cross, inbound to Guantánamo. Even at top speed, the destroyer was still nearly 2.5 hours from Guantánamo if the balloon had gone up. That was good planning on the part of the yet-unknown submarine's skipper."

"The apparent attempt to draw the destroyer into an armed confrontation with another nation-state's aircraft, could have easily escalated into an international incident. At the time, the ship's eyes and ears of necessity were on the horizon, not the submerged depths off Windward Passage. And remember, the AEGIS destroyer's mission was search out any 'surface' vessel capable landing a force on the beach."

Stalwart continued, "The Pentagon orders never mentioned the possibility of a submarine. The only submergible al-Qaeda has access to, based on our knowledge from the Pacific Northwest incidents in 2002 and other intelligence, is a small diesel Soviet-made diesel attack submarine. No one could have expected that the Russians would have modified these small, traditionally coastal-assigned submarines, so drastically. And you can be damn sure that they didn't volunteer that information to the world community, when they reported that two of them had 'gone missing' in 2002."

"Those AEGIS destroyers, post-attack, are still working rotating shifts out in the Windward Passage. But their patrol pattern has been tightened up a bit. There is a very remote possibility that al-Qaeda could come back to Camp Delta, finish the assault, and rescue more detainees. The Pentagon doesn't want to gamble on that possibility."

Commander Stalwart paused briefly to stretch her shoulders in a futile attempt to bleed off some of the stress she felt building there. The strain she and Agent Davis were under, having responsibility for attempting to second guess bin-Laden's next move, would have been considered by other warriors in their position to be 'above their paygrade.' But both FBI Agent Davis, and U.S. Coast Guard's Commander Stalwart, readily accepted the responsibility and the stress that came with it.

The commander, with a glance at Davis who was industriously making notes on the legal pad in front of her, now opened an entirely new area of discussion. She began, "Not five minutes after we went 'feet dry' here at Leeward Airfield, one of the Marine guards doubled-timed over to inform us that there was a urgent call from the Pentagon holding for Agent Davis. It had come over the control tower's only secure phone line. You can imagine how popular that made us with the enlisted ATC controllers. Here they are trying to run a military airport, only to have two ditzy girls tie up their only communication link with the stateside FAA."

At this, the entire room broke up into peals of laughter and snorts, including a few from the two General officers. The two women had just managed to do for the assembled staff, what they had been unable to do for themselves. They had reduced the tension in the room to a more manageable level. Once the frivolity has died down, Commander Stalwart continued.

"The phone call was from the OD at the Pentagon. Probably some aspiring admiral, which seems to be the type that hangs out in places like that." Again, there were a few brief chuckles. All of which abruptly stopped when the staffers noticed General Montrose twirling his finger in a circular motion over his head, telling the commander to dispense with the comedy, and get on with her briefing.

"To cut to the chase, the message the OD had for Diane was that the president was *really* unhappy that bin-Laden had the *cojones* to attack a U.S. Naval facility. In fact, the OD repeated that to Diane no less than three times, apparently to ensure the tone of the NCA's message wasn't being lost over the secure satellite phone link."

The commander paused to take a drink from the water glass that had thoughtfully been placed on the oak conference table in front of her, by some considerate soul. Then she continued, "Basically, the follow-on message from the president is that whatever it takes to run down the Al-Qaeda submarine, along with her on-board guests, is to be made available by any and all commands. One of those special dispensations was a one-time permission to use the Navy's new long-range sonar system, designed to detect submerged enemy submarines over thousand of miles of ocean.

"The Navy is assuming the kilo is heading east at its fastest submerged speed of seventeen knots, for what they will find to be the false security of the Atlantic Ocean. In that regard, the president ordered the Joint Chiefs, who notified the CNO, who ordered the Pentagon, that as the agreement with the environmentalists over the use of the Navy's new sonar hasn't yet been signed off by a Magistrate, he is going to declare a operational emergency."

"The president isn't going to permit the submarine to flee back to where ever it is that bin-Laden hides the boat between missions. He has informed the Pentagon that if we cannot locate the fleeing submarine through other means, he wants the new sonar spooled up and put into use until it has been located, and the sub's identity and GPS position absolutely established. If the environmentalists want to take the Navy to court again, so be it."

Stalwart, in an aside, said, "Now this is my personal opinion. I doubt that actor Pierce Brosnan, or Jean-Michel Cousteau, both of whom claim to have been behind that lawsuit, will want to show their faces in court. Because there they might have to explain why they are willing to let a submarine, an armed hunter/killer boat at that, equipped with God knows what weaponry, escape just so they can again get their pictures into the newspaper."

"It is well-known that Cousteau never misses a chance to align himself with the fishes. He hopes that someday he will be considered to be in the same class as his accomplished father. Brosnan has starred in a couple of the spook flicks about James Bond, 007. But I imagine *that* is a role, movie producers won't offer him again, following his new found interest in anything that even collaterally puts nearly 400 million American lives at-risk," Stalwart stated.

"Just locating those alpha hotels isn't going to be enough, naturally. We have to insert an obstacle in the kilo's way that will force her to surface. Hopefully that will enable us to terminate the pursuit without any additional loss of life. As you will note from the briefing sheets Agent Davis passed out to you earlier, the Soviet-built kilos, until the our Los Angeles-class hunter/killer submarine came on-line, were stealthy enough to go almost anywhere in the world's oceans they wanted, just so they operated inside the operational envelope around which they were designed."

"Now that the U.S. Navy admits to having at least fifty-three of the LA-class boats active, those days are over. This is not to say our SSNs have zero trouble locating the kilo. That isn't the case. But a reasonably disciplined search by one of the large nuclear hunter/killers will net a kilo every time. The LA-class SSN is much larger, much faster, can dive much deeper, is much more stealthy, more heavily armed—the list goes on and on."

The Coast Guard Commander turned to a young yeoman seated along the wall, asking him to dim the room's lights. Stalwart picked up a electronic 'clicker' off the conference table in front of her, and hit the sequence of buttons that resulted in a four-by-six-foot plasma screen dropping out for the situation room's ceiling. She punched a few more buttons, and a full-color electronically-created screen, depicting the world between Jamaica and the Bahamas south-to-north, and Havana, Cuba and Santiago, Haiti, west-to-east, displayed itself.

There were three blinking dots moving across the screen's surface. Just exiting the body of water identified as the Caribbean Sea, in a northeastern direction, was a rapidly flashing red blip, with a small 'd' and the numeral '17k' both keeping pace with the icon.

About a one hundred miles behind the red blip, was a even more rapidly blinking blue blip, with the same letter 'd' and the numeral '32k' pacing its movement toward the Atlantic Ocean.

Due north of the red blip, was a rapidly flashing green blip, this one with the little 'd,' and also the numeral '32k' keeping pace, as it progressed due south on an apparent collision course with the red blip. By manipulating another button, Commander Stalwart froze the visual, and turned her attention back to the group.

She resumed, "What you are looking at here is a real-time tracking of the fleeing kilo submarine, shown in red. The intelligence that the KH-11 satellite is beaming down to Langley, indicates the kilo is submerged (dived = d) and is making headway at seventeen knots (17k). Jane's Warship Recognition Guide says that is the Russian submarine's fastest possible submerged speed. She is only rated at ten knots on the surface."

"The blue blip is Uncle Sam's Navy. It is a LA-class hunter/killer submarine, the SSN 773 *Cheyenne*, which just passed north of Montego Bay in Jamaica, steaming at thirty-two knots submerged. Being twice as fast submerged as the Soviet-built submarine, she is cutting the kilo's lead, in half, every hour."

"The *Cheyenne* is trailing a ELF long-wire, low frequency display, which is being bounced off a satellite. She is reporting to Norfolk that she has a seventy percentile firing solution on the kilo in her attack computer. This, even though she still is currently one hundred miles astern of her. Our boat is outfitted with SLCM—GDC/Hughes Tomahawks, and SSM—GDC/Hughes Tomahawks. So even alone, she could get the job done if the terrorists want to go out with a bang."

"The green blip is our 'cousins' from across the pond. The British Navy boat is a Trafalgar-class hunter/killer submarine, the S-87 *HMS Turbulent*, also running at thirty-two knots, submerged. It was dispatched from a port call she was making, representing Prince Charles, somewhere in the Atlantic. The *Turbulent's* heading is almost magnetically due-south, about 125 miles away from the approaching kilo," reported Stalwart.

"Of course, with her intercept heading, she is closing the gap with the kilo much faster than the *Cheyenne*. The 'brits' are also trailing a ELF long-wire array, bouncing it first off a geosynchronous satellite, then to London, and back to Norfolk, reporting that the First Captain, their term, is adjusting his course as required to maintain a collision course with the kilo. He adds that his attack computer says it is one hundred percent sure it can take the kilo out with a single fish or missile."

Commander Stalwart reached over and clicked off the plasma screen, which promptly retracted itself into the ceiling. The yeoman flipped back on the room lights. Then the commander turned to Major General Montrose, then General Stark, and finally to FBI Agent Davis, asking if they had any questions or comments.

Neither general indicated he had any comments at that time. Then, General Montrose checking his watch said "I've decided that this meeting will be adjourned until 0800 hours tomorrow. We still have a lot of critical issues to address. However, none of you has gotten any rest in the last thirty-six hours. Considering the loss of life yesterday and this morning, I don't want to extrapolate any mistakes into an already tragic situation. Tired warriors make mistakes," he concluded.

FBI Agent Davis and Commander Stalwart thanked the assembled staff for their patience. The morning's meeting had lasted nearly four hours. However, Davis had one final observation to pass on, before the meeting adjourned. General Montrose nodded his approval.

She proceeded, "The president has ordered the Joint Chiefs, that if possible, the fleeing submarine is to be forced to the surface, and the occupants are to be taken alive. Too many intelligence questions remain about this morning's attack. Only live terrorists can provide the answers to those questions. The president said that while he certainly doesn't want any more American's lives lost, the administration's preference is to avoid having to kill the submarine. That action would only serve to guarantee that the al-Qaeda and Taliban occupants of the rogue submarine, become martyrs throughout the Muslim world."

"He has put the skippers of the *USS Cheyenne* and the *HMS Turbulent* on-notice to that effect. For that reason, the president has ordered the JCS to utilize the U.S. Navy's low-frequency transmission system that operates by use of long-wire trailing arrays. The president is to be consulted before *anyone* pulls the trigger on the fleeing submarine."

With this final point, the Guantánamo post attack damage control meeting adjourned until 0800 hours the following morning.

Back at sea nearly ninety minutes after the post-attack meeting had adjourned for the day at Gitmo, the American *USS Cheyenne* and the Brits *HRM Turbulent* caught up with the *Scorpion*. At the time, neither boat was aware of the name of the bandit submarine, only its probable type and class.

Both of the pursuing submarines had been continuously processing the *Scorpion's* sound signatures through their threat identification computers. The data the two Coalition submarines input into their on-board computers was being updated constantly.

The Russian diesel submarine was running at its maximum submerged speed. As a result, the fugitive boat was breaking every submarine law of stealth by doing so. The *Scorpion* churned frantically toward the Atlantic Ocean, with no regard for the sub's critically important, 'quiet-running' envelope. Much like a bull the proverbial china shop.

The pursuing submarines had been deferring their own ship's operational demands for computer time, to repetitively process the fleeing submarine's unique tonals, time and time again. It was repetitive simplicity in its most basic element.

Only by continual monitoring of the *Scorpion's* flight, could there be no question that this was the same submarine that had been used in the attack on Guantánamo Bay's Camp Delta, less than five hours earlier.

In the mind of the president of the United States; the four members of the American JCS; the multitude of 'star carriers' in the Pentagon; and the captains at the helm of these two hot-pursuit killer submarines, that fact alone justified the rapidly growing backlog of deficit computer-time, accumulating aboard each of the Coalition submarines.

Whether the captain of the fleeing *Scorpion* was aware of the presence of the two coalition submarines pursing his boat, was debatable. During the cold war, the Soviet-built, diesel-powered kilo, quiet by design, had occasionally managed to avoid the west's submarines. But today's Soviet equipment didn't match up to the latest state-of-the-art systems aboard the *Cheyenne* and the *Turbulent*.

Both pursuing captains were well aware that when two submerged submarines approach one another head-on, both in pursuit of a common target, a condition called 'target fixation' is born. The potential for a 'blue-on-blue' friendly fire incident goes up exponentially. It was a major concern, and had been, ever since a 'friendly fire' incident during the first Iraq war. Coalition Apache helicopter gunships, had mistakenly attacked an out-of-position Canadian ground detachment.

The American officers involved were courts martialed out of the service, and were considered fortunate to escape being sentenced to Leavenworth prison. Since then, every U.S. military organization had instituted primarily, secondary, and tertiary procedures to prevent any possibility of a blue-on-blue accident.

The First Captain of the British boat, due to his superior speed, had altered course, and scribed a fifty-mile wrap-around arc. This permitted his boat to safely bypass the heads-on-charging al-Qaeda boat. At the maximum submerged speed the *Scorpion* was moving, the small diesel boat's threat-detection sonar systems were almost blind. The fact that both the American and British nuclear-powered submarines were designed to be twice as fast, submerged, as the diesel submarine, meant their threat detection systems had been designed to operate more efficiently at the higher speeds.

The nuclear-powered boats were keying their depths off the fleeing diesel boat. It had chosen to hide below a 'thermocline' at a depth of eight hundred feet. In addition to the superior speed of the nuclear boats, they also could safety dive much deeper than the boat they were currently pursuing.

The *Turbulent* completed her clearing maneuver, then came about, and slid in to take up position one-mile behind the American submarine. The *Cheyenne*, moving along at barely one-half her maximum possible submerged speed, was still firmly in the kilo's baffles.

The 'baffles' on a submarine are located directly behind the ship's direction of travel. There, the propeller(s) of the boat churn the water mightily. And if the submarine is submerged, and traveling at high speed, those propeller(s) produce cavitations, which further disturbs the water behind the submarine.

Due to the 'noise' of the cavitations, the various sonar systems on-board a submarine who is running at high-speed, have great difficulty in translating the signals they are receiving back from the 'pings' they are sending out. So much so, it is said they are either 'deaf,' or 'blind' to what is happening in their 'baffles' behind the submerged boats.

The fleeing al-Qaeda submarine, with the two nuclear-powered boats loping along in pursuit close behind, had just passed southwest of Great Inagua Island, northeast of Cuba. Then the word had come over the extremely-low-frequency underwater communication system of the Coalition boats, giving them orders to fall back, take up defensive positions on the kilo, and attempt to contact her over the ELF underwater hailer system.

The enemy boat was to be advised in the strongest terms that two, 334-ton, 170-foot long, Cyclone surface patrol boats, PC 12 *The Thunderbolt*, and PC 3 *The Monsoon*, both dispatched at the request of the U.S. Southern Command, would be arriving on-station in less than ten minutes time. The U.S. Navy was ordering the kilo to immediately stop her forward motion, blow all ballast, surface, and prepare to be boarded.

The al-Qaeda boat was warned that she would be given the cease-and-surface order, no more than three times. She was to surface, lay down all arms, and prepare to surrender to the *Thunderbolt* and the *Monsoon*. She would be boarded, all her weapons secured, the submarine's occupants taken into custody, and the boat towed to the closest stateside U.S. Navy base.

If the kilo failed to surface as ordered within the next twenty minutes, she would be considered to be a threat to the American and British ships. In that event, the *USS Cheyenne* was ordered to blast the diesel submarine out of the water, on the orders of the president of the United States.

The Coalition submarines had long ago gone to 'battle-stations.' The *Turbulent* had taken a firing angle, sixty degrees off that of the *Cheyenne*. Both had Mk-48 torpedoes in their tubes, and were prepared to fire once their outer doors were opened.

The Cyclone surface patrol boats had both arrived, and taken up stations well north and south of the small, submerged submarine. They had positioned themselves in that combat spread, in case the kilo ignored the demand to surface, and attempted to make a dash for the perceived safety of the surrounding waters, to escape the 'box' she had been maneuvered into.

The American captain of the nuclear boat had blown a little ballast, and brought his boat up to a depth of six hundred feet, just above the thermocline the kilo continued to hide under. Both the *Thunderbolt* and the *Monsoon* had configured their Sperry RASCAR surface radar, Raytheon SPS-64 (V) 9 navigation radar, and the WESMAR hull-mounted sonar to electronically block any attempt, on the part of the submerged al-Qaeda submarine, to transmit or receive radio messages, other than those of the Coalition's boats.

"Skipper, we're at six hundred feet," Lt. Commander Johnson, the XO aboard the *Cheyenne*, reported to his captain. "COB reports once the water-tight doors on 'tubes' one through four, are opened, the fish will be ready to go, Sir."

"Okay, XO, keep us steadily as she goes," Commander Luther Pride, the captain, told him. The *Cheyenne* having risen above the thermocline, was no longer able to maintain sonar contact on the kilo, which still remained in motion just under the t-zone. The captain picked up the phone. "Sonar, Conn."

"Sonar, aye."

"Where is the *Turbulent*, Sonar?"

"He's holding back about eighteen hundred yards, Sir. He is following your lead and will hold until you tell him otherwise. He is under the thermocline, about two hundred feet below us, at the same general depth as the kilo, Sir"

"Where are the two Cyclones, sonar?"

"The *Monsoon* is now holding station about 2,500 yards to the south; the *Thunderbolt* is holding about the same distance to the north. Both of them are burning up the ozone with their jamming. Still no indication the kilo is headed for the surface—at least we haven't observed any vertical movement through the t-zone yet, Captain."

Captain Pride began to question whether his decision to surface before the kilo, had been the right one. Pride wanted to be on the surface, locked and loaded, when the kilo surfaced. Just in case those special operations troops she was carrying intended to make a fight of it. The down side of surfacing first meant that his electronic eyes and ears would be at a disadvantage, until the kilo got above the thermocline.

"Captain, Conn!"

"Captain here, Conn—what do you have?"

"Sir," the duty communication officer responded, "The captain of the HMS *Turbulent* reports that the kilo somehow managed to zero-in on his position, and approached at about seventeen knots apparently intending to ram him. The 'brit' dumped some torpedo decoys overboard, which gave the kilo second thoughts. But the kilo still got close enough to scrape down the side of his boat. While the kilo was getting turned around for a second shot at him, the British boat expedited his departure out of the immediate area. She has now taken up station five thousand yards to the north, Sir. *Turbulent* says he doubts this guy is going to surface, and feels he is hoping to take one of us down with him. The *Turbulent* has sustained unknown damage to her hull, Sir."

"Okay, Conn, standby," the American captain ordered.

"Captain, Sonar."

"Sonar, aye."

"Sonar, do you have an location on the kilo currently? He has just rammed the *Turbulent*. This surrender negotiation is getting out of hand!"

"Yes, sir, I have a some noise to the south, about four thousand yards from our current position, on a heading of one hundred-eighty degrees, magnetic. The kilo seems to be moving something metal around inside his hull. Could be loading a torpedo, Sir. Maybe he had empty tubes during the attack last night, as he was just providing the taxi service for the assault team. Ever since the Camp Delta guards reported that some of the al-Qaeda special-ops guys had managed to get away with a few detainees, and returned to the boat, the kilo has been running at top submerged speed for the Atlantic, Sir. She would have been porpoising and unable to reload her tubes at that speed, Sir."

COB, the Chief of the Boat, had joined Captain Pride in the control room, and ventured an opinion. "Intelligence tells us the kilo has been heavily modified to accommodate a large special operations team. Logically, that modification disrupted her aerodynamic hull configuration. I imagine it is rough as a pot-holed New York City street, riding that submarine at the seventeen-knots her captain has been maintaining all the way from Guantánamo. So maybe, faced with a command to surface, or be blown to a series of loosely connected blood spatters, he's decided to load a fish or two, and take one or both of us with him, Sir."

"Okay, COB, this is what I want you to do. First, get the *Turbulent* and us another twenty thousand yards away from this guy. Second, send a message to the NCA that this guy has been duly warned. He has refused to reply, let alone surface. The kilo just attempted to kill the *Turbulent* by ramming her. She is now making noises consistent with loading torpedoes. I damn sure want some orders, and I want them fast," the captain stated.

"Tell whomever is on the receiving end of the message, that if the kilo even opens one outer torpedo door, I'm going to roll him up under our existing rules-of-engagement. I'm permitted to shoot if he opens his outer doors, or makes any indication he is going 'offensive'. Now get that coded, and off to the satellite, most ricky-tick!"

"Aye, Aye, Sir. Consider it sent. May I suggest we open our outer doors? As long as we are already making a little noise by repositioning the boat anyway, Sir?"

"Make it happen, COB," Commander Pride, the *Cheyenne's* captain, ordered.

NEWS BULLETIN
Worldwide News Herald
Special Edition
01 December 2003

PRESIDENT ORDERS
NAVY TO SINK SUBMARINE
FLEEING AFTER ATTACK ON
U.S. NAVAL STATION—GUANTÁNAMO BAY!
Loss of life among invaders, detainees
and defenders reported to be heavy.

WASHINGTON, D.C.—The Secretary of Defense reports that the President of the United States, today ordered the sinking of a submarine that had only hours previously had landed a large, well-equipped terrorist assault team on the treaty-leasehold property of the United States at Guantánamo Bay, Cuba.

The President, in his constitutional responsibility as the National Command Authority (NCA), was forced to order the action, after all attempts to force the enemy submarine to surface, lay down its arms, surrender its combatants, and stand-by for boarding by warships of the United States of America, had been repeated ignored. The terrorist's only response to the American's surrender demand, was an attempt to ram a nuclear-powered British attack submarine, the *Turbulent*, which was assisting in their capacity of a member of the duly constituted Coalition, dedicated to stamping out terrorism throughout the world.

The name of the enemy boat was identified from debris recovered from the site of its all-hands sinking, as the *Scorpion*, a Soviet-made, Kilo SSK-class, diesel-powered, hunter/killer submarine. This boat was reputedly one of the two such submarines that al-Qaeda terrorists managed to steal from a far-northern Russian base, on the Russian's heavily-guarded Kola Peninsula, back in 2002. The other Kilo was sunk in 2002 by the U.S. Coast Guard, who sent it to the bottom of the Straits of Juan de Fuca, after the Kilo had participated in a numbers of devastating attacks on both civilian and military targets in America's Pacific Northwest.

Preliminary reports from Guantánamo Bay Naval Station indicate that between the terrorist invaders, and the detainees their collateral fire killed at Camp Delta, more than one-hundred eleven persons were killed-in-action, and another forty-eight wounded. American's losses have initially been estimated at eight killed, and twenty-seven wounded, but most of the defender's wounds are reported to be so critical, that additional deaths are anticipated by the spokespersons of the U.S. Navy Hospital located on-base.

The terrorists used a number of diversionary attacks in their unsuccessful attempt to draw members of the 2,000-person strong multi-service Joint Task Force 160, away from their stations safeguarding the detainees at Camp Delta. These diversionary attacks resulted in major disabling damage to one the bases' cross-bay transportation terminals; dining areas on the Windward side officers club; extensive damage in the base's general anchorage include disabling three civilian heavy-haul freighters, currently under contract to the U.S. Government; and the destroying of structures and supporting infrastructure at the over 50% of the newly-constructed, state-of—the-art, detainee Camp Delta.

Initial estimates, to replace the damaged transportation terminal, the Officers Club dining facilities, the infrastructure damage to Camp Delta, and the damaged in the bases' general anchorage, which includes having to tow three 300-foot long freighters from Guantánamo Bay to a shipyard in the United States for major repairs, is 314 million US dollars.

As the U.S. Naval Hospital, located on Hospital Cay on-base, has extremely limited bed-capacity, a full-service U.S. Hospital ship, will be arriving at the base within 48-hours. Until such time, the base commander reports that the detainee wounded are receiving care at Camp Delta's own full-service surgical and emergency care facilities. While the wounded detainee's injures will be treated at medical facilities on the 45-square mile base, the more seriously wounded members of the JTF-160 defenders have already been airlifted stateside, by C-130's modified to accommodate the handling of stretchers.

The Commander of the base's Joint Taskforce, reporting to the U.S. Southern Command HQ out of Miami, has ordered that each of the dead, regardless of whether invader, detainee, or defender, are to receive an in-depth post-mortem autopsy, which will be observed by a professionals from some of the nation's leading medical schools, trained to determine wound source origination.

According to surviving members of the Camp Delta guard force, six detainees, escorted by the six surviving terrorist assault team members, were observed leaving Kittery beach, located immediately below the camp, in a rubber inflatable and heading out into the Windward Passage, where a surfacing submarine picked them up, again submerged, and began a frantic attempt to escape east into the Atlantic Ocean. Coincidently, the nuclear-powered attack submarine, the USS *Cheyenne*, was in the Windward Passage at the time of the attack. The state-of-the-art U.S. submarine was able to acquire and maintain an end-chase on the fleeing Kilo submarine, keeping her under constant electronic observation at all times.

Shortly after the Kilo reached the eastern exit out of Windward passage, she elected to turn northbound, continuing her dash for her perceived safety of the Atlantic Ocean. The *Cheyenne* followed, all the while maintaining constant electronic identification surveillance, by concealing herself in the Kilo's churning baffles. Less than an hour later, the terrorists aboard the fleeing Kilo were interdicted by a coalition taskforce of warships consisting of the British attack submarine HMS *Turbulent*, and two U.S. Navy Cyclone-class patrol craft, the USS *Monsoon*, and the USS *Thunderbolt*, with the primary on-scene commander, the *Cheyenne*, immediately behind.

After being ordered three times, via low-frequency loud hailer, to stop, surface, and prepare to receive boarders from the American warships, the enemy submarine instead elected to fight, and proceeded to take offensive action against the *Turbulent*. The kilo, which was maintaining the same depth as the British submarine at the time, sought out and rammed the British ship, damaging her to the point where a sub-recovery vessel was required to tow the damaged submarine back into port for repairs. A total of seven British submariners were inured in the Kilo's attack seriously enough, to require being airlifted by helicopter to an unnamed U.S. Navy Hospital, stateside.

The Administration in Washington D.C., promises updates on the terrorist's attack on U.S.'s Guantánamo Bay Naval Station, as soon as they become available.

30—END OF BULLETIN

CHAPTER TWENTY-SIX

DAY 354—24 DECEMBER

HOOVER DAM

HIDDEN IN PLAIN SIGHT

NEAR BOUNDER CITY

NEVADA

It was Christmas Eve. The dam's day shift had already left for the day. They left following a brief ceremony and prayer in Edith Hammer's office to give thanks that none of the terrorist attacks that targeted the dam in the past twelve months had been successful. The swing and graveyard shifts had voted to forego a similar ceremony on their shifts, although the resident manager would have been willing to return to the facility for the observances.

Two of the day shift's salaried staff had apparently left for home immediately following the end of their shifts. They were not in attendance at the post-shift holiday ritual.

One of the absent staffers was Elizabeth Zubaida. She was a brilliant young Saudi who held a degree in Hydraulics. The woman had accepted a secretarial job in the dam's Press Relations department, just to get her foot in the door at the U.S. Bureau of Reclamation.

Personnel turnover at mega dams like Hoover is normally very low. However Zubaida appeared to have the utmost confidence in her career potential, if for no other reason, than her outstanding educational credentials. The only fly in the ointment, as far as Zubaida was concerned, was her boss, Jefferson Conduit. Conduit seemed to spend more time primping his carefully orchestrated physical appearance, than doing the job he was being paid to do. This invariably meant that Zubaida had to follow him around, putting out the forest fires caused by Conduits lack of attention to detail.

Conduit—a short, young African-American—had something in his psyche that manifested itself in his utter disregard of any other person of color. Persons falling into that category included any non-white, whose skin happened to be lighter than Conduits own charcoal-black epidermis.

The undercurrent of hostility, existing between Conduit and his assistant, was known to others on the dam's management team. But the unofficial 'personnel conflict' policy at the Bureau was to give the two feuding parties an opportunity to work it out between themselves. If that didn't work, then one or both of the employees were placed into the disciplinary process.

Also not attending the Christmas-ceremony-cum-prayer-offering was Mohammed Harket. He was one of the most popular young men in the dam's workforce. Mohammed was always quick to lend a hand to a co-worker. Harkat had been hired away from the Bechtel Corporation, when an apparent quality-control problem had surfaced at the dam, forcing management to make some unanticipated personnel reassignments.

Harket had been hired to oversee one of the most important departments at the dam, the Physical Inspection—Structural Service Unit. Few people were aware that even a grossly over-engineered hydroelectric structure, like Hoover Dam, leaked nearly 40,000 gallon of water daily. This seepage traveled from the reservoir-side face of the dam, through the structure, and out the downstream face. The constant dribbling of transit water could eventually cause erosion of the concrete structure, unless drainage channels were provided and maintained to accommodate it.

No one who was in Edith Hammer's office at the moment having punch and pastries, following the day shift change, was surprised that the two foreign-born engineers had elected not to attend. They were, after all, of the Muslim faith. And the customary recitation of the Christian prayer that the long-time Bureau of Reclamation employees expected possibly would have made the two middle-easterners uncomfortable. The Muslim community is not known for its tolerance of other religions, especially Christianity.

Both of the absent employees were popular with their peers, but for differing reasons. Mohammed's acceptance was because he never hesitated to offer to lend a hand to a fellow co-worker. And Elizabeth—well, her popularity among the mostly-male staff, was for more earthy considerations. That was another reason that she and her boss, who recently had come out of the closet, got along like oil and water. But the two engineers were not so popular that their co-workers would have abandoned the ritual Christian prayer of thanksgiving, before heading home on Christmas Eve, to accommodate them.

Meanwhile, elsewhere in the dam, the swing shift employees puttered along at the holiday-reduced pace, it being Christmas Eve and all. They made adjustments here, and took note of power readings, there.

The powerhouse at Hoover Dam had been designed in a three-section configuration. There were two wings, each dug into the opposite walls of Black Canyon. One each on the Arizona and Nevada sides, of the Colorado River. Each wing was six hundred feet long, with a graduated width ranging from sixty-four to seventy-three feet.

The interior ceiling of the two wings was nearly one hundred feet in height. The height was necessary to provide ample clearance for the huge 300-ton transverse bridge cranes, running along the underside of the roof in the two wings.

The mammoth bridge cranes were necessary to permit the removal and replacement of the gigantic turbine/generators, which provide a significant amount of the electricity that powers the western United States.

The process is impressive, but rudimentary. River water enters the 395-foot tall intake towers, located on the reservoir-side of the dam. The ingested water flows through thirty foot diameter penstocks to the powerhouse. This water is under immense pressure. Even a single intake tower produces a hydraulic head of water, six hundred feet in height. There are four intake towers, two dedicated to each powerhouse wing.

The force of the incoming gravity-driven water flow turns the turbines of the powerhouse's massive turbines. Each turbine's connecting shaft turns magnetic coils inside the generators, which creates electricity. That newly-born electricity is 'stepped up' by a transformer to 230,000 volts for transmission and distribution through the U.S.'s western electric grid.

There are nine generators in the Arizona powerhouse, and eight on the Nevada side. Each wing also had a 'service station' turbine/generator rated at 3,500-horsepower. Those smaller units are located at the far north end of each powerhouse. The service station units are one hundred percent dedicated to the intense, never-ending, maintenance requirements in both Arizona and Nevada powerhouses.

Hoover Dam can generate 2,080 megawatts of electricity, delivering an average of four billion kilowatt-hours each year, which is enough to serve the direct yearly needs of 1.3 million people. Indirectly, the electricity the dam generates impacts over twenty-five million residents.

The two wings are connected at the end closest to the seven hundred, twenty-seven foot high dam face, by a center section. It is approximately six hundred, sixty feet wide, and eighty feet in depth.

As there is no external road access available to the Arizona powerhouse, to permit the installation or removal of machinery, the center section also has a 300-ton bridge crane, which connects with the cranes in the powerhouse wings.

In other words, picture the hypothetic instance when a turbine/generator, such as Unit One, located in the far southern end of the Arizona powerhouse, breaks down. Powerhouse mechanics determine it cannot be repaired, in-place. This would require the dam's maintenance crew to remove the huge piece of inoperative machinery for repair.

The evacuation process starts when the unit is snatched—lifted up—by the bridge crane in the Arizona powerhouse.

At the far northern end of the Arizona powerhouse, the broken machinery is transferred to the center section's bridge crane, and lifted across that building's six hundred, sixty-foot width. The center section crane carries the damaged unit to the far-western side of its traverse. There, the machinery is transferred to the Nevada side bridge crane, and carried overhead to the far southern end of that wing.

There, the Nevada bridge crane would carefully deposit the broken equipment onto the trailer of a specially constructed heavy-hauler. That truck then transports the load out of the Nevada powerhouse, through a 1,900-foot tunnel that has been bored through solid rock, to the Boulder City access road. From that intersection, the truck turns left or right, depending on the eventual repair facility's location.

The broken machine is then re-built, repaired or replaced. When it is ready for reinstallation, it is trucked back through the rock tunnel, to the south end of the Nevada powerhouse. At that point, the Nevada side bridge crane will snatch it off the heavy-hauler, and it will begin its return to the location from where it was removed, along the same elevated route, sequentially using the three, three-hundred-ton bridge cranes.

With the intensive level of preventative maintenance each piece of equipment at the dam receives, inasmuch as some of the machinery is over seventy years old, it is unusual for the dam's maintenance team to have to extract and replace a turbine/generator using the 'snatch and carry' method. As a rule, rather than an exception, the 24/7 preventative maintenance program keeps the machinery in acceptable working order.

When even that fails, then a 'flying squad' of Bureau of Reclamation expert mechanics from around the country, supplemented by contractual experts from the equipment's manufacturer, is called in. Often these highly experienced 'breakdown' experts can effect repairs to get the device operational, without having to go through the laborious, tedious, time consuming, and potentially dangerous process that has been described here.

The last time a major piece of equipment had to be replaced at Hoover Dam, using the overhead cranes to snatch it out of its pit, and haul it out through the 1,900 foot long rock-hewn tunnel, was several year ago. Occasionally, if infrequently, a turbine/ generator housing, essentially just a metal casting, may have grown brittle with age, and found to be beyond cost-effect repair.

As Edith Hammer, the dam's resident manager would later recall, getting the broken Nevada powerhouse 'service station' turbine/generator, out and its replacement back in and installed, turned out to the simplest part of the entire operation.

First off, when a piece of electromagnetic machinery manufactured in the late 20's breaks, and for reasons that not even the manufacturer's experts can determine, you have trouble right there in river city. You aren't going to find a replacement for that piece of machinery sitting on a long-forgotten pallet in some warehouse.

Ninety-nine-point-nine times, out of a hundred, the broken unit of equipment is going to have to be 'as-built' to develop the necessary manufacturing specification. This requires a set of new drawings, laboriously prepared by taking the actual dimensions and measurements.

Even if original manufacturing drawings still do exist, seventy-years after the original unit was built, manufacturing techniques change, and tolerances are forever being tightened up. Meaning that an identical replacement isn't going to be the most efficient unit, now available.

No reasonable person builds a replacement machine that is just as inefficient as the decades-old original. Especially when the time to handcraft the replacement could take the better part of six months.

In the case of this particular breakdown, the workload the service station turbine/generator job had been fulfilling in the Nevada powerhouse, had been transferred to the Arizona-side unit, which was already was working at maximum capacity.

Therefore, the overall maintenance and preventative maintenance programs in both powerhouses, took a significant hit as the backlog of unprocessed preventive and routine maintenance work orders, increased daily. That meant the entire dam's operational capability was increasingly being threatened, each day the Nevada service station unit remained off-line.

Luckily, in this particular case, a new, more modern unit had been located. It was found coming off an assembly line in a factory in Central Mexico. According to the factory owner, the original customer had been forced into bankruptcy, and had defaulted on the order.

It would take several months, working 24/7, for the Mexican manufacturer to make the necessary modifications to the new unit. Those adaptations were necessary to insure the new unit, upon arrival, would drop right into the existing turbine pit in the Nevada powerhouse.

During that time, the over-worked Arizona-side service station generator was carrying a double workload. That meant letting over half of the critically-necessary maintenance jobs slide, as it, itself, edged ever closer to a major maintenance breakdown.

Arrangements had to be made, during the sixty-day retrofit period, to get the unit from Mexico to Hoover Dam, once it was ready for shipment. The unit would be shipped aboard a freighter, or moved by railroad, to the Long Beach Harbor. There it would transloaded onto a motorized heavy-hauler, especially designed for over-the-road travel, which would transport it from California to Hoover Dam.

Hoover Dam is considered one of a number of critical linchpins in America's national security. The reason behind that, is the vital electricity it provides the country's western power grid. And the irrigation water it pumps to tens of thousands of arid farms, throughout the western United States.

After 9/11, and taking into consideration al-Qaeda's on-going threats ever since, anything critical to national defense, which moved on the nation's highways, moves with a military escort. Regardless of cost or inconvenience.

As fate would have it, the shipment's departure out of Long Beach, en-route to Hoover Dam, came just as a unexpected, summer storm, with winds of near-hurricane force, and horizontally-driven rain, settled over the convoy's track. There would be plenty of time after the machinery finally reached the dam, for the National Weather Service to investigate how this massive storm slipped by their weather prediction computers.

The storm, growing off ground-generated thermals, slowed, then abruptly stalled directly over and along the heavily escorted convoy's only available route. The convoy was restricted to using the Federal Interstate Highway System, due to the dimensions of the heavy-hauler, and the weight of the replacement unit.

The storm birthed one microburst after another, each stronger that the one that had proceeded it. The military convoy escorting the shipment had its Humvees thrown about like matchsticks, including one tossed off an overpass. A number of military vehicles and the lives of several of the escorts were lost, before the convoy reached Boulder City, Nevada.

The storm, which seemed to have been bird-dogging the critical convey every step of the way, suddenly fled into the dark night as quickly as it had arrived, leaving behind a windless drenching rain. That continued to make the surviving members of the military escort, and the convoy's civilian drivers, miserable beyond measure.

The convoy pulled into Boulder City nearly three days late. After a brief night's sleep—the first in three days—the heavy hauler was slowly maneuvered up the narrow maintenance road, through the 1,900-foot rock tunnel, to the Nevada powerhouse and was finally installed.

After the unit had been wired and tested, it was put to work. Then for several hours, everyone sat around waiting for the other foot to drop. When it failed to do so, the mechanics went home to their families in Boulder City, and Las Vegas, for the first full, uninterrupted night's sleep they had enjoyed in months.

In the following weeks, the long-past-due maintenance workload began to return to its normal pre-breakdown levels. The new service station generator was exceeding all operational expectations.

None of the experts on the Bureau of Reclamation's crisis team, or the equipment manufacturer's hotshot crews, ever determined what had caused the original machine to self-destruct in the first place.

Some speculated it had been some type of explosion, which had thrown the magnetic coil out of balance, causing the generator to self-destruct. Unfortunately, the explosion had reduced the rotary portions of the shattered unit to nothing but small-to-medium fragments. Technicians judged it forensically impossible to determine the cause, if not the effect, of the equipment failure.

The dam's maintenance crew and supervisors had speculated that in order for a small but powerful explosive to be slipped into the high-speed rotations of the units magnetic coil, someone would have had to be physically present to introduce the foreign substance into the windings. But only Hoover Dam employees were permitted down onto the powerhouse floor, and never any tour visitors. Therefore, the possibility of internal sabotage was ignored, or overlooked, but in any case, never properly investigated.

By 8:00 p.m. on Christmas Eve, the generator floors in both powerhouses and the connecting center section were all but abandoned. The swing shift staff settled into their warm offices to reminisce about Christmas's past. Every hour or so, depending on the degree of supervision present in the dam's Risk Management department as the Bureau of Reclamation's security contingent was now called, a roving security guard would briskly walk through the powerhouse, possibly not bothering to look to either side of his assigned patrol route.

The guard would be in a hurry to get back to the warmth and companionship of the bullshit session he or she had been forced to leave, to make the security 'round' and hit all the computer-monitored keypunch stations.

It was exactly midnight on Christmas Eve, or rather the beginning of Christmas day, when a soft chirping noise began to emanate from the new service station generator, that had been installed in the Nevada powerhouse only months ago.

The guard for the Nevada powerhouse had chosen to walk his rounds in the opposite direction that hour. It made it possible for him to sit a few additional minutes in the warmth of the office. After all, those lucky stiffs with more seniority than he, had all gone home to their families hours ago. Despite how much coffee he quaffed down, he was having difficulty keeping his eyes open.

The excess coffee was making him run to the head every half hour, or so. If that wasn't bad enough, the Bureau of Reclamation's facility designers back in 1931 had located the rest rooms on the Nevada side, nearly one hundred fifty feet from the Risk Management office. But he knew that the other guards on this shift would by now be dutifully pulling on their parkas, and heading out visit their mandatory punch clock stations.

He would wait just a few minutes longer, and enjoy the warmth of the electric baseboard heaters. Then, he would leave and hurriedly walk the Nevada powerhouse route, backwards. He hoped that no one would later notice that his watch clock punches were out-of-sequence. While that was permitted, even encouraged, clustering the stops together was absolutely prohibited. The guard's procrastination served to delay his death that night by less than ten minutes.

A barely audible chirping noise was coming from the new service station turbine/generator, which was located in the north end of the Nevada powerhouse, directly under the visitor's balcony. The chirping began to increase in frequency, but not in audio volume. After about five minutes, the chirping had morphed into a buzzing noise, which again barely could be heard over the mind-numbing hum produced by the powerhouse's eight huge turbine/generators.

Exactly ten minutes after the chirping had begun, although there would be no surviving witnesses to document it, the new 3,500 horsepower service station generator fragmented with a deafening explosion, throwing red-hot chunks of fractured shrapnel in all directions! All the light fixtures in the powerhouse ceiling were blown out. Broken glass from the fixtures, rained down on the immaculately polished powerhouse floor. The glass dials of the instrumentation on the machines, was shattered and the sharp shards scattered across the floor.

The massive explosion, generated by two thousand pounds of enhanced Composition Four Plastique explosive, signaled the culmination of the most expensive operation that al-Qaeda had yet attempted to date on U.S. soil.

In the Pacific Northwest attacks back in 2002, the terrorists had used two submarines to attack the Naval Base at Everett, Washington, and bring down the Deception Pass Bridge. The bridge had been the only land link between Whidbey Island, the home of the Navy's submarine patrol airfield, and the U.S. mainland. But those underwater assets had been stolen from the Russians. The mission cost to al-Qaeda—a bribe to the submarine base commander's off-shore banking account—an amount of less than $20,000 USD. As the Americans would say, 'chump change.'

Nearly a year's worth of al-Qaeda planning, behind-the-scenes maneuvering, and the expenditure of literally millions of U.S. dollar equivalents, had just come to fruition. The new generator the Americans had purchased and installed less than four months earlier, exploded causing unbelievable havoc. The force of the detonation sought to vaporize everything within the 45,000 square foot Nevada powerhouse.

Al-Qaeda's chief planner, Ayman al-Jawahiri, had began forming the current scenario, nearly a year earlier. Immediately following the organization being instrumental in creating a highly disruptive, but fictitious personnel crisis at Hoover Dam. Through use of substantial bribes, and falsification of data management systems that al-Qaeda agents had managed to 'hack' into and insert in the databases, the erroneous crisis had been communicated to the Bureau's regional management.

Even though it could not have been farther from the truth, a small handful of contract efficiency experts in the Bureau of Reclamation's regional office became convinced that the dam's resident management was permitting the facility's mechanical reliability to degrade. The fake database suggested that dam management had permitted preventive maintenance, absolutely critical in a seventy-two year old facility, to regress to a point nearly beyond any amount of corrective action.

A small group of permanent staff, at the Bureau of Reclamation, had lulled into believing what their 'hacked' computer systems were telling them. The falsified accounting was being accepted as gospel, despite the contradictory due-diligence reports the financial mavens were receiving from the professionals who actually ran the facility.

The expected and proper action in a case such as that would have been for mid-level management to get off their collective asses and get out into the field. Only from that vantage point, could the decision-makers physically verify whether the conclusion they were receiving from the corrupted database was valid.

However, a newly promoted, highly egoistical member of the regional staff's management team, decided the Bureau wouldn't waste the time validating the information they were receiving. Instead, he launched a head hunting team to the dam, that very day.

All this caused personnel problems that mixed with the current overly competitive atmosphere created by a routine opening for a new resident manager thrust the dam's management team into conflict with one another.

The regional office dispatched experts, were given a number of simple instructions. Those instructions were that anyone 'believed' to be involved in the alleged mismanagement of the preventive maintenance program at the dam, or the personnel conflicts, was to be offered a lateral transfer, and given twenty-four to vacate their office at the facility.

Anyone who refused the transfer was to be put on paid administrative leave, escorted from the premises, and all identification and facility keys seized. They were verbally notified they were being recommended for termination, for "refusal to accept a valid reassignment transfer requested by management." The persons unluckily enough to fall into this latter category, were given seventy-two hours to present themselves at the personnel office at the Denver Regional headquarters, for out-processing.

These staged personnel actions, made possible by al-Qaeda's manipulation of the Bureau's accountability tracking system, meant that a number of staff openings immediately had become available on Hoover Dam's management team.

Al-Qaeda had been covertly grooming two degreed hydroelectric engineers for several years, just waiting for an opportunity such as had just presented itself, by the immediate technical and professional job openings at the dam.

These dedicated al-Qaeda operatives were Elizabeth Zubaida, who found temporary employment in the dam's Press Relations department, and Mohammed Harket, who had no problem being hired as a job-shop consultant. His resume said he had previously worked on some obscure project for Bechtel. Harket would take over the dam's Physical Inspection department, until the Bureau of Reclamation was able to mount the customary professional replacement search. As both engineers were working in the United States on tourist visas, they were not eligible for permanent employment under the latest Homeland Security guidelines, for employment of foreign nationals in sensitive positions in U.S. federal agencies.

Al-Qaeda had spared no effort or cost in fabricating believable backgrounds for both the two engineers. Thus, both were able to secure immediate, if temporary employment at the dam, with a full background investigation to follow, once the hiring paperwork could be processed through the bureaucracy.

The FBI's local SAC, whose job it was to assign the routine

applicant background investigations to street agents, claimed that all her manpower was tied up working terrorist-related investigations. However, she had promised, "the Bureau will get to the backgrounds as soon as the terrorist situation eases up, and more manpower becomes available." Like that was ever going to happen, post 9/11.

The dam's Human Relations Manager translated the FBI's statement to mean that the new employees could be brought on-board in a temporary status, in the meantime. After all, they had the biggest hydroelectric dam in the United States to operate.

Later, after-action investigations by the FBI and Department of Homeland Security, would bring forth shocking revelations. They would determine that the dam's new technical 'temporary' employees had worked together to plant the explosive charge that had destroyed the original Nevada-side service station generator.

The two al-Qaeda engineers had planted enough of the enhanced plastique explosive to guarantee there would be nothing left on which the forensic investigators could base any 'determination of cause.' Al-Qaeda's secondary requirement was that the generator was to be damaged beyond repair, thus requiring immediate replacement.

Meanwhile, long before the two spies managed to plant the explosives, which eventually caused the destruction of the old generator putting the dam's operational capability at-risk, Al-Qaeda had moved forward its master plan. Bin-Laden was ready when the Bureau of Reclamation began its frantic search around the world, for a new turbine/generator that more or less fit the dam's rigid specifications.

Over the months, al-Q aeda had bribed an official at one of the Mexico's largest power companies, to place an order for a generator. By design, it was to have a slightly differently-configured mounting frame, than the one being sought by the Bureau of Reclamation.

Orders for these large specialty generators were rare. And if suddenly a unit with an identical mounting-bolt pattern, matching the 72-year old unit it would be replacing, was located and found to be available for immediate sale, bells and whistles could start pealing and blowing in some alert U.S. government security agency. In order to avoid that risk, al-Qaeda made sure that the specifications for the new generator were slightly different. And that those differences would take several months to retrofit, so that the new unit would drop in and bolt into the old units 'pit.'

Hence almost immediately, following the two al-Qaeda saboteurs causing the destruction of the old unit, the government procurement office inexplicably learned of the existence of a new 'similar' turbine/generator. The purchasing agent learned the new unit had only just become available, following some financial reverses and the untimely death of the official who had placed the order. The Mexican government, in a routine post-audit of the murdered man's affairs, had come across the order for new generator.

Further investigation by the Mexican Federales, revealed that the shipping address that had been listed on the procurement order, didn't exist. Being a big believer in 'following the money,' as are all law enforcement agencies across the planet, the Mexican officers quickly uncovered an offshore savings account with a current balance of $100,000 U.S. dollars.

As the official in question did not come from a wealthy family, and to the best of the Federales' knowledge, had not just won the American Powerball Lottery, the money was confiscated, and the order for the generator, cancelled.

That had been the aim of al-Qaeda all along. Payment of the $100,000 had been generous enough to get the corrupt official to order the generator. Al-Qaeda had additionally given the official $20,000 more US dollars, to use as a deposit to the manufacturer, guarantying acceptance of the order. As the manufacturer assumed the order was backed by the strength of the Mexican government, he really didn't require the monetary deposit, but accepted it anyway.

On the day the new generator had passed through final assembly, and was being painted, the word came down about the Mexican official's unfortunate demise. The manufacturer, still incorrectly assuming the order was a valid procurement by the Mexican government, didn't panic. A few days later, however, two

Mexican officials accompanied by four vicious-looking Federales, arrived at the plant.

The men roughly escorted the manufacturing plant's owner to his office. *Then*, he began to panic! Several hours of intense questioning had taken place, with somber Mexican officials asking the questions, and the terrified plant owner answering them, when he was able. Finally, a series of looks passed between the two Mexican officials, and one of the Federales was told to bring the trembling man a glass of ice water. Once he had consumed that in a single gulp, he was assisted to his feet, and apologies were made.

The good news, the two officials told the manager, was that they had been ordered to find out if he was part of the conspiracy to acquire the illicit generator. After some admittedly rough interrogation methods, they admitted coming to the conclusion that he was not involved.

The bad news was that the order, being bogus, was now null and void. The government refused any responsibility for the hundred of thousands of dollars the manufacturer had borrowed from the National Bank in order to purchase the costly components required to build this one-of-a-kind generator.

Hearing that pronouncement, almost gave the manufacturer a heart attack—he was ruined—his plant was ruined—his employees, mostly members of his immediate family, would be thrown out on the streets without work and would be unable to feed their families.

Worse still, the Mexican National Bank, an arm of the Presidente Fox's government, certainly wasn't going to forgive the loan. Especially since the one-of-a-kind generator was of no value, except to a purchaser that had a specific need for it.

As the plant owner was changing his soiled trousers following the rough handling by the now-departed government officials, he never could have fantasized that a new buyer, the United States government, would figurative appear at his doorstep within days. Nor that they would offer to take the generator off his hands, at full retail, after some modifications to the mounting frame, data output ports, and load-monitoring instrumentation.

Had he known such good fortune was in his future, he likely would have gone home to his wife instead of his fifteen-year-old mistress, a extravagance that he and most of his professional colleagues maintained for the occasional dalliance.

Returning to real time. The devastation generated by the Christmas Eve explosion was rapidly expanding.

In the first nanosecond of the horrific explosion, Hoover Dam's highly sophisticated disaster-response computer (DRC) had blocked any responsive action by the powerhouse's human operators. It electronically seized control of the dam, and began to run the system itself, using its own artificial intelligence.

In less than six-seconds, the ten-million dollar computer system had assessed and measured no fewer than twenty-five hundred separate indices, to ascertain damage control. Following that action, the computer, in less than three-additional seconds, began to 'scram', or shut down, the dam's affected mechanic, electrical, and electronic operating systems.

In a scintilla of a second, the computer had notified the humans who were monitoring and controlling the United States' western power grid, the U.S. Department of Homeland Security, and last but not least, the U.S. Bureau of Reclamation, the dam's owner.

Even though water continued to flow through the dam on the Nevada side, the electrical power necessary to move the water, from Parker Dam, downstream, to the CAP—the Central Arizona Project which provided water for Phoenix and Tucson—was not, thus the computer also notified the human duty officer at that headquarters.

The various human operators at the multiple agencies that received the water that Parker Dam lifted over the mountains to Southern California, also received notification from the unemotional DRC computer.

From one end of the Nevada powerhouse to the other, up and down the well-maintained floor of the powerhouse, the mushroom crown-shaped generator/turbine combos came to a screeching halt, one after another. The vibrations from the rapidly expanding blast caused the heavy equipment to snap its lag bolts. As it racked out of position, the turbine shafts were thrown out of alignment, causing them to freeze up. In response, the DRC computer generated instantaneous remote commands that caused the uncoupling of each units connecting shaft. The shaft that connects the turbine to its uniquely-mated generator.

Simultaneously, the DRC issued a command which closed the intakes on two 395-foot tall towers upstream, on the reservoir-side of dam face, which had been funneling water to the Nevada powerhouse. The water already in the Nevada-side thirty-foot diameter penstocks, was bypassed downstream and returned to the river.

Emergency valves in the thirteen-foot diameter penstocks that connected the thirty-foot penstocks to the base of the powerhouse turbines, and ran between the larger penstocks and the Nevada powerhouse turbines, slowly managed to grind into place, blocking the massive water flow.

The complex DRC computer had detected no threat, as of yet, to or from the Arizona Powerhouse. Thus, it executed the emergency steps necessary to separate the functions of the two powerhouses, isolating the electrical feed from the Arizona side, and shutting down the Nevada powerhouse.

The 600-foot long Nevada powerhouse had immediately become inundated with smoke, turning the building's interior into night despite the feeble light that attempted to seep in from the wall-high now-glassless windows. Klaxons and alarms of all of all types began their shrieking, ear-splitting, mind-numbing warbling.

The shock wave from the explosion had occurred directly under the balcony, which normally was used as an observation point. It was from that ledge that a million tour visitors annually observed the operation of the Nevada powerhouse.

The explosion's shock wave rolled up and over the viewing balcony's edge. Then it sought out and found the rough-hewn, unfinished tunnel that had been bored between the balcony, and the visitor center lower elevator landing.

The fourteen-foot wide tunnel, gave the impression of just being temporary. It had been laboriously cut through the granite rock beneath the dam's visitor's center, only to be hurriedly rushed into use following September 11, 2001. The original visitor elevator entrances, by which the tours had previously accessed the near-mirror image powerhouses, by design, were located on the dam's crest.

However, the ease by which the terrorists had destroyed the twin towers of the World Trade Center, had made it abundantly clear that pre-2001 Hoover Dam was bomber-friendly. Almost overnight, the crest's two mammoth elevators had been deactivated, and taken out-of-service at least for their intended use, for the foreseeable future.

The tour management function, unusual inasmuch as it is financially self-sufficient, had to make a choice. They could restrict the revenue-generating tours to a totally above ground presentation. Or they could come up with an alternative means of descending the five hundred plus feet, down into the chilled interior of the dam, and provide access to the observation balcony, which was elevated seventy feet over the Nevada powerhouse floor. They decided on the latter.

The single, one-hundred-foot-long, by fourteen-foot-wide tunnel, running from the lower landing of the two, forty-two passenger elevators out onto the Nevada viewing observation balcony, had been bored through the hard rock. But the tunnel's inner face had never been finished. The sides and ceiling of the tunnel were unadorned and presented a rough rock surface. Since the tunnel roof leaked, as does any rock or concrete tunnel, a series of corrugated plastic panels had been erected overhead. This protected the tour visitors from getting wet, or more seriously, being beaned by the occasional stone that hydrostatic pressure still caused to occasionally 'blow out.'

The blast, still moving at hundreds of feet per second, gutted the tourist access tunnel, and smashed into the polished stainless steel doors of the two access elevator shafts.

The tremendous lateral pressure buckled the doors, as if Paul Bunyan had curled his hand into a fist, and punched it out. Both elevators had been taken out-of-service at the end of day shift, and there had been nothing to prevent the heavy doors from being punched into the shaft, were they fell a relatively short distance into the flooded equipment pits below.

The massive shock wave was created by the detonation of the two thousand pounds of highly enhanced C-4 explosives, which the terrorists had bribed an key employee of the Mexican manufacturer, to pack into the voids typically found in any metal casting.

Although al-Qaeda had exhaustively researched the location at which the replacement unit would be reinstalled in the powerhouse, the explosion had not been close enough or powerful enough to shatter Hoover Dam's downstream dam face.

The base of the dam measures six hundred, sixty feet thick by seven hundred, twenty-seven feet high. Nothing less than an twenty-five megaton, plutonium-enriched nuclear bomb was going to accomplish anything, other than slightly increase the dam's rate of seepage.

The procrastinating security guard had been vaporized. The heart and other vital organs of the personnel working within the powerhouse at the time of the detonation, ruptured, and were instantly turned into a reddish-gray colored puree.

Workers elsewhere in the mighty structure, within one hundred yards of the Nevada powerhouse, were knocked off their feet, landing in unceremonious heaps. Their ankles were broken as their stocking-clad-feet were torn from their steel-toed work boots, by the shock wave. Bodies were battered, bruised, mutilated and lacerated. More than a few died when they were struck by flying debris. Or their flying bodies were impaled on the sharp edges of the workspace in which they had been multi-tasking.

The combined effects of the massive explosion, coupled with the tremoring of some of the 115,00 horsepower generators now slowly coming to a halt, gave forth a human-like shriek. The spinning units were completely out of balance, and served to give birth to a deep, harmonic vibration that made workers in adjacent work areas instantly throw-up, and scream inhumanly. As the vibration increased in intensity, the workers who had been in areas close to the Nevada powerhouse, were blown off their feet, and screamed and screamed until their hearts ruptured from the exertion.

Up and down the massive room, electrical panels warped from the blast, massive amounts of heat were generated, and the electrical circuits shorted out. As the metal panels and distribution boxes crumbed under the effects of the man-made earthquake, fires erupted around each of the eight generators, as electrical shorts multiplied. The Nevada powerhouse had only seconds before become a human-free zone, after the last worker died screaming, asking God "Why?" Screaming a brief prayer that his wife and children would be taken care of, now that he was dead!

Shatter-proof glass—a composite of two sheets of glass with an intermediate layer of plastic—which had replaced the old-style plate glass panes years ago, throughout the seventy-year-old facility, exploded into cobbles. The clear plastic and glass faces of worker's watches, melted into their wrists.

The pipes feeding the overhead sprinklers in the powerhouse's high ceilings had been installed as a safety improvement back in the 80's. But they burst from the vibration long before any of the high-temperature sprinkler heads, activated. Literally thousands of gallons of water cascaded down onto the floor, drenching the shattered bodies of the deceased workers, and any first responders to the explosion. The infernos raging throughout the facility partially vaporized the falling water as it rained down upon the fiery conflagrations.

Finally, the disaster-response computer, now sensing the ambient temperature in the Nevada facility was rapidly increasing, and using its artificial intelligence to make the judgment call that all the employees had long ago ran for safety, or more likely were deceased, now dumped millions of cubic feet of toxic but fire-squelching Halon gas into the facility. The gas quickly suffocated every last flame in the 4,500,000-cubic foot powerhouse. Eventually, the computer also made the decision to silence the loud-to-the-point-of-being-nerve-racking alarms. But unfortunately, no one remained alive in the Nevada-side powerhouse, to appreciate the silence.

The strenuously lab-tested, but never proven in an actual emergency situation, DRC disaster-response computer, had avoided a great deal of normally expected collateral damage throughout the western U.S. By its spilt-second notification of the operators of the western power gird, a major blackout had been avoided. The grid operators had been given time to shift power loads, and obtain alternate sources of electricity, to keep things moving, albeit at a reduced outflow of power.

DRC's decision to sever operational interaction between the Arizona and Nevada powerhouses, kept the larger of the two powerhouses operating independently, permitting it to continue to feed power into the western power grid.

The disaster-response computer, by bypassing all the expected human emotional weaknesses inherent in an emergency shutdown of a major powerhouse, had saved the Arizona powerhouse, which was wired to operate independently of the powerhouse on Hoover Dam's Nevada side.

Although Monday-morning quarterbacking humans could and would endlessly argue over whether the computer waited too long to introduce Halon gas into the conflagration, it did the job it had been programmed for. The artificial intelligence of the computer had been pre-programmed with the specifications for this particular type of Halon, used in powerhouse applications nationwide by most industrial users.

The instructions that the human programmers had placed into its artificial intelligence circuits, directed that the DRC was not release the deadly Halon gas until its logic said that either the operators had fled, or were dead.

The DRC's damage control performance, had been proven to be within the parameters of its programming. The fact that it had sensed that the eight turbines in the Nevada powerhouse would almost immediately become non-operational, caused it to electronically uncouple the shafts between the eight Nevada turbine/generators, and close down the intakes of the two towers accepting water from Lake Mead reservoir.

Eight, 115,000 horsepower turbine/generators on the Nevada

side would have to be replaced. But they were of a more modern vintage, and replacements could be had in less than four month's time, plus shipping time en-route.

Replacing the 3,500-horsepower service station generator would again prove to be a problem. But the Bureau of Reclamation would this time spend a little more money, and have its installation 'pit' upsized, to accept an off-the-shelf model that would exceed the specifications of the old unit. The additional capacity would also provide additional flexibility, when the over-worked Arizona-side service station generator had to be pulled for a complete overhaul.

The overall cost estimated cost of getting the Nevada side powerhouse back on-line, was five billion in 2004 dollars. Hoover Dam was critical to the nation's national security, and that money would have to be spent. Experts speculated that if Congress passed an exception to the competitive bidding law, the powerhouse could be back on-line in eight to ten months, tops.

In the mean time, the operators of the western power grid were going to be kept busy locating, negotiating, and purchasing 16.8 million kilowatt hours of electricity, monthly, until the Hoover Dam's Nevada powerhouse was back up and operational.

In the more important consideration of human lives lost that Christmas Eve at the dam, the bodies of twelve mechanics and three security guards had been located in the Nevada-side rubble. Two additional mechanics, and four laborers were still unaccounted for. The search continued for those employees.

Two salaried members of the Hoover Dam management team also were missing. They were Elizabeth Zubaida, a temporary employee of the dam's Press Relations department, and Mohammed Harket, who also had recently been hired in the capacity of a consultant, to run the dam's Physical Inspection—Structural Services Unit. They being reported as missing had resulted in a team of FBI agents arriving at the dam without advance notice, and sealing the two employee's offices. Then a FBI ERT team— Evidence Response Team—carted the contents of both offices out the door.

Edith Hammer, the dam's resident manager, had called a brief meeting when the crew reported back to work, following the incident. She informed everyone that, "the FBI would be coming around to speak to each of you, individually."

She concluded the brief meeting, by thanking them all "for your much appreciated extra efforts before and since the tragedy. I want to stress it is important that the missing staffers not become the subject of the dam's rumor mill. We'll find out about the missing people, soon enough I suspect. I have to ask all of you to not respond in any manner, to questions and/or the baiting comments of the reporters, the FBI says to expect will be descending on us, later this week when the news is released to the media."

She continued, "The reporters are forbidden access to working spaces here at the dam. But I expect you may get some telephone calls at home, once the reporters find your names and addresses in the Boulder or Las Vegas phone books. Again, thanks for your cooperation. I know you've had a hellish year, but I know that we can look forward to a much more mellow New Year. That is if I have anything to say about it," Ms. Hammer concluded.

EPILOGUE

2003 marked a major shift in focus for America's War on Terrorism. Osama bin Laden's days were now totally consumed by his need to stay on the move to escape Coalition forces. Al-Qaeda's commander had turned most of the responsibility for the organization's planning over to Ayman al-Zawahiri, his chief deputy, and one of bin-Laden's elder sons, Saad. Actual field operations would continue to be the responsibility of al-Qaeda's surviving lieutenants.

The 2003 New Year's Eve ball had dropped in Times Square only hours before, when Saad met with Fidel Castro's brother Raúl in Havana on New Year's Day, to plan al-Qaeda's latest infamy. Bin-Laden secured Fidel Castro's involvement by promising the Cuban leader something he had wanted for decades. Fidel wanted the Americans out of their Naval base at Guantánamo Bay. He and his brother had been trying to accomplish that seemingly impossible feat, ever since the American embargo had been put into place back in 1961.

Bin-Laden knew the eviction of the American's forces from Guantánamo Bay would not be accomplished easily. Though he never said anything positive about the Americans, he had to acknowledge their bravery Such an ambitious undertaking would require an elaborate plan, coupled with multiple diversions, and a significant portion of the rapidly-shrinking al-Qaeda treasury.

To draw American intelligence agency attention away from Cuba, al-Qaeda had planned and funded two major diversionary attacks.

The first diversionary action was a multi-phase attack on Hoover Dam, located on the Arizona/Nevada borders. Destroying the dam would serve to bring hardship to nearly twenty-five million residents.

The second diversionary action was a multi-phase attack on the resort community of Lake Havasu City, in Northern Arizona. The City had a full time population of 50,000, however the swell of winter snowbirds, and summer visitors, individually, often doubled that figure. The Jihad brazenly attacking vacationing Americans in the southwestern U.S. community, would have the ancillary goal of attempting to restore some currently-lacking substance to al-Qaeda's boast that there was nowhere the Americans could go to escape the wrath of Osama bin-Laden.

2003 began as a threat-filled year for the Americans, as had the proceeding sixteen months since al-Qaeda and the extremist Muslim Jihad came out of the closet.

The primary and secondary attacks on Hoover Dam had been costly to al-Qaeda. The first phase, which had intended to destroy the dam's four intake towers instead was interdicted by alert law enforcement and dam personnel. The attack had been a complete failure, costing al-Qaeda nearly one million USD dollars, and the lives of a dozen believers. The Americans lost nearly a dozen first responders, collaterally, when the terrorist team had blown up their own vessel, apparently electing to commit suicide rather than be taken into custody.

The second Jihad attack on Hoover Dam, involved creating the circumstances under which the Americans had been forced to install a piece of replacement machinery in the Nevada powerhouse. A machine which al-Qaeda, unknown to the Americans, had booby-trapped, and was timed to explode on Christmas Eve.

That attack had been a technical success, costing the Americans fifteen lives, six wounded, and nearly three hundred million dollars in direct repair costs. Another one hundred million dollars had been required for interim operating costs, to avoid negatively impacting the country's western region Gross National Product revenues. Al-Qaeda's total out-of-pocket cost had been less than one million US dollars, and zero human capital.

The second al-Qaeda diversionary attack, this one against the resort community of Lake Havasu City, Arizona, had been timed to coincide with al-Qaeda's preparations for the assault on the American Naval Base at Guantánamo Bay.

In the resort community, an al-Qaeda team of hidden-in-plain-sight saboteurs had attacked the region's major tourist attraction, attempted to sink a shuttle boat loaded with casino tourists, tried to destroy an historic monument erected in honor of the memory of World War II servicemen, sought to topple an important communications tower, and force the temporarily closure of the area's municipal airport.

While the attack on the resort community provided the diversion al-Qaeda had been seeking, it proved to be costly in terms of human capital and monetary cost. Vigilant city, county and federal law enforcement personnel, aided by alert citizens, had caused the interdiction of the five Jihad attacks.

The Lake Havasu assault ended up costing al-Qaeda thirteen believer's lives, two captured operatives, and two million US dollars equipping and putting the team into place. On American's side of the ledger, was a facility repair cost of one hundred, eighty thousand dollars to repair-related damage to the area's landmark tourist attraction, London Bridge. An additional one hundred, twenty-three thousand dollars had been spent to replace vandalized electrical systems at the area's municipal airport. No American lives were lost. First responding police officers suffered injuries, which required a short period of initial hospitalization.

The terrorist's primary objective all along had been the American naval station located at the southeastern end of the nation-state island of Cuba. Al-Qaeda, using embedded spies, Cuban commando saboteurs, and Jihad SOF troops—which were delivered by submarine, had intend to attack at five locations on the forty-five square mile base, with the goal of dividing and diluting the American's security forces. But their primary objective of the campaign was always Camp Delta, the prison facility that contained nearly seven hundred al-Qaeda and Taliban detainees.

The Gitmo attack was costly to the Americans. A total of twelve American lives were lost, with thirty-two wounded. Repair/replacement costs, due to both direct and collateral facility damage, would eventually total just less than four hundred million US U.S. dollars.

Despite the enormous amount of money required from its waning treasury, and the human capital al-Qaeda spent on the total operation, including the two diversionary attacks, the Jihad only managed to rescue six al-Qaeda detainees from Guantánamo. It was the most inefficient, most cost per capita, rescue in the history of the planet. Al-Qaeda also lost its only submarine, when Coalition forces hunted the *Scorpion* down and sank her, on the president's orders for refusing to comply with the Coalition's order to surface and surrender.

President of the United States: George W. Bush
Continues to lead America's war on terrorism in 2004. Although stung by the failure to find weapons of mass destruction in Iraq, the president's approval rating still remains around forty-five percent as he comes up for reelection in November 2004, where he will face Senator John Kerry of the Democratic party, and Ralph Nader of the Independent party.

U.S. Secretary of State: Calvin Page
Despite rumors to the contrary, Secretary Page did not resign in 2003 as predicted to seek his own presidential ambitions. He continues to ably and honorably serve at the president's pleasure in 2004.

U.S. Secretary of Homeland Security: Ted Staples
Secretary Staples continues in 2004 to hold the most difficult,

misunderstood, and unappreciated position in the George W. Bush administration. The security organization he heads now employs nearly 185,000 persons in twenty-two agencies, nation-wide.

Federal Bureau of Investigation: Robert Mueller, Director
Director Mueller, as of late looking tired and over-burdened, continues to bear the brunt of not foreseeing the events of September 11th, 2001. In 2004, he has been repeatedly summoned by one Congressional committee after another, and quizzed about the FBI's role in the 'latest' domestic terrorist revelations. Director Mueller and Director Tenant of the CIA, profess to be fostering improved information sharing between the two agencies, difficult considering their diverse operating cultures.

Federal Bureau of Investigation: William "Bill" Savage, ADIC/ Counterterrorism
Assistant Director In-Charge Savage maintains responsibility for coordinating counterterrorism activities throughout the Bureau's nine divisions; four administrative offices; fifty-six field offices; over 400 satellite offices/resident agencies; four specialized field installations; and thirty foreign liaison posts, or Legal Attachés. He has a solid line relationship with the new U.S. Terrorism Threat Integration Center (TTIC) whose acting head, Supervising Special Agent Diane A. Davis, reports to him on paper.

Federal Bureau of Investigation: Diane A. Davis, Supervising Special Agent
Remains Acting Head of the TTIC in 2004. A fast tracked Special Agent in the FBI, whose multi-talents in all phases of law enforcement were demonstrated in the 2002 West Coast al-Qaeda attacks. Davis's continuing outstanding performance has been noted by her superiors, and acknowledged by the president of the United States.

Central Intelligence Agency: George Tenant, Director
Director Tenant is also spending a significant amount of his time appearing in front of Congressional committees in 2004. He is providing testimony as to why the CIA supported the administration's claim of weapons of mass destruction, prior to the beginning of the second Iraq war. Director Tenant appears to welcome the investigation into the matter, apparently confident it will exonerate the CIA from congressional accusations of 'lack of attention to detail,' and 'tweaking the facts' of its gathered intelligence.

Cuba Leadership: Fidel Alejandro Castro (Ruz), President-for-Life
President Castro in reportedly in poor health. He has shortened his traditionally long-winded speeches to the Cuban people, but remains staunchly anti-American in 2004. There is much concern in the American Intelligence community as to Fidel's successor. As poor a human rights advocate as Fidel is considered to be, his brother Raúl is considered worse by quantum leaps of cruelty.

Hoover Dam: Edith Hammer, Resident Manager
In early 2004, Edith Hammer submitted advance notice of her intention to retire from the Bureau of Reclamation in 2004. Pixel pundits report Hammer may be calling in an IOU the B of R made, guaranteeing her wish to retire within twelve months, if Hammer agreed to take over and resolve the management crisis that existed at the dam when she assumed its helm in 2003.

Hoover Dam: Mohammed Harkat and Elizabeth Zubaida
Both have officially been reported missing since early on December 24, 2003, when explosives detonated in the Nevada Powerhouse at Hoover Dam, gutting one half of the dam's power generation capacity. The matter is under investigation by the Federal Bureau of Investigation, assigned to the one of the Bureau's accomplished inspectors. The Bureau has discovered

that both employees left the facility seven hours prior to the midnight explosion. Search warrant-approved investigations of their residences disclose that a few of their more valued personal effects are missing, and their respective bank accounts, required by the Bureau of Reclamation for direct deposit of earnings, were emptied the previous afternoon before their monthly paychecks were electronically deposited.

Al-Qaeda Detainees held in Camp Delta—The Skagit Eight

Abdul Qayoon and Mohammed Oms were killed by combat gunfire during the terrorist's assault on Camp Delta. A face count of the surviving detainees, revealed that detainees Alghamdin, Alghmdi, Al-Haznawi, Alomari, Al-Sugami, and Barghouti apparently escaped the camp. This while al-Qaeda Special Forces troops, which landed on the beach below the facility, attacked the American facility. It is assumed that these six former-detainees were removed by the Jihad SOF troops, and were aboard the submarine *Scorpion* that was sunk when it refused to surface and surrender, per Coalition warship's orders off the Bahama Islands.

Al-Qaeda High Command:

Osama bin-Laden continues to spend the majority of his days fleeing capture by the Coalition. Members of the U.S. intelligence community report that his capture is, as always, "considered imminent." His son, Saad bin-Laden and the Al-Qaeda Lieutenant, Abu Hazim al-Sha'ir, are reportedly covertly traveling throughout the middle-east, seeking to generate monetary and political support for additional atrocities against the United States, and other member-nations of the War on Terror Coalition.

Joint Task Force (JTF) 160: Geoffrey Montrose, Major General, Commander

General Montrose continues to command JTF 160, which is charged with the safe keeping and security of the detainees at

Camp Delta in 2004. Work continues at Guantánamo Bay to rebuild facilities at the camp, the 'Dirty Shirt' mess, the bases' Leeway Ferry terminal, and improve security at the bases' Desalinization/Power Generation/727 UPS facilities. It is believed that General Montrose will receive another star, and be rotated to a staff billet on the JCS, before his planned retirement date in 2006.

JTF 160: Ahmed al-Halabi; Ahmed Fathy Hehalba; Yousef Yee
All have been taken into custody by the Naval Criminal Investigation Service (NCIS). Al-Halabi and Hehalba are being investigated on charges of Treason and Spying for al-Qaeda, while Yee currently faces far less serious charges, and reportedly, may be exonerated of those.

GLOSSARY

ADC: FBI Assistant Director In-Charge.
ADOT: Arizona Department of Transportation.
AEGIS: Means 'shield.' The Navy's most modern surface combat system. Designed and developed as a complete system, integrating state-of-the-art radar and missiles systems. The AEGIS Combat System is highly integrated and capable of simultaneous warfare on several fronts—Air, Surface, Subsurface, and Strike.
AH: STANAG ID for 120-foot and larger hospital ships.
AIR CAP: Umbrella of protection over a warship maintained by armed aircraft.
ALICE: Weight-bearing back pack harness used by the military.
ANDREWS AIR FORCE BASE: Home of Air Force One and SAM FOX. In 2003, Andrews celebrated its 60th year in operation.
ANFO: Ammonia Nitrate Fuel Oil Bomb.
ANG: Air National Guard or Army National Guard.
ANTIVAN: A paralytic substance.
AO: Area of Operation.
ASAC: FBI Assistant Special Agent In-Charge. (Reports to the SAC)

ASROC: Mod 5 Neartip torpedo.

BDND: Beginning of day, nautical dawn. A specified time of day when it is light enough to get dressed and prepare the morning meal, but not yet light enough to move out.

BINGO: When aircraft gauges say the engine(s) is out of fuel. Just before the engine ceases to function.

BLUE TEAM: Secondary alternating team.

BOOMER: A ballistic missile submarine.

BOQ: Bachelor officer's quarters.

BUCAR: An FBI vehicle.

C-17: Boeing Globemaster II air freighter.

C-4: Composition four, a plastique explosive compound used for demolition of military objectives.

CAMAGÛEY: An Cuban military airfield located towards the eastern midpoint of the island.

CAMP AMERICA: Barracks camp for assigned JTF 160 personnel at Guantánamo.

CAMP AMERICA-NORTH: A new extension of *Camp America* that provides expanded barracks capacity for the JTF guard force at Gitmo. It extends the existing *Camp America,* further west along Kittery beach. Construction of the camp expansion is currently frozen until higher authority had determined the fate of the detainees at *Camp Delta.*

CAMP DELTA: Gitmo camp where captured terrorist combatants are being detained.

CAMP X-RAY: Site of a former prison compound at Gitmo, abandoned when *Camp Delta* came on-line.

CAP: Central Arizona (irrigation) Project.

CARNIVORE: A software program developed by the FBI that permits the reading and tracking of each keystroke of any computer terminal in the world.

CAVITATION: The formation of fine vapor (air) bubbles on the surface of a propeller, when the propeller moves through the water rapidly. Cavitation produces a disruption in water flow, easily detected by sonar, and must be avoided at all costs by the crew of a combat submarine.

CIA: Central Intelligence Agency: World's best and most-principled intelligence agency.
CNRSE: Commander—Navy Region Southeast.
COB: Chief of the Boat. Senior enlisted man on a U.S. submarine crew. Usually a senior or master chief petty officer. Interfaces directly with the XO on issues that affect the enlisted personnel. The Royal Navy equivalent is the coxswain.
COCKPIT RAILS: The mechanical track to which a aircraft canopy mates.
CONUS: Continental United States.
CORDON SANITAIRE: Naval blockade.
CPG: A dam's central power generating department.
CSI: Crime scene investigation.
CUBAN MISSILE CRISIS: Happened in 1962, on President John F. Kennedy's watch.
DBR: Detainee behavioral reports.
DIA: U.S. Defense Intelligence Agency.
DIRT SHIRT MESS: Informal dining area where pilots and other military personnel can obtain meals without having to clean-up, and change into the designated Uniform of the Day.
DOD: U.S. Department of Defense.
DOE: U.S. Department of Energy.
DOER: An active participant in a criminal enterprise.
DOJ: Department of Justice.
DPB: Daily Presidential Briefing (An intelligence briefing by the CIA).
DRAUGHT: The depth of a vessel's keel below the water line.
DRC: Disaster Response Computer. A computerized emergency management system based on learned artificial knowledge, for use in times of paramount crisis, where human emotions may result in human operators failing to make logical decisions.
DRUM GATE: A 100-foot by 6-foot gate that controls access and egress to a spillway.
ECM: Electronic counter measures.
ELEMENT: When used in relationship to a military mission, refers to a function.

ELINT: Electronic intelligence.
ETA: Expected time of arrival.
F-16: Lockheed-Martin Fighting Falcon.
FAA: Federal Aviation Administration.
FBI HEADQUARTERS: J. Edger Hoover building—Washington D.C.
FBI: Federal Bureau of Investigation: World's premier law enforcement organization.
FEET DRY: When an aloft aircraft transitions from over water, to over land flight.
FEET WET: When an aloft aircraft transitions from over land, to over water flight.
FLAG: U.S. Submarine Command. Or when used in reference to an admiral.
FLIR: Forward looking infrared imaging.
FOLDER HOLDER: An organization or person's direct supervisor. The individual who has direct access to a personnel or unit's operations folder.
FRAGGED: An order that comes down the chain-of-command and is assigned. In combat, this could mean a particular target assigned to a specific group of aircraft.
FREEDOM HEIGHTS/CAMP BULKELEY: Both former barracks housing at Guantánamo Bay.
FULCRUM: NATO designation for Russian MiG 29.
GAO: Government Accounting Office.
GITMO: Military slang for Guantánamo Bay Naval Station.
GO FAST: Jet fighters, hi-speed off shore race boats, anything fast.
GOLD TEAM: Primary alternating team.
GP-M: A military type tent. General Purpose—Medium.
GPS: Global Positioning System.
GREAT SATAN: Fundamentalist Muslim extremist slang for America.
GREEN BENNIES: A term referring to the Army's Special Forces units.

HALOGEN LIGHTING: A very bright form of artificial light. A form of Halogen includes chlorine, which is a greenish-yellow gas at room temperature and atmospheric pressure. It is considerably heavier than air. It has a choking smell, and inhalation causes suffocation.

HALON GAS: A form of gas used in flame suppression that in itself, is deadly when inhaled.

HEADSUP: An alert or forewarning of things to come.

HELM: The steering station for a ship.

HOSTILES: Enemy combatants.

HRT: FBI's premier Hostage Rescue Team.

HUMINT: Human intelligence—information obtained from a human source in the AO—area of operations.

ICHI BON, NUMBER ONE: Slang meaning something is the best, or the first. From the days of Vietnam.

ICRC: International Committee of the Red Cross (called the Red Crescent in Muslim countries.)

IN-BURNER: Operating a military combat aircraft with the afterburner engaged.

IPCO: International Paper Company.

JAG/NCIS: A joint Judge Advocate General /Naval Criminal Investigative Service taskforce.

JAGUEY: A short, fat trunk tree with stocky branches that grows wild in Cuba.

JINKING: Maneuvering an aircraft in an erratic manner, to avoid hostile fire.

JTF 160 COMMANDER: Major General Geoffrey Montrose, USA

JTF 160: Joint Task Force assigned to Guantánamo Bay Naval Station (*Camp Delta*.).

KBS: Kellogg, Brown and Root—*Camp Delta's* contractor, a subsidiary of Halliburton.

KILLERY/WINDMILL BEACHES: Southern perimeter beaches at Guantánamo Naval Station located directly below the bluff on which *Camp Delta* was constructed. The northern shoreline of the Windward Passage which lies between Cuba and Haiti.

KLAXON: A loud signal device generally used in connection with facility security or in World War II, by destroyers on a depth charge laying run.

KM: Kilometer.

LAN: Local Area Network. A base communication system that permits all VTDs but the central computer to be a 'dumb' terminal.

LEEWARD FIELD: The active airfield at Guantánamo Bay NAS.

LEEWARD: In the lee of a hill.

LOURDES: Russian intelligence base in Cuba.

LST: Landing ship, tank.

LZ: Landing zone, usually for helicopters.

MARK ONE EYEBALL: The human eye.

1MC: Master ship-wide communications and PA system.

McCALLA: The inactive airfield at Guantánamo Bay NAS. Too short to handle jet aircraft without use of a naval landing hook system.

MG: Machine gun.

MICAP: Mission capability meeting.

MiG: Acronym for the Russian Mikoyan-Gurevich Design Bureau. Produced excellent aircraft when they had the materials, technology, and political support to do so.

MILSPECS: Military specifications.

MRE: Meals, ready-to-eat.

MSC: Medical Service Corps. A non-doctor medical administrator.

MSL: Mean Sea Level.

NAS: Naval Air Station.

NASA: National Aeronautics and Space Agency.

NCIS: Naval Criminal Investigative Service.

NCO: A non-commissioned officer.

NEEDLE VALVE: An eight-four inch valve that returns water from a dam's powerhouse to the source river.

NEWBIE: A new participant; a rookie; a FNG (a fucking new guy).

NO MAN'S LAND: An area directly beyond a military force's front lines, considered to be an open fire zone, possibly occupied by the enemy.

NOFORN: U.S. security classification. No foreign distribution allowed.
NORDEN: Top-of-line surface search radar.
NRMIUWU: U.S. Naval Reserve Mobile Inshore Undersea Warfare Unit, stationed at Gitmo.
NSA: National Security Agency.
NVG: Night vision goggles.
OD: Officer of the deck; Officer of the day; the Duty officer.
ONI: Office of Naval Intelligence.
OPERATION ENDURING FREEDOM: The global war on terrorism—Afghanistan.
OPERATION MARATHON/PRESENT HAVEN: 1996 program at Gitmo for Chinese refugees.
OPERATION SEA SIGNAL: 1994 program at Gitmo to provide humanitarian relief to refugees from Haiti.
OSHA: U.S. Occupational Safety and Health Agency.
OVERHEAD: A term referring to an aircraft currently flying over a carrier or other ship.
PBAU: FBI Profiling and Behavioral Assessment Unit.
PENSTOCK: A piece of piping, located between a dam's intake tower, and the powerhouse.
PHALANX MOD FIFTEEN: Six-barreled, fast-firing, antiaircraft gun on a military vessel, whose target acquisition function is slaved to radar.
PIC: Pilot-in-command.
PICKET LINE: Destroyer screen.
PIXEL PUNDIT: A newscaster.
POLITBURO: The political governing body in Russia.
POSIT: A position.
POWERPOINT: A stylized presentation format used by the FBI.
PPM: Parts-per-million.
PSHRINKS: FBI term for profilers. Also used by other federal law enforcement, military organizations, and intelligence agencies.
PSU 307: Port Security Unit at Guantánamo Bay Naval Station.
PUZZLE PALACE: Slang for the Pentagon. Also referred to as 'inside the ring.'

RCA SPY-ID(V): Air search/Fire control radar.

REGULAR PARTY: A military base's chartered and approved level of organizational staffing, broken down by occupational military occupation special (MOS) codes.

RICKY TICK: Vietnam era slang directing that something be done quickly.

ROE: Rules of Engagement.

RON: Remain over night—a military term.

RUMOR MILL: An informal and unofficial source for doubtfully accurate information that exists at every military base in the world. Also called 'The Word.'

SA: FBI Special Agent.

SAFED: Weapon's switch(s) on Safe setting.

SAC: FBI Special Agent In-Charge.

SAIL: The topmost section of a submarine.

SAM FOX: Originally used as a prefix to an aircraft tail number, formed a radio signal call sign to identify Air Force aircraft that were transporting high-ranking VIPS, typically on foreign flights. The call sign prefix was constructed of the acronym SAM (Special Air Mission) and the initial F (Foreign), which at the time was represented by the phonetic word "Fox."

SAT PHONE: Satellite phone.

SCREW SIGNATURE: A unique acoustical record of the sound produced by operation of a ship's propeller.

SCUD: Low, overhanging dark cloud cover.

SEA SPARROW: A shipboard defensive rocket.

SEAHUTS: The structures constructed at Gitmo's *Camp America* to house JTF personnel.

SEASIDE GALLEY: The JTF galley or mess hall at *Camp America*, which can serve up to 4,000 meals per day.

SH-60F (Lamps): Sikorsky ASW helicopter.

SITREP: Situation report.

SIX: The blind spot directly behind a combat aircraft.

SLICK BACK: An unmarked police cruiser.

SNAFU: Sure enough all fucked up.

SOF: Special Operations Force.

SOSUS: Sound Surveillance System—US. Used to detect and track foreign submarines.

SPILLWAY: A fifty-foot in diameter, bypass pipe or trough used in dam construction, or in day-to-day operations, depending on design.

SSBN: Submarine, ballistic missile, nuclear.

SSGN: Submarine, attack, surface missile, nuclear.

SSK: Submarine, patrol, diesel.

STANAG DESIGNATION: NATO warship identification classification system.

STAND THE SHIP DOWN: Secure from General Quarters.

STAR FIGHTER: A wannabe general or admiral assigned to the Pentagon.

STICKER BUSH: A bush that grows wild in Cuba that can get taller than a man.

TASKED: Assigned to a command.

TEXT MESSAGING: Use of a cell phone for non-verbal communications.

TFR: Terrain following radar.

TFS: Tension Frame System—A building structure used for support purposes, located at *Camp America* for the JTF at Gitmo.

TIERRA CAY: Former family housing quarters at Gitmo, now used for supplemental housing since Guantánamo is no longer a dependents-allowed billet.

TOT: Time on target.

TRUE ACTIVE SOFTWARE: Tracks all computer terminal keyboard-generated messages.

TSA: Transportation Security Agency.

TTIC: U.S. Terrorism Threat Integration Center. Headquarters is located on the Beltway in Washington D.C. Created by the order of President George W. Bush in January 2003.

TU: Tits up. Slang for something or someone who is broken.

UCMJ: Uniform Code Of Military Justice. Rules and regulations for US service personnel.

UPS: Uninterruptible power source.

USS DONALD COOK: An AEGIS guided missile-class destroyer designated DDG 075.

USS OSCAR AUSTIN: An AEGIS guided missile-class destroyer designated DDG 079.

VERSED, GHB, KETAMINE, BURUNDANG and ROHYPOL: Date rape drugs.

VLS: Vertical launch system.

WALLY'S WORLD: Headquarters and training area for the Army's quasi-secret Delta Force at Quantico.

WILLIE PETER: Phosphorous grenades. Used for trip wires and providing artificial illumination at night by military troops. Very dangerous to use for the inadequately trained. Once a speck of the material gets on the skin, it cannot be removed except by surgical means, and then only under water, which prevents air from providing the oxygen it needs for combustion.

WINDWARD: The windy side of anything, a passage, lake, or cove.

WSO: Weapons systems officer, also called 'Weaps.'

XACTIL: An involuntary muscle relaxant used in surgical applications.

XO: Executive officer.

ZULU TIME: Current UTC (or GMT) time used. UTC is Coordinated Universal Time. GMT is Greenwich Mean Time. For instance, UTC time in Cuba is Local plus five hours = GMT/Zulu.

REFERENCE MATERIALS

Afghan war detainees move indoors in Cuba, CNN.COM.
Albright, David, President of the Institute for Science and International Security.
Al-Qaeda Terrorist Sleeper Cells in the US . . . , The Washington Post Newspaper.
Bathurst, Robert B., *Understanding the Soviet Navy:* A Handbook. USGPO, 1979.
Bureau of Justice Statistics, Office of Justice Programs, *U.S. Department of Justice.*
Camp America/Camp Bulkeley, CNN.COM.
Carroll, Brian P, *Major Case Management*, FBI Law Enforcement Bulletin, The.
Comprehensive Database of Facial Expression Analysis, Kanade, Takeo, et.al.
DNA Crime Labs: The Paul Coverdell National Forensic Sciences Improvement Act.
DNA Profiling and DNA Fingerprinting, Epplen, Jorg T.
Douglas, John, *Guide to Careers in the FBI.*
Dr. Bill Frist, M.D. U.S. Senate, *When Every Moment Counts.*
FBI Agent Magazine.

Guantanamo Bay—Camp Delta, Global Security Organization.
Hoover Dam, U.S. Department of Reclamation.
Hoover Dam, Visitors' Bureau of Boulder City, Nevada
Janes Aircraft Recognition Guide.
Janes Warship Recognition Guide.
Lake Havasu City, Visitors' Bureau of Lake Havasu City, Arizona.
Michaud, Stephen G., and Hazelwood, Ray, *The Evil that Men Do.*
Prison Camp Sparks Protests, BBC News.
Rapid Start, Jefferson County Sheriffs Office, Case Management Techniques.
Ressler, Robert, and Shachtman, Tom, *Whoever fights Monsters.*
Special Coast Guard Unit Patrols Waters Around Gitmo, DefenseLINK, U.S. DoD.
The FBI Agents Association.
The History of Guantanamo Bay, www.gtmo.net/gazz
U.S. CIA Factbook—Cuba. U.S. Central Intelligence Agency.
U.S. Department of Energy: Washington D.C.

ABOUT THE AUTHOR

George H. Stollwerck is a former Chief of Police from a jurisdiction in the Pacific Northwest. Other law enforcement positions he has held include deputy sheriff, certified FBI Firearms Instructor, and member of a Presidential task force on nationalwide Cargo Security. He also has worked in public school administration, commercial and experimental aircraft design, and construction engineering.

During the Los Angeles Olympics, he served as a coordinator of planning for an airline with responsibility for interfacing between the transportation industry; the Los Angeles Olympic Organizing Committee; federal, state, and city authorities; and the print and television media.

Stollwerck is a commercial-rated aircraft and helicopter pilot and recently retired after fifteen years with a major international airline.

For the past five years, Stollwerck has lived in Lake Havasu City, Arizona on the Colorado River where he is working on his fifth novel.

Should you have questions or comments please feel free to direct them to the author at *ghstoll@rraz.net*.

BVG